DAMAGE CONTROL

NORTHSHORE STORIES

LYNN VAN DORN

Damage Control

Lynn Van Dorn

Copyright © 2017 Lynn Van Dorn
Editor: Courtney Bassett
Cover design: Soxsational Cover Art

All rights reserved. No part of this story may be used, reproduced, or transmitted in any form or by any means without the written permission of copyright holder, except in the case of brief quotations embodied within critical reviews and articles.

This is a work of fiction. The names, characters, and incidents are products of the writer's imagination or have been used fictitiously and are not meant to be construed as real. Any resemblance to actual events, locales, persons, or organizations is entirely coincidental.

This book contains sexually explicit content which is suitable only for mature readers.

www.lynnvandorn.com

Publisher's Note

This novel contains mature themes and elements which some readers may find upsetting. In particular, readers are advised that this book contains descriptions of self-harm and past instances of rape.

Prologue

Tyler at Not-So-Sweet Sixteen

July, nine years ago
Chicago Botanic Gardens
Glencoe, IL

Tyler, being a teenager, hated most Chadwick family functions, the one exception being the yearly picnic they held in summer for the families of everyone who worked at his father and grandfather's law firm. He wasn't expected to wear a stupid suit and tie, for example. And being outside at the Botanic Gardens with picnic foods like barbecue chicken, potato salad, and corn on the cob, all catered, naturally, was a million times better than something like the typical Chadwick and Chadwick affair. Those were always held at some hotel like the Drake or the Palmer House, with weird little hors d'oeuvres and wine he wasn't allowed to drink.

But aside from all that, today was special, one he'd been anticipating for months. Today Tyler would get to see Josh for the first time since December, and this time he was determined to do more than stare at him like a little creep. Today would be different, because Tyler was going to get Josh to finally notice him.

Tyler couldn't remember a time in his life before Josh. He knew that time existed, that he'd been four when Josh and Tyler's brother Ryan became best friends, but that pre-Josh period was hazy and difficult for him to recall. It felt like Josh had always been there, a dark shadow to Ryan's blond light, and that had been that. First Josh and Ryan had been friends, then not-so-secret boyfriends, then the Big Breakup that was Not-to-Be-Discussed had occurred. Now Josh sightings had dwindled to appearances at official Chadwick functions, accompanied as always by his father, who was head of accounting for the law firm, his mother, and his sister.

Tyler couldn't pinpoint when his obsession with Josh had started, but it might have been the summer Tyler was thirteen and he'd seen Josh strip to the waist while playing volleyball at that year's picnic. Or maybe it had always been there, just under the surface, waiting for puberty to come along and highlight how desirable his brother's ex was. Whatever the reason, Tyler had it bad and he was determined to do something about it.

He stared at Josh, standing with his sister Rachel and Tyler's other brother, Brad. Brad was eyeing Rachel and Tyler silently willed him to go for it already. Removing her would leave Josh on his own, allowing Tyler to sidle up to him and strike up a conversation. He would get Josh to go on a walk with him, they would slip away, then Tyler would be irresistible and nature would take its course. Tyler would be rid of his pesky virginity and Josh would at last get over Ryan. They could have a secret affair until Tyler was eighteen, then they would be free to live together forever in happy bliss, the end. Josh would be a successful doctor and Tyler would be a... something. Tyler wasn't sure what he wanted to do with the rest of his life. He just knew he wanted to do Josh. Often. And in a variety of ways that he'd seen presented in online porn. He wasn't sure if all of them were anatomically possible, but Tyler was willing to try anything once, no matter how unlikely or potentially uncomfortable.

He knew he looked good, even in the boring outfit of khaki shorts and polo shirt his father had insisted he wear. The shirt was teal, which brought out the green in his eyes, making them look almost turquoise. His hair was styled to perfection, currently colored platinum, which contrasted nicely with his dark brows and lashes. He'd tried for the same blond as Ryan, knowing that Josh had a thing for that hair color, but honey blond looked terrible on him, so he bleached all the color out and called it good. His father hated it, which was an added bonus. Unlike most of his peers, Tyler had perfect, pimple-free skin, and his teeth were naturally straight. The only thing that worried him was his size. He was short and slim and looked younger than sixteen. That wasn't always a problem when it came to attracting male attention, but he had a feeling it might be with Josh. Tyler would have to make up for his lack of height with gravitas.

He could do this. He *would* do this. He'd been waiting all year to do this. He'd been waiting all his life to do this. His hand dropped to his pocket. He felt the condom and lube packet he'd put in there this morning. They were little pieces of reality that reminded him that he had stepped out of his fantasies. This was real life, as real as it got. Maybe things wouldn't go precisely as he'd imagined, but nothing ventured, nothing gained, and nothing at all would happen if he didn't at least try. Not trying wasn't an option.

Josh was just so perfect. He had black hair that, left to its own devices, curled. Not horrible frizzy curls, either. Josh's curly hair made him look deliciously rumpled, like he'd just been fucked. Tyler wanted to twine one of those curls around his finger. He'd wanted to do that for years. Josh's gaze fell on him and Tyler froze, caught by his dark eyes framed by wire-rimmed glasses. Tyler adored those glasses. They made Josh look serious and intelligent and mature, which of course he was.

Brad finally separated Rachel from her brother, whisking her away to the picnic's prepared buffet. Tyler started forward, his heart pounding away in his chest. *You can do this you can do this you can do this.*

He stood by Josh and waited to be noticed. And waited. And waited. Running out of patience, he cleared his throat. Still nothing, so he reached out and touched Josh's shoulder. "Hi," he said.

Josh stopped scanning the crowd and looked down at Tyler. "Oh, hi there, Tyler. I don't think I've seen you in years. You must be in high school by now, right?"

You saw me six months ago, Tyler thought with irritation, but didn't let it show on his face. "I'll be a junior in the fall," he said.

Josh's eyes widened. "God, time flies. You make me feel old. I can't believe you'll be in college in a few years. Have you decided where you want to go yet? What you're going to major in?"

This was not going as Tyler had planned, and he fought to keep a frown off his face. "No, still keeping my options open. I'm very... flexible." Tyler peered up through his lashes at Josh, hoping for a response. Nope. Nothing.

"That's fine, you still have two years to decide."

Tyler shifted from foot to foot. What now? Josh kept looking away from him, scanning the crowd of people at the picnic. Tyler placed his hand on Josh's forearm to get his attention and loved the feel of muscle under his fingers. "Maybe you could help me," he said, making his voice into a throaty purr. "You could provide me with some guidance." He lightly touched his tongue to his upper lip.

Josh frowned down at Tyler. "I—"

"Josh! Long time no see!"

Tyler saw Josh start, then turn bright red. The cause was no surprise. Ryan had arrived.

"I had no idea you'd be here," Josh said, an uncertain smile on his face. "I thought you were spending the summer in California. It's great to see you."

Ryan beamed back at Josh, all tall and handsome and golden like a fucking Greek god. It was so unfair. "I had planned on staying the summer out there, but Dad talked me into coming home until school starts back up. How's med school treating you? You like U of C better than Stanford?"

"Yeah, it's great, being back home," Josh said. The smile had fallen from his face, but his eyes looked at Ryan like a starving man shown a feast he wasn't allowed to touch. Damn Ryan, anyway. He wasn't supposed to be home until next week. "How have you been?"

"Fine, fine."

The two of them stared at each other like they were the only two people in the universe and it was starting to piss Tyler off. "Ryan," he said, "Where's Missy?"

"Missy?" Josh asked, his eyes narrowed.

"His current girlfriend," supplied Tyler, ever so helpful.

"Oh," Josh said. "Well."

"Are you seeing someone?" asked Ryan.

"No. Well, I was, but not right now. We decided to see other people." Josh didn't seem particularly broken up about the breakup.

"I'm sorry to hear that," Ryan said.

Tyler wasn't sorry to hear it, but he already knew Josh was currently single thanks to Brad, the family gossip. "Ryan, I see Missy over there. It looks like Dad has her cornered. You should go rescue her. I can keep Josh company."

Ryan looked at Tyler as if finally noticing his presence, then he glanced over and saw that their father did indeed have his girlfriend cornered. He gave Tyler another look, this one dark and suspicious, then he gave Josh his sunniest smile. "Excuse me for a minute," he said. "Let me go save my date from Dad. We'll have to catch up later."

Josh frowned. "Maybe," he said. "I was thinking of taking off soon."

No! Tyler screamed in his head.

"No," Ryan said. "Stay. I've missed you. We should really hang out. It's been a long time."

Josh gave a noncommittal grunt. "You should go rescue your girl."

"So," Tyler said once Ryan had finally left, "you wanna ditch this place?" He touched Josh's chest with one finger. Josh's very solid chest. Tyler would have given up everything he owned, including his brand-new car, to see that chest bared again.

Josh looked at Tyler's finger, a slight frown on his face. "What do you—"

"Tyler! There you are!" Brad smiled at Josh. "Hey, Josh, you don't mind if I borrow my brother, do you?"

"No, of course not. I was thinking about leaving, anyway." His eyes tracked over to where Ryan stood with his dad and girlfriend. "You mind finding your own way back to the apartment?"

"Nope, I'm good," Brad said. "I'll get a lift back from someone. If nothing else, your sister can drive me. Go take off."

Tyler pouted. Well, fuck. There went months of hoping and dreaming down the drain thanks to his two shitty brothers.

"Come on, Tyler," Brad said. "Let's go take a walk."

"I don't want to," he said sulkily.

"Too damn bad," Brad said, and dragged him away from the picnic.

When they were out of earshot, Brad said, "What the hell do you think you're up to, Ty?"

Tyler was silent, his default mode when being lectured.

"You're sixteen years old, for fuck's sake. Just barely sixteen. Josh is twenty-five. You should not be flirting with him."

Tyler crossed his arms over his chest. "Who says I was flirting?"

"Cut the crap, Ty. You were so obvious that even Josh almost noticed."

"Really?" Tyler perked up. That sounded promising.

"Stay away from Josh, Tyler. Period. End of discussion."

"But—"

"No." Brad, usually the most easygoing of the Chadwicks, was channeling Dad today. "You're too young. And even if you weren't, he's still in love with Ryan."

"It's been five years," Tyler said. "He should be over Ryan by now. I could help him with that."

Brad gave a little shudder. "Ugh. No. No on so many levels. You. Are. Sixteen. You want him sent to jail?"

Tyler frowned. "No."

"Put Josh out of your head. Find some boy your own age."

"That won't make a difference. It's not like Dad would ever let me date a boy, no matter how age-appropriate."

Brad gave Tyler a one-armed hug. "Two more years and you can go to college. Pick something far away and live your own life. Fuck your way across campus once you're eighteen. Just don't forget to use condoms, okay? Two years. It's not forever, I swear. Hang in there."

Easy for Brad to say. He didn't live at home. He was Josh's roommate, and he didn't even appreciate it because Brad was straight and Tyler was pretty sure he wanted to bone Josh's sister.

"I hate it at home."

"I know," Brad said, but he didn't. Not really. "Look, Ty, playing Lolita is a really bad idea. You think you know what you're doing, but you don't. Let this Josh obsession you've got go, okay?"

Tyler bit his lip. "I won't always be sixteen."

Brad smiled at him. "True. You're going to look back one day on this year and wish you could go back in time and live it again. Enjoy being sixteen while you still can. This could end up as the best year of your life!"

As it turned out, Brad couldn't have been more wrong.

Chapter 1
Tyler's Sordid Past Rears Its Ugly Head

Thursday, September 15th, 3:24 a.m.
Ryan's overpriced condo
Chicago, IL

"Hon, you are about to get most righteously fucked and I don't mean that in a good way."

Tyler regretted not putting his phone in "do not disturb" mode. "Ethan, you realize that it's after three in the morning here, right? Shockingly, Chicago is in a different time zone than LA." He wouldn't have even answered, but it was Ethan, one of his closest friends, and the best ex-boyfriend a guy could ask for. He'd always answer when Ethan called, although that didn't mean he wouldn't be grumpy about it.

"Screw time zones. This is important. What part about righteous fucking did you not get?"

"Like any of it. What's going on?" A thin ribbon of worry started to worm its way through him. They'd wrapped up the filming for his latest movie, *The Silver Arrow,* in August, and he'd just gotten done with a fashion shoot for Hermes in Saint-Tropez on Monday, so he was currently free of any obligation for the next several weeks except being a groomsman in his brother's wedding. Everything had been going so well recently that he should've known it couldn't last.

"TMZ has gotten its hands on a certain video of you and two football players."

Tyler sat up in bed and fumbled for the bedside lamp. His heart started to pound and his stomach lurched. "What? No. Not possible."

"All too possible. It's not the best resolution, but in the video, it's pretty clear you are the adorable cheerleader who is eventually spit-roasted by two beefy football players. I'm both shocked and impressed. You're my new hero."

"No, I'm not." Tyler's mind spun, trying but unable to latch onto concrete ideas. "This isn't possible," he repeated.

Ethan snickered. "I can't believe your life. You were a cheerleader? Like with actual pom-poms? How is it possible I don't know this about you?"

Tyler groaned. "Yes, for part of one year. No pom-poms. I was cut after getting caught being fucked by one football player while fellating another. This was not my proudest moment, Ethan. For the record, the one pounding my ass was a pretty terrible fuck. The other one had a nice dick and decent-tasting jizz, though, so that was pretty much a wash."

"For the record, huh? Can I quote you on that?" Ethan asked. "My boss would shit himself."

Cold reality splashed over Tyler, washing away the last of his drowsiness. "No, you can't quote me, Ethan! What the actual fuck?"

"Just kidding, honest. No, you know I wouldn't do that. I'm the nice ex, since the role of dickbag ex was already taken. But if you do want to feed me something you *want* out there, you know I'm your man."

"Yeah, I know. Ethan, what am I going to do? The studio is going to murder me. Alicia is going to help them."

"Don't know, Ty. I love you, but my hands are pretty much tied over here. I had to give you a heads up, but if they find out I warned you, I'm also screwed."

"I know, and thanks again. When are they leaking the video? Or has it already happened?"

"That's above my pay grade," Ethan said. "But from what I understand, they're currently checking with legal. I think the main thing saving your ass at the moment is that they're afraid of child porn charges. I don't suppose you were all eighteen?"

A slight feeling of relief flowed through Tyler. "No. I was sixteen, not sure how old they were. Seventeen or under, though."

"I'll float the idea by the powers that be that the chances of any of you being of age is very slim, but Tyler, the story will get out. We've already put out a blind item, and there'll be more, and not just from us. I doubt we're the only ones with the video. None of the mainstream media is likely to show it, even if you were all over eighteen, because it's too porny. But if this thing isn't already all over the internet I'd be surprised, and everyone is going to report on it. Well, maybe not PBS, although you never know. My boss was talking about showing censored clips. Enough to show it's you and what's going on, but with enough blocked out to get by the FCC."

Tyler groaned. "Fuck me."

"Get ready to bend over, hon. The world is about to cram its dick up your ass, minus the lube and reach around."

"Shut up."

"You need to get your agent and brother on this right away. I'm serious, Ty. You're about to get spit-roasted again, and it won't be nearly as much fun this time."

It hadn't been all that much fun the first time. Tyler had come away from the experience with the opinion that threesomes were overrated, especially threesomes with supposedly straight teenaged jocks. In Tyler's opinion, sex with teenagers in general was overrated, which was probably why his next big scandal involved an adult. If people started digging, they might uncover that, too. The court documents were supposed to be sealed, but there weren't supposed to be any copies of the threesome video in existence, either. Tyler broke out in a cold sweat just thinking about it.

A low, throbbing pain started to pulse at the base of his skull. He felt like he was in a tiny boat cresting a huge wave. Any second the wave would break and he would plunge down, down, down. "Thanks for the heads up, Ethan," he managed to say through lips that felt numb. "I owe you big time."

"Yeah, you do, but you know I still adore you, even if you were a shitty boyfriend. And seriously. You didn't hear any of this from me."

"Of course not. I've gotta go. My agent needs to know what's going on, even if she does end up killing me." Tyler took a deep breath and let it out slowly. "And Ryan, too. The sooner, the better. Anyway, give Charlie a kiss from me."

"I'll kiss Charlie, but not for you. Good luck. I'm not sure what I can do from my end, but I'll try to help you. I can't be too obvious, though. Stay strong, and keep in touch. Pervert."

"You're such an ass. Bye, Ethan."

After he'd hung up the phone, Tyler sat on the bed and tried to process. The video in question was from a security camera set up in his high school's weight room. It hadn't occurred to any of the boys that it would there, but equipment had been disappearing from the room and the administration wanted to find the culprits. Instead they saw more than any of them had ever wanted to see.

All three boys had been suspended, and Tyler spent the next three weeks at Bridges to Salvation, a camp in Wisconsin that guaranteed results for special cases like him.

Just thinking about Bridges made Tyler twitch, and he fell back on one of the few things he'd learned from his years of therapy that ever helped him. He sat still and counted slowly until his breathing evened out and his heart no longer raced. Then he got out of bed and went to wake his brother.

Ryan would fix this for him, or do his damnedest trying. He would deal with his agent and the press and the studio, and in Ryan's eyes Tyler would be a child again. It didn't matter what Tyler did. He'd never be anything besides the little brother who was broken. The one who always needed fixing because, unlike his brothers, perfection always eluded him. He'd never be anything but damaged in his family's eyes. Even his mother's, which were mirrors of his own.

He picked his phone back up. Before Alicia, before even Ryan, the person he needed to talk to was Purvi Kapoor, his PA and BFF.

Tyler: You know how I always say don't panic?
Purvi: You do? When?
Tyler: Shut up. It's time to panic.
Purvi: What the fuck is going on?
Tyler: TMZ has a sex video of me when I was in high school w/ 2 guys. I told you about the video, right? Well, it's out there. I'm boned. Utterly boned.
Purvi: What video? You never told me about a video. I'm gonna quit if you don't call me right fucking now.
Tyler: Later. Need to talk with Ryan first.
Purvi: Fine. I see how you are. See if I save your ass this time.
Tyler: But you love my ass.
Purvi: Truth. Call me as soon as you can. Have Ryan call me, too.

With Purvi semi-informed, Tyler went to Ryan's kitchen and flipped on the lights. He fiddled with the complicated coffee maker and eventually got it to start brewing a pot. Then, knowing he couldn't put it off any longer, went to go get Ryan up.

It turned out to be unnecessary. When Tyler approached his room, he saw a tiny sliver of light shining beneath the door. He knocked softly and Ryan called out for him to come in, his voice sounding wide awake.

Tyler found him still dressed, only his suit jacket and shoes removed. He sat on his still-made bed, his laptop open and balanced on his flat stomach. He closed it and set it aside.

"Shit, Ryan, it's after three. Do you ever sleep?"

"You're awake," Ryan pointed out.

"Yeah, about that," Tyler said. "I just got a call from Ethan."

Ryan scrunched his face up in thought. "Ethan. He works for one of the tabloids, doesn't he?"

"Yeah, *TMZ*. And, um, they found the video. Somehow. I thought it was destroyed, but Ethan's seen it because he fucking described it to me in gory detail. I'm fucked, Ryan. I'm well and truly screwed."

"What video?"

"*The* video. The one from high school. You know, with those two football players. Ethan says they're thinking about showing it, at least a censored version."

Ryan's eyes went cold. "Like hell they are! They can't show that. You were all underage. I need to send a cease and desist immediately. Christ. The timing on this is atrocious. Brad and Rachel are getting married in two weeks. How could you?"

Tyler started to count.

"I told you that you were going to regret that little stunt of yours one day and here we are, aren't we? Won't Dad just eat this up? He's going to be impossible. More impossible."

Tyler continued counting.

"Okay, first, I need to call Alicia. Hopefully she'll help us rally and not drop you as a client. Even with a cease and desist this is going to get out. People have seen it. It's sure to have already been leaked. This is a nightmare! Tyler, do you have any idea of the mess you've caused?"

Tyler stopped counting. There weren't enough numbers in the universe to center him tonight. "I was sixteen in that video, Ryan. Sixteen! No, I wasn't thinking at the time about how I was going to inconvenience you in the future. I was thinking about getting laid, period. Besides, I think I was punished enough for what happened back then. I don't need shit from you now. I get that this is awful. That's why I woke you up. Or came to tell you, since you weren't asleep. But no matter how much this fucks up your life, it's fucking up mine more, okay? I really don't need a lecture from you right now. I made coffee. The least you can do is be civil."

Ryan banged his head against the headboard twice, then sighed. "Okay, okay. You're right. I just... let me deal with this. Why don't you go back to bed? I need to get started on damage control and there's not much you can do right now, anyway. Thanks for telling me right away, though. That was the correct thing to do."

Tyler slunk back to his room, dismissed like a small child. *Oh, let the grown-ups deal with this. They know better.* Right.

Tyler would never be grown up in his brother's eyes. He'd always be the one who needed to be rescued. Like a fucking little princess.

Screw that.

If Ryan didn't need him, then he didn't need to stick around. He went back to his room and packed his suitcase. Then he hunted for the keys he'd need. They were in the credenza by the front entrance to the condo, neatly labeled. Tyler pocketed them, then went hunting for Oliver.

He found him on Ryan's lap, the little traitor. So much for escaping undetected. "I'm taking off," he said. "I just need to grab my cat."

"Where are you going that you need Oliver?" Ryan stood up, cradling the cat. He was a scowling golden giant and Tyler felt a small jolt of panic. Ryan looked so much like their father in that moment. His frown, his eyes, even his hair was the same. He couldn't help but flinch back a little. "Hey," said Ryan. "Are you okay?"

"Yeah, fine. I'm just feeling jumpy tonight." He hated this instinctual cringing. He hated the weakness that he couldn't erase. At the best of times his brother made him feel physically inadequate—next to Ryan, Tyler's hair was too dark, his skin too pale, his stature too short, his features too delicate. At the worst of times Ryan triggered that primitive portion of Tyler's brain that had once belonged to prey, and he wasn't sure if he wanted to flee or fight.

It wasn't Ryan's fault. He was overbearing and bossy, and he was every bit a product of his upbringing as Tyler was. It was something Tyler reminded himself, often while counting.

"I'm about as fine as anyone would be in my situation, but I can't just sit here while you fix this. I'll go crazy. I need some space."

"Where are you going? To Brad's?"

Tyler barked out a laugh. "To play third wheel with him and Rachel? No thanks."

"Then where? Right now, a hotel isn't a great idea."

Tyler dangled the keys he'd grabbed in front of Ryan. "I'm heading north to the lake house and I need to borrow a car. Which one can I take?"

"If you take my brand-new Porsche," Ryan said in a mild tone, "I'll kill you."

"Figured as much. Which one can I borrow and still live?" *Not the Volvo. Driving that stupid SUV makes me feel like a soccer mom.*

Ryan considered. "Take the Volvo."

Tyler groaned. "Fine."

"You know, you leaving the city is probably a good idea, now that I think about it, and the lake house is ideal. It's so remote I can't imagine anyone finding you there. But you can't…"

"I can't what? Crash the Volvo? I wasn't planning on it, although I might be doing you a favor there."

Ryan frowned. "Please try and take this seriously, Ty. If you go up there, I need to know that I can trust you to keep your shit together. That you won't do anything stupid."

It was on the tip of his tongue to goad Ryan more, to force him to spell out what he was worried about, but it was getting on four a.m. and was either too late or too early for bullshit. "I'll try," he said.

"Promise me," Ryan said. "I have enough on my plate without worrying about your safety."

"I promise," Tyler said, even as he was planning on how he would break that promise. "Will you help me put Oliver in his carrier?"

Ryan smiled and it was like sunshine breaking out on his face. "Sure. No problem."

Later, after he'd helped Tyler load Oliver, his suitcase, and a ton of groceries in the car, Ryan said, "I love you, you know."

"I know." He did, too, but that didn't mean Ryan's love was an easy thing. It was a thick, woolen blanket on an already hot day. "I love you, too." *And I'm going to break my promise at the earliest opportunity because that's what I do.*

"Oh, and Ty, you might run into an old family friend up there."

"Who?"

Ryan grinned. "Rachel's brother, Josh. I don't think he's heading up until the weekend, though. He's rented a place on Blue Lake, but I'm not sure where, so you may or may not see him. If you do, maybe you can invite him over for a drink or something. You know, for old time's sake."

Tyler's jaw dropped. "Josh Rosen, as in the boy who was pretty much your shadow for years?" Like Tyler could have ever forgotten who Josh was.

His brother blushed, as well he should. "Yeah. I thought, what with him becoming a part of the family and all, I'd ask him to be one of my groomsmen when Stephanie and I get married. While we were talking he mentioned going up north for a vacation."

Wow. Tyler knew Ryan could be insensitive, but asking your childhood secret boyfriend to be in your wedding party was pretty impressively douchey even for him. "And you thought that asking him to be your groomsman was a good idea why?"

Ryan looked confused. "He used to be my best friend and his sister is marrying our brother. Why wouldn't I ask him to stand up with me at my wedding?"

Tyler gave Ryan a long look. "Think about it," he said. "An answer may come to you." Then he got in the car and backed out of the parking space, leaving a frowning Ryan in his wake.

Chapter 2
Josh Wallows in Nostalgia

Friday, September 16th, 6:20 p.m.
On the road
Blue Lake, WI

As he drove toward Blue Lake, Josh kept looking for familiar landmarks, but not much was as he remembered it. Granted, he hadn't been here in over fifteen years, and on most of the trips he'd been a backseat passenger sandwiched between Brad and Tyler. Also, he'd spent most of his time on the trips studying Ryan's profile and the back of his head, living for the moments when, goaded by Brad kicking the back of his seat, Ryan turned around to glare at his brother. So, in general, he hadn't spent much time looking at the scenery. Later, when it had been him riding shotgun as Ryan drove or vice versa, it had always been dark by the time they'd arrived.

Even so, it felt like much of the area had changed over the intervening years. As Josh drove into the town, he noticed that alongside the small touristy shops that persisted, there were stores that looked brand-new. A Walmart, a pharmacy, Starbucks, and a plethora of fast food restaurants had joined what had once been the sole Dairy Queen. The old IGA was still there, though, and he pulled in to pick up groceries.

Even that hadn't escaped the march of progress. Instead of the bare-bones grocery store he remembered, it had reinvented itself into a gourmet food mart. One that did carry hot dogs, though, and marshmallows. Organic marshmallows, which somehow seemed wrong, but Josh threw them in the cart anyway.

After buying groceries and getting gas for the pontoon boat that came with the rental, Josh headed for his temporary home for the next eight days. The sun would set soon and he wanted to get there before it was fully dark. As he drove closer to the lake, he noticed familiar landmarks, ending with the massive pine that no one could bear to cut down and so they had paved the road around it. Just before the tree was the driveway for the Chadwicks' house. Josh resisted the urge to turn left down that driveway, and continued past the tree and down the road to where the drive for his rental was marked with a sign that read "Connolly Hollow."

Built along similar lines as the Chadwicks' place, the rental was far too big to be called a mere cabin, but it had a facade of redwood logs to resemble one.

He wandered around the house, feeling out of place. It was just familiar enough to be disorienting. This had been a colossally stupid idea. He'd thought coming here as an adult would jog him out of his juvenile unrequited obsession with Ryan Chadwick. Instead Josh felt lonely in a way he never felt when alone in his own home.

His sister had told him he should have booked himself passage on a gay cruise ship instead of, as Rachel put it, "sulking in solitary splendor in the middle of nowhere." Maybe it wasn't too late to change his mind. Josh tried to picture a ship full of hot, horny men, but instead of the idea being attractive, the thought of being trapped on a boat with so many strangers made him feel claustrophobic.

Scratch that, no gay cruises. Perhaps there was a happy medium between solitude and utter chaos, and while Josh tried to think of what that might be, he could sit on the dock, look at the lake, and drink himself into oblivion. Grabbing the bottle of whiskey he'd bought from the grocery store and not bothering with a glass, Josh walked out through the screened porch, down the sloping lawn, past a clump of pines, and onto the dock right as the sun hit the edge of the tree line. The view was pretty goddamned amazing, all orange and red and gold against black trees. It was as gorgeous as his memories. The only difference was that this time he was sitting on a dock all by himself.

Josh watched the last of the sun's rays reflected on the water of the lake while he sipped at the whiskey and waited for the stars to come out. The mosquitos were going to chase him inside soon, which was just as well, since getting drunk and falling into the lake wouldn't be nearly as much fun in his thirties as it had been at fifteen.

Memories crowded in on him, thick and fast. His, for lack of a better word, relationship with Ryan Chadwick had been a clandestine one, to say the least. Josh understood why, but it had still chafed. It was only during their summers that loosened, at least a little. He and Ryan would take off in the boat and explore down the chain of lakes that went on for miles, much of it surrounded by uninhabited land. Away from everyone's eyes, the unspoken rules between them relaxed. Not as much as Josh wanted, but he'd been willing to take whatever Ryan would give him; Josh had been that pathetically devoted. He still was, after a fashion. Even after all these years, some part of him refused to give up on his teenaged dream of living happily ever after with Ryan Chadwick, as impossible as most of his brain knew that dream to be.

It had started out innocently enough. Ryan's father, Peter Chadwick, discovered that his accountant's son was a whiz in math, the subject his own son was close to failing. It had it made sense to their respective fathers to have Josh become Ryan's tutor. The boys, while not friends, had known each other through meeting at company functions over the years where family was invited. Josh had been nervous as hell to start the tutoring, because Ryan had never previously given him the time of day. Thanks to Josh skipping kindergarten and going straight to first grade, Ryan was almost a year older than him, despite being in the same grade, and besides, Ryan was charismatic and popular and Josh was a gawky nerd. Nevertheless, right from the start Ryan had made an effort to be his friend. And in return, Josh, who was beginning to figure out that girls would never be his thing, experienced his first, devastating crush.

At first, Ryan didn't seem to show any improvement in algebra despite all of Josh's efforts. As much as he didn't want to disappoint his father for failing to help his boss's son or to end his excuse to see Ryan on a near daily basis, Josh didn't think that Ryan was ever going to be able to keep up with the workload.

"I think you should drop the honors class and take regular algebra instead. You're not doing your GPA any favors," he'd advised.

But Ryan refused to drop the class, insisting that he'd get it eventually, he just needed to try harder, and that he needed Josh, as well.

Josh, despite his misgivings, agreed to continue to try and tutor Ryan. He thought it was only a matter of time until Ryan did poorly enough that he'd be kicked out of the class, but he decided that if Ryan wanted him to keep on, he'd help as much as he could for as long as he could, just to be able to spend time with him.

Josh was caught totally off guard a few weeks later when Ryan proudly showed off his algebra test with a B- grade on it, which for him was a substantial improvement from the previous test. "It's all because of you!" he'd said and hugged Josh hard, then punched him on the shoulder.

Josh had punched him back, and soon they were rolling around on the floor of Ryan's room, pretending to fight and laughing their asses off. They ended up with Ryan pinning Josh down. "I am a math God! You're my bitch now." He grinned.

"Am not!" Josh struggled, but he was a head shorter than Ryan and at least twenty pounds lighter. He was good and pinned. "You weigh a ton. Get off."

Ryan leaned down so his face was about an inch from Josh's. "Admit it. You're my bitch. My own personal math bitch."

Josh popped a boner and, mortified, prayed Ryan wouldn't notice. "Get the fuck off me, asshole. One B- and you think you're king of the freaking universe."

"Admit it and I will."

"Fuck you."

Ryan shifted his weight. He had to notice Josh's erection. How could he not? "Say it."

Josh started to panic and reflexively lashed out. He bit Ryan's lip.

"Ow, dammit! What'd you do that for?"

Josh bucked upward. "Let me go, Ryan. I'm serious."

Ryan leaned even closer, his nose brushing against Josh's. "Are you going to bite me again, or kiss it and make it better?" He moved closer, his lips only a breath away from Josh's.

Josh groaned and pushed his mouth onto Ryan's. He had no idea what was going on. It was like he was suddenly living out a wet dream and he didn't know how to cope with that.

Ryan pulled his lips away from Josh after only a few seconds. "Say you're my bitch," he said, then licked at the place on his lip Josh had bitten.

"You're my bitch." Josh wished Ryan would stop licking his lip like that. It wasn't helping his erection at all. "Now get the fuck off me."

Ryan stared at him, then started laughing. He rolled off of Josh and laid on his back, gasping for breath between fits of laughter. "Okay, you win that one. You wanna play some *Doom*?"

Josh felt like he'd been run over by a large truck. "Um, sure."

And, just like that, Josh became Ryan's bitch. Ryan said jump and Josh asked if that meant he wanted a hand job. Or a blow job. Or anything, really. Irrevocable as day following night. He could see that now, with the clarity of age and time and too much whiskey. Now he needed to figure out how to stop that reaction in himself every time he thought of Ryan.

It would help if he knew why. *Why did you make me want you? Why didn't you just leave me alone?* He'd never asked Ryan for an explanation. He'd been too afraid to disturb the fragile balance between them. He'd accepted that Ryan would have a string of girlfriends but that Josh would be the one constant. Forever in the shadows, but always there. He'd told himself it was enough.

After high school Ryan went to Stanford, like his father and grandfather had before him, and Josh of course followed, glued as he was to Ryan's side no matter what girl he was with that week, but resentment roiled beneath the surface of their perfect friendship. Josh had become tired of pretending he wasn't in love, tired of pretending he wasn't gay, and tired of pretending he wasn't having sex with Ryan. Eventually, in his junior year, Josh had snapped and given Ryan an ultimatum: give up all the women, or give up Josh. Ryan had looked puzzled and said he had no idea what Josh was talking about. They were not a couple. They had never been a couple. They were friends and nothing more. Ryan had said Josh was his best friend, and always would be, but that was all. Never mind that Josh had just sucked him off.

"Friends don't give friends blow jobs," Josh had said, among other, more embarrassing things, like "I love you" and "I've always loved you" and "why don't you love me, too?"

Ryan had looked irritated and refused to discuss it. There was no breakup, but it felt that way to Josh. He was heartbroken, and no one knew except his sister and his therapist. He and Ryan didn't stop being friends, but they grew apart. It made sense, anyway. Ryan started law school and Josh medical school. Ryan stayed at Stanford, and Josh fled Ryan and returned home after he was accepted at the University of Chicago. Then there hadn't even been any shadows for Josh. There had been nothing, just one guy after another who was never Ryan enough for him.

Back in high school Ryan had made out with girls in the hallways, but it had been Josh he'd kissed first, in secret, so that they could practice "for the real thing," as Ryan had put it. Although to Josh, kissing Ryan was as real as it got. It would have been better, he reflected, to have never kissed Ryan in the first place. That had been a huge mistake, and he wished he could go back and turn his head. To pretend disgust. To have never shown what he desperately wanted but knew he could never have. Better to have nothing and not realize what you're missing than to get part of what you want but never, ever enough because you, yourself, are not enough.

With that depressing thought, Josh decided to go inside and drink until he passed out, preferably in one of the bedrooms. Tomorrow he would face the day, probably with a hangover, and start to finally deal with all this shit, but not tonight. As Josh stood, he saw a light on in one of the nearby houses. It looked like he wouldn't be alone this week. Unusual for late September, but not impossible. After all, he was there. People probably came up to see the leaves start to change, or to close up their homes before winter. Except... he counted the docks. That had to be the Chadwicks' place, and it was supposed to be empty.

Who's in there?

It wasn't any of his business.

But checking would be the right thing to do. The neighborly thing. Right. Because it might be Ryan in there.

It wouldn't be him.

But it might, and either way, I should check it out.

Josh walked unsteadily up the dock, the contents of the bottle he held sloshing as he swung his arm. He remembered how he and Ryan had stolen whiskey from the liquor cabinet and gotten wasted one night while sitting on the dock. Predictably, they'd fallen into the lake, first Ryan, and then Josh, for solidarity's sake. They'd somehow ended up under the dock. Josh had pushed Ryan against a piling and kissed him, the liquor making him bolder than usual. Nothing had mattered, not clinging lake weed or that he was trying to make out in tepid water up to his chest with his feet buried in silty muck. Touching and kissing Ryan with impunity had been enough.

Josh wondered what he'd do if it was Ryan over there. Probably make a complete fool of himself, especially considering he was already half hard from his trip down memory lane. Not that it mattered. It wouldn't be him.

But it might be.

That refrain (*it might be him it won't be him but it could be but it won't and even if it is he's engaged and won't be alone yes true but he might be*) pounded through Josh's head as he walked over the grass through the first neighbor's lawn, which needed to be mowed, to the next neighbor's lawn, which didn't. He was about to head towards the Chadwicks' back door when he noticed a hunched figure squatting at the end of their dock, and it wasn't Ryan. Too thin, too small, and the hair was entirely wrong.

Well, hell.

He didn't recognize the person, but it, presumably he, had unusually dyed hair. It was hard to tell in the twilight, but he thought it might be green or blue. The figure was bent over, doing something, but it was too dark to see what.

"Hey," Josh shouted, "whaddaya think you're doing?" That came out far louder than he'd planned, and rather slurred as well.

The figure jumped, then cursed. "Fuck. Fuck fuck fuck fuck!" He, it was obvious now the figure was male, grasped his arm and shot to his feet. "Oh, Jesus, oh fuck."

Josh hurried over, his sluggish brain grasping that something was not right but unable to ascertain what. Then he saw the blood. So much blood, coursing down the young man's arm from the bend of his elbow. He looked up at Josh, his eyes large dark holes that bore through him.

"Can you help…" the young man managed to get out before he passed out, slipping sideways off the dock into the lake.

Chapter 3
Tyler Does Not Die Buried in Beaver Shit

Friday, September 16th, 7:00 p.m.
In the lake
Blue Lake, WI

I *am going to die here,* Tyler thought, sinking down through murky lake water, *and they are going to find my body buried in beaver shit.*

He considered trying to swim to the surface, but it seemed like too much effort. Each of his limbs felt as if it weighed about a million pounds, and none of them were interested in coordinating with each other or his brain. *Brad is going to say I told you so and Ryan is going to wish I wasn't dead so he could kill me himself and Oliver, what will happen to Oliver?* That last thought made him flail harder, for all the good it did.

Then he was yanked upward and his head broke the surface of the water. A voice panted in his ear, "Breathe, damn you. Goddammit, breathe!"

Tyler tried, but all he could seem to do was make shallow liquidy gasps. He'd sucked half the lake into his lungs when he'd fallen in. He didn't quite remember how that had happened. The last thing he remembered was watching the sunset while carefully cutting his left arm in the bend where the slice would be fairly easy to hide. Yes, he had promised not to, but the last few days had been particularly shitty and he just needed one tiny, insignificant cut, or so he'd told himself, crouched on the dock. He'd had two seconds of peace, of lovely uncoiling within, then some asshole had scared the everlasting fuck out of him and he'd cut too deep. Way, way too deep and far too long. His little slice had ended up going halfway down his arm. The next thing he knew, he was immersed in icy-cold water. Presumably he'd passed out and had fallen off the dock. At least the asshole who'd scared the piss out of him had had the decency to fish him out of the lake.

"It's pretty shallow here. Can you stand? I need to get us out of the water, but you're going to have to help me."

When he wasn't shouting and scaring the living daylights out of him, the stranger had a great voice. Deep and resonate. A voice you could trust. Tyler shivered.

"I know, it's cold, but I've got to get this bleeding stopped before I can warm you up. Come on, let's get you out of this water."

With much splashing and cursing, his mysterious killer/savior got both of them out of the lake and onto the grassy bank. The guy pulled his soaked t-shirt over his head, displaying what appeared to be a drool worthy chest, although the dim light might be helping to hide a multitude of sins. Besides, he probably shouldn't be having carnal thoughts about his rescuer. Inappropriate. Oblivious to Tyler's mental drooling, the man wrung the water out of his t-shirt, then bound it tightly around Tyler's now sluggishly bleeding arm.

"My phone's somewhere in the lake. What about yours? Did you have it on you or is it back in the house?"

Tyler tried to speak but could only cough wetly. He tried to stop but ended up vomiting lake water and the remains of his dinner—tuna salad he now deeply regretted eating—onto the grass. What had the guy said? Something about his phone, maybe.

"Are you okay?"

Tyler gave the other man an incredulous look.

"I meant other than nearly drowning and bleeding to death. Never mind. I need to find a phone."

Tyler reached in his pocket and pulled his out. Water sheeted off it. "I think," he said, then coughed some more, "mine's fubar."

"Well, fuck. So much for calling an ambulance."

"No!" Tyler shook his head vehemently. "No hospital."

"Dude, you need more than Neosporin and a Band-Aid for that. This is ER worthy. My first aid kit is not gonna cut it." He stood up and hauled Tyler with him as if he weighed nothing. It made a treacherous part of Tyler's heart flutter. Dammit. He ordered himself to stop having inappropriate thoughts about his rescuer, even if he did have that gorgeous voice. And that chest. There was something familiar about him, too.

"I need a phone. Is there one in your house? There should be, but—" and there the guy broke off. "Fuck it. I'll just take you to my place. It's not that far."

"No," Tyler rasped. He wanted to lie down on the grass and nap, not hike who knew how far to some stranger's cabin. He spoke, his words interspersed with wheezy coughs. "There's. A phone. In the. House. Call. My brother. Not. 911. Promise me."

The guy cocked his head to the side, was silent for a few seconds, then nodded. "Okay, fine. That arm of yours is bad, but I think I can stop the bleeding. You're going to need a tetanus shot, but we can worry about that in the morning."

"We" and "in the morning." Huh. His rescuer was taking his role of savior pretty seriously. In the grand scheme of things, that was hilarious. "I'm not due. For that shot. Yet. Next year."

The guy gave him a skeptical look. "You sure?"

"Positive," Tyler said, and coughed some more.

He was beginning to think he knew that face. Although it felt like too big a coincidence, it was probably him and besides, Ryan had warned him. This was how Tyler's luck went—spectacularly good or bad and very little in between. It was him. It had to be.

It wasn't far up the lawn to the house, but it felt like a million miles to Tyler. After a few steps, the stranger—*who am I kidding, I know who he is*—put an arm around his back and half-carried him the rest of the way. He pushed the back door open and sat Tyler down at the kitchen table.

"Keep your arm on the table. It needs to be elevated. Is there a first aid kit, or anything I can use to stop the bleeding that's not my shirt?"

Tyler's brain felt like it wasn't firing on all cylinders, and his rescuer wasn't helping much. Tyler's suspicions had been confirmed by the bright kitchen light and in a heart-stopping manner. The other man was familiar, but not. He was a stranger, if a known one, and he was perfect, except for one detail.

"You should have glasses," Tyler blurted.

"Yeah, I should, but they're in the lake with my phone. I lost them at some point while retrieving you, but I'm only half-blind without them. I'll get by for now. Anyway, first aid kit? Bandages?"

He had dark hair that was starting to curl as it dried, thick eyebrows with a slight arch, dark eyes, and strong cheekbones. His lips were elegant and his nose was a bit of a beak, but it fit his face. He had scruff that was more than a five-o'clock shadow but less than a beard, and Tyler wanted to lick it and feel the texture of it on his tongue.

Then there was the guy's chest. In the bright kitchen light Tyler could see that his savior had a trim runner's look to him. He was lean and muscled and looked like he could knock out a marathon with ease. His pectorals were lightly covered in dark hair with tan nipples that were currently erect, presumably with cold. There was a bead of water clinging to one of them. Tyler watched as the water droplet trembled then ran down in an uneven path to his navel, where a trail of more dark hair disappeared into his soaking jeans.

Despite being cold, wet, desperately tired, and in pain, all Tyler wanted to do was eat this guy with a spoon. This was a complication he did not need.

"Don't faint on me again. You still with me?" asked Josh fucking Rosen. Nine years older since Tyler had last seen him but still super yummy, and intoxicated to boot, based on the smell of his breath. And the absolute best part was that while he recognized and remembered Josh, it was clear Josh had no clue who Tyler was. There was some irony for you. Or maybe not. Josh had never really noticed him before. No wonder he didn't recognize him now, looking as he did like a blue-haired drowned rat.

"I'm... yeah. Sorry. Zoned out."

"That's not surprising. So. First aid kit. Is there one?"

A shudder racked Tyler and his teeth began to chatter. He hadn't thought he'd cranked up the A/C before going out to the dock, but he must have because he was freezing. How a wet, shirtless, inebriated Josh wasn't dying of hypothermia was a mystery.

Josh glanced at Tyler's injured arm. "Okay, one thing at a time. That arm'll have to keep for another minute. My shirt seems to be doing the job for now, anyway. Let's get you warmed up, then I'll see what I can do for that arm and I'll call—"

"My brother," Tyler insisted.

"Yeah, not 911. I got it, I got it."

He walked off down the hallway toward the bedrooms like he owned the place. In a short amount of time Josh came back with an armful of blankets, towels, and a pillow, which he shoved under Tyler's injured arm, elevating it.

"You need to take your clothes off."

Tyler blinked at him. "What?" He couldn't have heard that correctly.

"You're going into shock. Blood loss. The chill from the lake. Normally I'd call 911 and have them haul you to the hospital, but I promised not to. Hell, I would drive you to the ER myself, but I'm nearsighted and a little intoxicated, so that's out because I don't want to kill us both. Besides, considering how far we are from the nearest hospital, it's possible you'd keel over on me from shock before we got you there if I don't triage you. So that's what we're doing. Triage. Which means wet clothes off and warm blankets on. I've already turned the heat on. I'm Josh, by the way, and I'll be your rescuer this evening." He flashed Tyler a brilliant, toothy smile. "First course tonight is me getting you undressed and dry. If it makes you feel any better about this, I'm a doctor."

Tyler snorted. *Yeah, a dermatologist. Also, a* little *intoxicated? Ha.* "I can. Do it. Myself," he said. It was a struggle to talk with chattering teeth and lungs that felt like they were filled with wet cement.

"How? You've only got one working arm."

Tyler frowned down at his cut arm, swathed tightly in a t-shirt with a growing bloodstain. He wiggled his fingers and was grateful they all seemed in working order. Even so, it hurt. He supposed that feeling pain was a good sign.

"How about this? I'll turn my back. Get undressed and try to dry off. If you need help, just say something."

"Just do. My shoes. I think I'm good. Otherwise."

Josh knelt by his feet. He untied Tyler's drenched shoes, then pulled them off along with his sodden socks. He looked up at Tyler through his spiky eyelashes. "You sure you don't need help?"

Is Josh fucking Rosen flirting with me, or am I hallucinating? Of the two, hallucinations seemed more plausible. Maybe hallucinations were a symptom of shock. "I'm good."

"Okay, no problem. Yell if you need me." Josh stood up and turned his back to Tyler.

While it was difficult to do mostly one-handed and while shivering, Tyler managed to shimmy out of his soaked jeans and underwear. He let them fall with a wet plop onto the tile floor. The shirt was a little harder but he managed it, letting that fall on the floor, too. He grabbed a towel and started drying off.

"Still doing okay?"

"Fine. Still cold. Better, though." He took another towel and wrapped it around his waist, then pulled a cotton blanket around himself. "Okay. You can turn around now."

Josh turned around and a loopy grin spread across his face. "Your color already looks better and you're starting to lose that frozen popsicle look." Josh toweled Tyler's hair until it was only damp, then tucked a comforter around him. "So. First aid kit? Where should I look?"

"There's a couple of gauze pads. And tape. On the counter. For... you know. But my brother's a doctor. Pretty sure he's got more stuff in his room, maybe. Second door on the left."

Josh paused. "Your brother's a doctor. Of course! Damn, I'm so stupid. I mean, it's been a weird night, but I still should have realized it was you, even with the hair. I thought you were some sort of squatter or something and that's why you didn't want me to call 911."

Maybe it was the blood loss, but Tyler had a hard time following that. He focused on the most cogent point. "A squatter?" He could feel his hair standing up in damp clumps on his head and tried to finger comb it into submission.

"I'm sorry, it was a stupid mistake, but you look..." Josh paused, clearly trying for a diplomatic answer, "not like yourself. But, wow! You're little Tyler, all grown up, aren't you? I didn't recognize you with the blue hair. It's definitely different. Is it for a role?"

"Yeah, it's from my last movie. I was an elf. I'll have the blue bits cut off before the wedding. Promised Brad. Is it too Cookie Monster, you think?" Little Tyler. Right. Story of his life.

"Wrong shade for Cookie Monster. He's sort of your basic blue. Your hair is all Caribbean ocean. I think it's appropriately aquatic, Captain Negativity. So. Do you remember me? I haven't seen you in a long time."

All Caribbean ocean. Oh, my. That was... well, something. From anyone else that would for sure be flirting, but this was Josh Rosen, his brother's lovesick former shadow. Flirting was extremely unlikely, seeing as he was still pining for Ryan, at least according to Brad. And even if Josh was flirting with him, hooking up with him would be a terrible idea. Although... No. Terrible idea. Period. Josh belonged to Ryan, whether Ryan wanted him or not. That's just how things were and had always been.

His mind went back to one summer seventeen years ago. He'd been outside playing, pretending his G. I. Joes were hunting through the jungle rather than just overgrown grass. He'd been behind one of the large maple trees and out of sight of the house. He was Lying Low, because Dad was up for the weekend and it was best to be neither seen nor heard when he was around.

Ryan and Josh came flying out of the house, laughing. They were talking, but Tyler couldn't hear what they were saying. Then they ducked into the boathouse.

Tyler got up and followed them. If they were going to take the boat out, he wanted to go, too. Ryan had promised he'd get to go the next time they went out.

He pushed the door open and almost said something, but didn't. Instead of getting the boat ready to take out, his brother leaned against the wall, his friend kneeling between Ryan's spread legs. His hand pulled the waistband of Ryan's swim trunks down.

Tyler must have made some sound because Ryan's head turned his way. "Tyler! What do you want?" He pulled up his trunks and jumped away from Josh, who stood up and hovered behind him.

"You promised you'd take me out on the boat."

"Yeah, right, I did. Okay, let's go."

Josh bit his lip. "Is he... going to tell?"

"Tyler won't tell Dad anything, will you, Ty?"

Tyler huffed in offended disgust. As if.

"Seriously, you can't tell anyone. Promise me. If you want me taking you out on this boat ever again, you can't say anything. Not. One. Word."

Tyler rolled his eyes. Who was he going to tell? Mom knew but pretended she didn't. Brad knew, too. The only one who didn't know was Dad, and Tyler of all people wasn't going to be the one who snitched to him. Ryan was being dumb.

He mimed zipping his lip anyway because he really wanted to go out on the boat.

"Okay, good. Go grab your life jacket."

It wasn't until years later that Tyler understood what had been going on in the boathouse. The memory was tainted with seeing his brother's dick—seriously gross—but he'd be a liar if he said he'd never had fantasies involving boathouses, only instead of Ryan leaning against the wall with Josh on his knees it had been him looking down into Josh's eager eyes.

Tyler looked up, met the dark eyes he'd seen in his youthful fantasies, and tried not to think about boathouse blow jobs. "Dr. Josh Rosen, I presume," he said with a small smile.

"Yeah," Josh said. "At your service. Why don't I go and see what I can find?"

Tyler nodded and watched him walk back down the hall. Things weren't going the way they were supposed to. First, he'd promised not to cut himself. Then he'd promised himself that it would be just a tiny one, in an inconspicuous spot, and he'd do it on the dock, so he wouldn't make a mess. It had seemed like a good plan. Now everything was fucked all to hell and back.

Captain Negativity. Ha! He was really Captain Cautiously Optimistic Because This Time Might Be Different. Or perhaps Lieutenant No, Wait, I Can Fix This. Only those weren't particularly catchy. Maybe Corporal Let's See How I Can Fuck Things Up This Time.

Tyler was still trying to come up with a more appropriate title than Captain Negativity when Josh walked back into the kitchen, humming. He had changed into a dry pair of sweats and a t-shirt. Brad's, probably, based on the Cubs' logo. "Here," he said, and thrust a pile of clothing at Tyler. It looked like similar sweats and a t-shirt, with a pair of thick socks on top. "I'll even turn my back while you get in them." Then he put two tablets on the table. "Found some Tylenol, too. It's not much, but it'll be better than nothing for the pain. I couldn't find any first-aid supplies, though."

"Thanks. You've been great." Tyler was loath to drop the warm blankets wrapped around him, but couldn't figure out how to get dressed any other way. At least the clothes were relatively easy to put on, even with only one good arm.

"It's all part of the service we provide here, sir," Josh said, walking to the sink and filling a glass with water. He dropped his voice into a loud whisper. "I'm angling for a big tip."

Wait. Was that a double entendre? Hell, in anyone else that might have been a single entendre. But, no. This was Josh, and he was making a very slight joke to lighten the mood, that was all. Which, honestly, was almost worse than flirting.

Tyler had packed away his crush on Josh years ago, relegating him into Ryan's faithful shadow, Brad's fastidious roommate, and Rachel's fussy brother. Josh had a permanent stick up his ass and loved a man who would never love him back. He was sad and pathetic, like that weird bachelor uncle everyone avoids at family reunions. Tyler had forgotten Josh was also kind of funny and charming, in a daffy way, not to mention hot. Way fucking hotter than he had any right to be.

Tyler felt unreasonably irritated that no one prepared him for this version of Josh. "You can turn around now." He sounded sulky even to his own ears and tried to temper his tone. "I can't do the socks one-handed, though, and I need you to tie the drawstring on the sweats."

Josh walked back with the glass of water in his hand. He put it on the table next to the tablets, then pulled the ties at the waist of the pants. "You can let go," he said. "I've got this." Then he cinched them as tight as they would go and tied the cord into a neat bow. That done, he knelt at Tyler's feet again. "You can take the pain pills while I put on your socks."

Tyler didn't want to take the medication. The pain in his arm wasn't ideal, but somehow it felt deserved. Left to his own devices he wouldn't have bothered, but fighting Josh on this didn't seem worth the effort. He swallowed the pills, then drank the entire glass of water. He hadn't realized how thirsty he was. It tasted fantastic.

Meanwhile, Josh took his feet, rubbed them briskly, then encased each one in a sock. That shouldn't have been sexy but it kind of was. Josh had great hands. He picked the comforter off the floor, then stood and pulled it around Tyler's shoulders.

"Okay. Let's take a look at that arm, shall we?"

Chapter 4
Josh Gets a Tad Hysterical

Friday, September 16th, 7:18 p.m.
The Chadwicks' lake house
Blue Lake, WI

"Okay, let's take a look at that arm, shall we?"

Josh didn't notice the marks at first; he was too busy studying the crooked slice running from the bend of Tyler's elbow down his forearm to register the neat horizontal scars, and, thanks to the whiskey, he was having a hard time focusing on anything for more than a few seconds. He did his best to concentrate, though, because this was important. The bleeding had mostly stopped, which was a relief. Then, just as changing your eyes' focus turns a duck into a rabbit or two faces into a vase, the lines pushed past the fresh wound and were the only thing Josh could see.

"We need to get this cleaned up," Josh said, tearing his gaze away from the scars. He looked at Tyler's eyes. They were an unusual non-color that was blue and green and gray all at once. Perhaps under other circumstances they would be nice eyes, but right now they were just glassy and unfocused, reflecting back at him like still water. "Tyler?"

The eyes blinked at him. "Yeah?"

"We need to get this cleaned up," he repeated. "I can either scrub it with soap and water or I can hold your arm under running water for several minutes. Your choice. The running water will hurt less, but you'll have to stand by the sink. You up for that?"

"I'll take the sink option. I can stand. I cut my arm, not my ankle," Tyler groused, then he started hacking up a lung. He stood up, still coughing, and staggered to the sink. He gripped the edge with his good hand bent over it. His coughing turned into gagging, then he vomited into the sink.

Josh really wanted to get him to an ER, promise or not. The kid was a mess, and there were those lines. Too many to be mere accidents, and he hadn't even seen the other arm closely.

This wasn't the first time Josh had seen lines like those. He was a dermatologist working in a practice whose patients mostly lived in the affluent North Shore. Yes, he had his psoriasis and eczema and melanoma cases, but his bread-and-butter patients were the acne-prone teens brought to him by parents who demanded nothing short of perfection in everything from their macchiatos to the smoothness of their children's skin. It wasn't common, but he knew exactly what those lines were. However, right now they didn't matter, except to explain how Tyler had managed to cut himself while sitting on the dock. Josh could worry about the lines later. Or never. It wasn't any of his business.

Tyler filled a glass sitting by the sink with tap water and drank it down. He coughed a few more times, but seemed better. "Okay, Dr. Rosen," he said. "Let's do this thing."

Josh turned the faucet on and ran it until the water was blood-warm, then placed Tyler's wounded arm under the stream. "Don't move until I tell you. I'm timing you. Where's the phone?"

Tyler gestured with his head. "Right next to the fridge."

It was cordless. Thank heaven for small favors. Josh took the phone and walked into the living room where he could keep an eye on his patient while still being far enough to talk without being overheard. The running water would help, too.

Josh wanted, if he was being honest, to call up Ryan and yell at him, which was beyond pointless. Ryan was Tyler's brother, not his keeper. Slight as he was, Tyler was a big boy. But some of those marks were very faint and thus quite old. He wondered how long ago that had started and why no one had thought to warn him.

Why would anyone warn me? It's none of my business. Okay, good point. Besides, he couldn't call Ryan because, like most people, Josh had only a handful of phone numbers memorized: his own cell, work, his parents, and his sister.

Brad it was, then, and just as well. Yelling at Ryan would be temporarily satisfying but ultimately unhelpful. Brad was the one he needed.

It took several rings, but Rachel eventually picked up. "Hello? Fair warning, if you're trying to sell me something I'm just going to hang up."

"Rachel, it's Josh. Are you with Brad? I need to talk to him."

"Josh, what's up? Why aren't you calling me from your cell?"

"Long story. Can you get Brad?"

"Sure," she said. "He's right here."

A few seconds went by, then Brad's voice was in his ear. "What's up, sweet cheeks?"

Josh clenched his teeth. Right after Rachel, Brad was his best friend, but he still managed to grate on Josh's nerves on a regular basis. Josh loathed that ancient nickname, and Brad knew it, which was why he called him that whenever he felt he could get away with it.

Josh bit back a caustic remark. He wanted to yell at someone in the worst way, and Brad was a convenient target, but now was not the time. He squinted at the clock. Only a minute and a half had gone by. For some reason, it seemed longer. Tyler must have been thinking the same thing because he called out, "Am I done yet?"

"No. Stay put until I tell you."

Over the phone line Brad said, "Josh, why are you calling from our lake house's phone, and why does it sound like you're not alone?" Even over the phone, Josh knew that asshole was waggling his eyebrows suggestively.

For a few seconds he considered saying, "I've shacked up with your baby brother," just to get the inevitable reaction, but the situation wasn't funny. The problem was that the sobering effect of the cold lake water was wearing off but the whiskey remained in his bloodstream. Josh reminded himself he was a responsible adult.

"I'm calling from your lake house because there's been an accident. Tyler cut his arm and it's pretty bad."

There was no immediate reply from the other end.

"Brad? You still there?"

"Yeah," he said. All humor was gone from his tone. "How bad is pretty bad?"

"There's a fairly long gash on his forearm. It was my fault, though."

Brad barked out an unamused laugh. "Did you stab him?"

"What? No. What the fuck, Brad?"

"Didn't think so. Did you put a fucking razor in his hand and tell him to carve a new line?"

Josh flinched at Brad's tone. "No, but I did startle him. He was on the dock. I saw him there and didn't know who it was and shouted…"

"This isn't your fault, Josh. Not even fucking close. Does it need stitches?"

"Probably. Yes. Um. He kind of passed out for a second. Most likely shock, or maybe because I startled the hell out of him. Anyway, he fell off the dock and into the lake."

Brad started to swear. Josh let him run his course, then continued. "I got him out, but he inhaled a ton of water and he's coughing a lot. I got the bleeding mostly stopped and warmed him up. The house is currently like a fucking sauna but he's still shivering, which worries me. I have him holding his arm under the tap right now to clean it. He won't let me call 911, and I can't drive him to the hospital because when I jumped in the lake to rescue him, I lost my glasses, along with my phone. I just got that phone, too. Anyway, I need help and there's nothing here. No antibiotics, no saline, and I can't even drive to a fucking pharmacy because, newsflash, not only am I blind but I've drunk way too much shitty whiskey and I'm kind of drunk."

"Only kind of?" Brad asked.

"Shut up, I'm not done. Meanwhile, I mention 911 and your brother freaks out." Josh paused, realized he was getting hysterical, and tried to collect himself. "Even if I could see well enough to drive him to the hospital and wasn't risking a DUI to do it, I don't know how I could get him to go, other than knocking him unconscious and stowing him in my trunk, which would probably raise a few eyebrows. I need your help."

"Okay, Josh, you need to calm down."

"I am calm!"

"No, you're not," said Tyler and Brad in unison. It was eerie.

"Take a deep breath," said Brad.

Josh drew air through his nose then exhaled through his mouth a few times. "Okay," he said. "I'm okay."

"You can't call 911 and you can't take him to a hospital. The publicity for Tyler would be a nightmare. Yeah, I know, 'HIPAA,' but someone will talk. Someone always does, and before you know it, it'll be all over the internet. For now, just butterfly him up and wrap it in gauze. That stuff should all be in the house. Look in the guest room bathroom cabinet. Then when I get there, I'll sew him up."

"Sew him up? You can't give him stitches here. The area is far from sterile. Are you crazy?"

"This is not my first rodeo, Josh. You're bound to have seen his scars. There're more, all of them in places a lot harder to work with than his arm. I've sewn him back together so many times that he's practically my own personal voodoo doll. The ER isn't always the best solution, you know?"

"No," said Josh flatly. "I don't."

"He'll be fine as long as he doesn't bleed out before I get there."

"The bleeding's already slowed down a lot." Josh dropped his voice and walked farther away so Tyler wouldn't overhear him. "I got it all over me, by the way. Should I be concerned?"

"Tyler's a notorious man-whore, but no, he's fine, or at least he was the last time I had him tested, which was about a week and a half ago when he got into town. He says I'm worse than Ryan for fussing, as he puts it, but excuse me for making sure my brother stays healthy. I'd still wash it off, though, because, well, blood."

"Yeah, thanks. That would have never occurred to me," Josh said.

"You're the one who called me all freaked out. Josh, don't worry. We're on our way. Do you have a second pair of glasses or contacts or whatever? We can stop by your place and get them."

In the background, he could hear Rachel's voice. "Did he lose another pair of glasses? Tell him that I've got one of his old pairs here for emergencies."

"You get that?" Brad asked.

"It's hard to mistake my sister's dulcet tones. Thank her for me.

She's better prepared than I am, as usual."

Brad laughed again, but this time with genuine humor. "Are you nuts? Her head is swollen enough as it is."

"I heard that! You tell him my head is not swollen, Josh!"

"How long until you guys can get here?"

Brad grunted. "This time of night traffic won't be terrible, but I'll have to stop by a pharmacy to get a bunch of stuff. I'll write a few scripts for Ty and bring them with me. So, seven hours if we're lucky, eight if we're not."

It was a just a bit after eight, so Brad and Rachel probably wouldn't get there until around four a.m. "Bring food when you come. There's a Taco Bell in town. Rachel knows what I like. If I have to cope with this bullshit then you owe me tacos. Lots of tacos."

"You got it, man. Thanks for saving my baby brother. I'd ask you to give him a good smack for me, but you're way too nice. See you soon."

Josh hung up the phone and walked back into the kitchen.

"Am I done yet?" Tyler asked. He looked ready to collapse.

"A little longer would be better. Let me see." Josh went to stand behind Tyler and cradled his left arm. Cleaned of blood, it was easy now to see how Tyler had started a shallow horizontal cut that jumped, then went vertical and cut much deeper.

So, yeah, I didn't put the razor in his hand or tell him that cutting his arm on a dock in plain sight was a good idea, but it feels like it's my fault. If I hadn't drunk so much. If I'd just kept to myself. If I hadn't been wishing for the impossible. This is my fault.

"It's not your fault, Josh."

"What?" Tyler wasn't psychic, was he?

"I heard you in there, talking with Brad. Not all of it, but enough. Stop blaming yourself. You saved me."

"Are you sorry I saved you?" Josh wanted to take back the words as soon as they flew out of his mouth. What kind of question was that to ask someone who might be suicidal?

"Fuck, no! I hadn't planned on shuffling off this mortal coil tonight, believe it or not, and I appreciate you fishing me out of the lake. Thank you."

"You're welcome," Josh said next to Tyler's ear. "I wish it hadn't been necessary."

He felt Tyler's muscles tighten under his arm. It was like he was supporting a marble statue. Josh wished he could look at Tyler's face but he was afraid that if he let go, Tyler would fall over and shatter into a million pieces.

"I swear to God that this is taking forever. I should have picked the scrub option."

"I can still do it if you want."

Tyler tried to speak and started coughing instead. He gripped the edge of the sink with his right hand and rode it out. As the coughing fit calmed he took slow, deep breaths. "Jesus, I think inhaling all that water might be worse than this stupid gash in my arm. This sucks."

"Please tell me I'm done now," said Tyler.

"Yeah, it's been long enough." He reached around Tyler and shut off the faucet. "Hold your arm over the sink. I'm going to dry it off for you." He grabbed a few paper towels from the roll hanging under the cabinet and blotted Tyler's arm dry, being careful to avoid the area with the wound. Then he led Tyler back to the kitchen table, sat him down, and propped up his arm.

He raided the guest bathroom and found all the promised items, plus a half-full bottle of Betadine. Feeling somewhat better able to deal with the day's events armed with familiar medical supplies, Josh swabbed Tyler's arm with the Betadine, used every single butterfly bandage in the box to keep the wound closed, topped that with several gauze pads, then wrapped the whole thing with an entire roll of gauze.

"Okay, that'll have to do. Now guess what time it is."

Tyler had been passive under Josh's ministrations, sitting still with his eyes closed as if he was squeamish, which seemed incongruous for someone with that many scars. Now he opened his eyes just a slit. "Nap time?" he asked. "I vote for nap time."

"Even better. It's snack time!"

Chapter 5
Tyler Is Cranky and Needs a Nap

Friday, September 16th, 8:15 p.m.
The Chadwicks' lake house
Blue Lake, WI

Tyler tried not to feel things very much. Feeling things was dangerous and never worked out well for him. He had his way of dealing, though. Not necessarily a good way, and at some point, he'd have to come up with something better. Probably sooner rather than later, but for now, it would do. It wasn't perfect, but the last thing Tyler was interested in was perfection. He'd seen the price Ryan paid for their father's version of perfection, and it had soured him on the concept permanently. Perfection was fine for other people, but not him. Today, however, had been about as far from perfect as one could get, unless you were going for perfectly wrong, perfectly awful, or perfectly fucked-up.

He'd spent the day doing very little, conspicuously not looking at the internet. He'd felt a lurch of worry with each new notification on his phone, answering only texts from Ryan and Purvi.

Purvi: You hanging in there?
Tyler: More or less. Is it really bad? No, I don't want to know. Never mind.
Purvi: You're such a fucking baby. Put on your big girl panties and google yourself.
Tyler: Come on, just tell me. It's your job to assist me. Assist already.
Purvi: You said I was on vacation. Besides, you freaked out the last time I tried to tell you. You wanna know, you look.
Tyler: Is it bad?
Purvi: Define bad
Tyler: FUCK FUCK FUCK FUCK FUCK FUCK FUCK FUCK FUCK FUCK
Purvi: That's it. I'm done
Tyler: No, wait.
Purvi: DONE
Tyler: WAIT. YOU CAN'T QUIT ME.
Purvi: Sure, I can. You're no Heath Ledger.
Tyler: Good. Heath Ledger is dead. I'm merely fucked.
Purvi: Go away, Tyler. I'm on vacation.

Tyler: YOU'RE SWIMMING IN MY FUCKING POOL, PURVI!
Purvi: You need to chill. It's going to be fine.
Tyler: No, it's not.
Purvi: Yes, it is.
Purvi: I love you, Ty.
Tyler: You're the only one who does
Purvi: This is true. Tell Big O I said hi and give him pets from me.
Tyler: You only love me for my cat.
Purvi: Duh

Eventually he gave even that up and put his phone on "do not disturb" and stuck it in his back pocket. If it was truly important, Purvi would get ahold of Ryan, and Ryan would call the lake house phone.

He'd held out for a few more hours, but the tension coiled within him became too much and he'd gotten a shiny new blade out of his secret stash, then he'd gone outside to the dock to watch the sun go down.

He'd almost gone back inside, promise and skin still intact, but that brand-new blade called to him. It was so sharp he'd barely feel the slice. All he'd feel was blood trickling down his arm and release as everything inside him clenched tight like a fist let go.

Only that hadn't happened. Things had gone awry, to put it mildly. This wasn't the first time, either, which is why Ryan had given him that preachy little warning (that of course he'd ignored) back in Chicago. This was the first time that he'd nearly simultaneously bled out and drowned, though, which had to be a life achievement of some sort. Tyler and accidents were two things that went together a little too well, but tonight had been a whole new level on the catastrophe scale. Usually he just cut a little deeper than he'd intended and needed stitches. Or, that one time, a blood transfusion.

Sometimes he got a bit too Zen while bleeding and forgot to stop it. It wasn't intentional. Most of the time he coagulated all on his own, but there were a few times where things had gotten away from him. He knew what he was doing was risky and foolish and all kinds of wrong, but it worked for him, and he was still alive to do it. That was the important thing.

As vices went, Tyler figured it could be worse. He didn't drink to excess, smoke, or take illegal drugs, and was a firm believer in condom usage. He didn't gamble, spend money like water, or cheat on his taxes. He always wore his seatbelt, avoided trans fats, and exercised regularly.

Besides, he was going to give up the cutting. One of these days, soon, he would find a psychiatrist he didn't hate and he would show up at appointments he made and he would get his problem fixed, for good this time. But that would have to come later, after this current crisis was over.

Tyler didn't have the wherewithal to deal with any of his personal failings right now. He was too tired and his head throbbed with a sick headache. He could barely deal with his current circumstances. He would deal with everything else later, after he'd slept, gotten rid of the pounding in his head, and was properly alone. He couldn't think with Josh buzzing around him.

He wanted Josh to leave. He wanted the cavalry not to be on their way. He wanted to crawl into bed and maybe not wake up for several days. He wanted to go back in time and fix things. He wanted to cut himself. Just a little.

Tyler felt cheated by what had happened. He hadn't had a chance for the catharsis he normally experienced. He'd had one small moment of uncoiling, then just fear and pain and being hauled out of the lake. He felt wrung out and washed up and still ready to snap, and Josh was not helping. Oh, he thought he was. Josh had put on a brave face and was zooming around the house like a cross between a 1950's-era housewife and a bumblebee on meth. It was exhausting just to watch.

Plus, there was the flirting, which might or might not be in Tyler's imagination. Josh kept standing too close and touching him. It was pushing him over toward the other thing Tyler sometimes did to deal with stress, as appalling an idea as that was right now. Nearly as terrible as bleeding out while drowning in a beaver shit infested lake, but not bad enough to keep his mind from thinking about it.

If it weren't for his brother and soon to be sister-in-law's imminent appearance, Tyler would have offered to blow Josh by now just to get him to stop. As attractive as he was, it would've been no hardship for Tyler to take that bullet, but no. While there was more than enough time for a blow job in and of itself, they didn't have time for the sheer volume of seduction it would no doubt take to get Josh out of his sweat pants. He seemed so unaware of what he was doing. Tyler could imagine that conversation.

"Josh, I'm super stressed right now and you're kind of driving me crazy with all the touching and such, so could I please suck your dick? I really think that would help."

"No, Tyler. I'm sorry to have led you on. I'm only attracted to huge, hulking blond men who claim to be straight. I'm not into skinny, blue-haired, femme former twinks, especially almost-famous ones who are getting a little too old to play teenagers convincingly."

"Seriously? Because I am offering one blow job, free of charge, just to cut the tension. Also, skinny? I am not skinny. I am slender. Svelte. Lithe, motherfucker. As for aging, old man, you are one red convertible away from a midlife crisis."

"It's a nice offer, Tyler, but I'm fine. I'll be over here, fantasizing about your brother while I come up with new ways to torture you while we wait for our *siblings to show up. How does that sound?"*

Ugh. A world of no.

Tyler thought he had enough energy to suck Josh's dick, especially if he could do it sitting in this chair. But talking him into it? No. That was not on tonight's menu.

No blade. No sex. What did that leave?

For him, tonight? Orange juice followed by Oreos and a lot of silent counting. It made him feel stabby.

"I need to lie down," Tyler said, trying to keep his tone pleasant.

"You should eat more cookies. Or at least drink more juice," chirped Josh.

Oh, dear God. Death might have been preferable. It certainly would have been more peaceful. "Drinking orange juice with Oreos is inhumane. I'm pretty sure it's in violation of the Geneva Convention."

Josh started ticking points off on his fingers. Tyler got the impression he did that a lot. He seemed like the kind of guy who enjoyed making lists and crossing items off as they were accomplished. "One, you have no milk, and speaking of violations, since this is Wisconsin, being out of milk is probably at least a misdemeanor, if not an outright felony. It's a good thing your brother's an attorney. Two, you need to replace fluids and calories. Losing blood is one hell of a weight loss program and you don't have any to spare. Three, if you'd like something else to eat, just tell me and I'll find it."

"Are you done?" Tyler sounded bitchy even to his own ears, but he'd ceased to care. He wasn't happy hearing that the pushy doctor thought he had no weight to spare losing. It hit a little too close to his imagined conversation with Josh for comfort.

Josh looked a tad hurt at Tyler's tone. "Sure, I guess."

"Well thank fuck for small favors. Look, I really don't want to come off as ungrateful, but I'm tired and sore and no, none of that is your fault, and aside from the orange juice and Oreos you've been a peach. But right now, I would dearly love for you not to be here. It's not you, it's me."

Tyler gave Josh his smile with knives in it but that didn't seem to faze him, which was a shame. It worked on most people. Maybe Josh was too drunk to notice.

"Tyler, are you breaking up with me?" Josh gave him an exaggerated and downright pathetic version of sad puppy eyes. It was embarrassing to witness, and almost endearing in its own terrible way.

I guess we're back to flirting, which is weird but still better than you mothering me. Tyler adopted a regretful tone. "Yes. I hate to break this to you, but I've fallen for Ramon, the pool boy."

Josh pursed his damned sexy lips. "Really. The pool boy. Not Simone, the saucy French maid?"

That threw him for a second. He wasn't sure how Josh could be unaware Tyler had a profound attraction to dick, especially considering that he'd all but propositioned Josh at that one summer picnic when he was sixteen. It was depressing to think that he'd been so insignificant that Josh didn't even remember it. Although maybe that was for the best. In retrospect it was exquisitely embarrassing, and the first of many incidents that made his sixteenth year his annus horribilis.

It was probably also too much to expect that Josh paid any attention to his public persona, such as it was, because even without him being officially out, it should have been obvious to anyone with a grain of sense he was gay. Granted, he'd gone out to events with women, mostly quasi-famous actresses and models. Some had been at the studio's urging and some because he was friends with them. He'd also been photographed with various men, including his ex Ethan, and most recently Chris Steward, who played the rather virile questing prince in *The Silver Arrow*. Chris was straight, more's the pity, but a fun guy to hang out with, and there had been a few online gossip sites that speculated on whether he and Tyler were a couple. While there was rampant speculation about Tyler's sexuality in the tiny corner of the universe that existed as his fanbase, no one meeting him in person would get the impression he was anything even approaching straight. Still, it had seemed safer for him not to be publicly out and let people draw whatever conclusions they wanted.

Thanks to the fucking video, any lingering ambiguity regarding his sexuality would be gone, and he was going to be famous, just not for the right reasons. Tyler's stomach gave an uneasy flip at the thought. He felt all the things careening beyond his control and he grasped for anything solid. He couldn't cut and Josh was beyond his current meager powers of seduction, so he started to count while Josh looked at him, curious yet patient. He stared into Josh's dark eyes and found he didn't have to count very high before he was able to speak in a light, flirtatious tone.

"No," he said. "Definitely not Simone. It's pool boys all the way down."

Josh raised his eyebrows. "I thought that was turtles."

Tyler felt his lips twitch in an involuntary smile. "Not for me," he said.

"So, what does Ramon have that I don't?" asked Josh, deciding to be a good sport and play along.

"Ramon lets me sleep."

"Ramon sounds like he's no fun, but if you insist, I'll make you a bed on the couch."

Tyler leaned his head back and stared at the ceiling. He counted to ten. "I have a bed. It's in my bedroom. Where one usually finds a bed."

"Um, yeah. About that. I think the couch would be better. More convenient."

This time Tyler counted to twenty. "You aren't going to leave me alone, are you?"

"No, I'm not. You need to be monitored, so it's either nap on the couch in the living room where I can sit comfortably, read a book, and we can pretend that we're just being companionable, or you can lie down in your bedroom and I can sit on the side of your bed and stare at you."

"You win. Couch it is."

"Excellent choice, sir. And might I also recommend finishing the juice while you're waiting?"

It appeared that the obsequious server was back. "Bite me."

"Sir is probably hypoglycemic, and therefore cranky," Josh said as he gathered up the blankets and comforter.

Cranky. Like he was a little kid. It made Tyler want to lash out, but he restrained himself because he was not, in fact, a toddler. "Fine. Fine. I give. I'll drink the fucking juice." Tyler picked up the glass and finished it off. "There. You can stop nagging now."

"You still cold?"

"No, Mother. Actually, it's pretty warm in here."

"Oh, thank God. I've been sweating like a pig waiting for you to warm up. I'm turning down the thermostat." Josh bustled about, finishing with laying blankets down on the couch and retrieving more pillows from one of the bedrooms. "Okay. Your bed's ready."

Tyler stood and there Josh was, right beside him. "I can walk twenty feet."

Josh didn't reply. He didn't back off, either. After Tyler lay down, Josh fussed about him, making sure his arm was elevated and that he was sufficiently propped to facilitate an adequate oxygen supply. Then he went back into the kitchen. A short time later Tyler heard the washing machine start, and Josh came back. "You need anything?" he asked.

"No. You are disgustingly domestic, Dr. Rosen. You clearly need a boyfriend. Or a kid. Or even a dog."

Josh sat in an adjacent chair and put his feet up on a footstool. "How do you know I don't have any or all of those things? Or a girlfriend, for that matter?"

Tyler snorted. "You couldn't keep any of that secret from Rachel, and what she knows, Brad knows, and what Brad knows, everyone knows. As for a girlfriend, well, I suppose anything's possible, but I've known you my whole life, remember? My brother is marrying your sister. You dating a woman would've been front page family news, mister. Besides, unlike yours, my gaydar is accurate as fuck and you register on my equipment like a man who's never even gotten to second base with a girl."

"You're not wrong," Josh said, his voice clipped. "Your brother had more than enough girlfriends for both of us. I was twenty by the time I called it quits with him, and by then I was positive I was not into women. No experimentation required."

Josh wasn't bitter. Nope, not at all. Tyler sympathized, but he thought that carrying a torch for his brother after all these years was beyond pointless. Hell, loving Ryan in the first place had been Josh's first mistake. Ryan was so screwed up he practically inhabited his own separate reality.

Josh cleared his throat. "You seem to know all about me, and here I know next to nothing about you."

Well, that was super flattering to hear. Nice to know he was so obscure even someone he'd grown up with was clueless about him. "You clearly aren't following my illustrious career."

"Sorry, but not really. I've seen two of your movies, though. You seem to have the plucky teenaged sidekick shtick down."

For now, sure, but Tyler's ability to play teens had a fast-approaching expiration date. Possibly one that had already passed. If he couldn't transition he was fucked. *The Silver Arrow* was supposed to be his ticket to bigger roles that didn't involve him playing a high schooler. Now it looked like he'd be lucky to be doing infomercials by this time next year. The orange juice and Oreos sat uneasily in his stomach. "Yeah, you bet," he said. "I'm surprised you also escaped Brad's big mouth."

Josh chuckled. "Over the years I've gotten very good at tuning him out when he gets going."

"Try being related to him." Tyler closed his eyes, hoping Josh would take the hint.

He didn't. "You could tell me about yourself."

Tyler opened one eye. "Weren't you going to read a book?"

"I was, yeah, but I'd forgotten that my book is somewhere in the lake now."

"Are you trying to guilt me into talking to you, Josh?"

There was silence for several moments. Tyler closed both eyes, thinking he'd finally gotten Josh to shut up.

"Maybe," Josh said. "Is it working?"

Tyler huffed out a frustrated breath. "No, it's not."

"Is there anyone—what the hell is that?"

Tyler opened his eyes again. Oh. Look who'd decided the coast was clear and it was safe to come out. "It's a cat," he said.

"Why is there a random cat in here?"

"Oliver is not random. You should be honored he's graced you with his presence. He's pretty skittish."

Oliver padded farther into the room, assessing the perimeter for danger. When no one shouted at him, he took that for tacit permission and jumped up onto Tyler's chest. "Oh, man, right in the diaphragm," he wheezed, and started coughing. That naturally startled Oliver, who used Tyler's rib cage for a springboard and launched himself across the room. He scrambled up the bookcase and glared down at both men in accusation.

Meanwhile Josh vaulted out of his chair and started fussing again. "Are you okay? Can I get you anything? More juice?"

Tyler grabbed the front of Josh's borrowed shirt and pulled him closer until Josh was hunched over nearly double and their faces were inches apart. "You know what you can get me?"

"What?" asked Josh, his voice breathless.

"A big can of chill. The fuck. Out."

Josh stared at him.

"Look, Josh. It's been a long day. As you so helpfully pointed out, I'm cranky. I could use some space that doesn't have you hovering in it. Is that too much to ask?"

He was rewarded by Josh looking at him like a kicked puppy, and this time it seemed genuine.

Josh cleared his throat. "No, that's not too much to ask. When Brad and Rachel get here, I'll take off." He tried to straighten up.

Tyler tugged him back down. "Oh, no you don't. You do not get off that easy. You called them in, you don't get to just escape when they show up."

"But—"

"This," said Tyler, "is the deal. You're going to sit in that chair, with or without a book, and you will be quiet. You will not even think loud thoughts. I will lie here on this couch and maybe I'll take a nap. My cat might unbend enough to come down from the bookcase. Stranger things have been known to happen. And when Brad and Rachel get here, you do not get to abandon me. Oh, no. Your penance for scaring the fuck out of me on that dock is to run interference when they get here. My penance for being on that dock in the first place is to take the lecture I'm sure to receive with the proper humility of one who has fucked up for the nth time. Then, and I cannot stress this enough, when Brad is done giving me stitches and throwing drugs at me, *you will make them go away*. Is that clear?"

"Me, too?"

"You, too, what?"

"Do you want me to leave after they do?"

There was something in Josh's eyes that stopped Tyler from automatically saying "yes." It was not dissimilar from the look Oliver had given him as a kitten when Tyler had found him mewing under his car. That look said, "I'm hungry but I don't trust you." He'd been patient, blowing off an audition for a role he hadn't wanted in the first place, and eventually he'd lured the kitten out.

Josh was giving him the human version of that look. Well, fuck. He already had one stray cat with issues. He had a pile of his own issues. The last thing he needed was a stray dermatologist with issues.

Josh pulled away. "Don't worry about it. I'll make sure you're left alone."

Tyler grabbed him by his sweats. "Wait."

Josh looked down at him. "What?"

"You can stay if you want, but on one condition."

Josh raised his eyebrows.

"You have to share your tacos with me."

Josh went back to the recliner. "I'll think about it."

Chapter 6
Josh and the Big Bag of Crazy

Friday, September 16th, 10:50 p.m.
The Chadwicks' lake house
Blue Lake, WI

It didn't take long for Tyler to fall asleep, based on the soft wheezy snores that Josh could hear coming from the couch. After a while, the dark gray cat came down from his perch on the bookcase and jumped up onto Tyler's legs. He curled up and also fell asleep.

Josh tried, but sleep evaded him. He sobered slowly as the night ticked by, and grimly drank glass after glass of water to try and stave off his inevitable hangover.

Tyler was not what he expected, to put it mildly. Not even close. From the things that she'd said over the years, Josh got the impression Rachel thought that Tyler had been spoiled rotten, but that wasn't how Josh remembered him. All he could recall was a quiet, watchful kid. The boy he remembered barely talked. He certainly had never thrown a temper tantrum.

The Tyler sleeping on the couch wasn't the near-silent boy Josh remembered, but he wasn't the spoiled diva Rachel implied he'd become, either. He'd been a bit prickly tonight, sure, but Josh could see how he'd probably been irritating Tyler without even realizing it. Josh had been thrown, while drunk, into a stressful situation. He'd responded by being bossy, obnoxious, and, worst of all, flirty. Josh cringed just thinking about it. It was no wonder Tyler had lost his temper with him.

It was funny to think how intimidating Tyler had seemed when he'd finally lost patience with Josh. Physically, he was about as threatening as his cat was. It was all in the personality, Josh supposed. Somehow it superseded Tyler's physical presence, and Josh forgot that Tyler was roughly the size of your average high school student.

He couldn't help but contrast Tyler to his brothers, both who'd topped six feet while still in middle school and were naturals for the football team. As a freshman in high school, Ryan had constantly been mistaken for a senior. In comparison, Tyler was considerably shorter, and at his age wasn't going to grow any taller. He resembled his small, beautiful, fine-boned mother, and if he stuck with acting, Josh was willing to bet he'd be able to get teenaged roles into his early thirties.

Tyler puzzled him. Josh found himself attracted to him, hence all the drunken flirting, but he wasn't sure why. Tyler wasn't like the men he normally dated. Josh liked… okay, fine, he liked Ryan. No secret there. Most of the men he'd been with over the intervening years weren't exactly like Ryan but still tended to be of a similar type, which was nothing like Tyler, who, if you weren't wearing your glasses, could easily pass for someone too young to drive, let alone drink. Even at the advanced age of twenty-five, Josh thought Tyler still looked like a textbook twink: short, thin, pale, pretty, and with all the appearance of jailbait. Elfin jailbait, at that. All he was missing was pointy ears.

That was, until you got a closer look at him. When Tyler had grabbed his shirt to pull his face down, details that had been blurry thanks to Josh's nearsighted vision snapped into focus. He saw the crease between Tyler's eyebrows, the beginnings of dark stubble on his otherwise smooth skin, and his eyes, which were not the eyes of a teenager.

They weren't the eyes of a fuck-up, either. There was no weakness there. Only steely certain will behind irises that weren't sure what color they wanted to be. They were disconcerting: strange and beautiful and scary all at the same time.

Tyler had enough force of will that after he'd snapped out his demands, Josh hadn't even considered refusing. Not only that, but Josh had asked to stay, although he wasn't sure why. He should be itching at this point to escape to his rental sanctuary, but he wasn't. Right now, the thought of going back to that empty house held zero appeal. Tonight had been stressful and terrifying and uncomfortable, but also exhilarating and almost fun.

He found Tyler fascinating. Perhaps not in an "I'd like to fuck you" kind of way. Even if seedy-looking elves were Josh's type, which they decidedly were not, sex with Ryan's younger brother—his much younger brother—couldn't be a good idea. It was more that Tyler drew him in an "I can't look away from this glorious train wreck" fashion. Staying and watching the Tyler show currently sounded more appealing than sulking in solitary splendor. He'd planned on taking the boat out and going fishing today, but he had several more days to fish. This promised a lot more entertainment value.

※

Saturday, September 17th, 4:53 a.m.
The Chadwicks' lake house
Blue Lake, WI

Josh woke when Rachel touched his cheek. He opened his eyes, saw her, and smiled despite having a bit of hangover even after all that water he'd forced down. He also had to take a piss in the worst way. His eyes cut over to the couch. Tyler was no longer there.

"How was the drive?" he asked.

Rachel yawned. "Long. Really, really long. Here are your glasses. I was wondering if you'd take a walk with me."

Josh put the glasses on and turned his head toward the window. The night had gone from pitch black to dark slate gray, the color of Tyler's cat's fur. He looked at the clock and saw it was almost five. "When did you get here?"

"Just before four, so we've been here awhile. Tyler made us let you sleep, though, and just so you know, he ate half your tacos."

"That's okay. At least he didn't eat them all." Josh got out of the chair and stretched his stiff muscles. "I'll go for a walk with you," he said, "but I'm starving and I need to use the bathroom. That first, then tacos, something for my head, then I'm all yours."

When Josh walked into the kitchen, Brad and Tyler sat at the table. Brad was beginning to close Tyler's wound with small, meticulous stitches while Tyler sat with his eyes closed, head resting on the chair's back.

"Is the lecture over? Did I miss the whole thing?" Josh asked, making a beeline to the counter where a Taco Bell bag sat, waiting just for him.

Tyler said, "Yes," at the same time Brad barked out, "No."

"You're pretty much down to repeating yourself."

"Maybe if I say it enough it'll sink in," Brad replied.

"You keep telling yourself that," Tyler said.

Josh dug out a taco and unwrapped it. "So," he said. "What'd I miss?"

Tyler tipped his head forward and stared at Josh. "You're lucky," he said, "that I only ate half of your tacos. Don't forget your promise."

Brad snorted. "Oh, you're a fine one to talk about keeping promises, Ty."

Rachel tugged on Josh's arm. "Come on. Walk with me."

"Sure," Josh said, stopping himself from asking Tyler if he'd be okay. He finished the taco, took some Tylenol, then put on his shoes. They were still wet, but better than walking in just socks. He grabbed another taco and unwrapped it to eat while he walked.

"We'll be back," Josh said to the kitchen just before he closed the door behind him. "I won't forget."

Tyler didn't respond, but Josh thought he saw his eyelids flutter as if he was looking at Josh through his lashes. Not even sure if it would be noted, Josh nodded, then shut the door behind him.

The predawn light was hazy and fog clung to the lake. There was just the smallest tinge of pink on the horizon.

"How close is the place you rented?" Rachel asked. She was quiet, but with a sense of underlying simmering tumult that would spill out once it found an outlet. Figuring she'd unburden herself when she was ready, Josh didn't remark on it.

"There are two places between it and this one, so fairly close. You wanna see it?"

"Sure," she said. "You can give me the grand tour."

Josh waited for Rachel to speak, but she kept her silence. It wasn't an easy one. He could nearly hear the commotion of her thoughts, even if he was unsure what they contained. It reminded him of last night and how Tyler had ordered him to think quiet thoughts. Apparently the Rosens had noisy brains.

He hadn't locked the house last night, but everything was undisturbed. Josh flipped on the kitchen light and got out the coffee he'd bought. He handed the container to his sister. "Here. Make a pot and feel free to poke around the place. I'm taking a shower."

"I'll make it super strong, just like you like it. Please tell me you bought creamer."

"None of that flavored shit you like, but there's milk in the fridge and sugar on the counter."

She shrugged. "When in Rome. Go take your shower. You smell awful. We'll talk when you're done."

When he came back to the kitchen, showered, shaved, and dressed, the delicious scent of coffee greeted him. Josh poured himself a cup and didn't bother putting anything in it. He joined his sister at the kitchen table, where she fiddled with her own mug. "You want to take our coffee outside?" he asked. "Or to the porch, at least?"

Rachel took a few sips out of hers so it wouldn't slosh when she walked. "Yeah. The porch sounds great."

The gray outside had gone from slate to pearly. It was cool, but Wisconsin was in the grip of an Indian summer and the day was supposed to get warm. Reflexively Josh reached for his phone to check the weather, then remembered with an unhappy thought that it was in the lake.

"Okay," Josh said, hoping his sister was ready to spill whatever beans she was holding in, "let's talk."

"Tonight was my night for learning Chadwick family secrets," Rachel said. "I feel like I should be pissed at Brad for not telling me until now. On the other hand, it's not the sort of thing you would bring up in casual conversation."

"Yeah, how does that go? 'So, Rach, I've got a brother who cuts himself. A lot. You wanna catch a movie later?'"

Rachel laughed. "I know, and that's just the half of it. It's why I'm only a little bit pissed at him. Technically, I guess it wasn't his secret to tell, but Brad has made it his business, so now it's mine, too."

"And mine?" asked Josh.

Rachel shrugged. "You probably saved Tyler's life last night, so yeah, I think it's your business. There's more than just the cutting, though. The whole thing is, well, super fucked-up. I want you to brace yourself."

"Noted," said Josh. "Consider me braced."

Rachel looked at him over her coffee mug. "I don't think you are, but don't say I didn't warn you. Let me see. I need to condense five hours of discussion into something coherent. It's not easy."

"Begin at the beginning."

"Easy for you to say." She took a deep breath. "Okay. Tyler and his dad have never had an easy relationship."

"That I knew. Whenever Mr. Chadwick was around, Tyler always made himself scarce. It's the thing I remember the most about Tyler as a kid. He was quiet and watchful. He's not quiet anymore."

"That he is not," Rachel agreed. "Okay, so Tyler and his dad didn't get along, which you know, but Brad says it got much worse after he came out." Rachel paused. "Did you know he was gay? It's not a secret, exactly, but it's not publicly known, either. Mostly because Tyler hasn't been in a relationship since his last two movies started filming, and before *Blood and Water* no one really knew who the hell he was."

"I didn't know he was gay until tonight," Josh said, "but you know I don't really pay attention to Hollywood stuff. Brad may have mentioned it at some point, but most of the time I only listen to him with half an ear. It came up in conversation with Tyler last night, though."

"Oh?" Rachel raised her eyebrows.

"Tyler made an offhand remark about him running off with a hypothetical pool boy named Ramon. That was a pretty big clue."

"Okay," she said, drawing out the word, "that must have been an interesting conversation. Anyway, Brad told me that when Tyler was thirteen, his dad found a bunch of gay porn on his computer. Tyler eventually admitted he was gay, and his dad put him into therapy."

"What kind of therapy are we talking about?" Josh asked, apprehensive and afraid to hear the answer.

Rachel sighed. "Various types, including conversion therapy."

That's what Josh had been afraid of. "They sent him to one of those pray away the gay places?" He thought back. He remembered that the Chadwicks went to some church—he forgot which one, but he thought it was maybe in Lake Forest. In the summer, though, when it was just Mrs. Chadwick and the boys, they never went. Peter must have been the religious one, although he'd never seemed like the holy roller type to Josh. He'd thought Mr. Chadwick's religion might have been less about God and more about social standing. "I didn't realize the Chadwicks were like that. Shows what I know."

Rachel shrugged. "Brad said it's more that Tyler was defective and his dad was trying various things to fix him, including some places recommended by people at their church."

"Clearly it was super effective."

"Yeah, well, Tyler's been in and out of therapy and treatment centers since he was a teen. Brad said that's when Tyler started acting out. Instead of avoiding his dad, he started arguing with him. He dyed his hair everything from pitch black to bleached blonde, and tried out a variety of interesting hairstyles. He pierced his ears, then his eyebrow, and he started wearing makeup. Eyeliner, painting his nails, that sort of thing."

"I bet he made the prettiest little emo goth ever," Josh said. He could just imagine teenaged Tyler, looking approximately the same, only maybe a little smaller; a pocket-sized Cure groupie with black hair instead of blue, kohl-rimmed eyes, and black nails. With that pale skin of his, he really would've made a great goth. That scary smile of his wouldn't have hurt, either.

Josh also pictured Tyler with bleached blonde hair and that jogged a memory loose: a pale-haired Tyler with his finger on Josh's chest. Oh, yeah, that had been at the last Chadwick picnic he'd gone to, and Tyler had been a teenager then. Josh, for the life of him, couldn't remember why Tyler was touching Josh's chest in that memory.

Rachel gave him a look with skeptical eyes and raised eyebrows that was so like their mother it gave Josh a nasty start. It was a look to inspire incipient guilt, even if you were sure you hadn't done anything wrong. "Anyway," she continued, "Peter Chadwick's answer to all that was to demand he join a sport, so Tyler became a cheerleader."

Josh snorted a laugh and Rachel gave him the look again. "Sorry," he said. "I'm just picturing Mr. Chadwick telling his friends that his son was an emo goth cheerleader."

"Yes, Josh, I'm fairly certain that was the point."

"God, you're no fun this morning."

Rachel frowned. "This isn't a joke."

No, it wasn't. The problem was that thinking of emo Tyler and cheerleading Tyler was both amusing and charming and made him want to smile, even knowing that whatever Rachel was going to tell him was bad enough to have destroyed her sense of humor for the time being. He thought of the marks on Tyler's arms, and that was enough to kill his momentary levity. "I know it's not a joke. Go on, tell me what happened next."

Rachel looked uncomfortable. "Tyler was caught having sex on school grounds with two boys."

Josh sucked in air through his teeth. "Really? At the same time?"

"Um. Actually, yes."

"Actually yes, what?"

Rachel studied her coffee. "It was two boys at one time. Two of the football players, apparently."

"Wow. Just... damn. Give me a second. Two football players." Josh started to picture it, then tried to stop. He was not going to imagine Ryan's little brother in a three-way. No. Although it was a bit like trying not to think of a pink rhinoceros.

"Are you done thinking about it?" Rachel asked. "I thought you were taking this seriously."

I am seriously trying not to think about a teenaged threesome with Tyler in it. I am seriously trying very hard. "I am. Go on."

"Okay, so all three boys were suspended from school. Tyler's dad found this program here in Wisconsin to put him in called Bridges to Something-or-other. I forget now what Brad called it."

Josh stilled. "Was it Salvation? Bridges to Salvation?"

"Yeah, I think that was the name," said Rachel. "Have you heard of it?"

"Unfortunately." Bridges was infamous, at least among the gay community in the Midwest. They promised a cure to homosexuality, and it was rumored they used torture to get it. "They supposedly use aversion therapy," he said. "Nasty shit."

"Brad said it was a bad place, a really bad place, but he didn't go into detail, which for him is unusual. I meant to google it when I got a chance." She gave him a weak smile. "Just haven't had that chance yet."

"This is all second and third hand," Josh said. "I've never met anyone who's been through there, except Tyler, I guess, but I've talked to people who've had friends and loved ones sent there, or know someone, or heard it from someone else. Hard to say how accurate any of the stories are, but the general theme is sort of *Clockwork Orangey*."

"*Clockwork Orangey*?" Rachel asked. "I don't think Orangey is a real word."

Josh gave his sister a look. "So, the story is that they take in homosexuals, mostly teens and some young adults. First, they give them all these lectures about how they're evil and corrupted and defective people, but there's a cure. Then they show them homosexual pornography and torture them while they watch. You know, to erase the gay."

"Okay, that's pretty fucked-up." Rachel had gone pale. "What do you mean by torture?"

"I've heard the gamut: electrical shocks, beatings, immersion in ice-cold baths, giving them drugs to induce nausea, sleep deprivation. You name it. Supposedly rape, too." Josh turned and looked out at the lake, which was still and pretty and peaceful. "All or none of which might be true. I don't know, but the stories are consistent enough to make me think it can't all be made up. There've been a few attempts that I know of to get the place shut down, but so far no one has managed it." He shrugged. "I'm not sure if that means the allegations of illegal activity are false, or that they have really good lawyers. Do you know how long Tyler was there?"

"A few weeks, I think. The first time."

Josh felt sick. "There was more than one time?"

Rachel nodded. "Yeah, but again, I'm getting ahead of myself. Tyler came out and they said he was cured. And, for a time, his behavior seemed pretty normal, at least as normal as any teenager gets. He went back to school and concentrated on his classes. He got kicked out of cheerleading and the other boys got kicked off the football team, but Tyler tried out for the school play and got the male lead. He and the lead actress went out a lot, so the family, or his dad at least, thought they were dating. Brad said he was pretty sure the girl was Tyler's beard, but he wasn't any more interested in setting his father straight than Tyler was. Brad figured that whatever it took for Tyler to be able to get through high school was fine by him. He had no idea how bad things were until he came home from college during Christmas."

"Wait, I think I remember this," Josh said. "That was the year Tyler was in the hospital, right? I'm trying to remember. There was some sort of accident. I just remember that Brad wasn't around much that break."

"It wasn't exactly an accident. Brad came home to an empty house. His parents had gone out and Ryan was still at Stanford for a few more days. Tyler was supposed to be home, though. At first Brad thought he'd gone out, too, but his car was parked in the garage, so he checked around the house, thinking he'd find Tyler napping. Brad had this great plan of waking him up by dumping water on him."

"Your fiancé is an asshole," Josh said, reminded of the water balloon incident.

"Yeah, but he's my asshole. And it's a good thing he's an asshole, because he found Tyler, not sleeping, but bleeding out on the floor of his bedroom."

Even knowing where the story was inevitably headed, Josh winced. "He'd cut his leg, high up, and way too deep."

"Don't tell me he cut his femoral."

Rachel shrugged. "Brad didn't say, and I haven't had anatomy since high school." She smiled then. "But, speaking of anatomy, after Tyler and his mom moved out to San Francisco, you know, after the divorce, Brad made Tyler memorize the major arteries and veins to better avoid them. But don't tell Ryan, because he would kill Brad for enabling Tyler."

"Yeah, because Ryan and I talk so frequently," Josh said. "Get back to your story. You've left poor Tyler bleeding to death in his bedroom."

"Well, Brad tied a tourniquet and called 911. Supposedly it was a suicide attempt, although Tyler to this day denies it and claims he just cut too deep, but regardless, he started seeing a psychiatrist. She prescribed some anti-anxiety and antidepressant medications and he got more therapy. Meanwhile Brad says his parents had, out of nowhere, started fighting a lot."

"I don't know if I'd say out of nowhere," said Josh. "Granted, I was around a long time ago, but I thought their marriage was pretty much a cold war situation. I got the impression Mrs. Chadwick spent summers up here to get away from her husband. She always came up right after school ended and didn't return until a week before school let back in. He sometimes came up on the weekends, but rarely, and those were the worst. No one was happy then."

"Okay, maybe not out of nowhere, but the cold war definitely went hot. Then there was the incident with the guidance counselor. That was pretty much the beginning of the end."

"What incident?"

"Tyler got caught again, this time giving a blow job to his guidance counselor. The one who was supposed to be helping him deal with the fallout from what had happened with the two football players."

"You've got to be kidding me."

"Nope. His actual guidance counselor. Young guy, apparently. Not too long out of college, in his first job, according to Brad." Rachel shrugged. "Doesn't make it any better. He was still a creep who took advantage of a teenaged boy."

"And there was no trial for statutory rape? Because I'm pretty sure I wouldn't have missed that."

"It never went to trial. In the end, the guy lost his job and got a reduced sentence after pleading guilty. He got time served and put on the sex offender's registry, and I'm sure that put the kibosh on his career. Tyler got sent back to Bridges. He was there all of one day and tried to kill himself. He was found by staff in time and was sent to the hospital. Then Mrs. Chadwick asked for a divorce and sole custody of Tyler. Things got ugly for a while, but you already know most of that. Eventually she got custody of Tyler, I think he was seventeen by that point, and they moved to San Francisco where she's from. Tyler finished out high school there, went to UCLA, started acting, and everything was presumably rosy. Well, except for Tyler's little habit of slicing himself up, that is."

"Does Brad know what set him off this time?"

"Yeah, about that. You remember that thing I told you about the football players?"

"Trust me, that's not the kind of thing a person forgets," Josh said.

"Well, there's a video of it, and it was sent to several tabloids and leaked to the internet. That's what I mean about the porn aspect. Tyler found out about it on Thursday and came out here to hide away from pretty much everybody."

"Holy shit."

"Pretty much. And in answer to your next question, no, I don't know how it was leaked or why it even exists. I just know it does, and that Ryan is working with Tyler's agent to fix the situation because it has the power to tank Tyler's career, and Tyler's brilliant idea to make things better was to come out here and carve himself up on a dock. Because things weren't bad enough already. Thank God you were here."

Josh frowned. "I think you're being too hard on him. If I hadn't been here, I wouldn't have scared him and he wouldn't have needed saving."

Rachel snorted. "Even without you startling him, Tyler still might have ended up dead."

"We all make mistakes," Josh said. He wasn't sure why he felt the need to defend Tyler, other than it seemed wrong to attack him when he wasn't around to defend himself. "Some of us more than others, true, but no one's perfect."

"Yeah, I know. I just find Tyler frustrating. He has this amazing opportunity that most people would do anything for, and he's pissing it away through bad decisions and a weak will. It bothers me. I can't help it."

Josh remembered Tyler's eyes, though. "Tyler isn't weak," he said. "He's got issues, no argument there, but weakness isn't one of them."

Rachel gave him a hard look.

Josh squirmed under her gaze, feeling guilty but not sure why. "What?"

She shook her head. "Nothing."

"Sure, be that way. You ready to head back?"

Rachel looked dubious. "You don't have to come back with me," she said. "You've been officially absolved of any blame or responsibility. This is a family problem. I've been drafted because I'm almost a Chadwick, but you're a free agent. This is supposed to be your vacation. Have fun vacating."

"I could go out on the boat today, like I planned, and do some fishing. Or I can go back with you and throw myself into the big bag of crazy."

She wrinkled her brow. "Is there a third option that involves video games? My money's on door number three."

"This is interesting, and I'm not in the mood to fish. I'm sticking my nose in whether it's needed or wanted. End of discussion." That, and he'd promised Tyler he wouldn't abandon him.

"All right, it's your funeral," Rachel said. "For the record, I think you're making a mistake, but whatever. Let's head back."

Chapter 7
Tyler Ponders Fratricide

Saturday, September 17th, 7:30 a.m.
The Chadwicks' lake house
Blue Lake, WI

Brad was almost done with the last of the stitches when the kitchen door opened and Tyler's morning got a little more irritating.

"Oh, great," he said, "you, too."

Ryan flashed a sunny grin at Tyler. "I can feel the love from way over here." He wore dress slacks and a button-down shirt, both sadly creased. He looked exhausted, despite the wattage he put into the smile.

Tyler's agent, Alicia, walked in right behind him. She also looked exhausted and creased, and she didn't smile at all. Not a good sign.

"Fuck me," Tyler grumbled. Now that Ryan was here he would be lovingly bullied in stereo. Add in his agent and suddenly it would be overwhelming concern and disapproval in surround sound. *I am going to have to do so much counting today.*

Ryan came over to the table to inspect Brad's work. "Excellent job on the stitches," he said.

"Naturally," Brad replied.

"I assume you've already read him the riot act?"

"Yup," said Brad as he tied the last stitch and snipped the nylon thread. "You're done," he said. "Repeat back my instructions so you can't pretend later that you didn't know."

Tyler rolled his eyes and recited in a sing-song voice, "Use the waterproof thingies when I shower for the next two days, take the bandage off after three, no soaking it in water until after the stitches come out." He turned to his agent. "I can't believe Ryan pried you out of LA, Alicia, but thanks for coming. What did he bribe you with?"

"Jesus, I'm knackered. My flight got in late last night, your brother picked me up at the airport, and we drove straight here. As for my bribe, you probably don't want to know, but it was expensive. I can't believe I'm in Wisconsin. It's so… rural."

"That's part of the charm," Ryan said. "Too bad you couldn't see it in a few weeks. When the leaves fully turn it's gorgeous."

"If I'm still here to see the leaves change color, just shoot me, okay? Thanks." She swiveled back to Tyler. "How's the arm? Ryan told me about the accident. It's not like you to be clumsy, but it could've been worse, I suppose."

Tyler had no idea what Ryan had told her, but it didn't matter. "I was drunk," he said, and Alicia nodded as if he'd confirmed her suspicions. Drunk was always good as an alibi.

"It's just as well Brad had to come up here and give you stitches. This way I won't have to fill him in later." Ryan held out a chair for Alicia at the kitchen table. "Can I get you anything before we start?"

"For the love of God, give me coffee, the blacker the better."

"Yes, ma'am," Ryan replied and set about pouring some for her.

"Alicia, how boned am I?" Tyler asked, trying to keep how truly worried he was out of his voice.

She grimaced. "It's not looking great now, kiddo, but we'll see what we can do. The situation is by no means hopeless. When I first started in the business, back in the stone ages, it would've been a different story. Now we've got a chance."

Ryan brought Alicia her coffee, then took a seat next to her. He cleared his throat and steepled his fingers. "First things first. We've hired you a publicist, Ty. It's past time we did so. I know you've been dragging your feet on this, but we've run out of time."

"Fine," Tyler said. He knew he'd probably need a publicist eventually, he just didn't think it would be before he'd actually starred in a movie. So far, he'd played bit parts and some decent supporting roles. Even his part in *The Silver Arrow*, while the largest role he'd had to date, wasn't a lead. Of course, all that had been assuming his sordid past wouldn't be splashed all over the internet in video form. Now it was possible *The Silver Arrow* would be his last film and not a springboard toward an eventual starring role. "You're right. We need a publicist."

"I've got one of the attorneys from the firm serving several tabloids and websites with injunctions to keep them from showing the video or any stills obtained from it. We also have people working on how it was obtained in the first place," Ryan said.

"But that's going to mean jack shit in the grand scheme of things," interrupted Alicia. "All the legal maneuvering in the world isn't going to make this disappear. It would take a damn time machine to contain it at this point."

Ryan continued, unruffled. "The video has already been posted and removed from the more legitimate image and video posting sites on the internet several times in the past day and a half. It goes up faster than we can have it removed, and those are just the sites that care if they're hosting a sex video with underage participants. In short, we can close the barn door as tight as possible, but the horse has already escaped."

"What about the other thing?" Brad asked. "You think there's any danger of that getting out?"

"What other thing?" asked Alicia. "There are more things? No one said there were more things."

Yeah. What other thing?

Ryan raised an eyebrow in inquiry at Brad. Brad sighed. "Spring of his junior year in high school."

Oh, that other thing. *My "two boys didn't do it for me, so let's fuck a grown-up and see how that works for us" phase. There better not be video footage of that floating around.*

"Oh. No, I wouldn't think so," Ryan said.

Brad and Ryan looked at Tyler, and he held up his hands. "Don't look at me," he said. "I have no idea how buried any of that shit is. I was a minor at the time and no one told me anything, aside from Dad instructing me that there'd be hell to pay if I testified. I wasn't even at the hearing."

Alicia's voice sharpened to a knife point. "Testified about what? What hearing?"

Tyler ignored her for the moment. "You two were both in college at the time, and while Brad was in Chicago, he wasn't at the hearing, either, and he wasn't told any more than I was. Unless I'm wrong?"

Brad shook his head.

"And you," continued Tyler, turning to Ryan, "were still in California, probably studying for finals. Even so, of all of us, you'd have been the one most likely to know the answer. Dad talks to you."

"Dad didn't tell me much," Ryan said, "but we did discuss it a little."

"That's one hundred percent more than I got. I didn't get told anything other than to keep my mouth shut. Oh, and what a horrible excuse of a human being I was. After a while, I tend to tune it out. The only one who would know exactly how well all that shit got buried would be Dad, and good luck getting it out of him, although he might talk to Ryan. Maybe."

Brad and Ryan looked at each other and Ryan shook his head. Then he perked up a little. "Mom might know. I'll give her a call later."

Alicia looked around the table. "What the fuck have I gotten myself into? Someone better explain what's going on, or so help me I'm going to fuck you all sideways with something pointy and uncomfortable. I did not fly all the way here just so you assholes could jerk me around."

"We're all here for the same reason—to try and salvage what we can of the situation," Ryan said, his tone soothing. "I apologize, Alicia. We'll explain if we need to. Let me speak to my mother first, and then I'll decide if there's more you need to know. But I'm sure you'll understand when I say that we'd like to keep what is truly buried right where it is."

"I don't understand a damn thing about what you just said, and it's really starting to piss me off. If you're not going to be honest with me, I can't keep Tyler on as a client, especially if he was involved in something illegal."

Ryan sighed. "I'll have an NDA drawn up, then we'll fill you in. I'm sorry, but it's necessary. I can tell you ahead of time that Tyler was the victim in this incident, and he himself did nothing illegal. We don't wish you to go anywhere, but I understand Tyler can be a difficult client…"

Tyler, tired of being talked about like he wasn't there, started singing. "How do you solve a problem like Tyler? How do you catch a cloud and pin it down?"

Across the room someone laughed. No, not someone. Josh.

Alicia and the brothers swiveled toward the sound of Josh's laughter. Rachel stood next to him, grinning, and Tyler was struck by how alike they were—curly dark hair, expressive brown eyes, beautiful smiling mouths. Her hair was long, though, her nose was smaller, and she didn't wear glasses. Even so, they might have been mistaken for twins.

"When did you come in, hon?" asked Brad.

"Just now," Rachel said.

"This nice lady was threatening to fuck someone sideways with something pointy and uncomfortable. Which, for the record, is redundant," Josh said. "Hi, Ryan, when did you get here?"

Tyler looked at his brother. The beatific smile was back. It was as if he couldn't help himself. "Not long ago. I want to thank you for saving Tyler. I owe you. We all do."

Tyler looked back at Josh. He was blushing like a little girl, the sap. "No, you don't," he said. "You don't owe me anything. It was the least I could do, and I was, at least partially, to blame."

"Don't be ridiculous. You've gone above and beyond and we're all deeply grateful," said Ryan, earnest sincerity bleeding from every pore.

Tyler exchanged a disgusted look with Brad. It was like watching a soap opera. Then he locked eyes with Alicia. She raised her eyebrows in question at him and he shrugged. Explaining Josh and Ryan was beyond him, especially non-verbally.

"So, what's going on? Is there anything I can do to help?" Josh asked.

"No," Tyler said, turning back to frown at him. He wanted to shake Josh until he lost that look of eager helpfulness. It grated on Tyler's nerves.

"But—"

"I said no. Thank you," he added curtly.

Josh scowled back. "I just want to help."

You're an idiot. Go away before you get sucked into this insanity. "No," Tyler said. "You don't. Trust me on this."

Josh's lips thinned, and he looked mutinous, but he shut his mouth. He didn't leave, though.

Ryan cleared his throat. "Do you mind if Rachel and Josh are here for the rest of this discussion, Tyler, or would you prefer privacy? It's up to you."

Alicia made a disgusted sound.

Tyler started counting, got to twenty, then gave up. "You know what? Fuck it. Like it matters at this point. You heard him. Josh wants to *help*. And Rachel's practically family. No point in keeping all this fun shit to ourselves. Sit down, guys. Might as well make yourselves at home. Rachel, Josh, this is Alicia Peters, my agent. She's come all the way here to try and save my bacon. Rachel, can I assume Brad told you the whole story and then you told Josh?"

"Every embarrassing detail," she said.

"Great, then we don't need to backtrack. Alicia, this is Rachel and Josh Rosen. She's Brad's fiancée and he's—" Tyler paused, trying to be accurate yet tactful, "—been a friend of the family for pretty much forever."

Rachel pulled out the chair between Ryan and Brad, and Josh took the last chair remaining, which was between Brad and Tyler. Josh sat up straight and looked attentive, as if he'd be graded later on the material presented.

"Fabulous," Alicia said, deadpan. "I can't wait to see who shows up next."

"Is there any sort of plan yet, or are we waiting for the publicist?" Tyler asked, eager to get what was rapidly turning into a farce over and done with. "Although I have no clue what a publicist is going to do to help me overcome the world seeing me being fucked by two guys."

Alicia clucked her tongue at him. "What this needs is spin and good behavior on your part. The incident on the video happened many years ago. Youthful indiscretion. That the video was captured by CCTV and not filmed deliberately is a point in our favor. We can stress the invasion of privacy issue. That you and the other participants were underage is also helpful. Technically possession of the video is a crime. We're already pursuing that angle, as your brother said."

"But..." said Tyler, who could hear it in her voice.

"I just want you to know, before I tell you the proposal, that this wasn't my idea. I'm not opposed to it, if you aren't, but..."

"Oh, just spit it out, Alicia. How much worse could things get for me?"

"All right." Alicia drummed her perfectly-manicured nails on the table. "Are you in a relationship? Male or female, doesn't matter, but male would probably be easier to spin at this point, based on the nature of the video."

"What? No. Although, for the record, I'm gay, not bi. The women I've gone to events with were either friends or chosen by the studio. In the last couple of years, I've dated, but casually. My last actual boyfriend and I broke up over two years ago, and I haven't really wanted a new relationship. Being single is just easier. I have it on good authority that I'm annoying and high maintenance."

Alicia made a face. "Well, hell. The publicist we hired, Tom Harvey — he's fantastic and he'd better be for the money you'll be paying him — wants to play up that you're currently in a serious, committed relationship. The American public has become much more accepting of gay celebrities in the last decade or so, but you'll note that all the most successful and popular ones are one-half of a monogamous, nauseatingly happy couple. This is going to be a lot harder if you're single."

"Well, I'm sorry my personal life isn't cooperating," Tyler said. "And here I thought keeping my love life private and discreet was a good idea. Silly me." He felt a kick under the table, and looked up to see Ryan glaring at him.

"For the foreseeable future, you've lost the right to a life that's either private or discreet, kiddo," Alicia told him. "Get used to it or I wash my hands of you."

"A relationship," Ryan said. "You said male would be easier?"

"Tom says anyone who's either seen or heard about the video won't believe Tyler is straight. That ship has sailed. He was willing to work with you being bisexual if there was a girlfriend in the picture, but he told me gay was a much easier sell at this point. While Middle America has just about wrapped their heads around homosexuality, they are a lot shakier on anything more... exotic."

"Exotic like teenaged threesomes?" Tyler wasn't bi, but he still felt offended. He looked at Ryan, wondering how he was taking being labeled as exotic, but there was nothing but bland interest on his face, as if the conversation had nothing to do with him at all.

Beside him, Josh reached under the table to briefly squeeze his thigh. Whether in warning or in solidarity, Tyler had no clue, and Josh's face wasn't illuminating.

"So, this Tom person wants Tyler to be in a committed relationship yesterday?" Brad asked. "Is there a plan in place to make this miracle happen?" He gave Ryan a look, like somehow this was his problem to solve.

Alicia's nails tapped the table like rapid fire gunshots. "Any exes who would be willing to take you back?"

Tyler considered, then shook his head. "The only one I'm even on speaking terms with is engaged. I've either lost touch with the others or we didn't part well. Sorry." He thought of David and shuddered. No way in hell he'd try and reconnect with him. Tyler thought he'd rather fade into shameful obscurity first. As for the rest, Jeremy wasn't as bad as David, but still an asshole, Carlos had gone overseas somewhere, and Tyler had no clue where Ron was.

"What about friends? It doesn't have to be a real relationship. It just must seem like it for long enough for this to die down. Probably until after the premiere of *The Silver Arrow*. We can hire someone, but that's a last resort. A known quantity would be better."

Tyler was considering whether Purvi would let him borrow her boyfriend for a few months (doubtful) when Ryan said, "There's Josh. What about him?" Tyler felt Josh tense beside him.

Alicia lasered in on the man being offered up on a platter and looked interested. Tyler felt impending disaster press down on him and tried to forestall it. "No," he said, and if possible, Josh's posture became even more rigid.

"Why not?" asked Ryan. "It seems like the perfect solution. He's gay and out, so that isn't an issue. You already know him and our families are already connected. Faking a relationship would be easier with him than anyone we could find or hire. We can trust him implicitly. He would never betray us." He looked at Josh. "Are you currently seeing someone?"

Josh shook his head.

"Great," Ryan went on. "That's perfect. He isn't currently involved with anyone else, so that won't be an issue." Ryan looked back at Josh, and how he could miss the man's tension was anyone's guess. "I know it's a lot to ask, but you'd be doing us all a huge favor. For old time's sake, would you consider it?"

Tyler could sense Josh quivering like a bowstring pulled back too far. A little bit more and he'd snap. Tyler glanced at him and saw that Josh's face had gone as pale as a sheet of paper, and he'd made his expression into a blank mask. Tyler could have cheerfully murdered his brother in that moment. He kicked Ryan hard and felt a mean stab of pleasure when he winced in pain.

"Ryan, that's enough. More than enough," Rachel snapped. "Stop it."

Ryan got a look of hurt confusion on his face that clearly said, *what did I do?* "I have no idea what you mean, Rachel."

"Leave. Josh. Alone," she said through gritted teeth.

"Maybe you two should go," Brad suggested. He glanced at Josh and frowned, looking concerned. "Josh, why don't you and Rachel go into town? She said you needed to get another phone. No time like the present, hey? You don't need to be here. Rescuing Tyler isn't your responsibility."

Josh took a deep breath and relaxed by degrees. "No," he said. "It's fine. It... the suggestion. It took me by surprise, but it makes sense." He laughed, and it sounded fake as shit to Tyler. Rachel looked, if possible, even more pissed off.

Alicia folded her arms across her chest. "What the hell is going on?" Everyone ignored her.

"No," said Tyler. "It's a terrible idea."

"Why?" asked Ryan, who was too stupid to live.

Tyler opened his mouth, then closed it. He looked at Rachel, who was livid, but offered up no suggestions other than the promise of bloodshed he saw in her eyes. Then he looked at Josh. He'd gone from white to full flush, and his eyes studied his hands on the table.

"Josh doesn't owe this family a damn thing," Tyler said, "and he deserves better than to be saddled with me for what could be months. It'll be a non-stop circus and it's not fair to ask it of him. I won't disrupt his life like that."

"I could use some excitement in my life," Josh said, speaking to his clasped hands.

"Not like this. You're a doctor, for fuck's sake. You can't have people hanging about and constantly taking pictures."

Josh shrugged. "They'll see how boring I am and lose interest quickly enough. Especially after you go back to LA."

Alicia cut in. "About that. We need the two of you together. A long-distance relationship will not cut it. We need you to seem like a happy couple, or at least a reasonable facsimile. That means staying in the same zip code."

"There you go," Tyler said. "Josh can't leave his practice. This won't work."

"It can if you stay here," Alicia said. "In fact, that's a much better idea than Josh following you back to LA. The paparazzi will find someone more interesting to bother in a few weeks, especially when the weather in Chicago starts getting bad. You can make brief trips home if you need to, but it would probably be for the best if you're not in LA for a while. At least until the sharks find someone else to circle."

"Stop talking like this is a done deal, Alicia. We'll find some other way. I am —" Tyler felt Josh's hand on his thigh again and stopped talking mid-sentence. He looked Josh's way.

"I'll do it," he said. "We'll do it." His face, while still blank, was at least back to a normal color.

"But," Tyler began. Before he could list more reasons why this insane idea wouldn't work, Josh cut him off.

"Tyler." His voice was as sharp as a razor.

"What?"

"Shut up." Josh looked first at Alicia, then at Ryan. "We'll do it. Tyler can move in with me. It'll look better, and I have the extra bedroom. It won't be difficult. I'm pretty sure being in a pretend relationship will come naturally to me."

Tyler couldn't help but study Ryan's reaction. He smiled pleasantly back at Josh, unfazed by the hurt radiating off of the other man. Tyler considered kicking Ryan again, but there wasn't any point.

Alicia looked around the table, as if giving everyone a chance to object. When no one said anything, she settled her gaze on Tyler. "That little declaration is the best offer you're going to get. I'd advise taking him up on it. You'd be a fool to turn him down."

"Fine," Tyler said, giving up in the face of Josh's determined martyrdom. "The role of fool is already taken, anyway."

Chapter 8
Josh Is a Bone of Contention

Saturday, September 17th, 7:52 a.m.
The Chadwicks' lake house
Blue Lake, WI

One of the things about growing up Jewish in the United States is that there is a sad lack of holiday specials that feel relevant. It's hard to get enthusiastic about Santa and Rudolph when your living room houses a Hanukkah bush and a menorah, and instead of a huge pile of presents, you get eight days of decreasingly shitty presents until the last pretty good one. Still, Josh watched all holiday cartoons when he was a kid. He wasn't sure why. They came on and he was compelled to view them, from the Grinch to Peter Cottontail.

The best ones were the ones for secular holidays, though, Halloween specials being his favorite, and the acme of them all was the *Peanuts'* Great Pumpkin episode. Josh loved it from his first viewing as a toddler, but as he got older, something about it bothered him more and more. The joy Josh felt when watching it, knowing that in the next day or so he'd be out trick-or-treating, was mixed with a melancholy that he couldn't articulate.

It wasn't until he was much older that Josh realized what it was: the cartoon was a perfect metaphor for how life was often more shitty than not. There was no Great Pumpkin; instead of candy, you mostly got rocks; and for every sad sack Charlie Brown there was a corresponding bitch of a Lucy, holding out the football and yanking it away every single time.

When Josh was very young he'd never understood why Charlie Brown always went back for more. He knew Lucy was going to yank the ball away. She always did. Why on earth would he think that things would ever be different?

Then Josh met Ryan and he understood.

There had been so many times that Ryan had yanked the football away from Josh he'd lost count, yet still he remained, taking what crumbs fell his way and thinking, every time, *this time will be different,* but it never was. Witness now, here he was, figuratively lying flat on his back as his very own grinning Lucy held the football out of his reach while simultaneously working out the minutia of having his little brother move in and pretend to be in a relationship with his former... whatever Josh had been to him

Not boyfriend, even though they had been friends at the time. Best friends. Lover? The word felt wrong. Sex slave felt right, but sounded melodramatic even in the privacy of his own head, and fuck buddy was the most accurate and yet was too flippant.

Josh had just been Ryan's. That simple, that profound, that hopeless, and apparently there was some part of him that still felt owned. Nothing else explained why he'd dived headfirst into this mess. Josh had wanted to make Ryan feel something, even if it was just the smallest shred of regret, but there had been nothing on his face but the complacent knowledge that Josh would do what he wanted because Josh always had.

"I want you to pay off his school loans," said Rachel, and that snapped Josh out of his reverie.

"What?" Josh sputtered. "No."

Ryan tipped his head a fraction. "Half," he said. "Contingent upon this working."

"All," Rachel said, "period. Don't even think about trying to bargain with me, Ryan. Not today. I know you have the money. I'm your goddamned accountant. I know what you're worth to the last penny and I know where every single financial body is buried. Consider the fuckery your dad and grandfather used to get up to. Roll it around in that pretty head of yours and realize I know all of it, every questionably legal detail, and right now I'm so angry with you I can barely see straight. Do not fuck with me."

Brad shook his head. "Just agree to it, Ryan. You're being an ass. Although honestly, Rachel, I don't know what you think throwing money at the problem is going to accomplish."

Rachel looked at Brad, and some sort of nonverbal communication went on between them. It ended with Rachel taking a deep breath. "Josh, are you good with all this? Really? Because you don't have to do anything you don't want to."

"I know," Josh said, but even to his own ears he sounded uncertain. "It'll be fine. No problem." He smiled to show just how fine he thought everything was. Rachel winced, and he dropped the smile from his face.

Ryan tried to catch his eye, but Josh wouldn't look at him. Looking at Ryan wasn't going to fix anything. It never had and it never would.

A knee nudged his. Tyler. Josh met his eyes, now a chilly gray. Josh was surprised to see that Tyler was as angry as Rachel, but while her anger was hot, his was ice cold. He wondered if Tyler was angry at Josh for waffling or at Rachel for going into attack mode or at Ryan for being Ryan or just at the general situation. Maybe it was all the above.

"I'll pay it, Rachel," Tyler said, not looking away from Josh. "The whole thing, regardless of what happens. If this doesn't work, it won't be Josh's fault."

"No, that's crazy," Josh said. "I mean, do you have any clue how much money that is?"

Tyler looked unconcerned. "A lot?"

"I still have over a hundred thousand left to pay off," Josh said. "That's a lot of money for a fake boyfriend."

The agent laughed. "You might be surprised. Tom warned me that if we had to hire someone it wouldn't be cheap. Discretion is expensive. It's why that was the least desirable option."

Rachel frowned. "Tyler, this is your brother's idea, he should have to pay for it, not you."

"This entire discussion is absurd," Ryan said. "Rachel, you and your demands are totally out of line, and Tyler, you should be letting me negotiate for you, not just agree to any random dollar figure without an argument. That's why negotiating is my job and acting is yours."

Brad groaned. "Christ, Ryan, you are not helping. I don't know what's gotten into you, but you sound just like Dad and you need to cut it the fuck out."

"I'm just looking after Tyler's best interests," Ryan said, sounding both pompous and wounded.

Ass, Josh thought, and surprised himself. He'd never felt this disgusted at Ryan before. Hurt, yes. Angry, often. Disgust, however, was new. Maybe he was finally getting over him. If that was the upshot, perhaps this wasn't such a terrible impulse decision after all.

"I'm not stupid," Tyler shot back, "and this is my mess. I'll pay for it. Not you. Me. I have the money. Yeah, I'll have to liquidate some stock, but whatever."

"That's not the point," Ryan said.

"That might be the only thing Ryan and I agree on," Rachel muttered, loud enough for the entire table to hear.

"Rachel, find some other way to punish Ryan, because we all know that's what this is," Tyler said, his voice rising with his irritation. "He hurt your big brother and you want to kneecap him. Look, I get it. We all get it. I think even Alicia gets it. But extorting money from him isn't going to fix anything, okay?"

Rachel didn't look like she agreed in the slightest, but she didn't say anything. Josh still wasn't looking at Ryan, so he had no idea what his reaction was, other than hearing him let out an exaggerated sigh.

Tyler continued in a softer tone. "I agree that Josh should be compensated for agreeing to help me. This is more than just a favor. I'm asking him to turn his entire life upside down for what could very well be several months. I understand what that means, probably more than anyone in this room. Doing that for me free of charge would be insane. But if he's willing to go through with it I'll pay for it, not Ryan, and not anyone else.

You two," he said, pointing to Ryan and Rachel in turn, "can butt the fuck out of this. Josh isn't your bone to fight over."

Rachel turned on Tyler. "He isn't your bone to do anything with."

Tyler's tone turned sharp. "Really? Because two seconds ago you were negotiating with my brother like you were Josh's fucking pimp."

Tyler's agent watched the scene play out with wide eyes.

"Could we not do this?" Josh asked, and everyone looked at him.

The agent cleared her throat. "This has been entertaining as all get-out, but I have a serious question for our potential boyfriend: are you having second thoughts? I need to know ASAP, because if you're not on board we need to find someone who is, and we have very little time in which to do it. And, if my opinion means anything, I hope you say yes. Finding someone to do this who can be trusted not to spill the whole thing to the media won't be easy, and it could easily be as expensive as you've turned out to be. It's a large part of why I'm not fully behind this plan."

"No," Josh said. "I said I'd do it, and I will."

"Fantastic. You're practically tailor-made for this. Apparently trustworthy, respectable, and handsome enough. Hopefully you'll photograph well." She looked back and forth between Josh and Tyler, squinting a little. "I think the two of you will look okay together. How tall are you? Stand up."

Feeling like a small child, Josh stood obediently.

"You, too, Tyler. Let's see the two of you side by side."

Next to him, Tyler also rose. His head came to just above Josh's shoulder. It brought home how short Tyler was, especially since Brad and Ryan were both a few inches taller than Josh. He wondered what it was like to be the little brother who never grew out of being little.

"Not terrible," Tyler's agent said. "Tyler's 5'9 —"

Brad coughed, "5'8."

"I'm 5'8 and three quarters, thank you so very much," Tyler said, sounding peeved.

Alicia narrowed her eyes. "We have him listed as 5'9. You're what, six feet or so, um… Josh?"

Josh nodded.

"Don't wear any shoes or boots with thick soles or any kind of heels to them and you won't loom over Tyler too much. Yeah. You'll do."

"Thanks, I guess." Josh sat, then massaged his eyes, his headache having returned with a vengeance. "Tyler, are you okay with living with me and going through with this? It's what everyone here seems to want, but it's your life, not theirs. Also, you don't have to pay me."

Tyler rolled his eyes. "Living with you and pretending to be madly in love? It's just acting. It's what I do, like Ryan so helpfully pointed out. You're the one with your work cut out for you, not me, and you'll earn that money putting up with me. Trust me on that."

"I can pretend. I pretended for over half my life not to feel something. I'm pretty sure I can figure out the reverse." He looked at Tyler so he wouldn't see Ryan's reaction, or lack thereof, to his words.

Tyler stroked Josh's thigh like one would pet a strange animal that was injured and might bite. His smile was flirtatious. "You keep telling yourself that. But don't worry, I can be infatuated enough for both of us. You just hang around and be handsome. Making people believe I'm crazy about you will be a piece of cake."

Josh snorted. "So, we're doing this?"

Tyler's fingers on his thigh traced a lazy line up his leg and over his hip. "Looks like it," he said.

Josh narrowed his eyes as Tyler's fingers traced over his ribs. "I still can't accept the full payment of my school loans. It's too much money."

"Fuck that," Tyler said. "I'm a notorious pain in the ass. Consider it combat pay. Also, there's Oliver." His fingers drifted lower over Josh's stomach.

"Who's Oliver?" the agent asked.

"My cat," Tyler said. "And we're kind of a package deal."

"The cat's fine," Josh said. "For the amount of money you're proposing, I could throw out every piece of furniture I own and buy brand-new."

Tyler smiled and it reached his eyes.

Josh didn't want Tyler's money, but he was sick of arguing about it. He was also beginning to think that Tyler was going to be more trouble than he'd originally thought. Tyler's fingers ventured a little too low, so Josh caught his hand and placed it on Tyler's knee while he looked at Alicia. "Can we go over what exactly will be expected from me, I mean us?"

"That's Tom's call, not mine. Once I give him the good news that we've got someone willing, he'll be in touch." She reached over and patted Josh's arm. "You seem like a good sport. Please don't stab Tyler in his sleep, okay?"

"Um, sure. I never stabbed Brad, and he's a lot more annoying than Tyler."

"Thanks a lot," Brad said, not seeming offended in the slightest.

"In the meantime," the agent said, "practice on the whole pretending to be a couple thing. Work on being relaxed in each other's company, okay? Josh, stop looking at Tyler like he might bite you. Tyler, don't bite him."

A wicked grin slid onto Tyler's face. "No promises."

"Behave," Alicia said. "That's an order. You cannot afford to screw this up."

"Yes, ma'am."

"Watch it. No one likes a wiseass. Now, Ryan, take me back to Chicago. I need to see about getting a flight home out of this hellhole. I've got a ton of work to get done."

Josh found it was easier to breathe and think with Ryan gone. The first thing he noticed was that beneath layers of painted-on charm and flirtation, Tyler looked like death warmed over. It was as if he'd been wearing a pretty disguise for the agent, and with her gone he felt safe enough to let it slip.

"We should consolidate to one house," Josh said, "and it should probably be my rental. While it's unlikely that you'd be tracked down to your family's vacation home, it's even more unlikely that you'd be tracked to an unrelated house down the lake from it. Until we hear from this publicist guy, we should probably keep you out of sight."

Tyler shrugged. "Okay with me," he said, then yawned. "I can start packing."

"You need more sleep, Ty," Brad said. "We can take care of packing and moving your stuff. What do you have, one suitcase and groceries? Pretty much the only thing I need you to do is to crate Oliver."

"I'll carry the cat over and get Tyler settled," Rachel said. "You and Josh can go into town and get his phone replaced. That way, at least they'll have one working cell phone between the two of them. Meanwhile, I'll clean this place up. By the time you guys get back, I should have everything taken care of."

"Okay," Brad said, but he gave her a long look. "I guess we can just about handle that."

Tyler went up to Josh and looped his arms around his neck. "Do I get a goodbye kiss?"

Josh froze and Tyler chuckled. "That's what I thought." He gave Josh the barest whisper of a kiss on his cheek. "You need to loosen up," he said. "This is your life for the foreseeable future."

"Give me more than a minute to adjust."

"Start working on it," Tyler said, then he went looking for his cat, Rachel trailing behind him.

Once in Brad's car, headed toward town, Josh felt some of the tension that had been building all morning start to ease. "This has been one hell of a start to the week. I'm going to end up needing a vacation from my vacation."

Brad snorted. "I hate to put another thing on your plate, but I need to ask you a favor."

"In addition to pretending to be the love of your brother's life? I can't believe I just signed on to be Tyler's boyfriend. Fake boyfriend. Although I was kind of Ryan's fake boyfriend, too."

Brad snorted. "Being my brother's fake boyfriend seems to be your fate, doesn't it? Seriously, though, yes. Something besides that. If I leave you supplies, would you be willing to sew Tyler up if he needs it while Rachel and I are on our honeymoon? It would be a huge load off my mind knowing that base is covered."

"Sure, I guess. I could've given him stitches last night if I hadn't been drunk and minus everything needed to do the job properly."

"Excellent. I really appreciate it."

Josh frowned. "How likely is it that I'll need to perform this service?"

Brad shrugged. "Depends. When he's stressed, Tyler seems to fall back on one of two shitty coping mechanisms. Either he cuts or..."

Not sure what could be worse, Josh asked, "Or what?"

Brad's cheeks burned pink. "Um. Normally I wouldn't say anything, but..."

"Come on. Since when do you have discretion?"

"You'd be surprised," Brad replied. "Okay. His other coping mechanism is sex."

"What?"

"You heard me. Tyler either cuts or gets laid when he can't deal. And since getting laid is currently off the table, he's going to cut if things get bad enough. I just thought you should be prepared."

Josh remembered Tyler's hand sliding down his abdomen and heading for his groin, and the kiss that he could still feel the ghost of on his cheek. He began to think he was in way over his head, and there didn't seem to be a life preserver in sight.

"Okay, yeah. I'll make sure that you come home to two brothers. Don't worry." Josh figured he could worry enough for both of them.

Brad spared him a glance. "You're the best, Josh. Forget everything I've ever said about you. So, speaking of being worried, should we be at all concerned about leaving Tyler and Rachel together?"

"What's the worst that could happen?"

"Um, mutual homicide. I think they'll refrain, though, for our sakes if nothing else. Josh, thanks for doing this. Really. You are a literal lifesaver."

"I'm just volunteering to be your brother's roommate, more or less. Probably more, but it's not that much different than when I let you be my roommate when U of C screwed up your dorm assignment. If I can survive living with you, I'm sure I can handle Tyler."

"You know, I wasn't that bad of a roommate."

"Three words," Josh said. "Water balloon incident."

"Oh. Yeah. Well, I guess you've got me there," he said with a snicker. "Maybe I am a tough act to follow. At least I never tried to kiss you."

"All things considered, that's a relief. I'm not sure I want a Chadwick trifecta. That, and I'm pretty sure my sister would murder us both."

"Who do you think she'd kill first?"

"You. She'd save me for last because I'm family."

Brad was silent for a while then said, "I hope we don't come back to find she's dumped Tyler's body in the lake."

"Nah," Josh said. "He's safe, at least until he hands over the money. She's got her priorities."

"That she does," said Brad, sounding fond of his fiancée despite all her mercenary and potential homicidal glory. That was love for you. Good luck making any sense of it.

Chapter 9
Rachel Speaks Her Mind

Saturday, September 17th, 8: 37 a.m.
Back and forth between the Chadwicks' lake house and an unnecessarily large rental house
Blue Lake, WI

"Grab your cat," Rachel said as soon as Brad and Josh were safely out of her way. "You and I need to talk."

Tyler looked at her and raised an imperious eyebrow. She'd seen the same look on Ryan's face at the firm when he felt someone was overstepping his or her bounds. It was the sort of thing that his — likely aristocratic — ancestors had used to quell peasants on their vast estates back in England or wherever. It didn't work on her when Ryan tried to use it, and it didn't work on her when his shrimpy brother tried it, either.

"Great," he said. "I can't wait." Sarcasm and condescension radiated off him, but he did go get his cat and put it inside the carrier for her.

Rachel grabbed it and set off for the house Josh had rented, figuring Tyler would follow his cat, if not her, and she wasn't wrong. He caught up with her on the patio.

"So, is this the point when you ask if my intentions toward your brother are honorable?" he asked.

"Depends on what you mean by intentions," Rachel said.

"Let me rephrase, then," said Tyler. "Are you worried about your brother's virtue?"

Rachel glanced at Tyler and snorted in disbelief. "His virtue? You're joking, right?"

Tyler shrugged. "What do you think?"

Rachel shifted the carrier to her other hand. "I don't know what to think," she said, "which is why I'm going to try and shake you until something satisfactory rattles loose."

Tyler eyed her. "Not literally, I assume."

"Hopefully it won't come to that." Rachel gave Tyler a bright smile.

Tyler gave her back an unimpressed expression. "Stop trying to intimidate me," he said. "Scarier people than you have already tried and failed."

"Ditto," she said. "You're nothing but a little baby snake. I used to work for your father, don't forget. You aren't nearly the bastard he was."

"Is, not was," Tyler said. "He's retired, not dead."

They were almost to the rental and he walked a little faster so he could get to the door before she could. He opened it and held it for her. "Not a fan of my father, I take it?"

"Not even a little," Rachel said, putting the cat's carrier down on the floor.

"We have that in common, at least. Just leave him in the carrier. He'll yowl, but that's normal. I can't let him out until we've got his litter box set up or he'll go and pee on one of the beds just for spite."

"Lovely," Rachel said, and followed Tyler out of the house.

"What are you worried about?" Tyler asked. "Since I'm just a little baby snake. I hope I'm something venomous."

"Of course, you are." *Baby snakes still have fangs.* "Tyler, I'm worried that Josh is going to get fucked over by yet another Chadwick. He doesn't have a good history when it comes to your family."

"He and Brad seem to get along."

"Yeah, because Brad doesn't want to have sex with him."

Tyler was quiet. Dammit. That's what she thought. It would've been nice to be wrong.

"This is a weird conversation," Tyler said. "Have I mentioned how weird this is? Because it's really fucking weird."

They reached his family's house and he stomped inside, snagging Oliver's water and food dishes. "The litter box and litter are in the back bathroom," he said, pointing. When Rachel came out a few minutes later balancing the bag of litter on top of the tray, she saw he had gotten a bag of presumably cat stuff together and was holding it.

"This is heavy," she said.

"Be grateful I had Brad scoop it this morning." Tyler indicated his stitches. "I'd help you carry it, but Brad will have a fit if I tear these."

"No," she said. "I've got it. I'm stronger than I look. I'm probably stronger than you." Rachel ignored his huff of disbelief as she lifted the pan higher to get a more secure grip on it. Tyler held the door for her as they left the house.

They didn't talk this time as they walked to the rental. Tyler seemed to be lost in his own thoughts, and Rachel found that carrying a litter box and forty pounds of cat litter left very little breath for speaking. She was out of shape. Josh was always nagging at her to exercise and she always ignored him. Rachel was glad he wasn't here to witness this, because he would be full of smug and retaliation would be necessary.

Rachel panted a little and shifted the litter and litter box in her arms. "God, this is heavy," she bitched, realizing she was repeating herself.

"I thought you were stronger than you looked, Xena."

"Just get the door," she said.

Tyler gave her a snappy salute and held the door open. Rachel set the pan and litter down with a grunt of relief while Tyler let his cat out and filled the food and water dishes.

"Are we done?" Tyler asked. "I'd really like to take a nap now."

"No, we're not done," Rachel said.

Josh was her older brother, but there were times when it felt like she was five years older than him, rather than the other way around. In many ways, it was like he was in a sort of emotional perpetual holding pattern that had frozen fifteen years ago when he and Ryan parted ways. Throwing him and Tyler together felt wrong, like letting your dumbass roommate's pet baby cobra play with your huge but clueless black lab. Things were not going to go well for anyone involved.

Tyler had that eyebrow of his raised again, waiting for the lowly peon to get to the point.

"Come on," she said. "Let's go sit on the porch and talk."

Tyler made an "after you" gesture. Rachel took a seat on a small couch that let her look at the lake and was a bit surprised when Tyler sat next to her.

"I've been here before," Tyler said.

"Been where?"

"Here," he replied, giving her a look like he doubted her intelligence. "This house."

"Oh. When?"

Tyler shook his head. "When I was a kid. I think my parents were friends with the people who used to own it. Maybe they still own it." He gave a little shrug. "Most of the houses on this side of the lake were built by people my parents knew. They used to call it the North North Shore." Tyler let out an unamused laugh. "Brad played with most of their kids. And Ryan had Josh, of course."

What about you? Who did you have? she wondered, but didn't ask. Instead she just said a very noncommittal, "Of course."

"I've always rather liked you," he said, surprising her again. "Or approved of you, I guess. You're good for Brad. Good with him. He's lucky to have you." The last sentence sounded almost wistful, but maybe that was her imagination. She was starting to feel bad for Tyler, and she didn't want to.

"I... thank you," Rachel said. "I always thought you were a spoiled, attention-seeking brat." Tyler gave her a look that was equal parts anger and resignation, so she hastened to add, "I'm sorry, Tyler. I was wrong. About a lot of things, as it turns out. I want to apologize to you for assuming that about you, well, except for the brat bit. I think that one's accurate."

"I love you, too," Tyler said. "Bitch."

Damage Control

"Okay, fine, I deserved that. You know, Brad should have told me the truth about you a long time ago, but he's as protective of his brothers as I am of mine." Rachel gave Tyler a wan smile. "But I wish I'd known, because I tend to think the worst about people. Dealing with money and lawyers all day is part of it, maybe, but I think that's just how I am. I see the worst in people before I think to look for their best. But my brother, Josh, he's not like that."

Tyler gave her a noncommittal grunt.

Rachel decided to take a different tack. "You know he's a dermatologist, right?"

"I am aware," Tyler said, and smiled at her. Even knowing Tyler was gay, even being thoroughly in love with his brother, Rachel reacted to that smile, her heart tripping in her chest. She had to pause a second to gather her wits about her. If Tyler ever used that smile on Josh he'd be toast.

"Dermatology wasn't his first choice. Josh wanted to specialize in pediatric plastic surgery. In the abstract, he found it fascinating. He was halfway through his residency when he had to stop. Not because he couldn't do it. He was an excellent surgeon. He had to stop because of the toll it was taking on his health. He couldn't detach himself enough from his patients' trauma. It was so much more than birth defect repairs. It was burns and mutilations and—"

"I get it," Tyler said. "Trust me. I get it."

"He had stomach problems. Lost a lot of weight. He started compulsively cleaning things, which we didn't find out about until later. He did a pretty good job of hiding what was going on for months by avoiding me and my parents and what few friends he has."

"What about Brad?"

That made Rachel smile, but it was bitter. "He'd moved in with me by that point, and that year I monopolized his time. It made it even easier for Josh to avoid scrutiny, since two of the people most likely to notice were pretty much oblivious to everything at the time. Anyway, Josh went to work and the gym and played video games. Then one day in the middle of a surgery he was assisting, he started vomiting blood. He spent that night in the ICU as a patient. That's when we found out all this was going on." Rachel realized she had her fists clenched and relaxed them. "It was decided that it was in his best interests not to pursue plastic surgery at all. I think it was pediatrics that was the problem, but he and his advisor and the hospital all agreed that he needed something less stressful, so he took some time off until his health recovered, then he switched to a more general dermatology residency. It must've worked because he got better, but he still has the cleaning thing, which is mostly under control. I think he's got it under control, anyway."

"Okay," Tyler said. "So, he's fragile. Don't break him. Check."

"You know," Rachel said, beginning to lose what little patience she had, "I figured not breaking my brother was kind of a given. He's a person, not a toy."

Tyler's face went glacially haughty. "I'll make sure to put him on a shelf and only bring him down for special occasions."

"Dammit, Tyler, just... please stop. I am trying to..." Rachel should not have tried to tap dance around what she wanted to say. She'd attempted to be diplomatic, even subtle, and that had been dumb. She wasn't good at subtle, and she suspected her pathetic attempts at it were wasted on Tyler. It would have been better to just say what she meant in the first place. "I'm trying to protect him, since he's not good at protecting himself. I'm worried about him. You, Tyler, worry me. A lot."

"What if I promise to play with him really carefully?" Tyler gave her a look of poisonous irritation.

Rachel forced herself not to react. "Josh has a hero complex," she said. "He's going to want to save you."

"Fuck that," Tyler snapped.

"I know," she said patiently. "Brad already warned me this was going to be a problem after Josh called us, all panicked because of you. My brother has a hero complex and you ... well, in Brad's words, are a resentful and ungrateful shit who hates being rescued even when he needs it."

"Right." Tyler spoke through a clenched jaw, and Rachel wondered if maybe she shouldn't have repeated that. Oh, well. Too late now.

"I'm just warning you ahead of time," Rachel said. "That's how he is."

"I'm not some princess in a fucking tower." Rachel could tell from Tyler's tone that she'd hit a nerve. Great. Just great.

"I didn't say you were." She made her voice as placating as she could.

"What else?" Tyler snapped. "I can tell there's more."

"He supposedly came out here to get over your brother," Rachel said. Tyler gave her a skeptical look. "I know, I know. I don't get it, either. I don't understand thing one about him and Ryan and why he can't seem to let go. I've given up long ago trying to make sense of it. It's not rational."

"Josh isn't over him," Tyler stated. It wasn't a question.

Rachel shrugged. "At this point, I don't know. Ryan was his first love, and Josh doesn't do anything by half measures. It's why that surgical rotation almost did him in. He isn't good at letting things go. Do you see?"

"Maybe." Tyler looked unhappy about it. Good. That was two of them.

"Josh isn't going to let you down if he can help it, Tyler. He wants to be someone's hero; if you let him he'll try and slay your dragons."

Tyler made a disgusted noise. "While still carrying a torch for my brother."

"Probably. Some habits are really hard to break. Unless you replace it with a new one."

"Meaning?" Tyler sounded suspicious.

"Meaning he'll never get over Ryan until he has a good enough reason to do so. I think he's been looking for a replacement and is doomed to failure because only Ryan is Ryan. And all of that is neither here nor there. I don't want you, Tyler, to become the new Ryan."

Tyler looked at her like she was crazy. "Seriously?"

"Yeah, Tyler. Seriously."

"Me? You think your brother is going to throw away two decades of... whatever he feels for Ryan for me?" Tyler looked skeptical and something else that Rachel found worrying.

She turned and looked Tyler full-on. "You interest him, Tyler. *Nothing* interests him except work and his Xbox and now you. So, yeah, I'm worried."

"What do you expect me to do about it?" Tyler asked.

"Option one is to make him go away."

"Is that what you want me to do? Be the bad guy? Take the hit and go down with the ship?"

"Option two," she said, forging ahead, "is to go through with this insane plan and keep your distance from him. Be the professional I know you're capable of being."

Tyler chewed on his bottom lip. "The problem with that is everyone will see at once he's not my boyfriend. Josh isn't a good actor."

"No, he's not," Rachel agreed. "What are you going to do about that?"

"You and I both know that there's only one way this is going to work. Option three is me seducing your beloved brother, right?"

"Unfortunately, yes. Option three is you seducing Josh."

"I can tell you're not a fan of option three." Tyler looked resigned to her not liking it.

"No, not so much. But there is option four. I am holding out for this one."

"Okay, lay it on me. What's option four?"

Rachel grabbed Tyler's hand and squeezed it. He gave her a startled look. "Be his friend."

Tyler blinked at her. "His friend?"

"Yes," Rachel repeated, becoming exasperated. "Is it a difficult concept? He could use a friend. Maybe you could use one, too."

Tyler continued to blink at her. It was like he was trying to give her a message in Morse code. Too bad she'd never paid much attention when they were learning it in Girl Scouts. He could be blinking "help me" or "eat at Joe's" or "two boxes of Thin Mints" for all she knew.

Tyler didn't say anything for a long time, but he did at least get his eyelashes under control. "Okay," he finally said. "Four options. I'll think about it."

"And if you fuck him over, I will gut you." Rachel gave Tyler her sweetest smile.

"You are going to be such a fun addition to the family," Tyler said.

Rachel eyed the baby cobra that was her future brother-in-law. "Likewise," she said.

Chapter 10
Tyler and Josh Have Their First Fight

Saturday, September 17th, 6:57 p.m.
A bedroom in an unnecessarily large rental house
Blue Lake, WI

Tyler was not in general a fan of napping, but the past day had been a lot even for him, and after having Rachel talk at him while Brad and Josh were off in town, he'd been more than willing to snuggle down in a strange bed in a strange room and sleep until he couldn't sleep anymore.

When Tyler woke, he had a dull headache pounding in his temples. Everything felt overwhelming. The video still existed and was out there being watched by who knew how many people. He would be expected to perform like a circus animal for the paparazzi, and the man he was supposed to perform with was a terrible actor. Josh couldn't pretend his way out of a paper bag. Something would have to be done about it. An option would need to be chosen. Tyler just had to figure out which one.

Alongside that, Rachel's warnings chimed in his ear: *don't fuck him over or I will gut you* and *he wants to be someone's hero, if you let him he'll try and slay your dragons*. Like Tyler was some helpless princess in need of rescue.

Fuck that.

And like he needed some dermatologist in a shining white coat moping around, trying to fix things for him. Another Ryan, only one not bound to him by blood and love.

Fuck that even more.

Without even realizing he was doing it, Tyler pressed down on his stitches. It helped to bring things into focus. The pain was good and bad, but it worked, and that was what mattered. He wasn't sure what he would do if cutting was no longer an option. Just thinking about the loss of that comfort, even knowing it was wrong to crave it, made him feel trapped.

Maybe he still could. If he was careful. Maybe.

Tyler ordered his mind to focus. Wallowing here wasn't going to accomplish anything. He'd get up, take the medication Brad had left for him, and see what could be done with Josh. This would work. Things would be okay. They had to be.

He rolled out of bed, staggered to the bathroom, and realized he was starving. His headache might be from too much blood lost and not enough fuel to replace it, something Brad nagged him about so often it was a familiar refrain. Tyler left the bathroom and made his way through the house and into the dim and deserted kitchen.

He opened the fridge and found milk in there. Then he rummaged in the cupboards until he found one with boxes inside. There was Raisin Bran and next to it was his favorite: Strawberry Frosted Mini Wheats, which was so weirdly specific that Brad, bless him, had to have bought it for him while he was in town.

Tyler made himself a bowl and went out to the screened porch. There he found Josh, sitting and staring out at the sun as it set over the lake. He sat in shadow but was bathed in the orange and pink sunset glow, beautiful like he was being filmed in chiaroscuro lighting. Then Josh looked up at him and he was just himself again.

"Did you sleep well?" he asked. "I'm glad you're eating something."

"I slept fine. Anything exciting happen while I was dead to the world?"

"Yeah, I talked to that publicist guy. Tom something or other. Ryan gave him my number. He's sending a photographer to take pictures of us tomorrow. Supposedly candid shots of us in town having a blast on our romantic getaway that'll be leaked to the internet. You and I are also supposed to take a shit-ton of selfies and upload them to Twitter and Instagram."

Tyler frowned. "I'm not on Instagram. At least, I don't think I am. I'll have to ask Purvi, since that's pretty much her thing. Well, I have to get a new phone, then I'll ask her."

"Who's Purvi?"

"My personal assistant." Presumably Ryan had told her he wasn't dead in a ditch somewhere. Even so, it must be bugging the shit out of her to have him incommunicado for so long. "I'm kinda shocked Ryan didn't give her your number, too, but count yourself lucky. Purvi can be a bit overwhelming. That, and she would have thrown herself at you shamelessly."

"Why?"

"It's what she does. She's harmless, though. Especially since her current boyfriend is nuts about her and is proving to be remarkably resistant to homosexuality."

"What?"

Tyler smirked at Josh's bafflement. "Okay, here's the thing. Purvi's a great girl. My absolute best friend in the whole world. But she tends to date guys who are bi-curious, because she finds them attractive for whatever fucked-up reason, and they tend to leave her for men. But so far, her current victim hasn't thrown one pass my way, and I'm pretty sure this one is legit straight. I mean, he might still leave her, but if he does, it won't be for a guy. I've got my fingers crossed for her with this one. He seems really into her. That said, some habits die hard and when you two meet, which is pretty much inevitable if you're going to be my fake boyfriend, she's bound to flirt with you." Tyler shrugged. "I don't think she can help it."

Josh's lips quirked but he nodded gravely. "I'll be sure to let her down gently, if and when we meet and she throws herself at me. You want to know the rest of what Tom told me?"

"Sure, go ahead."

"Okay, so someone from *Entertainment Weekly* wants to do a phone interview with you for an article. They want to have one of their photographers take pictures of you in Chicago on either Tuesday or Wednesday. We're supposed to get you a phone tomorrow and Tom will tell you more."

"Christ, that guy moves fast. I can't imagine what I'm paying him."

"Hopefully not more than you're paying me." Josh flashed him a smile, but he seemed uneasy.

Tyler swallowed the cereal he was eating, then grinned back. "You're worth every last penny. Or you will be. Did he say what they'll be interviewing me about? I can't think they'd just do a piece on who I'm dating, as fascinating as you are."

"He said that they're going to touch on the video for sure, and what it's like to be a recently outed gay actor in Hollywood, and also a bit about that movie you're going to be in. The arrow thingy."

"*The Silver Arrow*," Tyler said automatically. "So tomorrow we get to go to town and be all coupley? That means homework tonight, you know."

"What kind of homework?" Josh asked, sounding dubious.

"The fun kind. But we should start by doing what all couples do, even fake ones. Get to know each other."

"Tyler, I've known you your whole life."

"Sure, but how much do you know about me now? You couldn't even remember the name of the movie that I just got done shooting."

"Okay, fine, you're probably right. And we need to..." Josh stopped and cleared his throat. "Get more comfortable with each other. Physically, I mean."

"Well, yeah. That's the homework." It was impossible to tell in the fading light, but Tyler would bet anything that Josh was blushing. He ate his last Mini Wheat and put the bowl down on a side table. "Josh," he said, deciding to ask him what he'd earlier asked his sister, "Are you worried about your virtue?"

"My virtue, no." Josh shot him a puzzled look. "I am kinda worried that you'll cut yourself in the bathroom, though. I'll never get the blood out of the grout, and then I'll lose my deposit on this place."

So. Subject change. That was telling, but Tyler let it slide for now. He knew this discussion was inevitable, and they might as well have it out now, even if he'd rather it was later, preferably when he didn't already have a headache. "You're worried about the grout. I suppose that's a valid concern."

"Have you seen the bathrooms? White marble tile with white grout in every damn one. In a lake house that they rent out. What were they thinking?"

"Living with you is going to be… different," Tyler said. "I've never once had a roommate who worried about grout."

"You bleeding out would probably stain the marble, too. It's very porous. Impossible to know if they sealed it properly."

Tyler tried to catch Josh's eye, but he was staring out at the lake. "I'd hate to ruin perfectly good marble," he said. "That would be a shame. I'm pretty sure the kitchen has dark grout and granite."

Josh stopped pretending to look at the lake and faced Tyler. "Did you go through the house looking for appropriate places to cut yourself?"

Tyler made an irritated noise in the back of his throat. "No, but it sounds like you did. Tell me, Josh, on a scale of one to ten, one being a Xanax-induced stupor and ten being shit your pants terror, how worried are you about me bleeding to death on you?"

Josh looked grim. "Eleven."

"Eleven," mused Tyler. "Not good."

"Look, don't take it personally. Worrying is what I do. Rachel claims that it's my main hobby. I worry about everything, pretty much. Global warming, losing my hair, Republicans, spiders, antibiotic resistance, super volcanoes, insurance companies, and this spot on my right elbow. I'm pretty sure it's just a freckle, but I like to keep an eye on it."

Tyler wasn't sure if he was supposed to laugh at that or not. "But you're not worried about your virtue?" Rachel hadn't mentioned worrying as a hobby, but he supposed it had been implied.

Josh snorted. It was almost exactly the sound his sister had made. "You're about two decades too late. It was gone by the time you were in first grade. God, that makes me sound old. Hell, I am old."

"You are not old, Josh."

"I'm too old for you."

Tyler rolled his eyes, even if it was probably too dark for Josh to notice. "I have an ex who's older than you are," he said.

"Then maybe you're too young for me," Josh said, sounding fretful and full of second thoughts, which was not good.

Tyler got up and sat next to Josh so their legs touched. He threw on a pouty expression. "Well, I guess that puts me in my place."

"Yeah, I can see your ego and self-confidence crumble from here. Or I could, if it wasn't so dark."

Tyler pounded his right fist against his heart. "A direct hit," he said. "Aren't you worried that you're putting the marble in danger?" His shoulder brushed against Josh's.

"For now, I'm pretty sure it's safe. Also, while you were asleep I went over the place with a fine-tooth comb and hid everything sharp."

Tyler wasn't sure if Josh was joking or not, but either way, he began to drift from amused to annoyed. "How enterprising of you. Even the kitchen knives?"

"They're not all that sharp. It would take you ages to break the skin with those things."

"So, you pretty much babyproofed this place just for me. You really are disgustingly domestic, Dr. Rosen. Did you lock up the chemicals, too? Gotta make sure I don't chug the Drano."

"Were you planning on drinking the Drano? I'd advise against it. It is not a nice way to die."

"I was not, in fact, planning on drinking a Drano martini," Tyler said, preparing for the inevitable "just because I like to cut myself on a regular basis doesn't mean I'm suicidal" speech. He had a lot of practice delivering it.

"That, I believe," said Josh.

"You... do?" That wasn't in the script, and it took Tyler a second to follow what Josh was saying.

"Well, yeah," Josh said. "I mean, besides admitting to me that you're no planner, you don't strike me as being suicidal."

He was right, which rankled a little, although why it rankled Tyler couldn't have said. "Maybe you failed to notice these," Tyler said, brandishing both inner wrists. He wasn't even sure why he was bringing it up. Usually he took pains to hide them from people. Explanations were tedious and best avoided, so why he was shoving them in Josh's face was anyone's guess.

Josh's thumb brushed lightly over Tyler's wrist, right where there had once been a horizontal slice and now there was just a slightly raised scar. Tyler remembered vividly how the blood that day had come out much faster than he'd expected, but not fast enough, because he'd survived. He'd learned later that cutting your wrists, especially the way he went about it, wasn't a very good way to try and kill yourself. Gunshot, hanging, and jumping were much better bets, but a razor was all he'd had available to him at the time. He hadn't even thought to slit his throat, which might have worked better. In retrospect, he hadn't really wanted to die. He'd just wanted *out*, and that, at least, he'd achieved.

"These are several years old. You were a teenager?"

Tyler nodded.

"You want to talk about it?"

"No. Like you said, it was a long time ago. The circumstances were... unique. I don't want you thinking I'm going to go all Sylvia Plath on you now. I'm not."

"She stuck her head in an oven."

"I know that," Tyler snapped, starting to lose his temper.

"You're not the first cutter I've met, you know," Josh said, and his voice altered, now sounding both pedantic and condescending, reminding Tyler of a particularly annoying history professor he'd despised. "I see a lot more of them as patients than you'd think. Usually teenagers, but not always. Some cut for attention, and some because they want control, and some are trying to commit suicide and just haven't managed it yet. I always advise a psych eval. I'm friendly with a psychiatrist who specializes in self-harm and I try to send people to her because I know she's good. But a depressing number never go and there's another scar or wound the next time I see them, and then it's just one more round of scar reduction therapy. Based on my other cutters, I'd lay odds you fall in category two: the ones who do it for control. How am I doing so far?"

His accuracy was kind of freaking Tyler out, and he hated it. It was awful that he was an open book to Josh Rosen, of all people. Irritated, he pulled his wrist away from Josh's grasp. He felt every one of the years separating them and didn't like it one bit, so he plastered on his sharp smile and said, "Oh, this is riveting. Do go on."

And the idiot did just that.

"Right. Definitely category number two. But whichever, you're clearly self-destructive, based on your history of self-harm and indiscriminate sex. You already know cutting is dangerous as hell and sex has its own inherent risks. I think we'll have to work on that. If you're not already seeing a therapist, I can give you my friend's number. She really is very good." He let out a little nervous laugh, so maybe Tyler's smile was starting to get to him. "Not that I'm one to talk. My response to stress is to obsessively clean or kill demons. The two of us are pretty much crazy and crazier. It's a good thing we're not really dating." This little speech was said with such a complacent pomposity that it made Tyler see red. He felt his temper, already roiling like a pot filled too high and given too much flame, boil over, and he strove to keep a lid on it.

"Wait. What?" When Josh started to answer, Tyler put a finger to Josh's lips to shut him up. "No. You need to stop talking. Give me a second."

Tyler counted to ten, then he counted to twenty. It wasn't all Josh's fault. He couldn't know that the phrase "we'll have to work on that" was something they'd said over and over at Bridges while hurting him. Josh would have no way of knowing that. It wasn't fair to want to rage at him for saying those words and dredging up those memories.

But the rest. Laying his weaknesses bare in that patronizing tone. Like Tyler was Josh's patient, his project, his soul to save, his child to correct, his fucking princess in a fucking tower to fucking rescue. Yes, Rachel had warned him, but Tyler still felt like he'd been blindsided. That Josh, as fucked-up as he apparently was, had the gall to give him a lecture on his faults pushed Tyler past irritated and angry and into the land of righteous fury. He wanted to scream at Josh for that alone, and he couldn't, because he needed him. Even if he was being a horrible, pompous ass, right now he was Tyler's horrible, pompous ass, and they needed to be able to deal with each other or it would all be for nothing.

Options, Tyler. You need to choose an option, and option one is the shittiest choice of the bunch, he reminded himself. Tyler grabbed his feelings tight and held on for dear life, focusing on the one thing Josh had said that didn't make any sense.

"Okay, let's start with the easy one. To relieve stress, you kill demons?" Tyler removed his finger from Josh's mouth, dragging it downward slowly and pausing to give his lower lip a light stroke. "Please explain."

Josh dragged in a breath. He seemed a little apprehensive now. Good. That was smart. "Just video games," he said. "Nothing exciting."

"How disappointing. And you obsessively clean? Again, so domestic. You'll make some man a fine husband one day." Okay, his emotions were leaking a little, because there was broken glass embedded in those words.

Josh flinched back a little at Tyler's tone. "There are worse habits to have."

"Like cutting and fucking, do I have that right? Josh, do you mind telling me how, despite only knowing me, well, the adult me, approximately one day you feel qualified to draw that conclusion?" Josh opened his mouth, but Tyler gave his head a vicious negative shake and Josh shut his mouth again. "Answer: you don't know me and you have no right to judge me, so fuck you, fuck your armchair psychology, and fuck your holier-than-thou condescending attitude."

And crap, there it was. So much for reining in his temper. Tyler seethed, and he wanted to stop, but he couldn't seem to. *Let it go,* he thought. *Just let it go. Like that damn Disney movie.* He resumed counting.

Tyler felt Josh retreat both physically and emotionally behind a solid wall of frigid detachment. Josh had gone somewhere, far away, and what was left was a block of stone.

"I'm sorry," the block of stone said. "I didn't mean to offend you."

"No," Tyler said. "You do not get to just nope out of this conversation."

Josh's warm eyes had become chips of obsidian glittering in the fading light. "This isn't a conversation. This is you having a temper tantrum."

"Who the hell do you think you are, my father?"

The block of stone turned into ice. "I thought I was the one who was here to save your career."

"Yeah, for a hundred thousand dollars."

The ice cracked and satisfyingly angry heat poured out. "You know what? Fuck your money, Tyler. Take it all and shove it up your tiny, ungrateful ass. I didn't agree to help you for the money."

"Yeah, you agreed to it because you want to fuck with my brother and I'm as close as you're going to get." Josh recoiled, and Tyler felt a stirring of something in his gut. Possibly remorse. Probably shame. Also, a little worry. Tyler might have gone too far with that last remark. Oh, well, too late to take it back now. He pressed the wound on his arm to clear his head and braced for Josh's inevitable response. When there wasn't one, Tyler relaxed by degrees. He still wasn't feeling friendly, but he was able to drain most of the venom from his tone. "Not so fun when some virtual stranger lays bare your secrets, is it? Although in your case, it's not really a secret so much as a big flashing sign that we mostly ignore to be polite."

"I don't think this is going to work," Josh said. His hands were fisted on his lap and he now resembled a not-so-dormant volcano. Tyler was struck by a feeling of déjà vu, remembering Rachel sitting there in the same way that morning, fists also clenched, describing her brother landing in the ICU.

Tyler kept an eye on those fists, took a deep breath, and tossed Mount Josh a virgin sacrifice to try and appease him. "I'm sorry," he said.

Mount Josh stopped smoking. "What?"

"You heard me. I apologize. I'm sorry I blew up at you. You said something that set me off. That thing about trying to fix me and my problems—it's not your job, okay?"

Mount Josh was back to being stony and silent, but at least he wasn't erupting, so Tyler soldiered on. "But I still shouldn't have lost my temper, and I'm sorry for that."

Still no reaction from Josh.

"I could get down on my knees to apologize if you want."

"How the hell would that help?" Ah, finally a response. Thank God.

"Generally, getting on my knees tends to smooth over most arguments."

Josh eyed him. "You are trouble."

"Yes, Josh. I did warn you. It's kinda my thing."

"It doesn't have to be," he said, all sanctimonious again.

"Look, I need to stop cutting and possibly get a better attitude, and you need to stop obsessing about my brother and pull that huge stick out of your ass. I think we can agree that we're both pretty screwed up. I mean, I'd definitely give the edge to me, but you aren't that far behind. Like you said—crazy and crazier—that's us in a nutshell. So, spare me your so-called grown-up advice. I need you to be my pretend boyfriend, not my parent, not my savior, and absolutely not my knight in shining armor. Fuck that noise."

"Tyler ..."

"It's easy to go around fixing other people's problems, isn't it? I mean, you're a doctor, it's what you do, I get that, but I'm not your damsel in distress or your case to solve." *He wants to be someone's hero; if you let him he'll try and slay your dragons.* It wasn't like Rachel hadn't warned him.

"In the morning," Josh said, "we can call your agent and the publicist and tell them that it's not going to work out and they'll need to find someone else."

"No, dammit. Just stop. If I don't get to cut, you don't get to go run and hide. Because that's what you do when you can't or won't deal, isn't it? Cleaning and playing video games is just how you pass the time."

Josh looked like he'd been slapped, and Tyler wished he'd kept his mouth shut for once in his life.

"You've known the adult me all of one day and you know that how, Tyler?" Josh asked, his voice back to being icy, and Tyler was torn between feeling shame for being caught out as a hypocrite and relief that he still hadn't pushed Josh too far. Not watching what he said while angry was nearly as bad a habit as cutting.

"No doubt the exact same way you know about my issues: Rachel and Brad. They both talk a lot. Sometimes I can't help but listen."

"What else did she tell you?" Josh shook his head. "No. Wait. I don't want to know."

"Good call." Tyler nudged Josh with his shoulder. "I really am sorry. You just pushed my buttons a little, or a lot, and I pushed yours back. Which, when you think about it, is something couples do all the time when they fight. I should know. Maybe there's hope for us."

Josh held himself stiffly beside him. "I don't know. I'm not sure we can do this. That I can. I thought that I could, but look at us. We couldn't even have one conversation without getting into a fight. That can't be a good sign."

"Josh, I can't promise to be the best fake boyfriend ever. There's a reason I agreed to give you a shitload of money to do this for me. You should not expect nonstop sunshine and roses from me. I'm not that nice a person, and having that stupid video leaked, then dealing with the siblings, hasn't helped my mood any. Also, I have one fucker of a headache. But if you try not to be a condescending prick to me, I will do my best not to be a bitchy asshole to you. And I promise I won't open a vein and stain the marble, so you can stop worrying about it. Is it a deal?"

"Um... Tyler?"

"Yes, Josh?" Tyler leaned his head lightly along Josh's unyielding stony shoulder. Despite the nap, he still felt very tired.

"I'm not..." Josh started to say, then stopped. "I'm probably going to say and do the wrong thing again without realizing it," he continued. "You're kind of a walking minefield, so you're going to have to be more patient with me or this will never work. But you're right, I was being condescending. For that, I apologize."

Tyler huffed. Exchanging awkward and stilted apologies was better than trading barbs and insults, but only marginally. The way they were going, option four wouldn't be achieved any time this century. The idea of being friends with Josh seemed very far-fetched right now. Even option three, by far the easiest one of the bunch, was looking like a steep uphill climb. How on earth was he supposed to seduce a block of stone? "I've lost count, but I'm positive we've both reached our daily quotas for apologies, so enough already. Let's bury the hatchet, at least for now. No hard feelings?"

"Sure. No hard feelings," Josh said, although he didn't sound conciliatory.

"You wanna kiss and make up?" Tyler threw that one out there because he figured it was worth a shot.

Josh didn't reply but, if possible, his body became even more rigid. Tyler lifted his head to look at Josh's face, but all he could see in the dim light was a blank expression and glassy eyes. He smirked and took a guess. "You're thinking about kissing me right now, aren't you?" Maybe there was hope for option three after all.

"No," growled Josh. Except he was. Despite everything, Josh was not indifferent. Not completely.

"Liar. Do you feel the sudden urge to go clean the bathroom? Maybe go dust something?"

"Shut up," Josh said. He looked pissed, but the corner of his mouth twitched like he wanted to smile despite himself.

"Or maybe you just want to go hide somewhere." Tyler leaned up so he was whispering in Josh's ear. "Fight the urge. Be strong. I believe in you." Then he bit Josh's earlobe just hard enough so he could feel the press of his teeth. Tyler felt a shiver go all through Josh's body. Okay. Now they were getting somewhere.

"Fuck you, Tyler," Josh said, pulling away from him. "Fuck you redundantly sideways. You should check out the steak knives in the kitchen. I could've been wrong about how sharp they are. Just don't do it in one of the bathrooms."

With that bit of snark, something eased within Tyler. Josh was back to making jokes. Dark, unfunny ones, but that was okay. It was a start.

"Nice!" Tyler clapped his hands together, then rubbed them briskly. "Okay, that's all sorted. First fight out of the way and no bloodshed. Go us."

"Tyler, I think it's safe to say that you're the strangest man I've ever known."

Tyler patted Josh's thigh. His very nicely muscled thigh, Tyler couldn't help but notice. "You need to get out more. I feel sad for you. You are the saddest gay man in existence. Lucky for you I tumbled off a dock and into your life. This is practically going to be community service."

"Fuck you," Josh said again, this time with more resignation than heat.

"Perhaps one day," Tyler said, "but not tonight. We do have homework, though, and the day isn't getting any younger. Tell you what, why don't I go take a shower and put on my jammies? I feel like ick and I smell worse. You can start a fire in the fireplace, and then we can drink booze and have a proper slumber party."

"Jammies?" Josh asked. "Are you sure you're not a preteen girl? Are we going to paint our nails, too?"

"We can if you want to," Tyler said. "What do you have to drink in this place?"

"Besides anything you brought over, there's beer in the fridge, though none for you. Not with the antibiotic you're on."

Tyler sighed. "Fine, Dr. Rosen. While I'm in the shower, go build that fire and drink a beer for me. Hell, drink two." A drunken Josh had had no problem flirting with him last night. Tyler figured a few beers might help things along this evening.

Next order of business: attempting to seduce one grumpy, self-righteous, and possibly not indifferent dermatologist. How hard could that be?

Well, let's see. On one hand, he's mad at me and still pining for my brother. On the other hand, Brad let it slip that he hasn't had a boyfriend in over half a year. My odds are not spectacular, but I've gotten less likely prospects to fuck me.

Tyler went to go arm himself for battle.

Chapter 11
Josh Is Not Seduced by Tyler

Saturday, September 17th, 8:55 p.m.
Living room of an unnecessarily large rental house
Blue Lake, WI

Like the dutiful man he was, Josh went to the kitchen, got a beer out of the fridge, then set about lighting a fire in the fireplace using wood the owner had thoughtfully stacked outside. He hoped the chimney had been swept recently. Then he wondered if there was a carbon monoxide detector in the house. He looked around and found it, but figured he should crack a few windows just in case.

That done, he went and sat on the couch and put his feet up on the coffee table. Both Rachel and his mom would have yelled at him for that, but neither was around. Then it occurred to him that anyone who thought white marble bathrooms were a good idea probably wouldn't want his feet on the table, either, so he took them down.

Josh realized he was nervous, which was silly. He had no reason to be nervous of Tyler. On the other hand, he seemed to have a hair-trigger temper and, with all that talk about "homework," apparently was hell-bent on seducing him. Josh still wasn't sure how he felt about that, other than worried. The idea seemed all kinds of wrong, seeing as how Tyler was Ryan and Brad's baby brother. Even thinking about sex with Tyler was a bad idea. Yes. But.

That "but" was the problem. There was a bit of Josh, centered around the part of his brain that controlled his dick, no doubt, that couldn't help but wonder if being seduced by Tyler would be so awful. He was attractive, if not conventionally handsome, and Josh hadn't gotten laid in months. Maybe...

No, I am not going there.

Well... perhaps.

This is an extremely stupid, terrible idea. He's Ryan's *brother, for fuck's sake.*

Yeah, and Ryan had pretty much said, "Here's my brother, please use him to get over me," or at least it had felt like that at the time. The raw hurt Josh had experienced earlier had since peeled away and left irritation underneath, like dead skin sloughing off a healing burn. At this point Josh felt angry enough with the entire situation he'd put himself into that he was giving serious consideration into letting Tyler try his hardest, just to see what would happen. Hell, you could even argue it was rude not to at least let the kid give it his best shot.

Josh heard the shower turn off and he looked at the clock. 9:17. He mentally went through how long it should take to dry off and dress. He wondered if Tyler would shave, then got his answer when he heard the buzz of his electric razor and then a hair dryer. That puzzled him for a second, because Josh didn't own a hair dryer, and the last time he'd heard one it had been when he'd still been living at home with his parents. Eventually there was silence, but the door to the bathroom remained closed. Josh noted it was 9:35. He decided he'd wait ten more minutes, then knock on the door and hope that what was behind it wasn't stained marble and a still, pale figure collapsed on the floor.

Why the hell had he agreed to this insane plan again? Boredom and pissiness and prurient curiosity, pretty much, not to mention some of that savior crap Tyler had accused him of. This was shaping up to be one of the dumbest things he'd ever gotten himself into, and that included having Brad as his roommate.

Josh finished his first beer, then went and got another. As he drank it, he clicked the bottle lightly against his teeth to the rhythm of his anxiety.

9:40.

9:41.

9:42.

The bathroom door creaked open and Josh straightened up, pulling himself out of the slouch he'd fallen into on the couch. Trying to appear casual, he took off his glasses, rubbed his eyes, and yawned. It was far too early to go to bed, but he was exhausted from the previous night. He closed his eyes, glasses held in one hand, and stretched. He felt something settle on his left thigh. He wondered if Oliver had come out of hiding and decided to be friends.

He knew the answer to that almost at once, even without opening his eyes. The weight was too heavy, too hard, and besides, Josh could smell him. Soap (Josh's) and aftershave (not Josh's) and sandalwood from his shampoo.

Josh put his glasses back on and looked down at Tyler's head in his lap. "Hey," he said. "Make yourself at home already."

Tyler gazed up at him. "Thank you, I have. Are you ready for your homework? Fair warning, there is a distinct possibility that I might fall asleep on you. I didn't realize how tired I was until I got in the shower. Also, if I haven't said so earlier, I really like your glasses." He made a throaty noise that was a fair imitation of a purr.

Josh figured that Tyler hadn't bathed since his dunking in the lake last night, but hadn't realized how ridden hard and put away wet Tyler had previously appeared until seeing him now, clean and shaven and dressed in clothes that weren't three sizes too big for him. He still didn't look precisely bright-eyed or bushy-tailed, but he no longer looked like a disreputable, grubby elf, either. He was transformed, or so it seemed. Josh's brain scrambled to make sense of it while his mouth moved on autopilot.

"I like my glasses, too," he said, "because they allow me to see."

"Always so serious," Tyler said with a pout. Josh reminded himself that there were sharp teeth behind those sulky lips, but it was easy to become distracted. Tyler's mouth should, by all rights, be illegal, or at least come with some sort of Surgeon General's warning: beware, staring too long at Tyler Chadwick's mouth may cause serious lapses in judgment.

"Are you trying to seduce me?" Like it wasn't obvious what Tyler was up to.

Tyler gave him a Cheshire grin. "Possibly. Is it working?"

Josh wobbled his hand back and forth, and Tyler snorted a laugh. "What am I going to do with you, Tyler?"

"I'm sure you'll think of something. People always do." Josh didn't doubt that one bit. He was in trouble. Lots and lots of trouble.

Tyler might not have been Josh's normal type, but that didn't really matter, because all cleaned up and lying like a present on his lap, Tyler was stunning in a very literal way. Just looking at him, Josh felt like he'd been hit on the head with a brick.

Tyler wasn't handsome, like Ryan or the men he normally dated. Not merely cute, either. He'd been wrong about that. Tyler was even a step beyond pretty. The word that sprang to his mind was lovely, and even that wasn't quite right, but it was all his muddled brain could come up with, and it seemed wrong to toss Tyler off his lap just to go find a thesaurus.

Tyler's hair fell softly around his finely boned face and onto Josh's lap, now silky instead of clumpy with product and lake water. His brows were a rich brown and gracefully arched. His chameleon eyes, now a soft bluish-gray very like the fading strands of his hair, were framed by dark curling lashes. The kind of eyelashes that made women frown and say they were wasted on a man, but Josh begged to differ with them on that. Tyler's mouth was curved into a sweet smile, his lips looking like they'd taste of sugar and sin. But what drew Josh's eye, more than any other feature, was Tyler's skin. It was clear and pale and perfect. Josh figured Tyler must bathe in sunscreen to live in California and still have skin like that. He wanted, more than anything he'd wanted in a very long time, to stroke it.

Tyler was well on his way to seducing him, and they'd barely touched each other. This was bad. Josh's heartbeat felt heavy and ominous in his chest.

I am in so much trouble.

How had he not noticed this before? First there had been surprise, then fear, and of course he'd been more than a little drunk. Then this morning there had been Rachel and Brad taking up his attention, and finally Ryan, who tended to eclipse anyone and everyone. Meanwhile Tyler had been there, all the time talking, but appearing smaller and drabber in Josh's memory. Ordinary despite the hair. Small and unremarkable and cute in his too large borrowed clothing. Josh had looked at him but not seen *this*. How was that even possible? But here was the man who was in movies, the one who could maybe one day be a star.

"Hey, are you okay?" Tyler asked.

No. No, I am not.

"Yeah, I'm fine," Josh said, and drank more of his beer. "You look like a pretty princess," he said, aiming for derisive but not quite making it.

One fine dark brow rose. "You think so?"

Josh shrugged. "You clean up well. Also, the t-shirt helps." Along with gray plaid pajama bottoms, Tyler now wore a pink shirt that spelled out "Self-Rescuing Princess" in rainbow glitter.

"I wore it just for you. I'm not the type to wait in a tower for my Prince Charming," he said. "Just so you know."

"Okay, your highness, I'll try and remember that," Josh said, then yawned, even though sleeping was the last thing on his mind at that moment.

"You seem pretty tired. We could go straight to bed. Even if it is a shame to waste this fire."

"Separate beds?" Josh asked, and Tyler shook his head. "That's what I thought. I'm not sure I'm ready for that level of coursework."

"That's what I'm here for," Tyler said. "You've got a big test tomorrow, and I'm your tutor. We are going to study *so hard*."

That made Josh laugh, even if it was mostly from nerves. He took his glasses off to rub his eyes again, and felt them plucked out of his hand. He leaned his head back and sighed when he felt Tyler straddle his hips and perch on his thighs. "You're far too old to sit on my lap," he said, and opened his eyes.

Tyler was close enough that he wasn't blurry even without glasses. His lips curved in a slight smile. "I am the perfect age to sit on your lap," he said. "Now, let's get to know each other better." He leaned forward and kissed Josh.

The kiss was strange and careful and cautious until Josh thought, *okay, sure, why the hell not?* and licked his way into Tyler's dangerous mouth. Then it became just carnal. His hands drifted to Tyler's back, stealing underneath that ridiculous shirt. Tyler's skin was like every metaphor Josh had ever heard: smooth satin, soft silk, warm velvet. He didn't want to stop touching it. Ever.

So much trouble.

He moaned, and Tyler growled in response. Tyler cupped Josh's face and held it still. He kissed Josh's closed eyes, the tip of his nose, and his chin. Then he took Josh's lower lip between his teeth and bit it. Josh's cock, which had been at half-mast since Tyler laid his head on his leg, now hardened to full attention.

"You like that, don't you?" Tyler murmured. His hips rocked forward and their erections ground against each other. Josh groaned and resigned himself to coming in his jeans for the first time since leaving adolescence.

Josh pulled the silly pink shirt off Tyler and tossed it across the room. Tyler's chest was as gorgeous as the rest of him, with sleek muscles, a slender waist, and a narrow trail of brown hair low on his abdomen. His skin smelled wonderful. Josh bent forward and drew one small, hard nipple into his mouth while his thumb caressed the other, making Tyler shudder. "You like that, don't you?" Josh echoed. Tyler groaned, then laughed, then groaned again when Josh lightly bit the other one.

Josh kissed down Tyler's chest, bending him backward as he did so. When he got below Tyler's sternum and saw the marks etched there, Josh stopped and hauled him upright.

"What?" Tyler asked, his eyes now dark and sleepy like the bottom of the sea.

"I need to see you," Josh said. "Now. Everything."

"That sounded a lot less sexy than it should have," Tyler said. He folded his arms over his chest.

Josh knew he had ruined the moment, but he was helpless before the need to see how extensive Tyler's scars were. Still, he tried. "I can't do this—I mean, I can, and I will—but I have to see your scars. All of them."

Tyler frowned. He seemed to be debating it in his head. "Why? Why now?"

"I can't just turn off the doctor," Josh said, trying to articulate something he didn't really have words for. "He's always there, noting suspicious moles and cystic acne and eczema and psoriasis and, well, scars. I can't make him stop just because there's the possibility of a blow job in my future."

"Until about a minute ago there was way more than just the possibility. Now, not so much."

"Please, Tyler. Let me see them. Let the doctor in my head get this out of his system. And then I promise that'll be the end of it. I won't bring it up again."

"You're going to owe me for this, Dr. Rosen. Big time."

"What do you want?" Not that it mattered. Josh wouldn't quibble. He grabbed the glasses Tyler had stolen from him and put them back on.

"To be determined later," Tyler said. He stood and slid the gray pants down his slim hips. He paused after he'd revealed an inch of closely trimmed pubic hair. "Are you sure you're ready for this?"

"Tyler, I've seen your penis before."

Tyler's jaw fell open. "You watched the video! You perv."

Josh shook his head. "There was that one summer when you kept running around with no pants on."

"That's worse. I think I was six!"

"And I was fifteen and completely uninterested in you or your lack of modesty. I'm sure you have a very nice penis, but right now it's not my main concern."

Liar.

Tyler gave him a sharp look. "Your odds of getting a blow job are getting less likely by the second," he said, but he pushed his pants down until they puddled at his ankles. He stepped out of them and then went around the living room, turning on every lamp. "Where do you want me?" he asked, his voice snapping with barely leashed anger. He wasn't just put out, Josh realized. He was furious. Josh was going to have to make amends for this, but it couldn't be helped. Above and beyond his natural medical curiosity, he had to know what he was getting into.

Watching Tyler stalk about, Josh's mind went two places at once. The doctor wanted Tyler to stand still so he could make a mental note of each white or pink line, red mark, and half-healed wound. The man just stared at Tyler as he moved, each light bringing more of his nude body into stark relief. Josh first thought of Michelangelo's David, but that wasn't right. David's muscles were all wrong, and his expression too smug. No, Tyler was more Canova's Perseus, the one he'd seen while visiting New York with his family when he was a teenager, only minus the stupid hat, with his sword and the severed Gorgon's head implied. Josh suspected that if it were up to Tyler, the implied severed head would be his instead of Medusa's. Tyler, like Perseus, was exquisite: all slim, elegant lines with fine bones, and the most perfect ass Josh had ever seen, period. Tyler's ass deserved odes written in its honor.

"There... there's fine," he said, his mouth dry as he went to where Tyler posed in the middle of the room as if he were indeed a marble statue. Josh started to catalog the scars that covered Tyler's body like graffiti, but it became evident that it would be nearly impossible to count them all. There were too many, going back too many years, and they weren't all neat and even. At first Josh stood, then he took a seat on the coffee table when his mapping brought him to the lower regions of Tyler's body.

He'd seen worse. He'd seen much worse. Josh had to keep telling himself that. On Tyler's arms, most of the scars were old and pale pink or white. Hard to see unless you were looking for them. Easy to hide if he just folded his arms. The majority were in neat, small horizontal lines, and Josh's fingers lightly traced the ones in the bend of Tyler's right arm. Nearly all were smooth, but a few had a slight ridge to them. He looked up and Tyler's eyes were cold and distant. Each wrist had one single horizontal slash that had been deep enough to require stitches, but otherwise he'd left his wrists alone. Tyler had been lucky not to have severed a tendon. Or maybe he had, and they'd been able to repair it. The slashes on his wrists, as old as they were, made Josh internally wince.

Tyler's chest was unmarked until his lower abdomen, where there were a few scars and one healing wound below his navel that looked more like a scratch than a cut. Tyler's hips were heavily marked, though, each one crossed and recrossed so many times that picking out individual cuts was difficult. The tops of his thighs were relatively unscathed, the only scars showing being very old and faint. His legs from the upper knees down were perfect, except for what looked like an old and strangely shaped burn scar on his calf where no hair grew. There were marks on the tops of his feet as well, but like the thigh scars, they were faded and old.

The pattern was clear. He'd been careful, so very careful, to keep his new marks where they wouldn't be easily seen. "Part your legs," Josh said, and Tyler made a face but did as he was asked, putting one foot up on the coffee table and cupping himself, revealing scarring as crossed and recrossed as that on his hips. There were a few areas that looked like they'd had stitches at one point. "My God," Josh muttered before he could stop himself.

"Did you know that you're starting to get gray hairs, Dr. Rosen? Not many yet, but I can see them all in this light."

Josh tilted his head up to peer at Tyler, who stared down on him with impassive eyes.

"Am I past my sell-by date?" Josh asked, keeping his tone light, because if discussing Josh's handful of gray hairs removed that blankness from Tyler, they could talk about them all night. Hell, Josh would let Tyler name each one if it just took that look off his face.

Josh wanted to kick something. He wanted to curse. He wanted to put bandages and antibiotic ointment on the few healing cuts. He wanted to pull out every trick in his arsenal to make the visible scars fade. He wanted to fix Tyler and he'd already been forbidden from trying. Instead Josh gave him a small smile.

Tyler scrunched his nose, temporarily dispelling his resemblance to a marble statue. "Maybe. Are you done looking?" he asked, his tone bored.

Josh stood and took Tyler's face, as cold and still as Perseus himself, and cradled it. "I'm done," he said. "I'm sorry, but I had to see. I had to know. But I'm still sorry."

"I think that's enough studying for tonight," Tyler said. "At this point I don't care if we fail tomorrow. You can call my publicist and tell him

Damage Control

that I'm sick or dead or whatever you like." He started to pull away from Josh.

"No, wait. Just a second."

"What?" Tyler asked. "What more is there?"

"I..." Josh said, and stopped. He wasn't sure what to say to make Tyler feel better, but there must have been something of his thoughts on his face because Tyler flinched away from him.

"Don't you dare pity me," he said, making a disgusted noise. "Just don't."

That surprised the breath out of Josh. Tyler's body inspired many things in him, but not pity. He thought, *I am struck by your body's beauty and I am frightened by how little you seem to care for it.* He didn't say that because he was afraid it would only make everything worse, but he had to say something, even if it wouldn't be the right thing, so he repeated, "I'm sorry."

Tyler closed his eyes. "Josh, I can't do this. Not now. Maybe later. But I'm tired and I just can't."

Josh turned around, bent over, and retrieved Tyler's pajama bottoms. He handed them over. "Here," he said. "Put these on. You'll feel better." Then he walked over and grabbed Tyler's t-shirt from the floor and turned it inside out so the glittery design on the front was visible: "Self-Rescuing Princess." He presented the shirt with a flourish and a bow. "Your highness," he said.

"I should go to bed," Tyler said, putting on the shirt.

"You just woke up three hours ago," Josh protested. He went around the room and started turning off all the lights until only the fire lit the room. "Come sit beside me," he said. "You promised me a slumber party. There's even marshmallows we could roast once the fire dies down."

Tyler looked at him, his eyes tired and ancient.

Part of Josh wanted to roll back the clock to where he was kissing Tyler and everything was still fine, but he had to know, he had to see, and he didn't regret that, even if he did regret this withdrawal.

"Please," he said, and Tyler allowed himself to be pulled down to the couch and tucked beside Josh, who pulled a soft throw over them both. After a while Oliver came in and joined them, settling onto Tyler's lap. Tyler slowly petted the cat and relaxed by degrees until his head came to rest on Josh's shoulder.

While he sat beside Tyler, Josh worried, as was his habit. Part of him was disappointed that he was no longer being seduced, but a larger part was doing a pretty good job of convincing him that this was better. It was safer, certainly. Sex with Tyler would just cause problems he didn't need. Better to keep this casual, informal, and platonic.

But!

No buts. This was for the best.

Sometime later Tyler lifted his head. "Did you say something about marshmallows?"

Chapter 12
Tyler Demonstrates His Talent

Saturday, September 17th, 11:07 p.m.
The living room of an unnecessarily large rental house
Blue Lake, WI

Josh got up to go to the kitchen and Oliver followed him, probably hoping for a handout. Tyler sat alone and drew the throw around himself. Josh's absence made the left side of his body feel unnaturally cold, and he shivered.

Tyler had become, over the years, an expert at not showing all his body. He had a whole routine down pat that involved staying mostly dressed while he got his partner naked. A lot of men dug on the contrast.

If that failed, he would remove his shirt when the light wasn't too bright. If he could get away with it he didn't remove his pants, allowing stiff folds of denim to frame his erection. In a pinch, boxer briefs covered the worst of his secret. The last time he'd gotten completely naked for someone who wasn't a doctor was when he was still with Ethan and they'd still been bothering to fuck. Toward the end that had been rare and the marks on his hips and thighs had multiplied. Both things had featured prominently in their breakup. Ethan needed a better top and someone who didn't practice personal scrimshaw, and really, who could blame him?

Tyler should have never allowed Josh to remove his shirt in the first place, but he'd gotten carried away. Josh blurred all the lines and it was breaking something inside of Tyler. A lover, but not; a doctor, but not. He had asked to see, had pleaded for it, in fact. Tyler had given in, albeit with reluctance, because he needed Josh's cooperation, and because, if he was being honest, it was Josh, his long-ago crush, who'd been doing the asking. Maybe all those old feelings weren't as well stowed away in the attic of his emotions as he'd thought. Tyler drew his right leg up, hugged his knee, and pondered the implications.

Josh hadn't run screaming. Just that one phrase, "my God," was the only indication that he'd felt anything other than professional detachment. It made Tyler simultaneously want to carve several new lines while wishing he didn't have a single flaw on his body. He'd wanted, under the scrutiny of Josh's eyes, to be perfect. He'd longed for it so hard that it had hurt, the imperfections covering him aching in phantom pain. He'd yearned for the very thing he'd accused Josh of — to hide in his room and lick his wounds in peace away from Josh's observant and clinical eyes.

But no. Josh was persistent and dogged and wouldn't leave him alone. It shouldn't have been a surprise. For six years he hadn't left Ryan alone, either, until the Big Breakup occurred, and even then, Josh would have no doubt dropped everything and gone crawling back if Ryan had said the merest word.

Josh returned from the kitchen, his arms full. He laid everything down by the fireplace, then came and stood by Tyler. "Come on, your highness. Your dinner awaits." He held out a hand in a courtly gesture.

"I already ate dinner," Tyler said, but he put his hand in Josh's and let himself be pulled off the couch and drawn closer to the fire, which had burned down to mostly banked coals.

"Cereal is not dinner," Josh said. "It's barely breakfast. You need to eat." He placed another small log on the fire and sparks danced up the chimney. "Go get some pillows off the couch so we can sit on the floor."

"Yes, Mother." Tyler made a face at Josh, but went and grabbed two pillows. He put them down on the floor, then sat on one, his legs folding themselves, after years of practice, into an effortless lotus position.

"You're bendy," Josh observed. He opened a package of smoked sausages and put two on the tines of a toasting fork.

"Seven years of yoga. It was supposed to cure me. It does help my stress levels somewhat, and it has improved my flexibility. I wouldn't say it cured me, though."

"But you enjoy it?" Josh held the sausages over the coals and slowly rotated them. The smell was mouthwatering.

"Yeah, I guess. I like being flexible. It's come in handy a time or two."

"Oh?" Josh asked, acting for all the world like he didn't give a shit when it was clear he was curious as hell.

Tyler scooted back, then curled his body upward into a shoulder stand, then folded down into the plow position, at first keeping his legs straight, then bending them so his knees ended up next to his ears. "My ultimate goal is to be able to deep throat my own dick," he said, his voice somewhat muffled. "I can almost do it."

"What? Why?"

There was a smell of charring sausage. "Just to say I can," he said, and rearranged himself, first back into a shoulder stand, then to lotus on the pillow. He reached over and turned the handle of the fork that rested in Josh's slackening hands. "Like you wouldn't do it if you could. Watch out. Your sausages are burning."

Josh's attention snapped back to the fire. "I think they're about done." He grabbed a slice of bread and extracted the first sausage, then handed it to Tyler.

He rummaged through the stuff Josh had brought back from the kitchen looking for mustard, found it, and squirted it on his sausage. Tyler waited until Josh started to bite into his own sandwich to purr, "I just can't wait to get my mouth around your hot sausage," and was rewarded when Josh choked.

Tyler smiled, feeling pleased with himself, and Josh, and things in general. Amazing. He took another bite of his sandwich. Maybe he'd just been hungry.

Afterward they fed small bites of sausage to Oliver, then ate roasted marshmallows and drank root beer and it was, perhaps, a little like a slumber party, not that Tyler had any personal experience with them. Chadwicks didn't do slumber parties. The closest he'd ever come was every summer of his childhood at this lake with his brothers and Josh. Until that also ended.

When the fire died down to mere glowing embers, Josh closed the glass doors of the fireplace and stood, taking their dinner things back to the kitchen. Tyler glanced at the living room clock and was surprised it was almost one in the morning. Where had the time gone? He slouched down so that he lay on the floor with his head on one of the pillows. Oliver came to butt his head against Tyler's hand, so he petted his cat. He would go to bed. Any minute now.

He roused when he felt Josh pulling him up. "Come on, time for bed, princess."

"Don't call me that. I know you think you're funny, but you're not."

Josh smiled down at him and tugged on his arm. "Come on, your majesty. It's late, and we have a big day tomorrow."

Tyler yawned hugely and let Josh pull him through the house, too tired to argue. There was a bed in front of him so he crawled onto it, on top of the comforter. He probably would have slept like that, but he found himself moved this way and that until he was ensconced under the covers. He couldn't remember the last time he'd been tucked into bed. It was kind of nice.

He was drifting past the first layers of sleep when the bed dipped behind him. A warm body curled around his from behind, one arm going under his pillow and the other snaking around his waist.

Tyler crawled upward toward consciousness enough to say, "I thought you weren't ready for this level of coursework."

He felt Josh's lips against his ear as he murmured, "Just go to sleep."

Tyler knew he wouldn't now. He never slept entangled with another person. He'd always been a light sleeper, and the older he got, the less he liked or tolerated being touched while he tried to sleep. It was virtually impossible for him to relax this close to another person.

He was too exhausted to protest, though. Tyler decided he'd stay put until Josh fell asleep, then he'd slip out and find the bedroom he'd claimed earlier. For now, he lay in Josh's arms, listening to his soft breathing, let his mind drift, and dozed, knowing that Josh's first snore would be enough to wake him.

ೞ೦

Sunday, September 18th, 6:32 a.m.
Josh's bedroom in an unnecessarily large rental house
Blue Lake, WI

When Tyler woke to misty morning light, it was as he usually did, sprawled half on his side and half on his stomach, legs curved, his right arm underneath his pillow and his left curled in front with his hand under his chin. What wasn't usual was the large warm body draped over his, morning wood pressing against his ass.

Tyler eyed the digital clock by the bed. It was early, just after 6:30 a.m. He thought he'd get up, make coffee, and regroup, but edging out of bed went nowhere. Josh was heavily asleep and just plain heavy. Abandoning subtlety, Tyler heaved on the arm and chest that pinned him down, using his own body for leverage. Josh flopped onto his back, but his arm tightened around Tyler, and he was hauled backward until he rested on Josh's chest with his face shoved into the crook of Josh's neck.

"It's too early. Go back to sleep," Josh mumbled, hanging onto Tyler like he was a damned stuffed animal.

"If you don't let me go," Tyler said, "I'm going to bite you."

"Shh. Sleep."

Tyler opened his mouth and put his teeth on Josh's throat. He'd intended on sinking them in just enough to prove a point but was distracted by Josh's response, which was to go from sleepy torpor to rigid attention in less than five seconds. Josh let out a small moan, and the erection that lay along Tyler's thigh twitched.

Coffee didn't seem so important now. Tyler sat up, then straddled Josh's waist. Josh had his eyes shut tight and was biting his lip, but he brought his hands up to cradle Tyler's hips. Josh had beautiful hands. Large, with long tapered fingers, and strong, but they held onto Tyler like he was fragile. Tyler rolled his hips so Josh's erection slid along his pajama-clad ass. Underneath him, Josh shuddered.

Tyler felt a rush jolt through him. His cock ached, but he ignored it for the moment. It could wait. He slid down Josh's body, over his erection, and down his legs. Josh had gone to bed in a t-shirt and shorts, and Tyler thought that was way too much clothing.

"Take off your shirt."

Josh opened sleepy, bewildered eyes and looked at him like he'd spoken in a foreign language.

"Now," he ordered.

Something sparked in Josh's eyes and his lips formed a crooked half-smile. He sat up and slowly peeled off his shirt, then tossed it aside. Josh started to lean toward Tyler, but he was stopped by one finger pushing on his chest.

"Lie down," Tyler said. Josh obeyed, all those lovely abdominal muscles first contracting, then relaxing. Josh's chest was nearly enough to distract Tyler, but he contented himself with running his index finger from the ridge of Josh's Adam's apple down to his navel. Josh squirmed under the touch, his skin flushing, and his responsiveness made Tyler's cock throb harder.

Josh was gorgeous, full stop. Even in the morning. Maybe especially in the morning. His dark hair was a messy riot of loose curls. His eyes were warm and inviting like a hot drink on a cold day. Everything about him screamed, "take me," and Tyler thought, *don't mind if I do.*

He scooted further down Josh's legs and took a moment to appreciate them. They were long and lean and hard with muscle. Tyler remembered Josh had been a runner in high school, and he would bet money Josh was still a runner, with legs like those. He ran his hands lightly over the crisp hair on Josh's thighs, eliciting a shiver from him, then Tyler pulled Josh's shorts off and tossed them on top of his discarded shirt. His exposed erection was long and curved slightly up and to the left. It was dusky against the paler skin of his abdomen, the head glistening with precum, and it made Tyler's mouth water. He bent down and licked at the salty fluid with just the tip of his tongue. Josh let out an inarticulate growl and fisted his hands in the sheets. Tyler looked up at him along the length of his body and liked every inch he could see.

"I am going to suck your cock," Tyler said, his voice pleasant and conversational. "I'm going to take it all the way down into my throat because I can. You are going to lie there and keep your hands to yourself." The last three words were punctuated by small licks of his tongue along the vein that ran along the underside of Josh's cock. "Do you understand?"

Josh groaned and his hands clutched the sheet tighter.

Tyler leaned down and took Josh's cock into his mouth, easing it down his throat until his lips brushed the black hair curled around its base. He swallowed around it and hummed a little. Everyone liked humming, and Josh was no exception.

Josh bucked under him and let out a gusty breath. "Oh God, oh God, I…"

Tyler pulled up with exquisite slowness, applying suction as he did. Then he swallowed Josh's cock again and got down to business, although in his case it was all pleasure. Tyler adored giving head. He loved the movement and the wet, obscene noise, and the feeling of fullness and stretched lips. He enjoyed the taste and smell and the texture of cocks — salty and musky, smooth and silky, hard and hot, sweet and bitter. It had been a long time since he'd given a blow job without a barrier between him and the other man, and this was so much better than sucking over latex. There was something about that thought that bothered him, but he shoved it down where it wouldn't interfere with how fantastic this was, because what Tyler craved, even more than the smell, or the taste, or even the sensation, was the reaction he got. Getting a man to the point of babbling incoherence using just his mouth was what he needed, maybe even more than his own release, and Josh fed into all of that with every moan, sigh, and twitch of his body.

Josh was a treat. He bore his arousal so beautifully, keeping himself mostly still as he'd been directed with his fists at his sides, clutching the sheet, his back slightly bowed, his breath coming out in short pants. He was quiet, though, and Tyler thought they should remedy that.

He pulled his mouth off Josh's cock and curled his hand around the base. Josh gasped, "Please, don't... don't..."

Tyler pumped Josh firmly and tongued the head. "Don't what?"

"Don't stop. Suck me, please."

"Like this?" Tyler sucked him in deep again.

"Oh God, yes, please, please."

Tyler lifted his head again, eliciting a plaintive moan from the man underneath him. "I want to hear you, Josh."

"Please!" Josh raised the volume of his voice several notches. It wasn't quite a shout, but it was close.

A thrill shot through Tyler and went right to his aching erection and balls, making his body squirm involuntarily. He went back to concentrating on sucking Josh's dick while his hand caressed Josh's tightened sac, his short, manicured nails lightly scoring along it. Tyler could sense Josh was close to coming. Very close now. His loud cries were music to Tyler's ears.

"I'm going to come, please, I'm going to —" Josh's voice grew raspy.

Tyler held Josh's hips as he bucked helplessly. His cum flooded Tyler's mouth and throat and it was a pleasing mix of salty and bitter, with an edge of sweetness. It figured that Josh even had semen that tasted good. Dr. Sensible probably had an excellent diet, smoked sausages and marshmallows aside. Josh lay beneath him, his chest heaving, looking wrecked. Tyler wanted to crawl up his body and mark him, bite him, somehow declare ownership. *Mine.* It seemed fitting with the taste of Josh in his mouth.

That thought stopped him in his tracks, and he sat back on his heels.

Oh, shit. What did I just do? We're supposed to have a fake relationship. Not real. No one should be possessing anyone else. No matter how cute their bed head might be or how good their jizz tastes and oh, shit, I should not know what Josh Rosen's jizz tastes like. Fuck.

He'd just spontaneously blown his brother's more or less ex-boyfriend. So not right. Tyler's adrenaline high crashed and he was smacked in the face with unpleasant reality. He and Josh weren't in a relationship, and he'd had no right or business doing to Josh what he'd just done.

Tyler didn't know what he'd been thinking—sex with Josh this morning wasn't required to further the plan. He'd lost his flinchy politeness in Tyler's company by the time they'd gone to bed. Enough that Josh would've been able to hold his hand and even kiss him in public today without being freaked out. The blow job this morning had been stupid, reckless, and above all, unnecessary.

We were doing fine with option four but I couldn't leave things alone because, let's be honest, I've wanted to blow Josh Rosen since I was a teenager, and at the first opportunity I took what I wanted without even asking. Classy, Tyler, as always. Way to go.

"Shit," he muttered to himself.

"What?" Josh asked.

"Um... so. That was a thing that just happened."

"Tyler?" Josh propped himself up on his elbows to look at him. He was frowning. Crap.

Tyler wasn't sure what to say. *First you got me to strip naked in bright light, which I don't do, then you were relentlessly nice to me, and then you tucked me into bed. You didn't even snore on me. So, in return, I used your admittedly amazing body so I could live out a teenaged fantasy. I'm sorry. Is there a Hallmark card for that?* "I shouldn't have done that," he said. "I'm sorry. It was a huge mistake. Which I'm good at making. Naturally. So. Crap. I'll just shut up now and leave you alone and go take a shower."

Well, that's just great. One blow job and I've turned into a complete idiot. It's middle school all over again, like when I sucked off Justin Davis and thought it was true love forever. Tyler cringed at the memory of Justin beating the shit out of him to make him stop following Justin around like a lovesick stalker. He wasn't sure what had hurt more at the time—Justin's rejection or his fists.

On the heels of that fabulous memory came the stark realization that Tyler had just sucked off a man and let him, no, held him down and *made* him come in his mouth. No condom. And while Tyler knew, thanks to mother hennish Brad, that it was far less risky than raw anal, it was still something Tyler didn't do. Not on a first date, at any rate.

But Josh isn't a stranger. I've known him my whole life.

Bullshit. Tyler knew Josh, but he didn't *know* him, other than from the family gossip that trickled his way, mostly through Brad. He racked his brain for bits and pieces of stray information to try and reassure himself that what he'd just done wasn't as boneheaded as his wiser self knew it to be.

Nothing Brad had ever said indicated Josh was anything other than boring, responsible, dependable, and still stuck on Ryan. He didn't seem like the type of guy who would blow his wad in another guy's mouth without warning him of the potential danger, if said potential danger existed. No. If Josh had anything, he would've said so right off the bat, Tyler was sure. Well, fairly sure.

Things are fine. You're fine. Probably fine. Maybe fine. Right. Fine.

What he wasn't sure about was how Josh was going to react now that his orgasm was over, and his brain caught up with the idea that it had been delivered by the wrong brother.

Tyler looked at Josh, whose expression had gone dark and threatening like a smoking volcano. Tyler didn't think he would react with violence, but he wasn't completely certain of that any more than he was certain Josh was disease-free, so Tyler decided discretion was the better part of valor and fled the room. He wished with a desperate fervor that he already had his phone so he could talk to Purvi. She was bound to know the etiquette for this type of situation. If nothing else, she'd call him a dumbass, then remind him that she loved him.

Unable to contact Purvi, Tyler made a beeline for the shower. Still hard despite everything, he jerked himself off while letting hot water beat down on his shoulders. Pretty much any satisfaction was ruined by guilt and worry, especially since flashes of Josh kept intruding. It was enough to make Tyler wish he had a blade handy, but his only option was cuticle scissors and he wasn't that desperate, so he finished washing and braced himself to deal with his brand-new fake boyfriend, who he'd just used like a very elaborate sex toy without regard to any potential consequences or Josh's feelings.

Tyler stood in the shower and banged his head against the white marble, wishing he could go back in time and make the previous hour not have happened. He had a feeling it was going to be a long day.

Chapter 13
Josh Considers Throwing Tyler Back into the Lake

Sunday, September 18th, 7:10 a.m.
Josh's bedroom in an unnecessarily large rental house
Blue Lake, WI

Josh decided he was in favor of any morning that started out with an unexpected blow job, especially one given by a bossy elf with blue hair. It hadn't occurred to him that Tyler would be toppy, but it probably should have. Everything he'd seen thus far screamed of someone who craved control. There was no reason to think sex would be any different. At any rate, both Josh and his dick had approved. Even the part of him that had been all for keeping things platonic had been silent while Tyler sucked his dick. Josh was congratulating himself on what a great decision he'd made by not taking Tyler back to his own bed last night, when the man opened his mouth and ruined Josh's morning.

"I shouldn't have done that."

There was Lucy, that little bitch, snatching the football away again. Josh felt a familiar wave of frustration crash into him. History was repeating itself. He was back to presuming things, only this time with a different brother, and it was unfair because it wasn't like he'd asked for oral sex this morning. It had just sort of... happened to him, and he'd gone along with it with enthusiasm. As Tyler had blown him, he'd thought that the next few months might have compensations unrelated to the shit-ton of money he had no intention of taking, no matter what Tyler and Rachel thought. He'd pictured sex with Tyler in every room in his condo, because why not? Then Tyler answered the question for him.

"It was a huge mistake."

With every man he'd been with since Ryan, Josh had been the one pursued. Men, and even some women, threw lures at him all the time. Generally, he ignored them because he often wasn't interested, and when he did show interest, the men chased him, not the other way around. Josh hadn't gone after anyone since Ryan, because he hadn't cared about anyone enough to bother. The last time he'd really put himself out there had been that disastrous day almost fifteen years ago when he'd gambled and lost by trying to force Ryan's hand, and that day he'd sworn off men who didn't want him. Yet here he was, again, with expectations regarding a Chadwick, and here he was, again, being shut down.

Josh buried his head under a pillow, flooded with embarrassment and irritation. He couldn't hide forever, though, so he got up, put on his discarded clothes, made the bed, then stomped off to use one of the other unoccupied bathrooms. Afterward he went to the kitchen, still stomping like a petulant child, and poured himself a bowl of Raisin Bran that he had a hard time choking down. Josh had agreed to endure months of Tyler's company. Tyler would be in his home, underfoot, inescapable, and Josh would be in his old, uncomfortable position of wanting when he wasn't wanted back. And again, like it had been with Ryan, Josh hadn't even started it. He was beginning to think there was something wrong with the Chadwick boys, or at least two-thirds of them. It made him wish that he hadn't rashly decided to help one of them to spite the other, for what little good that had done him.

To hell with them both. The sentiment rang more hollowly than he would have liked, and that did not improve his mood.

Josh stirred his mushy cereal and felt acid burn in his throat. Ryan hadn't wanted him because he wasn't female. Tyler didn't want him because... well, there were so many possibilities there. Far too many to nail down just one. Maybe he was too old, or dull, or just not Tyler's type, whatever that might be. Probably this morning's blow job was some sort of obligatory, then instantly regretted, pity fuck.

There had been something in Tyler's voice right before he'd left to take a shower. Some note of obvious chagrin that even Josh's blood-starved and sex-addled brain had caught. Tyler hadn't just left the room this morning; he'd fled like it was the morning after an awkward and poorly thought out one-night stand.

Oh, and here's a fun thought. What if he's doing more than showering in there?

Josh could picture Tyler in the bathroom carving a line on his hip or thigh that had Josh's name on it. He'd promised he wouldn't do it anymore, but Josh held few illusions that the promise would be kept. Breaking away from any type of self-harm was, while possible, very difficult. Tyler, even with all the best intentions in the world, would start cutting again. It was pretty much inevitable, and Josh had no idea how much or little it would take to trigger him to cut. Like he'd said last night, Tyler was a minefield, and Josh hadn't the first idea where it was safe to step.

Josh wondered how many of those new lines he'd end up seeing, how many more Tyler would hide from him, and how many of them would be because of him. It made him feel ill, but even the nausea didn't stop the frustrated want that coursed through him. Josh still wanted Tyler, even with the very real possibility that Tyler didn't and wouldn't ever want him back.

He stirred his cereal and wondered if he could make it living with Tyler for what could be months. Maybe this attraction he felt would fade. In his experience, it generally did. Time and familiarity were bound to dull Tyler's shine into something more ordinary. Or maybe he'd only imagined it in the first place. Perhaps he'd take one look at Tyler after he got out of his shower and see just a normal guy, rather than the heart-stopping creature who'd laid his head on Josh's lap last night and then bewitched him this morning. The post-orgasmic light of clear day was good at dispelling that sort of thing. Then living with Tyler would be like rooming with Brad, except he'd never wanted Brad.

Josh looked up from his ruined cereal when he heard Tyler walk into the kitchen. He was wearing boots, tight jeans, and an even tighter blue Henley that was the same shade as the navy streaks in his hair. Tyler was as lovely as he'd appeared last night, smothering that small hope, although he looked less elfin with his hair styled to sleek perfection rather than just falling in soft waves around his face. Josh felt a stab of lust and then hated himself and Tyler and even Ryan a little bit for it. Fucking Lucy and her fucking football.

He'd be damned before he'd run at it this time.

"Um, about what happened this morning..." Tyler began, not looking at him.

Josh dropped his bowl in the sink with a clatter. "What about it?"

Tyler fidgeted, discomfort rolling off him. "I thought we should talk about it," he said, looking like talking about what they'd done — what Tyler had done — was the last thing he wanted to do.

"Forget about it," Josh said. "It's not worth talking about." He stalked off to take his own shower before he gave in to the impulse to strangle his fake boyfriend.

ଔଃଓ

Sunday, September 18th 9:15 a.m.
Josh's Lexus, on the way to town
Blue Lake, WI

Tyler kept chewing his lower lip on the drive into town. About halfway there he asked, "Are you mad at me? Stupid question. I can tell you're mad. Dammit. I should have known this would happen."

"Why would I be mad?" Josh replied, knowing that wasn't an answer and not caring.

Tyler worried his bottom lip some more. "This won't work if you're angry with me. We have to fix it, and it needs to happen before we get somewhere public."

Josh huffed. "What do you want to do about it?" *You started it, you fix it, hotshot.*

"Going back in time and unsucking your dick isn't an option, unfortunately."

Josh lay on the ground, the air knocked out of him, and Lucy stood above his wheezing form. She spiked that stupid football of hers right into his face.

"No," was all he managed to say, his voice coming out thready and weak.

"Pull over. We need to talk while you're not driving."

"There's nowhere to pull over. Your timing sucks." Forest lined the edges of both sides of the road and there was no shoulder.

"I tried to talk about it back at the house but you shut me down," Tyler said. "There. Pull in there." He pointed to a dirt and gravel road marked only with a wooden sign made unreadable by lichen.

Josh turned onto the little road. There was just enough room for his car before a locked gate with a "no trespassing" sign blocked the rest of the gravel drive that curled out of sight through the trees. "This is someone's driveway," he said. "I can't just park here."

"They're clearly not home. This is fine." Tyler unbuckled his seatbelt and bent himself like a pretzel, drawing his knees up to his chest, hugging them tight, and resting his chin on them. It looked uncomfortable as hell to Josh.

"Fine for what?" Josh put the car in park and turned off the engine. Tyler's posture made it clear they weren't going anywhere any time soon.

"Our inevitable argument," Tyler said, sounding resigned. "Okay, let's hear it. I know you're pissed off."

"What exactly do you want me say, Tyler?"

"It'll be better if you yell at me and get it out of your system. If you let it fester it'll get worse, and when you do finally break, you'll want to break me, too, and I'm rather fond of my face. I kind of need it to stay intact."

Tyler's words were insouciant but his whole body was tense. Was he expecting Josh to haul off and hit him or something? "What do you want from me?"

"Your cooperation would be nice."

"Is that what this morning was all about? Trying to get my cooperation?"

Tyler flushed and looked guilty as hell. Great. Nothing better than to experience one of the best blow jobs of your life only to find out for certain it was actually a combination bribe and pity fuck. Not to mention that it had been so awful that Tyler wished he'd never done it. Josh had had all sorts of sex ranging from fantastic to mediocre. This, however, was the first time he'd ever had what he'd thought had been awesome sex and it turned out instead to have been terrible for the other party. He wasn't even sure what he'd done wrong, but it made him want to punch something. Or someone.

"Come on," Tyler said. "Scream at me. You know you want to."

Josh eyed the man next to him. Tyler looked miserable and defiant and something else. Like he was waiting for that punch, knowing it was coming, dreading it, but not doing anything to avoid it, either.

"I never asked you to suck anything," Josh finally said, not screaming. He tried to keep his tone even, but as he went on his voice got harsher and louder despite himself. "I was sleeping, minding my own business, and you announced you were going to deep throat me. Was I supposed to refuse? Did I fail some sort of test? What the hell, Tyler?"

Tyler flinched a little at that and Josh felt glad, then guilty for feeling glad, then angry for feeling guilty. He glared at Tyler and continued his tirade, this time not raising his voice.

"This blowing hot and cold shit has got to stop. You need to make up your mind what you want from me and this… thing between the two of us. Now. I'm not driving anywhere until we settle it."

Tyler leaned his head back on the headrest and stared out the car's sunroof. "I'd like to go back in time and fix things, but I can't. What I did this morning was wrong and stupid, but I can't undo it. And now you're pissed at me, and we can't go around being a happy sappy power couple because you look like I pissed in your cereal. Everything I did to try and establish a rapport with you was all for nothing. We're back at square one because I fucked up. No, worse than square one, because at least yesterday you didn't hate me. I really am sorry, okay? I warned you ahead of time that I'm difficult. And you…" he waved his hand around, "…discombobulate me." He gave Josh a weak smile. "I need you. I fucked up. I'm sorry. Please don't hate me."

"I don't hate you," Josh said. "I'm currently annoyed and frustrated by you, but I don't hate you."

"Sure, you do," Tyler said. "Don't sweat it. I'm used to it. And I deserve it." Tyler radiated sincere contrition that might have fooled someone who wasn't used to that tactic, but the only one of Josh's relatives who didn't employ it on a regular basis was Rachel.

"Stop trying to guilt me into not being angry with you. I'm not going to magically stop being mad just because you say you're sorry and give me big, sad eyes. Unlike you, I can't change my emotions like flipping a switch."

Tyler scowled at him, which was infinitely preferable to his guilty hangdog expression. "Fine. I still need us to look like we're an actual couple that doesn't hate each other if we're going to go out in public. If you can't manage that, just drive me back to the house now. Fuck, go ahead and toss me in the lake if it makes you feel better. Maybe we can try again tomorrow. Or not. I told everyone this was too much to ask of you, but did anyone listen to me? No. Because no one ever does."

Josh thought about it. He could give up. Saving Tyler's career wasn't his responsibility. Although wasn't there that adage about being responsible for the life you saved? He'd always thought that was nonsense, but if he threw up his hands and walked away now it would prey on his mind once his anger dissipated. That was just how he was wired. In his heart, he felt committed to this lunacy, like it or not, and while he didn't like it very much at the moment, he would do his best to help Tyler, even if that meant sitting in this car until he was no longer mad enough to want to drown him. Or at least get him really wet.

"You want to give up?" Josh asked. "I didn't peg you as a quitter."

Tyler looked frustrated. "I'm trying to give you an out, you ungrateful idiot. Take it and run away like a good boy."

"If I quit on you, what's your plan B?"

Tyler shrugged and looked away. "Obscurity. Community theater. Porn. I don't know. There are so many options open to me."

"Stop feeling sorry for yourself. It's not helping."

"Fuck you, Josh. How did you put that? Fuck you redundantly sideways."

"If we're going to make this work," Josh said, ignoring him, "we'll need to have some ground rules. I won't make it even a week without murdering you if I have to spend all my time trying to figure out you mean A when your mouth is saying B and your actions tell me C. Life is too short for that shit."

Tyler just looked at him, unblinking.

"Are you paying attention to me, Tyler?"

"I'm hanging on your every word. This is fascinating. Truly. Do go on."

"And you wonder why people hate you," Josh muttered.

"No," Tyler said, "I don't wonder about it at all. Again, you were warned I was a pain in the ass. You should have listened."

"Do you really want me to give up on you and take you back to the house?"

Tyler was silent for several moments. "No," he finally said, "but I'm fucked if I know how to fix this. I've already apologized. I'm sorry I'm not Ryan. I'm a terrible person. I don't deserve your help. Yadda yadda. What good does any of that do?"

That threw Josh for a loop. "What does Ryan have to do with any of this?"

Tyler gave him a curious look. "Last time I checked you were still gone on him. Or did that change and no one gave me the memo?"

"My feelings regarding your brother have nothing to do with what happened this morning," Josh said, still not sure where Tyler was going with this.

Tyler gave him a skeptical look. "Right," he said, stretching the word out.

"They don't. I'm still pissed with you about this morning, and I fail to see what Ryan has to do with it. I don't remember him being there in the room with us."

Tyler raised an eyebrow at him. "Are you sure about that?"

"Um, yeah. I'm pretty sure I would've noticed if he'd been there."

"I don't think you and I are participating in the same conversation," Tyler said, "so I will try to be clear and use words of one syllable. Considering how many years of college you've had, I think you should be able to follow along."

"How is it possible that no one's ever smothered you in your sleep?"

"It's one of the great mysteries of the ages," Tyler said, looking away.

Josh sighed. This was going nowhere. "Okay, Tyler, please explain to me why you ran out after sucking my dick like I was the worst one-night stand you'd ever had and how that has anything to do with Ryan, who, as far as I know, was in another state at the time. You can use words of multiple syllables if you like."

Tyler turned back to stare at him. "I didn't run out like you were the worst one-night stand I'd ever had."

"Yes, you did. I was there. You said it was all a mistake and ran out like your ass was on fire. What was I supposed to think?"

Tyler covered his face with his hands. "Jesus Christ, I am an idiot. Or you are. Or it could be both of us." He dropped his hands from his face but looked away so Josh couldn't see his expression.

"Probably," Josh said. "Care to share your insight with this idiot? Because I have no idea what you're talking about."

"Josh, I said it was a mistake because getting a random blow job from your ex's brother who you barely know is weird and skeevy and I shouldn't have done it at all, let alone without a condom or at least a conversation about if you have something I could catch," Tyler said like he was explaining gravity to a small child. "I did not say it was a mistake for any other reason. Do you get that? I was being weird and gross, not to mention stupid and reckless. You were just... collateral damage."

"Collateral damage?" That stung. "And that's it?"

"No, that's not it." Tyler looked at him for several long moments as if searching for something. "If you must know, you were..." He seemed to consider several different ways of ending the sentence, discarding each one until he ended up with a wistful, "...perfect, really." Tyler groaned and closed his eyes. "How the hell did we manage to get here? Although in my defense, I still think you're mad for the wrong reasons."

"In my defense," Josh said, feeling less angry but still confused, "I think you might be insane. This is what living in California does to people. It makes them crazy."

"Fuck you."

"No, thank you. I'm sure it would end up being another mistake."

"Look here," Tyler said. "If we ever have sex, it will be premeditated and on purpose."

"So, what was this morning, then?"

Tyler shook his head. "Oh, no, I am not answering that. You tell me, Josh. What do you think this morning was?"

Josh itched to say something caustic but restrained himself. One of the two of them should probably act older than twelve. Also, Tyler had said he was perfect. It put him in a far more amiable frame of mind and lessened his desire to throttle Tyler. "I think it was one of the top ten best blow jobs I've ever received, if you must know. Although I might be mistaken. You took me by surprise and I wasn't fully awake at the time."

"Only top ten? I think you're insulting me now."

"Okay, maybe as good as top three," Josh said, deciding to be generous. "You're remarkably skilled and if things don't work out, porn is probably your best backup option. I think you could have a very lucrative career."

"Thanks for the vote of confidence," Tyler said dryly.

"No problem. I'd be willing to write you a letter of recommendation. 'He's bendy, has no apparent gag reflex, and is extremely fuckable.' What do you think?"

Tyler gave him a bemused look, pursed his lips, then opened his eyes wide. "I think you want to fuck me."

Josh froze. "What?"

"I thought... well, never mind what I thought. I was wrong, because you totally want to bone me and the real reason you've been pissed at me all morning is that you thought I didn't want you back. That's it, isn't it? Wow, how did I miss that? I really am an idiot. This is like a red-letter day for me in the getting shit wrong department."

Josh felt his cheeks burn. This was when Tyler would laugh at him, at the whole situation. It was absurd when you thought about it. A cliché, even. Age and supposed experience making an ass of himself over youth and beauty.

"Don't look at me like that," Tyler said. "Christ, I'm surprised, that's all. It's not like I think wanting to fuck me is a bad thing. I just wasn't expecting it from you, of all people. I was sure you still weren't over Ryan.

My bad. Please, feel free to desire my toothsome self." Tyler finished with a flourish of his hand like he was a game show model showing off a fantastic prize.

"Are you mocking me?" Josh asked.

"Not in the slightest. Well, maybe a little." Tyler looked like he'd solved one of the world's trickiest puzzles. "Don't get me wrong, I still think you're all kinds of freaky for wanting to fuck your ex's baby brother, but far be it from me to turn you down, especially seeing as how you're here to save me. Okay, this works. You'll continue to be my fake boyfriend and we'll have sex and that'll fix the awkward. Problem solved."

Josh stared at Tyler. He felt outraged and insulted and, God help him, tempted. Damn Tyler, and damn him for being even the least little bit interested in the now happily grinning evil elf sitting in the passenger seat of his car. "So, let me get this straight. In return for me agreeing to keep on being your fake boyfriend, you're in turn agreeing to have sex with me. Do I have that right?"

"You know, when you put it that way, it sounds like a pretty conventional relationship."

"No, dammit, conventional relationships are less transactional. My God, Tyler, this is probably the reason you're on speaking terms with only one of your exes." Getting involved with Tyler was such a terrible idea.

Tyler made a face at him. "There's no need to be nasty. I'm just trying to figure out how to make this thing between us work because I really need it to work, no lie. The only thing I'm any good at is acting. Well, that and blow jobs and looking pretty, but selling blow jobs is illegal and I'm too short to model for an actual career. Anyway, I'm still processing the idea that you want to have sex with me. Bear with me while I shift my world view. I never thought I, of all people, would break through the Ryan wall. Give me a moment to take it all in, will you?"

"The Ryan wall? What is it with you and him?"

Tyler threw on a superior expression, complete with raised eyebrow. Ryan used to do the same damn thing and it wasn't any less irritating when Tyler did it. "I'm pretty sure that's my line, honey. Which is to say I know you have a thing for him and this thing has been going on for over two decades. Excuse me for not realizing that you've finally moved on and want to plow my not-so-fertile but extremely well-toned fields."

"There is so much fucked up about what you just said that I don't know where to begin. Plow your fields? Really?"

"Too poetic?" Tyler fluttered his eyelashes.

"I haven't been anything to your brother for nearly fifteen years, Tyler. Do you really think I was celibate the whole time, keeping myself pure on the off chance he'd renounce being straight and take me back?"

Tyler stopped pretending he was a shameless flirt and appeared to consider that. "It does sound unlikely when you put it that way. Exactly how much sex are we talking here?"

"That's none of your business," Josh snapped.

"You just came in my mouth, so, yeah, I kinda think it is my business," Tyler said, his tone light but his posture tense.

Josh thawed. "If it was an issue I would've stopped you and said something, I swear."

Tyler gave him a hard look, then nodded once.

Josh ran a hand through his hair. "Tyler, I really don't want you to have sex with me just because you think it's what I want. That's... awful."

Tyler squinted at him. "Isn't that why most people have sex?"

"No, Tyler, they don't. Most people have sex because both parties, except in your case, where one must allow for the possibility of an extra person, mutually wish to have sex with the other person. The mutual part is key."

Tyler laughed, and it sounded like he was genuinely amused. "Did you just try to slut shame me, Josh? I think you did, but luckily for you I'm feeling tolerant right now. Anyway, here's a newsflash for you: I did not suck your dick this morning out of pity or charity or what-the-fuck-ever you're thinking. For the record, I sucked your dick, you moron, because you're handsome and you were nice to me and I wanted to and also because you have a nice dick. I felt bad afterward because I thought I'd taken advantage of you, and believe it or not, I don't make a habit of randomly sucking men off without a condom or their consent. I do have some standards."

Josh leaned his head back. So, if Tyler was to be believed, this morning had been an aberration for him. Interesting. He'd have to consider that later and decide what it meant, if anything. In the meantime, he wanted to address the issue that seemed to be bothering Tyler the most. "My consent should have been obvious when I followed your royal decrees, Tyler. If I hadn't been with the program, I'd have told you to get off my dick. I could've stopped you at any time, had I wanted to. Hell, I could probably pick you up and throw you across a room. You weigh hardly anything. You're tiny."

Tyler frowned. "I am not tiny."

"My sister is taller than you, Mr. Five-Foot-Eight-and-Three-Quarters."

"Your sister," Tyler growled, "is an Amazon and an unfair comparison. She's like Wonder Woman if she'd taken up accounting."

Josh snorted a laugh. "Thanks for that image. I needed that. I want you to know that this has been one of the most uncomfortable conversations I have ever had in my entire life, surpassed only by confessing my love for your brother and telling my parents I was gay."

Tyler held his arms up while he hummed the theme from Rocky.

"God, I hate you." Josh shut his eyes so he wouldn't have to look at Tyler gloating at him.

"No, you don't." Tyler cackled. "I have your number now. You think I'm fuckable and you're helping me despite being given several opportunities to back out. You're a knight in shining armor, just looking for a dragon to slay and, as irritating as I would normally find that, I've decided to overlook it, at least for now."

"I take it back. I don't hate you. I loathe you."

Josh felt a finger run up and down his arm. "Just how much do you loathe me?"

Josh opened his eyes and Tyler had done something, God knew what, and had put on his "I want to eat you like a hot fudge sundae" face. It was the same expression he'd been wearing that morning when Josh had opened his eyes to see Tyler straddling him. It was a dangerous look.

"Put that away," Josh said. "It's lethal."

"What?" Tyler opened his eyes wide in mock innocence.

"Stop it. You look like a cross between the big bad wolf and a lovesick teenager. It's weird."

"You like weird," Tyler shifted closer.

"No, I don't," Josh said and it sounded unconvincing even to his ears. "I am boring with a capital B. I have a type that I stick to and you are not that type."

Tyler rearranged his legs so he was kneeling on his seat. "Maybe, but for some reason I turn you on. Despite being me. And not your type. And not my brother."

Josh swallowed. "You need get over this Ryan obsession you have."

Tyler leaned into him. "So do you."

"You know, that's why I'm here. Not in this car. Here in Wisconsin. I came here to get over Ryan once and for all."

Tyler ran his index finger along Josh's jaw, then turned his face so Josh had to look at him. "How's that working out for you?" he asked.

"Pretty well until your morning freak-out," Josh said.

Tyler waved his hand. "Unnecessary attack of conscience," he corrected. "I can help you work on your issues. Think of fucking me as being therapy. Only more fun and much cheaper."

"No one ever screwed their way into better mental health," Josh said. "I know. I've tried."

"Okay, how about we have sex because we both want to?"

"Just like that? I've known you, the adult you, all of two days now." Josh gave Tyler what he knew was a smug grin.

A slow smile spread over Tyler's face. It made him look heartbreaking. Josh knew it was all a facade and he still felt the irresistible pull of that smile.

"Yeah," Tyler said, his voice husky. He leaned forward and ghosted a kiss on Josh's cheek like he had yesterday. "Why not?" His lips barely touched Josh's jaw. "You think I'm hot." Lips grazed his neck. "I think you're hot." Tyler's thumb ran along Josh's bottom lip. "We're both single." Tyler cradled Josh's jaw, licked his lip, then bit it. "I'm negative and you implied you were, too. Are you?"

It took a few seconds for Josh's brain to process that. "Um, yeah. If you need proof, I can get it for you."

Tyler sat back, seductive face gone and amused one back in place. "Of course you can. I don't know why I was ever worried. You're the poster boy for responsibility and Brad can vouch for me. There's no reason we can't fuck each other silly during this whole..." Tyler waved his hand around, "...charade."

"This is, by far, the strangest proposition I've ever received. You want to be longtime acquaintances with benefits?"

"Yes," Tyler said, "but I have high hopes to upgrade to friends with benefits at some point. You're fun. I think I'm going to like you. No, scratch that. I already like you."

"I'll think about it," Josh said.

"Let me help you make up your mind." Tyler slithered onto Josh's lap, which was fine, if unexpected, until his ass hit the car horn. Josh's hand scrambled for the power seat button, then made the seat go back as far as it could, which was just enough to stop the honking. Meanwhile, he had a lapful of Tyler, who was convulsed with laughter.

"Be my fake boyfriend and have actual sex with me," Tyler said, between what Josh uncharitably thought were not particularly masculine giggles. "Come on, it'll be fun, I promise. At least before the inevitable heartbreak and tears, but we can worry about those later."

"Heartbreak and tears?" Josh ran his hands up and down Tyler's back. He was a little fuzzy on how he'd gone from wanting to strangle the man on his lap to wanting instead to just touch him all over, but his hands had already decided they were down with that development.

"Oh, yeah," Tyler said. "That's when I go back home to the West Coast and crush your delicate little spirit, leaving you shivering in chilly Illinois, a hollow shell of a man who is unable to even look at another pretty boy without suffering pangs of thwarted, frustrated longing. It will be very sad."

"I think I'll manage to struggle through somehow," Josh said, and kissed him. "And you can keep California all to yourself. I lived there for four years and wasn't a fan. I'll stick with chilly Illinois, thanks all the same."

"California is awesome and you're clearly insane to prefer Illinois," said Tyler, then kissed him back, slowly, sweetly, like a lover would. "Keep that in mind when you start to pine for my very fine ass."

Josh cupped that very fine ass in both hands and groaned when Tyler pulled back to scatter small kisses down his jaw and neck. "Okay, fine, I surrender. You win. Congratulations, Tyler. We can go out in public and they will see you and one extremely horny boyfriend. But you need to stop rubbing on me like a cat in heat or we're going to have to go back so I can change my jeans, and we've already wasted enough time today."

Tyler let out a frustrated huff, but he climbed off of Josh and buckled himself back into the passenger seat. "We are going to need to buy lube and condoms," he said. "Lots."

"Whatever you say, your highness," Josh said, and started the car. "Let's do this thing."

Tyler reached over and grabbed his right hand as Josh started to shift from park to reverse. He gave it a squeeze, then released it.

"Thank you," he said, and Josh thought that he might be sincere, but with Tyler it was almost impossible for him to tell.

"Thank me later," he said, backing onto the empty road.

"Oh, don't worry," said Tyler. "I will."

Chapter 14
Tyler Goes to Town

Sunday, September 18th, 10:20 a.m.
Horrible touristy shops and a phone store
Blue Lake, WI

"This isn't going to work. I'd forgotten how boring this place is."

Blue Lake had a small downtown populated with touristy shops, specialty food stores, a few bars, and some restaurants. There were also several places that rented watercraft or took people on boat tours, but most of those were closed for the season. It was late morning and while the town wasn't deserted, it wasn't thronged either, and everyone Tyler had seen so far was at least forty years old and most were far older. He, and to a lesser extent Josh, stuck out, and not in a good way.

"It's off season," Josh said, "but this place was never particularly interesting even in summer. Ryan and I used to come here and get ice cream sometimes, but mostly we stuck to exploring in the boat or swimming or hiking in the woods."

Also fucking, Tyler thought. *It's a minor miracle neither one of you ever got poison ivy on an embarrassing place.* "I have no idea what I'm doing here," he said, looking at a store window display filled with rustic-esque knickknacks. End tables with bears painted on them. Table lamps where the base was a ceramic moose. There was a lot of plaid, and things with buttons glued on for obscure reasons, and pine cones. It was awful. He wanted to firebomb the place out of a sense of aesthetic decency.

"Why don't we go and get you a new phone?" Josh suggested. "Then you can call your publicist and figure something out."

"Oh, thank God, yes." At least at the phone store was unlikely to be decorated in plaid.

After getting back in the car Josh said, "You're going to have to stop looking like you stepped in dog shit. It's not attractive."

"I hate this place," Tyler said. "But I'll work on my expression."

Josh glanced at him for a second. "If you hate this place so much, then why did you come here?"

"I've always liked the lake house, but this town and the people, not so much. Here, I'm strange and wrong. Even as a kid I never fit in, not really. Ryan had you. Brad had a whole gang of kids that he ran with. Me? I had no friends. Who wants to be friends with the weird little boy who can't keep up with the other kids his own age? I pretended I didn't care, was nasty and snide, which I excel at, and I got beat up a lot when Brad wasn't around."

"I'm sorry," Josh said, and Tyler thought he probably was. That crusader spirit of his likely wanted to figure out time travel and either be pals with poor little lonely Tyler or fight everyone who was mean to him, or both. That was cute, but not particularly helpful or even necessary.

"Forget about it. It taught me how to take a punch, and being a pariah to the other kids here was the least of my problems growing up. The main reason I hate Wisconsin is because of that shithole Bridges to Salvation existing in it."

"Oh," Josh said, and there was a wealth of meaning in that word. "You know, the entire state isn't responsible for that place."

"My dislike doesn't have to be rational or fair. It just is. Besides, I don't see the rest of the state doing anything to make it go away. I think I'm justified in being pissed off for that reason alone."

"Okay, I guess." Josh sounded deeply disappointed, like Tyler had let him down in some way. Tyler wanted to growl at him and tell him to stop acting like his parent, but he locked his jaw and kept his mouth shut. He'd already had one stupid fight with Josh today and didn't have the will or energy for another.

"You know, the first place Dad sent me to, before Bridges, wasn't so bad as those places go. It was called Better Tomorrows, of all stupid-ass things, and was run by these religious hippy types. There were prayer circles and lots of hugging, because their theory was that we thought we were gay because our fathers hadn't given us enough affection as little kids or some shit. I don't think their theology or psychology was particularly sound. It was all kinds of fucked-up, but fairly benign in the grand scheme of things. I mean, it's hard to hate a place that uses hugging as therapy."

"Hugging. They wanted you to hug away the gay. Your father paid money to send you to a place that thought homosexuality could be cured by *hugging*."

A spontaneous giggle escaped from Tyler. It was funny in retrospect. "Yeah. I mean, there was also a lot of one-on-one counseling to try and convince you that being gay was something you could opt out of, and group sessions where we were encouraged to share our stories so we could all learn to rise above our baser urges, but also hugging. A surprising amount of hugging."

"How does that even work?"

Tyler smirked at Josh. "Spoiler alert, it doesn't."

"You know what I mean, Tyler."

"Well, you'd be assigned to another dude and you'd stand there and hug each other."

"That doesn't sound too terrible."

Tyler shrugged one shoulder. "The worst part was getting paired with some other horny teenaged boy who was into you when you weren't into him. Having to hug and be hugged while simultaneously having an unwelcome boner rubbed into your stomach is awkward. Anyway, I had a pretty good thing going there. I'd act out just a little too much at home and then get a stint at Better Tomorrows. It was almost like a vacation. I could've kept that shit up until I graduated from high school, but I lost my temper."

"You, lose your temper?"

Tyler gave Josh a side-eyed glance. "I know, it's shocking. One day when Dad pissed me off I made the mistake of taunting him, telling him their theory on why I was gay. He wasn't too thrilled with that, naturally, so that's why he picked Bridges for my next incarceration. Someone from church recommended it, probably. Bridges was definitely not run by hippies. They were more the 'spare the rod and spoil the child' type."

Josh didn't say anything, so Tyler looked over at him again. He just drove, silent and looking grim. "But I survived and that's all that matters," Tyler finished, feeling like he needed to reassure Josh for some reason.

Josh clenched his jaw, then relaxed it. "Sure," he said. He pulled up in front of the phone store and parked, but made no move to get out of the car.

"You all right?" Tyler asked.

"Yeah," Josh said, although he looked ill. "Let's get you a new phone."

When they walked inside the store, Tyler was happy to see it was a perfect example of corporate conformity. It soothed his soul somehow to see that even in this tourist trap some things resisted rustic woodsy twee cuteness. It made Tyler think that maybe there was hope for the world after all.

"Hi, can I help you? Omigod, you're him, you're him!" This was squealed with such delight that it startled Tyler enough to freeze him in place.

Standing at the kiosk right by the door was a boy so sparkly he might have been special ordered directly from Twinks R Us. His hair was bottle blond and styled into a gravity-defying quiff. He had big brown eyes highlighted by smoky shadow and expert eyeliner that Tyler couldn't help but admire, a perfect smattering of freckles on his likewise perfect nose, and full, glossy lips. His nametag announced he was Arik, and if he was legal it was only by the skin of his shiny, white teeth. Seeing him was a little disorienting. They were still in Butt Fuck, Wisconsin, right?

Tyler rallied and threw on his most supercilious expression. "The guy who needs to get his phone replaced? Yeah, that would be me."

"I'm sorry," Arik said. "I know I'm being all gushy on you, but you were awesome in *Blood and Water* and the best in *Pretty in Pink*, the new one, obviously, and I just saw the new trailer online for *The Silver Arrow* which is my favorite book in the whole world and oh my God, your hair, you're going to be the best Druindar and he is my absolute favorite. I totally ship him and Prince Florian, even if I know it's completely hopeless." He let out a gusty sigh.

Tyler smiled with genuine pleasure. "Thank you," he said, at once deciding that Arik deserved a hug and maybe a pony. He was adorable. "You're right, by the way. Florian and Druindar can't possibly be a couple. His one true love is Sandor. Duh. You know those two are fucking in every broom closet in that stupid castle of his."

Arik let out a snort of a laugh, then clapped a hand over his mouth. "I can't believe it's really *you*. And, well, I'm sorry about the whole sex video thing. People suck."

Tyler's face stilled as reality crashed down on this heretofore wonderful fan experience. "You saw the video?"

"Yeah, on Reddit the other day before the mods killed it. Just a gif, but damn. I mean, sorry. But," he lowered his voice to a whisper, "you are like totally my hero now."

Tyler stilled. "What?" *What the actual fuck is wrong with people?*

"I have no idea what you're doing in here in Blue Lake of all places, unless you like to fish," Arik made a face that spoke to how doubtful he found that idea, "but maybe, if you get super bored, I could show you some of the prettier spots. If you don't have plans."

Great. To top it off, now he was being flirted with by this child in the most obvious way possible, despite being with his fake boyfriend who Arik didn't know was fake. Tyler decided the kid didn't deserve a pony after all.

He opened his mouth to say God knew what, although it was bound to be unkind, but Josh saved them both by cutting him off. "Arik," he said, having checked out his name tag, "Tyler is always thrilled to meet one of his fans, but we really do need to get his phone replaced. It fell into the water and I'm afraid it didn't survive." His voice was deep, pleasant, and professional, what Tyler suspected was his doctor voice. It probably made all the pimply teenaged girls wet their panties just listening to it.

Arik wrenched his gaze away from Tyler. "Oh, right. I remember you from yesterday. Your phone fell into the lake, too." A tiny frown marred his smooth brow. Oh dear. He was thinking. It looked like it might be a bit of a struggle, too.

Tyler decided to help the poor boy out. "It sorta happened at the same time. Josh and I got a little carried away on the dock. Okay, maybe a lot carried away." Tyler beamed up at Josh, pouring every bit of manufactured devotion he was capable of into his expression.

Arik looked back and forth between Tyler and Josh, his eyes wide.

Tyler could practically see the wheels in his wee brain turning.

"Hi," said Josh, deciding to put Arik out of his misery, "I'm the boyfriend." He'd put on a toothy grin while he held out his hand for Arik to shake, which the kid did only out of sheer reflex. "Now. About that phone."

Arik's face flamed as he realized that he'd just made a fool out of himself in front of someone he idolized and that idol's handsome, charming, and much larger boyfriend. Clearly rattled, he stuck to business for the first half-hour of figuring out what phone Tyler wanted, then getting everything set up. Tyler, for his part, was on his best behavior, and Arik started to calm down when he realized that Tyler wasn't going to scream at him and Josh wasn't going to take him outside and beat him up, or worse, call corporate.

Tyler played up his role of besotted boyfriend, referring to Josh as "honey" and snuggling next to him. Josh seemed to tolerate it fairly well, which Tyler thought was a good sign.

As Tyler stood on tiptoe and whispered in a bored-looking Josh's ear, "When we're done here we need to go to the drugstore next," he heard the electronic shutter noise of a digital camera. Tyler focused on the source of the noise and saw Arik holding his new phone.

"I took a picture of you two," he said, and shrugged. "You looked cute together." Homeboy was working to dig himself out of the hole he'd made.

Tyler took the phone and looked at the picture. In it, Josh's eyes were unfocused behind his glasses but he was smiling, as if he and Tyler shared a private joke. Tucked against him was Tyler's face in profile, his lips close to Josh's ear. No one seeing it would think they'd pretty much been at each other's throats mere hours ago.

"I love it," Tyler said, and gave Arik a real smile. "Thank you."

Arik beamed with pleasure, and if he'd had a tail he would have wagged it. "Can I take one with my phone?" he asked. "And another with you and me?"

"Sure," Tyler said. "No problem." He made Josh pose with him again. This time he whispered, "When we go to the drugstore, make sure you buy enough condoms and lube to shock the cashier." The result of that picture was even better than the first, with Josh blushing a bright pink as Tyler's lips touched his ear. Then he had Josh take a picture of him and Arik. In that one, Tyler looked a bit smugger than he would have liked while Arik grinned like an idiot.

"Oh my God, the people in the forum are going to all shit themselves when I post this." Arik sounded like this might be the pinnacle of his short life so far.

"Forum?" Josh asked. "What forum?"

Arik handed Tyler a bag with the new phone's box and other

accessories in it. "Uh, the Tyler Chadwick sub on Reddit." At Tyler's blank look he added, "It's a place online where people who are your fans can post things about you. It's not a big sub, but it's pretty active, especially lately. You know, because of the new movie and video and all." He gave Tyler a beseeching look. "I don't suppose you'd be willing to do an AMA about it. I think there'd be a lot of interest."

"A what, now?" Tyler was lost. Apart from the bare minimum that Purvi bullied him into doing, Tyler largely avoided social media. He didn't have the attention span required for it and left most of it up to her. That was why he paid her and put up with her, after all. Well, that and her being his best friend and managing his life like she was a four-star general for Team Tyler. He looked down at the phone in his hand. He'd need to call her soon. He couldn't remember the last time he'd gone this long without at least texting her.

Meanwhile, the kid, unaware that his attention had wandered, had launched into some sort of spiel. Too bad Purvi wasn't here. She ate this shit up. "It stands for ask me anything. A lot of celebrities do them: actors, writers, politicians, that sort of thing. Seriously. Check it out. Here." Arik wrote on a card and handed it over. "This is the name of the site. Also of your forum, if you want to check it out. If you contact the mods and offer to do an AMA, I can't imagine they'd say no."

Tyler grabbed Arik's hand and brought his fingers to his lips and gave them a brief kiss. "I'll mention it to my publicist now that I have a phone on which to call him. It was lovely meeting you, Arik," he said. "A pleasure." Tyler smiled at the dazed expression on Arik's face. It spoke of never wanting to wash that hand ever again.

☙❧

Sunday, September 18th, 12: 30 p.m.
Sitting in Josh's Lexus in a pharmacy parking lot
Blue Lake, WI

"Are you sure this is a good idea, sweetheart?"

"No," Tyler said, unable to lie to his mother. "I think there's a more than a fifty-fifty chance it's going to be a disaster, but what choice do I have?"

"You didn't need to drag that Rosen boy into it. He's been through enough, hasn't he?"

That Rosen boy was currently shopping for condoms and lube

while Tyler sat in his car and made phone calls, first to Tom the publicist, then a brief one to Purvi, and now to his mother. Tyler had been joking when he'd said that they needed to buy enough stuff to shock the cashier, but with as long as he was taking in the store, it looked like Josh had taken him at his word. Not for the first time, Tyler wondered if perhaps he was biting off more than he could chew. Oh, well, the die was cast and all that. The chances of Arik not posting the pictures he'd taken of Tyler and The Boyfriend were so small as to be microscopic.

Tyler huffed. "This is not my fault! It was Ryan's plan and I'm pretty sure Josh agreed to do it mostly as a big fuck you to him, not that that jackass even noticed as far as I can tell. You know how Ryan is."

His mother clucked her tongue in disapproval. "Yes, I know how he is, but you still could have said no."

Yes, he could have, but he hadn't wanted to. Saying no would've meant either finding a stranger to pose as his boyfriend, trying to weather the scandal alone, or just giving up on his career, none of which were palatable options. Saying yes meant he'd have a reliable, trustworthy pseudo-boyfriend who was a known quantity. That he wanted to climb said pseudo-boyfriend like a tree was beside the point.

"I'm kinda backed into a corner here, Mom."

She sighed. "You'll do what you want. You always do. But if things go sideways, which no doubt they will, I'll be here. You know that."

Tyler swallowed past the lump in his throat. "I know," he said. "But it'll be fine. You'll see."

"You always say that," she said.

"I'm not always wrong," he replied.

His mother laughed. "No, not always. I remember Josh as being such a nice boy. Is he still?"

"He's a nice man. When he's not angry with me, of course. Actually, he's pretty nice even when he's mad."

"Try to behave, Tyler."

"People keep telling me that," he said.

"Then maybe you should listen to them."

"Yes, Mother."

"That was advice, sweetheart, not an order," she said, and he could hear the smile in her voice.

"Okay. Mom, I should probably go. He's walking back to the car. I'll call you later, promise."

"I love you. Bad decisions and all."

"I love you, too, nagging and all."

Tyler didn't need his mother to remind him that he had a bad track record when it came to making plans and decisions. He sometimes thought his life was one long series of bad ideas and worse decisions. Not protecting his laptop with a good password. Dyeing his hair blond that first time so he would match his brothers. Talking two horny JV football players into a threesome. Making that first cut. Allowing himself to ever be alone with Mr. "Please Call Me Michael" Koenig in his office. Not kicking David out sooner. All the shitty things he'd done to Ethan to push him away. Cutting in the dark at the end of a dock.

This "long-time acquaintances with benefits" plan was bound to be another one to add to an already lengthy list. Tyler didn't care, though, because he wanted Josh with every cell of his selfish body, consequences be damned. He'd deal with the fallout later, in his own way.

Josh opened the driver's side door, slid in, and tossed a bag onto Tyler's lap. "The cashier didn't seem shocked. Either I didn't buy enough, or she's already seen it all and has ceased to care."

"You were in there long enough."

"I had to weigh my options," Josh said with a crooked grin.

"I'm sure you did." Tyler said.

"You get anything accomplished while I was comparison shopping lube?"

"As a matter of fact, I talked to Purvi, who is delighted I'm still alive, Tom the publicist, and my mother. You should call yours, by the way, unless you want your parents to get one hell of a surprise."

Josh ran a hand through his hair and closed his eyes. "I know. That just isn't a conversation I'm looking forward to."

"Yeah, I'm not the type that men want to bring home to meet their parents." Or their friends, or coworkers. Of all the guys Tyler had dated, the only one who had taken him home to meet his family was Ethan, who, tellingly, was just like him.

"Tyler, you've already met my parents. That's part of the problem. They know I've known you pretty much your whole life. That first summer I came here you wanted everyone to carry you around everywhere—your mom, Ryan, even me. One should probably never date someone they carted around on their shoulders when he was a kid. It's weird. And then there's the other thing."

Tyler had zero memory of being carried piggyback by Josh, but he could see how that might be weird. "Hopefully not too weird or you just wasted," he looked at the receipt, "almost fifty bucks. Damn. You are not fucking around."

"Yet."

"Ha ha," Tyler said. "What was the other thing about bringing me home? Other than it being weird."

"Okay, so I came out in college. I think my parents have come to terms with it now, but at the time there was this sort of unspoken expectation from them that was like, 'let the boy get this out of his system, then he can settle down with some nice Jewish girl and give us grandkids."

"And I'm about as far from a nice Jewish girl as you can get."

"You are a princess," Josh said, and Tyler threw a box of condoms at his head.

"They are aware you're thirty-four, right?" Tyler pointed out. "They have to have figured out by now that you're not going to get being gay out of your system."

"Yeah. Mom has gone from trying to set me up with this nice girl she knows to that nice boy. Or boys, because she's relentless, no matter how many times I ask her to stop trying to set me up. As for Dad…"

"What?" Tyler asked.

Josh looked away. "It's complicated. They're my parents. They don't have to make sense. I'll call them this week, I promise. I just need to work up to it. Anyway, what did your publicist say?"

"He said that the photographer he had come up here is already bitching up a storm about how impossible the place is, duh. Tom wants to cut his losses, so at the photographer's suggestion we've been ordered to go eat lunch at The Pier and make sure we sit outside so our lunch date can be documented. Then the photographer is going to meet us back at the lake house and get some supposedly candid shots of us on the boat."

"So, the plan for the rest of the day is more of me playing devoted boyfriend. You know, never in my wildest dreams did it occur to me that I'd end up as some actor's arm candy."

"I am not just 'some actor,' I'll have you know."

"Well, I'm not just any old arm candy," Josh huffed.

"That you are not," Tyler said. "Let's go get some lunch."

❧

Sunday, September 18th, 12:57 p.m.
The outside seating area of The Pier restaurant
Blue Lake, WI

Purvi: I'm bored. What's happening now in the soap opera that is your life? Have you fucked the doctor yet?
Tyler: We're eating lunch, so no.
Purvi: Send me a picture
Tyler: Of my lunch?
Purvi: NO! Of Dr McDreamy.
Tyler: It's Rosen. Josh Rosen.

Purvi: Like a Jewish James Bond?

Tyler tried to picture Josh as a secret agent and failed.

Tyler: Heh. A decided no.

If there was a photographer taking pictures of them, he was being damn subtle about it. Tyler didn't care, though, because he was having a fine time eating lunch with Josh while at the same time carrying on a text conversation with Purvi. The lake was pretty, the sun was shining, and there was a nice breeze. It felt like he was on an actual date, only without the awkwardness of having to get to know the other person while being on his best behavior.

Between eating their house salads and waiting for their entrées, Josh reached for his hand and held it while they talked. That elicited a look from their waitress, but that was all. The other diners didn't seem to either notice or care. Not that he'd expected stoning or anything, Tyler supposed, but he thought maybe they'd encounter more hostility, even if it was of the passive, evil death stare from outraged moral citizens variety.

Then he thought of the kid at the phone store whose gayness was screamingly obvious and who just as obviously didn't care who noticed. It had been a little surprising for Tyler to see, but in a good way. He was used to it in San Francisco and LA, where being gay was just another thing that made you *you*, like the color of your eyes or the size of shoe you wore. In his memories of growing up in Highland Park and spending summers here, things had never been so easy or open. Everything had been a struggle. But maybe that was more because of his father, rather than where he'd been living at the time. Escaping his father had made him feel free to be anything, including himself. Here and in Illinois, even though he'd never really hid his sexuality, his openness had always been defiance rather than pride.

On the table, Tyler's phone vibrated, and he looked at it like it was a bomb about to go off. He missed his pre-video life, when phone notifications were usually from Purvi because she was bored or wanted to nag him about something. Today Purvi was almost drowned out by a wave of people wanting to talk to him, harass him, insult him, or just bother him. Tom kept telling him to stay positive, that they'd turn this all around and the video would be nothing but a fifteen-minute wonder. Tyler doubted it, but he was trying to keep his doubts to himself.

"Smile," Tyler said, "and try to look less constipated."

Josh made a face and Tyler took a picture of him like that. "Nice,

Ty. Very mature."

"Are you going to give me a real smile or not?"

Josh gave him a plastic smile, so Tyler leaned forward and tickled his ribs. He laughed reflexively and Tyler took the picture. "What was that for?"

"Tom texted me. Among other things, he's ordered me to take pictures like we're actually happy people on a happy date."

Josh looked put upon.

"This is what you signed up for, remember? That means you get to help me generate fodder for my Instagram account, which thank fuck someone besides me is maintaining. God bless Purvi. One more selfie of both of us and I'll leave you alone. For now."

Josh allowed himself to be selfied with good grace. They were probably garnering dirty looks by this point, but it couldn't be helped.

Tyler: Would you like to see what Dr McDreamy looks like?
Purvi: YES!
Tyler: Here. [attachment]
Purvi: Holy shit. He's hot.
Tyler: I know, right?
Purvi: Wow. I would totally bar his mitzvah.
Tyler: That doesn't even make sense.
Purvi: He's like what you'd get if Adrien Brody and Hugh Jackman had a baby.
Purvi: Can I have him when you're done with him?
Tyler: You're mental. He doesn't look like Hugh Jackman.
Tyler: Well, maybe a LITTLE. If you squint.
Purvi: I can see it.
Tyler: You're insane. And no, you may NOT have him.
Purvi: Why not?
Tyler: So many reasons: 1) gay 2) no, really, I'm not kidding, there is no converting this one, forget about it, you'll only embarrass yourself, gay 3) good luck getting him out of Illinois 4) what about Kevin?
Purvi: :(Good point.
Purvi: Kevin says he would totally go gay for Dr McDreamy.
Purvi: Correction: bi. Kevin claims no man is hot enough to make him forsake pussy entirely. Not even you. Isn't that sweet?
Tyler: I think Kevin's a keeper.
Purvi: Don't forget to send pictures to your publicist. Sheesh, do I have to do EVERYTHING for you?
Tyler: :P

Dutifully, Tyler sent the pictures he'd taken to Tom, who texted him back approval, which was a relief, and another update.

"Josh, you remember that kid who sold me my new phone?" he asked.

Josh frowned. "The twink who hit on you like an hour ago? Yes, I think I remember."

That gave him an odd burst of pleasure. "Why, Josh, are you jealous of that precious little baby gay?"

"No," was his curt reply, which Tyler found suspiciously snippy for someone who wasn't at all jealous.

"Well, you needn't be. Not only am I devoted entirely to you, but I've already gone through my 'fuck the pretty fellow twink' phase, and I have to say that I wasn't a fan. It felt far more incestuous than it would be fucking you, and you and I are practically related."

Josh inhaled some of the water he'd been drinking and choked a little. "What?" he gasped.

"Yeah, my last boyfriend was like me, only a less pretty version, which is why he went into journalism. In my experience putting two twinks together is just asking for trouble, even if one is more of a former twink. Dating someone almost exactly like me was exhausting."

"Former twink?"

Tyler sighed. "Alas, my elderly yet still fine ass has graduated from twinkdom. I'm just a queen now."

"Royalty, certainly," Josh said.

"Aren't you sweet? Such a gentleman." Tyler leaned over to kiss Josh's cheek, making him blush. Tyler decided that making Josh blush was his new favorite hobby.

Josh cleared his throat. "I don't think I ever had a twink phase. I was too self-conscious and awkward. Besides, even at eighteen I was far too tall, dark, and hairy."

Tyler grinned at him. "I remember you at eighteen. I think you're selling yourself short, but you're right. You were never a twink. You're one of those, 'I had no idea he was gay' gays. You're a stealth gay."

"I told you I've been out since college," Josh said with a frown.

"Oh, don't be all offended. I get it. You have a profession and being all out there isn't helpful, even if you were the type to be all out there naturally, which you're not. It's fine. We can't all be inherently fabulous."

"God forbid. So, what about Arik, anyway?" asked Josh. He pronounced the kid's name like it personally offended him.

"What about him?" Tyler asked, just to mess with him.

"You brought him up!"

"Oh, right! Sorry, I got distracted. You're very distracting. What I was going to say was that I mentioned that website the kid talked about to Tom. He apparently has had other clients do the answer questions thingies before and thinks it might be a good idea. He's looking into it."

"Okay. So, that's good, right?"

Tyler shrugged. "Maybe. I haven't googled myself since I got the phone. I'm afraid to. The shit I'm getting from people I know is bad enough. I'm not ready to see what the rest of the world thinks of me, too. But I can't put it off forever, can I?"

Josh squeezed his hand. "You can put it off for a little while longer," he said, then took his hand back when the waitress brought their lunches.

ଓଃଠ

Sunday, September 18th 3:56 p.m.
On Blue Lake in the Chadwicks' sexy speedboat
Blue Lake, WI

"You need to stop frowning," Tyler said. They'd ended up taking out the Chadwicks' speedboat because it was a million times sexier than the pontoon boat that came with Josh's rental. Tyler sprawled in the back while Josh manned the helm. He'd stopped the boat at the agreed-upon point so photos of them could be taken, but hadn't moved from his seat behind the wheel.

"I'm not frowning." But at least he got up and joined Tyler in the back of the boat.

"Yes, you are. What's wrong? I've been on my best behavior and everything."

"I'm not mad at you." If anything, Josh's frown deepened. Just great. "There are other things in this world besides you that irritate me."

"Aw, you say the sweetest things, Josh."

"Don't pout." Josh smoothed his thumb over Tyler's mouth, catching in a delicious way along his lower lip. "I don't like the photographer your publicist sent out. He's an asshole."

"He's pissed off to be sent into the wilds of northern Wisconsin on what he considers to be a bullshit assignment. Don't take it personally."

"It's hard not to take it personally when the first thing he asked me was how much they were paying me."

"You know, he's not going to be the only person making that assumption, Josh. It's part of the reason I need you to work with me. No matter how much you're pissed off, you can't show it in public. It's not fair, and I'm sorry that it's not fair, but I did warn you this wasn't going to be easy."

"You're not the one pissing me off, that jerk is, and how he looked at you."

Tyler squinted up at Josh. "Yeah, he looked at me. He's a photographer. That's his job."

"You know what I mean."

Tyler did. He had an effect on some people, almost always men who were not quite as straight as they claimed to be or thought they were. They were the guys in high school who wanted to hit him because it was their only excuse to touch him. The ones in bars who said ugly things with hungry eyes. The men who wanted to fuck him five ways to Sunday but weren't interested in going on an actual date, not that Tyler would date anyone like that. Not now, having learned that hard lesson.

Tyler made some men itch like a burr under a saddle and he knew it. Sometimes he even did it on purpose, but not today, and he had been irrationally glad that Josh had been with him. Like he needed some sort of champion. Like he wasn't perfectly capable of taking care of himself. He'd been both dodging and egging on assholes like the photographer for as long as he could remember.

Tyler wondered what Josh had seen, though, so he lied and said, "Not really. I wasn't paying attention."

"Like you were an insect he wanted to squish," Josh said, and there was a cold anger in him that Tyler knew had to go.

"As cute as I find you when you're grumpy, please try to look as if I'm the light of your life," Tyler said, and leaned up to kiss the side of Josh's firm mouth. Josh deepened the kiss and Tyler pulled back slightly. "Just remember to keep it PG," he reminded.

Josh also pulled back and plastered a pleasant smile on his face. "How long do we have to do this?" he asked.

Tyler grinned back and held his head at a fetching angle. He gave Josh a few subtle nudges to adjust him into a more photogenic posture. "Long enough for him to get some decent shots of us in nicely intimate yet also tasteful poses. You know why the guy was looking at me like he wanted to squish me like a bug, right?"

"He's an asshole."

Tyler laughed, throwing his head back to show the line of his throat. It was time to employ some misdirection. "He's an asshole who's hot for you."

"You are so full of it, Tyler."

Tyler brushed away a curl of hair that had tumbled across Josh's forehead. "No, really. He wants you bad. It means you're going to look great in these shots and I'm going to come out looking like hammered ass, but as long as it looks like we're in happy la-la land, that's all that matters."

"He is not hot for me."

"You keep telling yourself that, Romeo." Tyler said. "What do you say to me cooking dinner tonight?" He repositioned them again, this time with Josh leaning back and Tyler almost, but not quite, sitting on his lap.

"You can cook?"

"No, I just figured I'd offer and then kill us both with food poisoning."

Josh leaned toward Tyler and touched their noses together. "You've got a smart mouth on you, your highness."

"You're getting good at this, Rosen. I bet our friend is over there rubbing one out instead of taking pictures."

Josh snorted in disbelief then asked, "What are you going to cook for me?"

Tyler batted his eyelashes at Josh. "What do you want to eat?"

"Is that a trick question?" Josh brought his hand up and stroked Tyler's cheek.

"No, but we could invite our photographer friend over there to dinner and ask *him*. I'm pretty sure I know what his answer would be."

Josh snorted.

Tyler felt a vibration in his pocket and pulled out his phone. There was a text from the photographer saying that he'd gotten all the shots he needed and they were off the hook. "We can stop the displays of affection," Tyler said. "He's done. He asked for your number, too. I hope you don't mind, but I told him he could go find his own dermatologist."

"God, Tyler, what am I going to do with you?"

"You keep asking that. I can give you a list if it would help."

Josh sighed and shook his head. "How about take you for a ride?"

That remark hit a little too close to home for comfort and Tyler faltered. They weren't being serious and they weren't being sincere and they were being upfront about it. No one was taking anyone for a ride. They were both going into this with their eyes wide open. No expectations. No strings. But still, Tyler's mother's warning from this morning repeated in his head.

No. It would be fine. It would. Really.

Tyler needed to remember that Josh was not, and would never be, his Prince Charming. He didn't need a prince, in any case. He didn't need anyone. He was fine. Everything was fine.

Even so, Tyler started to feel that craving within himself and he strove to stomp it down. Not now. Maybe not ever again, although that idea was tinged with unreality. He couldn't quite believe in a Tyler with only fading scars on his body.

"Okay, Captain," he said with a brilliant smile. "I'm all yours. Take me for a ride."

Chapter 15
Josh Gets a New Boathouse Memory

Sunday, September 18th, 6:17 p.m.
The Chadwicks' boat house
Blue Lake, WI

"Do you remember when I caught you and Ryan in here?" Tyler asked as Josh secured the speedboat in the boathouse.

"Yeah. You scared the crap out of me that day." Josh joined Tyler where he leaned against the wall in the exact spot Ryan had been standing all those years ago. "And we probably scarred you for life. How old were you then? Seven?"

"Eight, and I was mostly baffled by what you were doing, but the whole thing made a lot more sense by the time puberty hit."

"I was worried that you'd tell everyone what you'd seen and that would be the end of me and Ryan." Josh's mouth kicked up in a half-smile. "Such as it was. Might have been for the best if you had. In the long run, I'm not sure you did me a favor that day by keeping our secret."

Tyler made a disgusted noise. "What secret? We all knew."

Josh stilled. He knew that Brad knew now, but he figured that was because Rachel had told him, since those two shared pretty much everything, and he knew Tyler knew because he'd seen him and Ryan together that day. The idea that everyone knew what had been going on the whole time was an entirely new concept for him. "What do you mean you all knew?"

"You two were pretty fucking obvious. I knew what was going on since I was, I don't know. Six? Seven, maybe. Something like that. Not the specifics, of course, that came later, but both Brad and I knew to stay out of your way and leave you and Ryan alone. Mom covered for you two all the time. That day I came in here, I knew better, but Ryan had promised to take me out on the boat and I just barged in without thinking."

"I can't believe you all knew. My biggest secret for years and everyone knew."

"Well, everyone except for Dad. Ryan knew there was no way in hell I'd say anything to him, so that little warning he gave me was for your benefit, not mine. He knew damn well I'd never go running to tell Dad what his perfect golden son and his best friend were getting up to."

Josh leaned against the wall next to Tyler. "So, except for your father, everyone knew."

Tyler gave him an exasperated look. "Are you not paying attention? Yes. We all knew."

"Everything?"

"It wasn't like we had secret cameras trained on you guys. It's just that you were... I don't know... all you could see was him and all he could see was you. You were this self-contained unit. It was some epic shit, let me tell you."

"No," said Josh. "That's not right. We were never a unit and we sure as hell weren't self-contained. There were all those girls. One after another. I hated every one of them, too. Even the nice ones."

Tyler shook his head. "I can only tell you what I remember. I'd say you should talk to Ryan about it, but I don't think it'd do any good. He's like the mayor of Denialsville."

"Ryan and I were not epic." Saying that was automatic, but hadn't he always, deep down, thought that very thing? A bit of him was convinced that what he and Ryan had had was special. Different. Important. It was why he'd had such a hard time letting go.

Tyler gave Josh a thoughtful look. "I've spent my whole life searching for someone to look at me like you two used to look at each other. Haven't found him yet, though."

"But..." Josh combed his memories, wanting to see what Tyler insisted had been there, and still knowing in the end it didn't matter. "It wasn't enough. *I* wasn't enough."

Tyler shrugged. "Not many people end up happily married to the person they were epically in love with as a teenager. It's not the end of the world." He pivoted and stood in front of Josh. "If it would help, I could get on my knees and give you a whole new boathouse memory."

Josh ran a hand up and down Tyler's spine, feeling the slight bumps of bone and planes of muscle under the rough weave of his shirt. He welcomed the change of subject, although he noticed that Brad had been right: Tyler's default response to difficulties seemed to be to fuck his way through or around them. It would bear watching. "You already gave me a blow job," he said.

"I didn't realize you had a once-in-a-lifetime limit. Silly me."

Josh felt adrift, unsure what was expected of him. Had today, from the end of their argument in the car until the end of their boat ride, been a real first date, which it almost felt like, Josh would've kissed Tyler and gone home alone, but it hadn't been a first date. They'd woken up in the same bed that morning. Josh already knew the feeling of Tyler in his arms and he liked it, rather more than he should. It had probably been a mistake to tuck Tyler into his bed last night. He wasn't even sure why he'd done it, only that it hadn't occurred to him to take Tyler back to his own room, and lying next to him had felt right.

The sensible portion of his brain told him in calm and measured tones to smile and step away from Tyler and go back to the house. The other portion, the part that kept reminding him that it had been six months since he'd had sex with another person, screamed at him that Tyler was *right here, right now* and that he'd be a fool to pass that up.

You already feel like today was a real date when it wasn't. Adding sex on top will not help matters, said the sane portion of his brain.

Fuck that and fuck him, urged his dick, which shouldn't get a vote but wanted one anyway.

Oh, go ahead. What harm could it do? said the rest of his brain. Tellingly, Josh heard that in Tyler's voice.

Sorry, sanity. You've been outvoted.

Josh grabbed Tyler's hips, then swiveled them both so Tyler's back was to the wall. "You're being greedy," he said. "It's my turn."

"All right," Tyler said. "Fair's fair." He smiled his siren's smile and even the sane portion of Josh's brain shut up.

Want. That thought pulsed through him, drowning out everything else. Just *want* and *now.*

Josh bent down and captured Tyler's mouth with his own. His tongue licked along Tyler's lips until his mouth opened with a sexy little moan that shot straight to Josh's dick. Josh's tongue slid inside and he resumed learning Tyler's mouth and how he liked to kiss and be kissed. Tyler seemed hesitant, almost fastidious, which Josh found intriguing. For someone who had hopped up on his lap with no prompting and gave blow jobs like an expensive whore, Tyler kissed like a shy virgin. It made Josh want to kiss him more, to see if that reticence was real or another act. Josh felt like he could kiss Tyler for hours, just trying to figure him out, but at the same time he wanted to taste every inch of him.

I have time, he assured himself. *More than enough time.* But there was an urgency inside himself that denied that. *Hurry,* it whispered back. *Hurry before he changes his mind. Hurry before the ball is snatched away.*

Josh's lips trailed down Tyler's jaw, catching on the slight roughness of the late-day stubble there. His thumbs ran along the ridges of Tyler's collar bones, then he traced each one with his tongue before sucking at the hollow of Tyler's throat. He started to remove Tyler's shirt to give him better access, but Tyler stopped him.

"Touch me," Tyler said. "I swear to God I will die if you don't touch me right fucking now." He made begging sound like a demand.

Josh's hands smoothed down Tyler's sides, then reached behind to squeeze Tyler's ass and cradle his narrow hips. "I am touching you."

"I want you to touch my cock, you ass," Tyler said, his voice edging toward a whine. He bucked his hips, held as they were in Josh's loose grip.

Josh widened his stance and lifted Tyler and shoved him against the wall, then leaned in so he could rub their erections together. Even through layers of cotton and denim it was almost too much. "Was that what you wanted?" Josh asked.

"Fucking tease," Tyler panted. His legs encircled Josh's hips and he clung on like a barnacle. Tyler grabbed Josh's face and pulled him in for another kiss, this time with a feverish ferocity that was the polar opposite of his earlier diffidence. The contrast drove Josh wild. When he pulled back, Tyler demanded, "Get on your goddamn knees and suck my cock."

"You're such a bossy little bastard," Josh said, pretending like the orders coming out of Tyler's mouth weren't hot as fuck.

"Do it," Tyler hissed, sliding his legs down Josh until he was standing on his own feet.

Tyler gave Josh a little push, then leaned back against the wall. Josh sank down obediently, first into a squat and then down on his knees. He undid the button on Tyler's jeans and unzipped them carefully. Then he pulled the jeans and underwear down Tyler's thighs.

Tyler had exquisite hip bones, the iliac crests creating delicate ridges that Josh traced his thumbs over. The skin was stretched taut there and Tyler shivered under Josh's touch. His thick erection was a deep rosy hue that was a stark contrast to his milky skin. It jutted out, seeking contact, so Josh closed his fist around it. Tyler thrust into Josh's hand and moaned.

"Suck me, dammit."

Josh leaned forward and licked the slit, gathering the precum there onto his tongue. Tyler hissed in a breath.

"Ask me nicely, princess."

"Fuck. You," Tyler bit out and bucked his hips again.

Josh let go and Tyler groaned. "Try again," Josh said. He took first one, then the other, of Tyler's testicles into his mouth and sucked. Tyler's head hit the back of the wall with a bang that had to have hurt.

"Jesus," Tyler moaned.

"Wrong Jew. Keep trying."

Tyler let out a short burst of laughter. "God, you win. Please, suck my cock, Josh. Pretty please with sugar and whipped cream and a fucking cherry on top."

"Your wish is my command." Josh took Tyler's length into his mouth as far as he could. He sucked hard and fast, wanting Tyler to come quickly. Later he would do this again and take the time to savor it, but right now he just wanted to taste Tyler's orgasm.

He loved the sounds that Tyler made as he surrendered to Josh's mouth. They were so needy, so abandoned, and so different from the very controlled man who'd sucked his dick this morning. Josh also loved it when Tyler's fingers sank into his hair, gripping tight and holding on for dear life.

Tyler started to fuck his mouth and Josh let him, curling his fist around the base of Tyler's cock to keep him from going too deep since he didn't have Tyler's apparent complete lack of a gag reflex.

"I wanna come on you," Tyler said. That wasn't really Josh's thing, but before he could even think to register a protest, Tyler pulled out of his mouth, curled his own hand over Josh's, then came on Josh's face and chest. Some of it hit his glasses and slowly dripped down the lens.

The sane portion of Josh's brain recovered enough to be both irritated and a bit grossed out by the semen on his glasses. The rest of him thought it was kind of funny, at least until Tyler reached down and rubbed his cum into Josh's skin and lips with a dreamy look on his pretty face. Then everything went back to *want*.

"Fuck, that's hot," Tyler said. His pupils had swallowed his eyes, making them look black and bottomless. "You're filthy and gorgeous and m—" he paused, frowned, then continued, "messy. You need a shower now. And a change of clothes." He gave Josh a lopsided smile. "That was intense," he said. "I got a little carried away. There's some in your hair, too. Just a little. Right here." He gently pulled on a curl that fell over Josh's forehead. "Sorry." Tyler took Josh's glasses off his face and licked them clean, then dried them with his shirt.

Josh got to his feet, then leaned against the wall next to Tyler. He brought his shirt up and wiped off his face. "Damn," he said. "You're just one surprise after another, Tyler."

"I aim to please." Tyler handed the inadequately cleaned glasses back to him.

"Your aim is terrible," Josh corrected, making Tyler snicker.

Josh was torn between wanting to shove Tyler against the wall and fuck him and a near-desperate longing for a shower. While he debated the merits of each option, with the shower being in the lead, Tyler knelt at his feet in one fluid gesture.

He looked up at Josh with a roguish glint in his eyes. "Let me make it up to you." He undid Josh's jeans button and fly.

Josh opened his mouth to tell Tyler it wasn't necessary—he could take care of it himself in the shower and that would be for the best—but then Tyler's mouth was on him and he forgot what he'd been going to say.

Tyler held his hips and swallowed his cock, making it disappear like a magic trick. Then the trick was explained when he felt Tyler's throat convulse around him.

"Fuck. Fuck." It seemed to be the only word his brain was capable of making his mouth say. He'd thought the blow job this morning had been intense, but this was beyond even that. Tyler's mouth was hot and wet and tight around him. As he bobbed his head along Josh's length, Tyler let his teeth graze him, just a little, and Josh teetered on the edge. "Oh, fuck."

Tyler pulled his mouth off him, making Josh shudder with need. "You're about to come, aren't you?" His hand jerked Josh, but it wasn't enough.

"Fuck, please." Oh, good. His brain was capable of two words.

Tyler ran one of his fingers along Josh's slit where he leaked copious amounts of precum.

"So polite, even in extremis," Tyler murmured. His lips grazed the head of Josh's cock, making it twitch with frustrated need. "Well, since you asked so nicely…"

Tyler swallowed his cock down again and Josh's hand went to the back of Tyler's head, fingers tangling into his blue hair. Tyler hummed, his throat gripping Josh's cock with impossible tightness, and Josh was right there on the edge again. If Tyler pulled back this time, he thought he might die. But instead of another retreat, Tyler's hand went between Josh's legs and Tyler's slick finger pushed inside his body. The sensation of Tyler fingering his ass was enough to push Josh over the precipice he'd been teetering on and he came hard. His knees were replaced with jelly, and after Tyler slowly pulled his mouth from his softening cock, Josh slid to the ground in an inelegant heap next to Tyler, who grinned at him.

"Wow." His brain had come up with a third word. Progress.

"Feel better?" Tyler asked. "Did that make up for your messy glasses?"

Josh moved his legs so they were in a more comfortable position and leaned his back against the wall. Tyler sprawled next to him, looking like a debauched fairy prince with his regal air despite his mussed hair and red, swollen mouth.

Give me a half-hour and I could fuck the shit out him. That was Josh's dick, so no surprise there. The sane portion of his brain started to chime in with post-orgasm fretting. *Do you know what you're doing? Are you sure? Also, I think a half-hour is being optimistic.* The rest of his brain was still too blissed-out to function and had nothing helpful to contribute.

Tyler let out a low, soft laugh and dabbed at his lips with his tongue. "I'll give you a minute for your IQ to normalize." He straightened his clothing, then stood with graceful ease. He leaned against the wall and gazed down at Josh with amusement evident in eyes that had gone the blue of a tropical sea.

"Fuck you," Josh said. He also got to his feet, his movements considerably less elegant than Tyler's. He pulled up his jeans, refastened them, and thought about how much he wanted a shower.

Tyler clucked his tongue. "Such gratitude."

So Josh kissed him, his lips and tongue saying everything without needing to utter a word.

A distant warning—*are you sure, are you certain*—sounded again in the back of his brain, and Josh pulled back. "Thank you," he said, "for the new boathouse memory."

"My pleasure," Tyler purred at him in full-on lash-fluttering shameless flirt mode. Then he turned it off, like one would a faucet, and gave Josh a more guarded, neutral expression. "Is there anything you won't eat?" When Josh just stared at him, he added, "Food. Is there any food you won't eat?"

Oh. "I don't keep kosher and I don't have any food allergies, if that's what you're asking. If you're serious about making dinner, go nuts."

"Great. Let's get back to the house so you can clean up and I'll make dinner."

⊰⊱

Sunday, September 18th, 7:42 p.m.
An unnecessarily large rental house
Blue Lake, WI

Before getting into the shower, Josh made the mistake of checking his email. There was one from his father with the subject: *your upcoming birthday.*

> *Your mother and I want to know if you have plans for your 35th birthday. I know it's a few weeks away, but coming so soon after Rachel's wedding, we thought perhaps you should start thinking about it now.*
>
> *Your mother would like to go to Wildfire, so it would be nice if you could tell her that's where you want to go. It would make her very happy.*
>
> *Your mother also wants to know if you're bringing a date to your sister's wedding so she can plan the seating chart for dinner. She says you aren't currently dating anyone, and you're running out of time to secure a date. If you don't find someone, you know your mother will find someone for you. I was thinking perhaps you could ask someone from your office. Perhaps one of the nurses?*
>
> *Which reminds me, I was golfing the other day with Peter and he told me that his son Ryan is engaged. Had you heard? I know you two used to be friends. Maybe Rachel told you, although she didn't say anything to me about it. I hear Ryan's fiancée is a lovely woman. He's bringing her to Rachel's wedding, so you'll get a chance to meet her then.*
>
> *You should take this as your wakeup call. Being single at 30 is*

one thing, but at 35, people start to talk. Your mother and I worry that you'll end up alone, with no family of your own.

Make 35 a new beginning. Hopefully you can start a new relationship, and maybe even your own practice. I know you'd like having your own office, and it would be beneficial if you had someone to come home to at night. And maybe you should consider buying a house instead of living in that condo.

Just promise me you'll at least think about it.

Josh wanted to ignore his dad's email completely, just delete it and forget about it, but if he didn't reply his dad would just send another, even more annoying version of the same message.

He gritted his teeth and sent a terse reply.

re: your upcoming birthday

Dad, tell Mom Wildfire is fine. We should make sure Rachel and Brad are back from their honeymoon so they can join us. My date to the wedding is all taken care of. I'll discuss it with Mom tomorrow.

He wasn't sure which part was the worst: not getting to choose where he had his birthday dinner (fairly minor, but still irritating), the suggestion he buy a house (even though he loved his condo), being told that he should open his own dermatology practice (he'd rather stick needles in his eyes than have his own office), being told that he should find someone as his date for the wedding (with the unspoken threat of his mother setting him up with someone she thought would be 'just perfect' for him *again*), or being flat-out told he would die bitter and alone while having Ryan's fiancée shoved into his face.

Probably the last was the worst because it hit closest to home.

He was a little surprised Rachel hadn't said anything about him already having a date to her wedding to their parents yet. Maybe she was waiting for him to break the bad news. His father would not be happy when he learned that his son's date was not the suggested nurse, but instead his former boss's twenty-five-year-old son.

Josh sighed. That was not going to go over well at all.

He never said so out loud, but Josh thought that his father was hoping one day his son would spontaneously stop being gay. If asking his son to bring a nurse from his office to the wedding wasn't code for 'please date a girl for a change,' Josh didn't know what was. The thing was, two of his office's six nurses were male, and if Josh wasn't already committed to being Tyler's fake boyfriend, he would have had half a mind to bribe one of them to be his date just to see the look on his father's face.

However, as Tyler was his date, his mother didn't need to worry about the seating chart or setting him up with God knew who and his father would just have to deal. Both he and Tyler were at the head table already, since both were groomsmen. Problem solved.

Tomorrow Josh would have to call his mother and tell her what was going on, or at least some of what was going on. She could break the news to his dad, because that was not a conversation Josh wanted to have. Things in his life were stressful enough right now. Tyler was a huge ball of trouble in an extremely appealing package. Pretty soon they would be in a public spotlight, and Josh wasn't sure how he would handle that. Going back to work was going to be interesting. He was probably going to get all kinds of shit from his coworkers about dating someone both notorious and so much younger than himself. And now he got to look forward to seeing Ryan at his sister's wedding with his apparently beautiful fiancée.

The whole mess was enough to give him indigestion, but there was nothing he could do about it right this second. Josh ate a few antacids, then stepped into the shower. Today had been long and emotionally tiring. His life for the foreseeable future would be far more chaos than order. Josh just wanted to eat dinner, shut his brain off, and hope tomorrow was less stressful, although he didn't have high hopes. He had a feeling he was going to need more antacids.

When Josh stepped out of the bathroom, freshly showered and dressed in sleep pants and a t-shirt so old and faded he couldn't remember if the original color was blue or gray, his nose was assaulted with the delicious scent of coconut and lemongrass and spices cooking. He followed the scent to the kitchen where the smell of cooking rice joined the party.

"Is that curry? It smells great. Where did you get curry?"

Tyler turned and gave him an arch look. "Some of us buy actual food when we go grocery shopping and not just sausage, beer, and marshmallows."

Josh folded his arms across his chest. "I bought more than just sausage, beer, and marshmallows."

Tyler ignored his protest. "The rice is almost done, then we can eat. I've got a bottle of wine chilling, too."

"No alcohol for you," Josh said. "Remember?"

"Really? Not even one glass?"

"No. Not until you're done with the antibiotic."

"God, you're no fun," Tyler complained.

"I'm the king of no fun. If you wanted fun you should have picked someone else," Josh said.

"I'll remember that next time I need a pseudo-boyfriend." Tyler checked on the rice.

Josh sat down. The idea of Tyler with another man, even a hypothetical one, sent a sharp stab of jealousy shooting through him, jealousy he had no right to feel. That wasn't good. Worse was the thought that of course there would be other men, ones of the non-pseudo variety. Probably several. The hypothetical here was Josh; not a real boyfriend, not quite a lover, not anything really but an overpaid companion. Two days into their fake relationship and he was already getting attached. It was insane. It was Ryan all over again.

He could hear his brain saying *I told you so* in a smug way, like that was at all helpful.

Added to all the other things he'd been worrying about, this seemed like one problem too many. The one that might push him over the edge. He couldn't get attached to Tyler. That was unacceptable. Period. End of discussion.

Tyler brought two plates of curry and rice to the table and set one in front of Josh. "I hope you like it," he said. "You know, just because I can't drink doesn't mean you can't. You might as well have some wine."

Josh didn't reply, but he got up and found an opener for the wine bottle, then poured himself a glass. It was a semi-sweet Riesling that paired perfectly with the dish. Tyler had thought of everything. It reminded him of his father's email and the insinuation that he needed to find himself a nice housewife. The thought made him surly. "Aren't you just the little Suzy homemaker? I'm beginning to think you're way more disgustingly domestic than I am," he said, and he gave an internal wince at the bitterness that escaped in his tone.

Tyler flashed him an annoyed glance. "What crawled up your ass and died?"

Josh closed his eyes. Getting pissed off at Tyler was unfair and he knew it. The person he was mad at was himself, and his father, but mostly himself for letting his father get to him. He was also a little scared. Everything Tyler did drew him, and that attraction, with all its implications, made him want to reach for more antacids. He opened his eyes and gave Tyler a smile he didn't feel. "I'm just old and cranky," he said, "and it's been a very long day."

Tyler's face was unreadable, scrubbed blank of any expression. "Are you going to eat my food or not?" he asked.

Josh looked down at his plate of fluffy brown rice, chicken, and vegetables in a pale green sauce. He took a bite and tasted lime and coconut, lemongrass and ginger, garlic and basil. "Holy shit," he said, feeling even worse about being grumpy. "This is delicious, Tyler." He shoved another bite in his mouth and closed his eyes again, this time in sheer appreciation.

"I make it a lot, so I've gotten good at it. I'm glad you like it." It almost sounded like he was bashful. Tyler. Tyler and bashful were two words that didn't belong together.

"I love it," Josh said, and was rewarded when Tyler smiled and turned pink. He was adorable, and that was a word that suited Tyler down to the ground.

A bolt of longing pierced him. His stupid brain thought: *Him. I want him.* Josh tried to stop the thought but it kept banging around in his head, refusing to shut up, refusing to go away.

Josh wanted Tyler to blush, but only for him. He wanted his sharp smiles and sharper words; his dark humor and dancing eyes; his graceful body covered in scars. In that moment, he wanted Tyler so much it was hard to breathe.

His rational brain rushed in and tried to salvage the situation. *That's just lust speaking. I want sex, not forever. This feeling will fade. It will.*

It had better, because Tyler would leave, and Josh's life would go back to what it had been—comfortable and sterile and lonely, just like his father had pointed out. Tyler would be famous and Josh would watch his movies and tell some other guy, "Hey, I used to date him," and even that would be a lie because they were only fake dating.

Two days. It's been two days. Get a fucking grip, Rosen.

Losing Ryan fifteen years ago had been like losing a limb. It had left a gaping wound in his psyche that he thought of as the not-Ryan, and over the years it had become almost an old friend, one he'd nurtured and let grow into unreasonable proportions. He'd coddled his rejection to the point where he'd started seeing a therapist again to try and deal with it. Soon the not-Ryan would be joined by a not-Tyler. He needed to nip this in the bud now, or by the time he left the not-Tyler would be enough to swallow him whole.

"You okay?" Tyler asked.

"Yeah," Josh said, wishing it was the truth. "Why don't I do the dishes?" His life might be chaotic and messy, but he could at least get the kitchen under control.

Chapter 16
Tyler Takes Charge

Sunday, September 18th, 8:22 p.m.
An unnecessarily large rental house
Blue Lake, WI

Tyler: Oh holy crap.
Purvi: What now?
Tyler: I gave Dr McDreamy a facial.
Purvi: With semen?
Tyler: No, we just got back from a spa day.
Purvi: Really?
Tyler: No. FFS. Not that sort of facial. But now that you mention it, my face could use the other kind. Are there spas in Wisconsin?
Purvi: I'm sure Wisconsin has spas. Back to Dr McDreamy. You shot your load on his face?
Tyler: Yep. That I did.
Purvi: Well? Did he like it?
Tyler: I don't think he was a huge fan but he didn't punch me or anything. I'm not even totally sure why I did it, but it was super hot. I wonder if he'd let me do it again.
Purvi: You could, oh, I don't know, ASK HIM, maybe. Also, are you sure sex with this guy is wise?
Tyler: It was his idea. He thinks I'm fuckable.
Purvi: That's because you ARE fuckable. You make me wish I had a penis so I could fuck you. I mean, I've got the strap-on, but it's not the same.
Tyler: I can't decide if that's sweet or creepy. Either way, ew. Stop fantasizing about sex with me. Or Josh.
Purvi: Try and stop me. I'm doing it right now.
Tyler: Gross.
Tyler: By the way, I cooked him dinner.
Purvi: Wow, you must really like him.
Tyler: It was just curry.
Purvi: Uh huh. You keep telling yourself that.
Tyler: Anyway, he's cleaning the kitchen now.
Purvi: I like him already. Can we keep him?
Tyler: He's a person, not a stray cat.
Purvi: So? What's your point?
Tyler: Go away and bother Kevin. I'm busy.

ෆඃඣ

Sunday, September 18th, 8:39 p.m.
The pristinely clean kitchen of an unnecessarily large rental house
Blue Lake, WI

Josh insisted on doing the dishes, something Tyler generally appreciated in a person. Josh, it seemed, was a bit of a cleaning dynamo, not only scrubbing every dish, pot, and utensil Tyler had used by hand, but he also pulled everything off the kitchen counters and cleaned the granite, wiped down all the cupboards, scrubbed the stove, scoured the sink, then swept the floor. Tyler sat in the kitchen and watched him, only lifting his arms when Josh came over to wipe down the table.

Josh kept up a steady stream of conversation while he cleaned, requiring only the occasional agreement or disagreement from him, which was just as well because Tyler was too busy studying Josh to pay close attention to what he was saying. The whole thing was starting to worry him. Not the cleaning so much as the desperate, overzealous way he went about it. This wasn't housework. This was a coping mechanism gone horribly wrong.

Both Josh and Rachel had told him that Josh cleaned when he was stressed, but this was beyond what Tyler had imagined. He'd pictured Josh in an excessively tidy and spare home, with nothing left out or out of place, free of dust and clutter and life. And maybe that was the case. What hadn't occurred to him was Josh cleaning a refrigerator that was already spotless, then pulling it out to clean underneath it. That was a level of crazy even Tyler didn't aspire to.

Tyler wanted to stop Josh but he felt like a big fat hypocrite after all the shit he'd given Josh for daring to suggest that Tyler's little cutting habit needed fixing. Which, to be fair, it did. And which he would, one of these days. But hypocrite or not, Tyler thought he should intervene. He couldn't imagine Josh allowing him to cut himself open without trying to stop him, and this was almost the same thing.

"Josh, what's bothering you?" he asked.

He paused in the act of moving the fridge back in place to scowl at Tyler.

"Who said anything's bothering me?"

"Well, let's see, you just cleaned under a fridge in a rental property you don't own. That's not normal. Tell me what's wrong." Maybe he was having second thoughts. Maybe the idea of sex with Ryan's baby brother was just too strange and it had all hit home after dinner. Or, rather, after his shower. Something had happened between the boathouse and Josh coming to eat dinner, because that was when this had started.

Josh looked at him but didn't say anything, then he finished moving the refrigerator back. "Why would you think anything's wrong?" he asked, then started rummaging under the sink for God knew what.

This was going nowhere. "You said you clean when you're stressed. Rachael said you clean when you're stressed. Clearly, you're stressed. What's going on? Is it me? The arrangement? We can stop. The friends with benefits thing isn't necessary." Only now that they'd agreed to it, the idea of no more sex with Josh felt like all kinds of awful. It was a much longed-for treat dangled in front of his eyes only to be snatched away.

Josh started cleaning the coffeemaker. "I'm fine. Don't worry about it. I just can't stand when things are dirty. It's nothing personal. If it bothers you, don't watch."

Right. Like he was going to leave the room while whatever this was went down. "So, you still want to bone me."

"Yes, Tyler, I still want to bone you." Josh continued to go at the coffeemaker. "Just not right this second."

Ouch. Nice to know that sex with him ranked underneath cleaning minor kitchen appliances. Tyler let Josh do his thing, wanting to step in but not particularly wishing to get slapped down again for his efforts. Then Josh got on his hands and knees to scrub the tiled floor with a scouring pad, and Tyler decided that enough was enough.

"Okay," he said. "You're done for the night."

Josh looked up at him with a frown. "What?"

"You are done," Tyler said. "The floor isn't dirty, and, Christ, look at your hands."

Josh did, then let out a long sigh. His beautiful, elegant hands were red and chapped and looked irritated as hell. "Damn," he said. "I forgot to put on gloves." Josh slanted a look Tyler's way that was both guilty and exasperated, twin spots of color high on his cheeks. "I... um... there's cream in my room," he said. This didn't surprise Tyler in the slightest.

"Do you want me to get it for you?" he asked.

"No." Josh got to his feet and put the scouring pad by the sink. "I can get it." He washed his hands, then walked out of the kitchen.

Tyler went out to the living room to wait for Josh. He sat on the couch and Oliver joined him, demanding to be petted. "We're quite the pair, aren't we?"

Oliver mewed in response.

"I mean, I probably still win the most-fucked-up prize, but he's giving me a run for my money. Mom's right. This is going to end in disaster."

"Merow?" Oliver asked.

"Oh, you know. Heartbreak and tragedy. What always happens."

Oliver butted his head on Tyler's chin.

"Except from you, Ollie. You're my fuzzy love, aren't you?"

Oliver agreed.

"I should probably leave him alone. It's just that he's just so…"

"Maow," said Oliver.

"Yeah," said Tyler and sighed.

Tyler sat with Oliver for a long time before realizing that Josh wasn't coming out to join him. Which was fine. And totally his right. The deal they'd struck was for one fake boyfriend and the possibility of sex, not the guarantee of such. He should be content with Josh's public performance today, which had been better than he'd had any right to hope for, especially considering how angry Josh had been when they'd left the house this morning. As for what went down in the boathouse this afternoon, that hadn't been a top ten best blow job, let alone a top three, but it had been pretty good. It would've been better, he suspected, if he hadn't been so perilously close to coming even before Josh had gotten his mouth on him.

Tyler didn't feel content, though. It had been well over two years since Tyler had contemplated anything beyond hand jobs, blow jobs, or using one of his favorite toys. Toward the end of their relationship, sex with Ethan had become much less fun and more of a chore, and therefore rather infrequent.

The problem, Tyler had decided after much grumpy vodka-fueled introspection and discussion with Purvi, was that physically he wanted to bottom and mentally he wanted to top, and God forbid he ever find a guy who liked both, was attractive, not a sociopath, unattached, and willing to put up with Tyler for more than five minutes at a time.

He tended to desire men who were overwhelming but who he couldn't trust himself with, and settled for men who were safe but ultimately not what he wanted. Ethan had been the latter, and David, who was before him, was the former, and both had ended badly. Ethan had left him feeling smothered and tired and in need of freedom. David made him feel unsure and anxious and in need of a restraining order. It was stupid, and he knew it, and it kept happening, so after Ethan he stopped dating. Relationships were too fraught with drama that he didn't have time or energy for. Picking up random guys for a no-strings quickie was a hell of a lot less stressful for everyone involved.

Then Josh had fallen into his lap. Josh, who might be neither too much of this nor too little of that. Like Goldilocks, Tyler was always hoping to find the one who was just right. He wanted some middle ground between safe/dull and scary/exciting, someone sexy, who made his heart beat a little bit faster, and who didn't either bore or frighten him. It shouldn't be so hard to find a man who didn't need to be constantly bolstered, or who didn't feel the need to put Tyler down to feel better about himself. Someone he could trust. Tyler was beginning to think Josh might possibly fit the bill, and for the first time in a very long time he wanted more. So much more.

And what then? Quit Hollywood and become his little house husband? Why bother trying to save my career, then? And what about Ryan? Do I really want to compete with my brother's memory? No, thank you.

Tyler had no idea how to answer any of those questions, and he felt stupid for sitting around and mooning like a teenaged girl for a man who was hiding in his bedroom down the hall. It was like he'd been cast into some sort of unfunny gay farce. The kind that bills itself as being arty and you know going in that at least one of the leads was going to die before the end of the movie. Probably him, in a beautifully filmed scene with his blood flowing across a floor or down a drain or into bathwater. "Look at the pretty fag, dead because the pressure of life was too hard for him to bear. Boo hoo." Well, fuck that.

Tyler moved Oliver from his lap and went to go take a shower then go to bed. It wasn't that late but he could probably use the sleep, or at the very least, rest.

Showering didn't help his mood any. Tyler felt overwhelmed with doubts and wanted, very much, to cut himself, probably because he'd been thinking about it earlier, fetishizing it in a way that he knew was dangerous. He could imagine the blood as it swirled out of him and down the drain—so red, so pretty—just like he was watching it on a movie screen. It would be nice if he could shut off his damn brain for a while and just be pain and blood. Nothing else. He could stop obsessing about Josh and get some sleep.

There was the other option, though. There was always the other option, and it was almost as exhilarating and dangerous as cutting, if not as straightforward. Could it be worse than staining the tile in this pretty bathroom? Probably not. Hopefully not. He let go of his mental razor blade and instead grabbed the very real soap and put it to good use.

After his shower, Tyler went to his room and pawed through his clothes. He couldn't go in there naked, no matter what his intended outcome, but getting fully dressed seemed counterproductive. In the end, he chose the pajama pants he'd worn the night before and nothing else. They were easy to remove if things got that far, and enough protection if things went south.

Lastly, he went through the plastic bag Josh had dropped then forgotten in the living room after they'd come back from lunch. He took what he needed, then went to beard the lion in his den.

Tyler knocked softly on Josh's door but didn't get a response. He took a deep breath, then let it out. He hoped like hell the door wasn't locked. If this didn't work, Tyler would slink off to his own bed, but he had a sinking feeling that he'd end up looking in the house for something sharp, or going back to his house to plunder his secret stash. Maybe not tonight, but soon. It was inevitable.

Tyler turned the handle and it gave under his hand. Opening the door eased something inside him, and he felt better. Enough that he thought sex with Josh felt a lot less like something he needed and a lot more like something he wanted, and the Josh part of the equation might be more important than the sex part.

Tyler wasn't sure if that was better or worse.

Inside, the room was pitch black and Tyler had to rely on touch to tell him where everything was. He put the items he was holding onto the nearest bedside table and then climbed onto the bed.

Josh was either asleep or sulking with extreme determination. Tyler gave his eyes time to adjust to the dark and could just make out Josh huddled in on himself at the far edge of the bed, facing the wall. He reached out a hand and encountered the soft, worn fabric of Josh's t-shirt stretched over warm, taut skin. Tyler's hand slid under the shirt and stroked Josh's back, learning the contours of it. He loved the strength evident in the muscles of his wide shoulders, the dip of his spine, and the elegant line that ran from chest to waist to hip.

The muscles moved under his hand, and then light flared in the room. Only a table lamp, but it seemed very bright after the darkness.

"Tyler?" Josh turned over and lay on his back. "Is everything okay? Did you need something?"

Tyler noticed that Josh's hands were covered in white gloves. It made him look oddly formal, but also a bit like a cartoon character. It was a little surreal.

Everything isn't okay and I need you. Tyler leaned over to kiss Josh.

Josh's eyes widened and he pulled back. "Tyler, I don't think this is a good idea."

Tyler's heart plummeted. "Why?" he asked, and Josh's face closed down.

"I'm not in a good mood right now," he said. "Also, my hands are covered in goop."

"Is that a technical term, Dr. Rosen?"

"It might be."

"What if I asked very nicely?"

Josh smiled at him then, the skin around his eyes crinkling in a way that Tyler found charming. "I didn't know you did nice."

Tyler pouted at him because it was expected. "I can do nice. It's a strain, naturally, but with the proper inspiration, I can be downright angelic."

The smile fell from Josh's face, leaving a wary expression in its wake. "Tyler, it's been a long day and I'm tired. Can we cut to the chase? What do you want from me?"

Josh's tone was not encouraging, but there was something in his eyes that kept Tyler from stammering out an apology and leaving. Josh's eyes wanted him to stay, Tyler was certain. Well, nearly certain. Certain enough for him to forge ahead.

"What I want," Tyler said, "is my promised possibility of boning. You don't even have to exert yourself. You can lie there with your snazzy gloves on and just enjoy it."

Josh frowned. "I don't think..."

"Don't think. It's okay to shut that brain of yours down sometimes." Tyler gave a lock of Josh's hair a gentle tug. "Your hands. How messed up are they?"

"Not bad, just red and irritated. I shouldn't have gone into a cleaning frenzy without protecting them. I know better. Some dermatologist I am."

Tyler shrugged. "We all have our moments. My most recent one involved a dock." That brought a small smile back to Josh's mouth. "Josh, I need this tonight, and maybe you do, too. So, please? This is me being nice, in case you weren't sure."

Josh's face showed both resignation and desire. "Okay," he said. "Yeah. Sure. Why not? Go on, do your worst."

"With that ringing endorsement..." Tyler straddled Josh's waist, and a wave of relief washed over him. He hadn't wanted to slink out of Josh's room and back to his own. The handsome man underneath him was all his for the taking, he thought with a combination of wonder and glee, then his conscience had to piss on the parade with the added, *for now*.

That was fine. For now, was good enough. More than good enough.

He tugged Josh's shirt off and threw it on the floor, then he took Josh's hands, still in their gloves, and placed them above his head. "Leave your hands here. Don't move them. Do you understand?"

"Yes, Tyler." This was the correct answer, but Josh looked and sounded more tolerant than obedient. That was also good enough, though.

Tyler leaned forward to give Josh a light kiss of approval. "Such a good boy," he said, kissing him again just because he could before sliding off him and the bed. He dragged the comforter onto the floor so it would be out of the way, then pulled Josh's sleep pants off.

Underneath he wore a pair of forest green briefs with white edging that did very little to preserve any modesty. "These are amazing," Tyler said, "and frankly unexpected, but they've got to go." Then he pulled them slowly off of Josh. He wasn't fully erect yet, but they'd get there.

For a moment Tyler considered leaving his own pants on, but Josh had already seen him naked under brighter light than this and seemed to still want him. No point in fucking around at this stage, he supposed.

Josh's eyes followed him as he shimmied out of the soft gray pants. He shook his head.

"What?" Tyler asked, freezing in place, wondering if Josh had changed his mind.

"You're just so damned beautiful, that's all."

Beautiful. Tyler flinched a little at the word. He wanted to be handsome, but knew his face couldn't quite achieve it. He wanted to be tall, as well, and that was another thing that was never going to happen. Not in this lifetime, at any rate. He told himself to be grateful that Josh, for whatever reason, said the word "beautiful" in a way that didn't come out as either condescending or mocking. Josh seemed to mean it, to think that Tyler would want to hear it, and maybe there was a part of him that did. Even after all these years, he latched onto any praise thrown his way like a starving dog snatching at scraps of food. It was a failing he thought he'd stamped out, but apparently not, because he wanted to hear Josh say it again, and again, and again.

Tyler smiled for Josh, then slowly pivoted for him, giving him a show because he seemed to appreciate it. "You like what you see?" he asked. He basked in the heat of Josh's gaze.

"Too much." Josh shook his head again. "You have dimples above your ass," he added, apropos of nothing. "Two perfect dimples that I want to run my tongue over."

Tyler grinned. "You approve, I take it."

"Too much. Far too much."

"There's no such thing as too much," Tyler said, and crawled first back on the bed and then onto Josh. He tucked his ass against Josh's groin, then leaned forward to properly pay homage to Josh's body, something he had wanted to do for a very long time. Longer than he was comfortable admitting to.

That morning Tyler had gone straight for Josh's dick, but tonight he wanted to explore everything like a greedy kid set loose in a toy store. He cupped Josh's face and kissed him. Josh tucked his gloved hands behind his head and kissed Tyler back with the ardor of a man who wanted to grab hold of him and reverse their positions but was nevertheless managing to restrain himself.

Tyler ran his hands down Josh's upraised arms and was delighted to learn he was ticklish, even if he did have to remind Josh not to move his hands.

"Don't tickle me, then."

"Spoilsport," murmured Tyler. He licked at Josh's lower lip until he opened up and let him inside. Josh sucked on his tongue and Tyler curled his hands into Josh's hair. He sighed as Tyler's lips trailed down his neck, then gasped and twitched when Tyler bit his earlobe.

"More," demanded Josh.

"I want to bite you all over," Tyler whispered in Josh's ear. Josh's skin flushed at that, starting at his chest and moving upward. Ah, the good doctor liked that idea very much. Tyler moved lower and drew one of Josh's nipples into his mouth. He sucked, then bit it, and Josh's spine bowed in response.

"This is harder than I expected," Josh said, his voice a little ragged. "I think I want to touch you even more because I can't."

Tyler looked up at him through his lashes. "That's the whole point." Then he licked a line down Josh's chest to his navel.

Josh had lovely, defined muscles he would no doubt know all the names for. Tyler, whose anatomy knowledge began and ended with the major blood vessels Brad had made him memorize, nevertheless knew a nice specimen when he saw one. He ran his hands and lips and teeth over firm ridges and along smooth lines until Josh's breath came out in short gasps. Then Tyler trailed his mouth down to Josh's cock, which he licked from base to tip.

"Are you trying to fuck me or kill me?"

"So impatient," Tyler chided, and moved so that he sat between Josh's legs rather than straddling them. He caressed Josh's thighs and felt the muscles quiver under his fingers as Josh trembled. At the same time, he sucked Josh's cock. Not enough to get him off but enough to keep him interested.

Josh groaned. "So much for being nice. Are you going to make me beg?"

"Not tonight," Tyler said. He moved so he could grab the bottle of lube from the bedside table. He poured a good amount onto his hand and coated his fingers.

"Tyler, what are you doing?"

He started to finger his entrance as he knelt on the bed beside Josh. "Prepping myself." He slid one finger in, then two. This was his first time ever doing this to himself with an audience, he realized. Ethan, God love him, couldn't top to save his cute little ass, so Tyler had never bottomed for him. It had been mostly tops before Ethan, though, and Tyler had learned the hard way to prep himself ahead of time. Relying solely on your partner, in his experience, was a recipe for a sore ass, so lubing himself up beforehand just was good sense. He should've done that tonight, but he'd been too impatient and too eager. Not like his normal self at all.

Tyler's fingers knew just what to do from years of practice, but he felt vulnerable with Josh watching. His skin burned under the other man's steady gaze. It was frustrating, especially as getting his fingers to press that magic place inside him in his current position was possible but awkward as fuck.

His own erection started to flag a little. Maybe this was a bad idea. Scratch that. Of course it was a bad idea. He was pretty much a walking collection of bad ideas.

Then Josh said, "I... that's... I want... fuck, Tyler," and his incoherence washed away Tyler's momentary uncertainty. He took fingers slick with lube and stroked himself while Josh watched him. "You're killing me. I want..."

Tyler reached for the condom and unwrapped it. "Me?"

Josh nodded, apparently beyond speech. His cock stood at attention, and Tyler slid the condom down his length and added more lube. He straddled Josh and reached between them to position Josh's erection at his entrance. "Okay," he said, "here goes nothing." He took it in slowly, letting his body adjust to Josh's size. The initial feeling was as he remembered: first discomfort, then a lovely fullness, then pleasure with the tiniest edge of pain that evaporated as he began to move.

Oh, God, he'd missed this. It was so fucking hot. Not just sexy hot, although it was that, but a cock attached to an actual person was so much better than even the best dildo money could buy. The cock inside him was alive. It twitched and throbbed with heated blood and was attached to a man who seemed to be slowly but surely losing his mind.

"Fuck me, please fuck me, please," Josh chanted. His hips surged upward as Tyler rolled his hips down, and *there*. Pleasure arrowed through him like a bolt of electricity, pooling in his balls and radiating outward. His hips undulated, making Josh hit that spot over and over. The feeling built into an overwhelming crescendo that loomed just out of his reach and he moved faster, chasing it, wanting to be broken under it.

Tyler dropped his hand down to his cock and stroked it in time with the movement of their bodies. Josh growled at him, sounding both frustrated and crazed, his gloved hands clutching the headboard.

"Come for me," Josh demanded.

Usually being ordered to come had the opposite effect on Tyler, but tonight it worked somehow and he came hard onto Josh's chest and his own hand. He sank, boneless, onto Josh and clung to him, shuddering with his release.

For a few moments Josh lay under him, only his hips moving, thrusting upward, then he muttered, "Fuck it," and rolled them both over, slipping out of Tyler's body. "Now it's my turn." He stripped off his gloves and threw them aside.

Tyler, still floating on a pink, fluffy post-orgasmic cloud of contentment, sighed as Josh leaned down to kiss him. He could feel Josh, still hot and hard, against his leg. "You didn't come," he said when Josh lifted his head.

"Not yet." Josh kissed his neck and trailed his hands up and down Tyler's body. At first it just felt nice, then it was more than nice. Tyler's dick stirred, having not gotten the memo that the body it was attached to had run out of bones, strength, and the wherewithal to move.

Josh kissed down Tyler's neck and chest while he stroked his semi-erect cock, which had decided it was not done for the evening, no matter what the rest of Tyler's body thought. He moaned, the sensation almost too much.

"Oh, to be still twenty-five," Josh said.

"Then I'd be sixteen, you perv," Tyler gasped out, and remembered his plan to lose his virginity at that summer picnic all those years ago. What a terrible, idiotic idea that had been, but holy fuck, it was a good thing his sixteen-year-old self hadn't known the reality of how good fucking Josh Rosen would be, because he would've been persistent in his pursuit of Josh to the point of mortification for everyone involved. "Oh, Christ. Besides, there's something to be said for the stamina of thirty-four if you're planning on fucking me twice tonight. God. Please."

Josh stopped stroking him, pushed his legs apart, and knelt between his bent knees. "Good point. You ready for round two?"

Tyler nodded and felt Josh lifting his legs up, then thrusting into him. Tyler grabbed his knees, arched his back, and pushed back against Josh. He was still sensitive and let out an embarrassing yelp as Josh slid all the way in.

"You okay?" Josh asked, his hands gripping Tyler's thighs tightly as if that was the only thing holding him in check.

"God, yes. Fuck me."

Tyler found himself folded in two, being fucked right into the mattress, and it was amazing. Better than he would have imagined so soon after coming.

That upward curve in Josh's cock hit his prostate at the perfect angle and the pleasure built again, this time more quickly and with more of an edge of pain to it from the intensity of the sensations and his already overstimulated nerves. Tyler started to moan, but as Josh fucked him it grew louder and louder, until it was a good thing they were alone in the house. He wasn't sure his body could come again, let alone untouched, but it wanted to, and then it did, although it was less in his balls and dick and more inside his body and brain, which went white and blank for a moment as it short-circuited from a surfeit of stimulation. In the aftermath, his hole clenched spasmodically around Josh, who swore and moved faster.

Josh groaned as he thrust, making almost as much noise as Tyler had. His hips stuttered in their rhythm as he thrust forward the last few times, holding Tyler in place by his legs. Then he slumped forward, letting go. Tyler slid his legs down and around him as Josh buried his face in Tyler's hair and panted for breath. "Oh, Ty," Josh sighed, his lips against Tyler's temple, the words more felt than heard.

"You cheated," Tyler said. "You weren't supposed to use your hands."

Josh raised his head and cupped Tyler's face with hands that were, perhaps, a bit goopy. Tyler didn't care. "Sue me," Josh said, then kissed Tyler long and deep. He removed the condom and threw it away, then disappeared into the bathroom and came back with a warm, wet washcloth that he used to wipe Tyler clean. "Will you stay and sleep with me tonight?" Josh asked, grabbing the comforter off the floor and wrapping it around them.

Tyler wasn't sure how much he'd sleep but he would stay, at least for a while, if for no other reason than he didn't think his legs were currently functional. "Okay," he said, and let Josh pull him close.

෴

Monday, September 19th, 3:05 a.m.
Josh's bedroom in an unnecessarily large rental house
Blue Lake, Wi

Tyler: We have DONE THE DEED.
Purvi: Is he a top or a bottom?
Tyler: That's my girl, always asking the important questions.
Purvi: Well?
Tyler: Not 100% sure, but he let me ride him like a cowboy so currently he's my favorite person in the whole wide world.
Purvi: Even more than me? <pout>
Tyler: No comment.
Purvi: Asshole. So???
Tyler: I'm willing to bet that the good doctor pitches and catches, but we'll see.
Purvi: Hmmm. Are you going to give me the dirty details or what?
Tyler: I came twice.
Purvi: YOU DID NOT!
Tyler: I totally did. Hand to God.
Purvi: His dick is that amazing?
Tyler: His dick is definitely that amazing.

Purvi: I'm jealous.
Tyler: You should be.
Tyler: I had the dream again, tho.
Purvi: Oh, hon. Are you ok?
Purvi: Ty? You still there? You want me to call?
Tyler: No, don't call. I don't want you to wake him up.
Purvi: You're still in bed with him???
Tyler: He's surrounding me like a boa constrictor. Not sure how he's sleeping with my phone's light on or with every limb around me, but he's dead to the world, the fucker.
Purvi: Hold on. You, Tyler Harrison Chadwick, are allowing a man to spoon you. Do I have that right?
Tyler: Fuck you, P
Purvi: Hahahahahahaha
Tyler: FUCK. YOU. SO. HARD.
Tyler: He doesn't snore.
Purvi: That explains why he's still alive. Have you gotten any sleep?
Tyler: Since the dream? Not so much. I feel like I'm going to jump out of my skin.
Tyler: Him being here is kinda nice, tho.
Purvi: That's adorable. Like rainbow sparkly unicorn poop adorable.
Tyler: I swear to God I will fire your ass.
Purvi: No, you won't. What time is it there? I'm about to go to bed.
Tyler: Just after 3. Jesus, you suck at math.
Purvi: Fuck you, it's too late for math. Or early. Put away your phone and try to get some more sleep. In the morning, do your yoga. That always helps. Just take it easy on the arm.
Tyler: Yes, Mom. Night.
Purvi: Night.

Chapter 17
Josh Puts Safety Measures in Place

Monday, September 19th, 7:58 a.m.
Josh's bedroom in an unnecessarily large rental house
Blue Lake, WI

Josh woke to an empty bed and a note.

I didn't run out on you with my fine ass on fire this time. Just couldn't sleep. Ty

Josh was grateful for the note. Last evening had been so strange that the whole thing felt unreal, part wet dream and part nightmare. First there had been Tyler in the boathouse, then the irritating email from his father, his stupid and embarrassing cleaning frenzy and the subsequent toll to his hands, Tyler stealing into his room and pretty much fucking his brains out, and lastly being woken in the middle of the night by a nightmare-panicked Tyler.

The harsh light of morning found him angry and disgusted with himself over falling apart last night. Josh had lost his shit in front of Tyler, and for what? Not much in the grand scheme of things.

Josh felt like burying under the covers and hiding in the bedroom, but all that would just be more evidence of him being a useless, whiny, pathetic—

Is any of this helping?
Not really.
Then stop it. Man up and stop wallowing in self-pity. Be happy you got laid last night. That was pretty awesome. Now get out of bed and go for a run. Your ass could use it.

Josh let out a gusty sigh, looked at the clock, and saw it was almost eight. When he opened the bedroom door he smelled coffee and it drew him with its irresistible lure to the kitchen. The reward for not hiding in bed: coffee. Sweet, delicious coffee. And possibly sweet, delicious Tyler, if he could figure out where he was.

After pouring himself a mug of coffee, Josh went looking for Tyler. He had supposedly not run, or at least he'd left a note before doing so. At first, he was nowhere to be found and Josh thought maybe he actually had disappeared, but he found Tyler at last when he went out to the empty screened-in porch and looked out at the lake. Tyler was on the dock, crouched just like he had been on the Chadwicks' dock the first time Josh had seen him.

Josh's heart leapt into his throat and coffee sloshed onto his hand when he couldn't hold the mug steady. He put it down and sucked at the coffee spilled on his hand. He was about to charge out the door when he saw that Tyler had changed position, and Josh realized with a touch of chagrin that Tyler was doing yoga on a folded blanket he'd laid over the boards of the dock, and not slicing himself open like he'd first thought.

Josh drank his coffee and watched as Tyler twisted and contorted his body slowly and with beautiful precision, a few poses not seeming physically possible, or at least highly improbable. Several times Josh expected him to overbalance and fall into the lake, but he never did. He transitioned gracefully from one pose to the next with no apparent thought or difficulty. It was, without meaning in the least to be, exquisitely erotic.

You'd think I hadn't had sex last night. Or that I was still twenty-five. Or fifteen. I need a cold shower and a long run, not necessarily in that order. Josh finished what was left of his coffee, then went back inside to change. He got dressed, grabbed his phone and earbuds, then left his own note below Tyler's:

I'm out running, but will return.

Running tended to help Josh focus and clear his mind, but he had a hard time achieving that this morning. What he needed was to get some sort of grip on his feelings. Josh felt like he was teetering on the edge of a cliff and the tiniest push would send him tumbling over the edge. He needed to install a safety railing. At the bottom of the cliff was him hopelessly in love again and doomed to heartbreak. That was unacceptable, so what he needed was a nice tall barricade on the edge of the cliff that you couldn't accidentally fall over. Even if you, say, fucked a really hot wannabe elf right up against it.

It would need excellent reinforcements.

Josh ran, his muscles burning, as he constructed his mental barrier. He posted signs warning to *stay behind the yellow safety line* and *do not climb on the railings*. On the safe side of the barrier was rationality. He could see Tyler in all his impossibilities. He was an actor and he belonged in another life in another state. He could not ever be a permanent part of Josh's life in Evanston. It wasn't feasible.

What was going on right now, pressed right up against those safety rails, was a brief interlude. Like a vacation, and vacations weren't meant to last forever. On the other side of the railing was the abyss. Signs posted there read *here be dragons* and *abandon hope all ye who enter here*. Beyond the barrier was chaos—a churning mass of unfettered emotions running around free and getting into trouble.

The problem was that all he wanted to do was cling to the edge of that guardrail, past the yellow safety line, and look down, his heart in his throat. He thought about climbing over, standing on the very edge with the wind of desire rippling around him. He thought about jumping. There would be no net to catch him. Nothing to save him from the inevitable crash, but part of him craved the fall even so.

Josh ran harder and made himself mentally come back from the edge. He made himself stand behind the yellow line. He took a step back from the beautiful boy who leaned against the railing, hips canted forward, head tipped back with throat bared.

"Don't you want me?"

Too much.

"There's no such thing as too much."

That was a lie. Too much was what got you over the rail and onto the edge. Too much tilted you off-kilter and pushed. Just one finger would be all it would take.

This wasn't helping.

Maybe I should worry about this later.

Probably.

Maybe I worry too much.

Just a bit.

Let's look at the bright side. At least now I'm obsessing about someone new.

Which was true and a bit strange. His not-Ryan was still there, as he always was, but becoming faded and cast into the shade next to Tyler, who stood out in his head like he was crafted from neon light.

Josh wasn't sure trading one obsession for another was a good idea, but he promised himself that this time it would be different. He wasn't fourteen and being kissed by his secret, desperate crush. He wasn't twenty and sick with hopeless love for his best friend and determined to make his best friend love him back.

Tyler was fascinating and sexy and unlike anyone he'd ever been with. It was no wonder he was attracted. Being attracted was healthy. Everything would be okay as long as they stayed on the cliff but behind the railing. They didn't have to go over the side. It wasn't necessary. And one day, weeks or months from now, Tyler would go one way and Josh would go the other, back to his comfortable life. He would have postcard memories of his vacation that he could take out and look at from time to time.

Everyone would be okay and no one would be going over any cliffs.

Monday, September 19th, 10:16 a.m.
The road just outside an unnecessarily large rental house
Blue Lake, WI

Josh was nearly back to the house when his phone rang. He slowed to a jog and checked it. His mother. He'd been planning on calling her today anyway, might as well take this and get it over with. He leaned against a tree, steadied his breathing, and pushed accept.

"Hello?"

"Joshua," his mother said, and he knew he was in trouble, "do you have any idea what I just saw?"

"No clue," he said, thinking that whatever it was, it wasn't good.

"Sharon just sent me a picture she found online of you and some Hollywood actor. She asked me if it could possibly be my Josh in that picture and I told her not to be ridiculous, that you were on vacation in Wisconsin, and then she texted me the picture and it's you, Josh. I would know my own son anywhere, even if he is kissing some young boy who looks half his age. What on earth do you think you're doing? What will everyone think?"

"First of all," Josh said, "he's not half my age."

"That's it? That's all you have to say for yourself?"

"Do you want an explanation or an apology, Mom?"

"Don't take that tone with me. I need to know what's going on. God knows what I'm going to say to your father."

Josh took a deep breath. He wasn't sure if he should tell his mother the truth or not. In the end, it seemed best not to. There was too great a possibility that she'd let the truth slip to one of her friends and it would get out. It would make the local gossip rounds, which would spread like wildfire, and before they knew it there would be online rumors about Tyler having to buy himself a relationship. So, no. A big fat no on the whole truth. Still, best to stick to as much of the truth as possible, leaving out only the fake bits.

"You've met him, Mom. That's Tyler Chadwick."

His mother sucked in her breath. "He is not! Tyler's just a child."

"That 'child' is twenty-five. He's in town visiting his family, and he's staying for a while after the wedding since he just got done making a movie and wants a break. Anyway, we reconnected."

"That doesn't explain the picture I saw, Joshua. There was more than reconnecting going on. And twenty-five is still too young for you."

Josh sighed. Might as well just spit it out. "We're... sorta... going out."

"That looked like more than going out to me."

"Mom, we're both adults. What we do is our business. I was planning to call you today, anyway. I figured you might end up seeing something. I just didn't think it would be this soon."

"Your father won't be happy." His mother tsked.

"When is Dad ever happy about anything I do?"

"Josh!"

"Tyler is my date for the wedding," he said. "Dad's going to have to get over it."

"Isn't this awfully sudden?"

Yes, as a matter of fact. It was extremely sudden. "Well, you know how it is. I've known Tyler since pretty much forever, I just haven't seen him in years. When we met again, we clicked."

"And what about Ryan Chadwick?"

Josh didn't like where this was going. "What about him?"

"Do you think dating his brother is a good idea? I don't think you've thought this through."

"It's not serious, Mom. It's not forever. Don't worry."

His mother was quiet for a few moments. "Josh, honey, that's why I worry. They're never serious, are they? You're not serious about anyone you date. You haven't been serious about *anyone* since dating Ryan Chadwick."

"Ryan and I never dated. We were friends. Just friends."

His mother huffed. "A mother knows her son, Joshua. I saw how you looked at him."

Oh, God, kill me now.

"I... Mom, it was years ago. It doesn't matter. And Tyler is..."

"What?" she asked.

Beautiful. Bewitching. Beguiling.

"Only temporary. He's going back to California soon. He's not my happily ever after, Mom. Sorry."

Why did it hurt to say that? It was only the truth.

"That reminds me. The other day at temple I was talking with Carol and she said she had a nephew."

Oh, boy. Here we go. "Mom, I'm not—"

"He's a doctor, and he just broke up with his boyfriend—"

"Mom!"

"The only downside is that he lives in Hinsdale."

"Hinsdale? You have *got* to be kidding me. You want to set me up with a doctor in Hinsdale?"

Josh thought of the last doctor he'd dated. He'd been nice, good-looking, and single-mindedly interested in his career. It had been like trying to date a carbon copy of himself. Josh hadn't bothered trying to take him to bed. His own hand was less boring.

"It's closer than California," his mother snapped back. "Stop being so negative. You haven't even met the man."

"Mom. Stop. I'm dating Tyler. End of discussion."

He heard his mother sigh on the other end of the line. "Okay, okay. It's just that I worry about you. I just want you happy. That's all I've ever wanted for you."

"I know."

"I only want what's best for you."

"I know, Mom."

"You'll always be my little boy, Joshua, and I won't always be able to be there for you. I'm not getting any younger."

Josh grimaced and was glad his mother couldn't see his face. "Mom, you're only sixty. Bubbe is eighty-nine. Zayde is ninety-two. Your health is excellent. You are in no danger of dying."

"I could be hit by a truck tomorrow," she said, indignant.

"Look both ways when you cross the street, then."

His mother huffed. "I see how you are. Making jokes at my expense."

"I'm sorry."

"No, you're not. But I love you, Josh, and I'll see what I can do with your father."

"Thanks, Mom." Josh did his best to keep the sarcasm out of his tone. "Oh, and Wildfire is fine for my birthday."

"Only if you want to go there."

It wouldn't have been Josh's first choice, but he didn't care enough to protest. "No, it's fine. Great, even."

"If you're sure…"

"I'm sure. Go ahead and make the reservations. Don't forget to add in Tyler."

His mother sighed again. "I still think he's too young for you."

"Mom!"

"Okay, okay, I'm done. I'm only looking out for you. You know that, right?"

He did, of course. His parents drove him crazy, but they loved him, even if they showed it in irritating ways. "I know," he said. "Love you."

Josh leaned his head back against the tree after he disconnected the call. That could've been worse. He hadn't lost his temper and she hadn't cried. He'd count that as a win.

When Josh walked into the house, he could hear Tyler talking to someone. He found him in the living room on his phone, perched on the coffee table, his back to Josh.

"Do you think it's significant? I think it might be."

A voice came out of the speakerphone, but it was too muffled to hear from across the room. Josh crept up behind Tyler, wanting to surprise him. He felt more copacetic after his run and the better-than-expected call with his mother, and feeling good apparently translated to fucking with Tyler. He bent and bit Tyler's neck.

Tyler jumped, but not as much as he'd hoped, and he didn't squeal like a little girl, which was a huge disappointment. He did grip Josh's face with the hand that wasn't holding the phone. "Good morning," he said, and pulled Josh in for a kiss. He bit at Josh's lips until he opened them, then his tongue coaxed and lured Josh's into his mouth. Instead of shy sweetness, this time his kiss was of the eat-you-alive variety. Josh fell into it and forgot all about Tyler being on the phone until he heard a throat clear.

"I see you two are getting along," said Ryan. Josh's eyes flew to the phone and saw that Tyler and Ryan were on Skype. Fuck.

Josh sprang away from Tyler but didn't get very far because Tyler's free hand grabbed his and pulled hard. "Like a house on fire," Tyler said, tugging Josh down to sit next to him on the table. Feeling trapped, Josh gave in.

"Hi, Ryan," Josh said, seeing his bright-red face in the tiny corner window on the phone. Next to him, Tyler looked cool as a cucumber. Meanwhile, Ryan's face was as handsome as ever and filled with concern. "I just got back from a run."

"Yeah," Tyler said, "you're all sweaty now. And shirtless, too. Be still my heart."

"Tyler," said Ryan, a warning note in his voice.

"What?" Tyler asked, sounding as innocent as a newborn baby.

"I could call back at a better time, since you seem busy. Or better yet, you should come home so we can talk in person. You have to be back in Chicago to have pictures taken in the next day or so, right? Come by my place and we'll discuss this. Call me when your plans are firm so I'll know when to expect you," Ryan said, then disconnected.

"Passive-aggressive bastard," Tyler muttered.

"There's a lot of that going around today," Josh said.

"Hmm?"

"I just got off the phone with my mom. She makes being passive-aggressive into an art form. Anyway, was that necessary?"

"Was what necessary?" Tyler fluttered his long lashes at Josh.

"Kissing me when you knew Ryan was watching."

Tyler's tone went crisp. "After you crept up on me and bit my neck in the middle of what might have been an important phone call? Yes. I think you got what you deserved there."

"Still not cool, Tyler. Are you going to tell me what that was all about?"

"Later. It might be nothing." He grabbed Josh's face and kissed him again. "Although there is a lot of appeal to a sweaty, shirtless man, you stink. Go shower. I have to do this whole Reddit thing, and it starts in about an hour, so I need to be ready."

"How are you doing this without a computer? Did you pack a laptop?"

Tyler waggled his phone. "Behold the future, old man. I've got it all under control. I hope. They said I need a picture with me holding up a sign with my brand-new username." Tyler handed the phone to Josh, then held up a piece of paper with /u/HRHTylerChadwick on it with the date. Josh took the picture and gave Tyler back the phone. "Excellent, now go shower. You stink."

Dismissed, Josh went to go and clean up. He refused to think about Ryan watching him suck his brother's face. It was too embarrassing and it got shoved in his mental box of things he pretended never happened. He then tried, with much less success, to keep his mind off the idea of taking Tyler against the white marble in the shower.

He told himself that it was normal to desire Tyler and it was nothing to worry about. Touching himself while thinking about doing filthy things to Tyler was also normal, or at the very least unlikely to shock the star of his fantasies. Josh tried not to think that maybe he was standing a little too close to the edge of his mental cliff.

Please step back for your safety and the safety of others.

Chapter 18
Tyler Is Internet Famous

Monday, September 19th, 8:30 a.m.
An unnecessarily large rental house
Blue Lake, WI

Tyler came inside after doing yoga to find Josh's note, and his first thought was to wonder how long Josh would be gone on his run. Then he left the house and started walking.

Things felt like they were spiraling away from him again. Last night he'd quieted the urge with sex, and that had been fine at the time, but then he'd had the damned recurring nightmare and the need to cut had come rushing back. Luckily, he still had the keys to his family's lake house. He just needed a little insurance, and having it didn't mean he had to use it. Just knowing he had it would probably be enough.

Tyler tended to have the nightmare when he was overly tired or stretched too thin or anxious. He'd been all three lately, and while sex with Josh had been great, it still hadn't been enough to keep that stupid dream at bay. He'd woken from it, heart pounding, and found himself naked in a strange room and a strange bed. He must have made some sort of sound because a strong arm had hauled him back against a hard chest. That had made him struggle in earnest panic, only to stop when Josh's worried voice rasped in his ear, "It's okay, it's okay. I've got you."

Tyler had calmed, his racing heart slowing as the warmth of Josh's non-threatening body with its already comforting scent had seeped into his consciousness. Josh, whom he'd known his whole life. Josh, who would never hurt him. At least not like that. He was safe. He was fine.

"Was it a nightmare?" Josh had asked.

"Yeah, just a bad dream. I'm okay now. Just need to take a piss," Tyler had replied, and it was only a partial lie.

Josh's arms had let him go, if somewhat reluctantly, and Tyler had scooped his pants off the floor and put them on before he went to the bathroom.

Tyler had sat on the side of the tub and counted his way past memories that were better left buried. The urge to cut had screamed through him and he'd pushed it down hard. He'd taken the bandage off his arm and looked at his healing wound, then had run his fingers along the stitches. It didn't hurt like it had a few days ago, but the bits of nylon were still a potent reminder of his promise to leave himself alone. There was too much at stake right now.

Nevertheless, he wished he could hold a blade. Not necessarily use it, but having it in his hand would help.

After a minute or so he'd flushed the toilet, washed his hands, and had gone back to bed, knowing he wouldn't sleep again. Only he'd fallen asleep after all, something about Josh's warmth and scent lulling and soothing him past his insomnia.

Tyler had felt better this morning after doing his normal, if somewhat modified, yoga routine. Even taking it easy, his left arm was currently singing in agony and Brad would have yelled at him for putting any weight on it, but the stitches had held and the pain was helpful. It wasn't what he needed, but it would do for now as a reminder of why he couldn't — or shouldn't — cut.

Then there was Josh, and Tyler's promise to him that he wouldn't cut himself, at least not during their arrangement. Part of him dreaded the months ahead, when he would be under constant scrutiny. He didn't think Josh would take it well if he reneged on his promise, and yet his feet kept walking.

Tyler felt he was becoming too much invested in a relationship that was at best temporary, and he wasn't thrilled at the prospect. Even if things were perfect, if Josh found that he had room in his heart for only Tyler, Ryan be damned, there would still be the need to go home, and the North Shore was no longer his home and never would be again. Tyler could only ever leave Josh behind and he had no hope that Josh would follow him. Josh's entire life was in Illinois. It was as ingrained in him as California had become for Tyler. Any fantasies Tyler had of Josh ever being anything to him other than a sort of brother-in-law were just that: fantasies, and far-fetched ones at that. Better to put it out of his mind.

Tyler unlocked the house and went to his bedroom. He found the box, hidden high in the back of his closet, and got it down. In it was a package of razor blades, Band-Aids, gauze pads, and tape. He didn't dare snag the whole box, but he did take two blades before putting it back. The blades were unused, wrapped in cardboard, and small. He slipped them into his pocket, locked the house up, and walked back, hoping Josh had still not returned.

He already felt better with them in his pocket, and it wasn't like he was necessarily going to use them. It was just good knowing they were there.

It was enough that he felt like he could face googling himself while waiting for Josh to get back. What he found after only a cursory search was a train wreck that would have been bad enough if it was happening to someone else, but it was happening to him, and the horror was all too personal. The reactions he saw ran the gamut, but the most common response was mockery. So many Twitter and Facebook jokes. He had become a meme—someone had cut an image of just his face looking shocked, and it had become the template for all sorts of hilarity.

There was also a surprising amount of sympathy and outrage over the video being leaked—some on his behalf, some of the latter directed at him for having participated in such a disgusting display, as well as a dismaying number of people convinced that he or his people had leaked the video on purpose to garner attention and buzz.

He'd survived taunts before. He could handle insults and name-calling, had been doing so all his life, but this was a huge step beyond. This wasn't ridicule from a few high school bullies. This felt like it was coming from the entire world. Tyler put his hand in his pocket.

No. Not the entire world. A tiny, bored part of it who will not dwell on this forever. I just need to ride this out and not panic. They want me to fall apart, to be broken under this wave. Not because they hate me, but because it's interesting and entertaining.

Tyler hadn't heard that voice in his head for a while, the one he thought of as his backbone, maybe because he hadn't needed it since it had screamed at him one morning that David had to go and this time for good. It was the voice that held his hand when things got a little shittier than he thought he could bear, saying, *I am better than this,* and *I will not let him break me,* and *one day I will twerk on their fucking graves.* It was the voice that had gotten him through beatings and taunts, rejection and humiliation, and Bridges. It had whispered to him during every lecture from his father when he was told he was useless and wrong and dirty and unlovable: *I'm nothing at all like what he thinks. One day I will be free and he will have no power over me.*

That voice had been right on every count, and he listened to it now. It had never steered him wrong before. The solution seemed obvious. He'd been allowing things to happen to him. Today, however, he was going to start fighting back. Not by opposing the wave of morbid curiosity that surged around him. No. He was going to ride that motherfucker back to shore, starting today with his scheduled internet Q and A. If people wanted to be entertained, Tyler was going to be their man. He was going to entertain the hell out of them. As for everyone else, fuck 'em. Cowering wasn't helping, hiding wasn't an option, so the only way forward was to brazen it out.

With that in mind, Tyler watched the video, or at least the most common clip that was going around, to refresh his memory of how bad it was. It was both better and worse than he recalled. It was obvious what was going on, but it was still far less pornographic than he'd remembered. They weren't being videotaped by a person, but by a stationary camera the boys hadn't known was there. The angle was odd and made things difficult to see. But, like Ethan had said, Tyler's face, largely the same now as it had been at sixteen, was easily recognizable, at least before he started sucking on Robbie Marchant's dick.

The odd thing was that he couldn't say the same of either Robbie or Jason. The faces of the football players had been obscured in the video by being cropped away or fuzzed out.

Tyler was puzzled by that. It was possible the person hosting this clip had done the alteration, but why try to protect the other boys? Tyler started searching for any video footage where their faces weren't obscured and couldn't find anything. The only reasonable explanation was that they had been scrubbed before the video had been put online, but the question was why. And on the heels of that, who. It seemed unlikely that someone unconnected with Tyler would have bothered to scrub out the other faces but leave his recognizable.

Not that it seemed to have protected them. The video had been posted less than a week ago and internet detectives had already outed the two other participants, the poor bastards. He wondered how they were weathering the storm. Tyler thought he should probably reach out to them and maybe try to apologize or commiserate or something, although how did one even go about that? Was there some sort of "sorry that our videotaped threesome ended up on the internet" protocol? Maybe he could send an Edible Arrangement. Nothing said, "I hope this hasn't ruined your life" like pineapple slices cut into daisies.

Tyler texted Ryan, who immediately Skyped him. Tyler hadn't gotten much beyond explaining that the video had been altered from what he remembered when he felt teeth on his neck and saw Ryan flinch. Not a lot. It was just the smallest twitch. And it was followed by a frown.

The frown was probably what made him do it, pulling Josh in and thoroughly kissing him while Ryan watched. He wanted to prove something to Ryan, although he couldn't say exactly what. It felt like he was expressing ownership, which was absurd. But the more he thought about it, the more that kiss felt like he was marking his territory. So, he sent Josh away before he did something humiliating like prostrating himself at Josh's sweaty, sneakered feet.

Safely alone, Tyler put his hand back in his pocket and fingered the blades in there. He would worry about Josh later. Now he just needed to worry about saving his career.

Okay, Tyler, let's do this.

He opened the Reddit app he'd downloaded onto his phone and familiarized himself with how the site worked. At first it seemed like a confusing free-for-all, but he perused a few threads to see how the interface worked, then went to the sub IAmA, where Tom had arranged for him to be on in about half an hour. First Tyler reread the instructions he'd been sent by the site's liaison, then he looked at some of the current threads to see what he'd be getting himself into.

The people answering questions over the past day were quite the spectrum. There was an employee at Home Depot, a few athletes, a neuroscientist, an indie film director, a comedian, two politicians, some person with a poop fetish, a Japanese astronaut, and the weatherman from the *Today Show*. Tyler looked at some of the questions being asked, and they were all over the place, too. It did give him a pretty good idea of how to answer his questions, though.

When it was time, he created his thread like the liaison had told him.

I am Tyler Chadwick, actor, occasional model, and the star of that underage gay threesome sex tape that's being circulated illegally on the internet. AMA.

Okay, if that didn't bring people in, nothing would.

Next, he posted a link to the picture Josh had taken of him, a link to his IMDb page, and the following bio:

Hi, I'm Tyler Chadwick. I grew up in a Chicago suburb, but moved to San Francisco with my mother when I was 17. I studied theater at UCLA and started doing work in commercials shortly before graduation. That led to a few spots in TV shows, bit parts in a few movies, then my first big role as Andy in Blood and Water, *and later Duckie in the remake of* Pretty in Pink. *My latest role is Druindar in* The Silver Arrow, *which is scheduled for release on Christmas Day (note my glorious blue hair). I've also done modeling for Yves Saint Laurent and Hermes.*

Today I'm here to answer questions about video footage that was leaked less than a week ago to the internet of a very jailbaity 16-year-old me and two equally underage football players. Shame on you for watching something so expressly illegal. Naughty. Chris Hansen would like for you to please take a seat over there. For those of you who haven't seen it, spoilers: I am the cheerleading meat in that football sandwich. There, now you don't have to risk the wrath of the FBI by watching underage accidental porn.

I'll be here for 90 minutes and I'm hoping that people ask some questions because I am easily bored. Okay, Reddit, ask me anything.

The questions started pouring in right away and every time Tyler refreshed the screen after answering one, it seemed like there'd be three

Allthepie
Okay, I'll go there. Why the weight room at your school?
HRHTylerChadwick
I didn't care if I got caught. I was going through a rebellious stage at the time. Just didn't realize I was going to get caught on tape.
Allthepie
Was it worth it? Did you get into trouble?
HRHTylerChadwick
I got into so much trouble. I was suspended and had to drop cheerleading, but later I tried out for the school play and that's when I fell in love with acting, so it must have been fate.
tacocat
But was it worth it?
HRHTylerChadwick
Not really. It wasn't the end-all, be-all I thought it would be when I talked them into it. Don't get me wrong, it wasn't the worst sex I've had, but it was a long way from being the best. The problem with seducing straight boys is that they often have no clue what they're doing. Especially as teenagers.
tacocat
They were straight? Because it looked pretty gay to me.
HRHTylerChadwick
Well, I thought they were straight at the time. There is very little more attractive to an oversexed gay teenaged boy than a straight jock. Or maybe that was just me. Anyway, if they were gay, they weren't out at the time. For the record, I never had any intention of outing either one. The only thing I wanted was to get off.

Banana4Scale
Is Aaron Goldberg as awesome in real life as I hope he is?
HRHTylerChadwick
He's amazing. Great director and super nice guy. I'm really hoping this crap doesn't blow back and drag down *The Silver Arrow*. Neither he nor the film deserve that.

PM_MeYourPerkyTits
Are you a fan of *The Silver Arrow* and the rest of the books?
HRHTylerChadwick

Fuck, yeah, I'm a fan. I was so excited when I got the part of Druindar I about creamed my jeans.
The_Puffin
Do you think there'll be any sequels?
HRHTylerChadwick
Depends on how well *The Silver Arrow* does. Hollywood loves a franchise, though, and there are two more books. I'd love to do the whole trilogy.

UsernameRemoved
Has the leaking of the video affected your life much?
HRHTylerChadwick
It hit while I was on vacation with my boyfriend. His vacation, really, not mine, since I just got done with shooting *The Silver Arrow* less than a month ago and haven't been up to much. But he's got a real job, being a doctor and all.
dankmememaster
Your boyfriend is a doctor? How did you meet?
HRHTylerChadwick
I've known him forever. His sister is getting married to my brother in a few weeks. It's only been somewhat recently, though, that our relationship turned into a romantic one.
dankmememaster
You say he's an old family friend. Does that mean he lives in Chicago, where you grew up?
HRHTylerChadwick
Yes, in the area.
asciinoquestions
Your boyfriend is a doctor in Chicago and you live in LA? How does that work, exactly?
HRHTylerChadwick
We're still working it out. I'd planned on spending the next month or so in Chicago visiting my family. After that, we'll see, but I'm sure it'll involve racking up tons of frequent flyer miles. And lots of Skype. I'm hoping I can talk him into moving to LA.

Fat chance of that ever happening, Tyler thought. *I don't think you could pry Josh out of Illinois with dynamite. The only reason he went to Stanford was because of Ryan, and when that didn't work out, where did he go? Right back home.*

LumpyPotatoPrincess

What's it like waking up and finding out you're a meme?
HRHTylerChadwick
Not great, to be honest. But at least it's a funny meme. That's some comfort.

Its_a_tumor
Is Chris Steward hard to work with? I've heard he's a raging egomaniac.
HRHTylerChadwick
Compared to me, not so much. Seriously, he's a great actor and a good person. It was a privilege working with him and I learned a lot from him. Hopefully I'll get to work with him again (fingers crossed for sequels). We got to be good friends during the filming, so even if there aren't any sequels, I'm sure we'll still hang out.
Its_a_tumor
Good friends? Like how good?
HRHTylerChadwick
Get your mind out of the gutter. Chris is straight and has a lovely girlfriend. Besides, even if he wasn't taken, I am.

DarkPastamancer
Is your boyfriend hot?
HRHTylerChadwick
Give me a minute and you can judge for yourself.
DarkPastamancer
Oh, we'll judge the fuck out of him. Buckle up.

    Tyler called Josh over. He was engrossed in playing a game on his phone, so it took a few seconds for Josh to even acknowledge him.
    "What?" he asked, sounding pissy and not getting out of the recliner.
    "The internet wants to know if you're hot. Hold this and I'll show them."
    Tyler handed Josh a sign that said: *I am /u/HRHTylerChadwick's boyfriend. Envy me.*
    "You have got to be kidding me," Josh said.
    "Come on, old man. Time to earn your salary. Give me a smile."
    Josh smiled the fakest smile ever and Tyler frowned.
    "Wait. I've got a better idea." He climbed onto Josh's lap and kissed him. "Okay, now say 'cheese.'" He snapped a few pictures of the two of them and decided to post the one that had Josh looking like he was thinking of doing unspeakable things to Tyler. "Oh, yeah, that'll do."

He thought about sliding off Josh's lap and then decided to stay. He was nothing if not capable of multitasking.

HRHTylerChadwick
Okay, here's a picture of the two of us. Is he not fine?
NarwhalBacon
I think my ovaries just exploded. Would you two be open to another threesome?
HRHTylerChadwick
I think we're good, but thanks for the offer.

squattingslav
How do we know this isn't a publicity stunt?
HRHTylerChadwick
I'd like to claim I'm the sort of evil genius mastermind to engineer a threesome at age 16 to be filmed by my school's CCTV just so I could use it 9 years later to promote myself after getting a supporting role in a film that's probably going to make a ton of money, but I am just not that crafty. Thanks for the vote of confidence, though.

2brknarms
Do you think being gay will affect you getting future roles?
HRHTylerChadwick
Maybe. I hope not. But if so, fuck them. I'm not ashamed of who I am and it doesn't have any impact on my ability to act.
Banananananana
What about the threesome footage? Are you ashamed of that?
HRHTylerChadwick
I'd love to be able to go back in time and have that not exist, but I can't. I can only move forward and hope people realize that I was a teenager there. So were the other two kids there with me. This was something that should have been destroyed nine years ago, but wasn't. Then it was put out there to hurt me, and others have gotten hurt in the process.

Essentially, it's cyberbullying, and while I can weather it, the two guys with me shouldn't have to. I know they've been identified, but I sincerely hope that people will leave them alone. How many people would like bad sex from their adolescence all over the internet?
ApothosisAvocado
Bad sex? That's disappointing.

HRHTylerChadwick
Meh. Okay, maybe not bad. Mediocre, though. Threesomes are overrated. Take it from me. I know.
ApothosisAvocado
Man, that's just depressing.
HRHTylerChadwick
That's me, Tyler Chadwick, destroying all your illusions. There is no Santa Claus, Columbus did not discover America, and threesomes are overrated.

Tyler lost track of how many questions he got and answered. He addressed a few of the negative ones, but ignored the outright insulting ones. There were so many questions that he could have kept going for at least another hour, if not longer, but Josh finally grabbed his phone and held it above Tyler's head until he promised to stop so they could eat lunch and then do something that didn't involve the internet.

"Like what?" Tyler asked.

"I'm sure we'll think of something if we apply ourselves. Sign off on this thing, and we'll see what we can come up with."

"I thought you wanted to eat lunch," Tyler said, snatching his phone away from Josh and editing his bio to read that he was done answering questions and thanking everyone who participated.

Josh took the phone back and put both his and Tyler's phones on the side table. "Lunch can wait a few minutes."

Lunch ended up waiting a bit more than a few minutes, and between answering all those questions, then being distracted by Josh, Tyler forgot until much later about what he had in his pocket.

Chapter 19
Josh Does Not Condone Dragon Murder

Monday, September 19th, 12:43 p.m.
The dock outside of an unnecessarily large rental house
Blue Lake, WI

They made sandwiches and ended up eating them while sitting on the dock. Tyler pulled up his jeans to mid-calf and dangled his feet in the water.

"I talked to my mom this morning," Josh said. "Told her you and I were dating."

Tyler nudged Josh's leg. "Look at you, the dutiful son."

"Not really. She called me while I was out running. Our pictures from yesterday are already circulating. A friend of my mom's sent her one because she recognized me."

"Oh," Tyler said. "Well, that's what we wanted. The pictures circulating, I mean."

"Yeah, the plan seems to be working," Josh agreed. "Didn't stop her from trying to set me up with some guy in Hinsdale, though."

Tyler looked up from his sandwich. "Really?"

"Yeah, the nephew of some woman she knows from temple. A doctor, apparently."

"A Jewish doctor, huh? That sounds like a much better prospect than a temporary fake relationship with a currently unemployed actor." He gave Josh an unconcerned, cocky grin, but his fingers picked restlessly at his sandwich, then threw part of the shredded crust into the lake.

"I am not going to fake break up with you over some guy I haven't even met, if that's what you're insinuating."

Tyler flicked Josh a glance, then went back to studying his now crustless turkey on whole wheat. "That's a relief. It's a little late for me to find a new boyfriend at this point."

"Happy to be of service."

Tyler threw a leer onto his face. "Oh, I'm more than happy to let you service me." At Josh's grunt of disgust, his leer morphed into a smirk. "You can always keep the doctor from the south 'burbs in reserve, you know. Save him for later."

Josh didn't want to think about later. Not on this pretty day, sitting on the dock with this pretty boy. The wind ruffled his blue hair and Tyler brushed it out of his face. Josh found himself wanting to run his fingers through it. "I think I'll pass." Josh had dated enough doctors to staff a clinic and enough lawyers to start a practice to rival Chadwick and Chadwick. The last thing he needed was his mother setting him up with yet another "perfect man."

Tyler shrugged, clearly not caring one way or the other, and took a bite of his sandwich.

"Mom wants me settled." Josh found himself needing to fill the silence that stretched between them, the words coming out of his mouth before his brain had a chance to vet them. Then, once started, he couldn't seem to stop. "Her greatest ambition is for me to find some nice, professional man, plan a wedding, have two kids, preferably through a surrogate, and buy a house in a suburb that's either Highland Park or within close proximity. As for my dad, well, he wants that for me, too, but... I don't know. It's hard to explain. He knows I'm gay, I had the whole big coming out conversation with my parents ages ago, but sometimes it's like he pretends that I'm not. I know he does that with his friends. Maybe because it's easier? He never says anything, but there's this underlying current in every conversation I have with him that..."

Tyler stopped staring out at the lake and looked at him. "That what?"

That I'm not good enough and that I'll never be good enough. "That I'm not the son he expected to have, I guess. Not that he's ever said it to me in so many words." Josh shoved the last bite of his sandwich in his mouth and thought while he chewed. "Our family is all about the passive-aggression. Except Rachel. She's some kind of recessive throwback. With me and my parents, though, it's all veiled insinuations and talking sideways around our issues. I think it's because we don't want to disappoint each other but are sure we will, anyway. You'll see for yourself at the wedding and then when my parents take me to dinner for my birthday."

"You sound like a fun family," Tyler said. "You know, if you think it's going to be a problem, I can bow out from your birthday dinner. I do have to attend the wedding, though."

"No," Josh said, "you're committed now. You know, you'll be the first man I've ever brought home to meet my parents. Well, except Ryan, and he doesn't really count, since they thought the only thing we were up to in my bedroom was studying." Or maybe not, based on what his mother had said that morning. Josh decided to forget his mother had ever insinuated she'd known he and Ryan had been more than friends back then. It was too embarrassing to contemplate. He gave Tyler a little grin. "You probably don't count, either, since they already know you, too."

Tyler blinked at him. "Josh, are you serious? You've never once brought a guy home to meet your parents? How is that even possible?"

"There's been no one who seemed worthy of taking home," Josh said.

Tyler looked indignant. "Oh," he said. "You're one of those." He curled his lip.

"One of what?" Josh asked, baffled.

"I've seen it a million times, Mr. Stealth Gay. You find guys good enough to fuck, but not good enough to date. Or you date, but you never introduce him to your friends or family. When you go out, it's across town in places where no one knows you, and if you do meet someone you know, you pretend to just be friends with that cute boy who's half your age." Tyler had torn the remainder of his sandwich into tiny pieces while saying this. Now he threw the mess into the lake, then scooted back, bringing his wet feet onto the dock.

"God, Tyler, project much? What did I do to piss you off this time?"

With no sandwich to destroy, Tyler ran his thumb over the uncovered stitches on his left arm.

Josh grabbed Tyler's right hand and held it. "Stop that. And stop blaming me for shitty things I haven't done to you. I told a stranger in a phone store I was your boyfriend and let him take a picture of us, knowing he'd be posting it to the internet. You already know my family. And here's a depressing thought. Aside from Rachel, your brother is my closest friend. Rachel's right. I have no social life. But what I'm getting at is that you know my friends and family already. Even if I wanted to keep you a secret, Tyler, who would I keep you a secret from?"

Tyler looked horrified. "Ryan is your closest friend?"

"God, no. Brad."

"Brad? My brother Brad? Instigator of the often mentioned but never fully explained water balloon incident?"

"Yes, that Brad. I might tell you about it someday, but you'll probably have to get me drunk first."

"I'll keep that in mind," Tyler said. "I had no idea you were besties with Brad. Huh."

"Yeah, since we've been roommates. He's the one who always talks me into golfing with him, even though I don't particularly like to golf. And he's always inviting himself over, even though we usually just end up playing video games. I mean, don't get me wrong, he's even more mouthy than you and annoying as hell, but I like him. Most of the time. Not when he calls me sweet cheeks, though."

Tyler stared at him, mouth agape. "Uh, I think I'm going to need an explanation for that nickname."

"I don't think so," Josh said.

Tyler opened his eyes very wide so he looked like an anime character. "Please? Pretty please with sugar on top? I'll do that thing you like..."

Josh gave Tyler a skeptical look. "What thing would that be?"

Tyler's expression slid toward lascivious. "Anything. Everything."

Josh sighed. "God, you're trouble."

"Yes, but I'm worth it." Tyler traced the Superman logo on Josh's t-shirt with his index finger. "Come on. You still owe me a favor of my choosing, remember?"

The scars, right. If Tyler could strip himself naked for Josh, Josh figured he could do the same. "Okay, here goes. One night, back when we were roommates, Brad went out with friends and I stayed home. I had an early night and fell asleep. When Brad came home he found a dark, quiet apartment, so he thought it would be hilarious to wake me up with a huge water balloon dropped on my head for the edification of his guests."

"Yep, that sounds like my brother, all right."

"So, I was woken up by this huge splash of cold water. I jumped out of bed and ran after Brad, who headed for the living room, laughing his fool head off. There were a whole bunch of drunk idiots who got an eyeful that day."

"An eyeful. Wait. Don't tell me that... Oh my God. You were naked, weren't you?"

Josh felt the blush, equal parts remembered embarrassment and fury, crawl up his face. "Yes, I was naked."

Tyler stuffed a hand in his mouth to stifle his laughter, but his eyes danced with unholy mirth.

"So there I was, in my living room, naked, wet, and surrounded by strangers. It was like I was in a nightmare. Then I came to my senses and ran out of the room. As I fled the scene, I heard one girl call out, 'Wow, that is an amazing ass.'"

"She was right. You do have an amazing ass," Tyler observed. "Not as good as mine, but you have other compensations."

"Thank you, I think. Right after the amazing ass comment, some dude shouted, 'Yeah, seriously sweet cheeks, man.' The rest is really embarrassing history."

"I'm surprised you're still speaking to Brad, let alone that you consider him a close friend."

"I made him grovel. A lot. Which he did, because groveling to me was his best option. It was a long time before he brought up the sweet cheeks thing. By that time, he'd already started dating Rachel and probably thought he was safe from my wrath."

"I think you're a big softie and you wouldn't have kicked him out regardless. But if you want to irritate Brad, you can call him Bradley. He hates his full name, although that's no match for sweet cheeks."

"Call me that, by the way, and we are never having sex ever again."

Hopefully Tyler wouldn't figure out that was largely an empty threat.

"Gotcha. I still can't believe Brad's your best friend, after your sister, and you just now figured that out. That is the most pathetic thing I've ever heard, Josh. You really are the saddest man in existence. For real."

"Now you sound like my sister," Josh said.

"Christ. I'm not sure whether to be flattered or insulted. Your sister's a barracuda. I can only dream of being that scary when I grow up."

"Tyler, my sister is only four years older than you. Which reminds me, you are not half my age. Although I guess you could pass for seventeen, maybe. In the right light. And if the other person was high."

Tyler frowned. "Did your mom give you shit about the age difference?"

"Yeah. She demanded to know why I was making out with some child in a boat."

Tyler's frown deepened into a scowl. "I'm not some child."

Josh reached over to smooth the line of Tyler's angry eyebrows. "I know. Stop looking like that. You'll get wrinkles."

"Great. Then maybe I won't look half your age. Tell me, Mr. Stealth Gay, why am I the first man you're introducing to your parents? Although you're right—I've already met them, so I shouldn't count. How do you explain never having done the whole family meet and greet thing with anyone else? Are you only doing it with me because you have no choice?"

"It wasn't because I was ashamed of any of the guys I was dating, if that's what you're thinking. If I'm ashamed of anyone, it's my parents. They'd scare off just about anybody. The first thing out of my mother's mouth would probably be to ask how he felt about adoption versus surrogacy, then my father would grill him endlessly about financial minutiae and his golf game."

"Um, I'm far too young to think about children, your sister does my taxes, and I don't golf. Ever. There. That wasn't hard."

Josh shook his head. Well, it wasn't like he hadn't tried to warn him.

"It's not like I keep the guys I date a complete secret. Rachel and Brad have met most of them, at least the ones that made it past the first few dates, but my mom and dad are a lot to inflict on an innocent person. There's never been anyone who was important enough to put them through all that."

"No one important enough. Hmm. That seems..." Tyler pursed his lips, gave Josh a long, considering look, then continued. "Okay, you've been pining after my brother since the breakup that you claim wasn't a breakup, so we're talking fifteen years, right?"

Tyler paused, waiting for acknowledgment, so Josh shrugged. "I'm not sure I'd use the word 'pining.' It makes me sound like a character from a Victorian novel."

"Uh huh. And despite all your not-pining for Ryan, you're okay with getting freaky with me. And, as you took great pains to explain to me yesterday, I am one in a long line of men you've gotten freaky with since you and Ryan split." Tyler shot him a look, complete with one raised eyebrow. Josh longed to put his thumb on it and push it down.

"That's not exactly how I would have put it," Josh said, "but yeah. Like I said yesterday, I haven't been celibate since Ryan."

"Okay. So, my point is that I find it hard to believe that in fifteen years you couldn't find one guy you liked enough to introduce to your parents. You seem like the type who'd be all about having a committed, monogamous long-term relationship. I mean, you stuck it out with my brother for six years. But it turns out that you're, like, the exact opposite. You're a worse man-whore than me." Tyler poked him in the chest and demanded, "Explain."

Josh knew there was something wrong with him. Ryan had shattered him years ago, or maybe Josh had done it to himself, but either way, he was broken and he'd never put the pieces back together correctly. Every time he dated someone new, he hoped to recapture some of that magic that he'd felt with Ryan, and in the beginning, there was always the bright and shiny possibility, but days or weeks would go by, and he'd just be going through the motions with a man who was never quite right. An itchy, unsatisfied feeling would creep up on him, and Josh would find a reason to break it off. Then he'd be alone until sheer horniness drove him to date again, and the cycle would repeat like it always did.

"I think the problem is me," Josh said, his eyes on his lap. "It has to be me. I have no trouble finding men to date and have sex with, but when it comes to the sticking point, when dating is supposed to morph into something more permanent ..." He shrugged. "I just can't. No one is ever... I don't know... it never feels right. And I've dated a lot. A *lot*. So, it's definitely me. I just don't know how to fix it. Maybe I don't want to, and that's the problem. So, hey, you've probably found the best man you could have to seduce into being your temporary boyfriend, because you can pretty much guarantee I won't become attached. I don't do attached."

Tyler looked skeptical. "If you say so."

"Anyway, that's why I don't take guys home. Why get my mother's hopes up when I'll just break up with him in a few weeks, or give my dad more ammunition in his 'why can't you be more serious' campaign?"

"Josh, you are the most serious person I know, except for Ryan. You should not make being more serious a goal."

"It's not. I..."

"What?"

Josh looked out at the lake. He didn't know how to finish the sentence. He wanted his father to take him seriously and to stop insinuating that his life needed fixing. That made him think of Tyler, and he realized he'd done the same thing to him. Josh felt his cheeks burn with embarrassment and guilt. "Nothing," he said. "My dad is who he is. There's no changing him."

Tyler laid his cheek on one knee and gave Josh a long, considering look. "At least you still talk to your dad."

"Mostly through emails, though. Why aren't you and your dad speaking? Was it the divorce?"

Tyler's hand went to the burn scar on his calf and rubbed it. "You know he sent me to Bridges after the threesome incident," he said.

"Mm hm." Josh was relieved that the conversation had veered away from how fucked-up he was. It was bad enough discussing it with his therapist. He wasn't even sure why he'd said any of it. There was something about those eyes of Tyler's. Josh gazed into them and forgot himself, finding all sorts of unexpected things falling out of his mouth. Now that Tyler had started talking about himself instead, Josh didn't want to say anything that might derail him.

"After I came back from that shithole I told my dad that if he ever sent me back there that I'd never forgive him. Also, I said..." Tyler trailed off and shot a look Josh's way. He looked guilty, but of what, Josh had no idea. "Well, I said a lot of shit that boiled down to 'I'm not going back, you can't make me.' He sent me back anyway, over my mother's protests, and I haven't forgiven him. I'm sure I've been disinherited, but I don't care. Ryan and Brad can have his money. The movies I've been in have paid fairly well, and while my modeling won't ever make me rich, it all adds up. My investments are well-managed, and even without that, I've always got the trust fund. It's not 'fuck you' money, but I'm in no danger of starving." He looked up and gave Josh a heartbreaking smile. "Which is a good thing, since I am not doing porn. That probably means I'm doomed to starring in dinner theater productions of *Evita* in Fresno or something."

"Can you sing?" Josh asked.

"Sure. I can dance, too. I am a total triple threat."

"Fresno won't know what hit it," Josh said. He ruffled Tyler's hair, then smoothed it back down. "Why do you still have a trust fund? Your father didn't take it away?"

Tyler gave him a satisfied smirk. "He couldn't. It was set up by my grandfather and it's untouchable, at least by Dad. I'm sure it pisses him off, though."

"Do you have any plans to reconcile with your father?" Josh asked.

"God, no. Why would I want to?"

"Because he's your father."

Tyler wrapped his arms around his knees. "I don't care. I spent my childhood terrified of him. On good days, he ignored me. On the bad ones, it was all insults and yelling and smacking me around."

Anger simmered in Josh. He'd had no idea. He'd never liked Peter Chadwick, but that was because Ryan's father was the one he and Ryan had to hide from. Josh had been scared of him, frightened of what he'd do if he found out about him and Ryan. Forbid him to ever see Ryan again, that was certain, but Josh had also been scared that his father might lose his job. He didn't know for sure if it would or could have happened, but it was something he'd always worried about. It had never occurred to him to be frightened of what Mr. Chadwick would do to Ryan himself if they were found out. That Peter Chadwick might have been physically abusive had never crossed his mind.

"I didn't know," Josh said, his voice soft. "I'm sorry."

Tyler shrugged. "I don't need him. I'm better off without him in my life."

"And your mother?"

"I love my mother," Tyler said. "She was as much his victim as I was. He had something on her, I have no idea what, but she couldn't leave him. Not until he sent me back to that place. At that point, whatever he was holding over her mattered less than getting me out. Luckily my California grandparents took us in. My trust fund didn't start until I was twenty-one, and we literally had nothing but clothes when we left Illinois." Tyler shivered, even though the afternoon was unseasonably warm.

"Did your dad hit your mom and your brothers?"

"My mom, sometimes, when he got really angry, especially after Brad moved out. Never my brothers, as far as I know, but Ryan was always the perfect heir and Brad the extraneous yet inoffensive spare. I was the whipping boy."

"And your mom allowed it?"

Tyler clutched his knees tighter. "I asked her once why we didn't leave after I came out. Everything got exponentially worse then, and both Brad and Ryan were off at college by that point, leaving zero buffer between me and Dad."

"What did she say?"

"Pretty much the typical Chadwick response: she couldn't talk about it."

"Do you have any guesses?"

Tyler shook his head. "No. I figure it had to be a good reason, though. Right?"

Josh rubbed Tyler's leg and encountered the burn scar. "Sure. How did you get this, anyway? It's one hell of a burn."

"I don't want to talk about it."

"Being a typical Chadwick, Tyler?"

Tyler gave him a small, unhappy smile. "You know how you said

Rachel is the family rebel against the Rosen passive-aggressiveness? Well, Brad is the only one in the family who talks about shit. I think that's his form of rebellion. It's probably why he and Rachel get along so well. They really are soul mates."

"You can talk about things with me, if you need to. Unlike Rachel and Brad, I can keep a secret. Anything you tell me won't go anywhere."

"Thanks, but talking about the past doesn't help. It's over and done with. Dad no longer has any power over me. That's all that matters. I appreciate you trying to help, really, but this isn't something you can fix. This is not your dragon to slay."

"I don't think I'm the knight in shining armor type," Josh said, feeling hopelessly inadequate.

"Yes, you are. I bet you even have a shiny white lab coat."

Josh shook his head. "Nope. No coats at work and no ties. They spread germs. I'm just a dermatologist in a nice Oxford shirt. I don't think I'm up to dragon slaying."

"Then it's lucky I'm not asking for dragon murder, isn't it?" Tyler smiled but it didn't reach his eyes, which were blue today, the same color as the sky reflected in the lake, and as chilly as the water despite the heat of the day.

"Yeah, that's good, because I'm pretty sure dragon murder isn't something I can comfortably condone."

Josh rubbed Tyler's burn scar again. Brad would tell him, if he asked, but Josh wanted Tyler to give him the story, not Brad, so Josh let it go, at least for the moment.

෬෨

Monday, September 19th, 7:23 p.m.
Living Room in an unnecessarily large rental house
Blue Lake, WI

Later that evening Josh was back in the recliner reading when Tyler came in and climbed up to sit on him, his back to Josh's chest.

"Can I help you?" Josh asked. He opened his legs and bent his knees so his thighs cradled Tyler's narrow hips.

"I'm trending on Twitter," Tyler said, twisting his neck to look at Josh. He was flushed and excited.

"I take it that's a good thing."

"In this case, it's fucking fantastic. You need to see this." Tyler took

Josh's phone and laid it aside so they could both look at Tyler's phone. "Check out this trending hashtag."

It was **#threesomesareoverrated**. "That's you?"

Tyler nodded. "That is indeed a reference to me. There's also some discussion about me in **#fuckcyberbullies**, and **#tylerchadwick** is trending, too. Some of these conversations are nuts. You're in here, too. There's a lot of weighing in on the hotness of my boyfriend."

"You're making that up."

Tyler grinned at him. "No, I'm not. Strangers on Twitter are drooling over you. There's ugliness, too, but you'll get that. Trolls, obligatory gay bashers, the holy rollers. But there's a lot of people who are saying that I'm a victim of cyberbullying and are rallying behind me. You don't even want to know how many people heard something somewhere about me being in Chicago for a wedding and now think you and I are getting married."

"That's great," Josh said. "Well, except for the wedding thing. That's just weird."

"Yeah," Tyler said absently, looking at the phone again. "Weird." Then he looked up and turned around again, a dazzling smile back on his face. "But mostly this is more than great. It's amazing. A damn miracle. My bacon might be saved."

"That's great, Tyler. This is really good news."

"Yeah, it is." Tyler thrummed with excitement as he went back to staring at his phone.

"We should celebrate," Josh said and kissed Tyler's neck, then licked a trail to his ear and bit the lobe.

"Hey, I'm trying to read this," Tyler said, engrossed now in the same phone that yesterday he couldn't look at without flinching.

"Too bad. If I can't read, then you shouldn't be able to either." Josh's hands slipped under Tyler's shirt. He ran his hands over his skin, loving how it felt under his fingers.

"What do think you are? A cat?" Tyler squirmed under Josh's touch. "The role of my cat is already being played by Oliver, and he's on the couch napping."

"Shut up, Tyler. Let's finish what we started before lunch." Josh brushed his thumbs over Tyler's nipples, then pinched them. Tyler hummed his approval in response.

"Oh, I suppose. If we must."

"It's imperative," Josh murmured into Tyler's ear, his lips grazing it.

"You're doing a fine job so far," Tyler said, a little breathless.

Josh plucked the phone from Tyler's slack hand and put it on top of his own, then he undid the button on Tyler's jeans and lowered the zipper.

He ran his hands over Tyler's abdomen from just under his ribs down to his navel, where there was a line of hair that ran down into Tyler's briefs. Josh ran his fingers up and down through the hair, loving the little sounds of enjoyment Tyler made. Gone for the moment was his bossy elf. Right now, Tyler was pliant and almost soft under Josh's hands, or at least as soft as Tyler ever seemed to get.

Josh slipped a hand under the elastic of his briefs and found Tyler's more than half-erect cock. He groaned and bucked his hips when Josh's hand encircled him, his ass rubbing against Josh's own erection. Under his firm strokes Tyler became hot and fully hard as well as desperate, based on the sounds he was making.

Tyler felt perfect in his arms, fitting him just right. All the things he'd never thought he wanted in a man—a pretty face, a slender form, blue hair, and an over-the-top attitude—he now found irresistible in Tyler. He couldn't have explained why, but decided explanations were unimportant. The only thing that mattered in that moment was the desire he felt and Tyler's enthusiastic response to it.

Josh stroked Tyler's cock with one hand and his chest with the other. He bit at Tyler's neck and shoulder. Under his attention, Tyler came undone. He arched his back and his hands sought purchase, eventually reaching back to grip Josh's hair. Tyler pulled on it and they both moaned. With his arms above his head, Tyler's torso lengthened and further tightened, making him into one sweet long line of silky skin over muscle and bone. Josh wished he had more hands to touch him with.

What am I going to do when this is over?

The answer was obvious, of course. Find someone like Tyler and fuck him until he got it out of his system. Well, maybe not exactly like Tyler. That might be mission impossible, but he wasn't the only slim, pretty man in existence. Josh would find someone else who fit him like this, even if he had to go through every single one in Chicagoland.

And how well did that work out for you with Ryan? How many tall, muscular blonds did you fall into bed with? How many made you forget Ryan?

Too many, and none, really.

Told you.

Josh ordered the rational part of his brain to shut up.

Don't say you weren't warned.

Tyler started pleading with him, and Josh's heart gave a lurch. With Josh's rationality silenced, his desire started chanting: *Mine mine mine.*

He needed to step back from the precipice. He was edging into dangerous territory.

Josh's hands and lips and dick begged to differ. *Mine.*

Josh gave up arguing with himself. *I'll make him come, then I'm going to drag him to the shower and—*

Tyler's phone suddenly played some song Josh didn't recognize. "Fuck," Tyler groaned. "Fuck my fucking phone."

"Make it stop," Josh demanded.

Tyler let go of his death grip on Josh's hair and picked up his phone. "Hell," he said. "It's Tom. I should take this."

He pulled away from Josh's arms and hopped out of the recliner. Tyler put the phone between his ear and shoulder so he could pull up his underwear and jeans. Something fell out of his pocket as he was struggling, but he didn't notice. He walked out of the living room, talking as he went.

If that wasn't proof positive that Tyler wasn't his, Josh didn't know what was. He wondered how much more time he'd have. He'd thought months, but now Josh was beginning to wonder if everything was as big a disaster as they'd feared. Maybe all Josh would have was weeks.

Most of Josh's relationships only lasted a few weeks before he got bored. Maybe that's all he'd need to get Tyler out of his system. Infatuation was all this was and infatuation, in his experience, was a fleeting thing.

Somewhat reassured but still feeling more than a bit thwarted, Josh got out of the recliner so he could go to the bathroom and jerk off. Otherwise he was likely to do something stupid, like take Tyler's brand-new phone and throw it in the lake.

When Josh stood he saw something glint on the floor. It must have been the thing he saw fall out of Tyler's pocket. He bent and picked it up, and the bottom fell out of his stomach.

It was a razor blade, thankfully still wrapped in its cardboard sleeve, but it had no business being in Tyler's pocket. Looking at it was enough to kill Josh's erection.

Josh wrapped his fingers around it and followed Tyler down the hall. He found him in one of the bedrooms. Not the one Josh had claimed and the two of them had slept in the past two nights.

"No, of course we can be in New York on Thursday... I'll talk to my PA and have her buy tickets... yeah, that's fine... no, he's free until next Monday, so as long as we're back by then... oh, that would be great. Tom, thanks so much... yeah, I guess, but I couldn't do this by myself... okay... okay... All right. It'll be good to finally meet you... okay, bye."

Tyler turned to Josh, stars shining in his eyes. "Guess what?"

"What?" Josh turned the blade over and over in his hand.

"Tom's got me booked on *Late Night with Seth Meyers*. I mean, it's not *The Tonight Show*, but it's still awesome. We're going to New York! I'm going to be on the show on Thursday, so we can drive into Chicago tomorrow, meet with Ryan, then fly to New York out of O'Hare. I just need to tell Purvi and have her arrange everything."

"Purvi, your PA, right?" Josh wasn't sure what to do about the blade. He'd come in here ready to accuse Tyler of... what, exactly?

Premeditated mutilation? Now he couldn't say anything. He didn't have the heart to piss on Tyler's happy little parade. He stuck the blade in his own pocket. They could discuss it later. Or not. Tyler had already warned him that Chadwicks didn't talk about things, and Josh was worried that pushing him might trigger the very thing he wanted to avoid. He'd just keep an eye on Tyler, hope for the best, and brace for the worst.

"Yep. Technically she's on vacation, but she won't mind. You okay getting dragged to New York, aren't you?"

Josh shook his head. "I was a mopey teenager the last time I was in New York, depressed because my parents made me go with them and Rachel instead of letting me stay home by myself, which is what I wanted. The only thing I enjoyed was going to the Met. I'd love to go see it again."

At the time, he'd been pissed off that he'd had to spend an entire week away from Ryan. If he'd been able to stay home, he and Ryan would have had an unprecedented opportunity to fuck with impunity. Being horny, sexually frustrated, and unable to explain why he was so unhappy to his parents, he'd made the trip miserable for everyone, and he had few pleasant memories of the city or that vacation. At least on this visit he was probably going to get laid.

"Okay. We can spend the weekend and do touristy shit or visit some museums, then fly home Sunday. If you're okay with that."

Josh thought about it. "Sure, but let's plan on heading back Saturday. That gives me another day before going back to work."

"No problem," Tyler said. "Whatever you want."

"Oh, really? Anything I want?"

Tyler stood up and walked over to Josh. He reached up and curled his fingers into Josh's hair. He pulled Josh's ear down to his lips and said, "Anything you want. I am in a particularly generous mood."

Josh ran his hands down Tyler's sides. He thought about making good on what they had started earlier, but lunch was a distant memory and getting Tyler to eat was higher on Josh's priority list than getting into his pants. "Good, because what I want," he paused, then bent to whisper in Tyler's ear, "is pizza."

Tyler pulled back. "Pizza?"

"Yes, Tyler. Pizza. Food needs to occur."

Tyler made a face. "I could cook. We have a ton of food here."

"Can you make me pizza?"

"Probably not with the stuff we have on hand," Tyler said.

"Then let me find someone who can, and who also delivers. You can call Purvi in the meantime."

☙

Monday, September 19th, 8:40 p.m.
The immaculately clean kitchen of an unnecessarily large rental house
Blue Lake, WI

"I'd almost forgotten about it being cut into squares," Tyler said, grabbing an edge piece. "Pizza in California is great, but it's not the same as this. And pizza in New Zealand is weird. Not terrible, I guess, unless you count the shit with Marmite on it." He took a bite of sausage and mushroom and sighed. "Okay, Rosen, you win. Pizza was a good idea."

"So, we're going to see Ryan before we fly to New York?" Josh asked. He grabbed one of the middle pieces, which were his favorite.

"Yeah, we need to, or at least I do. I have to talk to him about the video."

"The threesome one, I assume," Josh said.

"Of course, that video. It's not like there are multiple incriminating videos of me out there. As far as I know." Tyler grabbed another piece and hummed with pleasure as he ate it.

Watching Tyler Chadwick eat pizza should not be turning me on, but it kinda is.

"Well, what about it? Or are you going to keep me in suspense?"

Tyler dropped the narrow crust onto his plate. "It's been altered. The video I saw when they made me watch it in front of my parents in the principal's office is not the same version that was leaked to the internet. While you can see who I am, the other two guys either have had their faces cropped out or they're blurred so you can't make them out. Not that it helped — they've been outed — but someone thought they could hurt me and keep those two out of it."

"So, you think whoever did this has a personal axe to grind."

Tyler shrugged. "That makes the most sense to me. Ryan wants to investigate it. He's got some flunky at the firm he wants to put on it. He figures that while we can't stop people from seeing the video at this point, at least if we find out who released it then Ryan can see about getting criminal charges filed. At the very least we can sue the pants off him. Or her, I guess."

"Okay," Josh said. "Works for me. I'm just along for the ride, anyway."

Tyler frowned. "Are you sure you're okay going with me to see Ryan? You don't have to go. I need to return Ryan's car to him, but I can get a taxi to your place."

"No, unless you don't want me there, I'll tag along. When are we meeting the infamous Tom?"

"He's flying to Chicago to meet up with me and Ryan to discuss strategy, and he'll be joining us in New York with Sydney."

"And Sydney is?" asked Josh around a bite of pizza.

"My stylist. I have a whole entourage. Ryan's my lawyer, Alicia's my agent, Purvi's my PA, Sydney's my stylist, and now Tom's my publicist. And you, too, of course."

"Your arm candy."

Tyler gave him a salacious grin. "Among other things."

"When are we leaving tomorrow? I have to do a few things to close up the place, since we're not coming back."

"In the morning after we've packed our stuff, I think. It's a long drive back."

Josh stood and went to Tyler, holding out his hand.

"What?" Tyler asked, but he put his hand in Josh's and allowed himself to be pulled to his feet.

"If we're leaving in the morning, then tonight is my last opportunity to fuck you in the shower. That white marble calls to me."

"What is it with you and marble? You're fixated. Besides, like threesomes, sex in the shower is overrated."

"Not the way I do it," Josh said.

Chapter 20
Tyler and Ryan Have a Difference of Opinion

Tuesday, September 20th, 5:25 p.m.
Driving way too fast on the interstate
Chicago, IL

Over the past few days, Tyler had reached a few conclusions regarding Josh. He did not snore, but he was a relentless cuddler, which was less annoying than snoring, but only by a tiny margin. He was a neat freak who disliked disorder and tidied compulsively, but all cleaning did not make him go mental. Rather it seemed that being upset made him clean more. He had a thing about making sure Tyler ate on a regular basis. He was a good kisser, far above average. He was clearly good people because Oliver liked him and had deigned to sit on his lap twice. And he'd been right about shower sex.

Tyler had gotten up close and personal with that white marble last night. He'd braced his hands against it as the hot water of the shower fell on his back, and Josh, on his knees behind him, ate him out. Then, when he thought he might go insane from the sensation of Josh's mouth, Josh had made use of the water-resistant lube he'd picked up at the store and fucked Tyler with one hand and jerked him off with the other. Tyler wasn't sure he'd look at white marble the same way ever again. He'd become an unresisting pile of goo that Josh had had to dry off and practically carry to his bed, where Tyler got fucked again, this time by Josh's dick. The upshot had been an exhaustion so bone-deep that even the dream had not intruded on his sleep, so that was a win, and Tyler had changed his opinion on shower sex.

On the way back to Chicago, Tyler added one more item to add to his growing list: Josh was quite possibly the only resident of Illinois who bothered to drive the speed limit. It was just as well they had two cars. Tyler decided that being a passenger in a car with Josh for that many hours would have driven him insane.

It was a good thing Tyler had programmed Ryan's address into Josh's phone before they left because while Josh was content to putter away in the right-hand lane, getting passed by everyone, Tyler had a difficult time keeping his speed under eighty, and spent most of his time in the far-left lane going faster than that, at least until he hit Chicago proper, at which point traffic slowed to its usual crawl, although it was still much better than the freeways at home.

When he got to Ryan's neighborhood, he called Josh to let him know the best streets to look for parking and to see how far out he was.

"You're already there? How is that even possible? The expressway's been a damn parking lot ever since I hit the Kennedy."

"Come to LA and I'll show you what a real traffic jam is."

Josh snorted. "I've been to LA and I lived near San Francisco for four years. Traffic there does not make me want to rush back. Look, I need to concentrate on driving here. Based on how fast I'm going, I think I'm maybe a half-hour away. It's going to depend on how bad the side streets are. Just go hang with your brother and I'll get there when I get there."

Way to sell your city, Tyler. Great job. How about next I go on about how fabulous the smog is and then wax poetic about the drought? I am an idiot.

Then he thought, *why am I worrying about how Josh feels about LA?*

Still grumbling to himself, Tyler pulled into the garage under Ryan's building and parked the Volvo between Ryan's Mercedes and his new Porsche. He grabbed Oliver, who was the world's best travelling cat and still asleep in his carrier, and headed to the elevator.

He let himself into the condo with his key, opened the carrier door for Oliver, then went looking for Ryan.

"Did you hear that? I thought I heard something."

The voice was male and unfamiliar to Tyler. Ryan had company? It didn't sound like Tom. Maybe it was the office flunky.

"It's probably one of my neighbors coming or going down the hall. I haven't heard from Tyler yet, so we have plenty of time." That was Ryan.

Plenty of time for what, exactly? Tyler wondered. He belatedly remembered he was supposed to have texted Ryan when he arrived, and he'd forgotten. Oops. Tyler was dying to know what his brother was up to, so he crept down the hallway as quietly as he could. Before he even got to the living room, though, what Ryan was up to became clear. Based on the sounds Tyler heard, Ryan was receiving an enthusiastic if rather messy blow job from someone who was not his fiancée.

"So, what the fuck do you think you're doing?" Tyler demanded as he entered the room. Exactly as he'd predicted, there was his brother, pants open and dick out. His partner in crime scrambled backward at an impressive rate of speed, considering he'd recently been on his knees with his own dick out. Tyler, who couldn't help but play up the scene, covered his eyes with one hand and gave a theatrical shudder.

"It's not what it looks like," stammered the man who'd been sucking Ryan's dick, and it was all Tyler could do not to laugh.

He uncovered his eyes and stared at the guy, who was perhaps around his own age or maybe a bit younger, with tousled black hair and wire-rimmed glasses. He'd zipped and buttoned up his pants with remarkable speed and was even now buckling his belt.

"Really?" Tyler said, hands on his hips. "You're going with 'it's not what it looks like,' despite being caught in flagrante delicto? You must have massive balls or be massively stupid. Either way, color me impressed."

"Leave him alone, Tyler," Ryan said. He sat there, unruffled and immaculate, as if he hadn't been having his dick sucked thirty seconds ago.

"You leave him alone," Tyler shot back. "Or did you recently become unengaged?"

"This doesn't concern you," Ryan said.

"Really, Ryan? This is the boathouse all over again. You going to swear me to silence this time, too? Only instead of Dad, who am I supposed to not tell? Stephanie? Although I think she's mostly interested in you for your looks and your money, so for all I know she's cool with your extracurricular activities. I guess there's still Dad, but you know we don't speak. And, of course, there's Josh."

That last one got a reaction from both men. Ryan twitched, then stilled, and the other started asking questions. "Josh? As in Josh Rosen, Rachel's brother? The one we're paying to be Tyler's boyfriend?"

Tyler turned to face Ryan's new chump. "The very same. Only I'm paying, not you."

"Why would he care?" The young man looked very tense and his eyes darted to Ryan, seeking reassurance he was unlikely to find.

"Josh is the proto-you," said Tyler, ignoring the warning growl from his brother. "The first, and until now I assumed the last. I caught him and my brother doing this very thing once upon a time. Let me see. I was eight, so it was seventeen years ago. But don't worry, new boy. They haven't been a thing since you were in elementary school. You should ask my brother why they stopped being friends one day. I think it would be edifying."

"Tyler." Ryan sounded threatening, but Tyler did not give a single fuck and he didn't look away from the guy sitting on the floor.

"What's your name?" Tyler asked.

"Patrick. Patrick Malone. I… uh… work with your brother."

"I thought he could be of assistance," Ryan said.

"I'll just bet you did," Tyler replied, not taking his eyes off the furiously blushing Patrick.

"That's enough, Tyler. You've had your fun, but Patrick isn't yours to toy with."

"Right," he said, drawing the word out. "That's your job."

"I said that's enough!" Ryan shouted, making both Tyler and Patrick jump. "I'm sorry I raised my voice," he added.

Since Ryan rarely lost his temper enough to shout, Tyler thought it was time to back off. For the moment, at least.

Tyler went and sat on the other end of the couch from Ryan. "So,

Patrick," he said, "With zero innuendo, what exactly is it that you do for my brother?" He smiled wide and it made Patrick look uncomfortable as hell, poor boy. Tyler could almost feel sorry for him, except he had to know about Stephanie, so he couldn't be completely innocent.

"Patrick's a legal secretary for the firm. He's currently studying law at Loyola."

Tyler arched an eyebrow at Ryan in the bitchiest way possible. "Is he also incapable of speaking for himself?"

"No, he's not incapable of speaking for himself," Patrick said, standing up. He sounded less mortified and more pissed off.

"Excellent," Tyler said. "Glad to hear it. And, aside from the obvious, you're here to do what, exactly?"

Patrick shrugged. "Ryan said he had a project I could help him with. I have classes during the day so I do a lot of after-hours work."

Tyler was opening his mouth to say something that would no doubt get him shouted at some more when his phone vibrated. He pulled it out and tapped a quick message on it. "Looks like Josh is here. He must've gotten lucky with the parking. I'll go down and get him."

"Sit," Ryan barked. "I'll let George know to send him up."

Tyler huffed. "Fine." He waited for Ryan to move out of earshot, and then went over to Patrick. He leaned in close and whispered, "Do you have any idea what you're doing?"

Patrick glared at him. "Yes," he hissed. He ran a hand through his hair, making it look even messier. "No."

"Little piece of advice, pro bono: you should run. Just get out while you can."

He looked miserable. "I can't."

"Then you're an idiot. He's going to break your heart. Unless you're just in it for the sex and what you can get out of him, in which case enjoy the sex and don't think you'll get anything else, because you won't."

He waited for a response from the kid, but all he got was a look of pure misery that might've made Tyler feel guilty if what he'd said hadn't been the truth. He gave his head a little shake and went back to sit on the couch.

Not long after, Ryan walked back in with Josh, the two of them laughing at something. They looked right together, like old and familiar lovers, which they were, Tyler thought. Something twisted in his gut at the sight. He looked over at Patrick and saw his own dismay mirrored on the other man's face.

For all that Tyler loved his brother, sometimes he hated him just as much. He wanted to go and snatch Josh away from his brother. *Mine. Not yours. Mine.* As if Josh was a possession to be squabbled over, like the action figures he and Brad had stolen back and forth from each other when they were children. As if Tyler even had the right to make a claim.

Ryan sat back down on the other side of the couch and Josh took the chair nearest to him. Of course. Patrick stood there and looked uncertain. Tyler thought the kid probably wanted to sit next to Ryan on the couch, but he ended up deciding against it and sat instead in the chair next to Tyler.

Well. Wasn't this cozy? Ryan, two of his lovers, and his brother, who had fucked lover number one last night. He ought to do the same to Patrick, just for parity. He wondered what Ryan would think of that notion. Then he wondered what Josh would think. If it meant he could have Ryan in exchange he'd probably be all for it.

"So, who's your friend?" Josh asked Ryan. Ryan didn't even have the grace to blush.

"Patrick Malone. He works for the firm. I'm going to have him do some of the legwork needed to get to the bottom of this video situation. Patrick, this is Josh Rosen. You know his sister, Rachel."

"Of course," Patrick murmured. "I'm pleased to meet you. I hear you and my boss go way back."

Josh turned pink. Ryan shot Patrick a disapproving frown. Patrick radiated defiance back at Ryan. Tyler wished he had popcorn.

"Josh has been a part of the family for pretty much as long as I can remember," Tyler said, loath to leave well enough alone. "He and Ryan were inseparable for years. And then they broke up—I mean, stopped being friends. And now he's my hired pookie bear. Life is strange."

Now Ryan frowned at Tyler, Josh looked confused, and Patrick seemed worried.

"Yeah," said Josh. "Extremely strange. So, about the video. Tyler told me that he thinks it was altered before it was leaked."

Ryan visibly relaxed. "Yes, the video. I never saw the original, but Tyler did, right after it happened."

"More than once, actually. First the principal played it with me, the other two guys, and all our parents watching so everyone could see what bad boys we'd been. Then later, after the police were called, it was shown in front of them as well."

"And everyone's faces were visible?" Ryan asked.

Tyler nodded. "Yes, at various points. But when I watched it yesterday I couldn't find one version of that damn thing where their faces aren't blurred or cropped."

"For now, we'll go with the assumption that the video was altered before its release, but we'll do more digging to make sure. If we assume that the video was altered before it was leaked, we must ask ourselves why," said Ryan, steepling his fingers.

"I think the more important question is how," said Patrick.

"How it was altered?" Tyler asked. "Why would that matter?"

"No," Patrick said. "How did they get the video in the first place?"

Tyler shrugged. "I have no idea. I thought it no longer existed. Last I heard the cops had it, and after no charges were brought, it was supposedly destroyed."

"Obviously it wasn't, or a copy was made before it was. Who could've gotten it or made a copy?" Josh asked.

"One of the cops could have," Patrick suggested.

"Possibly, and you guys should probably consider that, but this happened almost ten years ago. Why would anyone steal a tape out of evidence, sit on it for years, alter it so only Tyler's face is identifiable, then release it anonymously? It must be personal. Someone who has some sort of grudge against him. Someone who also had access to the tape." Josh's serious face broke out into a smirk. "You piss off any cops in your wild youth, Ty?"

"No. My only other run-in with the police, I was the victim. Other than that, the only trouble I caused was..."

"What?"

Oh. *Oh.*

Tyler looked at Ryan. "Should we discuss this privately?"

Ryan narrowed his eyes. "Why?"

"Let me rephrase that. We need to discuss this in private. Now."

Ryan heaved a sigh. "All right. Will you two be okay?"

"Of course they will," Tyler said. *They have so much in common.*

Once in they were in his bedroom Ryan asked, "What didn't you want to say in front of them?"

"So many things. But specifically, I think it was Dad."

"You what? That's crazy."

"He's crazy," Tyler said. "Who else had motive and opportunity? Who else hates me and has hated me my entire life? You know how chummy he was with the police in Highland Park. Are you telling me that Dad couldn't have gone in there, paid someone, and suddenly instead of being destroyed the video mysteriously disappeared? And the faces of those football players. Dad was friends with the father of the one I was sucking off. He might be friends with the other kid's dad, too. I didn't know him as well."

"Yet you were okay with having his dick up your ass."

Tyler wanted to punch his brother. *Oh, you sanctimonious ass.* "Ryan, I was sixteen, and being fucked by two football players seemed like a pretty good idea at the time. Unlike you, I didn't have a dedicated lap dog who was there whenever I needed a quick fuck. And look. History is repeating itself. Isn't it funny how that works out?"

Ryan glared at him. "Did you have a point to make, or did you come in here to lecture me about something that's none of your concern?"

Tyler closed his eyes and counted to twenty. "Okay, Ryan, fine. It's your life and you can fuck it up however you choose. I just want you to consider that Dad could have been the one to have released the video. Although if his intention was to protect the other two guys, it didn't work. The internet has outed them both. This is bad enough for me, but worse for them, I think. They didn't ask to be infamous."

Ryan frowned. "The entire situation is unfortunate for everyone involved. As for Dad being the one to blame, I suppose it's possible, but I think it's highly unlikely that someone at the police station let Dad waltz in and take the video."

"I think it's probable. Dad was a good one for getting people to do what he wanted. You know that," Tyler said. "Besides, I know I'm irritating, but I'm not 'steal a video and sit on it for ten years' irritating. Only Dad hates me that much."

"Dad doesn't hate you," Ryan said, "and it's within the realm of possibility that someone at the school made a copy before the police got ahold of it. Because I'm not a crazy person, my money is currently on Michael Koenig, that sleaze ball school counselor of yours."

Tyler thought about it. "Maybe. I don't know, though. What reason would he have had to make a copy? That happened months before he tried anything with me."

Ryan gave Tyler one of his "I am the all-knowing big brother and you are just an idiot child" looks. "He was a pervert, Tyler, who got off on having sex with minors. It was probably wank material. It wasn't like he was too concerned about breaking school policy or the law, either, considering what he did to you."

"Technically it was what I did to him, and it wasn't exactly against my will," Tyler said.

Ryan gave him that look again. "He was an adult and you were not. And he's got a motive, too. You were the thing that ruined his life. It makes sense he'd hold you responsible. Releasing the copy of the video now is logical. You're about to potentially make it big. Now is the perfect time to try and bring you down. I'm not saying it's necessarily him, just that he makes more sense than Dad. You and Dad have had your differences, but he's still your father and he loves you."

"Right. He just sent me out to be tortured for my own good."

"He couldn't have known..."

"Maybe not the first time, but after I came home covered in bruises, an infected burn on my leg, and half delirious from fever, you'd think that maybe a caring parent wouldn't have sent me back."

"That was... Dad said you were burned in an accident."

"Dad says a lot of shit. It was not an accident. None of it was an accident."

Ryan paled. "I... Tyler. Why didn't you ever tell me?"

"Yeah, well, you were off at Stanford at the time. And later..." Tyler shrugged. "Brad knows, and I would've figured he'd have filled you in, since being the family gossip is his calling. He was here after I came home and thank God he was, because he was the one who made sure I went to the hospital. It was Dad who came up with the accident story for the doctors."

"I'm sure he was doing what he thought was best," Ryan said, but even he didn't sound like he completely believed his own words.

"Sure, Ryan, if that's what you want to think, but what Dad thought was best referred to him, not to me or Mom. She was pretty pissed at Dad after my first stint in Bridges, and things got worse for both of us at home. I had to account to him for every second of my time, and Dad took all of Mom's money. Closed her personal account and confiscated her jewelry. After that, even to buy groceries she had to ask him first for the money, and she had to produce a receipt for every purchase. Don't tell me that Dad wasn't a bastard, because he was, and he still is."

"He's still our dad, Tyler."

"I don't give a shit. He was a terrible father. He forced you into being his version of a perfect son while pretty much ignoring Brad and me. Then he found out I was gay and it was open season as far as he was concerned. But at least I can see how he fucked me over. He fucked you just as hard and you can't even see it, can you?"

"I don't know what you mean," Ryan said, but he sounded uncertain. "He never hurt me."

"Not physically, no."

"What are you getting at?"

Tyler sighed. Ryan was going to make him spell it out. "Years ago, you were in love with Josh. It probably wouldn't have lasted, but who knows, because you didn't lose him because you grew apart or fell in love with someone else. You lost him because Dad convinced you that you couldn't have him in the first place, that anything aside from being completely straight was just as unacceptable as bad grades or not being a varsity football player or any future that didn't lead to law school and taking over the firm. You let Dad make every choice for you, you idiot, and you're still letting him do it."

Ryan shook his head. "We are not discussing this."

"Yes, we are. This is about Dad, and how he screwed us over when we were kids and how he's never stopped doing it. Why are you still in the closet? Why are you engaged to a woman you don't love?"

"Stephanie has nothing to do with this."

"Are you serious, Ryan? You're engaged to a woman and I just caught you having sex with a man."

"It wasn't..."

"Yes, it was, and if he went to his knees that readily, I sure as shit know it wasn't the first time for you two."

"Tyler, we're supposed to be talking about the video, not my sex life and your unwanted opinions about it."

"Then you shouldn't have tried to get in a quickie before we arrived." Tyler shook his head. "Does Stephanie know what you're doing?"

Ryan only stared at him.

"And Patrick. What is he to you?"

"What is Josh to you, Tyler?"

"My temporary fake boyfriend. I think we've established that."

"You two seem awfully friendly for a temporary fake relationship," Ryan said.

"You practically pushed him into my arms. What did you expect would happen? I'm not made of stone."

Ryan looked mulish. "And what happens when you go back to California?"

"Why do you care? It's not your business. Not anymore. You made that clear fifteen years ago."

"Likewise, neither Stephanie nor Patrick are any of yours."

Tyler sat down on the side of Ryan's bed. "You don't have to keep making the same mistakes," he said. "Make some new ones. If you feel anything for that kid, you need to either keep him or let him go. But if you keep him, that means he's not a secret. You admit what you feel is real and not wrong and go with it. Hell, you wanna fuck both him and Stephanie, I don't care, if they both know what's going on and are okay with it. But stop pretending to be something you're not, and if you can't, then let him go. You hurt Josh. Really hurt him. I don't think you meant to, but you did, and he still has the scars. Don't do the same thing again."

Ryan stared at him and said nothing for a long time, then he finally spoke. "How hard would it be, do you think, for me to get Josh back? He lives in Evanston, I'm pretty sure Rachel told me that. That's not far. It can't be even ten miles. I don't think it would take much—"

Tyler stood and faced his much-larger brother, his hands fisted unconsciously. "You leave him the fuck alone or I will hurt you, Ryan. The things Rachel will do to you will pale in comparison."

Ryan laughed, and it was ugly. "That's what I thought. Relax, Tyler. I don't have any designs on Josh. I see you do, though. That's interesting."

"Fuck you. God, you're such an asshole." Tyler sat down on the bed again, rage drained from him and replaced with a sick feeling of dread. He felt far too possessive of a man who did not in any way belong to him.

"You're awfully high and mighty for someone poised to break a man's heart," Ryan said, glaring down at him and looking like the spitting image of their father. Tyler had to give himself a little shake to dispel the image.

"Who's to say he won't break mine?" Tyler asked, thinking it was looking to be far more likely.

"I never said it didn't cut both ways," Ryan said. His expression changed, his face showing what might have been sympathy.

"Right. Right." Tyler didn't want to think about the future either, so maybe it wasn't fair to give Ryan such a hard time. Only he and Josh had gone in with no illusions. If either of them fell foolishly in love, they had only themselves to blame. It wasn't the same. Still, he began to feel like he'd purchased a brand-new glass house and a rock chucker to go along with it.

"You know," he said, with a small smile for his big brother, "at least I'm not fucking Harry Potter."

Ryan snorted. "Patrick doesn't look like Harry Potter."

"Okay, I'll grant you the glasses are the wrong shape, but he's got messy black hair and pretty green eyes. Nice wand, too."

"Shut up, Tyler."

"All right, fine. Do whatever. Just don't come crying to me later."

"Ditto. What about the video?"

"I still think it was Dad. What do you want to do about it?"

"We can't do anything without proof. I am not confronting anybody with something like this on just your hunch. My hunch is as valid as yours at this point."

"Then prove it one way or the other," Tyler said. "Use your boy—since I know you're going to anyway—and see what he can dig up. Don't tell him who he's looking for, if you're worried about it. Maybe we're both wrong."

"And if it is Dad?"

"Can you recommend a good litigation lawyer?"

Ryan shook his head in exasperation. "You want to sue our father."

"What if I asked for either an apology or a million dollars? Which would he choose, do you think?"

"This isn't going to end well," Ryan said.

Tyler folded his arms across his chest. "Then he shouldn't have started it."

Chapter 21
Josh Avoids Making a Scene

Tuesday, September 20th, 6:16 p.m.
Ryan's overpriced condo
Chicago, IL

"So," Josh said.

"So," Patrick replied, scowling.

"What's that about?" Josh gestured toward where Ryan and Tyler had disappeared. Josh knew the kid was mad about something, although he wasn't sure what, and Tyler was upset with Ryan, again for unknown reasons. As for Ryan himself, he was... well, Ryan. Josh had never been great at reading him. Even when they'd been just kids, Ryan had always been a puzzle for him to solve, not always correctly. Today Ryan was irritated with Tyler, but there was something else there, too, and Josh had no clue what it was. Too many years had passed, and what small ability he'd had to read Ryan's moods had long since evaporated away.

The kid shrugged. "Don't look at me. I'm just the hired help."

"Me, too, I guess. So. You think the Cubs will make it in the playoffs this year?" Josh gave the kid a tentative smile.

Patrick gave him a disgusted look in return. "Screw the Cubs. What's with you and Ryan?"

"I don't see how that's any of your business." Josh had no idea why this kid was so hostile, and even less idea why he was asking about him and Ryan. There was no him and Ryan, and even if there had been, who the hell was this kid to demand information about them like he had every right to know?

"Tyler said—implied—that you and Ryan were a couple. Had been one, I mean. Is that true?"

"Again, I fail to see how that's any of your business." Why would Tyler have shared anything about him with a stranger? A cute stranger, it occurred to him, and one who worked with Ryan. Maybe he wasn't a stranger after all—at least not to Tyler. They were about the same age. It wouldn't be all that surprising that they knew each other, perhaps well. Josh's stomach filled with acid, and his hand went to his pocket before he remembered that he no longer carried a roll of antacids around with him everywhere.

Patrick's mouth folded into an angry line. "Stephanie's bad enough, but at least I have an idea why he's marrying her. But you're one step too far."

"What the hell are you talking about?" Along with his acid reflux, Josh was starting to get a headache. He rubbed the back of his neck and wished the kid would shut up.

The kid drew himself up. "Me and Ryan. We're together." Then he wilted. "At least, I thought we were."

Josh froze, the pain in his stomach and head temporarily superseded by the kid's revelation. "No," he said. "That's not possible. He's straight. He always said so. I thought..." Josh couldn't finish that out loud. He'd thought that he was Ryan's only exception in his very straight life because he'd been special. Important. Unique. This kid had to be mistaken or delusional. He couldn't be Ryan's... whatever. Josh was supposed to have been the only whatever in Ryan's life.

Patrick gave him a puzzled look. "Ryan isn't straight. He's deeply closeted, I'll give you that, but not even close to straight. I mean, he came on to *me*. The only thing I did to encourage him was exist and not freak out the first time he kissed me."

Josh's world began to tilt at a nauseous angle. "No," he said. "You're making it up. You have to be."

The anger seemed to drain out of Patrick. "There's a mark," he said. "Birthmark, scar, something—high on Ryan's hip that looks a little like—"

"A flower," Josh finished with a sense of inevitability.

"More like a star, I think," said Patrick.

With that, the elaborate fantasy world in which Josh and Ryan shared a tragic, doomed *special* love shattered into a million pieces, flinging shrapnel throughout Josh.

For over half of his life Josh had constructed and kept alive a make-believe and utterly false scenario in which the otherwise straight Ryan had one exception, Josh, and the two of them would live together one day in perfect bliss once Ryan admitted to himself he'd been in love with Josh all along. Josh knew it was a stupid fantasy, had always known it deep down. He was by no means the first guy to fall for someone straight and hope to turn him gay out of sheer love and willpower, but it was his stupid dream and he'd clung to it forever. He'd even been making great strides at letting it go recently. Josh thought he'd almost gotten to the point where he was ready to bury his stupid dream for good and replace it with a bit of refreshing reality, one in which he was happy with someone who wasn't Ryan.

But now this. As it turned out, his dream wasn't just stupid. It was the wrong dream. Ryan wasn't straight. He'd never been straight. Of course, he hadn't been. It had all been a lie. Every goddamned thing about his relationship with Ryan had been a lie.

Josh remembered all the times as a teenager that he'd thought, *if only I was a girl he'd really love me.* What a colossal joke. Then he'd hated himself for wanting the wrong things, only Ryan had wanted them, too, he just hadn't had the guts to admit it out loud. It wasn't until college, when Josh had started seeing a therapist, that he had begun to accept himself as he was. And when he'd done that, he'd wanted the same for Ryan. They could both come out, and who would care? Only that had been a disaster, and Josh had felt terrible for loving his best friend and destroying their friendship because he'd wanted things Ryan couldn't give him. Now this. Josh was overwhelmed by a feeling of utter betrayal. He wondered how many men there had been over the years, then decided he didn't want to know. One or a hundred, it was all the same.

Instead of Ryan not wanting Josh because he was a man, it turned out that Ryan hadn't wanted Josh because he wasn't the *right* man. Why couldn't Ryan have just said that fifteen years ago? *"It's not me, Josh, it's you."*

Except, no. That hadn't been true. Josh remembered that last afternoon they'd been together vividly. Ryan hadn't ended things because he didn't desire Josh. No. Not by a long shot. It had been because Josh was no longer willing to hide, and Ryan wasn't ready to admit that he wasn't straight. He still wasn't, based on his current engagement despite this boy who radiated both possessiveness and frustration.

If Josh had never said anything, would he be in this kid's shoes now, still Ryan's unacknowledged shadow? The idea had a horrible feeling of rightness to it. He could imagine it in his head: leaving work and heading to this beautiful apartment where he'd never be allowed to spend a whole night. He'd never share his love with anyone in his life, other than Rachel and Brad, who already knew. Other than the time Ryan allowed him, he'd be alone.

It struck Josh with a sickening jolt that he'd spent the last fifteen years essentially as Ryan's secret lover without the benefit of having been his lover. He'd never fallen in love with any of the men he'd dated because he hadn't allowed himself that possibility, and he'd ended up living the very life he'd been trying to avoid. The whole idea made him want to vomit. At the same time, he felt for Patrick, who seemed caught in the same trap.

"How long?" Josh asked him. "Have you two been together, I mean."

"Since January."

According to Rachel, Ryan had asked Stephanie to marry him in August. Josh felt a stab of pity for Patrick. "And Tyler knows about you two?"

Patrick gave a bark of unhappy laughter. "He walked in and caught us. Just now."

"Are you in love with Ryan?" Josh asked. Josh's stomach roiled with an uneasy mixture of envy, anger, sympathy, and exasperation.

Patrick looked away. "I don't know. I..." He looked down and studied his hands, folded tightly in his lap.

"You are, aren't you?" Josh said, exasperation winning.

"Maybe. Tyler said I should leave, but I can't. I need this job."

"Tyler's probably right. Does the job require screwing the boss?"

The kid looked startled. "No, of course not. I know if I broke it off Ryan wouldn't fire me. For one thing, I'd sue him for wrongful termination so fast his head would spin."

Josh snorted. "But you don't want to end it."

"No. I don't want to end it, and I can't imagine working with Ryan if I did."

"Yeah," said Josh. "I hung in for years, hoping he'd acknowledge he had feelings for me, then I finally gave up. What are you going to do?"

The kid shrugged and looked miserable. "I have no idea."

The intercom buzzed, snapping them out of their moment of painful and awkward almost bonding over loving the wrong man. Patrick got up and went over to answer it.

"George says there's a Tom Harvey here to see Tyler and Ryan. Should I let him up?"

"Yeah, that's Tyler's publicist. Have him come up. I'll go get them."

Josh had no idea which door off the hallway was the right one, so he started knocking until he got an answer at one.

"What?" asked both brothers in unison.

"Tyler, your publicist is here. He's on his way up right now."

The door was yanked open. "Excellent," Ryan said, and looked at his watch. "He's right on time."

"You didn't think to mention Tom was meeting us here?" Tyler asked. He frowned, and the expression was a mirror of Ryan's familiar look of disapproval.

"You need to meet with him to discuss strategy," Ryan said. "I thought you'd find this convenient."

"Sure, fine," said Tyler, and they all walked out to meet the man who would hopefully save Tyler's career. "Although it would have been nice if I'd been consulted."

Tom Harvey was younger than Josh would have expected, maybe in his late twenties or as old as thirty, dressed with exquisite casualness in jeans and a perfectly tailored blazer over an argyle sweater. He had mahogany-colored skin with traces of old and faded acne scars on his face, a smooth, freshly shaven bald head, and he wore heavy-framed glasses. He had an infectious smile and a good handshake, and Josh felt he was probably worth every bit of whatever outrageous sum he was being paid. Tom oozed confidence, charm, and the ruthlessness of a shark.

Josh took a different seat when they all settled back in the living room. Ryan and Tyler took up their respective positions on the couch, Patrick made sure he was in the chair next to Ryan, sitting down like they were playing a game of musical chairs with deadly stakes, and Tom took the chair next to Tyler. Josh sat apart, joining in the conversation only when asked a direct question. This was all beyond him, and he let their plans wash over his head while he drifted as if underwater, mostly deaf to his surroundings and partially blind.

In a twisted way, he'd achieved what he'd desired for years — he was sitting in Ryan Chadwick's living room. How many times had he daydreamed about running into Ryan somewhere and being asked to come home with him for a drink and to catch up on old times? It was such a plausible scenario. All this time they'd lived less than ten miles apart, both of them close to the lake, looking out every day to the same view, although Josh couldn't help but notice that Ryan's view was much nicer than his. His sister worked for him. Brad was his de facto best friend. Yet for years, despite proximity and the many ways in which their lives overlapped, they'd never run into each other. Not until Ryan had called him up last week to ask him to be his groomsman.

Now here Josh was, drink in hand while sitting in Ryan's home. Only in his fantasies it had been just the two of them. Ryan smiling just for him. Shining just for him. There should have been no younger version of himself with nicer eyes. No charming publicist, who talked even more than Tyler, which scarcely seemed possible. And, of course, there had been no Tyler in his fantasy. His fantasy had been realized, and it was shit.

And is that so bad? He looked at Patrick, his attention riveted on Ryan, but glancing over at Josh occasionally, as if to make sure he was still hiding in his corner. Like a dog guarding his food, Patrick wasn't going to let any potential rival get too close.

Ryan was still his youthful dream. Still heartbreakingly handsome. Still as fascinating and enthralling as ever.

But.

There had never been a "but" before. There had never been qualifiers. Now Josh considered the reality of being Ryan's secret, and knew it would have entailed far more than his self-induced near-solitary existence. There would have been the constant fear of being caught. The self-loathing from living a lie. Not to mention constant insecurity and jealousy. He remembered the doubt and despair and all that glorious darkness of forbidden love that had seemed so attractive in its romantic bleakness at nineteen. At nearly thirty-five, the idea made him feel tired and sad. Josh looked at Patrick, sitting by Ryan, his face set in lines of resentful anxiety, and a novel thought surprised him: *better you than me.*

Josh switched his gaze over to Tyler, with his filthy mouth and magical eyes and a body that fit perfectly with his. He wasn't radiant like Ryan. He was far more abrasive than charming, and had a smile that a piranha would envy. You couldn't bask in Tyler. You could only hold on and hope you wouldn't be maimed in the process.

But. Again, that but.

Josh noticed everyone standing so he stood as well. He moved forward to shake Tom's hand as he left. He'd barely registered the plan for New York, and right now he didn't care. All that mattered right now was the promise of escape.

"You can stay here tonight, of course," Ryan said, "and leave from here to go to O'Hare tomorrow. When's your flight again?"

"Early afternoon," Tyler said.

"I have two guest rooms, it'd be no trouble to put you up," Ryan said.

Patrick looked unhappy. "I should go home. I have studying to do. I can start working on the video mystery tomorrow after classes."

Ryan frowned. "I shouldn't be keeping you from studying. You know you need to keep your grades up."

Patrick pasted on a sick grin. "I'm aware, but thanks for the reminder. It was nice to meet your brother. And Josh, too. But I should go."

"Don't feel the need to leave on our account," said Tyler with his toothy grin. "We're all friends here, aren't we?"

"Besides, we're leaving," Josh said. "I need to go home. There are things I need. At home." He looked at Tyler, pleading with his eyes for him to understand that he had to get out of Ryan's home, the sooner the better. Staying even another ten minutes was not an option. If he didn't get out of there soon, he'd explode.

"Ryan, do you mind if I leave Oliver with you while we're in New York? I can usually leave him alone for a few days, but better with you than by himself in a brand-new place. We'll come get him when we get back. The rest of his stuff is in the back of the Volvo."

"Sure," Ryan said. "No problem. Are you taking off right away?"

"Yes," said Josh before Tyler had the chance to answer.

"Have a safe trip and good luck, both of you. Make me proud."

Josh said nothing. Tyler grunted.

Ryan looked at Patrick. "If you can wait a few minutes to leave, I have some things I'd like to discuss."

"Of course," Patrick said.

Of course. Watching Patrick jump to Ryan's command made Josh feel ill. Patrick's eager devotion was palpable, and it was like looking back through time and seeing his younger self through a new and strange set of eyes. He couldn't stay and watch it.

Josh marched to the door, hoping Tyler was behind him, but when he turned, he wasn't. He waited there, feeling awkward with Ryan and Patrick staring at him. "Tyler, are you coming?"

Tyler appeared, holding Oliver. "Sorry," he said, "I was just saying goodbye to my cat." He kissed him between his ears, rubbed his face along his fur, then put him down. "Okay," he said. "I'm ready."

They left Ryan's condo and walked down the hallway to the elevator. Josh pushed the down button several times just to make sure. The doors opened for them a few seconds later.

"We need to go down to the garage—"

As soon as the doors clicked shut, Josh shoved Tyler against the elevator wall and attacked his mouth with lips, teeth, and tongue. Tyler was stiff with shock for a second, then he fisted his hands in Josh's shirt and opened his mouth, inviting Josh inside. This kiss was hot, desperate, and needy.

The elevator dinged and the door opened. They were still on the same floor. "We'll never get anywhere if we don't push a floor," Tyler said with a shaky laugh, and selected G. The door closed again. "Now, where were we?"

Josh buried his face in Tyler's hair. "Oh, God," he said.

"Hey, are you okay?" Tyler rubbed his back, moving his hand in small, comforting circles.

"No. Give me a minute." Josh held tight to Tyler until the elevator reached the garage level, breathing in the sandalwood that clung to his hair, the tang of his fading cologne, and the scent below that, which was just Tyler. Josh slowly drew air in through his nose and let it out through his mouth and felt the desperate, trapped feeling inside him start to fade as the elevator took them farther away from Ryan's door. By degrees he felt better. Steadier.

"Come on," Tyler said after he stepped out into the garage. "No falling apart on me. Not yet. Let's get you home first, then you can fall apart all you want. All over me, if necessary. Okay?"

"Yeah, I'm fine now," Josh said. "I just needed—" *air, space, escape, you*—any and all of those fit. "I had to get out. I couldn't stay there."

"I know," Tyler said. "It would have been—"

"Intolerable," Josh said.

"Yeah, I get it. You all right to drive?"

"Sure. It's not far."

"Okay," said Tyler, sounding dubious. "Let me get my suitcase out of Ryan's car, then you can take me home."

Josh felt he should qualify the statement and reiterate that it wasn't Tyler's home, it was his temporary pseudo-home. He couldn't muster the energy to say it, though.

"Yeah," Josh said. "Let's go home."

Tuesday, September 20th, 9:10 p.m.
Josh's perfectly adequate condo
Evanston, IL

"And here's my view of the lake," Josh said. "It's better during the day, of course. You can't really see anything much now."

Josh had given Tyler a tour of the building's facilities—Tyler had been especially interested in the lap pool—then of the condo itself. He'd left Tyler's suitcase in the spare bedroom, then dragged him to his favorite part of the condo: the balcony. Though several blocks from the lake, his building was tall, or at least tall for Evanston. His condo was on an upper floor and it faced east. His balcony was just big enough for a small table, two chairs, and two grown men.

"I think the view is fine," Tyler said, looking at him and not the water.

"You're not even looking at the view."

"Sure I am." Tyler reached his hand up and stroked Josh's hair much like he stroked Oliver's fur. "Is it a safe bet that you figured out what Ryan's been up to with his boy Patrick?"

"Yeah, he staked his claim on Ryan while you two were off discussing... whatever you were discussing. You going to tell me about that?"

"We'll get to it," Tyler said. "How did you not lose your shit in there?"

"I did," Josh said. "In the elevator, remember?"

"No, I mean I kept expecting you to erupt all over Ryan's living room. You were really quiet in there—too quiet. That was my first clue something was brewing. You're like a volcano when you get upset—all silent and broody and eerie, then, boom! Explosion! Lava everywhere. Then you cool off and it's okay for the natives to come out from their huts."

Josh had never thought about it in those terms, but he supposed it was a decent assessment of his temper.

"I, on the other hand," Tyler said, "wouldn't have waited to leave before I made a scene. I did make a scene, actually, before you got there. I'm so angry at Ryan right now. I can't believe he had the gall to rub your nose in his new boy toy. I'm sure it's my fault because I kissed you in front of him while we were on Skype."

"He's been with that kid since January," Josh said. "Whatever Ryan feels for him, it's got nothing to do with you or me." He sighed. "What a mess."

"That kid can't be more than a year or two younger than I am. Is that what you think of me, Josh? That I'm some kid?"

"No. You're definitely not a kid," he replied. There was a sheen of youth and innocence that still clung to Patrick that had been burned out of Tyler. If age was determined by cynicism, worldliness, and guile, Tyler would be eligible for a senior discount. He might almost look like jailbait in the right light, but often he made Josh feel as if he were the naive and inexperienced one.

"Good," said Tyler. He stepped closer to Josh and fit their bodies together. Josh's arms went around Tyler of their own volition. It felt so right to Josh that it hurt a little. He didn't want to let go. He was standing on the wrong side of the yellow safety line, and this was not a good idea. He was now able to see a world in which there would never be a Ryan and Josh, and that was okay. Painful, yes, but okay, and the ache he felt wasn't so much loss as it was betrayal. He felt foolish, stupid, and blind. He also felt adrift, as if he'd lost a few of his tethers, or as if a part of him had been scooped out and forcibly removed. Not a necessary part, nothing he needed to function, but it left a gap that his psyche desperately wanted to fill. Putting Tyler there would be a terrible idea, no matter how well he seemed to fit.

His therapist would not approve.

His body didn't care, though. His arms wanted to hold Tyler. His lips wanted to kiss him and his tongue wanted to taste him. His nose craved Tyler's scent, and his eyes desired every lovely perfection and imperfection of his face and form. His ears longed to hear Tyler's voice and his fingers to trace across Tyler's skin. His cock just ached to be inside of Tyler in any way it could be.

Had it ever been quite like this with Ryan? Yes and no. Yes, that overwhelming craving had always been there. But no, because Tyler wanted him back and had been quite frank about it. The illicit note that had been in every interaction with Ryan was absent. Josh had always felt with Ryan that he needed to steal and fight for every bit of affection, both physical and emotional, that Ryan doled in miserly dribs and drabs.

In contrast, Tyler just gave and gave and gave—his body, if not his heart. Not that Josh wanted or needed that, because nothing between them was real or permanent. Tyler said over and over that he needed Josh to appear to be his devoted boyfriend and he was willing to do whatever it took get what he wanted. Even so, Josh thought there might be more there beneath the pretense. A bit of affection that had nothing to do with obligation.

As he held Tyler in the cool September night, Josh closed his eyes and thought, *you have Ryan and Tyler in front of you. No Patrick or Stephanie. No forced temporary arrangement. Just the two brothers, side by side, yours for the asking. Which do you pick?*

The answer came to him easier than he would have thought. Ryan might have loved him once, but not enough, and it never would be enough. Tyler might never love him, but for now that didn't matter. Tyler was the one in his arms, the one with his head nestled against Josh's shoulder. It was Tyler's heartbeat he felt.

In Josh's mind, he saw the barrier before the abyss. He stood there, his feet on solid ground, then he lifted one foot and began to climb onto the railing.

Josh bent and kissed the side of Tyler's neck where his carotid artery pulsed. "I want you," he said.

Tyler started walking backward and Josh followed, the helpless moth to Tyler's brilliant flame.

"Of course, you want me," Tyler said. "How could you not? Look at me. Who wouldn't want to fuck me? I practically need to beat people off me with a stick. You have no idea how lucky you are that for some reason the only man I can think about is you." Tyler backed himself against the sliding glass door, a small, mocking smile on his face. "I can't wait to show you off to the world," he said. "How crazy is that?"

Josh opened the door and pushed Tyler inside. He shoved Tyler up against the wall and kissed him hard to shut him up, because the more he babbled sweet, utter nonsense at Josh, the more Josh wanted to blurt out something stupid like *I love you*, and he didn't. He couldn't.

But he could and did acknowledge the desire that thrummed through him. Love was out of the question. Impossible after such a short period of time, but lust was different. Lust was safe and convenient because it let him take the thing he found that he most wanted.

Tongue still thrusting inside Tyler's mouth, Josh fumbled with the clasp of Tyler's belt, then the opening to his pants, his fingers clumsy in his haste. He felt the button give way and his hand found Tyler's cock, covered only by a thin layer of stretchy cotton, and curled around it like it was meant to. Like his hand had been formed for just that purpose.

"You tore off my button," complained Tyler. He pushed himself against Josh's hand while he licked and bit at his neck. "These were my favorite pants, too."

"Fuck your pants," Josh said. He worked his hand inside Tyler's boxer briefs and pulled them down just enough to expose his stiffening shaft and tight balls. Josh stroked him with one hand and brought the other up to Tyler's face, skimming his thumb along his cheekbone and the ridge of his brow.

"What do you want?" Tyler asked, his tone uncharacteristically gentle. "What do you need?"

You. I need you. "Everything," he said.

Tyler stilled for a moment, then said, "You don't ask for much, do you?" He cradled Josh's face and kissed him, his lips soft and sweet and promising the world.

"Go big or go home." Josh sank down to crouch at Tyler's feet.

"I like where this is going," Tyler observed.

"Unbutton your shirt," Josh said. He needed to see Tyler stripped of clothing and pretense, if only just for now. He wanted to peel back every layer of protective coating that Tyler had shellacked himself with over the years like an oyster creating a pearl. At the same time, he wondered if there was anything left under those layers anymore, or if the boy Josh had known had suffocated long ago under all the artifice. Josh wanted to know, to see, what was real. Just for tonight. "I want to see all of you."

Tyler obeyed, but in his own fashion, making each undone button into a small, seductive production. When he finished with the last, he swept the shirttails to each side like parting stage curtains and held them back behind hands he splayed on his hips, framing his erection. "Now what?" he asked.

Josh unlaced Tyler's boots, then removed them with their respective socks. His pants were rolled above the boots and now showed Tyler's sharp ankles and narrow, elegantly arched feet. Josh licked the delicate skin stretched tight over the lateral end of his fibula where it nestled into his heel bone.

"Christ," muttered Tyler. He gave his erection a lazy stroke. "That is way hotter than it has any right to be."

Josh tugged on Tyler's pants to draw them down his legs. Tyler assisted by pushing away from the wall. Tight as his pants were, they revealed Tyler's thighs in slow, teasing increments until they slid past his knees, when he could shake them off. That left him in his pale pink unbuttoned shirt and black skintight boxer briefs, pulled down to the tops of his hips. Tyler hooked each thumb under the elastic band.

"This is as naked as I've been in any kind of light with anyone in a very long time," Tyler said. "Except my doctor. And you." He arched his arms and back, letting the shirt fall off and settle on the floor behind him. Then he pulled his underwear down and kicked out of them.

Josh's heart thumped painfully. This was what he'd wanted, but there was a rawness to Tyler, hiding under his outward seductive charm, that scraped at Josh's conscience. Maybe he was asking too much, expecting too much. He stood and covered Tyler's nakedness with his own fully clothed body. "Thank you," he said, pressing Tyler back against the wall and kissing away the wry twist of his lips.

"You, sir, are overdressed," said Tyler. He thrust Josh back by an arm's-length. "Strip."

Josh couldn't help but grin. "You're such a bossy little elf," he said, peeling his sweater and t-shirt off in one motion.

"Really?" Tyler leaned against the wall and tipped his hips forward, just like he had against the imaginary barricade Josh had erected in his mind, only now wearing less clothing. "That's how you see me? A bossy *little* elf?"

Josh reached his hand out to stroke Tyler's length. "Maybe not so little. Do you want to know what my first impression of you was? As an adult, I mean." He stepped away from Tyler, unbuttoned his jeans, then pulled down the zipper.

"Sure," Tyler said. "Why not? Take off your jeans."

"In a second. I thought you looked like a grubby juvenile elfin prostitute."

"Charming," Tyler said, sounding insulted, but his eyes sparkled with humor.

"Yeah. Like you'd suck me off in a back alley and expect to get paid in Pixy Stix and Skittles."

Tyler pushed away from the wall, the look in his eyes both amused and dangerous. "Liar. You thought no such thing."

"Then you went and took a shower, and when you came to me and laid your head on my lap you were so goddamned beautiful it was like you weren't even real. Which one is you, Tyler?"

"I'm not telling. Take off your pants. Now."

Josh pulled his jeans down and stepped out of them and his loafers so he stood wearing only a very small and very tight pair of dark gray and red briefs.

"God, Josh. I thought the green ones were nice, but these are better. Worse. I don't know. Who did you pack these underwear for? You were supposed to be on vacation alone." Tyler trailed his fingers over and down Josh's chest to the briefs in question.

Josh stepped back out of reach, then pulled them off and down his legs. "Maybe I was hoping to meet a cabana boy," he said.

"On a lake in Wisconsin?"

"You never know." Josh moved forward to push Tyler back against the wall. He cupped Tyler's balls in one hand and his shaft with the other. His thumb glided along the head, coating his fingers with the wetness there. "I found you."

Tyler's eyes squeezed shut and he moaned. Josh kissed along the side of his jaw and neck. He swallowed the words *Mine mine mine mine* before his mouth could say them. He leaned back and drew Tyler away from the wall. "Let's go to bed," he said. "I'm far too old and you're way too short for us to do it in the hallway."

"Good plan. I'm all for doing it on a bed like a civilized person. Carpet burns on my knees are not fun," Tyler said. "I will ignore for the moment that you said I'm short, old man."

Josh laughed softly and led Tyler to his bed. Tyler hopped back and fell onto it, his legs and arms spread wide.

"Tell me what you want," Tyler said, his entire body an invitation.

Josh climbed onto Tyler and pinned him with his weight, sitting on his thighs. "I already told you. I want everything."

Josh pictured his constructed safety railing. Tyler sat on it, his legs dangling over the edge as he kicked his heels. Josh climbed up to join him. He peered into the abyss below. It was a long way down.

"Okay," Tyler said, and drew him down so that their lips nearly touched. "Tonight, whatever you want, whatever you need, it's yours. Everything." Instead of pulling Josh down the rest of the way, Tyler lifted his head to kiss him.

On the barricade in his mind, the man sitting next to him reached out, took his hand, and held it tight.

Chapter 22
Tyler Might Be in over His Head

Wednesday, September 21th, 12:21 a.m.
Josh's extremely tidy bedroom
Evanston, IL

Tyler: You are never going to guess what I walked into today.
Purvi: Tell me! I'm bored, anyway.
Tyler: Ryan getting his dick sucked in his living room by a dude.
Purvi: What. The. Actual. Fuck. EXPLAIN NOW.
Tyler: Okay, so got to R's place earlier than I expected and caught him getting a bj from this kid. I mean, I'm pretty sure he's old enough to drink, but not by much.
Purvi: OMG!
Tyler: Yeah. My "I'm not into dudes at all, never mind my six-year relationship with Josh" brother is definitely into dudes.
Purvi: Wait. Josh as in YOUR Josh?
Tyler: He's not MY Josh, but yes. That Josh.
Tyler: That's right. You wouldn't know. When they were teenagers Josh and my brother were A THING.
Tyler: And by THING, I mean they fucked a lot. Pretty much in secret, because supposedly my brother is straight.
Purvi: Um... that doesn't sound straight.
Tyler: Preaching to the choir.
Purvi: Isn't he engaged? To like a girl?
Tyler: Yup.
Purvi: Huh.
Purvi: So bi?
Tyler: Maybe? He's still going with straight.
Tyler: Anyway.
Tyler: Things were like all kinds of fucked-up and awkward around here tonight. Josh's been broody all evening, natch, then as we were leaving he attacked me in the elevator.
Purvi: Attacked?
Tyler: Tried to give me a tonsillectomy via mouth suction.
Purvi: Ah.
Tyler: And then we
Tyler: Never mind.
Purvi: NEVERMIND??? Oh, no you don't. You fucking TEASE.

Tyler: We'll talk tomorrow, promise.
Purvi: I hate you.

⊰❦⊱

Wednesday, September 21st, 12:36 a.m.
Josh's extremely tidy bedroom
Evanston, IL

Josh had made love to him. Tyler lay in Josh's bed, surrounded by Josh's scent, naked in Josh's arms, and pondered the implications. They were troubling.

Tyler had expected a hard ride, and had been okay with that. After Josh's mini-meltdown in the elevator, he'd been willing to throw his body at Josh if it would get that shocky look out of his eyes or prevent another cleaning incident. Josh's master bathroom was tiled in a million little squares of blue and gray glass, and Tyler could just see him in there cleaning the miles of pristine white grout with a toothbrush.

Instead of the angry fucking he'd been expecting, Tyler had just been cherished within an inch of his life. Instead of bites and bruises, Josh had covered every inch of Tyler's skin in kisses, licks, and caresses. Even the scarred bits. Especially the scarred bits. Josh had held him down and kissed and licked along the scars on his hips and thighs until Tyler had begged Josh to fuck him already or suck his cock or just do something, anything, please. It had been lovely and terrible and frankly, a bit disturbing. Tyler wished he knew what was going on in the head of the man curled around him. He was afraid he might know the answer, though, and that was largely the problem.

A heartbroken Josh would have made sense. An angry Josh would have been better. What he'd gotten instead was sweet Josh. Seductive Josh. Adoring Josh. It was as if he'd switched his allegiance from Ryan to Tyler in one fell swoop, starting with that desperate kiss in the elevator. Even if it wasn't ill-fated rebound affection, and Tyler was nearly certain it was, he needed Josh's actual devotion like he needed a hole in his head. Unless, that was, he could pry Josh out of Illinois for longer than a week or two.

Would that even be possible? Tyler let his mind, safe here in the slight unreality of late-night drowsiness, imagine it. Josh in his house, in the pool, drinking coffee in the morning, pestering Tyler to eat breakfast. Eating dinner, just the two of them, or maybe with Purvi and her boyfriend. Snuggled together watching TV. Taking Josh to a premiere. Josh in a tux, on a red carpet, smiling and holding Tyler's hand. Josh in his bed every night, curled around him like he was right now.

Then he imagined Josh despising California and everything about it, missing home and his family, especially his sister, resenting Tyler and the often-relentless paparazzi. He saw Josh retreating into himself, alternately fighting and sulking. Tyler pictured his immaculately clean house and the new marks on his legs. The look of accusation in Josh's eyes, his patience with Tyler having worn tissue-thin.

Tyler remembered all the ways he'd been hurt before. He knew that people, if pushed hard enough, were capable of anything. He knew just as certainly that he would push because pushing was what he did best. He pushed and pushed and pushed until people snapped. He thought of that last party with David and shivered.

Josh would never... I'm pretty sure... but what if I'm wrong? And on the heels of that thought, *But what if I'm right? What if he's everything he seems to be? Is that better or worse?*

None of this was supposed to be real. Tyler hadn't signed up for that, or the inevitable disaster that would result. For that matter, neither had Josh. If he was a better person, Tyler would back out now and leave Josh alone, damn the personal and professional consequences. It was too bad that Tyler wasn't the tiniest bit noble. He didn't want to give up either Josh or their arrangement, and was in no way ready to do so, no matter how selfish that made him.

Tyler had enjoyed the hell out of Josh's attentions tonight. Rather more than he would have thought, and quite a bit more than he was happy admitting to himself. He wasn't sure how he would feel about a steady diet of adoration, but last night had been wonderful, and right now his body felt fantastic. His muscles were warm and liquid, his ass had a pleasant ache, and he was comfortably tired. Tyler felt well-used and, if he was being honest, well-loved. He liked that as well, likely too much.

Tyler had told Josh there was no such thing as too much. He might've been wrong about that. *I shouldn't get used to this. It's not real and it's not mine. He doesn't belong to me and he never will.*

Stop it, whispered the part of him that never, no matter what, gave in to despair or hysterics. *Stop borrowing trouble and just chill the fuck out. It was sex, great sex, fantastic sex, but just sex. Not a marriage proposal. Not forever. There is no need to freak the fuck out. But if you want him, take him. It's as simple as that.*

Simple, maybe, but not easy. Not by a long shot. It would be far easier, and safer, to keep pretending that what they were doing meant nothing. It was a fling. Just a way to pass the time before they went their separate ways. No claiming needed to occur. No feelings needed to be acknowledged. This was all temporary, and Tyler would be wise to keep that firmly in mind. Dreams of Josh in his future were just that: dreams and nothing more. Fantasies he should have long ago outgrown.

Tyler rubbed his cheek along the arm he was using as a pillow and breathed in the scent of Josh's skin. He decided to worry about it all later, when he was alone and could think without Josh's very distracting presence. He was likely overreacting. It was, after all, just sex.

"Has my 'everything' expired yet?" Josh whispered in his ear.

Tyler rolled over so that he faced Josh and his warm eyes, messy hair, and hopeful smile. Saying no to him would be like kicking a puppy. Hell, a whole basketful of puppies. How Ryan had ever managed it was a mystery beyond Tyler's comprehension.

"Depends. I'm a little sore," Tyler said. "The spirit might be willing, but I'm not sure anything else is."

Josh's hand dipped under the blankets, found Tyler's cock, and stroked it. "I don't know about that. I think something besides your spirit might be willing."

Tyler arched his back and thrust into Josh's fist. "Are you seriously telling me that you're up for more? Because my spirit and dick might be on board, but my ass is not." Josh let go of his cock, so Tyler pouted.

Josh laughed at him, the jerk. "Wimp."

"When I go on national television tomorrow night I do not want to wince when I sit down, thank you so very much. It's been a long time for me, you know. Give me some time to get back in the saddle, so to speak. Oh God, stop that, you horrible man." That last was said in response to Josh pushing him onto his back and pinning him down. Then Josh took one of his nipples into his mouth and sucked hard. "Never mind. Forget what I just said. Keep on doing that."

So of course Josh stopped, because he was indeed a horrible man. "Just how long has it been for you?" Josh asked, then he redeemed himself by applying his attention to Tyler's other nipple.

Tyler counted back. "It's hard to think when you do that. No, I didn't say stop. Uh, almost three years."

Josh reared back to look at him. "Are you serious? Brad made out like you were some sort of notorious man-whore and you didn't deny it."

Tyler huffed. "You know, not all sex ends in my ass getting pounded. Shocking concept, but there it is."

"Oh," Josh said, looking somewhat contrite. "Well. I had you pegged as a dedicated power bottom. I stand corrected and apologize for impugning your honor, your majesty."

Tyler shoved on Josh's shoulder, pushing him off and onto his back. He leaned over and frowned down at him. "And you pegged me as a power bottom why?" he asked, his voice silky but with a sharp edge underneath.

"Um..." Josh said, looking a bit concerned.

Tyler flopped back to lay on his side. "I'm just fucking with you," he said. "Yes, I'm a bit... assertive." Josh snorted at that. "Yes, I like to be fucked. But not exclusively. That's just dull."

"Oh?"

There was a wealth of prying curiosity in that one tiny word, and Tyler struggled to answer it without letting every secret he had pour out of his mouth. Until last week, Tyler had been happy enough making do with blow jobs and hand jobs from random hookups. He didn't want that brain of Josh's, even hampered as it currently was with an erection, to puzzle out why Tyler had so easily fallen onto Josh's dick after what amounted to a long drought. The answer was far too revealing.

"I haven't bottomed since I broke up with my evil ex, David," he ended up saying. "That was three years ago. After David, I ended up dating Ethan, who's the most bottomy bottom who ever bottomed. He wouldn't fuck me with a dildo, let alone his own dick, so that's probably why we didn't last. Well, that and we're too alike. Being with him was like having sex with my lazy and less-attractive twin. Don't get me wrong. Ethan is a great guy and one of my best friends. We just don't work as a couple. Too similar in some ways, too different in others. Now he's with this guy in his forties and I think Ethan calls him daddy, which, ew, but they're in lurve, so more power to them. And if you even *think* of trying to get me to call you daddy, I will cut you."

Josh laughed. "I wouldn't dream of it, princess."

Tyler glowered at Josh. A tiny part of him might not hate that awful endearment, but that didn't mean he had to acknowledge it. "Don't push it," he growled at Josh, who responded by smiling and kissing his nose, which only made Tyler scowl harder.

"Okay," Josh said, like a dog with a bone, "so you don't always bottom." He stroked up and down Tyler's back with one of those lovely hands of his. "Good to know."

"What about you, Dr. Rosen? Do you always top?"

"No," Josh traced abstract designs along Tyler's spine with his fingers. "Depends on who I'm with."

"Ha. Called it. Oh, man, don't stop doing that."

"Called what?" Josh, that lovely man, kept petting him as ordered. He really was perfect, damn him.

Tyler grinned up at him. "That you're vers. I had a feeling you were all things to all men, so to speak. It's so very *you*. Thank you, by the way, for taking one for the team. I couldn't have asked for a nicer man to break my ass back in."

Josh's fingers traced down to Tyler's ass, then squeezed it. "Yeah, like topping you is any kind of hardship. God, your ass is amazing."

"I'm glad you noticed."

Josh snorted. "Yeah, I noticed." He leaned in and nipped Tyler's bottom lip. "Although you are the most toppy bottom — or mostly bottom, I suppose — that I have ever been with, there is just something about you that makes me want to stick my dick into you. Repeatedly. I want to fuck you any and every way I can, so it's a good thing you're okay with that."

"Yes, that is convenient, isn't it?" Tyler said. He reached up and stroked Josh's hair.

Josh shrugged the shoulder he wasn't lying on. "Yeah. But…"

"But what?"

"I wouldn't mind if you…" Josh blushed and trailed off.

"You want me to top you?" Tyler pushed Josh onto his back and climbed on top of him, rubbing his ass along Josh's erection. "I did tell you I was flexible. Let me demonstrate. Bossy bottom? You seem to like that one a lot, but wait, there's more." Tyler arranged himself artistically on the bed, hands above his head and legs spread, a look of pure innocence plastered on his face. "Sweet submissive? No? Moving on, then." Tyler's expression slid into a knowing leer, then he moved again so he knelt between Josh's legs. He pushed them up and apart, spreading his ass cheeks. "Hold your legs like this," Tyler said in a tone that brooked no disobedience. He fingered Josh's hole, making him gasp then bite his lip. "Or demanding lover?" Tyler reached up for Josh's cock and jacked the hard length a few times before bringing it to his mouth. He licked along the length, tasting salt and warm skin and smelling Josh's sweat and musk. He traced his tongue along the vein running down it and lathed the head.

Josh let go of his legs to bury his fingers in Tyler's hair. He pushed Tyler's face down. "Suck me," he half-ordered and half-begged.

Tyler fought the pressure of Josh's hands long enough to pull up and say, "Obedient boy, coming right up," then sucked Josh's cock as told. When Josh tasted close, Tyler worked saliva-slicked fingers into him, found his prostate, and stoked upward until Josh came, his body jackknifing, Tyler's name on his lips. Tyler swallowed and slowly pulled his mouth from Josh's softening cock, causing him to squirm from overstimulation.

"God, Ty. That was…" Josh sounded shaky.

"What?"

Josh panted for breath. He put a hand over his heart. "Just… wow."

"So articulate," he murmured, but Josh's response caused a thrill to course through Tyler, making him feel both weak and powerful. He moved up Josh's body, leaving a trail of wet, bruised skin from the suction of his mouth. "I can fuck your mouth," he said, and did just that. Josh's hands grabbed his hips and controlled the movement, keeping Tyler from going too deep, but Tyler didn't care, mindless from the sensation of sweet, hot suction and Josh's incredible tongue. Looking down at Josh was intoxicating, watching this mostly proper and normally fastidious man suck his dick with a blissful expression on his face while saliva wet his cheeks and chin. In what seemed to him hardly any time at all Tyler came, gasping for breath, one hand grasping the headboard for dear life.

Yes, it was only sex, but nevertheless it was so damn good. Good enough to almost forget that it meant nothing at all.

Tyler pulled out of Josh's mouth and slid down his body. "I can fuck your ass until *you* wince when you have to sit." Tyler kissed the corner of Josh's mouth, liking the look of his wet, swollen lips. "I can be whatever you want."

Josh wiped his face on a corner of the sheet. He was quiet for several moments, then he finally said, "Just be yourself. Don't be or do what you think I want. Be what you want. Do what you want."

Tyler's heart stuttered in his chest. He wondered if Josh had any idea what a gift those words were. Probably not. He gave Tyler a serene smile and waited, patient as a saint, for him to speak.

Tyler took a moment to consider. He wanted to be free of the video, to have the scandal behind him in the form of old, boring news, to have a new and larger part in a movie that would be a hit. But he also wanted Josh, who was sweet and sexy and earnest and handsome, and was also hopelessly mired in a life so different from Tyler's that they might as well live on different planets.

Tyler wanted to have his cake and eat it, too. That was what came of being an intrinsically selfish person. However, there wasn't anything he could do now about any of his wants except for Josh, so he bent down and kissed him with all the sweetness he could muster, his tongue sliding with careful delicacy into Josh's eager mouth. He tasted his semen on Josh's tongue, and a wave of possessiveness swamped him. God, how he wanted this man. *Stop it. Just stop.* He rode out the wave of want and need and brought himself under control.

"I want to fuck you, and I will," he said, making his voice sound light and carefree, "but not tonight. It's late and I'm tired and nervous about the interviews, and what I want, since you asked so very nicely, is not to be alone."

Josh ran a hand through Tyler's sweat-dampened hair, brushing it away from his forehead. "I think I can manage that," he said, reaching past Tyler and turning off the light. Then he lay on his side and tucked Tyler in front of him. "Don't worry," Josh said into his ear. "You'll be great. I just know it." He was quiet for a while, then he added, "I've been meaning to tell you. I don't want the money. I'm not going to take it."

"I just fucked your face and you want to discuss finances? Your pillow talk sucks." Tyler didn't want to talk about the money. The promised salary was a combination barrier and safety net, reminding them both that what they were doing was in no way personal.

Even if maybe it was.

"Tyler, I'm serious." Josh tugged on him so that they faced each other again, even if it was difficult to see much in the darkened bedroom.

"So am I." Tyler more sensed than saw Josh's frown. He ran a finger over Josh's lips to try and reverse it. "You should take it. It's yours."

"No. I can't—won't—accept it. I never meant to. Even before we started... whatever this is that we're doing."

Tyler was afraid to think too hard about the implications of that. "But—"

Josh leaned forward and kissed him. "No. Shut up and let me say this. Firstly, I don't want the money in any way, shape, or form. And secondly, I was thinking about something Tom said."

"What? Or am I still not allowed to talk?"

Josh kissed him again, nipping at his lower lip. "Smartass. I wasn't paying attention to everything he said, but I did catch that he wants you to attach yourself to a charity."

Tyler made a face. He hated the idea of using charity for publicity. It seemed super sleazy to him. It wasn't that he didn't donate to several charities, he just preferred them being anonymous donations.

"You want me to donate the money to charity so I can be all 'look at me' about it? You donate it to charity if you feel so strongly about it."

"I was thinking that instead of donating to a charity, you could maybe start your own. What about a legal fund to work on getting places like Bridges banned or shut down, or something like that? It would be a better use of that money than handing it over to me. I don't need it."

Tyler thought of how he had tried, and failed, to get Bridges shut down. How Brad had tried, and failed, to help him. They had been too young, probably, and no match for their father, who had a vested interest in keeping what had happened there to his son quiet. It was one thing to pay a nice, stiff fee to ensure your troublesome son was discreetly tortured "for his own good." It was quite another to have that dirty laundry aired in public. Peter Chadwick had made sure they failed. Bridges stayed open and the torture kept on happening. But not to him. Not anymore.

Closing down Bridges and places like it would go a long way to assuaging his guilt that he'd managed to escape after having spent only twenty-two days there. Some of the boys had been there for months and months. Like Trev. Tyler shoved that thought away. No. He was not going to think about that tonight.

"Well, if you're determined to reject my generous compensation, I can't force you to take it," Tyler said. "The money wasn't my idea in the first place, you know. I just wasn't going to have Ryan pay you to be with me."

Josh winced. "No. I don't know what Rachel was thinking. That was beyond... it was..." He made a sound of disgust.

"Yeah," Tyler agreed. "Okay, I'll talk it over with Ryan and Tom. See what they think. Hell, I'll get Ryan to fork over matching funds. I think you're right. Fucking with places like Bridges would be money well spent."

"Good. Now try to get some sleep." Josh let Tyler turn and arrange himself into a comfortable position. When he'd settled, Josh's arm went around his waist and his lips brushed the back of his neck. He let out a hum of what Tyler could only think was contentment.

Tyler allowed himself to be held and thought, *I might be in serious trouble here.* But even that thought wasn't enough to pull him away from the warm, solid body at his back.

What I really want is to have my Josh and eat him, too, Tyler thought, *and that isn't possible.*

ଓଓ

Wednesday, September 21st, 5:46 a.m.
Josh's extremely tidy bedroom and very boring guest bathroom
Evanston, IL

Tyler woke sweating and shaking, his heart pounding like it wanted to escape his chest. Between the recurring nightmare he'd just experienced and the uncertainty of the future, he needed solace, release, and escape. He'd put it off as long as he could, but he'd reached a tipping point. He was going to break his promise.

He glanced at the red numbers of the alarm clock and saw it was 5:46 a.m. He eased away from Josh, snagged his underwear that had been discarded in the hallway, and crept to the guest bathroom. Instead of beautiful blue and gray tiny glass tiles, this bathroom was done in generic but inoffensive beiges and browns. Tyler turned on the shower, setting the temperature as hot as he could stand, then recovered his blade from its hiding spot.

It bothered him that there was only one. He'd grabbed two, he was nearly certain, but later he'd found only one in his pocket. He wondered if he'd lost one and if Josh had found it, but if he had, why hadn't he said anything? Tyler added this on top of his already heaping pile of potential disasters.

In the shower, Tyler let the water beat down on his head, and he contemplated his options. In the end, he chose a spot in between his groin and thigh. He made a careful cut, less than an inch long and no more than a quarter inch deep. He couldn't see the blood well up, but he could imagine how it looked — dark, thick maroon beads that became lighter and thinner as they mixed with the water from the shower. The blood from the cut ran down his leg and then hit the water pooling in the tub, making bright red swirling designs that slipped down the drain.

Watching it, his mind went blank, forgetting the nightmare and his nerves and his anxiety. His hand went to the cut and worried it a little, coaxing both more blood and stinging pain from it.

Stop. I should stop. I will. In just a second. Stop.

It wasn't until he started to feel the water cooling that he came to his senses. He turned off the shower, grabbed a wad of toilet paper and wedged it over the cut. He dried himself off and when he checked his makeshift bandage, there was only one tiny spot of blood on it. That was good.

He dried his hair, shaved, slathered on moisturizer, and thought about getting dressed, but after the blood and the shower he felt relaxed and sleepy. They didn't have to be at the airport for several hours, so Tyler put on his black boxer briefs (*all the better to hide blood, my dear*), carefully slid the cardboard sleeve back onto the blade and hid it with his things, then went back to the master bedroom and Josh.

The sun was just starting to rise, but the room was still shrouded in darkness. Tyler felt his way over to the bed and slipped under the covers. Josh's arms found him and folded around him, enveloping him in heat and comfort and the illusion of safety, as if nothing could ever touch him or hurt him in that space.

It was a dangerous fantasy, but Tyler allowed it to wash over him and pull him back down into, if not sleep, at least a comfortable doze.

He pretended that the drowsy word Josh whispered against his neck was just his imagination. "Mine."

Then he added that, too, to his growing pile of anxieties.

∽∗∽

Wednesday, September 21st, 1:50 p.m.
O'Hare Airport
Chicago, IL

Purvi: Talk to me. How was it? Dish the dirty details already.
Tyler: I don't want to talk about it.
Purvi: :(that bad?
Tyler: NO!
Tyler: Yes.

Tyler: No.
Tyler: Maybe.
Tyler: It's complicated.
Purvi: Since when did your life become a Facebook status?
Tyler: Screw you. This isn't funny.
Purvi: It's a little funny.
Purvi: Stop sulking.
Tyler: I had the dream again. And
Purvi: And what?
Purvi: Tyler?
Purvi: Dammit. Fuck you. Fuck you very much.
Tyler: Sorry. Had to go through security at the airport.
Tyler: Purvi?
Purvi: Sigh. I'm still here.
Tyler: P, I did it again. It's a really small one, though. Barely an inch long. But if Josh finds out he's going to be pissed. I promised him I wouldn't.
Purvi: You dumbass.
Tyler: I know, I know.
Purvi: Why, ffs?
Tyler: Shit, if I knew the answer to that, I wouldn't do it. Why do you eat chocolate even though you're supposed to be on a diet?
Purvi: Fuck you.
Tyler: I rest my case.

○৪○

Thursday, September 22nd, 11:00 a.m.
An expensive hotel suite
Manhattan, NY

"We're going to have to do something about your hair. It's a disaster. You look like a fairy fallen on hard times." Sydney, Tyler's stylist, made a disgusted face. She looked a bit fae herself, with her small stature, blond hair cut in a pixie style, and huge blue eyes. Tyler thought she resembled Tinkerbell minus the wings, but had enough of a sense of self-preservation to never say it out loud in her presence.

Josh laughed at her assessment because he was an asshole. "Skittles and Pixy Stix," he chimed in, then snickered. Tyler wanted to toss something at his dark, curly head.

"No one asked your opinion." Tyler turned back to Sydney. "What do you suggest?"

"I've got a friend who lives in the area and does hair. I'll give her a call and get her to come here."

"Good idea," said Tom.

It felt like a million years since they'd left Josh's condo. Yesterday had passed in a disorienting blur of airports, dodging paparazzi, taxi rides, and finally collapsing into bed in the suite at the hotel Purvi had booked them into. Even Josh had been too exhausted to do more than snuggle into him last night.

When I leave, I'm going to have to get that man a giant teddy bear, Tyler thought.

"*TMZ* has pictures of you on their website," Tom said, looking up from his laptop.

"Are they flattering?" Tyler asked.

Tom turned the laptop toward him. It was a photo of Tyler and Josh sitting in the first-class lounge in the airport, waiting for their plane. Tyler's head leaned on Josh's shoulder while Josh rested his cheek against the top of Tyler's head.

"There's a few more, mostly of the two of you walking through the airport. Here's what they have to say: '*Despite the recent scandal over a certain video leaked showing Tyler Chadwick in a compromising position, Dr. Joshua Rosen, a dermatologist in the Chicago area and longtime family friend, is staunch in his support of his boyfriend. Here the two are seen traveling together to New York. When asked about the video, Dr. Rosen said that it was ancient history and had no bearing on his relationship with Chadwick.*'"

"Well, that explains the plethora of emails I've been getting," Josh said. "How do these people even get my email address, anyway?"

"Have you answered any of them?" Tom asked, his sharp gaze lasering in on Josh.

Josh gave Tom a look like he thought the other man was crazy. "No. Why on earth would I?"

"Can you show me the emails? Some of them we might not want to ignore."

Josh looked a little sick. "We? Does this mean you're my publicist now, too?"

"You and Tyler are effectively a unit, at least for the foreseeable future. This is what you signed on for."

Josh opened his mouth, probably to say something along the lines that he hadn't signed anything, and if Tom realized that Josh wasn't on contract he'd probably have an aneurysm. It was interesting, now that Tyler thought about it, that Ryan hadn't insisted on there being a formal contract drawn up. What with the flurry of activity that had gone on, Tyler hadn't even considered the idea until now, and it seemed very out of character for Ryan to have ignored such a detail. Granted, Josh was Josh. Practically family, but it would be for the best not to let Tom know that Josh was helping Tyler merely out of the goodness of his heart.

"I did warn you that helping me would be a pain in the ass," Tyler told Josh. He leaned down and said near his ear, "But I'd like to think there are compensations."

On cue, Josh blushed. "The thing is, though, that I never talked to *TMZ*. I have no idea where that quote came from."

"Oh, about that," Tyler said. "Ethan, my ex, works for them. He texted me last night and I might have mentioned that we were flying to New York, and I might have mentioned Josh, and I might have given him a quote from Josh."

"Might?" Josh asked.

Tyler grinned at him, momentarily forgetting his nerves. "Ethan really is the best ex-boyfriend a guy could have."

"Should I be jealous?" Josh asked, not looking in the least threatened.

"Let me see. Should my fake boyfriend be jealous of the guy I broke up with almost two years ago and who is so happy with his fiancé that it's borderline gross? That would be a big fat no."

"Can you trust him?" Tom asked.

"Of course. He's the one who called me in the middle of the night to tell me about the video in the first place. Also, that blurb is all him. Totally his writing style."

"All right," said Tom. "Ryan has gotten a start on your foundation idea, Tyler. You need a name for it, though."

"That's easy. Call it The Chadwick Foundation. That'll piss my dad off, plus it sounds very official. Like the sort of thing that would sponsor programs on NPR."

Josh snorted, but Tom nodded. "Good. I'll contact your brother about it and make sure to start getting the word out about it."

"Tyler," Sydney said, "I want you to try on a few things for me that I brought so I can see what's going to work best with the blue hair. Does it have to stay blue? I can have Sam color it when she comes to cut it."

"The studio wants it to stay blue for now, at least until the interview with *Entertainment Weekly*, since they're planning on taking pictures," Tom said. "They want the visual reminder that he's portraying a well-loved character from an extremely popular series of books. The blue stays, at least for now, end of discussion."

Sydney sighed. "If we have to keep the blue, can I at least have Sam freshen up the color? The navy bits still look okay, but the lighter areas are going grayish-green and right now it's all very fairy crack whore."

"She can blue me up, I guess. You're right, my color is fading, but I'm sick and fucking tired of blue hair, so hands off my roots. I promised Brad that I'd cut the blue off for his wedding and I can't wait." Tyler turned toward Tom. "After tonight, if the studio wants me in blue hair for anything short of filming *The Golden Key*, they can eat a bag of dicks, okay? Or get me a wig. A wig would be acceptable."

Tom made a somewhat affronted face but didn't comment.

"Now that's settled," Sydney said, "let's see what I have that works with blue hair and doesn't make you look like a fairy junkie."

"Elfin prostitute," Josh corrected.

Tyler glared at him, but Josh had gone back to playing with his phone. "I hate you," Tyler said. "You are a terrible fake boyfriend."

Josh shook his head but kept his eyes on his phone.

Tyler flipped him off, not that Josh even noticed, then headed for the bedroom. When he opened the door, he looked back and Sydney was still in the suite's living room, staring at Josh. "Do you want me to try on clothes or what?"

"Right," Sydney said, and grabbed everything she'd brought with her. She pushed past Tyler and laid it all on the bed before pulling him into the room and shutting the door behind her.

"Okay," Tyler said. "What do you want me to try on first?"

Sydney smacked the back of his head.

"Ow! What the hell, Syd?"

"I might ask you the same thing, Tyler. What the hell do you think you're doing?"

Tyler eyed her. "In what way? That is way too unspecific a question for me to answer."

Sydney tapped her foot. "That man out there. The one who is crazy about you in a way so painfully obvious as to be embarrassing. The one who is apparently a fucking doctor from fucking Illinois and is a fucking friend of your fucking family. And if you aren't fucking him, I will eat every stitch of clothing I brought."

"And your point is?" Tyler felt like tapping his own foot back at her. "Last time I checked, I hired you to make sure I looked good, not to be my moral compass."

"Look, when Purvi told me that you'd found some sort of boyfriend for hire, I was pretty dubious, but I figured it was harmless enough, and I could see the logic behind it. But Ty, my dearest darling idiot, that man is not faking anything."

"All he's done all day is give me shit," Tyler said. "You heard him. He just said I looked like an elfin prostitute."

She rolled her eyes. "He's been flirting with you and you've been flirting right back. But really, even if he'd never opened his mouth, the way he looks at you is enough. He's been eye-fucking you all morning. So, what's the plan? String him along and then break his heart?"

Tyler shrugged. "I'm supposed to be joined at the hip with him until my career either stabilizes or tanks, so who knows how long that will take. And I swear I had zero intentions of having Josh fall for me or whatever. He knew from the outset what this was. I needed him to be less jumpy around me, and then we figured sex was fine as long as it was no strings attached fuck buddy shit. But it turns out he can't sleep without pretending I'm his stuffed animal and he's got this astounding body and I actually like talking with him and I'm pretty sure I'm just a rebound fling anyway, so you could make a case that fucking me is almost therapy for him."

Sydney gave him a skeptical look. "It's worse than I thought. You like him, don't you?"

Tyler sat on the bed with a huff. "Maybe."

"Uh huh."

Tyler folded his arms across his chest. "Okay, yes, I like him. He's impossible not to like. He's just so…"

"Hmm? He's a looker, that's for sure."

"He's… nice, and a good person. Even when I piss him off, he just closes his eyes, takes a deep breath, and is all reasonable at me."

"That monster!" Sydney exclaimed. "How dare he?"

"Shut up. I know it's only a matter of time before he snaps. That, and he's devious. He talked me into getting naked for him. In the light."

Sydney blinked. "No way. I *dress* you and I've never seen you naked. It's one of your things. I know what you're trying to hide and couldn't care less about your junk, and you still make me turn my back when you take your clothes off. And you let that man out there, your supposedly fake boyfriend, see you naked. Were you replaced by a pod person?"

"I've known Josh for over twenty years. There was also a precedent for seeing me naked. Apparently, I used to run around with no pants when I was six."

Sydney looked appalled. "That's disgusting."

Tyler couldn't help but smile. "I'm guessing you don't have any younger brothers."

"No, thank God. And all that aside, I still can't get over that you let him see you naked. Willingly. As an adult. I'm not sure whether to be proud or disturbed."

"Feel free to experience both. God knows I am. You wanna know what he said afterward?"

"Did he say 'ow' because you'd just disemboweled him?"

Tyler let out a pained laugh. "Oh, no. It's way worse. I let him look his fill at all my… you know… and first he said that he was sorry, and then later he said I was beautiful. How am I supposed to cope with that shit?"

"Oh, hon." Sydney ruffled his fairy crack whore hair. "You do realize that this is a doomed relationship, right?"

Tyler flopped backward, lying on top of his clothes. "It's not a relationship. It's all fake. Josh agreed to pretend to be my devoted boyfriend who is noble and steadfast enough to overlook the public embarrassment of having a sex tape from my adolescence be seen worldwide. Any feelings on his part are totally incidental and not my fault."

Sydney sat down on the side of the bed and patted Tyler's leg. "What about your feelings?"

Tyler waved a hand in the air. "Immaterial," he said.

"You're doomed," she repeated.

"I know, trust me. When all this blows up in my face, you and my mom can throw an 'I told you so' pity party while I drown my sorrows in Chunky Monkey ice cream. I'm going to get so fat."

"Don't eat so much that your ass won't fit into those new Valentino trousers we just got."

Tyler made a face at her and Sydney gave his shoulder a squeeze. "Okay, now that we've established that you're an emotional dumbass bent on a collision course with heartbreak, let me show you your present from Purvi."

It was a t-shirt and it was perfect. "I want to wear this tonight," he said.

Sydney looked dubious. "Are you sure?"

"Oh, yeah. Dress it up however you like. I am your willing Ken doll, but I am wearing that shirt. Purvi deserves a raise."

Sydney sniffed. "You wish you were Ken. You're more like Skipper." She started pawing through the clothes on the bed, selecting a few items and tossing others aside. "Let's try and make you not look like an elfin prostitute. I think I can manage that much, at least."

When Tyler and Sydney left the bedroom, they found Tom and Josh looking furious and grim, respectively.

"Um... I think I'm going back to my room, okay? I'll come back when Sam gets here to cut your hair." Sydney beat a strategic retreat.

"What happened?" Tyler asked. "What the fuck now?"

Tom flipped his laptop around and there was a picture of Tyler's stitches. "Someone in the airport snapped this. Care to elaborate how this happened? I don't appreciate being blindsided."

"It was an accident," Tyler said. "I..."

Tom started reading. "'*Tyler Chadwick has been seen with a serious wound that we can't help but speculate on. No word from his camp on where it came from, and it's in an interesting location, especially when one notes the scars on his wrists, according to one source. Is Tyler feeling the pressure from a certain sex tape that surfaced recently? Our source hints at something else, that Tyler has a history of cutting himself, to the point where he has had to get stitches more than once. As our source pointed out, it's convenient for Tyler that his brother is a surgeon. For right now, all we can do is speculate on the origin of Tyler's wound.'"*

"Fuck," Tyler said.

"Yeah, that about covers it." Tom closed the laptop. "Now we just have to figure out how to spin this. I wish you'd said something earlier. Instead of days to think up a strategy, I've got hours."

"Is this going to be a big problem?" Josh asked.

"It's not ideal, that's for sure. I'm going to need some time to think. Tyler, are there any more skeletons in your closet I should know about?"

Tyler thought about being told a million times to shut his mouth and say nothing. It hadn't helped in the end, though. If the past few weeks had taught him anything, it was that secrets wouldn't stay buried forever. Might as well come clean. "I got caught giving my high school guidance counselor oral sex when I was sixteen and then I tried to commit suicide." He held up his wrists. "Poorly. That's it, I swear."

Tom massaged his temples. "'That's it', he says," he muttered. "What about this allegation that you cut yourself? Is there anything to that?"

Tyler froze, then nodded stiffly. There was no point in continuing to deny it.

"Okay, fine. Actually, no, it's not fine. Not even a little. I'm going to my room to figure this out. I'll have something for you before the EW interview." Tom left, closing the door behind him carefully, which was somehow worse than if he'd slammed it.

Tyler felt Josh take his hand and squeeze it. He squeezed back.

"Are you okay?" Josh asked.

"No. 'I am pretty fuckin' far from okay.'"

"That's *Pulp Fiction*, right?"

"Got it in one. 'Check out the big brain on Brad.'"

"Come here, Tyler."

Josh tugged on his hand and dragged him into his lap, drawing Tyler's head to his chest and resting his chin on the crown of Tyler's head. Tyler both hated it and loved it. He hated, in fact, how much he loved it, so he snuggled into Josh and frowned while he did it, up until the girl Sydney had called came to cut his hair.

"It'll be okay, I promise," Josh whispered into his ear before he let Tyler stand up.

Tyler didn't respond but he tried, very hard, to believe him.

Chapter 23
Purvi Watches Late Night TV

Thursday, September 22nd, 12:47 a.m.
The TV room in Tyler's very nice house
Burbank, CA

Purvi sat on Tyler's couch with her latest project, as Tyler liked to call him, curled up with his head on her lap.

Purvi's superpower, according to her employer, was the ability to find pretty boys and convince them, after weeks to months of dating her, that they were gay. Occasionally bi, but usually gay.

It was how Purvi and Tyler had met. She was dancing with friends at a club and there'd he'd been, all shiny and irresistible. She hadn't been able to stop herself from trying to get him to leave with her. He, in turn, had started laughing so hard that he'd begun throwing up, pausing in between retching to say, "You can't be serious," then "Maybe if you had a dick," then "Maybe not even then," then "There is not enough tequila in this world," and lastly "I shouldn't have had that last drink."

Purvi had dragged him to the ladies' room, cleaned him up, and gotten him home without once trying to molest him. They'd soon become thick as thieves, and eventually he'd hired her to be his PA. Since she'd been running his life prior to that, it made sense to put her on the payroll. Together they'd gone through hundreds of auditions, dozens of bad dates, several boyfriends, as many breakups, gallons of ice cream, and countless text messages.

Her latest project, or Kevin, as he preferred to be called, was proving to be remarkably resistant to homosexuality. They'd been together over six months, and so far, he appeared to be some sort of miracle: adorable, smart, employed, and virtually no interest in any dick except his own. Purvi would worry that she was losing her touch if she wasn't so happy.

Kevin, a teacher who had to be up early the next day, had fallen asleep on her at some point earlier in the evening. Purvi shook him awake when it was time for Tyler to be interviewed.

He yawned and sat up with his head on her shoulder.

"He does look like a hipster elf," Purvi said. "All he needs is a pair of fake glasses and a beard."

"That's not a bad style on him. I like the buzzed sides with the length on top. I could do that with my hair. I could even grow a beard. What do you think?"

Right now, Kevin's dark blonde hair was long and held back with one of Purvi's ponytail holders. He had fine, somewhat sharp features, green eyes with a gold ring around the iris, and a dimple in each cheek when he smiled, which was often. Every time Purvi looked at him her heart stopped. Granted, he wasn't as pretty as Tyler, but then, who was?

"I like it long," she said, tugging on it.

Seth started by asking Tyler about *The Silver Arrow*. Boring. "Come on," she said to the TV. "Get to the good stuff."

"Nice," Kevin commented.

"Eh. If I wasn't at least a little horrible, Ty and I wouldn't be friends."

"Did you watch the video?"

"Hells yeah," Purvi said. "How could I not?" She prodded him. "How about you?"

"Of course I watched it."

"And?"

Kevin shrugged. "I don't see the point of a threesome without at least one girl. I mean, Tyler's pretty and all, but he's still a dude."

"I love you," Purvi said. "Now, shush. They're going to talk about the video."

On the TV, Tyler explained how he'd been on vacation with his boyfriend when the video had leaked, like the champion liar that he was.

Seth gave Tyler a half-grin. "I'm sure that was a fun conversation. How did he take the news?"

"He's been great through this whole thing. I couldn't ask for a better boyfriend. He's totally been my rock."

"What's it like becoming notorious overnight? It must be hard, but you seem to be handling it surprisingly well. How are you coping?"

Tyler flashed Seth and the audience his killer, panty-wetting smile. "Not losing my sense of humor has helped. Something I said online the other day kind of went viral. Check out what my best friend had made for me."

Tyler stood up, his back to the audience, and unbuttoned his blazer. Seth cracked up over what he was wearing underneath. "Can I show the people at home?" Tyler asked, his voice all flirtatious purr.

Still laughing, Seth waved his hand in a "be my guest" gesture. The shirt, which was tight enough to be indecent, said "Threesomes Are Overrated" in a looping, cursive script.

"Oh my God, Kevin. I can't believe that marvelous bastard wore my t-shirt on national television."

"I think it's kind of brilliant," Kevin said. "It's like a big fuck you to everyone giving him crap about this."

"That shirt is great. I think I want one," Seth said.

"That can probably be arranged. I could've used something like this right after it happened." He laughed. "Not that they would have let me wear it in school, though."

"Yeah, this initially happened when you were in high school, right? Did it get out then? Were you bullied at all as a consequence?"

"Right after it happened my dad put me into a gay conversion therapy program for a few weeks. It was… awful. But by the time I got back to school the video was old news. I got crap from the same people who'd been giving me crap before it happened. It was worse for the other guys, though. Everyone in school already knew I was gay. No one knew about the football players. They had a much harder time than I did."

Tyler paused, bit his lip, and projected what Purvi thought of his "earnest and adorable" look. It was like Anderson Cooper and Mr. Rogers had the world's cutest blue-haired baby.

"Those guys are grown up and have lives that are being ruined because someone decided it would be fun to dig up ancient history and post it illegally online. People online have been hounding those guys. I just want to say that I'm sorry, and it makes me angry. This was obviously done to hurt me, and I can take it, but those guys don't deserve any of this."

"You seem to have a good attitude about the situation."

"I'll be honest, Seth, it's been hell. A lot of stress. I… had a rough adolescence. The whole poor little rich boy cliché with a disapproving father thrown on top. He was not happy about me being gay."

Seth put on his serious face. "So, you didn't get much support at home?"

Tyler looked pained. "My mother did what she could, and my brothers have always accepted me, but my father was the opposite of supportive. I felt very powerless as a teen, especially when I was put in conversion therapy. I tried to commit suicide at sixteen. I cut myself, quite a lot, as a way of dealing with stress. I got help, but it's a struggle. It'll always be a struggle." Tyler looked into the camera, brave face in place. "Because of what happened to me as a teenager, I'll always have scars."

"Holy shit," Purvi said. "Dude went there."

"Shh," said Kevin.

"Is that why you model for Hermes and not Calvin Klein?" Seth asked with a smirk.

Tyler smirked back. "I'm never going to model underwear. I'm not that kind of exhibitionist. That's why suits. Just not of the birthday variety."

Seth laughed. "So, no nudity in future films? You know how popular showing your… um… assets is these days."

Tyler pursed his lips. "I might consider it for the right role, but it's not something I feel comfortable with. I can act, and I would like to think I can do that without flashing my... assets." He gave Seth a roguish look. "Besides, my face is up here." With that, Tyler smiled and looked breathtaking.

"Wow," Kevin said. "He is good at that."

"I know," agreed Purvi. "It's kinda much if you aren't used to it."

On the TV Seth laughed. "Good point. So, Tyler, tell me about this foundation you've started. I understand it's related to what you had to go through as a teen."

Purvi perked up. "What? No one told me we were starting a foundation. Great. Like I need more work."

"...will work on helping teens who've been put in conversion therapy and getting legislation passed to eliminate it in the US. Currently it's only banned for minors in ten states, including my home state of Illinois and California, where I live now. I'd like to see it illegal nationwide."

"Definitely a worthy cause." Seth reached out and shook Tyler's hand. "Thank you so much for coming on. It was great talking with you, Tyler. I can't wait to see you in *The Silver Arrow*."

"Christmas will be here before you know it. I think they've already got stuff out in Costco."

Seth laughed. "That's true..."

They went on for a bit longer, generally bitching about Christmas taking over the entire calendar, then there was a commercial break.

Purvi looked down at Kevin. "I think that went well," she said.

Kevin gave her a sleepy smile. "Yep. Can we go to bed now?"

"Sure thing."

Right as they were about to go to the room Purvi slept in when she stayed over, the home phone rang. "Dammit. I need to get that. Go. I'll be up as soon as I deal with whoever this is."

She picked up the phone. "Hello?"

She heard breathing on the other end of the line, but no one spoke.

"Hello? Look, if this is a crank call, your technique could use work. This is pretty—"

The caller disconnected.

"—boring." Purvi hung up the phone. That was the third call like that she'd gotten this week. People were such assholes.

As she walked up to the guest room, she started texting Tyler.

Purvi: You do look like a hipster elf. The interview went well, I thought.
Purvi: About this foundation. How is this the first I'm hearing of it? You're going to expect me to do everything, aren't you?
Purvi: I better get a raise or I'm going on strike.

Purvi: Oh, and I think it's time to get the home number changed again.
Purvi: You were great tonight. Really. Give me a call later.

Chapter 24
Josh Wants to Know; Tyler Wants to Forget

Friday, September 23rd, 11:00 p.m.
An expensive hotel suite
Manhattan, NY

Tyler came out of the taping of the interview with Seth Meyers higher than a kite on adrenaline. From there they had gone to dinner at a Japanese restaurant, where Tyler had eaten his body weight in nigri, then to a nearby bar, where he'd consumed a similar volume of extra dirty vodka martinis. He was all over Josh in the taxi on the way back to the hotel, retracting his tentacles only long enough to pay the driver when they arrived.

"I'm sorry," Josh murmured to him as he and Tyler got out of the car.

The driver shrugged and looked unimpressed. "No mess to clean up, then I don't care what goes on back there. I seen it all, believe me. That was nothing. The stories I could tell..."

"I will give you twenty dollars not to," Tyler said, and that seemed to satisfy them both.

Josh and Tyler ended up sharing one of the hotel's elevators with an exhausted-looking couple with two small children and a mountain of luggage. Josh was relieved that Tyler limited himself to a death grip on Josh's hand and several significant glances.

Back in the room, Tom and Sydney waited for them with iced champagne. Tom made a toast to a successful day and then discussed the interview with Tyler in what Josh thought was exhaustive and excruciating detail. After what seemed like an eternity, Tom and Sydney finally returned to their own respective rooms, and they were at last alone.

"I think you're drunk," Josh told Tyler.

Tyler gave him a loopy smile and batted his eyelashes. "Merely tipsy, my dear. 'Take me to bed or lose me forever.'" He slipped out of his jacket and tossed it onto the sofa, leaving him in the "Threesomes Are Overrated" t-shirt and his slacks.

"Did you just quote *Top Gun* at me? You weren't even born when that movie came out."

"After I was cast in the remake of *Pretty in Pink*, I went on a glut of watching eighties movies, including *Top Gun*, which might be the most unintentionally gay movie I've ever seen, with the possible exception of *Fight Club*. And *Fight Club* might have been intentionally gay. I haven't made up my mind."

"Was this what you were studying at UCLA?"

Tyler frowned at him. "Yes, among other things."

Josh decided to sidestep the "wanna make something of it?" look on Tyler's face. "So. *Top Gun*, you were saying?"

Tyler narrowed his eyes at Josh, then dropped his scowl. "Yeah. *Top Gun* is still my blue-ribbon winner for gayness. The sexual tension between Val Kilmer and Tom Cruise in that movie is a fine, fine thing." He smiled, pique apparently forgotten or at least shelved.

"'Show me the way home, honey,'" Josh said in an effort to retain that smile.

"Oh, that is unfair, quoting back at me like that." Tyler toed out of his shoes and socks.

"I watched that movie enough times as a kid that I wore out the tape."

"Who did you want?" Tyler asked. "Maverick or Iceman?"

"Definitely Iceman." Josh had jacked off to more fantasies of sex with a sort of Val Kilmer/Ryan hybrid than he cared to admit.

"A man after my own heart," Tyler said. "Although I'd be okay with Maverick, too. Now that I think about it, I could go for a Maverick/Iceman sandwich. You know, to get the taste of that last one out of my mouth." His smile was wolfish. "So to speak." He grabbed Josh by his tie and tugged him in the direction of the bedroom. "But only if we're talking late eighties Val Kilmer. Otherwise, no deal."

Josh felt his lips twist in a rueful smile. "I'm not really an Iceman or a Maverick type. Sorry."

"Stop fishing. It's unattractive and unnecessary for someone who looks like you do. You know, Purvi thinks you look like Hugh Jackman fucked Adrian Brody and got a nearsighted baby."

"Your friend is strange."

"That she is. Personally, I think you're closer to *Independence Day* Jeff Goldblum. Less dorky, though. Like this much." Tyler held his thumb and index finger about an inch apart. "And better looking. Maybe Purvi's right about her Jackman/Brody theory. I can kind of see it." Tyler peered up at him, considering.

"I'm not sure how to feel about that." Josh pushed Tyler against the bedroom door and fumbled for the doorknob while he kissed Tyler's neck.

Tyler rubbed himself against Josh. "Flattered. You'll still be super hot in twenty years. Hell, probably indefinitely. Jeff Goldblum is a total gilf. I would absolutely fuck him now and he's practically paleolithic. As for Val Kilmer, have you seen him recently? There's a reason for that. Iceman has

Damage Control

not aged well. Tom Cruise, on the other hand, has made some sort of deal with the devil. He probably bathes in the blood of virgins."

Josh had a feeling Tyler would be the same, barely aging, looking like thirty when he was fifty. Josh would hate him if he wasn't so crazy about him.

I shouldn't be standing so close to the edge of this cliff. I should probably back up. Carefully, so I don't trip on something and fall anyway.

Josh pushed the thought away. He wouldn't be jumping off any cliffs tonight. "I want you."

"Mm hm," Tyler agreed. "Yes, please."

"So polite. Who are you, and what have you done with Tyler?"

"Bite me," Tyler said, his voice affectionate. "You're going to miss my fine yet surly ass one of these days."

The thought of life after Tyler presented itself and Josh shrank away from the thought. *No, not yet, not for a long time.* He needed more time to glut himself sick on Tyler's body, to tire of his sly humor and lovely face, and to start craving his freedom and peace and solitude. One day he'd be ready for Tyler to leave.

Just not today.

"Not a chance," he said.

"Talk to me, Dr. Rosen," Tyler demanded. He pulled his t-shirt off and tossed it aside, then unbuckled his belt and started to remove his slacks. Tyler slipped his hand under the elastic of his boxer briefs and palmed his erection. "I want to hear everything you plan to do to me." He pushed his underwear down far enough to expose his cock and he stroked it.

"I'm going to take you apart, piece by piece, then put you back together."

Tyler's eyes opened wide and his hand stilled. "Oh," was all his talkative elf could manage as a response. Josh couldn't help but feel a little smug that he'd managed to surprise Tyler into at least brief silence. It didn't last long, however. "That's the cliché you're going with? Really?"

Josh ignored that and drew closer to Tyler. He tugged on his boxer briefs. "Off," he said, and watched while Tyler slid them down his legs.

"Are you going to stay dressed or what?" Tyler asked as he hopped onto the hotel bed and got comfortable. "While you take me apart and put me back together." He said that last with an exaggerated roll of his eyes.

Josh rushed through taking his clothes off, nearly falling in his haste as he tried to remove his pants before taking off his shoes. Tyler laughed so hard he snorted.

Naked at last, Josh climbed first onto the bed, then onto Tyler, who at last stopped laughing and went back to stroking himself. Josh recalled what Tyler had said the other night, that he hadn't had anything but sex toys in his ass for almost three years. Josh imagined him, alone and naked, fucking himself with a dildo. He wanted to see that, to watch Tyler pleasure himself, abandoned and stripped down to raw need and desire, but not tonight. His need to touch Tyler hadn't been slaked quite yet.

"Done laughing at me?"

Tyler stopped touching himself and ran his hands over Josh's stomach, tugging lightly on the hair there. "For now."

"Do you want to know what I'm really going to do to you?"

Tyler's fingers stilled for an instant, then trailed lower. "Oh, yeah. Lay it on me."

"I'm going to possess you, Tyler. I'm going to kiss you and lick you and bite you anywhere and everywhere I want. I'm going suck your dick until you come in my mouth, then I'm going to let you taste yourself on my tongue. I'm going to fuck you, first with my fingers and then with my cock. I'm going to make you scream. And you are going to lie there and let me do it all. Do you understand?"

Tyler's breathing went shallow and rapid, his skin flushed a delicate pink, and the head of his cock leaked precum. His eyes sparkled like jewels. He was a filthy elven whore. He was a perfect fairy prince. He was a flawed man in a scarred body. He was a work of exquisite art. Josh felt his heart lurch in his chest and it was like he was flying, or maybe falling. It was hard to tell the difference.

"Fuck, yeah," Tyler said. He ate Josh alive with ravenous eyes.

It took what seemed like mere minutes and at the same time several hours to reduce Tyler to a desperate jumble of sensitized nerves, trembling muscle, and heated blood poised on his hands and knees, that gorgeous ass on display as he waited to be filled. Tyler was temptation incarnate.

When Josh slid on a condom and pushed inside Tyler's body, he swore he could feel Tyler's sigh of aching relief. "Yes," Tyler hissed as he flattened his back and met Josh's initial, shallow thrust. "Fuck. So good."

It was. Tyler was perfect. So lovely, so hot, so needy, and so damned tight around his cock that Josh wasn't sure he'd ever get enough.

"Harder. Come on, fuck me!"

Yes, your highness, Josh thought, then allowed his body to take over and let his mind drift on a tide of lust and pleasure and satisfied desire.

He didn't ever want it to end.

෴

Friday, September 23rd, 3:35 a.m.
The bedroom of an expensive hotel suite
Manhattan, NY

Josh lay in bed alone, his thoughts on the man who should've been sleeping beside him but wasn't. Over the past week they'd slept together every night, and more often than not, Tyler had startled awake from a panicked dream. He'd allow Josh to hold him, but he always got up afterward and went to the bathroom. In and of itself that shouldn't have been concerning, but Josh had seen a new wound on Tyler's leg tonight, and he couldn't help but wonder if he was adding a matching one to the other leg while he hid from Josh in the bathroom.

Josh wrestled with his conscience while he waited for Tyler to return, going back and forth over if he should say something. He did have the right, he didn't have the right. It was his business, it wasn't his business. Round and round it went in his head, going nowhere, and it all boiled down to one question he both wanted and didn't want to ask.

What made that wound in you, Tyler, that you're trying to fill with sex and blood? It scares me and I don't know how to help you, and I can't stand not trying.

The door to the room opened and Josh shut his eyes. He felt Tyler get into bed, and at first, he thought he'd leave it alone for a little while longer. Maybe Tyler would tell him without prompting if left to his own devices, and maybe Josh should leave well enough alone.

Josh felt acid trying to crawl out of his stomach and into his throat and realized he couldn't live that way. Not again. Tyler could tell him to fuck off, and likely would, but Josh couldn't pretend that something wasn't wrong when he knew it was. He needed to say something, if only to get the weight of it off his chest.

"Tyler, tell me about this nightmare you keep having."

While cocooning himself in the hotel's duvet, Tyler stiffened. "I thought you were still asleep. I didn't mean to wake you up."

"Tell me what keeps waking you up every night," Josh persisted.

"Not every night," was Tyler's sulky reply.

"Most of them. Is that normal for you?"

"It's... it's nothing."

"Liar."

Tyler flipped around so he could glare at Josh, although the effect was mitigated by the darkness in the room—Josh could just make out the glitter of his eyes. "I don't need to talk about it. Talking about it does nothing. It doesn't help. Go back to sleep. If it's an issue, I'll go sleep in the living room."

That should've been Josh's cue to back down and leave Tyler alone, but instead Tyler's dismissive tone pissed him off. Josh rolled them so he was on top of Tyler, pinning him down. "No. Hiding is my thing, not yours. You going to start cleaning, too?"

"Get off me," Tyler hissed.

"I guess I'll have to take up using sex to avoid my problems, then, since you still have a lock on cutting, don't you?"

Tyler's body went rigid like stone. Like the marble statue of Perseus he reminded Josh of, the one he wanted to look at again at the Met to see if it was as beautiful as he remembered, like the man he had lying underneath him.

"Tyler, did you honestly think I wouldn't notice a new cut? Don't get me wrong. You did a very nice job there. It's quite small. Very neat. Very precise."

Tyler squirmed, although Josh didn't think it was with embarrassment. Even in the dark, Josh could see his anger. "Let. Me. Go."

"Are you going to run?" Josh asked. "Avoid me and my inconvenient concern for you?"

"Get off me. Now. You don't... you need to... move, dammit! Get the fuck..." In the middle of speaking Tyler started struggling in earnest, and his voice gained a frantic edge. Josh realized with a sick sense of horror that Tyler was on the verge of a panic attack. He rolled off him and to the side, leaving Tyler lying on his back, chest heaving, to say the last two words in a weak mutter. "...off me."

Josh started rooting on the floor for his underwear, found them, and put them on.

"What the hell are you doing now?" Tyler asked, his voice gone back to peevish.

"I'm leaving you alone. I shouldn't have trapped you like that. I'll go out to the couch." Guilt stabbed through Josh. It was easy to forget how much smaller Tyler was sometimes. *I'm inches taller than him and I outweigh him by at least forty pounds. What the fuck was I thinking?*

Tyler groaned. "This is blackmail, you know that, right?"

"How the fuck do you figure that, Tyler?" Josh asked, annoyance creeping past and overtaking contrition.

"Simple. You want me to open up. To share my *feelings,*" he sneered the word, "with you for some fucked-up reason. Then you act like an asshole about it, and when I have the gall to get pissed off after you try to intimidate me, you decide to go pout and sulk in another room, making me the bad guy. Nice job. Bravo. You win, I lose." Tyler's voice dripped with disdain.

"This has fuck-all to do with winning or losing, Tyler. It isn't a contest." Josh dug a hand through his hair. "Look, I'm sorry already! Do you want me on my knees? I hear that smooths over a lot of arguments."

"Screw you," Tyler said. "I don't need this."

"Really? Because you just told Seth Meyers and whoever might have been watching you on national television that I'm a fabulous boyfriend. It'll look great when we're broken up before we can even get back to Chicago."

Tyler crossed his arms over his chest. "We're back to blackmail, then. What do you want this time, Dr. Rosen? Clearly not money. You're already getting sex from me on pretty much a daily basis. What else is there?"

"This isn't tit for tat," Josh snapped. "Not everything or everyone is so transactional."

Tyler's tone was pure ice. "Says the man holding me over a barrel."

"Tyler, please."

"Please, what?" Tyler sounded exhausted and Josh almost let it go, but he just couldn't.

Josh should probably back up and allow Tyler his secrets and protective layers, but it wasn't enough for him that Tyler gave his body to him freely and without apparent thought. Josh found that he wanted more. Of course, he wanted more. What good was knowing every inch of Tyler's physical form while being shut off from everything else? Josh wanted it all, even the scars.

"Tell me about the nightmare, Tyler."

"This is not a good idea," he said. "That is a can of worms you do not want to open."

"Just tell me. The things I can imagine couldn't be any worse than reality." Josh settled himself so he was on the other side of the bed, as far away from Tyler as he could get without falling onto the floor.

Tyler brought up his knees and hugged them. "You want to fix me."

Josh wanted to deny it. "Yeah," he said instead. "I kinda do."

"You can't."

Josh swallowed. "I know. I can't say if talking to me about it will help you or not. I hope it does. But it'll help *me*."

"I hate you," Tyler said softly.

"That's okay."

"I can't... oh, fuck it." Tyler snapped on the bedside lamp. "I can't do this in the dark. And come here."

"Uh, are you sure?" Josh didn't think he could stand seeing Tyler in a panic again because of his proximity.

Tyler sat up and spread both his arms and legs wide. "If I have to do this, I'll do it my way: my back to a wall and you in front of me."

Josh moved so he lay in Tyler's lap, the back of his head on Tyler's shoulder, Tyler's bent legs cradling his torso, and Tyler's feet tucked under his thighs.

It seemed strange that Tyler wanted to hold him like this, and it wasn't until later that it occurred to him that rather than cradling him, Tyler had positioned Josh like he was a shield.

November, nine years ago
Bridges to Salvation
Springtown, WI

Tyler lay in bed, shivering, and hoped he wouldn't be one of the unlucky ones to be singled out that night. You never knew. They liked to keep you guessing. You would lie there, hearing the muffled sounds the chosen ones made, and hope that your door would be the one that got passed by that night.

He'd been counting the days as they passed, keeping track. His father had paid for three weeks of what this place had the gall to consider treatment. There were eighteen marks in Tyler's notebook. He'd be able to go home soon. He just needed to hold on a little longer.

The sounds began to taper off, only the low, constant of Trev's crying remained, and Tyler was so used to the sound that it might as well have been white noise. He started to breathe easier. It was going to be okay. One more night endured, and tomorrow would be one more day to get through.

Then the handle to his door turned and he knew the night wasn't over yet.

Friday, September 23rd, 4:04 a.m.
The bedroom of a very nice hotel suite
Manhattan, NY

"You were raped?" Josh asked, feeling sick and yet unsurprised.

"Yeah." Tyler's voice was quiet but steady. "Four times while I was there. There didn't seem to be a rhyme or reason to it. Some of the boys were never touched as far as I know. There was one kid they… visited… every damn night. Christ if I know why. I've wondered about it for years. There were rules. So many rules, and just as many punishments. Each one was a tool they used to modify our behavior. That was the line they fed us from day one. But the night visits were something else. Extracurricular, if you know what I mean."

"Not sanctioned by the staff?"

Tyler let out a mirthless laugh. "Depends on the staff. Certainly, the ones who came at night sanctioned it. As for the rest, I don't know if they knew and turned a blind eye or what. Only that I never knew why they came or didn't come. They were a law unto themselves, and they knew none of us would complain. Who would we complain to?"

Part of Josh wanted to apologize for making Tyler tell him any of this, but he decided that if Tyler was willing to talk, the more chivalrous side of himself could go fuck off for a bit. "And that burn on your leg?"

Tyler ran his fingers idly through the hair on Josh's chest, the touch seeming to provide him with some measure of comfort. "Of course you want to know about the burn."

"Professional curiosity," Josh replied.

"Professional curiosity, my ass. You're just a nosy fucker." Tyler let out a gusty sigh. "Also manipulative. You think you can manage me."

"I don't want to manage you," Josh said. "I want to know you. The real you. Not one of the roles you play: shameless flirt, bitchy diva, charming actor, arrogant smartass, etc. That's just window dressing."

"You don't want much, do you?" Tyler let out a low, unhappy laugh, but his hand didn't stop stroking Josh's chest. Josh wasn't even sure if Tyler was aware he was doing it.

"How did you get the burn?" Josh persisted, keeping his tone calm and even.

Tyler sighed. "You aren't going to give up, are you?"

"No."

"Fine. If you must know, each time they came into my room I fought them. I knew it would've been easier if I didn't, but I had to, you know, even knowing it wouldn't do any good. That fifth time they tried to… I kicked out, blindly, and got one in the kneecap. Matt. As I found out later, I dislocated it. All I knew at the time was that he started to scream and it brought others. The staff who weren't involved in the nightly visits. I thought I was saved."

Josh could hear the "but" in there. "What happened then?" he asked, his voice not much louder than a whisper.

"They saw I was naked and I was told to put on my pajamas. Then they said I would see the head pastor in the morning." Tyler gave another of those unhappy laughs. "I didn't have pajamas. To the best of my knowledge none of us did. It wasn't part of the uniform I was given when I got to the camp. I was told by Matt and Greg that very first day I was to sleep naked, that any deviation from that would be punished. I was sixteen, far from innocent in any sense, and not stupid. I knew what that meant. I knew it from the start. I counted myself lucky that they'd only come four times. I didn't know what punishment they would have given out for wearing anything to bed, and I hadn't been willing to find out. But I didn't think either Matt or Greg would be making a repeat visit that night, and it was wonderful sleeping in my clothes for a change. Even with Trev still crying." He was quiet for a long time, then he said, "I sometimes wonder what happened to some of the other guys there, especially him. He was so broken. I wonder if he got better. If he ever got help, and is okay now, with a nice boyfriend and a passel of corgis. Trev had this thing for corgis."

"That's a nice thought."

"But not fucking likely. I know the statistics. I looked them up when I got home. I got all kinds of information on how what happened to me was forty flavors of fucked-up, not to mention illegal as shit. I had all these ideas about getting that place shut down, although in the end it came to nothing. You know who helped me with that, who did the most to confirm that what had happened to me was wrong in every way? You'll laugh. My guidance counselor, the one I ended up having sex with. Well, oral sex. I didn't let him near my ass. I didn't let anyone near my ass for a very long time."

Josh didn't laugh. He made a movement and Tyler stilled him, his arms holding him in place. "Anyway, I was lucky. I had this place I could go to in my head, a place that they couldn't touch, and I never, ever bought into their bullshit. I knew they were the wrong ones, not me. But some of the others, especially Trev, weren't like that. They drank the Kool-Aid. They believed what they were told. Or maybe they were just too tired to fight it. I don't know. They nearly broke me, though. They came very close. And they left scars."

"Like your leg."

"Yeah. And…" Tyler stopped, then took a deep breath, "the dreams. Can't forget the dreams, as much as I'd like to. One of these days, maybe my subconscious will get the memo I'm safe. Until then…" Josh felt Tyler's shrug as it traveled through his body, lifting then dropping his pectoral and external oblique muscles, sliding satiny skin along his bare back. "I've learned to live with it. It's not always this bad, you know. I sometimes go months without having one. It's been a stressful week."

Josh turned his head to try and see Tyler's face but Tyler used his unoccupied hand to stop him, holding his head in place by the simple expedient of running his fingers through Josh's hair. "Do you want to get dressed?" Josh asked, wishing he could see Tyler's expression. "Put on something besides just underwear?" It occurred to him that when Tyler woke from a nightmare he always got up, and when he came back to bed he'd no longer be naked. Josh had noticed, but hadn't attached any significance to it.

Tyler bent to place a soft, chaste kiss on Josh's cheekbone. "Sure, but it can wait."

Tyler was quiet for a few minutes, the only indication that he wasn't asleep the slow movement of his fingers in Josh's hair and on his skin. Josh was beginning to think that he was going to have to prompt Tyler again, but then he continued.

ೞ೦

November, nine years ago
Bridges to Salvation
Springtown, WI

Tyler followed Mrs. Roth (no first name for her) from his room to Pastor Steve's office the next morning. He wasn't taken to eat breakfast with the others, but that was just as well because he didn't think he could eat a bite.

They would ask him about those nights when Matt and Greg came into his room. He would have to talk about it and he wasn't sure he could. The words would lodge in his throat and choke him.

"Mr. Chadwick," the pastor said. "Your time with us is drawing to a close, and I am extremely saddened to be having this conversation this morning."

It's not going to be a picnic for me, either, Tyler thought.

"Your punishment for your loathsome attempted seduction of two righteous men will be branding. You may take the rest of the day to reflect on your sins. There is still time for you to repent."

"What..." Tyler was thrown. *Loathsome seduction? Branding? Repent?* "My what?"

The pastor touched the intercom button on his desk. "Please send them in," he said.

The office door opened and several members of the male staff trooped in. Apparently, it took six men to subdue one scrawny teenaged boy. He was made to kneel on a wooden prayer bench, his hands secured behind his back, his head held down, and his ankles restrained with his pant leg on the right side rucked up to his knee. Something was stuffed into his mouth and then he heard Steve say, "This is your punishment for being the tempter, like Lucifer."

Tyler could smell something strange (hot metal, he realized later), then his leg was a screaming white mass of pain. Unbearable, impossible pain. He fainted.

When he woke, he was in his room. His bandaged leg burned like a million molten needles pierced it. At other times, it burned with what felt like electric current. At others, it was like a paradoxical freezing, bitter cold seared him. In between was blessed numbness.

Tyler lay on his bed, involuntary tears leaking out of his eyes, and endured. Two more days. Instead of marking the days, he started marking the hours.

ఆ∞

Friday, September 23rd, 4:25 a.m.
The bedroom of an expensive hotel suite
Manhattan, NY

"It's a snake," Josh said, "isn't it?"

"The serpent that tempted Eve," Tyler confirmed. "Always there so I can't forget it."

"That's just bullshit. How is that place not shut down?"

"Of course it's bullshit!" Tyler's voice was as sharp as a cracked whip. "Even at sixteen I knew it was bullshit. That it was fucked-up and evil. And my parents *sent me there*. Twice."

"Your mother..."

"Look," Tyler said fiercely, his fingers tightening in Josh's hair. "I love my mother and she let that happen to me. I don't like to think about it much, because I love her, and she loves me, and she was *stuck*. She tried to stop him, I know, but yeah, I wonder if she could have tried harder. I wonder why she didn't leave and take me with her earlier. But it doesn't do any good, you know? If I blame her, too, what do I have left? Nothing."

Josh rubbed his head against Tyler's shoulder. "It's okay," he said. "You can blame and forgive whoever you want. Okay?"

Tyler was quiet for several minutes. "I guess," he said eventually. "Anyway, I came home, sick, feverish, the burn on my leg infected. Mom and Dad argued the whole drive home. She wanted to take me to the hospital. Dad said I could go to our family doctor in the morning. Mom called Brad, and he came over and took one look at my leg and said if they didn't take me to the ER then he would and fuck them both. His actual words. It's one of my few clear memories from that day. So, that was another hospital visit, and Dad made up some story about how I burned my leg. Some fictional accident that happened on a fictional vacation. It's always some accident, isn't it?"

Josh thought back to his residency, the one that had ended with his own ass in the ICU. It was indeed amazing how many accidents you saw.

And wondered about. Wondered and worried and agonized and second-guessed until you started vomiting and found you couldn't stop. "Yeah," was all he said. His mouth felt dry.

"I told Mom and Dad, later, that I would kill myself before ever going back to Bridges. When I found myself back there and was handed my uniform — and still no pajamas — by Greg, I knew absolutely I couldn't do it again. Not when Matt looked at me and told me that I already knew the rules and he better not see anything covering my ass that night. And how I better not fight them, either."

Josh was afraid to say anything. He just gave Tyler's fingers a slight squeeze.

"I'd smuggled in a razor blade. By that point I'd been cutting off and on for a few months. Mostly off, because I almost died that Christmas, on accident that time. But since I nearly died not trying, I figured it wouldn't be too hard if I was going to give it a real go. So, I had my plan in place, and I'd decided that if I was going to go through with my threat, there was no point in killing myself at home. Especially since everyone would think it was because of Mr. Koenig, and this had nothing to do with him. No, I was going to do it at Bridges, because I was pretty sure even they couldn't hide a dead body. Maybe there would be an investigation. Maybe they'd get shut down. Maybe... I don't know. I was a kid, and a big grand gesture like leaving my dead body around to inconvenience people seemed like a good idea."

"But you didn't really want to die," Josh said.

"No, not exactly. I was trapped and felt there was no way out for me. Dying in a spectacular fashion was the only escape I could think of. And if I was going to go, I was damned well going to try and take those fuckers down with me. Anyway, that night I sat on my bed, clothes still on, and slit my wrists."

"What happened? Since you didn't die."

"No, I didn't die, Captain Obvious. What happened is that my dumb ass did it wrong, which you already know, because I cut across, not down. But I sat there, and watched my blood well up and flow down my arms and it was... hard to explain. Beautiful. Terrible. Powerful. Mine. Those two asswipes came in to mess with me and found me giggling my ass off while I watched myself bleed. Apparently, it freaked them out. Can't imagine why. Anyway, I ended up at the hospital and then in more therapy, but of the conventional sort, with a psychiatrist. There was an investigation, but nothing happened. Bridges is still open. Pastor Steve is still there. But Mom decided I was more important than whatever had kept her chained to Dad, so there was that. I cut myself and everything got better. You see?"

Josh shivered. He couldn't help it. "Yeah." It seemed that was all he could say.

Tyler leaned his head against Josh's. "So now you know. Does it help any?"

"No. Yes. Tyler?"

"What?" Tyler buried his nose in Josh's hair and breathed in. "God, I love the way you smell," he said.

"Like sweat and sex?"

"Mmm," Tyler agreed. "Sweat and sex and you. I could bottle it and make a fortune."

Josh doubted that. "Tyler, I know I'm being all Captain Obvious again, but sleeping naked has got to be a trigger for you."

"Maybe. Probably."

"Well, don't do it, then. I mean, if putting on some pants keeps you from having a nightmare, put on the damn pants. Okay?"

"You're oversimplifying things. I'm still going to have the nightmare. I'm still going to have the urge to cut. Telling you my sad and pathetic story didn't fix dick."

"No, you're wrong, there." Josh moved so he could look into Tyler's eyes. "Things are different because now I know and you don't have to wonder: what will Josh think? He thinks you're brave and amazing. He thinks that you're strong and you're always selling yourself short." Josh made himself stop. Too many dangerous words wanted to fly out of his mouth. "He thinks that you should probably put pants on so we can both get some sleep. I still want to go to the museum in the morning. There's a statue I want to show you."

Tyler smiled. It was small and tired, but it was better than nothing. "Okay," he said. He got up, padded to his suitcase, then found a pair of drawstring cotton pants and put them on, then threw on a t-shirt as well.

Josh scooted over to his side of the bed, leaving room for Tyler to get back in. Tyler turned off the lamp, and instead of staying on his side of the bed, he burrowed into Josh's side.

"Come on, Rosen. Snuggle me. You know your clingy gay ass wants to."

Josh was too pleased he wasn't getting the cold shoulder to mind any teasing. He folded his body around Tyler's. "I think you secretly kinda like it," he said into Tyler's neck. "You're a closet snuggler."

"No comment," Tyler said, but he nestled his back against Josh's chest and sighed, if not with contentment, then at least with acquiescence.

As he held Tyler, Josh's brain churned. That Tyler had been raped he found terrible, but not shocking. He knew there'd been trauma in his past, he just hadn't realized the extent. Josh wished there was something—anything—he could do. Feeling helpless and a little lost, he tightened his grip on Tyler and thought that, while he couldn't change the past, he could be the absolute best fake boyfriend that money didn't have to buy. It was the very least he could do.

Chapter 25
Tyler Regrets the Existence of Siblings

Friday, September 23rd, 2:36 p.m.
The Metropolitan Museum of Art
Manhattan, NY

Tyler looked up at the statue of Perseus Josh had been bursting at the seams to see all day, "because it reminds me of you," and felt something resonate in his chest like a warning. *Careful: proceed with caution. Rocky shoals ahead.* Josh thought he looked like this beautiful statue, depicting a warrior, no less, holding an unsheathed sword and Medusa's severed head. He was also virtually naked, wearing nothing but a helmet and sandals, which struck Tyler as a poor choice for battle.

"My dick is much larger than that," Tyler said, pulling Josh's head down so he could whisper in his ear.

"True," Josh agreed, and led him around the thing so they could look at his posterior. "But the rest of his anatomy is pretty spot-on. Especially that ass."

"It is a great ass," Tyler agreed.

"You can say that again," said a middle-aged woman as she took a picture of said ass with her phone.

Josh tapped his lip with his finger. "Your hair isn't curly and your face is prettier. Or maybe just less vapid," he said. "Still, I think it's a decent likeness."

Tyler flashed back to when he'd sat next to Josh in his car in an anonymous driveway in Wisconsin, having that senseless fight. Tyler had had the sudden epiphany that Josh was angry because he wanted to fuck Tyler and was feeling thwarted because he thought Tyler wasn't interested. This was like that, but worse. A lot worse.

Tyler was almost sure that Josh was in love with him, or thought he was, which amounted to the same thing. Despite everything Tyler had told him last night, or maybe because of it. The good doctor seemed to have a huge hard-on for lost causes. There was that small margin of doubt, though. Tyler could be wrong. He could be reading far too much into what amounted to a nice chunk of carved rock.

He made himself smile. "So, what would you like to see next?

Saturday, September 24th, 3:40 p.m.
Sitting in first class
JFK to O'Hare

On the flight back to Chicago, Tyler composed and deleted three email drafts to send to Purvi. Every time he tried to explain his problem, it sounded beyond stupid. *I think this guy I've simultaneously known my whole life but also only one week is in love with me because he showed me a marble statue. Oh, and up until two days ago he'd been in love with my big brother for like two decades.* Right. That didn't make sense, no matter how many times he tried to write it out. He needed to call and talk with her, but he wouldn't be able to with Josh both underfoot and always within earshot. Maybe Monday, after he'd gone back to work, but Tyler would explode if he didn't talk to someone before then, and it had to be Purvi. Sydney had already given him her two cents, talking to Ethan was out of the question, ditto either Ryan or Brad, and his mother would just give him one of her gentle and unhelpful lectures. Purvi was his best option for a confidante. Tyler was still working out whether her not knowing Josh was a point for or against her.

He deleted another email draft and dropped his phone onto his lap in disgust. Josh, engrossed in reading something on his own phone, reached over the armrest between the seats to rub Tyler's thigh.

Saturday, September 24th, 4:52 p.m.
O'Hare Airport
Chicago, IL

Tyler: Need to talk to you. Hard to do it by text or email, but can't call.
Purvi: Srsly, wtf is up?
Purvi: Stop being attention whore. Spit it out.
Purvi: Fucking drama queen
Tyler: FINE.
Tyler: I'm like 90% sure Dr McDreamy is in love with me.
Purvi: Oh. Um. Marry him and have gay babbies
Tyler: Babbies?

Purvi: Babies. Asshole. Yes.
Tyler: Wait. Why are our babies gay?
Purvi: No. The babbies arent gay. Tho they might be. BUT. What I mean is they're from you and Dr dude so they're YOUR gay babies. Your pretty gay babies. So pretty.
Tyler: Are you drunk?
Purvi: Maybe
Purvi: Little bit
Purvi: Sorry
Purvi: I'M ON VACATION
Tyler: You're no help. Anyway, I see Ryan. Gotta go
Purvi: I can help! WE CAN FIX THINGS YES
Purvi: Sorry so shouty
Purvi: Fix later sooooo drunk

⊗

Saturday, September 24th, 5:05 p.m.
O'Hare Airport
Chicago, IL

Ryan offered to pick them up at the airport and drive them home. Tyler would've turned him down, but he missed Oliver and this was the most practical way to fetch him. Even so, he couldn't suppress a groan when the airport valet brought out the Panamera.

"Really, Ryan?"

Ryan gave Tyler a look of blank innocence, then he raised an eyebrow.

"At least you didn't drag the boy toy along," Tyler grumbled as the valet wedged their carry-on suitcases into the Porsche's tiny trunk, not sure if Ryan heard him, but hoping he had. "I guess I'll take the backseat," he announced in martyred tones.

Josh smirked at him. "Oh, does sitting in the back offend your royal sensibilities, princess?"

Tyler gave Josh a disgusted eye roll, then sat in the backseat after the valet opened the door for him. Before the valet closed the door, Tyler noticed the look of incredulity mixed with speculation that Ryan shot at Josh, and didn't like it one bit.

"Princess?" Ryan asked.

Josh shrugged and got into the passenger seat. Ryan stared at him for a few seconds, then paid the valet and got in behind the wheel.

"I thought the interview with Seth Meyers went well," Ryan remarked as he pulled the car into traffic. "Although I was surprised you brought up the cutting and suicide attempt. What was that about? Dad is furious, by the way."

"Fuck Dad," snapped Tyler. "Like I give a shit what he thinks." He paused, took a deep breath, then went on. "Someone got a photo of my stitches and put it out there. I must have pushed up my sleeve at some point without thinking, and it got photographed. There were insinuations about the truth in the tabloids, and Tom thought it would be best if we could garner as much sympathy as possible out of it. Am I happy about it? No. But I did what he told me to do."

"I hope your publicist knows what he's doing, but Alicia seems to trust him, so I guess we have to as well. I'll see what I can do with Dad. How did the *Entertainment Weekly* interview go?"

"They dressed him up like a slut for the photo shoot," Josh said, sounding grumpy.

"So, like a normal Thursday for him, then," Ryan said.

Tyler kicked the back of Ryan's seat. "Oops, sorry. My foot slipped."

"If there's a mark on the back of my seat, Tyler, you're a dead man."

There wasn't, but Tyler made a face at the back of Ryan's head anyway.

Josh cleared his throat. "They gave him this arrow someone had covered in silver glitter and had him pose with it. Suggestively. It was like fully clothed porn."

Tyler couldn't stop the giggle that burst out of him. "God, for someone who told me I should consider doing porn as a backup plan, you're such a prude. The pictures were completely tasteful. It's *Entertainment Weekly*, for fuck's sake."

Ryan sounded like he stifled a laugh, but when he spoke, his voice was level. "We've been making some progress on the video front. Patrick has a friend who's trying to track down the initial ISP that released the video. In the meantime, he's been researching Michael Koenig to see what he's been up to in the past nine years."

"Who's Michael Koenig?"

Ryan shot Josh a quick look. "Tyler's high school guidance counselor. The one who—"

"Oh, that guy," Josh interrupted. "You think he released the video?"

"It's a possibility. There are others as well."

"Like who?" Josh asked.

"Dad," Tyler said. "My money's on Dad."

"Really?" Josh said.

Ryan said, "No," at the same time Tyler said, "Yes."

"Well, that clears things up," said Josh.

"Never mind. For now, it's all speculation. Tell me about your trip. How was New York?"

Tyler let them talk while he went through his voicemails.

"I've got to fly back home," he announced, excited.

"But we just got... oh, you mean California. Why now?" Josh didn't sound thrilled at the prospect of his defection.

"The wedding is less than a week away," reminded Ryan, as if Tyler could have possibly forgotten.

"When? I was going to take your stitches out on Monday," Josh added.

"I have an invitation to read for a part in a movie on Monday," Tyler said. "Alicia left me a voicemail. Brad can come over and remove the stitches tomorrow morning. I'll get Purvi to book me a late-afternoon flight."

"That's great news," Ryan said. "What's it for?"

"Some movie. I haven't seen the script yet. Alicia emailed it to me, and I'll look through it tonight. According to her, this was set in motion the day before the video shit hit the fan and she was expecting them to want to cancel on us, but they called her today to confirm I would be there on Monday. I'm going to go and do the read through regardless of how good or bad I think the movie is going to be. I can't afford to burn any bridges right now. And don't worry. I'll be back in plenty of time for the wedding. It's not until next Saturday."

"Do you think I should come along in my official boyfriend capacity?" Tyler couldn't tell if Josh wanted to or not.

"Probably not, unless you're burning to come. I'll just be gone a day or two and will most likely be back by Wednesday at the latest. Anyway, you need to go back to work."

"I could take out your stitches tomorrow," Josh said. "You don't need Brad to do it."

"Nah, he'll get all grumpy if I don't have him do it. It's a professional pride thing. Tell you what. You can sew me up next time."

"There shouldn't be a next time," growled Josh.

Ryan cleared his throat. "Well, in that case, why don't I take you straight to Josh's condo? You can leave Oliver with me for a few more days."

"No!" Josh's response was loud enough to startle both Ryan and Tyler. "I mean, that won't be necessary," he continued in a more normal tone. "I'll watch him while Tyler's in California. That way he'll be used to the place by the time Tyler gets back. Okay?"

Tyler stared at the back of Josh's head, and even Ryan took his eyes off the road for a few seconds to glance at Josh. "Okay. No problem," he said. "One spoiled rotten cat, coming right up."

ೞಲ

Sunday, September 25th, 6:32 a.m.
Josh's very tidy bedroom
Evanston, IL

Tyler woke, curled up on his side, Oliver's warm body near his feet, an old and familiar comfort. Behind him was Josh, who was a new and increasingly familiar comfort. There was a part of him that wished he could stay in bed with Josh all day, but he also felt too excited to go back to sleep. He had an audition tomorrow, and from what he'd been able to read of the script so far, it wasn't terrible. No one would ever nominate the thing for an Oscar, but it would make a decent date movie and right now he couldn't afford to be picky.

Tyler glanced at the clock. It was just after 6:30. He left Josh in bed asleep and went down to the condo's gym. Thankfully it was empty except for two other people who didn't seem to give a flying fuck about who he was. Tyler found a mat and went through his yoga routine, then eyed the treadmill with distaste. However, he was banned from swimming until the stitches were out, so he got on the damned thing and started running.

"You hate running," Tyler heard Brad say after he'd been on the treadmill far longer than he was happy thinking about.

"No shit," Tyler panted, "but I can't swim yet. Doctor's orders."

"Oh, look at you, bucking for both patient and brother of the year. I had no idea you actually listened to me, let alone obeyed my orders."

Tyler would have sighed if he'd had the breath to do so. "Fuck. You."

"Come on. Get off that thing and come upstairs so you can take a shower and I can get those stitches out. I've got shit to do today that doesn't involve you. Rachel is going to need brunch and a gallon of mimosas after this, or she'll make my life intolerable."

Tyler stopped the treadmill with gratitude. "What now?" he asked Brad as they walked out of the gym and headed for the elevator.

"First, we had to wade through a bunch of reporters just to get near the building. The masses have figured out where you are, FYI. Then when we got here, no one would buzz us in, and Josh wasn't answering texts or his phone and neither were you. Rachel said, 'Fuck it' and used her key to get into the building and Josh's place."

Of course, she had a key to Josh's place. Of course, she would just use it. "Well, Josh is a heavy sleeper and I was down here."

Brad coughed. "Yeah. About that. Rachel marched into Josh's bedroom and there he was, dead to the world, in a bed that had recently had another occupant and I'm not referring to Oliver."

"Oh, God," Tyler said.

"And then she had me go into the spare bedroom to supposedly find you, but as we both know, no one had slept in there."

Tyler groaned.

"Meanwhile Rach woke up Josh. There was much shouting. Oliver's hiding somewhere. And I hoped you'd be down here and hey, here you were." Brad grinned at him. "So. It's been an eventful week for you, huh?"

"There are days when I envy only children," Tyler said. "How nice it must be not to have siblings."

Brad ruffled his hair like he was still twelve. "Oh, you love us. Don't deny it."

Tyler used the key Josh had given him to open the condo's door. "Some days it's hard to remember why."

They walked to the kitchen where Josh and Rachel sat drinking coffee and glaring at each other. At least until Rachel caught sight of Tyler, then she transferred the evil eye to him.

"You," she hissed. "You couldn't keep your little paws off him, could you?"

"Oh, for God's sake, Rachel," Josh exclaimed. "Mom took the news better than you have. Why do you even care?"

Rachel slumped. "I care because I never wanted this to happen. You're going to get hurt again, and it's going to be awkward if I have to despise my brother-in-law on your behalf."

"You know, maybe you should have thought about that before deciding to date Brad. How do you think I felt when I found out that my sister was in love with the brother of the man who I wanted but couldn't have? Shitty, that's how. But I sucked it up because you were happy and I happen to like Brad. I think you owe me, so let this go. Tyler and I will sort things out ourselves and it has nothing to do with you, or Brad, or Ryan for that matter."

Brad started applauding. Rachel transferred her death glare to him, but all he did was blow her a kiss. "Bravo, Josh. Way to finally grow a pair."

"Fuck off, Brad," Josh muttered, and stared into his coffee.

Rachel looked both hurt and murderous. Josh looked sullen and worried. Brad seemed completely unconcerned. "You," Tyler said, poking Brad in the chest, "keep the two of them from killing each other while I take a shower. You," he pointed at Rachel, "and I will talk after I clean up. As for you," Tyler grabbed Josh's chin and tilted his face up. "It'll be fine. Stop worrying." He leaned down to give Josh a brief kiss. "Okay?"

Josh looked dubious. "Sure," he said, but he didn't sound particularly reassured.

"Trust me," he said, and kissed Josh again.

Rachel huffed.

Tyler went to go take his shower. He rushed through it as quickly as he could, threw on the first clothes he grabbed out of his suitcase, and hurried out to the kitchen to rescue his...

Tyler's brain froze in its tracks. Not boyfriend. Not really. His... Josh. Yeah. He needed to rescue Josh.

Contrary to his worries, Rachel, Josh, and Brad seemed to be having a civil conversation, albeit one about him. No one was shouting or making threats, so Tyler relaxed and got Josh to go take his own shower.

"Okay, unsew me," Tyler said, then sat down at the kitchen table across from Rachel. Brad went to get his bag of supplies and then put water on to boil to sterilize the instruments he was going to use. While the water started to heat, he swabbed the wound on Tyler's arm with Betadine and let it dry.

"Don't mind me," Brad said. "Pretend I'm not here."

Rachel shot Brad a look, then focused on Tyler. "You just had to go for option three, didn't you?"

"Option three was your brother's idea, actually." Rachel glared at him through narrowed eyes. Josh sometimes got the same expression on his face when he was trying to figure out if Tyler was being sincere or not. "And, for the record, option four, too. It's hard not to like your brother. Even when we argue, he's got this core of decency that... well..." Tyler sighed. "I like him."

Having scrubbed his hands and sterilized his instruments, Brad sat down next to Tyler and started to snip and remove the stitches.

"So," Brad said as he worked, "what are options three and four? And are one and two relevant?"

"I thought we were pretending you weren't here," Rachel said.

Tyler snorted. "And you bought that?" He turned to Brad. "Rachel said I had four options to deal with her precious brother. Option one was to bail on the whole plan and go it alone. Two was to go through with the plan and keep our relationship strictly professional. Three was me seducing him. Four was becoming his friend."

"Okay. I can see how option one would have been unpopular with nine out of ten Tylers," Brad said.

"Josh ruled it out, too. I tried twice to bail on him, but he wouldn't go for it. He's got this whole knight in shining armor thing going on."

"See!" Rachel exclaimed. "I warned you."

"Yeah, that's Josh in a nutshell," Brad agreed. "He needs to be needed. Let's see here. Option two was to be professional and just pretend a relationship existed, huh?"

"But Josh can't fake shit," Tyler said. "Obviously."

"Too true. So, yeah. I can see why you went for option three."

"No, that's the thing." Tyler ran a hand through his still-wet hair. "He picked option three. Honest to God. Although I might have nudged him in that direction. A little." Tyler looked at Rachel and adopted an injured mien. "Your brother was hell-bent on using me to get over Ryan, and I'm sorry, but I'm not made of stone. Josh gave me these sad puppy dog eyes, and how was I supposed to resist that? If anyone got taken advantage of here, it's me."

Rachel started to look like she felt bad, but Brad spoiled it by laughing. "What a load of horse shit. You, taken advantage of. By *Josh*. That's hilarious."

"Thanks, Brad." Brad just kept laughing.

Rachel took a large gulp of coffee. "Do you have any idea what the two of you are doing?" She sounded more tired than angry now.

"Not really, but I'd still like you to back off." Tyler pasted on a smile he didn't feel. "I'm not planning on hurting your brother. I'm not planning on anything. I just need to get through the next several weeks and then—"

"You'll leave him here, alone."

Brad pulled out the last stitch and applied butterfly bandages to the wound. "He could move, you know."

"Who, me?" Tyler shook his head. "No. I am not moving back to Illinois. No way, no how, not gonna happen."

"No, dumbass. I meant Josh."

Tyler and Rachel both looked at Brad.

"All I'm saying is that Josh isn't required to live his entire life in Illinois. People do move. It's a thing."

"But, honey, this is my brother we're talking about, remember?"

Brad started cleaning up the table. "He followed Ryan out to Stanford," he reminded them.

"Yeah," Tyler agreed, "but that was Ryan. I'm not Ryan."

Brad grinned at him. "No, you're not."

"Anyway, it's been, like, a week. Josh is probably going to be sick of me by the time my publicist and agent decide that the current crisis is over, so stop worrying."

"Or you'll be sick of him," Rachel said.

Tyler made a noncommittal noise.

"Or, option c, none of the above," added Brad.

Tyler raised an eyebrow. "Meaning?"

"You'll figure it out," Brad said. "You're a bright boy." He ruffled

Tyler's hair again. "No matter what anyone says."

"I hate you," Tyler said with a scowl. "Now hit the road. Buy her mimosas until she stops being angry."

"There is not enough orange juice and champagne in this world," Rachel said, but she already seemed to have notched down from angry to resigned. "I'll see you at the wedding rehearsal on Friday. Five p.m. at the Field, then dinner afterward. Don't forget."

"We'll be there. Now get out. I have a grumpy dermatologist to deal with."

"Tyler—" Rachel began, a warning note in her voice.

"See you on Friday!" Brad said and strong-armed his fiancée out the door.

Chapter 26
Josh Stays Home

Sunday, September 25th, 8:15 a.m.
Josh's immaculate kitchen
Evanston, IL

The kiss burned Josh's lips after Tyler left to go take his shower, and Josh knew he was blushing. He cleared his throat. It was on the tip of his tongue to tell Brad and his sister, "It's not what it looks like," but that was a lie and all three of them knew it.

Brad took a seat at the kitchen table. "So," he said brightly, "I see you and Tyler are getting along." He waggled his eyebrows suggestively.

Rachel glared at her soon-to-be spouse. "This isn't funny."

"That's where you're wrong," Brad said, "because it really is. I've got to say, Josh, I'm kind of put out. I mean, what am I, chopped liver?"

"Shut up," Josh said, smiling despite himself.

"What? So, you never once looked at me that whole time we lived together and thought, 'hey, I could turn that straight boy gay.' That hurts."

Josh almost said, *Yeah, because that worked out so well for me with Ryan that I'd want to try it with you, too,* but stopped himself. Instead he held onto his smile and made his voice light. "Converting straight boys takes effort, and it's not like Chicago has a shortage of gay men. It's a whole cost-benefit analysis thing." Which was true, of course, but not the whole truth. At first, rooming with Brad had been exquisitely painful because of his physical resemblance to Ryan, but over time it got easier as he and Brad became friends. Brad shifted in his mind from the younger version of the man he'd loved into just Brad, his roommate, friend, and someone who was like Ryan only in very small ways, other than looks.

Brad sighed dramatically. "Even so, it'd be nice to know that you checked out my ass from time to time. Just so I don't feel like the Chadwick ugly duckling or something."

"Stand up. I'll check it out now, if it would make you feel better."

"You two are impossible," Rachel said with a huff. "This is serious."

Brad reached a hand out and rubbed her stiff shoulders. "Hon, you need to let this go. What Josh does with either of my brothers is his business, not yours. Not even by proxy, since I don't care beyond hoping that things work out and no one ends up not speaking to someone. They're grown-ups. Let them screw their lives up however they want."

Rachel bit her lip.

"I told you years ago that you and I dating might be a problem for Josh, remember? And you said it was fine, that we weren't serious and it wasn't like we were planning on getting married."

"He never..." Rachel looked at Josh. "You never said anything."

Josh opened his mouth, but Brad spoke first. "Of course not. He loves you and he has no spine."

"Seriously, Brad, fuck you. And it's fine, Rach," Josh said. "Really, it's fine."

"You just said it wasn't fine thirty seconds ago," Rachel said. "I just... I don't want you hurt. Although I'm not going to let Brad go for your sake." Rachel gave him a small, somewhat worried smile.

"Oh, like I want to make that phone call to our parents: 'Yeah, unfortunately the wedding's off. Rachel marrying Brad hurts my feelings because once upon a time I had a thing for Brad's brother. So. Sorry about your deposit and all.'"

"Once upon a time?" Rachel asked. "As in not now?"

Josh shrugged. "Ryan's moved on. Hell, he moved on years and years ago. Anyway, I have, too. As you've been telling me for ages, it's past time, right?"

"And what about Tyler?"

"Yeah, what about Tyler?" Tyler asked. His hair was wet and just combed back, he still hadn't shaved, and he wore a t-shirt and a pair of jeans that looked older than he was. There was a pinched, tense look on his face. He was a less-grubby version of the disreputable elf Josh had first encountered last week, and still beautiful enough to make Josh's heart trip a little in his chest.

"Tyler is..." he began, then stopped.

Tyler was a dream vacation. He was a gorgeous island in the tropics with crystalline beaches, surrounded by an ocean that was the same blue-gray-green of his eyes. The kind of place that you visit and fall in love with and fantasize about living on forever, but then you go back home to your cold Midwestern city and your sensible life and of course you never move there.

Tyler was a pipe dream, but Josh couldn't exactly say that out loud. "Tyler is none of your business. I didn't butt in when you started dating Brad. Keep your nose out of this."

Rachel frowned at him. "And when it all goes to hell?"

"I'll deal with it."

"Yeah, because you dealt with it so well the last time you dated a Chadwick."

Josh opened his mouth to say he and Ryan had never dated, then shut it. Instead he shrugged. This thing with Tyler was bound to go to hell, just like she predicted, but he wasn't going to give his sister the satisfaction of agreeing with her. Not today, at any rate.

"Buy stock in Ben & Jerry's," Tyler suggested. "Josh, why don't you go take your shower? While you're in there, Brad will take out my stitches."

⊂₃୧⊃

Sunday, September 25th, 9:13 a.m.
Josh's blue and gray tiled master bath
Evanston, IL

Tyler came into the bathroom and started shaving just as Josh was toweling himself dry.

"I've got more than one bathroom," he said.

"I know," Tyler replied, running a safety razor along his throat as he looked at a blurry image of himself in the mirror he had wiped free of condensation. Josh wanted to lick along the smooth, newly shaven skin that Tyler revealed stripe by careful stripe. Instead he watched and dried himself off.

"This is the first time I've seen you shave with a regular razor," Josh said, wrapping the towel around his waist.

"That's because you haven't babyproofed this place, thank God. Like I could do any real damage with this thing." Tyler snorted. "It's a good thing you didn't watch when Sydney's pal Sam came to cut my hair. She used a straight razor on me. I think you might've had a heart attack, Sir Worrywart."

"If she was wielding it and not you, I think my heart would've survived."

"I'm glad you keep regular razors around this place. Sometimes," Tyler said, moving onto the side of his jaw, "you just need something extremely sharp. Your electric razor gives a shitty shave unless you like being a bit scruffy, which I will admit is a good look on you. I need to buy you a better one, though. If you're going to be scruffy it should be intentional. And you do have a birthday coming up."

"You don't need to get me a birthday present." Josh watched the razor as it very carefully did not cut Tyler's skin. It made him nervous, but there was something sexy about it, too.

"Sure, I do. Thirty-five is a very important birthday." Tyler took a bit of shaving cream and dabbed it on Josh's nose. "Go get dressed. I'll be done in a minute."

Josh swiped at his nose, then went into the bedroom and threw his towel in the hamper. He walked to the dresser but stopped, looking at his bed and the rumpled covers, the obvious result of two people having slept together. He usually either made the bed or changed the sheets as soon as he got up, but today Rachel had happened. This morning had been hellish, his sister's shouting at him the aural equivalent of being doused with a huge water balloon.

Josh started to make the bed then stopped, suddenly exhausted despite a good night's sleep. He crawled facedown onto the bed and stewed on his messy, rumpled bedding.

"Hey, you feel okay?" Josh felt Tyler's hand caress his calf, ruffling the hair on it. "I can take a taxi to the airport if you're not up to driving me. It's fine."

No, it's not fine. Josh didn't want Tyler to go, or he didn't want Tyler to go without him, which was stupid. Tyler had an audition tomorrow and Josh had to go to work since he'd just had a whole week off. Besides, Tyler would be back before he knew it. Missing him before he'd even left was ridiculous. "No, I'll take you," Josh said, his voice muffled by the pillow.

Tyler's hand travelled higher, over the back of his knee and up his thigh. "You planning on wearing this? I must admit, it's a fetching ensemble. I hear it's what all the hippest emperors are wearing this year."

Josh sighed when Tyler's hand reached the crease where his thigh became his ass. "If you don't stop," Josh said, "we won't have time to get breakfast before your flight."

"To hell with breakfast." Tyler removed his hand and Josh felt momentarily bereft, but then Tyler was there, insinuating himself between Josh's legs. He kissed down Josh's spine from the nape of his neck to the upper cleft of his ass. "This is much better."

Tyler spread Josh's cheeks, then started to lick him with careful deliberation. It was too much, especially on this gray morning when Josh could almost taste in the back of his throat what the end of them would be like: all bitter and ashy and cold. "Oh, God. You don't... shouldn't..."

Tyler lifted his mouth and blew lightly on the damp skin, making Josh shudder. "Stop worrying for once in your life and just let me do this, okay? I've wanted to for... so long. You have no idea."

Josh's erection throbbed, trapped between his body and the bed sheet, leaking precum like it was a broken faucet, creating his own little personal wet spot. He tried to keep his body still, to relax and make things easier for Tyler, but he couldn't keep his hips from moving, even with Tyler holding onto him hard enough that he was probably leaving fingertip-shaped bruises on his hips. Tyler's mouth was molten hot on his sensitive skin and the sensation was nearly overwhelming. It was too stimulating, too pleasurable, and far too intimate. Tyler's mouth on him was exquisite torture and Josh wasn't sure how much more he could take, while at the same time never wanting it to stop. He was nearly mindless by the time Tyler lifted his head.

"Do you want me to fuck you?" Tyler asked, his voice husky and low. He ran his hands along Josh's sides from his ribs down to his thighs, his short nails dragging with a delicious pressure that was almost but not quite painful.

"Oh, God, yes."

Josh heard him undress, then open a condom wrapper, and he writhed in anticipation, the sound of clothes hitting the floor and the tearing of foil being enough to shoot bolts of aching need to his balls and cock. Tyler's fingers, cool and wet with lube, pressed inside him, first two, then three, fucking him hard and stroking along his prostate, but it wasn't enough. Josh groaned with frustration.

He felt Tyler remove his fingers, leaving him empty and wanting. "What position do you want?" Tyler asked in a blasé tone, like he was asking if Josh wanted chicken or fish for dinner. It was infuriating. "Like this, or on your back, or... you know, this is the thing with you being so much taller. It decreases our options."

Josh rolled over and out of the wet spot he'd made. He spread his legs and bent his knees, then shoved a pillow under his ass. He grabbed his aching erection and stroked it. "Shut up and just fuck me," he said. "God, you talk too much."

Tyler moved between Josh's spread thighs and ran his hands up and down his legs. "Just for that I should talk the entire time."

"Good luck with that. I bet you can't." Stupid bet. Tyler could, and would.

"Ooh, a challenge. You should know by now I can't resist a challenge."

Josh felt Tyler's cock nudge at his entrance. He pushed forward slowly. So very slowly. Josh gritted his teeth, keeping himself from shoving his body onto Tyler's dick, wanting to let it be slow so it would last.

Tyler moved inside Josh with shallow thrusts while he arranged Josh's legs so they rested against his shoulders. He bit the side of Josh's leg, then thrust all the way in, past the internal sphincter and deep inside. Josh loved fucking Tyler, loved claiming Tyler's body with his dick, but he loved this, too. Being taken in return, possessed, owned. As if Tyler wasn't planning on waltzing out of his life at the earliest opportunity.

"Whatever you're thinking, Dr. Rosen, stop it. Do you hear me?"

Josh closed his eyes, knowing he was lost and almost not caring.

Tyler increased his speed a fraction. It felt so good Josh could barely focus on what Tyler was saying. "Let's see here. Did you know that I am extremely fond of your hair?" Tyler flexed his hips and moved with careful deliberation.

"My hair?" Josh tried to concentrate on the feeling of Tyler inside him, filling him and fucking him. Meanwhile, Tyler kept talking, his voice as modulated and smooth as the precise movement of his hips and pelvis. Josh let his legs slide down from Tyler's shoulders, then he wrapped them around his waist.

"Yeah. You have amazing hair, Josh. I even like those gray hairs of yours. They're surprisingly sexy, you know. And your eyes are gorgeous, so dark and warm. It's such a cliché to say they're like chocolate, but start thinking about other warm brown things and you run into trouble. Yours are the color of really good, expensive dark chocolate. Wrapped in gold foil just like those gold flecks in your eyes. Open them up. I want to see your eyes, Josh. Now."

Josh opened his presumably chocolate eyes and stared at Tyler, wishing he had his glasses on. He couldn't make out Tyler's eyes at all, and wondered what color they were now, but his body was easy enough to see. Every thrust made his pale, slender form gyrate, almost as if he was dancing to music only he could hear.

"Your eyes right now, though, are black. Pupils completely blown because you want this, don't you? You want me. Touch yourself," Tyler demanded, his voice implacable. "I want you to come before I do."

"Uh..." Josh's brain, limping along on a limited supply of blood and oxygen, struggled to keep up.

"Hand on your dick, doctor. I swear you lose at least sixty IQ points when we fuck. If we ever play Trivial Pursuit we're doing it naked."

Josh stoked himself obediently. "I'll still win," he said. Then, "Fuck," as Tyler sped up his thrusting. He started to moan and whimper, unable to stop the incoherent sounds he was making.

Tyler panted with effort as he picked up his pace. "I love that... you seem like... this totally uptight guy. Full of... good manners and... all that... but underneath... you're..."

"What?" Josh gasped.

"Such a big needy slut." Tyler stopped moving. "Aren't you?"

"Tyler," he growled. He rocked his hips in frustration.

Tyler started thrusting again, but with glacial slowness. It was driving Josh insane. "My slut. Say it, Josh."

"God. Yes. Yours." No point in denying the obvious. "Please." That last came out as a desperate whine.

Tyler gripped Josh's thighs hard and his movement sped up again. "I'm so close. Are you close, Josh?"

"Almost... there... just fuck me, Tyler, please, shut up and fuck me."

"Come on, come for me," Tyler moaned, moving faster and with more force. "Come while I'm still talking. Come while I tell you... how...

fucking amazing... oh God... you're just so..."

Tyler's hips thrust hard twice more, then stilled while Josh rapidly pumped his cock. Tyler, still inside him, still hard, leaned forward and bit Josh low on his shoulder, right by his collarbone. It hurt, but it also arrowed pleasure right to his balls and he nearly came just from that. He was so close, skating right on the edge, and it was agony and bliss rolled together into one intoxicating package.

Tyler thrust one last time into him, shuddered, and sank onto Josh's chest, twitching a little with the pleasure of his orgasm. Josh wound the hand not buried between their bodies in Tyler's hair. "I win," he gasped. "What do I get?"

Tyler panted, "What do you want?"

You I want you I want you.

Tyler smirked at him. "Yeah, I know. Stupid question." He slid down Josh's body, pushing Josh's busy hand out of his way. He took Josh's cock in his own hand and ran his lips and tongue over his balls. The hot, wet glide of Tyler's tongue along his flesh while his hand stroked Josh's aching erection pushed Josh over the precipice and into orgasm, his semen pumping in helpless spurts on his belly and chest as his body exploded with white hot bolts of electric ecstasy.

"Ha!" Josh said after he got his breath back. "You came before I did. Age does have some compensations."

"I'll need to try harder next time. I won the other bet, though. I did manage to talk the whole time."

Josh looked down his body at Tyler. "What do you want?"

Tyler got up from the bed and removed then discarded the condom. "I think you, lying there covered in semen, is a damn fine reward. My tidy doctor, so messy. So *dirty*." He drew out the last word obscenely. Tyler came back to the bed and crawled up Josh's sated and slack body, licking sweat and semen as he went in delicate little laps that made Josh shudder under him. *Oh, my filthy, depraved elf. What am I going do when you leave me?*

When Tyler arrived at Josh's mouth he bit at Josh's lips and devoured his mouth in a seemingly endless kiss. Tyler finally came up for air and burrowed his face into the crook of Josh's neck, first biting then sucking at a spot just above where he'd already bitten. It made Josh writhe and arch his back. Tyler was going to leave a mark, more than one, in fact, but Josh couldn't bring himself to make him stop. It felt too wonderful.

"Wasn't that," Tyler asked after a while, "better than pancakes?"

"Well," Josh said, "it was messier. Now we both need to take another shower." How the hell was he ever going to let Tyler go? His sister was right. The rational part of his brain was right. He was in so much trouble.

"We can save time and conserve water by showering together,"

Tyler said. "It won't take long. A few minutes."

It ended up taking a lot longer than a few minutes. Breakfast was relegated to a protein bar eaten in the car in the way to O'Hare.

"Sorry there isn't time to stop and get you something," Josh said. "Grab some food in the airport, okay? Are you sure you don't want me to park and come in with you?"

Tyler leaned over when they got to departures and kissed Josh. "We don't have time, and this is fine. This morning was totally worth skipping breakfast," he said. "I'll let you know that I arrived safely." Then he was out of the car, carry-on in his hand. He disappeared through the sliding doors.

Tyler was gone and a feeling of unreality settled over Josh, like the past days were all a particularly vivid dream he'd been having. He drove home by rote, his mind a million miles away. He could almost believe that Tyler had been a figment of his imagination, except there was still a contingent of lurking photographers outside his building, and when he opened the door to his condo a dark gray cat waited for him. Oliver blinked solemn green eyes at him. Tyler wasn't the only one who'd skipped breakfast.

Josh went to the kitchen, Oliver at his heels. He fed the cat, then made himself a sandwich. Afterward he spent a few hours cleaning but stopped when he heard Tyler's voice in his head: *That floor isn't even dirty.* And it wasn't. His entire home was spotless and there was nothing left that legitimately needed cleaning. In need of distraction, he booted up his computer and started to make inroads into the demons making nuisances of themselves in his digital kingdom. Oliver sat by his side and provided moral support, occasionally batting at the screen to show he was doing his part.

∞

Sunday, September 25th, 10:30 p.m.
Josh's tidy bedroom
Evanston, IL

Tyler: Have landed at LAX, on my way home now. You want me to call later?
Josh: No, it's okay. Plan is to hit the gym, make some dinner, then bed. Work tomorrow.
Tyler: OK
Josh: Let me know how your audition goes.

Tyler: Sure.
Tyler: Night.

And if that felt a bit unsatisfactory, listening to Tyler's voice over the phone would've been too much right then. It would only remind Josh of the distance between them, the distance that was there even when they slept together in the same bed.

That night, Josh tossed and turned for a long time. He thought about breaking down, calling Tyler, and pretending that they weren't separated by several states, but Josh was afraid his voice would betray him. It would be better if he waited until tomorrow. Safer. Sleepless nights intensified emotions, he knew that from long experience, and the ache he felt from not having Tyler beside him was an overreaction. Right now, everything felt dialed to eleven, but it wouldn't last. Daylight was good at making middle-of-the-night monsters disappear like popped soap bubbles. Josh hugged a pillow against his chest, smelled Tyler's sandalwood shampoo, and waited grimly for sleep to arrive.

He was grateful when Oliver decided that, though he was a distant second to his beloved Tyler, Josh was satisfactory enough to curl into. He fell asleep at last with his hand buried in Oliver's fur, tangible proof that his elf was more man than fantasy and would be coming back, if for no other reason than to get his cat back. They were, after all, a package deal.

○§○

Monday, September 26th, 8:50 a.m.
A dermatology practice
Evanston, IL

Maria, his favorite partner in the practice, eyed Josh as he poured himself a cup of coffee in the doctor's lounge in the office. "Is that a hickey?"

Josh froze. "Uh…"

Maria yanked on his collar. "Oh my God. That is an actual hickey, and it's huge. You dog."

Josh jerked out of her grasp. "Is it that easy to see?"

She made a noncommittal noise. "You might want to button your top shirt button."

Damn. Josh buttoned it. He'd have to duck into the restroom and see how bad it was. It couldn't be too terrible, though, as he hadn't noticed it this morning when he'd gotten dressed. Luckily Maria couldn't see his chest, which still bore six yellowing bruises in the shape of Tyler Chadwick's mouth. "Thanks for the heads up," he said.

"Yeah, well, better me than Matt. He'd be more of a dick about it." Maria dropped her voice into a deeper register. "'You know, Josh, this doesn't set the kind of tone we want here at the practice. Our patients have certain expectations of us as medical providers and if we don't meet and even exceed those, they will take their patronage elsewhere.'"

"Having a hickey might count as exceeding expectations."

Maria laughed. "Possibly. Matt is such a tool. Anyway, is that," she pointed to his neck, "related at all to a certain actor by the name of Tyler Chadwick?"

Josh felt his cheeks heat, something he should have grown out of twenty years ago but still couldn't control. "Um, yeah, that is... he's... yes."

Maria gave him a playful shove. "So that was you? You're the boyfriend he mentioned on Seth Meyers? And that was you sucking face with him in a boat, wasn't it? Kick ass, I win the bet! I said it was you, but Marisol said I was full of shit and Nadia was on the fence. Nik didn't realize you had a boyfriend. That was an interesting conversation, let me tell you."

Josh shrugged. The blush didn't feel like it was going away anytime soon. "Yeah, it was me. Tyler and I are officially dating."

"How did you two even meet?"

Josh smiled. "If I remember correctly, he was building a castle out of blocks and wanted my help with construction."

"What?"

"He was a little kid, Maria. I've known him and his family pretty much forever. My dad worked for his dad. I just haven't seen Tyler since he was in high school. He's Rachel's fiancé's brother and he's in town for the wedding and... well... we kind of were thrown together and before I knew it he was my new boyfriend."

Maria seemed to do some mental calculations. "So, you're screwing your future brother-in-law. Kinky. Wait until Nik finds out. He'll probably faint."

"Does me being gay really freak Nik out that much?" He was their newest nurse practitioner. "It's not like I keep it a huge secret or anything."

Maria's lips twitched. "Nik has had a crush on you since the moment he met you. I'm pretty sure he's disappointed to see you making out with someone not him, but I don't think he's totally given up hope, especially since Marisol said you never date anyone for longer than a month or two, so heads up. It couldn't hurt to maybe have your Hoover vacuum come in and take you to lunch tomorrow so Nik knows you're off limits."

"Okay, sure, but not tomorrow. Tyler's in LA."

"Oh?" Maria gave him a skeptical look.

"He's got an audition thingy today. He'll be back later this week, though."

"Oh. Well, it's good to have you back, Josh."

"Did you miss me that much?"

"Nope," she said, and popped a bit of bagel in her mouth and chewed. "I just wasn't fond of all the extra work I had to do because your slacker ass was star fucking."

Josh gave her an evil look. Probably not nearly as effective as one from Tyler, but he hoped he'd do the man justice.

Maria just cackled and ate another bite of bagel.

ೞ๏

Monday, September 26th, 5:40 p.m.
A grocery store
Evanston, IL

Josh stopped by the store on his way home to restock his mostly bare fridge. While in the checkout lane, he was startled to see himself and Tyler on the covers of a few of the tabloids on display. That was beyond strange. One was a boat picture with, as Maria put it, him and Tyler sucking face. The other picture was of the two of them in JFK, holding hands. A third showed the incriminating stitches on Tyler's arm and speculated that he was being abused by his new boyfriend.

That made Josh look around him guiltily, like someone in the store would see him, point a finger, and scream, "That's him, the cradle-snatching actor abuser. Get him!" Of course, in reality no one seemed to realize or care that he was the guy in the pictures. It still made his heart pound thinking about his face there in tabloids all over the country. It was not a good feeling. He had no idea how Tyler stood it. Maybe it was something you learned to block out.

When Josh left the store to head home it had gotten dark. The crowd of paparazzi in front of his building had thinned out, down to a few diehard or desperate stragglers. They got a few pictures of him as he walked from his parking spot to the building's entrance, although he wasn't sure why they bothered, with Tyler not around. He was going to have to talk to security and see if there was anything that could be done about them.

Later that evening some asshole kept ringing his intercom buzzer to be let in, only he or she wouldn't identify themselves. This happened occasionally, sometimes by kids pulling pranks or by visitors who pushed the wrong button. But after the fifth time it happened that evening, Josh was good and pissed off. He'd already called his building's security, who said they'd investigate it, but that was a half-hour ago and the fucker had buzzed twice since then. Josh grabbed his phone and went downstairs.

A man stood in the condo's outer vestibule. Josh approached the glass door with caution. "Are you looking for someone?" he shouted through the glass. No way in fuck was he opening that door.

The guy was in his mid-thirties with dark hair and startlingly pale blue eyes. He hadn't shaved for a few days and it was not to achieve a purposeful scruffy effect. He looked rough, but as if he might be handsome, or at least attractive, under better circumstances.

"You!" Josh could see more than hear the word the man said. Then, "Stay away from Tyler."

Oh, hell. Creepy stalker fan, twelve o'clock. Hoping his flash wasn't on, Josh snapped a picture of Mr. Creepy Stalker.

"Go away or I'm calling the cops!" he shouted.

"You need to leave him the fuck alone!" Creepy stalker dude verged on hysterical. Josh dialed 911, then held the phone up for the guy to see. His finger hovered on the call button. Mr. Creepy Stalker's face filled with rage and he looked like he wanted to break through the glass door, but then he changed his mind, flipped Josh off, and hurried away.

Well, hell. That was fun.

Josh was almost to the elevator when the security guys finally showed up. Josh explained the situation to them and texted the photo of the guy to one of the guards. They promised they'd be on the lookout for him and call the cops immediately if he showed back up.

"We can call them now, if you like."

Josh was tempted, but it was already past eleven and he had to be up early for work the next day.

"Nah, what's the point? He's gone now. Hopefully he won't be back. But is there anything you can do about all the reporters that have been outside? They're a nuisance."

"We had the cops out today warning them to stay fifty feet from the building's door, but as long as they keep their distance and aren't physically harassing anyone, there's not a lot that we can do. Is this going to be a permanent thing?"

Josh ran a hand through his hair. "No. My boyfriend said they're bound to lose interest soon, and when he goes back home I'll expect they'll follow him. Honestly, I'm surprised there was anyone out there today."

"It's just that we've gotten complaints from the other residents. Heads up, I think they're going to bring it up in the next association meeting."

Josh groaned. "Thanks for the warning," he said, then headed for the elevator.

Once he was safely in bed in his condo, Josh got out his phone and reread through the texts Tyler had sent him while he was at work.

Tyler: Just got back from the read through with the casting agent
Tyler: I think it went okay.
Tyler: I know you're at work
Tyler: Talk to you later. Tonight.

Josh's fingers tapped idly on his phone. *What to say when what you want to say is all wrong? God, I miss you* warred with *I hate dealing with the crazies and assholes that follow you around.* So, he started with something safe.

Josh: Hey, there. So, your audition went well?
Tyler: Pretty good, I think. I won't know for a while.
Tyler: How was your day?

This didn't seem like a good time to complain about Tyler's creepy stalker fan or the annoying reporters. It wasn't like Tyler could do anything about either one from two thousand miles away.

Josh: Fine. Work knows I'm dating you and apparently the new nurse practitioner has a crush on me.
Tyler: Oh, really? Do tell.

Nik wasn't someone Josh would have looked twice at before Tyler because he wasn't Josh's type, or at least not Josh's previous type. Instead of tall, muscular, and hopefully blonde, Nik was of medium height, compactly built, and decidedly not blonde. His hair was brown and his eyes were brown. Chocolate brown, Josh supposed, although he'd never paid Nik's eyes much attention.

Prior to Tyler he wouldn't have—and hadn't—registered on Josh's radar. Now, however, Josh thought of his vow to get over Tyler after the dissolution of their association by fucking his way through every twink in the greater Chicago area until he found one that could fill that not-Tyler spot that was bound to develop. He couldn't imagine starting with Nik, however. Even if sleeping with a coworker was a good idea, which it wasn't.

Josh: What do you want to know?
Tyler: Male or female nurse?
Josh: Male
Tyler: Of course he's male. Is he hot?
Josh: He's no you, that's for sure.

Josh's phone rang. "Yes?" he asked.

"Do you miss me?" Tyler purred into his ear, the sound of his voice enough to make Josh's toes curl.

Yes, he missed Tyler, that was the problem. This was a preview of what things would be like later, when if he wanted to see Tyler he would have to resort to watching one of his movies.

"Yes, like a rash."

Tyler laughed, "Me, too." He proceeded to talk to Josh for almost an hour about nothing in particular, then he sent a picture of himself from the neck down wearing the world's smallest pair of neon pink swim trunks and nothing else.

"My God, Tyler."

"You like?"

Too much. Far too much.

There's no such thing as too much.

"Uh, yeah, I guess. You're very bright... and shiny."

Tyler's low laugh rolled over him, through his ear and into his brain, coating him like sweet, rich caramel. Josh was hard from that laugh alone. The picture hadn't hurt, either.

"That's my sunblock. Lots and lots of sunblock."

"You do know the way to a dermatologist's heart, don't you?"

"Yes, I do," he said, then veered onto another topic, telling Josh a story about Purvi and her boyfriend Kevin that had Josh laughing until he snorted, which set Tyler off into his own gales of laughter. By the time they both hung up, Josh felt better and had completely forgotten about Mr. Creepy Stalker.

Chapter 27
Tyler Goes Home

Sunday, September 25th, 6:19 p.m.
LAX airport
Los Angeles, CA

If Tyler made it out of LAX without punching either a tourist or a paparazzi in the face it would be a minor miracle. O'Hare without Josh had been a nightmare, at least until he'd gotten through security. LAX would be worse unless he figured something out.

There had been more reporters in the departure area of the terminal at O'Hare than he'd expected, like someone had tipped them off. Apparently, he was the flavor of the moment and he should've expected it, but hadn't. Hell, he should've had Josh come in with him to play the part of doting boyfriend seeing him off instead of dropping him at the curb in front of departures. All the way to security he'd been barraged by questions that he'd ignored. He'd moved grimly past them all and had refused to be baited.

"Where's your boyfriend?" *None of your business.*

"Are you two fighting? *Not in the way you think.* He and Josh did seem to bicker a fair amount, but Tyler enjoyed it. It was practically foreplay for him. He thought Josh liked it too, at least a little, based on how his favorite way of shutting Tyler up was to kiss him.

"Is it true you had an affair with Chris Steward?" *Christ, no. He's straight and we're friends. I'm allowed to have male friends and not fuck them.* "How has he taken the news that you're with someone new?" *Where do they come up with this garbage?*

"Do you think you'll be replaced with another actor for *The Golden Key*?" *The Silver Arrow hasn't even gone through the final edits. I think you're counting your casting replacements before they're hatched. At least I hope so.*

"Any comment on your injury? Is it true that you tried to commit suicide?" *It's a good thing I'm not suicidal because I swear to Christ you assholes would be enough to tip anyone over the edge.*

It was nothing but flashing lights and shouted questions until the TSA finally stopped sitting on their thumbs and ushered him through security. Bastards.

Tyler already missed Josh being close by, squeezing his hand or thigh when he tensed up, getting him to relax and pretend that everything was fine. Just being there and being himself. At least Tyler had had the script to distract him while waiting in the airport and on the long flight itself. He'd reread it compulsively and easily memorized the section they wanted him to read through tomorrow with the actors already cast, but he wanted more than to just know the lines. He wanted to own them, for them to come out of his mouth like natural speech.

Tyler was making good progress, and he thought tomorrow would be fine, but he couldn't help but feel the whole thing would've been easier if he'd had Josh next to him. If nothing else, he could have practiced the lines out loud and not just inside his head. Having a hand to hold would have been a nice bonus. Maybe he should've asked Josh to take a few more days of vacation.

Or maybe I could stop being a whiny little bitch and stand on my own two beautifully shod feet.

Tyler looked down at his gray suede boots. They really were fantastic footwear, but far too distinct.

What he needed to make it past the gauntlet no doubt waiting in arrivals was not so much a disguise as camouflage. It took a few different airport shops and kiosks, but he put together an outfit of oversized shorts and t-shirt, flip flops, cheap sunglasses, and the pièce de résistance, a Dodger ball cap. He shoved his stupid blue hair under it, put on the outfit in a bathroom stall, then slipped on a pair of sunglasses and went out through the security checkpoint and into the baggage area where Purvi had agreed to meet him.

She was easy to spot, her long, dark hair with its cherry-red streaks piled loosely on top of her head. Her skin was a few shades darker than its normal warm brown, meaning she'd been sunbathing without sunblock again, despite all his warnings about premature aging and ending up looking like luggage by age thirty. Maybe he could get Josh to put the fear of God and melanoma into her, since the fear of wrinkles wasn't working.

She didn't recognize him until he'd snagged her arm and brought her in for a hug. She smelled like sun and coconut and home. He gave her a tight squeeze. God, he'd missed her.

"Get me out of here," Tyler hissed, keeping his voice low.

"Holy Christ, what the fuck are you wearing?"

"Can we get the hell out of here, Purvi?"

"Sure thing, white boy. You know I live to serve. Kevin's bringing around the Tesla since you won't let me drive it, which I still say is unfair. I'm your best friend, but you'll only let my boyfriend drive your precious baby."

"That's because Kevin is a responsible adult who hasn't wrecked three cars in four years, P."

"Whatever."

Kevin pulled up to the curb and Purvi attempted to get in the passenger seat. "Oh, no." Tyler handed her his bag. "It's my car, I get shotgun."

"Hey, Ty," Kevin said. "Nice outfit. You want to drive? Purvi can take the front and I'll sit in the back."

Tyler reached over and chucked Kevin under the chin. "You are wasted on heterosexuality, sweetheart. Such a gentleman. But, no, I'm too tired to drive and Purvi will live."

"Paws off my man," Purvi said as she got in the back and shut her door.

"Speaking of which, I need to let Josh know I got here safe. He is a fretter." Tyler sent him a quick text. He frowned when Josh said not to call him, that he'd be having an early night. It made sense, but he still felt... what? Disappointed? Thwarted? Maybe Josh needed some space. Or maybe... a dozen scenarios flitted through Tyler's head to explain why Josh didn't want a phone call. Most were ridiculous, but there was one that could almost be plausible.

Tyler: I got home safe.
Ryan: OK.
Tyler: So... what are you up to?
Ryan: I'm busy.
Tyler: With what?
Tyler: Just so.
Tyler: You know.
Tyler: I can keep.
Tyler: This up.
Tyler: All day.
Tyler: If I must.
Ryan: Go away. I said I was busy.
Tyler: You're getting your dick sucked, aren't you?
Ryan: I'm going to block you.

Ryan was probably just working late. Possibly he was working late on Tyler's behalf. He and Patrick both.

Then Tyler remembered Ryan speculating how easily he could win back Josh. He'd said it just to fuck with Tyler, he was fairly sure about that. Ryan wouldn't really make a play for Josh after all these years. Not with a fiancée in one hand and a legal secretary in the other. And even if Ryan did, Josh wouldn't go for it.

Except Josh might, if given the right encouragement. It probably wouldn't even take much. Ryan was what Josh had always wanted. He wouldn't even be disloyal to Tyler because there was nothing between him and Josh but one week of no-strings sex and a non-binding verbal commitment. How could that compete with a six-year relationship and fifteen years of longing?

Tyler: Are you with the boy toy?
Tyler: Or someone else?
Ryan: I'm going to kill you if you don't stop texting me. I will let Patrick help. Go away.

Reading that was like having a weight lifted from his chest. Feeling much better, Tyler slipped his phone back into his pocket. His pleasure had zero to do with Ryan apparently still getting off with Patrick and leaving his doctor alone. Nope. Nothing at all.

"Before my audition tomorrow I need to lose the blue hair."

"Goodbye hipster elf," Kevin said.

"The sooner the better," agreed Tyler.

"I'll see what Sydney can arrange," Purvi said from the back seat. "Leave it to me."

"P, you are a lifesaver. What would I do without you?"

Purvi snorted. "Be sad. Without me, your life would be tragic."

No argument there.

03&0

Monday, September 26th, 1:22 p.m.
Tyler's very quiet house
Burbank, CA

Tyler came home after his reading to an empty house, which shouldn't have come as a surprise. Purvi had gone back to her own apartment to do whatever it was she did there during the day when she wasn't working. She practically lived in his nicest guest room, but she did maintain a separate residence for "sanity and fucking in privacy."

Tyler felt at loose ends. The read had gone well, or so he hoped. The lines had felt natural when he'd said them and everyone had seemed to respond very positively to him, but none of the other actors who were there reading had an anchor in the shape of a teenaged sex video tied to their ankles.

Tyler ran a hand over his newly cropped hair. Sydney had come through for him, as always. She'd arrived at the house early that morning, hours before the audition, to pick out an outfit for him, then taken him to get his hair cut. Sydney always knew the best people for everything and the guy she'd taken him to had been no exception. He'd done a fantastic job, cutting all the blue off and making Tyler's hair look elegant and classic, if very short, rather than leaving him resembling a newly shorn sheep.

His new hairstyle was far more appropriate for the role he'd read for today, that of a painfully shy and awkward college student, than his hipster elf hair would have been. Tyler smiled a little, thinking that if he got this part he'd get to at last play a character that wasn't jailbait. Well, unless you counted Druindar, who was quite old, but also immortal and forever young, so in Tyler's book that didn't count.

Tyler wandered through his house, looking for something to hold his attention and keep him from obsessing about his audition or thinking about a man who was two thousand miles away. Then he gave up and texted Josh, knowing he was still at work and unlikely to respond right away.

Tyler: Just got back from the read through with the casting agent

I miss you.

Tyler: I think it went okay.

I miss you.

Tyler: I know you're at work

I miss you.

Tyler: Talk to you later. Tonight.

It was pathetic. Tyler put his phone down and went to his room to get a swimsuit. He found his tiniest pair of swim briefs, the ones that were neon pink and only just this side of indecent, a gag gift he'd received from Ethan ages ago. He never wore them in public — he barely wore them at all — but today he put them on, along with a gallon of sunblock, and thought about his dermatologist as he rubbed it on his skin. He wondered if Josh would prefer watching the physical gyrations required to get his back covered adequately, or if he'd want to rub it into Tyler's skin himself.

He stood in front of his mirror, his pale skin gleaming wetly, and took a picture to send to Josh. He could say something like: "Look what a good boy I was today. I didn't forget to put on sunblock."

Tyler scowled at his reflection. "You are a huge hopeless idiot," he said to the man looking back at him. The scowling man agreed. *Yeah, we are all kinds of fucked, aren't we?*

Tyler turned his back on the mirror and went to the pool, determined to swim laps until his arms and legs were jelly and his brain turned off for a while.

Instead of counting the laps, as he normally did, Tyler's brain substituted *I'm fine* and *I don't need him* for the even and odd numbers. Tyler had no idea how long he swam or how many laps he managed, but he didn't stop until he'd exhausted himself, then he arched his back and floated on the surface of the water, letting his racing heart slow. Dusk had come and the water was cool but he didn't care. All the swimming in the world wasn't going to fix this problem. He had no idea what to do.

Purvi came out and stood by the edge of the pool. "You planning on getting out any time this century, Aquaman?"

"Maybe."

Purvi sat down and dangled her feet in the water. "What are you planning to do about this whole Josh situation?"

"Not talk about it," Tyler said. "You told me to go off and have gay babies. You are exempt from giving advice now."

"I was drunk. Allowances should be made. So, what's your long-term goal, here? Keep him, or play with him for a while then cut him loose?" Purvi was no good at taking a hint.

Tyler gave in and swam over to her. "I don't know. I'm not even sure he wants to be kept. Or if he does, I don't think he'd want to follow me out here. He doesn't like California much, and he's got his whole life in Illinois. I don't see him giving all that up just to be able to tap my ass on a regular basis. Besides, it's too soon for any of this shit. There's no point discussing it."

Purvi tipped her head to the side. "Of course, it's worth discussing. We always dish about the boys we're fucking. How is this any different?"

Because it's Josh, was Tyler's immediate, unhelpful thought. "It's all fake," he said.

"Is it?" she asked.

Tyler shrugged.

"Okay. Let's cut to the chase. Pretend I'm your fairy godmother and when I wave my wand you get what you want. What do you ask for?"

I want my happily ever after. How dumb is that?

"Him," Tyler said with a sigh. "I know it's fucking stupid, P, but I want him. I just don't know how to get from point a to point b, or if it's even possible."

Purvi tucked a hank of hair behind her ear. "All things are possible. My job is figuring out how to do it. I need to meet him first, though. When can I come out to Chicago? Probably sometime after the wedding, I'm thinking. That'll give me time to wrap up shit here."

"Wrap up what shit? I thought you were on vacation."

Purvi gave him a scornful look. "A PA is never on vacation. Luckily for you I can maintain your online presence while still working on my tan."

"About your tan—"

"I don't want to hear it. I look fabulous." Purvi consulted her phone. "How does Monday the third sound? I can get a flight that arrives late morning, then I can meet this Josh person and see what can be done. You think you can muddle through without me until then?"

"Fuck you. I can manage my own life, thank you so very much."

"Right." She looked unconvinced.

"You're my PA, not my fairy godmother. Bibbity bobbity boo is not going to cut it. I don't even know how he feels about me."

"I thought you said you were pretty sure he was in love with you. Or well on his way in that direction."

"I don't know. Sometimes he'll look at me or say something and I'm just *sure*. Then the next minute, I'm not. I've lost any sense of objectivity. I was hoping you could talk me down, but so far, you're doing a lousy job. You are, in fact, doing the exact opposite. Thanks for nothing."

"Talking you down is not my job. That's Ryan's gig. My job to make sure your life runs like a well-oiled machine. Let me work my magic."

"Whatever." Tyler had no idea what she thought she could accomplish, but clearly being on vacation wasn't good for her because now she was looking for things to do. A bored Purvi was dangerous. He hoisted himself out of the pool, sat beside her, and laid his head on her shoulder.

"Ugh, you're all wet and cold. Get off me."

Tyler ignored her. "I need ice cream."

Purvi rubbed his shoulder. "What you need is to dry off and eat dinner."

"I don't want dinner."

Purvi sighed. "Fine. I think there's Chunky Monkey in the freezer."

Tyler kissed her cheek. "You're the literal best, P."

"And don't you forget it."

෴

Tuesday, September 27th, 7:45 a.m.
Tyler's very vandalized house
Burbank, CA

Tyler had slept poorly the night before and was up at dawn with nothing to do for the day but pack what he wanted to take back with him to Chicago. He ate breakfast with Purvi, who had stayed the night. She left to run errands, saying Tyler could come with her if he wanted, but he wasn't in the mood to deal with people, so instead he decided to go for a swim. He hadn't gone more than the length of the pool and back, though, before Purvi was at the side of the pool trying to get his attention.

"Get out and put some clothes on. You need to see something." The tone of Purvi's voice put Tyler back in that little boat, balanced high on the edge of a wave that would crash and pull him under. His stomach turned over uneasily. Something was very wrong.

"What is it? And I'm wearing a suit. What more do you want?" Tyler climbed the ladder out of the pool and snagged his towel.

"You need to see this," was all she'd say. "Put something on you won't mind being photographed in. The vultures are outside."

"Then maybe you should tell me instead of showing me."

"Someone vandalized the front wall. We need photos and you need to actually see it. I'll try and stand between you and the assholes, though."

"Is it bad?"

Purvi looked uncharacteristically grim. "It's not good."

"Great, just what I needed," Tyler said, then went to get dressed.

Tyler's house was a corner lot surrounded by a tall stuccoed wall. The wall and the gorgeous pool had sold him on the property when he'd bought it several years ago. The only ways in or out were through the main gate and a small security door off to the side that was usually kept locked. Tyler went out his front door and headed toward the side security door, Purvi right behind him. He locked the door behind them and dropped the keys back in his pocket.

"Okay. What am I looking for?"

"It's out front," she said, and led the way.

In bright arterial-red paint, someone had written 'die faggot' in huge letters on one wall to the side of his front gate and 'die cocksucker' on the other. Tyler thought he heard something and turned toward the street. There were photographers taking pictures. Fuck.

"Is this it, or is there more?" Tyler asked. He took out his phone and took pictures of the graffiti.

"I think this is it. Come on. Let's go back in and you can call the cops. Your insurance company, too."

"It's just paint," Tyler said.

"It's not just paint," Purvi said. "That's malice and a threat. We are calling the fucking police, Tyler. We need to get the home phone number changed, too." She told him about the hang-ups she'd been experiencing over the past week.

"And you waited to tell me this why?"

Purvi gave him an irritated look. "I did text you about it. And hey, maybe they aren't related."

Things were spiraling out of control again. Tyler stamped down on the urge to lock himself in his bathroom and cut. That wouldn't help right now, there was too much to do for him to indulge in that right now. He needed to focus. "Okay," he said. "Cops first."

The police came and took their own pictures and took his statement. They asked if he had security cameras trained on the street and he had to confess that he did not.

"Might want to fix that," one of the cops said.

No shit, Sherlock.

"We'll keep an eye on the place for the next few days. Get those guys out there to disperse, too. You sure you've got no idea who did this?"

Tyler shook his head. He didn't think his father was responsible for this. It wasn't his style, and the idea of Michael Koenig caring enough after all these years to come to California and fuck up his wall seemed ludicrous. His first thought had been of David, because this shit was just like him, but he'd heard through David's friends that he'd moved back home years ago. Where, Tyler wasn't sure and didn't care, but it was somewhere back east.

"There's my ex," he said. "This shit is just his style, but he's a long shot. We had a bad breakup and I had to get a restraining order. This was about three years ago and I heard he moved out of state. His name is David Nowak, but I don't think it's him, unless he's moved back. I think it's way more likely that this was some random homophobic asshole."

The cops left, assuring him that they'd look into it. Tyler wasn't going to hold his breath. They weren't going to find the perpetrator unless he walked into the police station and confessed. Still, he'd had to make a report. That taken care of, Purvi made tea and sandwiches and frowned at him until he ate his.

It reminded him of Josh, and an overwhelming feeling of longing filled him. Tyler wanted Josh next to him, hand curled into his or resting on his leg, just sitting there next to him while Tyler dealt with this shit. Stupid. So stupid. But the desire to have Josh with him ached like a sore tooth.

Oh, right. My knight in shining armor, there to save me because I'm oh-so-helpless. Tyler stomped down on his irritation. He didn't want to need Josh. He could fight his own battles, thank you all the same. He did not need his hand held or a shoulder to lean on or any of that bullshit.

But I might want all those things anyway.

That was too damn bad. If wishes were horses and all that jazz. Tyler shook himself and got down to business. He called his insurance company. He called a company to come and paint over his wall. He called his security firm to order and install cameras. He called Ryan, then he called his mother.

"While you're making calls," Purvi said, "call your publicist, too."

"About the graffiti?"

"Nope, I've already talked to Tom about the wall. We've got some ideas about that, social media-wise, so you don't have to worry your pretty little head about it right now. We have that much under control. There's something else he wants to talk to you about, though."

"What?"

"You'd know if your lazy ass ever checked the internet," Purvi said. "Shit's been a-brewing."

The bottom dropped out of Tyler's stomach for the nth time that day. "What shit?"

She gave him a look so chock-full of pity that it made him want to toss something at her head. "Just call him. I don't want to be the bearer of more bad news. I'll be in your office if you need me."

Great. Tyler took a deep breath, then called Tom.

"When are you going back to Illinois?" Tom asked him.

Tyler went blank. It was Tuesday. Purvi hadn't booked him a return ticket yet since he hadn't been sure how long he was going to stay. "I don't know. There are still a few things I need to take care of here. With the house and all."

"Look, you need to either bring the doctor to you or you need to go back to him."

"What?" Tyler asked, lost.

"You should check the internet occasionally," Tom said.

"That's what I pay Purvi for," Tyler groaned. "Tom, just tell me what's up."

"There are pictures of you in O'Hare all by yourself looking extremely upset, all over the fucking internet."

"Um, yeah, I was at the airport. No one ever looks happy at the airport. And there were all these questions, stupid-ass questions, and I needed to get through security. Of course I looked upset."

"Just because you're feeling pissy doesn't mean you get to show it in public. Thanks to your lack of control over your emotions, there's now speculation that you and your boyfriend are having problems and that you coming home without him is a sign of relationship issues. It's all 'trouble in paradise' and 'lover's quarrel' and insinuations that your boyfriend dumped you because of the video or the cutting or both. We have to fix this and we need to do it yesterday."

"Oh, fuck them," Tyler said. "I had to come home to read for a part. Jesus fucking Christ."

"You look pissed-off in the airport photos and you declined to answer any questions. You're supposed to smile and be charming and evasive, Tyler. You know this. I shouldn't have to be having this conversation with you. You're making my job harder than it has to be."

Tyler throttled down his first instinct, which was to start shouting at Tom. He wanted to insist it was all so much bullshit, but this was what he'd signed up for, wasn't it? The price of becoming famous was fame. He knew that, had known it from the start. "Okay, Tom, what do you want me to do?"

"You and the doctor need to be in the same state as soon as possible and I want something spectacular when you're publicly reunited. You got me? Let me know if you're going to Chicago or if he's coming here, and I'll arrange to make sure there are plenty of people to witness and document it. I want something so heartwarming that even the most cynical pap will sigh and wipe away a tear. Are we clear?"

"Like fucking crystal." He hung up with Tom, then made the call he'd been both dreading and looking forward to all day.

വജ്ഞ

Wednesday, September 28th, 6:19 p.m.
O'Hare airport
Chicago, IL

Tyler went to Josh and not the other way around. It was what made sense. Josh had to work, and besides, there was the wedding. Flying Josh out to California at this point would be counterproductive. Even so, there was a bit of Tyler that felt like a dog slinking back to his master after having slipped his leash, and he hated it. At the same time, he resented every minute and mile that separated the two of them. If that wasn't fucked-up he didn't know what was.

Tyler hadn't lost that feeling of being very high up and about to fall with no net below to catch him. His stomach was in his throat, so all he could do on the plane was sip ginger ale and breathe slowly and count. He counted until the numbers ceased to have meaning, then he started counting from scratch all over again.

Tyler thought grimly that he should have given into the urge last night to cut himself, damn Josh and damn his promise. He'd already broken it once, why had he still clung to it last night? One tiny slice, one soothing trickle of blood, and he wouldn't be this tense right now. All the paparazzi Tom had promised him would be waiting for him at O'Hare would see how tense he was and more rumors would fly. No one would believe he was happily in love.

Happily in love. There was an oxymoron for you.

Part of him wanted to go into the airplane bathroom and slice something open, but with what? He didn't even have a pen on him, or nail clippers. Nothing. He wanted to claw himself with his own blunt nails, but instead he gripped his armrest with one hand and sipped ginger ale and counted.

"Don't like flying, do you?" asked his seatmate.

Tyler didn't think the man recognized him. Maybe it was his lack of blue hair, but more likely he was the type of guy who'd never read a celebrity gossip column in his life and had never seen any of Tyler's movies.

Tyler eyed the man seated next to him. He guessed he was most likely an executive of some stripe, based on his suit and tie, which were of decent quality but dull as dishwater. It all screamed vice-president of human relations.

"No, flying doesn't bother me normally. I'm not feeling well." Tyler's tone was not encouraging.

"Sorry to hear that. Going home or visiting?"

Tyler didn't want to talk to this guy, but he didn't want to count anymore, either. It wasn't helping. He wasn't even certain what was making him the most anxious: the "die faggot/die cocksucker" in blood-red paint, Tom's anger at him for forgetting to be professional and knowing full well he'd fucked up, or the realization that been quietly dawning on him over the past few days. Tyler felt like nothing under him was solid, which was apt, seeing as he was in an airplane.

"Both, I guess. I used to live there, but now I'm just visiting."

The man nodded. "I'm going home. I'll miss the Californian weather, that's for sure, but I can't imagine living there." He grinned. "I'm just too Midwestern at heart, I guess. You still have family in Chicago? That's who you're visiting?"

God, would the guy not leave him alone? "My brothers," he said. Then some devil made him add, "And my boyfriend."

"Oh." The guy seemed to think about that for a second. He shook his head with disapproval and Tyler braced himself. "Long-distance relationships are difficult. You think you'll move back or he'll move out to where you live?"

Tyler gaped at the man for a second, then shut his mouth. "Um, I don't know. I'm not sure."

"Well, good luck. I hope you work it out." Then the guy went back to reading his book.

"Thanks," Tyler mumbled. He looked out his window and saw nothing but an endless expanse of thick, white clouds. He sipped his ginger ale. He thought about Josh. He thought about falling.

After they landed and debarked, Tyler walked through the airport feeling like his skin was too tight and wanting to burst out of it. This was how he'd felt when he'd tried out for cheerleading, or the school play, or had his first audition. It was like when the principal said they were calling the police and his parents. It was the same as that morning when Mrs. Roth had marched him to Pastor Steve, or when Tyler had woken up the morning of an audition with a black eye, bruised ribs, and the realization that David would never, ever stop. There was a feeling of things on the cusp, of inevitable change, of uncertainty and hope and fear.

This shouldn't feel so important. It was just an orchestrated photo-op. It was a bit of theater, and Tyler hadn't had performance nerves in years. It was just Josh. There was no reason to feel this unsettled.

What if I fall?

Josh would catch him because that's what he did. He rescued princesses from towers, elves from drowning, princes from nightmares, and actors from censure. He didn't even condone dragon murder.

I don't want...

Not want. Not anymore. The pertinent word now was need.

I don't want to need.

It was too late for that, though.

Tyler took the escalator to the baggage claim area. He looked everywhere and saw only strangers, some hugging, some kissing, some shaking hands or waving. It was loud and chaotic and there were people everywhere.

Then there he was. Tall, but not too tall. Curly dark hair barely tamed. Fluorescent lights glinting off glasses that were perched on his beak of a nose, the one Tyler adored and had wanted to kiss since he was thirteen. Josh. Looking but not seeing, until he did, and then a wide grin spread across his handsome face. Seeing him was so good that it physically hurt.

Heedless of anyone around him, Tyler started running toward him. His fake boyfriend. His Josh. His. There were flashes of light in his peripheral vision, but he ignored them. All he saw was his target and he hurtled into his arms.

As he launched himself at Josh, Tyler's mind continued to fret at him. *What if he doesn't catch me? What if he lets me fall?* There were all those cameras waiting to document it, to snap wonderful pictures of Tyler sprawled in a miserable heap at Josh's feet

But his fake boyfriend had seen and was braced for impact. He took

Tyler's weight like it was nothing. Josh's arms went around Tyler and held him tight while his mouth found Tyler's lips and ate at them like he was starving. There were more flashes of light and questions that he didn't hear and wolf whistles.

Josh put him down and said, "Welcome home. I almost didn't recognize you." He ran his hand over Tyler's short, dark, no-longer-blue hair. "No more elf," he said.

No. Always your elf, and fuck me sideways, I am in so much trouble. We are in so much trouble.

"Not until they film *The Golden Key*," Tyler said. "If that ever happens. And if they still want me in it when the time comes."

"They will." Josh kissed him again. "I missed you."

"Like a rash?"

"Yep."

Welcome home. Only this wasn't his home. Not anymore.

"'Show me the way home, honey.'" Tyler took Josh's hand in his. "Although we should probably pick up my bag first. There are things in it."

"What things?" Josh asked.

Tyler gave Josh his sweetest smile. "Oh, you'll find out."

ଔଔ

Wednesday, September 28th, 11:21 p.m.
Josh's tidy bedroom
Evanston, IL

Tyler was in bed with Josh sleeping and wrapped around him when he got Tom's text.

Tom: Great job, kid. The gossip sites are already eating the pictures up like they're candy. If I didn't know better I'd swear you two were really in love.
Tyler: Thanks. All in a day's work, right?

Tyler put his phone down and closed his eyes. He reveled in the feel of Josh's arms around him and the smell of his skin. The feeling of utter rightness that filled him.

Welcome home.

Right.

Chapter 28
Josh and Tyler Have a Lunch Date

Thursday, September 29th, 11:30 a.m.
A dermatology practice
Evanston, IL

"I want to meet the Hoover vacuum that's sitting in our waiting room," Maria said. "Marisol told everyone, including poor Nik, that he's here to take you to lunch. He took one look at your pretty man out there and turned green." She waggled her finger at him and tsked. "Not nice."

"You suggested it!" Josh snapped, exasperated.

Maria gave Josh a lopsided grin. "True, although I was just kidding, but maybe it's for the best. You didn't even know Nik had a thing for you until I pointed it out, did you?"

"Nope. Had no idea he was gay, didn't care, still don't. Not sure why any of this is my problem."

"We were all tired of waiting for one of you to make a move. His palpable longing for you has been the source of much speculation around here."

"It couldn't be that palpable if I was unaware it existed."

Maria shook her head at him. "You're hopelessly oblivious to things like that. We all had bets going on about when Nik would finally get up the guts to ask you out. We thought about having a side bet to see if you got a clue and either shot him down or asked him out first, but no one wanted to take that bet, so we just picked dates for Nik. I chose the Christmas party." She sighed. "I really had high hopes for that, too. I figured if I got Nik drunk enough, he'd finally go for it."

"You're all awful. I should tell Matt you guys have a betting ring going on. It would serve you right."

"If you do, I'm telling Nik that Tyler's your brother-in-law and not your boyfriend, and that he should ask you out."

"I really wish you wouldn't, Maria."

She put a hand on his arm, her face turning serious. "I was just teasing you. Don't worry, I'm not actually going to encourage him. So, are you going to introduce me to this man of yours or not?"

Josh glanced over Maria's shoulder, past the reception desk, and saw Tyler sitting in the waiting room. He wore a dark-green sweater under a suede jacket, faded jeans, and boots. One leg was casually crossed over the other and he looked like he was rapidly texting someone. Probably Purvi, since those two were electronically joined at the hip.

Josh wasn't quite used to Tyler's hair yet, now very short in addition to being brown. He looked different. More serious, as well as older, and that at least was a bit of a relief. The new style emphasized Tyler's cheekbones and sharp, stubborn chin and made his eyes even more noticeable. Today, thanks to help from the sweater, they were a greenish-gray, and Josh thought he still looked like an elf, just not one of the crack whore or hipster varieties. Tyler had veered into yuppie elf territory, the kind that bought organic toadstools and mystic crystals at the fairy version of Whole Foods.

Josh realized he'd been staring at Tyler for far too long when Maria poked him to regain his attention. He felt his face flush, and led her out to the waiting room. Josh was a little nervous about introducing Maria to Tyler. It occurred to him that no one he'd ever dated had ever come to his work to take him out to lunch, and the last time anyone from work had seen someone he dated was at a Christmas party two years ago. That had been Gabe, he was pretty sure. Or maybe Jon. No, Gabe, because right after the new year they'd broken up when Gabe suggested they move in together and Josh realized he couldn't live with a man who, while extremely handsome, was incapable of carrying on a decent conversation or picking his socks off the floor.

Josh needn't have been concerned about what Maria would think of Tyler or vice versa. Tyler was in full-on charmer mode, and Maria fell under his spell in under thirty seconds of conversation. She held out a hand for him to shake and remarked that he had great skin and questionable taste in boyfriends. Tyler gave her a smile that could have melted a glacier and told her that he'd been trying his best to get into Josh's pants for years, which was a big fat lie, but Maria grinned back at him and agreed that it took a lot to get Josh's attention.

"I had to fall off a dock into a lake to get Josh to notice me," Tyler said. "He saved me from drowning."

"Really? Can't swim?"

"Oh, no, I swim just fine, but when Josh jumped into the lake to rescue me, I had to let him." Tyler looked at Josh and batted his lashes. "You know, so he could give me mouth-to-mouth."

"I did not perform CPR on his melodramatic ass," Josh pointed out, although both Maria and Tyler ignored him.

Maria laughed. "I like him, Josh. Before you guys take off, can I introduce him around? Everyone's dying to meet the first man who's ever come to take our elusive Dr. Rosen to lunch."

Now who's not being nice? Josh wondered.

Tyler raised a brow at Josh. "Really? That's just sad. Just when I think you're maybe not the saddest gay man in existence, you go and prove me wrong yet again." He turned to Maria, who was trying unsuccessfully not to laugh. "I'd love to meet Josh's coworkers," he said, his glacier-melting smile back in place.

Tyler was all gracious charm as Maria dragged him, with an embarrassed Josh in their wake, around the office to meet everyone. Tyler was greeted with interest, amusement, boredom, a frown (Matt, who made noises about staff wasting work time), and finally awkward silence when they got to Nik.

Nik sat and nodded a curt greeting at them. He glared at Tyler, which made Tyler in turn give him a narrow look. Even Maria frowned.

"Are you feeling okay?" she asked Nik.

"I'm fine," Nik bit out. "Just trying to work here."

Maria patted his arm and said, "Well, we'll leave you to it, then."

"Sure. So. How does the whole long-distance relationship thing work, anyway?"

Josh wasn't sure who the question was directed at, but Tyler stiffened, then flashed Nik his brightest smile. "We're still figuring it out."

"I'm sure," Nik said with his own toothy smile. "California to Illinois and back again is one hell of a commute, isn't it?"

Tyler's smile altered and became a little scary, but his voice oozed sweetness. "Luckily, it's not your problem, is it? Since he's my boyfriend and not yours."

Nik blinked and opened his mouth. Josh decided he'd better jump in before actual blood was shed. "If we're going to have any time to eat, we should probably go. Ty, you can meet everyone else another day."

Nik swiveled back to his computer screen, turning his back to them. Tyler's eyes sparked at Josh, a mixture of anger and irritation and something else—hurt, maybe—stark on his face. Then he put his mask back on, along with his most sugary smile. "Sure, no problem. What's good to eat around here?"

Josh led Tyler back toward the waiting room. "There's a place we can walk to that does good sandwiches. That okay?"

"Sure," Tyler said, sounding like more himself but still looking brittle. Josh grabbed his hand and tugged him outside, hoping that a walk on such a nice day would improve Tyler's mood.

There were a few photographers waiting for them outside of the office. Tyler's face lit up like a million lightbulbs as a full-wattage smile sprang across his face. He acknowledged them with a wave of the hand that wasn't holding Josh's in a death grip.

They shouted a few questions that Tyler answered. All super boring shit, in Josh's opinion, which was good, because he wasn't in the mood to watch Tyler tap dance across a minefield of barbed questions and innuendo. Maybe yesterday's kiss was responsible for the softball questions, or maybe they were all too dazzled by Tyler's smile to be mean. Josh didn't know or care, he was just relieved that the reporters seemed to be behaving themselves today. Josh smiled at nothing and no one and hoped he didn't look like too much of an idiot.

One of the reporters caught Josh's eye. Unlike the others, he didn't shout out any questions. He just took picture after picture of Tyler, while looking grim as fuck. Josh tried to make out his features but between the ball cap and aviator sunglasses he was wearing, it was hard to tell what he looked like, other than having a dark, neatly trimmed beard. Josh kept an eye on him and was glad when he eventually turned and left.

After answering what seemed to Josh to be entirely too many questions, the rest seemed to also lose interest and they started packing away their equipment. Tyler and Josh took the opportunity to walk away. Josh thought they might be followed, but for a wonder, they weren't.

"Is it always like that?" he asked.

"For me, no, thank God. Pretty soon someone far more famous than I am will do something interesting, and they'll swarm in that direction and go back to ignoring me. Either that, or the weather will chase them away. If I ever become legit famous, well, yeah, the real stars deal with that shit all the time, but they hire bodyguards. Also, there are ways to avoid most of this bullshit if you really want to. A lot of those pictures you see in the tabloids are staged. Way more than you'd think. Like when Tom sent the photographer up to Blue Lake, or the production he orchestrated at O'Hare. Right now, I've got orders to play it up and not avoid it, hence me allowing the Q and A. My life isn't like this all the time. Honestly, it's not."

Josh wondered which one of them Tyler was trying to convince. He squeezed Tyler's hand and kept his eye out for more people with cameras.

They walked the rest of the way to Josh's favorite deli in silence, but it wasn't a companionable one. Ever since he'd gotten back from California, Tyler seemed preoccupied and mopey, and the events of the past half-hour hadn't improved Tyler's mood any. The cheerful, sunny facade he'd shown the paparazzi was gone and it was replaced with a distracted gloom. There was something on Tyler's mind that was making him unhappy and he didn't want to talk about it.

At least not yet.

Tyler still wanted him, at least physically, so it wasn't that. The sex last night had been intense, to say the least. As for that kiss in the airport...

Tyler had told him ahead of time there would be a bunch of photographers waiting to capture their reunion with pictures and video. Why anyone cared so much about them was beyond Josh, but he was supposed to be playing the role of devoted boyfriend and that's what he was determined to be. Tyler had come flying at him and Josh had caught him and kissed him, simple as that. He hadn't been expecting precisely that level of enthusiasm, but it didn't matter. Tyler had leapt and Josh had grabbed for him and held on for dear life, a chorus of *mine mine mine mine* singing throughout his whole body. He hadn't wanted to let go. There had been no pretending on his part. It had felt all too real, which wasn't a surprise, because he already knew that Tyler had come to mean far more to him than he should. The only true surprise was how Tyler had clung to him like Josh was the only solid thing in his world. His eyes had shone like a brilliant summer sky and Josh had wanted to fall into them forever.

But now, while they sat in the restaurant and waited for their order to be brought out, Tyler's eyes were dark and ominous like the sky before one hell of a thunderstorm. Josh wondered if he was still irritated from his little dick-swinging competition with Nik.

Tyler seemed jealous. Josh knew he shouldn't find it flattering, but he kind of did anyway. Josh didn't think he'd ever had anyone be jealous because of him before. Certainly, never Ryan. And over the intervening years, no one else had, either, no doubt because none of them had ever been around long enough to be given the chance.

Having Tyler gone for the past few days had been sobering. His fake relationship with Tyler felt more real to him than any other relationship that he'd had in the past, including the one with Ryan. Hell, especially that one. The irony was not lost on him.

"I'm glad you're back," Josh said, putting down his sandwich. "I really missed you."

"Did you?" Tyler asked. There was an edge to his tone like he was spoiling for a fight. "Even with that cute nurse waiting in the wings?"

"Yeah, I did," Josh said. He didn't particularly want to fight, especially not about Nik. "I've gotten used to you being around."

That seemed to put a spike in the rising balloon of Tyler's temper, but instead of one of Tyler's wicked grins, or even better, one of his rare, real smiles, he looked wistful. "Have you?"

"Tyler, what the hell is wrong? Please, did I do something? Just tell me."

Tyler looked down at the sandwich he'd barely touched. "Was I in the wrong back there? Yeah, I was pretty rude, but he did start it."

How exactly did one say, "Yes, you were rude but so was he and it was super flattering and I kinda liked it because I want to be yours even though I'm not and I shouldn't like you being jealous over me but I do anyway," without sounding like a needy douche? Josh had no idea, so instead he said, "It's fine. You're fine."

"He started it," groused Tyler, more to himself than to Josh.

"He did start it, but Maria shouldn't have rubbed you in his face, even if I think she was doing it in a 'cruel to be kind' kind of way. Anyway, no harm done. Blood wasn't drawn."

Tyler huffed. "I'm pretty sure if you crooked your finger he'd be yours." Tyler picked at his sandwich, pulling off the crust.

"Why the hell would I want to do that? I'm not interested."

Tyler shrugged. "Among other things, proximity. It's doubtful your nurse lives as far away from you as I do. As he so helpfully pointed out, it is one hell of a commute."

Josh didn't want to think about that right now. "He's not my nurse and you're here now," he said.

"Yes. For now."

"Do you want to go back already? Is that it? Are you planning on going back to LA right after the wedding?" Josh felt a stab of panic. Not yet. It was too soon, wasn't it? It had to be too soon.

Tyler reached out and grabbed his hand and squeezed it hard. "Hey, calm down. I'm not going anywhere. Not yet. I still need you to be my knight in shining armor, okay? Keep on saving the day for me. You aren't getting off the hook that easily."

A wave of relief crashed through Josh. "Then why did you say you were here just for now?" As soon as the words were out of his mouth he realized how stupid they were, and he wanted to take them back.

"I don't live here," Tyler said slowly. "Not anymore."

"I know," Josh said, and he did. He just found it convenient to forget about that little detail.

"I can't stay here forever. Not if I want to work."

"I know," Josh repeated, and wished he didn't.

Tyler smiled at him and it was one of the real ones. "But I'm here now. Okay?"

"Yeah, of course." It didn't feel okay.

"I warned you there'd be heartbreak and tears," Tyler said, "but not today. I'm sorry I've ruined lunch. I'm in a mood, and now you're in one, too."

Josh leaned forward, cupped a hand behind Tyler's neck, and brought him forward for a quick kiss. He wanted to blurt out something insane and embarrassing like, "Please stay forever, don't leave me," but bit it back. This wasn't the time or the place, and he wasn't at all sure his feelings would be appreciated, let alone returned. Been there, done that, bought the t-shirt, wore it for fifteen years. Josh let the words stay safely lodged in his throat.

"It's okay," Josh said. "Really."

Tyler gave him a searching look. "Are you sure?"

"Yeah. Eat your damned sandwich. I have to go back to work soon."

Tyler looked down at his crustless sandwich and another smile slid onto his face, this one full of mockery, whether for Josh or himself or both of them was unclear. "Yes, sir," Tyler said, then picked it up and took a bite.

○ॐ○

Thursday, September 29th, 10:46 p.m.
Josh's perfectly adequate condo
Evanston, IL

Later that evening, after Josh had come home from work and eaten the dinner Tyler had cooked (*did you eat anything besides sandwiches while I was gone?*), after they sat on the couch watching Netflix (*no, seriously, put down your phone and watch this with me*), and after they'd gone to bed and done absolutely filthy things to each other using the various toys Tyler had brought back with him (*I knew you'd like that one, you kinky old man*), Tyler lay sprawled on top of Josh and seemed disinclined to move, and Josh was disinclined to move him.

"My coworkers liked you," Josh said, running his hand back and forth across Tyler's nape, loving the velvety feel of the short hair under his fingers. "At least the ones who got to meet you. The others were jealous and want me to bring you back. You are popular."

"Mmm?"

"Well, except with Matt. He gave me a lecture about time management when I got back from lunch. Dickhead."

"Who's Matt?"

"The office manager. Middle-aged guy with the terrible mustache."

"Oh." Tyler stretched sleepily, parts of his anatomy rubbing deliciously along Josh's. "I'm pretty sure Nate wasn't crazy about me, either."

"Nik."

"Whoever." Tyler's voice sharpened.

"You know, it's funny. Last week Dad sent me an email asking who I was taking to the wedding and suggesting I should ask one of the nurses in the office to be my plus one. Which is sexist as hell, by the way, because I know that was Dad's shorthand for 'bring a woman for a change', and there's a female doctor in the practice and two male nurses. Anyway, I thought that if I wasn't going to be there with you it would have served my dad right if I'd bribed one of the male nurses to be my date."

Tyler frowned. "I don't think it would have taken much bribery to get Neil to be your date."

Josh snorted. "Nik."

"You're enjoying this, aren't you?"

"Yeah, kinda."

"And your point is?" Tyler was starting to get irritated. Josh could tell by how his body stiffened.

"My point is that I probably would've asked Gary, who is happily married. I doubt he would've minded a night away from his twin toddlers. I would have only asked Nik if Gary said no."

"Oh," Tyler said. "Why?"

"Because I've known Gary for years, and Nik has only been with the office a few months and I've barely spoken with him about anything not relating to work. I don't know him. I had no idea he was gay, let alone had some sort of thing for me, until two days ago."

Tyler sat up and straddled Josh so he could look down into his face. "Your gaydar sucks."

"I don't need to use it very much. Mostly I figure out a guy is gay when he hits on me. Sometimes not even then, according to Maria. She says I'm hopelessly oblivious."

Tyler seemed to consider that. "I don't think you're really oblivious, you're selectively observant. You see the people and things that are important to you. Everything else is just background noise that you often ignore."

"So, I'm not hopeless?"

Tyler smiled and it was sweet and real and it made Josh's heart ache to see it. "You? Never."

"I see you."

Tyler leaned down and kissed Josh, his lips as sweet as his smile. "Maybe. A little." Then he kissed Josh again.

Later, while trying to sleep, Josh wondered what Tyler had meant. What was he not seeing? His mind worried at that thought as he drifted off, waking only when Tyler thrashed with the panic of his recurring nightmare.

"I've got you, I'm here," he said until Tyler calmed and relaxed again.

I see you, he thought. *I do.* But he worried that Tyler didn't think so.

Chapter 29
Tyler and the L-Word

Friday, September 30th, 7:25 p.m.
Alinea restaurant
Chicago, IL

Tyler: [attachment] Here. Put this on Instagram or whatever it is you do.
Purvi: Is that supposed to be your dinner?
Tyler: Yes
Purvi: Are you sure it's food?
Tyler: It's molecular gastronomy, duh. How do you not know that?
Purvi: I was making a thing called a joke. People with a sense of humor find them funny.
Tyler: Oh, that was a JOKE. Newsflash, if you have to explain it, it wasn't funny.
Purvi: Yeah. So, let's discuss why you're being such a little bitch lately. I suspect the answer has four letters and starts with a J.
Tyler: Let's not.
Purvi: Bitch.

"This is some pretentious bullshit right here," Josh whispered in Tyler's ear. "Not the food." He looked down at his plate, which was a sheet of glass covered with things that were pretty and presumably edible and only vaguely resembled food. "Well, the food, too. A little." Josh popped a mysterious gelatinous cube of something into his mouth. "Oh, man. That's amazing. But my point stands."

"That's my father for you," Tyler said. He was glad he'd been seated as far away from his father as was physically possible. He couldn't blow off the rehearsal dinner, but he could do everything in his power to avoid his dad.

"Alinea for twelve people. Really? Who the hell hosts a wedding rehearsal dinner for twelve at Alinea? This has got to be costing several thousand dollars. For one meal!" Josh sounded personally affronted.

"Plus wine. You should drink yours. You sound like you need it. Good. Now drink some more." The one being a little bitch tonight was Josh, for whatever reason. Purvi had no idea what she was talking about. "You sound like Rachel, you know. Booking this place was definitely not her idea."

Josh glanced at his sister, who sat next to him, animatedly discussing some sort of wedding issue with their mother. "She seems happy enough. Right now, that's all that matters." He picked up his wineglass and finished it off.

"Better?"

"It's such a stupid expense, but it's not my wedding and I'm not paying for it and yes, I think the wine is helping. Thank you." He smiled at the sommelier who came to pour more.

Tyler prodded something purple and crystalline on his glass sheet. "According to Dad it's the best restaurant in Chicago, therefore this is where we had to eat."

"What are you two whispering about over there?" asked Tyler's mother.

She sat across from him and Josh's parents sat next to her, Josh's mother gushing excitedly to Rachel about flowers or something. Josh's father divided his time between looking at his food with suspicion and looking at Tyler and Josh with barely concealed irritation. That man was not happy about how close Tyler was sitting to his son. Not happy at all. It made Tyler want to cuddle closer, which he knew was petty, but he couldn't help it. Tyler looked back at Dan Rosen and smiled. So. *I see you and you see me, and neither of us likes the other.* Tyler raised an eyebrow at him, just to show he wasn't cowed, then turned back toward his mother.

"Nothing, really. Just talking about the restaurant. Josh thinks it's a bit much." Josh smacked his leg under the table.

Cynthia rolled her eyes in a way that made Tyler grin. "Typical Peter," she said, and went back to studying her own sheet of glass before trying something squishy and green. She hummed in pleasure. "That one was really good."

To accommodate the size of their party, the restaurant had put a few tables together, half of the party on banquette seating and the other half in chairs across from them. Tyler and Josh were on the banquette side, with Tyler on the end and snuggled into Josh very close so they could talk without being overheard. Much. The entire party consisted of the bride and groom, both sets of parents, the three groomsmen, and the three bridesmaids. There was no Stephanie, but Ryan didn't seem particularly put out about it.

"Speaking of your father, he doesn't look well," Josh pointed out.

"No," Tyler said. "He looks like shit on toast." He ate the purple crystalline thing, which tasted of bacon and chilies and sugar. Tyler wondered if his dad was sick, then decided he didn't particularly care. He just needed to make it through tonight and tomorrow, and then he wouldn't have to be in the same room as his father until it was time for Ryan to get married.

Tyler glanced at his watch. Ryan said the limo he'd arranged to drive them and several of Brad's friends around for his bachelor's party was picking them up at the restaurant at nine. It was eight thirty. Tyler ate a few more things and drank more wine. He checked his phone and saw Purvi had sent another message. She was relentless tonight, damn her.

Purvi: Are you upset because you're still not sure if Dr. McDreamy is in love with you?

Tyler blanked his phone's screen and hoped Josh hadn't read that last text over his shoulder. In New York things had seemed so clear, but over the past week Tyler had become less certain. Josh was fond of him, yes. He desired Tyler, no doubt about that. But beyond that, he didn't know, maybe because Josh seemed far too serene and calm to be in love. Whatever he felt for Tyler, it wasn't the maelstrom that Tyler was currently experiencing. He wanted to stick his feelings for Josh back in the box he'd stuffed them into years ago, when he'd given up his crush as a bad idea. His emotions weren't cooperating, though, and it was making him grumpy.

Tyler: No. I don't think that's a problem. I think I might have been wrong there. You should cancel your ticket. You don't need to come.
Purvi: Fuck that. You're in dire need of my services. I want the old Tyler back. This new version is irritating. More irritating, I mean.
Tyler: I know you can't see it but I'm flipping you off so hard right now.

Tyler felt Josh's hand on his thigh, giving his leg a quick squeeze then rubbing back and forth. "It'll be time to leave soon," Josh said. "It's almost nine." He laced his fingers with Tyler's.

"Okay," Tyler said and looked up. Both of their fathers were staring at them. Tyler's father looked disgusted. He started to say something, but Ryan distracted him. Josh's father had a harder to read expression. He wasn't pleased, though, that much was clear. He frowned, and Tyler thought there was a warning in his eyes. A warning about what, though, was anyone's guess. Tyler imagined it was something along the lines of "stop corrupting my son, you little faggot." Or maybe he was projecting again.

Tyler: About to head out for Brad's bachelor's party. Maybe obscene amounts of alcohol will improve my mood.
Purvi: At this point I will take drunk Tyler over whatever the hell you are now.
Purvi: And that's saying something because drunk Tyler is a huge pain in the ass.
Tyler: I hate you
Purvi: You're just saying that to make me feel better.

CR80

Friday, September 30th, 10:30 p.m.
The Admiral Theater
Chicago, IL

Purvi: What's your damage? You're still all Eeyore mopey and shit. You don't seem to be having fun yet.
Tyler: Thanks for noticing.
Purvi: Cute.
Purvi: You need to drink more.
Tyler: I need to drink, period. This place doesn't serve alcohol.
Purvi: Titties and no alcohol. You poor boy.
Tyler: Tell me about it. If we don't leave to go to a bar soon, I may take a human life. Probably a stripper's.
Purvi: I'm pretty sure even Ryan and Dr. McDreamy couldn't save you from a stripper murder charge. Please refrain.
Tyler: We'll see.

Tyler glanced up from his phone and saw yet another stripper slink up to Josh, looking to give him a lap dance. Tyler caught her eye and shook his head. She frowned and moved like she was going to go for it anyway. She probably thought he was trying to cockblock her mark, which he sort of was, because her mark's cock belonged to him.

Wait. That didn't sound right, even in his head.

Okay, so it didn't belong to him, per se, but Tyler did have a proprietary interest in it. Not that any of the women here had a chance, Tyler did know that. Still. It was the principle of the thing.

It occurred to Tyler that once one started justifying one's actions with the phrase "it's the principle of the thing" that things had gone seriously sideways.

It wouldn't even be a problem except Sir Chivalry didn't have it in him to scowl at the girls to make them go away, and unlike Tyler, it wasn't screamingly obvious that he was gay and thus not up, so to speak, for a rather expensive and entirely unnecessary personal performance. The girls at the strip club had avoided Tyler like the plague the whole miserable time they'd been in the place. Josh, not so much. They also were avoiding Ryan, although in his case it was probably because of the dark and forbidding look on his face, like he was some sort of highly repressed Puritan minister bent on burning slutty witches at the stake, rather than him setting off any gaydar alarm bells.

At least the rest of the guys at Brad's bachelor party, including the groom-to-be, seemed to be having a great time. It wasn't their fault that two of the groomsmen batted for the other team and the third seemed to be leaning heavily in that direction as well. Tyler just wished the girls would leave Josh alone. For Josh's sake, of course, because he was way too nice to tell them they were barking up the wrong tree and was leaving it to Tyler to chase them away.

Tyler slanted another look Josh's way. He sat there, looking politely bored, but there was an underlying tension there that Tyler, if no one else, could sense. His body was in the club but his mind was a million miles away, thinking God-knew-what. For all Tyler could tell, Josh was cataloging skin diseases alphabetically in his head to pass the time. He seemed unaware of the woman stalking him.

This latest one was either bolder or more desperate than the rest, and ignored Tyler. She slithered closer to Josh, and Tyler had to restrain himself from doing something mental like scratching her eyes out. Instead he stood, and, being very careful to keep his hands clasped behind his back, leaned close enough to her so she could hear him over the loud music playing in the club. "Go away. Now."

She swiveled to look at him. It didn't help Tyler's temper any that in her occupationally appropriate stripper heels she was at least three inches taller than he was. There must have been something in his expression that was convincing, though, because she scuttled off without another backward glance like her shitty extensions were on fire.

Josh yanked on him and Tyler fell into his lap. "You need to stop scaring the young ladies," he said in Tyler's ear. "You're going to get us thrown out."

Good, he thought. Brad was going to owe him big time for making him come to see a bunch of female strippers. If it had only been that, it would have been fine. Not his thing, obviously, but he could tolerate it for a few hours. No, he drew the line at them all trying to mack on his boyfriend.

No, not my boyfriend. Fake boyfriend. Only pretend. I keep forgetting that, somehow.

Yes, because of that statue in the Met. Yes, because Josh had called Tyler amazing and brave. Yes, because he said, "I see you" and maybe, just maybe, he did. Tyler felt there had to be something more than pretense between them.

There doesn't have to be jack shit. Wanting something doesn't make it so. I know that. I've known that my whole fucking life.

There on Josh's lap in the middle of a strip club, Tyler felt paralyzed with indecision. He wanted to be a star, to win awards and make movies that were so good people still wanted to watch them fifty years from now, even if he knew the chances of that coming true were slim in the extreme. In reality, he'd be lucky to land a string of small supporting roles long enough to justifiably call it a career, and he wouldn't even have Josh by his side, his biggest fan no matter how insignificant he was. At the same time, he wanted to chuck it all and be Josh's stupid little disgustingly domestic house husband, even if he would end up bitter and miserable and always wonder "what if."

It was fucked-up and wrong any way he looked at it. He wanted too many conflicting things: fame, obscurity, legitimacy, anonymity, recognition, love. He wanted that last one most of all and despised how much he wanted it.

I need a do-over. One fucking ginormous do-over. Maybe starting from birth.

Tyler started to slide off Josh's lap but Josh stopped him. "Wait. Why do you keep chasing off the dancers?" Josh asked the question so only Tyler could hear it, his lips skimming the shell of Tyler's ear.

"Oh, I'm sorry. Did you decide that maybe you do like girls after all? Your parents will be thrilled when you bring home Chrystal." Tyler tried to wiggle out of the arms holding him and got nowhere. Part of Tyler clamored to thrash free, throwing sharp elbows and balled fists into Josh to escape. The other part relished being right where he was and wanted to melt into the man holding him. Unable to choose a course of action, Tyler held himself rigidly still. "You should let me go."

"Not until I get my answer."

Tyler stared straight ahead and said nothing. Josh had to know, he just wanted Tyler to say it, although Tyler was fucked if he knew why. He was also fucked before he'd sit here, on Josh's lap, and confess out loud that he was feeling jealous of a bunch of strippers that weren't even the right gender.

"It's not like they're allowed to touch," Josh's lips caressed his ear, then bit it. "It's all harmless, Ty. You have to know that."

Josh's condescending tone rubbed Tyler raw. "I'm sorry I spoiled your fun," he snarled. He tried again to wriggle free, but not hard enough because he remained on Josh's lap. "You should've stopped me sooner."

Josh's lips traced the ridges of his ear. "But watching you defend me from the scary girls is so hot," Josh breathed. "My hero. My knight in shining armor. If we look around, we might find a dragon you can murder."

"You are an asshole," Tyler said, not caring who heard him. "A gigantic, hemorrhoid-covered asshole."

Tyler didn't hear Josh laugh so much as he felt it. "Okay, let's stop playing, then. This should do the trick." Josh cupped Tyler's face and kissed him, his lips and tongue saying what Tyler had been telling the girls all night: "hands off, this one is mine."

Josh lifted his head and released Tyler. Dismissed, he went and sat back in his chair next to Josh with what even he recognized was a dramatic and petulant flounce. Ryan shot him a disapproving frown. Josh reached over and rubbed the back of Tyler's neck. The hand seemed to say, "Stop worrying, calm down, chill out, feel my hand, I'm here. Everything's fine. Just fine."

Doubtful. Really fucking doubtful.

Tyler picked up his phone and saw there were more texts from Purvi.

Purvi: Well?
Purvi: Do I need to come early and stage some sort of intervention?
Tyler: Go away and bother your latest project. Is he still straight? You could work on that.
Purvi: Tsk tsk. That was a pretty low blow. You're in a bad way, aren't you?

Josh's thumb caressed along his nape. Tyler tried not to shiver and failed.

Purvi: This isn't like you.
Tyler: I KNOW!
Purvi: OK
Tyler: OK, what?
Purvi: OK, you have two choices.
Tyler: Go on...
Purvi: Either you tell him or I will.
Tyler: YOU WOULDN'T
Purvi: Just try me
Tyler: I am firing your ass. Effective immediately.

Purvi: Right.
Tyler: I'm not kidding
Purvi: Right
Tyler: What if this is David all over again? The last time I was this messed up was when I was falling for his psycho ass.

There was a significant pause, then Ryan's phone rang. He stood up and walked away, the phone held to his ear.

Tyler: Purvi?
Tyler: Did you just call my brother, you traitor?

Ryan came back several minutes later, looking harassed. He tapped Tyler's shoulder and indicated he wanted Tyler to go with him. He stood up then glanced back to Josh. Josh smiled at him and flapped his hand, shooing Tyler away. Tyler hesitated a second, then followed his brother outside.

Ryan leaned against the side of the building. "I ordered a cab for you and Josh," he said.

"Why?"

"Your PA called me and asked what was going on because you are, in her words, acting all crazy pants. Also, you and Josh have got this 'get a room' vibe going on. It's hard to watch. Go back to Josh's place. Fix whatever's wrong with you, and fix it tonight. I won't have you and your big gay drama disrupting the wedding tomorrow."

"I swear to God I'm going to fire Purvi's ass."

"No, you won't," Ryan said.

"The hell I won't. And you have some nerve to bitch at me about my big gay drama since you're engaged to a woman and fucking a man."

"This isn't about me," Ryan said through gritted teeth. "This is about you and Josh making out in a strip club because you're so jealous of anyone who even looks at him that you can barely see straight!"

Tyler felt like he'd been slapped. He rocked backward. "You are not going to stand there and lecture me about Josh. You, of all people."

"Yeah, I think I am."

"Don't." Tyler started to walk back into the club. "You lost that right fifteen years ago."

"You should tell him how you feel," said Ryan so softly Tyler barely heard him. He swiveled to stare at his brother.

"What?" It came out sounding breathless, like Tyler had fallen and knocked the air out of his lungs. "Oh, that is *rich* coming from you, Ryan. Please, do go on about discussing my feelings, because that's something you know *so* much about."

Ryan winced and it made Tyler viciously glad.

"I'll admit that I may have handled things badly with Josh," Ryan said. He looked away. "You know how Dad was. Is. And Josh was so convenient for me. He kept our secret. He let me..." Ryan cleared his throat. "I took advantage of him. For a long time."

"You do know you're saying this to the wrong person, right?"

Ryan ignored that. *Typical, Ryan. Ignore what you don't want to hear or see.* It was the Chadwick way.

"Take Josh and go and make up your mind what you want," Ryan said.

"I want the impossible," Tyler said flatly, "so what's the fucking point?"

"God, stop being so dramatic. Have an actual conversation with him."

Tyler put his hands on his hips. "And what, exactly, should we talk about? Since you're apparently an expert now. Do tell."

Ryan eyed him coolly. "You're not stupid and I'm not blind. You know. You've known since you came back from New York, but this has been a long time coming. A hell of a long time."

Tyler opened his mouth, but nothing came out. Ryan couldn't know. It wasn't possible. He shook his head in denial.

"Yeah," Ryan said. "Ten years long, I think, and so does Brad."

Brad. Of course, Brad had blabbed about his little teenaged crush to Ryan. That made so much more sense than Ryan figuring it out on his own, but it didn't make Tyler one bit less angry, and so he lashed out.

"Chadwicks don't discuss things, or have you forgotten? How are things going with you and that kid you're fucking? You want to discuss that?"

Ryan threw up his hands in disgust. "Fine. I tried to help, but never mind. Don't show up at the wedding tomorrow acting like you are right now. I don't care what you have to do, but this ends tonight one way or the other."

"Or?"

"Or we'll just see if I could get Josh back." Ryan smiled at him like a shark.

"No, you wouldn't. You're just saying that to piss me off." Tyler wished his voice sounded more certain.

Ryan shrugged. "Or you could stop acting like a little baby."

"Fuck you," Tyler said, but absently. *I'm afraid,* he thought, and that was the lowering truth. Chadwicks didn't talk about things and the real reason, deep down, was that they were cowards.

And, fuck me, I am so afraid.

Tyler thought of Ethan, who'd wanted his love because he'd thought it meant he had someone who would always take care of him. And before him, David, who'd used Tyler's love like a rope to restrain and bind him.

Josh wasn't either Ethan or David, or any of the others who had come before, always too much of this or too little of that. Josh felt right, Goldilocks right, so right that it terrified Tyler. He was like a deer caught in oncoming headlights, dazzled out of his mind and braced for the inevitable impact, unable to move even if it meant saving himself.

The taxi pulled up to the curb. "I'll go get Josh," Ryan said, but it turned out not to be necessary.

"I came out to see if Tyler needed me. Were you going to leave without me, Ty?" Josh's lips curved and he looked so young in the soft peach glow of the sodium arc street lights that Tyler's breath caught. He could have been twenty-five and Tyler sixteen, still mostly innocent, still mostly untouched.

Only those years had happened. They had molded and warped him into what he was now, this man standing here on this sidewalk, hobbled by fear but still hopeful. Even after everything, still hopeful.

"No," Tyler said, his heart thumping wildly. "Let's go home."

ಞ

Saturday, October 1st, 1:21 a.m.
Josh's tidy bedroom
Evanston, IL

Tyler was curled into a tight ball and Josh's body curved around him.

"Stop pretending you're asleep," Josh whispered near his ear. "I know you're not. That was fun. Don't get me wrong. A lot of fun. But at some point, you need to acknowledge that sex won't fix your problems."

"Oh, and cleaning fixes yours?" Tyler both felt and sounded snarly. All he wanted to do was fall asleep, but if acrobatic sex hadn't tired him out enough to shut his brain off, nothing short of a hammer blow to the head would at this point.

Or bleeding. Bleeding always works.

No. Fuck that. Not now, not tonight. Perhaps not ever again.

You know it's only a matter of time.

Tyler wished that voice in his head would shut up, but he knew it wouldn't.

Josh sighed heavily, his warm breath caressing the back of Tyler's head. "No, it doesn't, but I didn't just wash all my windows or reorganize my pantry. I did, however, bring you home, where you practically attacked me and then begged me to fuck you until you couldn't see straight."

"Are you complaining? You seemed pretty into it at the time, or did I imagine the huge erection in my ass?"

Josh touched his shoulder. "No, I'm not complaining. But I think we need to talk."

Tyler's pulse picked up. "We should?"

"Yeah."

"Is this when you announce that you're leaving me for Ramon, the pool boy?" Tyler wanted to laugh but was afraid it might sound like he felt: ugly and jagged and frightened.

"I don't know any pool boys named Ramon."

"What about a nurse named Nik?"

Josh let out a soft chuckle. "You need to stop obsessing about Nik."

Tyler wasn't obsessed with Nik, he was concerned, and rightfully so. Nik wanted Josh and Nik lived here. When Tyler left, which he had to at some point, there Nik would be, waiting to swoop in and comfort a handsome, lonely doctor.

Not that Tyler should care. That he cared at all was the problem.

"Why do we need to talk?" In Tyler's experience, nothing good ever came from that announcement.

"You're not happy." But it sounded to Tyler like Josh wasn't happy. Fuck. Here it was, the beginning of the end. Heartbreak and tears, just like he'd predicted. Tyler hadn't thought it would come this soon and he was suddenly, profoundly grateful that he hadn't opened his big fat mouth and let that dangerous L-word fall out. It would've made everything so much worse.

"It's hard to be happy when your life is falling apart," Tyler said.

"Is it, though?"

Tyler had his back to Josh but he could picture his brows raised, the sincere concern evident in his eyes. Tyler wanted to turn on the light and flip around so he could see it, but he was worried it wouldn't be there after all. That instead he would see calm indifference, so he stayed where he was, in the dark, face hidden under his arm.

"Threesome video, remember?" Tyler said. "My career possibly in the toilet. Half the world has seen me naked and fucked by two guys. Oh, and…" Tyler stopped. He hadn't told Josh about the graffiti and this seemed like a bad time to bring up the oversight. "… you know. My life is a mess right now."

Josh ran a hand down Tyler's shoulder, then rubbed back and forth across the hair on Tyler's forearm. "No, it's not. You just had an audition. Tom thinks things are going well. Alicia is still your agent. The studio still wants you to do the promotion for the movie next month. Your career is fine, so tell me what's wrong."

"It's nothing," Tyler insisted. *You're driving me crazy, that's all. No big deal. Nothing to see here. Move along.*

"You've been moody and short-tempered since you came back from California. I know you don't want to be here, back in Illinois."

"I want to be here about as much as you want to be in LA," Tyler shot back. "I think we're pretty much even, there."

"Tom said we're supposed to stay together," Josh said, his voice even and measured, the opposite of Tyler's surly snarl. "He called me while you were in California and read me the riot act for dropping you off at O'Hare like I did. I have more vacation time at work. If you need to go home, I think I could swing maybe a month off, although it won't make me popular with my partners. And maybe a month is all you'll need, anyway. Like I said, things have been going okay for you. Well, except for the airport thing, but I think we overcame that just fine. I don't think it's impossible that things could stabilize for you within in a month. Enough for me to no longer be necessary 24/7. I can be available for public appearances if you still need me."

He was being so reasonable, so nice, that it made Tyler grind his teeth. No, he didn't want a paltry month, no matter how logical Josh made it sound. "I don't have to go home yet," Tyler said. "Like I told you yesterday, being here instead of LA is in my best interests, at least for now."

"For how long?" Josh asked.

Josh was already looking forward to being free. Tyler had known it would happen, had warned everyone, including Josh, that he would hate being in the spotlight, would hate everything associated with being Tyler's boyfriend. Fake boyfriend. Whatever. Besides, Josh had told Tyler he didn't do attached. Tyler hadn't believed him at the time. He'd thought Josh was fooling himself.

I guess the only one fooling himself was me.

"Tyler, for how long?"

"I don't *know.*" The words came out thick with frustration and anger. He wanted to be left alone. First Purvi, then Ryan, now Josh. They kept pushing him and pushing him and he wanted to explode. "Fix whatever's wrong with you," Ryan had said, like he had the first clue how to do that.

"What are we doing?" Josh asked.

"Pretending?"

Josh flopped onto his back, moving away from Tyler. "I'm sick of pretending. It's too hard." He sounded lost and tired and done. Done with all the hassles, done with the arrangement, done with Tyler.

Tyler's chest ached. That was almost word for word what Ethan had said to him the night they'd broken up. He turned so that he lay on his other side, facing Josh. "What do you want to do about it?"

"I want to stop. Can we just stop?"

Had anything hurt this much before? The brand on his leg, maybe. This was like a knife cutting and twisting through Tyler. "Stop? I... okay, sure, I guess. Now? Do you want me to leave?" He could call Ryan, he supposed. Ryan would take him in. Hopefully he wasn't too busy fucking his boy toy to answer his phone. Tyler could get a hotel room, except there was Oliver. He was going to have to find a cat-friendly hotel at one a.m. Tyler realized that he was edging toward panic and started to count. Ryan would take him and Oliver. Of course he would.

Josh tilted his head to look at Tyler. "Are you all right?" After Tyler's tight nod he went on, "Why would I want you to leave?"

"Because if you're not going to be my fake boyfriend, then why am I here?"

Josh was quiet.

Oh, for fuck's sake. Tyler turned on the bedside lamp, squinted in the sudden flare of light, and looked down into Josh's face. "If I'm not your fake boyfriend, then what am I to you?" He didn't really want to hear the answer — a burden, a no-longer-convenient fuck, an unwanted obligation — but he still needed Josh to say it out loud. It would be better than this choking uncertainty.

Josh took a deep breath. He held it for a long time with his eyes screwed shut, then opened them as he let the breath out. "I told myself I wasn't going to do this. Not ever again. But here I am anyway. Funny."

"What's funny, Josh?" Anxiety twined with dread coiled inside Tyler.

"Nothing. This the last time, I swear to God. I am never doing this ever again."

"Doing what, dammit?"

"This. I want to be with you, Tyler. I know I'm probably not what you're looking for and we're just together because I was there when you needed someone, but I really like you. I like you a lot and it's killing me that I'm pretending to belong to you but I don't. Not really. And if you tell me that I've gotten it all wrong then that's it. I... I'll stick around as long as you need me, but we need stop *this*. No more sex, no more sleeping together. I thought I could be detached, that I could divorce what I feel from this act that I agreed to, but I can't. Not anymore. It's too hard for me to pretend like you're everything to me in public and nothing but a willing body in private, because it isn't true and hasn't been for a while. I don't think I'm alone in how I feel, but acting is your thing and I'm not always good at reading people, so if it turns out that I'm nothing but a handy prop, then we will literally just be friends, okay? And I refuse to pine for your skinny ass for fifteen years, just so you know. I'm through with that, too. I'll find a way to get past this. But not with Nik, because he really doesn't do it for me."

Tyler stared down at Josh, trying to make sure he'd heard the words and processed them correctly.

"Say something. Anything. Tyler?" Josh looked at him, hope and fear naked in his expression.

All the impossibilities of a real relationship with Josh flew through Tyler's head, playing on the screen of his mind in full Technicolor. All the good and bad scenarios he'd come up with over the past week. Could this work? Was it possible?

Maybe. Maybe was such a shitty, selfish word. Maybe promised everything and so rarely delivered, but Tyler had built his entire life on maybes. This was just one more.

"Okay, ignoring that that was the craziest thing I've ever heard, am I right in thinking that you want an actual non-fake relationship with me?" Tyler asked.

"Yes?"

"Are you sure?" Josh hadn't sounded sure.

A smile broke out on Josh's face and he catapulted from handsome to breathtaking. Hollywood couldn't have conjured a more perfect hero. "Yeah, Tyler. Be my prince, my fairy tale, my happily ever after."

Tyler sat up and hugged his legs, grateful for the pajama pants he'd slipped on after they'd had sex. This was hard enough without being naked as well. "You know I'm difficult, Josh. My issues have issues. I'm not a fairy tale, I'm not your Prince Charming, and I'm not nice. I can't promise you happiness, let alone happily ever after."

Josh pulled Tyler's legs down, then straddled him with one knee on either side of Tyler's hips. He cupped Tyler's face, holding him like he was delicate and fragile and precious. "You're difficult and you have issues. I'm good with messes, though. You know that. And if you can't promise me happily ever after I'll take just ever after, as long as I get you along with it."

Tyler snorted, torn between exasperation and a desperate longing to have his cake and eat it, too.

Josh went on. "I tried not to fall for you, but you didn't make it easy, and now here we are. No, I'm not sure this is a good idea, but please jump off this cliff with me."

"It's supposed to be a relationship, Josh, not a suicide pact."

Josh let out a bark of laughter. "God, I love you," he said, then flinched. His entire face flushed bright red and he stilled. "I mean…"

Tyler thought his heart might explode inside his chest. Good thing the man on top of him was a doctor. He laid his hand on Josh's flaming cheek and stroked it. "Yes?"

"That was just a figure of speech…"

Tyler smiled. He would never have to worry that Josh was lying to him. He would always know. "Really?"

Josh sagged a little. "I didn't mean to say it like that, or so soon. It's crazy, right?" Josh let out about the fakest laugh Tyler had ever heard.

"Very crazy."

"I'm sorry. I'm getting way ahead of myself." Josh started to pull back but Tyler grabbed his wrists, holding him in place.

"This is crazy, like you said, and I don't know how it's going to work, but maybe we can figure it out, right?"

Josh nodded, his eyes wide with uncertain hope.

"And we don't have to figure it all out tonight, do we?" Tyler let go of Josh's wrists and instead held his hands, weaving their fingers together.

Josh shook his head, a slight smile on his face now to go with his hopeful eyes.

"Okay," Tyler said. "Yes."

"Yes? Yes, what?"

"Yes, I'll be yours. Yes, I'll jump off a cliff with you. Yes, I'll be your fairy tale, and your prince, and whatever else you want and probably a lot of things you don't. There may even be dragon murder if I ever find one. Yes, to everything."

"Everything?"

Tyler looked up into Josh's tense, beloved face. "Everything. Keep in mind that everything encompasses a lot. How about we see how things go and then start making plans for the future later? I know you think you love me, but it's only been a short period of time. I have so many more bad habits you've yet to experience."

Josh sat back, resting on his heels and Tyler's legs. He cocked his head to the side. "Do you know how many times I've been in love in my life?"

Tyler shook his head, not really wanting to know the answer. He already knew there had been a lot of men in the years stretching between Ryan and himself.

"Twice, and you're the second. Do you know how long it took for me to fall in love with Ryan?"

Tyler shook his head again. "I was too young at the time. I don't remember a time when you weren't in love with him."

"Three days. That was it. Three days and I was a goner. And the morning after you and I first had sex I spent a good half-hour talking myself down, thinking I was already half in love with you and that I had to stop it or else. But I couldn't. I tried, but I couldn't. So now we're at 'or else.'"

"Is my ass really that magical that you fell in love with me after we had sex?"

"No. Well, yes, your ass is magical, but the love part wasn't just about sex. If it had been, I'd have been in love dozens of times over the years and it never happened, no matter how hard I tried." Josh's shoulders drooped. "I spent fifteen years trying to replace Ryan and I failed miserably. The longer I went without falling in love again, the more I figured that he was it for me and I'd just fucked up my chance somehow. Then you came along, unexpected and unlike anyone I've ever been with, and that was it. Bam. Never mind that loving you is impractical and crazy and reckless as hell. Doesn't matter. I just do."

"And that's all I am? Ryan's replacement?"

Josh looked shocked. "No. Tyler, you're…"

"What?" It came out sounding terse.

Josh's sweet smile spread across his face. "You're everything." Then he blushed, predictably.

Tyler felt like he'd been shoved off the cliff Josh had mentioned earlier. He was in freefall with no parachute on his back or net below. He gripped Josh's hands tighter, afraid to let go. Josh loved him. He marveled at the impossible idea. Josh loved him. Or Josh *thought* he loved him. Was there a difference? Tyler had thought he was in love before, and look where that had gotten him. But what if this time was different? Tyler looked into Josh's dark eyes and wanted to believe that he could have this: Josh and love and forever.

Josh freed a hand and stroked Tyler's face. "Do you want me?"

Tyler nodded. "Too much."

"There's no such thing as too much."

"I was wrong about that." *It might have been the dumbest thing I've ever said.* Tyler felt too much right then and it hurt too much.

Josh leaned down to brush a soft kiss on Tyler's lips. The sort of kiss to wake a sleeping princess. "Do you think one day you might love me? At some point? It doesn't have to be today, or next week, or even a month from now. But do you think we have a future? Am I crazy? Can we both be crazy together?"

Tyler's heart lurched. "Yeah, this is crazy. We fit though, don't we?"

"God, yes," Josh said. "You—"

"If you say I complete you then I won't be responsible for my actions," Tyler growled.

A short burst of laughter escaped from Josh. "Your ragged edges mesh with my ragged edges. How's that?"

"Eh. Acceptable." Tyler found himself smiling. "Meshing our ragged edges together sounds dirty. 'Mesh my ragged edges! Mesh them so hard!'"

Still laughing, Josh swooped down to kiss Tyler into silence. "Are you done?" he asked when he pulled up.

"Temporarily."

"Good. So, are you okay with this? With me? With there being an us?" Josh hadn't lost his smile, but doubt had crept back into his eyes.

Tyler reached up and stroked Josh's cheek. "I don't know how this is going to work, but maybe we can figure it out. You know. Together."

"Okay," Josh said slowly. "Okay. And does this mean you think that maybe one day you could love me back?"

Tyler groaned. Josh was relentless, but he deserved to hear the words, as hard as they were for Tyler to say. "I'm already stupid with love for you, you impossible man. How could I not be? Some men give jewelry or flowers. You gave me a statue of a naked man holding a severed head. How could I resist?"

Josh collapsed onto Tyler, face snuggled into the crook of Tyler's neck and his weight smothering him for just a few lovely yet breathless moments, and then Josh moved off him, laying down beside him. Josh tugged at Tyler's shoulder and pulled him down so he rested on Josh's chest. "This really just happened," Josh said as he ran his hand up and down Tyler's spine.

"Yep."

"I'm not having some sort of dream."

"Nope. Don't think so."

"You love me."

"I'm afraid so." Tyler started to grin. He stroked Josh's chest. *Mine,* he thought, and for the first time he didn't feel the need to qualify the thought. *And I will find a way to keep you, by God. You are in for it now, Dr. Rosen.*

"I love you," Josh said. "It seems so strange to say it out loud."

"We are strange. This is strange. There is nothing normal about either one of us."

Josh moved his body under Tyler's hand, inviting more, so Tyler pushed up and kissed him.

"So, what?" Josh said. "Who needs normal? You love me."

"Yes, Josh."

"You really do."

"Yes. Even if you are annoying as fuck, I love your fussy, pedantic, neurotic ass. It's only fair, since you seem to love my mental, self-destructive, selfish self."

"I do," Josh said. "You also forgot high-strung."

"Thanks for the reminder."

"And princessy. Hot-tempered. Um... let's see, what else?"

Tyler raised an eyebrow at Josh.

"Oh, and bitchy! I forgot bitchy."

"Are you done?" Tyler asked.

"No. You're also sweet, loyal, smart, funny, brave, and strong. So strong. Stronger than you give yourself credit for. Also, the most beautiful person I've ever seen, and you give the world's best blow jobs."

Tyler wasn't sure if he could live up to all the things Josh thought he was, but maybe he could try. "Oh. Well. As for you..."

"Yes?" Josh asked. A shit-eating grin spread across his face.

Tyler sighed. "You're just Mary fucking Poppins, aren't you? Practically perfect in every way. It's a large part of what makes you so annoying."

"And you love me."

"You like hearing me say it, don't you?"

Josh nodded.

"Yes, Josh Rosen. I, Tyler Chadwick, do so solemnly swear that I am in fact, for better or worse, most emphatically in love with you. God help us both."

"Okay," Josh said. "That'll do for now."

෴

Saturday, October 1st, 2:02 a.m.
Josh's very tidy bedroom
Evanston, IL

Tyler: I should still fire you.
Purvi: But you won't
Purvi: Are you done being a little bitch?
Tyler: Maybe.
Tyler: Confessions of the L-word may have been exchanged
Purvi: Seriously?
Tyler: I believe I have just acquired an actual boyfriend.
Purvi: You sound like you've adopted a puppy
Tyler: There are similarities
Purvi: Is he at least housebroken?
Tyler: He's the neatest person I've ever met. It's pathological.
Purvi: Great. You snagged another crazy one. Tho R promised me this guy is no David.
Tyler: No. He's like the anti-David. You'll see when you meet him.

Tyler: I need to get him to California.
Purvi: You'll have to.
Tyler: I KNOW
Purvi: Leave it all to me.
Tyler: Leave what to you?
Purvi: Enjoy the wedding. Dance with your man at the reception. Piss off your father. Leave everything else to me.
Tyler: Purvi?
Purvi: Go back to sleep

"Put that damn phone down," Josh growled in his ear.

"I couldn't sleep." Tyler stretched, luxuriating in the feel of his naked back sliding along Josh's hairy chest.

"Do I have to exhaust you to get you to sleep?"

"You can try, old man."

Josh's hands stole under the waistband of his sleep pants. "Challenge accepted, your majesty."

Chapter 30
Patrick Crashes the Wedding

Saturday, October 1st, 5:45 p.m.
The Field Museum
Chicago, IL

Patrick had been expecting something much like the weddings he'd been to growing up in Ohio. They were always held in a church. There would be ushers at the entrance asking if each guest was there for the bride or the groom, even if the usher was someone you'd grown up with and knew damn well the bride was your cousin. During or before the wedding there might be a church service, especially if it was a Catholic ceremony. Afterward the reception would be held in the church basement, or rec center, or, if it was really fancy, in one of the town's banquet halls. At least half of the weddings he'd been dragged to by his parents had had a potluck dinner afterward, and instead of champagne there was punch made from ginger ale and frozen lemonade.

This was not that sort of wedding.

For one thing, it was being held at the Field Museum. Patrick wasn't sure if they'd let him in without an invitation, but he'd come wearing a suit and holding a present and he'd slipped in between two groups of invited guests who had arrived just as he had.

A rudimentary aisle had been set up with two groupings of chairs to either side. Patrick waffled about which side to sit on and finally chose the groom's side, if only because it put him closer to Ryan. Even so, he found a chair in the back and did his best not to look conspicuous.

Brad and three groomsmen stood in front of Sue, the museum's T. Rex skeleton, with their backs to the guests. First was Brad, then Ryan. From the back, the two of them looked very much alike, but Patrick would know Ryan from any angle, at any time. He was an inch taller than Brad and his hair was a shade more golden. Next came a shorter, slender man with closely cropped brown hair, and after him a tall man with black wavy hair that looked like it wanted to curl.

The man with the black hair had to be Josh. Patrick wondered where the vicious blue-haired tornado was when he realized with a start that Tyler was the man between Ryan and Josh, minus all his blue hair. He looked wrong up there. For one thing, he was taller in Patrick's memory. Seeing him from behind he looked impossibly too small, but it was an illusion.

Patrick knew Ryan was 6'4, Brad was nearly as tall, and Josh was somewhere around Patrick's height, which was six feet exactly. Tyler was maybe four inches shorter than Josh, which was short for a man, but combined with his small frame, standing next to Ryan Tyler almost looked like a child. The contrast in the brothers' coloring was striking as well, them being so blond and him the odd one out with his dark hair.

Patrick sat there, studying the back of Ryan's head, and tried to decide why he'd come. It was probably knowing Ryan would be there with both Stephanie and Josh in attendance and Patrick couldn't stand staying at home and trying to study, which was what he should have been doing. Crashing the wedding was a terrible idea and Ryan would be furious if he found out, but Patrick planned on remaining unseen. Unfortunately, it was a much smaller wedding than he'd expected. His current plan was to escape by slipping out between the ceremony and the reception, hoping no one would be the wiser. The entire fiasco was a waste of his time, but at least it had cemented something in his mind. Patrick didn't belong in this world, and he needed to break it off with Ryan. The sooner, the better.

Patrick thought the ceremony was unusual, but he had never been to a Jewish wedding before, so maybe that was it. He'd seen some things in movies, like the canopy thing held over the bride and groom, and at the end of the ceremony the glass being stepped on and broken. Brought up Catholic with mostly Catholic friends, Patrick found the whole thing somewhat bewildering, but interesting.

For a moment, he entertained the idea of a wedding between him and Ryan. He tried to picture his family and Ryan's family in one place and couldn't do it. Even if his relatives didn't freak out at the idea of him marrying another man, and they would, they'd be like fish out of water at an event like this one. The whole thing was hopeless, just like Tyler had warned him it was. Just like Josh had hinted.

Lost in his thoughts, Patrick was unprepared for the ceremony being so short, and missed his opportunity to slip away at the end like he'd intended. He tried to get away from the other guests, but due to how the chairs had been set up, the only way to leave was either past the reception line or climbing over a row of chairs. He wasn't sure which would be worse, and while he debated, he ran out of time and found himself in front of what had to be Rachel and Josh's parents. Their father looked like a fussy professor-type with salt-and-pepper hair cut military short and wire-rimmed glasses, visibly uncomfortable in his rented tuxedo. Their mother, who looked very much like Rachel, smiled and looked ecstatically happy.

Next was Peter Chadwick, an older, grayer, and frailer version of Ryan and Brad. Standing next to him, but simultaneously as far away as she could be, was a woman who had to be Ryan's mother. She looked equal parts happy and nervous, cutting glances between her sons and her former husband. Despite her age—Ryan was thirty-five so she had to be somewhere in her fifties at least—she was exquisitely lovely with only slightly grayed dark hair and enormous blue-gray eyes, but hers was a fragile beauty, like one wrong word would make her shatter.

Brad didn't give Patrick a second glance, but Rachel did. She narrowed her eyes at him but didn't call him out for his unexpected appearance. She only murmured in his ear how surprised she was to see him and said she'd see him later, which he tried not to think was ominous.

The bridesmaids passed by in a peach blur, but then he was before the groomsmen, and that's when his luck ran out. First was Tyler. The short cut of his hair somehow made him both less pretty and more beautiful, the resemblance to his mother marked, as they shared the same coloring. Then he opened his lovely mouth and the spell was broken. "Who the fuck invited your stupid ass to the wedding?"

Josh, standing next to Tyler, stiffened. Ryan, just beyond Josh, gave him a look of barely restrained fury. "Patrick? What the hell are you doing here?"

I have no clue. It seemed like a good idea this morning. He said the first thing that came into his head. "I brought a present."

Tyler gave him a disgusted eye roll. "Well, that makes it all okay, then."

Josh looked threatening. "If you make a scene and embarrass my sister I will murder you with my own two hands."

There was more eye rolling from Tyler. "Oh, the big, bad dermatologist. We're all so scared. Really, new boy, I am by far the one you need to worry about most. Josh likes to think he's scary, but really, he's the nicest man on the planet. I, on the other hand, will cut you and watch you bleed. You need to leave. Now." Then he gave Patrick a charming smile that still managed to convey imminent danger. Patrick had no idea how Josh felt safe enough with Tyler to live with him, fake relationship or not. He couldn't imagine being able to close his eyes and sleep in the same place as Tyler. Not without Kevlar pajamas.

However, Tyler was the least of his worries, because while his expression was lethal, the look Ryan gave him was full-on nuclear. "Go and wait for me by the south entrance. Do not leave before I've spoken to you."

He met Ryan's eyes. They were not the blue of summer skies. Right now, they were the color of concentrated flame. "And if I don't?" He'd meant to sound defiant, but the last word wobbled in his mouth.

"Do. It. Now." Each hissed word hit him with the impact of a bullet.

Patrick was toward the end of the receiving line, but there were other guests behind him who were wondering why things had ground to a halt. He had to do something. "Sure," he muttered. Dismissed, Patrick went to stand by the south entrance.

"I see I'm not the only one here uninvited," a man said.

Patrick looked up from the floor he'd been blindly studying, although he didn't have to look up far. The man who'd spoken was in his mid-fifties, slight, with graying dark hair with auburn highlights and hazel eyes. He had pale skin that was crinkled at his eyes and around his mouth, but was otherwise smooth and clean-shaven. He had fine features and was extraordinarily attractive. It struck Patrick that this was what Tyler would look like in thirty years.

He'd said he was uninvited, though. Maybe he was one of Ryan's maternal relatives. There was no love lost between Ryan's father and mother. That did make the most sense. Patrick grunted a noncommittal response.

The man leaned against the wall. "The trick to crashing a wedding where you are unwanted but known to the family is getting up to use the restroom right before the end of the ceremony. That way you completely bypass the reception line."

"That's a life pro-tip right there," Patrick said. "Where were you fifteen minutes ago?"

"In the restroom. Are you not paying attention?"

"Apparently not," Patrick said. *If I had half a brain, I would leave now.* "Are you a relative?"

The man tipped his head back and forth a few times as if debating with himself. "Something like that," he said. "What about you?"

"I work in the Chadwick firm with Ryan. And Rachel, of course."

"Hm," the man said. "Were you planning on interrupting the wedding ala *The Graduate*? If so, you're too late." He looked out through the glass door. "If you hurry and pry Rachel away from Brad you could make your getaway on the bus out there, though."

Patrick had never seen *The Graduate* so he had no idea what the guy was talking about. He remembered hearing or reading somewhere that the movie involved an older woman named Mrs. Robinson—he'd heard the Simon and Garfunkel song, at least—seducing a younger man. If so, Ryan was his Mrs. Robinson and he hadn't had to try very hard to get Patrick into bed with him.

"Oh, so that's how it is. Hm. I never thought he'd defy his father. Guess we can all be wrong."

Patrick looked up. The man he'd been standing next to gazed at the wedding guests milling about the hall, chatting, drinking, and eating canapés. Making his way through them like a bull storming through a china shop was Ryan, his brow low and a scowl on his face. *Defy his father.* That phrase caught at Patrick and he looked toward Ryan's father, who was occupied with Brad and his new daughter-in-law, but who still stared after Ryan with a similar frown on his face. Then Patrick searched for Stephanie and found her chatting with one of the bridesmaids. He saw her shoot an indecipherable look at Ryan—she might have been either confused or concerned or both—then she went back to her conversation.

"You shouldn't have come," Ryan said as he drew near. "I'm taking you home."

"Ryan, it's been a long time," said the man beside Patrick.

Ryan stopped short and looked away from Patrick. "Uncle Mike? I haven't seen you in forever. How have you been?"

The man smiled. "I've been better, honestly, but it's good to see you again, Ryan. The last time was... let me see... Gretchen was in eighth grade, so you would've been a freshman in high school. That was right after Sophie had her first relapse. But I don't want to talk about sad things. Not today. I'm glad to see Brad looking so happy."

"Yeah. It's great seeing you again, Mike, but I need to get my friend home. He's not feeling well."

The man—Uncle Mike—looked Patrick up and down. "Of course," he said. "I could tell the young man was feeling unwell and came over to keep him company. It's very kind of you to make sure he gets home safely." So, the man was a relative. Probably Ryan's maternal uncle. Not only did Tyler look like him, but they both had the uncomfortable ability to hide sharp objects into their smiles.

"See you later, Mike. We'll have to get together later and catch up."

"Sure, Ryan, I'd like that. Ah... good luck."

Patrick allowed himself to be dragged out of the museum and down the steps. They didn't go down to the bus stop, however, or hail a taxi. The family had hired a valet service for the wedding, and Ryan signaled to the attendant.

"Ryan," Patrick began.

"Not. One. Word." Ryan bit out. "Not until I have you in private."

The valet came back with Ryan's brand-new gray Panamera. It cost twice Patrick's yearly salary, even more than what Patrick's childhood home was worth. He'd heard Rachel giving Ryan a hard time about the purchase and had then googled the price out of curiosity. Patrick couldn't imagine spending that much money on a mere car. It was yet another reason why his relationship with Ryan was crazy and doomed. Even if Ryan wasn't engaged, even if he wasn't so deeply in the closet he'd require an experienced spelunker to find his way out of it, he and Patrick existed in completely different worlds.

Ryan got in the car and Patrick hesitated. He should've never gone to the wedding. It was a huge mistake. Getting in the car with Ryan was another. He was engaged. He would be at his own wedding less than a year from now. Was Patrick going to sneak into that one, too? Would Ryan also abandon it to take him, a supposedly sick friend, home? Of course not.

Better to back out now. The 146 bus was approaching. All Patrick had to do was wait for it to arrive, get on, take it back to the Red Line, ride it back to his stop, and walk three blocks to his apartment. He could picture it all in his head.

"Get your fucking ass in the fucking car," bellowed Ryan through the open passenger door, and Patrick jumped. It was unlike Ryan to curse, let alone yell.

"Why?" he asked.

The bus got nearer.

"Get in the car, Patrick. Now."

Patrick felt his legs wanting to obey but he locked his knees. "Why?" he asked again.

Ryan got out of the car, slammed the door, and went up to Patrick. "I just lied to my fiancée, my brother and his wife, and my parents. I told them that a friend I'd invited to the wedding was feeling very ill and needed to be taken home. I got Tyler to promise to keep his damned mouth shut. Now get in the car, Patrick. I am out of patience."

Patrick took one last look at the approaching bus, gave it up for a lost cause, then got into the Porsche and pulled the door closed. The seat enveloped him in undeserved luxury.

"Buckle up," Ryan snarled at him, throwing the car into first gear with more force than was necessary.

"Where are you taking me?"

"Home," was the short reply, and Patrick wasn't sure if he meant his apartment or Ryan's condo.

He should have gotten on the bus.

"What did you think coming today would accomplish?"

Patrick shrugged, and then realized Ryan couldn't see him while he was driving. "I honestly don't know. Please take me home. I think I'm done."

"No, you're not."

Patrick looked at Ryan. He stared straight ahead, his mouth set in a grim line.

"Yeah, I think I am. Look, if you give me a good recommendation, I'm sure I can find another job with hours that will work with school. Or I could maybe wait until next semester to look for something and then try and take more evening classes so working would be easier. I have some money saved. I'll figure it out. It'll be for the best."

"The best for who?" Ryan asked.

"Both of us. Hell. Ryan, there is no *us*. We have no future. You expect me to continue being your dirty little secret after you get married? I won't. I can't. I've crossed too many lines already, but that's one step too far. Let's end this now."

"No," Ryan growled.

"What do you mean, 'no'? You aren't the boss of me." Great. He'd reverted back to junior high taunts.

"Actually," Ryan said, "I am."

"You know what I mean. Ryan, why are you making this difficult? You know as well as I do that this had to end at some point. Now is as good a time as any."

Ryan said nothing and drove on. Not to Patrick's apartment, either. Instead, they ended up at Ryan's condo. Ryan parked under the building and looked at Patrick.

"Are you coming up or what?"

Patrick could get out of the car and walk to the nearest EL station. It wasn't that far away. Or he could go up and let Ryan fuck him, which he clearly wanted to do. One last time. Then he would go home and draft a letter of resignation.

"One last time," he said.

Ryan gave him a stormy look but didn't argue.

They rode the elevator up in silence, Ryan next to him nearly vibrating with some emotion Patrick couldn't identify. Lust? Rage? Frustration? Impossible to tell. Patrick reached out a hand to touch him and Ryan caught it. "No," he said. "Not here."

He stalked down the hall to his door, Patrick following. He should've been worried, but instead all he could feel was a rising anticipation. Stupid, stupid anticipation.

Patrick thought he'd take him in the living room, but Ryan surprised him by tugging him down the hallway and into a bedroom. Ryan's hands tore at his suit and tie, undressing Patrick while he remained in his wedding tux. "I want you," he said, kissing Patrick's shoulder. "I need you," as he caressed his bared hip.

Not enough. Not nearly enough, Patrick thought. *I should have taken the bus.* Then Ryan pushed him onto the bed and knelt between his legs, still fully dressed, even the boutonniere of coral roses in his lapel unmussed. Ryan took Patrick's cock into his mouth and Patrick stopped thinking for some time.

Later, Patrick lay next to Ryan on his bed, both naked and sticky and neither caring enough to do anything about it.

"In theory, I'm still angry you crashed my brother's wedding," Ryan said. "In practice, not so much." He leaned forward and kissed Patrick's neck.

"I promise I'll never do it again," Patrick said with a bit of a grin. *I am going to miss him so much. Miss this, too.* Not just the sex, but also this closeness afterward when Ryan removed more than his clothing. He was bare to Patrick, everything on display, and when he left, Ryan would close back up again, tunneling into himself like he was one of those Russian nesting dolls. Patrick felt a spasm of regret at that, but he couldn't lose himself to allow Ryan freedom. It wasn't fair and it was slowly killing part of him. It was why Tyler and Josh's words had resonated so strongly with him. He needed to leave, and soon, before it was too late.

Ryan was quiet for several moments. "What do you want from me?" he asked.

"I want you to let me go."

"No."

"Yes, dammit. Your brother was right. I can't stay."

"Fuck Tyler," Ryan growled, again uncharacteristically obscene.

"No, thank you," Patrick said. "I think he's psychotic. But still right. I should have never come back here. I'm an idiot."

Ryan's arm tightened around him. "My idiot," he said.

Not for much longer, Patrick thought absently. His mind had snagged on Tyler, and seeing him today without the blue hair. It reminded him of something he'd meant to ask Ryan before they'd become distracted. "Speaking of Tyler—"

Ryan groaned. "Do we have to?"

"Speaking of Tyler," Patrick continued, propping himself up on an elbow and looking down into Ryan's face, "I never told you, but before I interviewed to work for you, I had a terrible crush on him."

"What?" Ryan looked nauseous.

Patrick laughed softly and kissed Ryan's perfect brow. "I didn't know he was your brother until long after you and I started... this. Months before I applied at your firm I saw Tyler in *Blood and Water* and I fell in love with that character he played. He was so beautiful and sweet and sad in that movie. I wanted to tell him that there were other girls out there for him. Other boys, for that matter."

"Oh, really?" Ryan did not sound amused.

"Then I met you." *And you became the sun in my sky, damn you.* "One day at work I came across a contract of his and I asked about it. 'Oh, didn't you know? The boss's brother is an actor.' So that came as a bit of a shock. An even bigger shock was meeting Tyler in person. Do you have any idea what it's like to be caught sucking the dick of your famous crush's brother?"

Ryan smirked at him. "No. I can't say that I do."

Patrick frowned at him. "It's awful. I don't recommend it. First, I was drowning in embarrassment, then I saw what he was like and that was a rude awakening. All dregs of that crush, gone, smashed into smithereens the second he started screeching at us."

"I know there's a point that you're getting to," Ryan said, going into lecture mode, which was something he did in moments of uncertainty, "but you're being too reticent. You need to be more concise in your speech,

Patrick. State your point, add follow-up evidence as necessary. Don't give extraneous information if it will distract from your objective."

Patrick smacked Ryan's shoulder. "Cut it out. I told you all that so this would make more sense. That man you called Uncle Mike looks exactly like Tyler plus thirty years. It was the first thing I thought when I saw him. I knew him instantly as a relative, but he was really outspoken to me that we were in the same boat, meaning uninvited, and I'm curious as hell. Why was he crashing the wedding? Is he related to your mother?"

Ryan barked out a laugh. "Good lord, no," he said. "The uncle's an honorific. Mike isn't a relative, he used to be one of the attorneys with the firm. He left years ago to start his own practice. He's an old family friend, but he and Dad had some sort of falling out around the time Mike left. Anyway, he's had his own problems. His wife died recently from cancer that she'd been fighting for years. My mom used to be close with her, at least before she moved with my brother to California. As for why Mike crashed the wedding, I've no idea. I assumed he'd been invited when I saw him. And I have no clue what any of this has to do with Tyler, who you apparently have a thing for."

"Had. Past tense, and you being jealous is pretty damn ironic." Patrick leaned down to kiss Ryan's frowning lips, wondering as he did so when the last kiss would come, and whether he'd know it when it happened. The idea made him feel lost, so he pushed it away and kissed Ryan again. "Are you positive this Mike guy isn't a relative of some sort?"

"I am not jealous of Tyler, and Mike is not a relative. Mom's family all live in the San Francisco area to the best of my knowledge. That's where my parents first met. Mike was born and raised in Chicago and my mother is an only child. The resemblance is just in your imagination," Ryan's voice trailed into uncertainty. He closed his eyes. "Hell," he said after a while.

"Ryan?"

Ryan combed a hand through his hair. "He does look like Tyler, doesn't he?"

Patrick nodded. "Yeah, he does. I mean, Tyler's your brother, but if anything, that makes you less objective. You see your baby brother when you look at him. I see the actor I fantasized about for months. I was a little obsessed with him for a while."

"How obsessed?" Ryan scowled at him.

"Not that obsessed. I fell into your bed easily enough, didn't I?" *Like a stupid lovesick fool.*

"Yeah," Ryan said. "You're right, though. Mike does resemble Tyler."

"I think it's the other way around," Patrick said.

"Well." Ryan was quiet for some time, thinking, and Patrick left him to it. "This just complicates everything. Patrick, you can't quit. I won't accept it. I need you."

Patrick frowned at Ryan. "No, you don't. Use one of the other secretaries. I am not necessary."

"Yes, you are. Who else can I trust?"

"Trust with what?"

Ryan grabbed the sides of his face and brought him close enough that their noses nearly touched. "Oh, nothing. Just that I'm pretty sure I know why Dad hates Tyler and my mother and Uncle Mike."

Christ. It was bad enough that he was fucking the boss, now Patrick was being dragged into family drama as well. "And? So, Tyler's probably your half-brother. Does it really matter at this point? And what does that have to do with me?" *Other than that I'm doing a great job of keeping up your family traditions, of course. At least neither of us can get accidentally knocked up and pop out a bastard.*

"It would matter a great deal to my father. He is not a forgiving or understanding man. I need you to help me find out if he was the one who released the video to spite Tyler."

Patrick groaned and knew he wasn't going anywhere. Not yet, at any rate.

Chapter 31
Josh Gets a Lecture from His Father

Saturday, October 1st, 3:00 p.m.
A poorly secured parking lot
Evanston, IL

Josh stood next to Tyler in his building's parking lot, looking at his car in dismay. Someone had slashed tires and keyed the paint. "Really? All four? Those tires were almost new."

"Did they get any other cars?" asked Tyler. He started looking around at the other cars in the lot.

Josh joined him. "Doesn't look like it."

Tyler bit his lip and looked sick. "Do you know if there's any surveillance on the parking lot?"

"I'll talk to security and see." He looked at his watch. "It'll have to be quick, though. We need to get to the museum. Can you get a car to pick us up while I talk to them? Then I'll call my insurance company."

"Fuck fuck fuck," Tyler muttered as he got his phone out.

Josh handed his tux and gift bag with Rachel and Brad's present to Tyler, then jogged back to his building and reported the damage done to his car. As it turned out, there weren't any surveillance cameras on the lot, but the building's security was supposed to check on the cars once every hour and that had been done, according to their log books. Even so, no one had seen anything. Either the security was shit or the damage had been done since the last check at two in the afternoon. Possible, but unlikely. Josh cursed to himself and made a note to complain to the building superintendent and bring up security at the next condo association meeting, for what good that would do.

"You wanna call the cops?"

Josh looked at his watch again. "I've got a wedding that I have to be at. As it is, I should've already left."

"No sweat, Dr. Rosen," the security guard on duty said. Josh thought his name was Chris. Or maybe Craig. "We'll call the cops for you, show them the car, have them start a report, and give them your number. You can talk with them later." He lowered his voice. "This has happened before. Had a lady whose boyfriend was stalking her, kept fucking with her car. We finally caught him in the act. If this wasn't a one-time random act of vandalism, we'll get the asshole. Don't worry."

As if. Josh had to wonder if this had happened before to someone else why they hadn't tightened security then. But there was no point yelling at Chris/Craig, and he had to get going.

"Fine, call the cops, tell them I'll be available tomorrow to talk with them. I'll call my insurance company, too, and have them come out tomorrow to look at it."

"Sure thing, Dr. Rosen. We'll take care of it."

Josh left the building to see Tyler standing next to a taxi parked out in front of the building. He held open the back door of the car for Josh. Josh bent to kiss him before sliding into the backseat.

"Thanks for getting us a ride."

Beside him, Tyler bit his lip again and looked preoccupied. "I'm sorry it was necessary," he said.

"Don't be sorry. It's not your fault."

Tyler turned his head and looked out the window. Josh wanted to ask what was bothering him, but decided to let Tyler tell him when he was ready. The last thing Josh wanted to do was interrogate his new and now official boyfriend in the backseat of a taxi right before his sister's wedding. He took Tyler's hand into his and said nothing.

Tyler curled his fingers against Josh's and held on tight all the way to the museum.

⁂

Saturday, October 1st, 3:50 p.m.
The Field Museum: before the wedding
Chicago, IL

"You're late," Josh's father said.

"Only by twenty minutes," Josh replied. He kept his tone bland and hoped his dad would let their lateness go without an argument. "The wedding doesn't start until six. That's over two hours from now."

"On this day, of all days, I'd think you could bother to be here on time. Your mother has enough to worry about without adding a tardy son on top." His eyes flicked to Tyler and then to their joined hands.

Tyler bristled. Josh could sense him puffing himself up like an angry Oliver. If he'd had fur it would've been standing straight out, his ears laid flat. Josh squeezed his hand.

"We were late because—" Tyler started to say. Josh tightened his grip hard enough that it must have hurt, but it did stop Tyler talking.

"Because I had car trouble. We had to call for a taxi. Sorry, Dad, but we're here now with plenty of time before the wedding, so no harm done." He offered his father a smile which was not returned.

Josh glanced down at Tyler, who was giving him an "I will expect an explanation later" look.

"If you'll excuse us, I'd like a word with my son. Alone."

Tyler further stiffened. "Sure. I'll go find my brothers." He dropped Josh's hand from his and stalked off.

"Your mother has been worried sick. The least you could have done was call ahead to say you would be detained. Clearly you were... distracted... and couldn't be bothered."

Josh flinched but kept his silence. He didn't want to get into a fight with his father today of all days.

"This is your sister's big day and your mother wants everything to be perfect. We asked you to be here at 3:30. Not 3:40. Not 3:50. And here you are, not only late, but prancing in with that... that... boy."

Josh felt himself ice over. Retreating behind chilly reserve was the only way he knew how to cope with one of his father's lectures. Each time he was eight years old again and in trouble for breaking his great-grandmother's vase, the one she had brought with her when she'd come to Chicago from Germany, or thirteen and having to explain an unprecedented C in history.

"That boy," Josh said woodenly, "is one of the other groomsmen and has just as much right as I do to be here. Being Brad's brother and all." *And we were not fucking prancing, Dad.*

"And you see nothing wrong with your... association?"

"No, not particularly."

Josh's father curled his lip. "Can't you see how inappropriate he is for you?"

"Why, because he's a man? I'm gay, Dad. You seem to keep forgetting that."

His father gave him an annoyed look. "That boy is far too young for you, Joshua. He's mentally unstable, and he's done nothing with his life but squander every opportunity he's ever been given. Look at his brothers. Ryan's an attorney and now heads Chadwick and Chadwick. Brad's a surgeon working through his residency. And Tyler's an actor." Josh's father sneered the word, saying it like someone might say prostitute. "He has no future; can't you see that?"

"What?" Josh had been sure his father wouldn't be happy about Tyler because he was male. Not approving of Tyler because he was *Tyler* hadn't occurred to him. Not that it mattered to Josh. He was aware of their age difference (and had come to terms with it), had been witness to Tyler's questionable mental stability (which he felt was probably no shakier than his own), and he didn't want Tyler because of his future earning potential. Hell, had Tyler been penniless, things would have been easy for them. All he'd have to do would be to plunk Tyler down in his home and let him be that homemaker Josh's father wanted him to marry. But Tyler wasn't penniless or without resources, talent, or a career. All the things his father held dear, Tyler had in spades. His father was just too pigheaded to see that right now.

Josh let the litany against Tyler flow over and past him. It was a defense he'd been employing against his father for as long as he could remember, and it helped him keep both the peace and his sanity. Then his brain snagged on something his father was saying and he snapped back to attention.

"In addition, he's little better than a whore. I know about this video business. Everyone knows about it. As a doctor, you have a reputation to uphold, and he will drag you down into the mud with him. I raised you to be better than that."

Josh felt heat wash away his chilly reserve in a wave of fury. He wanted to hit something, but he restrained himself, fisting his hands but keeping his arms rigidly at his sides. "Do *not* call him that again. Ever."

Josh's father paused and looked baffled. Josh breaking into his lecture was not part of the accepted script. "I beg your pardon," his father said, not sounding at all like he was either begging or wanted Josh's pardon.

"Tyler is not a whore and I will not tolerate you calling him that. You don't have to approve of him, and you don't have to approve that we're in a relationship, but I won't let you insult him."

"Well," his father said, ignoring Josh's outburst like it hadn't occurred and certainly not apologizing, "be that as it may, you're nearly thirty-five and I can't tell you how to live your life, but I can tell you that I will not let you or that *boy* ruin your sister's wedding. I won't stand for either Rachel or your mother being unhappy. Not today."

"Ruining the day? How, Dad? Were you expecting us to trade our tuxedos in for rainbow spandex and glitter body paint? Did you think Tyler and I would start twerking on the Egyptian tomb at the reception wearing assless chaps?"

"This isn't a joke, Joshua, and I am not amused. I expect you to take this seriously." His voice had risen and several people who were setting up for the wedding looked their way. Josh's mother hurried over to smooth things over like she always did.

"Now, dear, that's enough. Josh wasn't so very late, and he still has plenty of time to get ready. Even more if you'll let him get dressed."

"Mom, can you go get me Rachel, or is she already changing?"

"I think she's arguing with the florist, honey. The wedding planner is trying to arbitrate. I could go get her. I'm sure the florist would thank me." She flashed him a worried smile, then scurried off in a flurry of Chanel no. 5 and peach chiffon.

"You will not upset your sister," Josh's father said. "Do you understand me? What the hell do you think you're doing?"

"I have no intention of upsetting Rachel, Dad," he replied. "I'm just taking this seriously, like you said."

"Oh, good, you finally got here. Tyler had better be with you," Rachel said after she'd marched over.

"He went to go find Brad and Ryan and he's probably already in his tux by now. I know it's your big day, but can you do me a little favor?"

"Sure," she said, looking between him and their father with ill-disguised unease.

"I know you do his taxes, so can you tell Dad how much Tyler's income was last year?"

Rachel gave him a questioning look but asked, "From his earned income, trust fund, or investments?"

"All together. A rough figure is fine."

Rachel thought for a few seconds. "Just under two million dollars. Gross."

"And expected earnings this year?"

Rachel grinned a little, probably seeing where this was going. "Just over two point five million, based on his current contracted pay from his most recent movie. He did very well this year, and next year will likely be better. After that, who knows, but he still has the investments and the trust fund, which are not inconsiderable. At his current rate of investment, I expect his income to only grow over time."

"And my income?"

Josh's father snorted and folded his arms.

"Last year's gross was just over 350K. I can't remember the exact figure off the top of my head. Is that close enough? I can look it up if you need me to."

"No, that's fine. I don't know, Dad. Suddenly it looks like I'm the bad financial bet in this relationship."

Rachel gave Josh a pointed look at the word "relationship" that he ignored.

"This isn't just about money," their father said. "Money can't buy respectability." Then, as if he couldn't help himself, he added, "Your income would be much higher if you'd listen to me and open your own practice."

Josh made a sound of disgust. With Dad, it was always about the money. It was all he'd heard growing up. Study hard and get good grades so you could be successful, success always being measured by what you did, who you knew, how much money you made, and what zip code you lived in. His father was always saying things like, "all the best people send their children to this school," or "all the best people belong to this club," like life was nothing but a petty game and some huge snob was keeping score. Josh knew his father still blamed him for not being able to complete his surgical residency. It was "my son, the dermatologist," not "my son, the plastic surgeon." Like anyone but his father cared.

"What the hell, Dad?" asked Rachel. "Can you not do this today? Is there a good reason why Josh felt the need to drag me over here—not that I mind, by the way, because I was this close to killing the florist—to defend Tyler's financial prospects to you?"

"I'm trying to keep your brother and that boy from ruining your wedding. Your brother can choose to interpret that however he wishes."

Rachel shook her head. "No, you're not. You just want to have your way. And, yeah, Tyler wouldn't have been my first pick for him, either, but it's not up to us. Besides, I'm pretty sure Tyler really does care for him, Dad, or at least Brad is sure, and that's good enough for me. Like it or not, that crazy little shit has added Josh to his extremely short list of people he gives a crap about. Brad is also on that list, and apparently, I am, too. Tyler has no intentions of ruining this wedding, okay? I mean, why the hell would he?"

"Calling Tyler a crazy little shit is not helping, Rach," Josh said. "He's not any crazier than I am."

"Thank you for that ringing endorsement," Tyler said, having decided that he was going to stick his nose in whether it was wanted or not, no doubt drawn over by the raised voices. He placed his hand at the small of Josh's back and Josh leaned into him.

"Was I wrong?" asked Rachel.

"No. My list is pretty short and you and your brother are both on it. His name is a lot higher up than yours, though." Tyler faced Josh's father, drawing himself up as far as he'd go, and said with exquisite dignity, "Mr. Rosen, if you're done with your son, I'd be more than happy to take him off your hands. Permanently, if necessary," he added and smiled. Josh winced.

Josh's father frowned. "Meaning what, exactly?"

"Meaning that I wouldn't dream of keeping Josh from his family. But at the same time, I will not allow you to berate him in public like he's a child. He's taking it from you because he's far too worried about what you think of him to tell you to go to hell, but I'm not."

"Excuse me?" Josh's father bit out.

Josh put a warning hand on Tyler's arm, which of course he ignored. "Sir, just like your daughter said, I have zero intentions of doing anything to ruin this day for either Brad or Rachel or even your wife, who's always been nice to me. Even if I wasn't on my best behavior because I love my brother and quite like and respect your daughter, I'd like to think that my mother taught me better than to make a scene at someone's wedding just because I can. And even without all that, I would do pretty much anything for your son, up to and including tolerating you. But I will not let you upset him, which you have. Am I being clear?"

Josh's father opened his mouth, seemed to change his mind, then shut it. "Who the hell do you think you are?" It came out sounding less angry and more bewildered than Josh thought his father would've liked.

"I am the man in love with your son," Tyler said in the same way one would remark that the sky was blue or water was wet.

Rachel sighed. "I guess that was inevitable." She looked at Josh. "Is it mutual? Stupid question, of course it's mutual. Even on Sunday I could see you practically worshipping the ground he swishes over. It figures you'd end up replacing one Chadwick with another. Honestly, I swear it's sheer laziness on your part."

"What on earth do you mean by that?" exclaimed Josh's father. At the same time Tyler spat out, "Swishes?"

Rachel got an "oh, shit, what have I said?" look on her face.

"I had a huge crush on Brad back when we roomed together in college," Josh blurted out while glaring at Rachel. He was not going to be the one who outed Ryan. Nothing Ryan had ever done warranted that. Brad would understand and condone this white lie, he was sure. Josh hoped that Tyler would go along with it. He probably would, but just in case, he gave Tyler a surreptitious pinch. "Totally unrequited, naturally, and I got over him years ago. Right, Rachel?"

"Oh, yes, definitely," she agreed, nodding vigorously. "It's okay. I get the allure of Chadwick men, believe me. I would never hold it against you."

"That's mighty big of you," Tyler spat, then he muttered, "Swishes," again in an aggrieved tone.

"And things have totally worked out for the best. I mean, at least Tyler's gay." She kissed Josh on the cheek, then she looked at Tyler. "If you hurt him..."

"Gross bodily harm. Got it. The last thing I want to do is hurt your brother. I like my kneecaps. I'm very fond of them. Of him, too. You, though, are tumbling from favor. I do not swish."

Rachel gave Tyler an insouciant grin, then turned to their father. "Enough, okay? Please? For me?"

He sighed. "Go get dressed, Rachel. Your mother will worry if you're not ready at least an hour early."

"Sure, Dad," Rachel said. She looked back at Josh, shrugged, and walked off.

Josh's father cleared his throat and gave Tyler a pointed look. "You're not good enough for my son."

Josh choked.

"Probably not," Tyler said, not sounding concerned.

"Dad," Josh said. "For the love of God, he's not my prom date. I'm too old for this."

Josh's father ignored him, which was nothing new. "This is a wedding, not a freak parade. We had to hire security because of *you* and the circus you've brought with you. Now you've got your hooks in my son and I can see it's no use to tell him to leave you alone like the bad piece of business you are, but I am warning you right now that if you hurt any of my family in any way, I'll see that you regret it." Then he did an about-face and left both Josh and Tyler alone.

"Well," Tyler said brightly. "That was fun."

"Come on," Josh said. "Show me where to get dressed."

"You okay?" asked Tyler.

"Sure. It could have been worse."

"From my point of view, I'm not sure how. He seems to be pretty firmly in the anti-Tyler fan club." Tyler smiled, but he looked worried to Josh.

"Eh. Don't fuck me over and he'll come around. Fifteen, twenty years from now, you'll see."

Tyler looked at him and raised that eyebrow of his. "That soon?"

Josh gave him what he hoped was a playful smile. "Don't tell me you're regretting being my not-so-fake boyfriend already?" And while his tone was joking, Josh felt real concern. Why would Tyler—or anyone, really—want him enough to put up with that kind of bullshit over the long term? He was forcibly reminded that by far the longest relationship he'd ever been in was the one he'd had with Ryan. He was going to fuck this up. It was only a matter of time.

"Whatever you're thinking, stop it. Your father loves you. He's a huge dickhead who probably wants me dead, but he loves you. Don't take that for granted." Then Tyler took Josh's arm and led him to where Brad and Ryan were getting ready.

☙❧

Saturday, October 1st, 7:50 p.m.
The Field Museum: the reception
Chicago, IL

In the end, it wasn't Josh or Tyler who made a scene at the wedding; it was Ryan and his little party crashing not-boyfriend. Ryan disappeared to "deal with him" and hadn't returned. Josh's mother was frantic.

"He's the best man! He was supposed to give a speech! It'll have to be one of you now."

"Josh should do it," Tyler said.

"What? No," said Josh, feeling a little panicked. "You're his brother. You should do it."

"You told me he's your best friend, right? This is a best friend sort of job."

"But talking is something you're good at. It's practically your calling. Besides, I have no idea what to say." Josh looked at Ryan's empty seat at the table in accusation, as if he could will Ryan's ass into it.

"Brad," Tyler called out, "who do you like better? Me or Josh?"

Brad swiveled in their direction. "Oh, Josh, by a long shot."

Tyler made a gesture that clearly said, "There you go." "Mrs. Rosen, if you can get us some paper and a pen or pencil, I'll help your son write a speech, okay?"

Josh's mother beamed at Tyler. "Thank you, Tyler. I'll go see what I can find."

"I think you've made a conquest there," Josh said. "She's likely already thinking about knitting baby sweaters."

Tyler gave a theatrical shudder. "Bite your tongue. But at least she's on our side, I'm pretty sure. I'll just never tell her that babies are not my thing and hope like hell my brother knocks your sister up soon. So. One Rosen down, two more to go. Although I think your sister is teetering in my direction."

"You think our dads are lost causes?"

Tyler shrugged. "Hard to say. Mine is, for sure. That's okay, it's not like you need his approval, anyway."

Josh's mom returned with paper and a pen she'd scrounged from God-knew-where. "Here," she said. She cupped Josh's cheek. "Thanks for doing this, sweetheart. Your sister will really appreciate it." She leaned down to kiss his forehead then went to sit beside his father.

"Okay," Josh said, "let's do this. And your brother owes me big time."

"Which one?"

"Both."

ෆ෨

Saturday, October 1st, 9:32 p.m.
The Field Museum: the dance floor

Chicago, IL

Much later, after dinner, all the speeches (including his own, which had been easier to make than he'd feared), champagne toasts, the cake was cut and eaten, and the bouquet was tossed and caught, the dancing started. Dancing. The worst part of the evening, as far as Josh was concerned.

"Come on," Tyler said, standing up from the table and holding out his hand. "Dance with me. I love this song."

He didn't want to dance with Tyler. Or, rather, he didn't want to dance at all. Josh hated dancing. He hated everything about it.

Josh had gone to every single school dance with Ryan. Not as his date, of course, but as his solitary shadow, and by the end of high school, no one had questioned his dateless presence. Where Ryan went, there Josh went as well: games, dances, movies, parties. Invite Ryan and you invited Josh, too. Everyone knew it. Josh remembered hearing a guy joke that Josh was probably there when Ryan lost his virginity, and of course he'd been there. They had lost their virginities to each other junior year after homecoming.

At that dance, Josh had done what he always did — stood on the edge, listened to the music, watched Ryan, and endured. Ryan would get tired, usually sooner rather than later, of dancing with his date, and then he and Josh would slip away. Usually just for a short time, but homecoming that year had not gone well. First, the football team had lost, and Ryan had taken the loss poorly, making it all his fault in his head somehow. Then, he and his date were not getting along. They had bickered all evening. It culminated with her giving Ryan a slap and him turning his back on her. She'd rushed after him, trying to apologize, but he'd shaken her off, grabbed Josh, and the two of them had fled, Ryan peeling out of the school parking lot and making the tires of his BMW squeal.

They'd gone back to Ryan's house because his parents had left for the evening. The au pair had already gone to bed, along with Tyler and Brad. Ryan dragged Josh to his room and had uncharacteristically grabbed him, borne him to his bed, then attacked him. Not that Josh minded in the slightest. He didn't mind any of it, not even that it hurt at first, despite the lube that Ryan had produced from a hidden spot under his mattress. Josh wanted to belong to Ryan too badly to let pain to stand in his way, and it got better. Much better.

Every dance after that, every party, every function that Ryan took a date to, Josh waited on the edges and hoped. Sometimes he got what he wanted. Usually he didn't. The worst nights were the ones where the person getting dragged off was Ryan's date, leaving Josh to find his own way home. Ryan always apologized, always made it up to him one way or another, but it was never quite enough compensation in Josh's book.

In the days leading up to a dance or a party, Josh's gut would churn and roil with acid. The uncertainty was the worst. Lady or tiger; would he be fucked or ignored? The possible outcomes would worry him all night as he stood and watched the boy he adored but could never touch. Not in public. Not where anyone could ever see.

That's why he hated dancing, but he couldn't explain that to Tyler. Not that Tyler wouldn't understand, of course he would, but he'd get that look on his face he always got when they discussed Ryan: a mixture of pity and fury. Josh didn't want to see it, not tonight, not so soon after hearing Tyler tell him that he was loved.

He thought of Tyler looking his father in the eye. *"I am the man in love with your son."* No doubt, no hesitation, no fear. Josh stood and put his hand in Tyler's. He allowed himself to be pulled onto a dance floor for the first time in his life.

"I suck at dancing," he shouted over the music.

"I don't care," Tyler shouted back, holding tight to his hand and refusing to let go.

Chapter 32
Tyler is Surprised

Saturday, October 1st, 9:45 p.m.
The Field Museum: the dance floor
Chicago, IL

Josh was a terrible dancer and Tyler didn't care. It was fun trying to make his oh-so-proper doctor gyrate his hips. If Josh ever managed to lose his self-consciousness, he might not be so bad. Tyler was cognizant of the looks they were getting and knew Josh had to sense them as well, which wasn't helping him relax. Not all, not even most, were hostile, but they all had a weight that could be felt.

Tyler hoped his father's eyes were among them, that he saw his son dancing with another man and realized there was nothing he could do about it, that nothing he had ever tried to "fix" Tyler had ever worked.

This moment had been inevitable since his birth—that Tyler would dance at his brother's wedding with another man. That it was Josh was an extra bonus. No matter how horrible he was at dancing, being with him was better than any other phantom hypothetical man Tyler had pictured himself with when he was younger and miserable and trapped in his father's house. Josh had always been his favorite hopeless fantasy. Being with him now seemed too good to be true. Tyler was still waiting for the other shoe to drop. As if on cue, Josh stepped on his foot.

Tyler glanced up at Josh, who was biting his lip in concentration. The music had changed from upbeat to slow and romantic, and Josh was attempting to slow dance with him while not stepping on his feet. He wasn't doing so well at that, but he was trying, and that was more than good enough for Tyler. He rested his head on Josh's chest so he could hear the beating of his heart like it was percussion for the music they swayed to.

Then someone screamed.

All heads swiveled to the woman, someone Tyler vaguely recognized. The wife of one of the lawyers who worked at the firm, he thought.

"Oh my God, a doctor, somebody, oh my God!"

Josh rushed over, Tyler trailing behind him. Within moments he saw a man crumpled on the floor. His father. Brad was already there, checking for a pulse. Rachel stood nearby, her eyes wide. Josh joined Brad on the floor. The two of them started CPR, Brad doing the breathing and

Josh the chest compressions.

"Has anyone called 911?" Josh called out.

"They're sending an ambulance," said someone. "They said they'd be here soon."

Someone, it looked like one of the Field staff, hurried over with a portable defibrillator. Tyler walked away. He couldn't watch. He wasn't sure if he wanted his father to survive or not, and it felt ghoulish to watch him teeter on the edge. He went and found his mother and held her hand.

"Have you called Ryan?" she asked.

"No, not yet. I think I should wait until the EMTs get here and see — " he almost said, "if he lives" and changed it to " — what hospital they take him to."

"I don't know what to feel," his mother said. "Isn't that terrible? He was my husband for twenty-eight years. You'd think I'd know... that there would be..."

"You're just in shock," Tyler said. "That's all. We all are." He said it for the benefit of anyone who might be listening to them. They didn't need to know that he viewed the possible death of his father with utter detachment. It was nothing to do with him, other than how it would affect his brothers. He hoped for Brad and Rachel's sakes alone that the old bastard wouldn't die on the dance floor of their wedding while Brad performed CPR on him. No one needed that kind of memory.

The paramedics rushed in and gave his father oxygen. *Good. If he has to die, let it be in the ambulance, or better yet, in the hospital.* Tyler found himself in the odd position of hoping his father wouldn't die solely so it wouldn't ruin Brad and Rachel's honeymoon. He stifled a very inappropriate laugh.

Josh started his way, looking grim.

"Well?" Tyler asked.

Josh ran a hand through his hair, disarranging the order Tyler had given it earlier. "They're taking him to Northwestern. Brad is going with him in the ambulance and Rachel said she'll follow, but wants to get out of her gown first, which makes sense. Cynthia, can you and my parents manage to take charge of the reception? I'm sure it'll start to break up since most of the wedding party will have left, but just in case, we need someone here."

Tyler's mother nodded and he was grateful for the excuse Josh had given to keep her away from the hospital. She didn't want to be there and his father wouldn't have wanted her to go.

"I'm calling Ryan," Tyler said.

"He picked a hell of a time to take off," Josh said.

"You can say that again," Tyler muttered while waiting for Ryan to pick up the phone.

"Tyler," Ryan said, "I'm glad you called. I need to speak with you about something. Can you and Josh come over to my place? I'd think that the reception has got to be winding down by now."

"Ryan, Dad's on his way to the hospital."

"What? What happened? Is he okay?"

"I think he had like a stroke or heart attack. He just collapsed. Josh and Brad did CPR until the paramedics came. They're taking him to Northwestern."

"How long ago?"

"They're taking him out right now. They've got him on oxygen."

"Okay. I'm on my way to the hospital. I'll meet you there."

෴

Saturday, October 1st, 10:25 p.m.
Northwestern Memorial Hospital
Chicago, IL

Tyler didn't particularly want to go to the hospital but it seemed expected. Josh had assumed they would go with Rachel and Tyler hadn't argued. There would've been no point. He let himself be swept along on the tide of concern that flowed around him.

On the drive there, he resigned himself to an interminable night spent in a hospital waiting room, drinking terrible coffee and surrounded by sick people. The prospect did not appeal. What he didn't expect was Patrick standing by the reception desk, wearing the same suit he'd been in earlier, only minus the tie. Likely it had been left back at Ryan's place. *Probably on Ryan's bedroom floor*, Tyler thought.

"Well," said Tyler, "you're just like a bad penny today, aren't you?"

Rachel narrowed her eyes. "What the hell is going on, Patrick? Why are you here? Why did I see you at my wedding? I'm positive you weren't invited."

Patrick swallowed hard, making his Adam's apple bob. "I, uh... Tyler, your father's in the ICU. Ryan's up there, too."

"What about Brad?" Rachel snapped.

Patrick looked uncomfortable but he soldiered on. "I haven't seen him, but I assume he's in there with Ryan. We got here a few minutes ago. Ryan told me to wait here for you to tell you where they were."

"And you're here why?" Rachel's fisted hands went to her hips and Tyler thought she looked to be currently at DEFCON 3.

At first Patrick looked panicky, then his expression went mulish. "Ask Ryan," he said. "Come on, I'll take you to the surgical waiting area since I just came from there."

They found Brad and Ryan having an argument. Based on the look Brad gave Patrick when they walked in, it was about him. Rachel went over to Brad and gave him a hug while Ryan left his side and walked over to Patrick, Tyler, and Josh. "Where's Mom?"

"Still at the wedding, directing traffic with Josh's parents," Tyler said. "She doesn't want to be here and Dad wouldn't want her here." Unsaid was that he wouldn't want Tyler there, either.

"I suppose," Ryan said.

"A better question is why you brought the boy toy. Rachel is pretty pissed, if you haven't noticed."

"It was Brad's wedding, not yours, Tyler, and I've already talked to him about it, and that's the end of it. I will not discuss it further."

"Oh, sure, last night it was all well and good to lecture me about my big gay drama, but yours is somehow sacrosanct?"

"Shut up, Tyler. I'm not going to tell you again."

"Or what?" Tyler taunted. "You'll tell Dad? Oh, wait, you can't, because he had a heart attack and you weren't there because you were too busy fucking Patrick."

"Look, you little piece of shit," Patrick spat. "A man's life is on the line, and right now that's more important than whatever issues you have with me and Ryan. I'm here because he's worried sick about his father, and I notice you haven't asked even one question about his condition. Maybe you need to figure out your priorities. Even if you don't give a shit about your father, your brother does."

Tyler cocked his head to the side and considered his brother's lover. While he hadn't defended himself, he had come right to Ryan's defense. Interesting. "This is probably a bad time to tell you that I'm kind of rooting for the bastard not to pull through, isn't it? Dad and I aren't exactly close, new boy."

Beside him Josh made an unhappy noise in his throat but didn't say anything. Not yet. Still, Tyler felt that maybe he should qualify that. "Okay, fine, I don't actively wish him to die. But I'm not going to fall to pieces if he does. Dad and I parted ways long ago. He's pretty much my sperm donor and that's about it."

Patrick and Ryan exchanged a look that spoke volumes, it just wasn't in a language Tyler understood.

"For the record, though, you," Tyler glared at Patrick, "crashing Brad and Rachel's wedding and you," he glared at Ryan, "leaving early 'to take him home' was pretty shitty and I'm still pissed at both of you because of it. Josh had to give the best man speech in your place, you ass."

Ryan cleared his throat. "Maybe I haven't behaved as I should have. I… wasn't thinking, and I apologize, Josh. I've already apologized to Brad.

I meant to come back to the wedding but something came up—"

"Really? You're going with 'something came up?' That's worse than 'it's not what it looks like.'" Tyler shook his head.

"Something came up, Tyler. I'm serious. It's what I need to talk with you about, so can we call a truce for now?"

Tyler gave an exaggerated sigh, then nodded. He'd gotten about as much remorse out of Ryan as he was likely to get.

"Good. So, here's what I know about Dad. They've taken him into surgery. They're going to do a bypass operation on two of the arteries in his heart. We're going to be here for a while, and we need to find somewhere we can talk."

"All of us? I have no problem with Josh taking part, so I guess I'll allow the boy toy to listen in." Tyler felt Josh give his arm a sharp squeeze, which meant he should probably try to rein himself in, at least a little. *Oh, the things I do for love.*

Patrick burned bright red. "Fuck you."

"That's enough," Ryan snapped. "There's a cafe not too far from the waiting room. Let's get some coffee and try to remember we're adults."

"Fine," Tyler said. Patrick was silent but stared daggers at him.

"I'll go tell Rachel and Brad where we're going and see if they want us to bring anything back," Josh said.

They stood for a few moments in awkward silence, then Patrick blurted out, "That man is way too nice for you. I have no idea what he sees in you."

"It's my ability to tie a knot in a cherry stem with my tongue," Tyler said, but that was just an automatic response. Really, he wasn't certain what Josh saw in him besides an admittedly fabulous ass, but there had to be something more. He just didn't know what that something more was. All Tyler could think of were the things he saw in Josh. "If you really want to know, ask him."

"Ask him what?" Josh walked up and gave them all a questioning look.

"Patrick wants to know what you see in me. Besides my fine packaging, of course."

Josh pinned an embarrassed and defiant Patrick with an annoyed glare. "What do you see in Ryan besides his fine packaging?" he asked. "That's a much better question."

Ouch.

Ryan stood there with thinned lips and said nothing while Patrick's skin went scarlet. Tyler gave Josh a mock chiding look.

"That was nasty. Clearly I'm a bad influence." He put a hand on Josh's neck and brought him close enough for a kiss.

"Hey," Tyler heard Ryan say. "You. What are you doing? Are you taking pictures?"

Tyler pulled away from Josh to see a man hastily shoving something into his pocket and backing away from Ryan, who stalked toward him like an avenging angel.

"Shit," Josh muttered and herded Tyler over to the corner where Brad and Rachel sat.

"Brad, I need you," Josh said.

Brad stood. "What's up?"

"I think one of the paparazzi followed us here from the wedding," Tyler said. "Ryan's gone over to deal with him."

"Tyler, sit down," said Josh. "Brad, you and I can block him from view."

"I will, too," Patrick said.

All three men stood like a living wall between him and the rest of the room, facing him with their backs outward, which wasn't awkward at all, having all three staring down at him.

"So," Brad said. "Care to explain why one of my brother's legal secretaries crashed my wedding?"

"No," Patrick said.

Tyler laughed. He couldn't help it. "Taking the fifth?" he asked.

"Yes," Patrick said.

"Good choice."

"You know this kid, Tyler?" Brad asked. "I don't suppose you'd care to fill me in. All I got from Ryan was a lame apology and zero explanation."

Tyler shook his head. "Nope. I am also pleading the fifth."

To his surprise, it was Josh who said something. "It's Ryan's business," he said.

"Yeah, but it was *my* wedding," Rachel complained.

"Nothing bad happened because he came, Rach," said Josh. "Let it go. This isn't the time, okay? I'll fill you in later, I promise."

Rachel looked like she wanted to debate the matter, so Tyler decided to make amends for his earlier nastiness by forcibly changing the subject. It wasn't Patrick he was really angry with, anyway, it was Ryan, and Ryan was off fighting a battle for him. Providing a little misdirection to take the heat off Patrick was the least Tyler could do. Especially as Patrick was currently acting as a portion of his shield.

"This was a bad idea," Tyler said. "I shouldn't have come. Dad won't want to see me, anyway. I didn't think. I'm sorry, Brad."

"It's okay," Brad said. "Ryan will take care of it. It's what he does."

"I know." Tyler looked up at Josh. "This is what life with me is like. It's probably only going to get worse. I'm sorry."

Josh frowned and didn't reply.

Ryan came over and joined their huddle. "Security was called and that asshole was removed, but I think we should go, at least for now. I'll take Josh and Tyler home, then come back later alone. Unless Dad asks for Tyler, of course."

Which he wouldn't.

⊗⊗

Saturday, October 1st, 11:30 p.m.
Ryan's overpriced condo
Chicago, IL

Ryan ended up taking them back to his place so they could borrow one of his cars. "That way you don't have to worry about a rental," Ryan said. "Also, we still need to talk, and my living room will work as well as yours, Josh."

Tyler sat on the couch in the same place he'd sat last time. This time, however, Josh sat in the chair next to him. Patrick sat in the opposite chair, leaving the other end of the couch empty for Ryan, who poured drinks.

Tyler found a glass with two fingers of what was probably scotch thrust into his hand. He took a sip and made a face. It was smoky and bitter and probably expensive as hell, and he hated it. He put his glass down.

Having distributed drinks, Ryan sat. "Okay, first things first. We can eliminate Michael Koenig as a possibility for uploading the video. He died in a car crash five years ago."

"Christ," Tyler said. It was strange. He knew, intellectually, that Mr. "Call Me Michael" Koenig had at best taken advantage of him and at worst raped him, but his memories of the man were more complicated than that. He'd had such a crush on him, daydreaming of climbing onto his lap and kissing him silent while he sat in the man's office and listened to him drone on and on about whatever-the-fuck. A lot of it had been useful life advice, but Tyler had listened with half an ear while wondering what the man's dick looked like. He'd studied Mr. Koenig's crotch, analyzing the folds of fabric, hoping for some clue.

The reality of sucking his guidance counselor's cock (cut, six or seven inches, decent girth) wasn't as great as the fantasy. Few things ever were, see also his disastrous threesome. But for all that, he'd, right or wrong, never felt violated by the man. His innocence had been gone long before Mr. Koenig had pulled out his dick for Tyler's rapt inspection.

Compared to what had happened in Bridges, what Mr. Koenig had done to him was less than nothing. It wasn't fair he'd been punished and the men at Bridges had not. It wasn't fair that Tyler had a huge scar on his leg as a souvenir from his stay there. But then life wasn't fair. It gave and it took without regard to who deserved what.

"What... do you know the details of the crash?"

"It happened during a heavy snowstorm," Patrick supplied. "He was driving on I-90 and somehow drove off the road in the storm and hit a snowbank. The car was plowed under. They found it days later."

"Was he killed in the crash or... later?" Tyler asked, taking another sip of the scotch, then grimacing.

"The article I found mentioned head trauma, so..."

Tyler hoped he'd died right away. Michael Koenig had had no business working with teenagers, but he hadn't been a monster. Or maybe Tyler had become so jaded to monsters by the time he had come around that, in comparison, he hadn't seemed so bad. In any event, Tyler didn't rejoice in the man's death and he hoped he hadn't suffered.

Tyler didn't think he'd have the same merciful thoughts had the man in question been Matt or Greg or that head fucker, Pastor Steve. No, he'd have hoped they died slowly, hungry and thirsty and cold and smelling their own waste.

He wasn't sure what that said about him. Probably nothing good.

"As for the video," Ryan continued, "we've been working with the Highland Park police to figure out what happened to it. They've had quite a bit of turnover since then, and they're tracking down people who had access to the evidence safe at the time."

Patrick leaned forward. "I have a friend who we hired to try and track where the video was uploaded. It's from an ISP from this area, which in the grand scheme isn't surprising. She thinks she might be able to get something more specific for us soon."

"Okay, great, I guess. That still doesn't eliminate Dad," Tyler said. He eyed his drink and wished he didn't hate scotch. "Not that I can go and accuse him of fucking with me while he's in the hospital recovering from a heart attack."

Patrick and Ryan looked at each other. "As to that," Ryan said, "I may have discovered something." He cleared his throat. "About you, and why Dad is the way he is with you."

Tyler sat up. "You mean besides me being gay and a massive disappointment to him?"

"Yes, I think so. Ty, do you remember Michael Connolly? We used to call him Uncle Mike?"

Beside him, Josh twitched with some sort of reaction. Tyler glanced at him, but all he got was an unhelpful puzzled frown. He looked back at Ryan.

"Vaguely. He used to work with Dad, right? Mom was friends with his wife, the one who was always sick. What was her name? Sophie, I think? Something like that."

"Yes, Sophie," Ryan said. "She had cancer. It kept going into remission and then coming back. Do you remember what Mike looked like?"

"I was a kid the last time I saw him. I'd probably recognize him if I saw him, though. I think he had reddish hair. Why?"

"I was going to go back to the wedding after I talked with Patrick." Tyler noticed the incredulous look Patrick gave Ryan at that and was not surprised. "But I didn't, because of that 'something' I mentioned in the hospital."

"Oh, right. That thing that came up that had nothing to do with you fucking Patrick. Right." Tyler said, not able to help himself.

Ryan didn't look angry, and that was a little worrying. "Not now, Ty. This is important. On way out of the museum, I noticed Uncle Mike waiting with Patrick by the door."

"He said that, like me, he was wedding crashing," Patrick added.

"And?" Tyler asked, wanting them to get to the point already.

"I thought he had to be your actual Uncle Mike because he looks just like you," Patrick said.

Tyler felt like he'd been thrown into icy water. "What? No. No, he doesn't." He flung a hand out and Josh caught it. Tyler curled his fingers around Josh's hand and hung on to it like it was the only thing keeping him tethered to the world.

Ryan took a sip from his glass, then set it down on a nearby table. "That's what I said, but Patrick made me really think about it, and there is a resemblance. So instead of going back to the wedding, I went to Dad's house and hunted down the old photo albums. I finally found what I wanted in the attic. Here, look at this."

Ryan held out a picture for Tyler to look at, and at first, his eyes refused to focus on it, possibly out of self-defense. Next to him, Josh swore.

"Fuck, that's creepy. Damn."

Tyler reached out, his hand shaking a little, and took the photograph. It was from one of the company picnics, and had been taken when he was three or four, based on what he looked like. He was standing next to his mother, his hand on her leg. She was talking with a couple. The woman was very thin and wore a scarf on her head. The man... the man...

The picture dropped out of Tyler's numb fingers and Josh bent and picked it up. He studied it more closely. "The resemblance is striking, especially taking into consideration how dissimilar you look from Brad and Ryan."

"I always thought I took after Mom," Tyler said. He marveled at his feeling of incredulity. Hadn't he always wondered why his father didn't love him? This was the explanation. He ought to feel relieved. Instead he felt utterly betrayed. "Mom. I need to speak with her. I need her to explain…"

Josh put down the photo and rubbed Tyler's hand. "Later. Rachel sent me a text while we were on the way here, saying that she and my parents joined her and Brad at the hospital. Now is not a good time to talk to your mom about this, okay?"

Josh was right. Tyler knew he was right. But there was a tearing, howling feeling of betrayal ripping through him and he could barely stand it.

"Take me home. Please. Take me home."

"There's more I'd like to discuss with you, Tyler. Regarding the video…"

"Fuck the video," Tyler snarled. "And fuck you."

Ryan recoiled. Tyler felt he should maybe apologize, but he couldn't.

"Later," Josh said. "It can wait, can't it?" He stood and pulled Tyler up with him. "Can we still borrow one of your cars?"

"Yes, of course," Ryan said, and he hurried to get them the keys to what would no doubt end up being the Volvo. Why he'd ever bought the thing was a mystery to Tyler.

Tyler bent and picked up the picture. He stared at the man by his mother and it was like looking into a mirror. It was him, with slightly longer, dark-auburn hair. That was his smile, or one of them, at any rate. It was the one Purvi called his "panty-wetting smile," and despite standing next to his wife, that smile was aimed right at Tyler's mother.

Chapter 33
Josh Takes His Boyfriend Responsibilities Seriously

Saturday, October 1st, 11:48 p.m.
In Ryan's Volvo
Chicago, IL

"I left my clothes at the museum. You did, too."

Josh glanced over at Tyler, who fingered the lapels of his tuxedo jacket absently.

"Rachel said that your mother grabbed everything that we left there—me, you, Brad, and Ryan. She gave my stuff to my mother. I'd guess she has your things. We can get them tomorrow."

"Yeah," Tyler said, his voice so low Josh could barely hear him.

"Do you want to talk about it? I mean, that's probably a stupid question, but as your official boyfriend, I need to ask. I'm pretty sure it's part of my duties and responsibilities."

Josh sensed Tyler looking at him and gave him another quick glance. Tyler had a half-smile on his face and looked a little less distant. "No one told me that. Please elaborate."

"Okay. For example, I'm required to not allow you to brood for too long without asking if you're okay and making an offering of some sort."

"What kind of offering?" Tyler asked.

"Oh, ice cream or a back rub or a blow job. Something like that."

"Hm. How about ice cream, a back rub, then a blow job?"

"Now you're being greedy. I'm also required to ask if you want to talk, but Chadwicks don't talk about things, so…"

Tyler let out a short, ugly-sounding laugh. "I'm not a Chadwick, though, am I? Maybe it's not Chadwicks who don't talk about things. It's probably a Foster thing instead."

"Foster?" Josh asked.

"My mother's family. And that seems a hell of a lot more likely, doesn't it? Ryan and I get it from Mom, not Dad."

Tyler's voice sounded thick, and Josh risked another look at him since they were stopped at a red light. As Josh watched, Tyler blinked and a tear fell from his lashes, down his cheek, and then dripped off his chin. Josh was about to reach out when a horn beeped behind him. The light had turned green.

"Stop worrying about me. Just drive. I'm fine." Tyler scrubbed his face with the heel of his hand.

Josh could no more stop worrying than he could stop breathing, but he could shut up and drive, if that's what Tyler needed, so that's what he did.

☙❧

Sunday, October 2nd, 2:03 a.m.
Josh's perfectly adequate condo
Evanston, IL

Josh woke and Tyler wasn't in bed. He squinted at the clock and saw it was just after two in the morning. He felt the blankets next to him but they'd lost any residual heat from Tyler's body. Josh got up and went to look for him.

Once he left the bedroom, Josh heard the water running in the guest bathroom. Oliver sat outside the door and pawed at it plaintively. Josh bent to scratch Oliver's head and called, "Tyler? Are you okay?"

No answer.

He tried the doorknob. It was unlocked, so he and Oliver went in. Through the foggy glass shower door Josh could see Tyler sitting in a huddled ball in the bathtub letting the shower's spray hit him. Josh slid open the shower door.

Tyler's right fist was clenched and blood dripped from it. He looked up at Josh, his eyes huge and glassy. "I didn't cut myself," he said. "I wanted to, so much, but I didn't."

Josh turned off the shower and took hold of Tyler's hand. "Let me see," he said, and gently pried Tyler's hand open. He was holding a razor blade, the cardboard strip still on it, but it had become soggy and flimsy with water. A corner of the blade was unprotected and had cut into Tyler's palm. It wasn't very deep, and Josh felt relief flood through him. It could have been so much worse.

Tyler looked at his hand. "Oh. Looks like I cut myself anyway. Does it count if I didn't mean to?" Then he laughed, and the sound was horrible. Josh couldn't stand it.

"Shh," he soothed. "Come on. Let's get you dried off and your hand bandaged up."

Tyler laid his forehead on his knees. "I'm sorry," he mumbled, and made no move to get up.

Josh stood looking down at Tyler. He considered trying to get him to stand up then changed his mind. He grabbed a towel, tucked it around Tyler's shivering body, and sat down on the floor next to the tub, folding his legs under him awkwardly. Oliver jumped into the bathtub and started rolling around in the water drops.

"You have a weird cat," Josh said.

"Oliver is not weird," Tyler said, "and I'm going to get blood on your towel." He made it sound like a bloody towel would be utter catastrophe. Josh didn't particularly care about the towel, but he got up, found an adhesive bandage, and sat back down.

"Here, give me your hand." Josh bandaged the cut, then kissed the back of Tyler's hand. "There, your majesty," he said. "Nearly good as new."

"Why are you here?" Tyler whispered. Oliver lay on his back, all four feet in the air, and Tyler rubbed his belly. Josh was impressed. He'd tried that the other day and had gotten clawed for his efforts.

"I woke up and you weren't in bed, so I came looking for you," Josh said. "Your cat was looking for you, too."

"No, I mean, why are you here, being my real boyfriend and shit? You said you love me, but I'm not sure what you see in me that you could possibly want. Besides the fine packaging, of course. What else worthwhile is there?"

"Tyler, you are way more than just fine packaging."

"Right," was his sardonic response.

Josh would be the first one to admit that he wasn't an expert when it came to relationships. He was nearly thirty-five and hadn't once had a normal one that lasted longer than a few months. What he'd had with Ryan wasn't even in the ballpark of normal, let alone healthy, and other than that, all he'd had was a string of short-term shallow relationships with enough men that he would have to get out pen and paper to keep them all straight. He'd never helped someone he loved to get through a tough time. He was so hopelessly out of his depth it was almost ridiculous. But leaving Tyler alone to wallow in self-pity in his bathtub wasn't an option, so Josh stayed put on the floor, his legs starting to go numb from having their blood supply cut off, and hoped like hell that what he was about to say wouldn't make things worse.

"It's not like you're full-on gorgeous all the time, you know. I've seen you look almost ordinary. Case in point, right now you're kind of a hot mess."

Tyler glowered at him. "Fuck you. If this is you trying to make me feel better it's not working."

Josh couldn't help but smile a little, because an irritated Tyler was a million times better than a miserable one. "And then you do this thing, I don't even understand how, and suddenly you're so beautiful that you take my breath away. You look, I don't know… photoshopped."

"Like Ryan Gosling in *Crazy, Stupid, Love*?"

"I guess. I never saw that one. But you look too perfect. Too lovely. Unreal."

Tyler rolled his eyes and favored Josh with a slight smile.

"But sometimes you stop. You drop it all like a discarded mask and I see the real Tyler underneath. Not ordinary. Not perfect. Not Tyler Chadwick: pretty boy, aspiring star, and tabloid fodder. What's under all that is something both more and less. The man I fell in love with."

Tyler shook his head, smile gone. "I'm not one of those people who're all beautiful rainbows and sunshine and sparkly glitter whatever-the-hell on the inside. If you think that, you're fooling yourself. You're seeing shit that's not there."

"No, I'm not. I don't want rainbow sparkle glitter crap. I'm not a rainbow sparkle kind of guy, if you haven't noticed. Glitter gets everywhere and you can never clean it all up. It's awful."

Tyler snorted, but it sounded almost like a laugh.

"I'll admit," Josh continued, "that I do love beautiful things. I love art. I always have. And the best art has depth. Layers. Nuance."

"And?"

"I've dated a lot of men. Lots of very attractive men. A few were better-looking than you, believe it or not."

"Hearing about the legions of handsome men you've been with is not helping," Tyler informed him. "I know I'm not your usual type. Brad told me that you've been dating Ryan clones for as long as he can remember."

"Yeah, and I didn't fall in love with any of them. You, on the other hand, I spend two weeks with and I can't imagine being with anyone else. You are interesting. You have depth. Nuance. Layers. So many layers I'm not sure if I'll ever uncover them all. You are art, Tyler, and I think I could spend the rest of my life studying you and not get tired."

"Stop. Just stop. I can't live up to shit like that. One day my ass will sag. I'll have wrinkles. Liver spots. Scary old man toenails."

Josh's lips quirked. "Where did you get the idea that art is only about aesthetics? You're not just a marble statue of a beautiful boy. I think you're like a Chuck Close painting," Josh said.

"A what?" Tyler raised that bitchy eyebrow of his and Josh knew he must have it very bad indeed, because he was starting to find the expression more endearing than annoying.

"He's this fascinating artist who paints hyper-realistic portraits that look like perfect photographs from far away but become unrecognizable colorful blobs up close. You're like that."

"What, like I'm incomprehensible unless seen from a distance?" Tyler asked. His tone was caustic but Josh thought there was more there, too. Buried beneath the self-denigration and gloom was a small spark of hope. Sort of like Charlie Brown and that football of Lucy's and how this time maybe, despite all evidence to the contrary, things might be different.

Josh could relate.

His fingers stroked the back of Tyler's head. "Not exactly. Perfect from far away, complex and beautiful and unexpected when up close, with shapes and colors you can't see until you stand near enough to not see the perfection."

Tyler sighed. "That's... dammit, Josh. I don't know what to say, other than maybe that prick Patrick was right. You do deserve someone better than me. So much better. The best."

"I don't want someone better, I want you." *Beautiful and scarred and sweet and sharp as a knife.* Josh rearranged his legs so he could kneel beside the tub. He leaned over to kiss the back of Tyler's neck and smelled alcohol that even a shower hadn't been able to wash away. *And apparently drunk as a skunk.* "What have you been drinking?" That explained a lot. It seemed Tyler was a maudlin drunk.

"I drank all the vodka and then there was no more," he said, making it sound like a tragedy. "I am merely a tiny bit intoxicated. I wish there was more vodka. Something not shitty. Would it kill you to buy Grey Goose? You're such a cheapskate. That and you have zero ice cream. How can you have no ice cream?"

"Oh, baby," Josh sighed. He tried to remember how much had been in the bottle. He thought maybe it had been between half and two-thirds full.

Tyler lifted his head and gave Josh a murderous look. "Do *not* call me that," he hissed.

"Okay, fine. No calling you baby. But princess is okay?"

Tyler heaved a great sigh. "Princess is what *you* call me, so it's acceptable. Annoying, but acceptable. I'd maim anyone else who tried it, but from you it's okay. *He* called me baby and I hated it, and he knew it, and he still called me it anyway, the fucker."

Josh rubbed Tyler's back and tried to parse that. "The 'he' in question is one of your exes, I take it?"

Tyler nodded. "The evil one. David."

"I know about Ethan. He's the failed twink experiment who's a journalist, right?"

Tyler nodded again.

"Okay, tell me about David. What flavor of gay is he?"

"The gaslighting, abusive kind."

Josh felt anger begin to curl within him. "Good to know, but that's not what I meant."

"Oh, I suppose David is a bit of a stealth gay. Like you, but not like you, if you know what I mean."

"Not really."

Tyler tipped his head back and gazed at the ceiling. "He's like you in that he can pass for straight. At first, he didn't even ping my gaydar and my gaydar is good. Like very, very good."

"So how was he not like me?"

"Um, you're not an evil sociopath, for starters."

"Tyler, that might be the nicest thing you've ever said to me."

Tyler huffed and almost smiled.

"Why was he evil?"

"Bad genes? Terrible parenting? Possessed by a demon?" Tyler shrugged. "Beats me."

Josh moved his legs again and tried to get the blood circulating in them before they cramped up. "Smart-ass. I meant what did he do to you? Besides call you baby."

Tyler poked Oliver with his toe and the cat responded by licking it. Josh didn't care what Tyler said. That cat was weird.

"It's so depressingly Freudian. Big surprise, I've got all these daddy issues and David saw that and capitalized on all of them. I met him when he was working security on a movie that I had a bit part in. I had just turned twenty-one and he was thirty-two." Tyler gave Josh a look. "I might have a thing for older men. Did I mention I have daddy issues?"

Josh tried not to smile, because it wasn't really funny, and failed. "I think I remember you saying something along those lines, yes."

Tyler also smiled, but his was full of bitterness. "David swept me off my feet. He was so… intense, I guess. So focused on me. I loved that, big surprise, but there were red flags right from the start that I ignored the shit out of. He separated me from my friends, or tried to. He and Purvi couldn't stand each other, and he kept trying to get me to fire her. When David and I disagreed, I was always the one who was wrong. He made all the decisions, from what we ate to how we had sex. And at first that was fine, because I didn't care, and because the sex was great—until it wasn't. And that was my fault, naturally, because I didn't want to do the things he wanted. He got off on hurting me, and he wanted to tie me up. And while I am not judgy about people's kinks, being tied up makes me…" Tyler's smile fell away.

Josh had a sick feeling in his stomach. He remembered Tyler mentioning that they'd tied him up at Bridges before branding him. "You're allowed to not be into bondage, Tyler. That's a pretty niche kink."

"I know," he said, but he didn't sound as if he believed it. "He wouldn't stop going on and on about it, and sometimes I gave in, but I hated it and he didn't care. He also knew about the cutting. I let him see my scars because I didn't know any better, and he seemed to think that gave him a pass to hurt me, too, whenever he wanted, however he wanted." Tyler pulled the towel tighter around himself. "He liked giving me bruises because of how pretty he said they looked on my skin." Tyler paused and frowned. "I shouldn't have drunk all that vodka. I'm going to regret telling you this in the morning."

Josh felt like he was going to be ill. He wanted to find this David guy and dismantle him. "I take it you're not referring to the fun sort of bruises."

Tyler flashed a grin and reached over to run his finger across the marks that lingered on Josh's neck and collarbone. "No," he murmured. "Not the fun sort. The 'I guess I'm just clumsy and fell down into someone's fist' kind of bruises."

"Fuck," Josh said. "God dammit, Tyler."

"Calm your tits, Sir Joshua. I got my shit together and left him. Or kicked him out, since he'd been living in my house. You know, I find it amusing that you feel the need to distinguish between bad bruises and fun ones. That's just adorable."

Josh said nothing, but he could feel his face flame.

Tyler made his expression very serious and gave Josh a poke to get his attention. When he spoke, it was as if he were imparting a great and solemn secret. "You like a little pain, don't you? The scrape of teeth. A little too much pressure." Tyler grabbed Josh's chin in a grip of steel and drew his face closer until they were only a breath apart. "Am I wrong?"

"No." Josh's cock twitched and he felt guilty because now was so not the time.

Tyler caressed his jaw. "Yeah, I figured that out pretty quickly. You like it when I boss you around and tell you what to do, too. It gets you off and I am more than okay with that, so it's all good." Tyler kissed him, just a soft whisper of lips barely touching, then he released Josh's chin. "David, though. He liked things I hated, and sometimes I think that the more I didn't like them, the more he did. Then one day I woke up with a black eye I couldn't see out of and bruised ribs, and that was it. I packed up his shit, had the locks changed, and then called the police and got a restraining order. I even got one of my friends to take his shit to his work so I wouldn't have to see him again."

"Good for you," Josh said, still wanting to dismantle David very slowly.

"That wasn't it, though. He ended up harassing and stalking me for months before he finally got arrested. Slashed all the tires on my car and keyed it, among other things."

"Huh," Josh said.

"Yeah, I know. Just like your car."

"So that's what was bothering you yesterday. Bad boyfriend

flashback."

Tyler clutched the towel tighter around himself. "What if it's him?"

"Is that likely? Didn't you date him in California?"

Tyler nodded. "Yeah, but after he got arrested he moved away. I don't know where. One of his coworkers told me that it was back where he grew up, but in all the time we were together, I never learned much about him. Didn't think about him for years, or at least not much, then my wall got painted."

"Okay, Ty, you've lost me."

Tyler blinked at him owlishly. "Fuck," he said. "So, here's the thing. And you can't get mad. Promise?"

"No, I do not promise not to get mad. It doesn't work like that. Now what the hell?"

"So, while I was back home someone painted 'die faggot' on one half of my wall and 'die cocksucker' on the other half. And now you're mad. No, you're disappointed. That's worse."

Josh let out a deep sigh. "Why didn't you tell me?"

Tyler buried his face again. "I'd planned on telling you when I got here, then shit happened and I forgot."

"Shit happened?"

Tyler turned his face so one pewter-colored eye peered at him. "Yeah, shit happened. That epic airport kiss, then the epic fucking when we got home. Then I was going to tell you at lunch on Thursday, but Nik happened. Then I was going to tell you Friday, but dinner didn't seem to be the right time, and the strip club wasn't conducive to conversation, then you took me home and there was more fucking and then you said you loved me, and I didn't think about it again until I saw your car on Saturday, but we were already late for the wedding, and then my dad had a heart attack and then I found out that he's not my real dad and my mom has lied to me my whole life. It's been a busy week."

Josh started to feel prickles of apprehension, because he'd also forgotten to share something. "So," he said.

"Are you mad?" Tyler asked. "Is this the portion of the evening in which I get yelled at?"

Josh ran a hand through his hair. "Well, here's the thing," he said.

Tyler lifted his head and now two pewter eyes peered at him. "What thing?"

"There was this guy on Tuesday night. He kept ringing the buzzer on the door. I finally went down to see who it was because security was doing dick-all about it, and there was this man trying to get in and demanding to know where you were. I threatened to call the cops and he went away. I figured he was just a creepy fan of yours."

"What did he look like?" Tyler asked. He gripped the towel so hard his knuckles turned white.

Josh closed his eyes, thinking. "About my height and age, muscular build, dark hair, beard, really noticeable blue eyes."

"Oh, Jesus. Aside from the beard, that could be David."

"It could be a whole bunch of people, actually. Hey, I took his picture. Let me get my phone."

Tyler nodded and Josh went to get it. When he walked back into the bathroom, Tyler had gotten out of the tub, dried himself off, and put his pajama bottoms on. He sat on the closed seat of the toilet with the cat on his lap.

Josh thumbed through his pictures until he found the one he was looking for. He turned the phone around and Tyler flinched back, clutching at Oliver.

"Oh, shit. It's him."

"Are you sure?"

"Oh, yeah. That's him. What the fuck is he doing here? How did he find your building? How did he know I was here with you?"

"I don't know why he's here," Josh said, "but the rest wouldn't be too hard to figure out from the internet. We've done everything short of taking out a billboard to advertise that we're a couple. Look, I've already given his photo to security. They know to call the police if he comes back, which he hasn't, and we'll tell the police about it when I talk to them about the car. If he keeps up this juvenile shit, he'll get caught and arrested again. Okay?"

Tyler nodded and said, "Sure," although he didn't sound sure.

"But if David's here, then it's unlikely he also painted your wall."

"Yeah. It was probably some other asshole who did that. Because that's what I need in my life. More assholes."

"We'll deal with them, Tyler. Together. Got it? And maybe when shit like this happens in the future you could mention it right away."

"Likewise," Tyler said, giving Josh his death glare, which paradoxically made Josh feel better.

"Agreed. Now, are you ready to come back to bed, grumpy boy? You can bring your cat with you."

Tyler gave him a long look, then said, "Yeah."

After they lay down next to each other and Josh pulled Tyler close, he said, "You're a depressing drunk."

"That's what Purvi always says, too. She likes it better when I drown my angst in ice cream, but you were all out."

"I need to meet Purvi, and I promise in the future to keep the freezer stocked, just in case. You still like Chunky Monkey?"

Tyler turned to face him. "How the hell did you know that? Have you and Purvi been talking behind my back?"

"Nope." Although Josh thought maybe they should. "It was your favorite when you were a kid."

"Oh. And you remembered." Tyler cupped his face and gave him a quick, hard kiss. "You realize you're stuck with me now, right? You can't keep comparing me to artwork and offering me ice cream and then decide later that you didn't mean it. I will go all Glenn Close on your ass."

"Charming," Josh said. "Lucky for both of us I don't have a rabbit. Or a wife."

"Shut up and make soppy love to my drunken ass."

"Even with the cat watching?" Josh asked, brows raised.

"I think it's too late to worry about corrupting him, and he's already left to go on kitty night patrol."

"Keeping us safe from intruders?"

"Who knows what his itty-bitty cat brain is thinking. Are you going to fuck me or not?"

Josh rolled so Tyler lay under him. "How about a blow job, since I didn't have any ice cream? I can follow it up with a back rub."

"Well, I suppose," Tyler said, making himself sound put-upon. "If that's my only option, I'll make do." He flung an arm over his eyes and adopted a martyred mien. "The things I have to put up with."

Josh stifled a laugh and kissed his way down Tyler's body, pulling off Tyler's pants as he went. The room was lit only by moonlight, so all Josh could see was the suggestion of Tyler's pale form. It stood out against the slate-gray sheets like an El Greco nude: shadowy velvet skin over defined dark ridges of muscle and bone. "So beautiful," he murmured, licking down a sharp hip bone to Tyler's groin.

"You're such a tease," Tyler bitched. "Just blow me already."

Josh's tongue lapped the crease of Tyler's sac, already drawn high and tight against his body. "Patience," he breathed along Tyler's skin, then bit his inner thigh, making him first jump then moan.

"Oh, fuck, Josh, please."

"Please, what?" Josh traced his tongue along Tyler's scars, following them like a road map back to his hip. He licked the skin adjacent to where Tyler's cock lay against his abdomen, so much larger and darker than you'd expect, and gorgeous like the rest of him.

Tyler groaned. "Fuck you, Josh. Fuck you so hard."

"Just for that..." he said, and pulled back.

"No, don't stop," Tyler protested. "You get back here, mister."

Josh reached over to turn on the bedside lamp. Tyler went from stark El Greco contrast to the warm, glowing tones of a Renaissance master. "Michelangelo would have painted the shit out of you," he blurted.

"What?"

"Nothing." He took Tyler's cock into his hand and pumped it, then lowered his head to lick away the precum that glistened at the head. "Just thinking out loud."

"No, wait, wasn't he gay? I think I remember hearing that somewhere. He'd probably want to actually fuck me, unlike certain cockteases I could name."

Josh gave Tyler's cock another slow lick, stabbing his tongue into the slit and making Tyler squirm under him. "Eh. There's no proof he was gay, and even if he was, he was a devout Catholic. He would've painted you as an angel on a cathedral ceiling, composed odes to your spectacular ass, felt guilty about the impure thoughts you'd inspire, and left your actual person untouched."

"How un-fun. Speaking of untouched..." Tyler thrust his hips up, fucking into Josh's hand.

Josh took the hint and lowered his head. He took Tyler's cock into his mouth and sucked, tracing abstract designs on it with his tongue.

Tyler moaned, made mindless but not silent (*never silent*, Josh thought) by a combination of vodka and Josh's mouth. "Oh, Jesus. Oh, yes. Yes. Fuck, yes." Josh pulled his mouth away, causing Tyler to whine. "I didn't say stop."

"I didn't say I was done."

Josh crawled up Tyler's body, only to have his face captured by strong hands and his lips devoured. Josh's heart pounded in his chest, the beats almost painful. He loved Tyler in all his incarnations, even the less-pleasant ones, but his favorite was the Tyler stripped bare of everything but base need and want, because it was for him, all for him.

I love you. God, how I love you. "Can I fuck you now?"

"You didn't finish my blow job, and what about my back rub?"

"Good point." Josh flipped Tyler over so he was facedown.

Tyler pushed up on his elbows and looked back at Josh. "Hey."

"Yes?" Josh rubbed Tyler's shoulders, then kissed the wing of each shoulder blade. He kneaded and kissed his way down Tyler's back, ending with dipping his tongue into the hollow of each perfect dimple that sat above each perfect cheek, just as he'd wanted to do from the first time he'd seen Tyler nude.

"Never mind," Tyler breathed. "Carry on."

Josh spread Tyler and even there he was beautiful, rosy and smooth and perfect. Josh bent his head to taste him, making Tyler hiss in through his teeth.

"Oh, Jesus, God, please, fuck, please!"

While Tyler uttered a medley of broken curses and pleas, Josh licked and nibbled, loving that he had the ability to make his elf lose himself so completely. Under his tongue, Tyler's sphincter softened and spasmed. He jabbed his tongue into Tyler's body and felt his entire body shudder.

"Please, Josh, please. God, please. I will do anything, I swear."

Josh gave Tyler's ass a playful bite. "Does that mean I can fuck you *now*, your majesty?"

Tyler moaned and raised his ass in the air and wiggled it at Josh. "Impossible man. Yes. Now. Or else."

Josh grabbed what he needed out of the bedside dresser. "I think Michelangelo doesn't know what he's missing out on." He pushed slick fingers into Tyler and desire pulsed through Josh. He was tight and hot and utterly exquisite.

Tyler cried out, then muttered, "Impossible man," again under his breath as Josh took his hand away so he could put on a condom.

"Your impossible man," Josh said as he slid his cock slowly into Tyler.

"Yes," Tyler hissed. "Mine."

Mine, repeated his brain in chorus, all the different aspects for once on the same page as he filled Tyler's body. *Mine*, with each thrust. *Mine*, with each moan from the man writhing under him. *Mine*, as he stroked Tyler to orgasm, then came himself in a surge of sizzling electric pleasure. *Mine*, as he cleaned a boneless and limp Tyler and helped put his pants back on. *Mine*, as Josh gathered him close and stroked the satiny skin on his back. *Mine*, as Tyler lay in his arms and snored softly in a way he shouldn't find adorable but did anyway. *Mine*.

"Love you," he whispered into Tyler's neck.

"Ugh. I was almost asleep," Tyler complained.

"Sorry," Josh whispered back.

A few seconds went by, then Tyler said, "It's okay." He nestled closer to Josh, and soon the soft snoring resumed.

Josh's arms tightened around Tyler. *Mine*, he thought as he drifted off to sleep.

ଔଓ

Sunday, October 2nd, 3:49 a.m.
Josh's perfectly adequate condo
Evanston, IL

Josh woke with Tyler's knee pressing hard onto his bladder. He extricated himself, went to go take a piss, and when he came back to bed, he noticed his phone's blinking light. Settling back into bed, he looked to see who had contacted him.

Unknown number: Hi, Dr. McDreamy. This is Purvi, Tyler's personal assistant. Any reason why he isn't answering his phone?
Josh: Purvi! I've heard a lot about you. Let me put you in my contacts.
Purvi: All good things, I hope.
Purvi: Who am I kidding? This is Tyler we're talking about. Forget everything he ever told you. I am AWESOME.
Josh: I'm sure you are. Is there something you need?
Purvi: Is Tyler okay? Why can't I get ahold of him?
Josh: He's sleeping.
Purvi: Since when is the King of Insomnialand asleep when you aren't?
Josh: It's been a long day. Do you know about Tyler's dad having a heart attack?
Purvi: Yeah. I got a message from Ryan. He said that I should try and talk with Ty so that's why I was trying to call. I know he hates that old buzzard, but he's still Tyler's dad.
Josh: There's more. I'll let him fill you in since it's all family stuff, but he drank over half a bottle of vodka, talked at me, then passed out. I'm not waking him up at 3:30 am just to chat.
Purvi: Wow. You got to experience the wonder that is drunken Tyler. You sure you still want to be his boyfriend?
Josh: Pretty sure, yeah. It was my fault for not having any ice cream, apparently.
Purvi: Ice cream is very important.
Josh: I've gathered that. It's like item one on the list of The Care and Maintenance of Tyler.
Purvi: I think I'm going to like you.
Josh: Good. I think you might be item two on that list.
Purvi: There is no shame in coming in second to ice cream.
Purvi: Seriously, how's my boy?
Josh: Things are kinda bad right now. Tyler's going to have a lot of shit to deal with. I'm glad you're coming on Monday.
Purvi: What the hell is going on?
Josh: I'll have him call you when he wakes up.
Purvi: Should I be worried?

Josh thought about how to answer that. The whole situation with Tyler's family was a mess.

Josh: I don't know. It's his family. He's taking things pretty hard. He worries

me, you know?
Purvi: Yeah, I do. I'm looking forward to meeting you.
Josh: Trust me, the feeling is mutual.

Josh put his phone down and pulled Tyler to him, a little surprised but grateful when he didn't wake. He needed all the sleep he could get. Tomorrow, or today, rather, was going to be another long and probably horrible day. In the meantime, Josh savored the quiet, the feel of Tyler in his arms, the soft sound of his breathing, and the scent of his skin. It didn't lessen his worry, but it did make it a bit more bearable.

Chapter 34
Cynthia Has Regrets

Saturday, October 1st, 11:40 p.m.
An upscale hotel room
Chicago, IL

Cynthia sank onto the window seat in her room, leaned her head against the glass, and looked down at the traffic below. Today had been one long wonderful, terrible ordeal. She intended to take a bath in the room's jetted tub before going to bed, but for the moment she was too tired to do even that.

Convincing Brad and Rachel to leave the hospital and not cancel their honeymoon travel plans had taken the last of her energy, but her worthless ex-husband had ruined their wedding reception and wedding night with his ill-timed heart attack. He sure as hell wasn't going to ruin their honeymoon, too. Not if she had any say about it. Thankfully, the Rosens had agreed with her and had thrown their weight behind her argument that Peter had come through surgery just fine and Brad and Rachel's absence or presence wouldn't affect his recovery.

So many thoughts had tumbled through her in the taxi on the way back to the hotel. Worry about Peter and an accompanying irritation that she was at all concerned about him, hope that the newlyweds would leave on their honeymoon as planned, concern over her disappearing eldest son, and more worry concerning Tyler and what he had going on with Josh Rosen. Cynthia liked Josh, she always had, but she wasn't sure he'd be willing to uproot his life for her son, and their relationship wouldn't work any other way, not in the long run. And lastly, Michael. Michael had come uninvited to the wedding. She probably shouldn't have ignored all his attempts at getting in touch with her. It was just that... he was... she wasn't prepared to see him. Even after all these years. Especially after all these years.

Later. She would deal with it all later. He wasn't going to give up. He'd made that clear before she'd insisted he go away, but tonight too much had happened and she was exhausted. Maybe tomorrow, after a good night's sleep, she'd be able to think clearly and decide what to do.

She was about to get up and draw herself a bath when her phone rang. Dread pounded through her. Was it Peter? Had something happened to him while he was in recovery? She looked at the phone's display. It was

Ryan, her problem child. Tyler thought that was his title, and he wasn't entirely wrong, but he at least knew he had problems and tried to deal with them. Not always effectively, but he tried. Ryan, on the other hand, pretended his life was perfect when it was obvious to her that it was anything but. He was exactly what Peter had molded him to be. Like mother, like son, and no big surprise there. She'd been little more than a child herself when Ryan was born—just barely eighteen—and Peter had made them both into the family he expected them to be.

"Hello, sweetheart," she said. "Is everything okay?"

"Mom, hi. I need to talk to you. Do you have a few minutes?"

"For you, I have all night," Cynthia said. "What is it?"

"It's about Tyler," he said.

"What about Tyler?" A sudden fear struck her. "Is he okay? Did he cut himself again? Is he in the hospital?"

"Whoa, slow down, Mom. No, he's not in the hospital and I assume he hasn't cut himself. I mean, I hope he hasn't. Josh is riding herd on him, so I imagine he's fine, all things considered. Which is—"

"I'm not sure how I feel about this whole Josh situation," Cynthia said. Tyler had told her it was a temporary, fake relationship, for media consumption only, but she'd seen the two of them at the wedding. She wasn't sure what Josh's feelings were, other than exhibiting a fond tolerance for Tyler, but she knew her son, and he was in deep. Way too deep for a supposedly temporary, fake relationship. When Cynthia had predicted heartbreak and tears she'd been joking, but now it looked like she'd been prescient.

"I was dubious, too, but Brad talked me around."

"Oh, really?" Cynthia said, now wondering if she needed to speak with Brad. Not that he'd listen to her. He'd never listened to her.

"Yeah, back in April."

That made her pause. "That was over six months ago."

"It was right after Brad and Rachel came back from visiting Tyler in New Zealand. According to Brad, he's been trying to make this happen since even before Tyler finally left David, but Ty and Josh haven't been cooperating. Tyler doesn't come into town all that often, and when he does, Josh was always dating someone or other, and of course for a while Tyler was with Ethan, even though we all knew that'd never last. I'm surprised they stayed together as long as they did. This time when he knew Tyler was going to be in town for the wedding, Brad talked Josh into taking time off work. The plan was to throw him and Ty together, which ended up happening in a way we hadn't considered, but it's all worked out, so there you go."

Cynthia felt a headache start to pulse in her temples. "Let me get this straight. Your brother has been trying to set up your other brother with your ex-boyfriend for over three years and you're okay with this. Do I have that right?"

"Josh was my friend, not my boyfriend, Mom," Ryan said, sounding sulky and put-upon.

"Oh, Ryan, stop it," she said. "Josh was your boyfriend for years and everyone knows it. Hell, I suspect even your father knows it. He's just as good as you when it comes to altering reality to suit his needs."

"Mom!" Her thirty-five-year-old son sounded like he'd reverted to being a teenager. She'd indulged him, her firstborn, letting him have his illusions that what he got up to with his teenaged best friend was a secret. She regretted that now. What she should've done was spoken with him and stood with him against Peter. It was too late to go back and fix things, though, as much as she wanted to.

"Don't 'Mom' me." Cynthia massaged one temple. "Oh, well, what's done is done. I hope you two know what you're doing."

"Talk to Brad if you want the in-depth explanation. The gist of his argument, though, is that Tyler needs a fully functioning adult boyfriend who won't screw him over, and Josh needs someone he can pour love into. I agree with the Tyler portion—he does need that. As for Josh, well, I'm just going to have to trust Brad's judgment. He's spent the most time with him over the years. I get the impression that he thinks getting Tyler together with Josh is killing two birds with one stone. Hopefully he knows what he's talking about. I wouldn't have thought Josh would want to be with such a high-maintenance pain in the ass like Tyler, but..."

"But?"

Ryan was quiet for a few moments. "I think it's safe to say Josh's little infatuation with me is dead and something else has taken its place. So maybe Brad's right, as much as it pains me to say that."

"Hmm," she said, still not sure Josh was a good idea for Tyler, but becoming convinced that Ryan did not, in fact, resent his brother and Josh getting together. Which reminded her. "By the way, who was the 'sick' friend you had to take home from the wedding?"

"No one," was Ryan's sullen reply. He'd definitely regressed to adolescence tonight.

"No one is very cute." And young. "Where did you meet him?"

"He works at the firm," Ryan finally allowed.

"And he's no one?"

"Just a friend," Ryan said. "A coworker, I mean. A friendly coworker."

"And you abandoned your brother's wedding to take him home," Cynthia observed. "Not to mention abandoning your fiancée."

"I didn't call to talk about this."

"I'm still your mother, Ryan, and I'd like an explanation."

"I'd like you to explain Uncle Mike," Ryan shot back, his voice icy and sharp.

Cynthia felt like the ground beneath her was shifting. "What do you mean?"

"I saw him at the wedding, Mom. He's Tyler's biological father, isn't he?"

She opened her mouth but nothing came out. Of all the things she'd expected him to say, that was dead last.

"Mom? You still there?"

Cynthia managed a dry, "Yes."

"Tyler knows. I told him. Showed him an old photo I found of Mike at one of the firm's summer picnics. The picture is from over twenty years ago and aside from having red hair, the man in the picture could be Tyler."

"Ryan, what have you done?"

"What have *I* done? How could you have kept this a secret from him? Tyler's extremely upset. Josh took him back to his place and is presumably dealing with it, but you need to fix things with him."

"Why did you tell him like that?" she asked, feeling panicky. "Couldn't you have come to me first?"

"I thought he deserved to know, that he would want to know. It would be one thing if he loved Dad, but I think he stopped years ago. And Dad, well, I used to tell myself that Dad loved Tyler in his own way, but he doesn't, does he? When were you planning on saying something? Were you *ever* planning on saying something?"

"It's complicated," Cynthia said. "I should've told Tyler a long time ago, but first I felt he was too young, and later... well. I have no idea how I'm going to explain this to him now."

"Try," Ryan said, as if he were the parent and she the child.

It wasn't until much later, lying sleepless in bed, that she realized she'd let Ryan get away without a proper explanation for his very young, very attractive "sick" friend or his current relationship with his fiancée. Ryan was headed toward heartbreak, and Cynthia wasn't sure if there was anything she could do to stop him.

Again, like mother, like son.

She looked at her phone and the numerous texts Mike had sent her over the past few days.

Mike: I hear you're in town. Can we get together?
Mike: I need to talk with you. We need to talk.
Mike: Please. I have something for you from Sophie. She said I had to give it to you in person, but I can't do that if you won't see me.
Mike: If nothing else, can I talk to you on the phone? I've tried, but you

won't return my messages.
Mike: Cyn, please.

Cyn. Only Mike had ever called her that. Peter never shortened her name, claiming that it made her sound vulgar.

Cyn was an appropriate name, sounding as it did exactly like what they did. She and Mike had done nothing but sin, lying to everyone: their spouses, their friends, and themselves. And for what?

"Happiness," Cynthia whispered out loud. "A little joy."

A little joy and so much harm.

It was nearly one a.m. by the time she gave up on the idea of sleep, got up, and convinced herself to call Mike. He answered the phone on the first ring, as if he'd been waiting on her.

"Cyn," he said, his voice making her shiver. "Thank God you finally called."

"Peter had a heart attack at the reception after you left," she said, ignoring the hope she heard in his voice.

"My God. Is he okay?"

"He's as okay as anyone could be in his position," Cynthia said. "He's in Northwestern Memorial recovering from bypass surgery. I'm sure he'll be fine. It'll take more than a measly heart attack to kill him."

"And you, Cyn? How are you?"

"Fine. My heart is just fine."

Mike made a noncommittal noise. "I'd like to get together and talk. I have something for you."

"Yes, you said that. Mike, we do need to talk. There's something important I need to tell you, something that I should have said a long time ago. I'm sorry, so terribly sorry I kept it from you, but I just couldn't and—"

"I think I already know," he said.

"You do?"

"Yeah, if what you're trying to say is that Tyler is my son, of course I know. He's the spitting image of me. I've known for a while. Sophie did as well, but we never talked about it. Not until just before the end. Cyn, why did you think Peter and I had that huge fight ages ago? It wasn't over me leaving the firm to go off on my own. It was over me trying to claim Tyler as mine. You know, after you left him, then ended up going back."

"I thought it was over me."

"It was, in a way. Peter didn't want me claiming Tyler. He said that if I acknowledged him as my son I'd have to take you, too. And that he'd see to it that you lost the other boys, his actual sons, as he called them. Cyn, I would have done it, taken you and Tyler and fought for Ryan and Brad, except you know I couldn't."

"No," Cynthia said. There was Sophie, who was lovely and sick and the mother of his two children. There was no way he could leave her and choose Cynthia. Even at her most selfish, she'd never wanted that.

"No," he agreed.

Cynthia leaned her head back and closed her eyes. "Stupid. I've been so damn stupid."

"Stop it." Mike took a deep breath. "The last few years have been nonstop caring for Sophie. I haven't had time for much else. But one night, a few months before the end, Sophie was feeling a little better. Enough to go to a restaurant, although she didn't eat much, and then to a movie. She chose what she wanted to see. We both knew it would be the last one."

Cynthia felt tears on her face. "I'm so sorry," she said again, wiping at her face and wishing she had a tissue. "I should've come back to see her. I know I should have, but I just couldn't."

Mike continued, ignoring her. "We saw that John Hughes remake, Sophie laughing and saying how fitting that the last movie we would see was a remake of the first movie we saw. And how nice it was that one of the stars was Cindy's little boy, now all grown up. Seeing him on the screen was, well, it's hard to describe how it felt. Wonderful and awful, because it was me up there. Me, with your eyes. Our boy, Cyn, and I don't even know him. Afterward, Sophie held my hand and kissed me and told me that she knew, she had always known. We talked, finally, about all of it. It was a relief to finally clear the air. Sophie wanted to do the same thing with you, too, but…"

"Oh, God," Cynthia said. "I don't… I'm sorry. I wouldn't return any of her calls." She felt like all the choices she'd made all down the line were wrong, every single last one, but at the time she hadn't seen any other path than the one she'd taken.

"She left you a letter," Mike said. "I promised her that I'd get it to you, one way or another."

"I sh-should've done everything differently," she said, starting to hiccup. She could hear Peter's sneer in her head, telling her that she couldn't even grieve with dignity. *Look at you, snot running from your nose. Disgusting.* "Everything."

"Not everything."

Cynthia thought of her three sons. First there was Ryan, who she'd let Peter mold into a carbon copy of himself. She'd helped Ryan, but in all the wrong ways, she could see that now. Instead of encouraging him stand up to his father, she'd taught him how to hide and pretend to be something he wasn't. Then Brad, the one who had never needed either her or her husband, her independent child who didn't care what anyone thought. He loved her, but she was afraid he didn't like her very much. And Tyler, who refused to either hide or pretend, no matter how hard she tried to teach him that lesson. She'd tried to protect him, but he'd ended up damaged anyway.

"Yes," she said. "Everything."

"Can I see you?"

There really wasn't any point in further avoiding him. She would do it, they would have their conversation and it would be painful, but then it would be over. Finally, over.

"Okay, sure," she said. "In the morning. We'll have breakfast. It'll be like old times."

ଔଞ

Sunday, October 2nd, 9:30 a.m.
An upscale hotel room
Chicago, IL

Instead of eating in the hotel's restaurant, Cynthia called for room service. What they had to say to each other was not meant for public consumption and it was possible that things would get ugly. At the very least she would likely cry. Again. Bad enough Mike would see that. She didn't need a roomful of strangers seeing it as well.

When Cynthia opened the door to his knock it was a bit like getting a punch to the chest. Seeing him at the wedding had been one thing. Here, in this hotel, the past eight years might as well have never happened. He had, perhaps, more gray in his auburn hair, and the lines around his mouth and eyes were a bit more pronounced. He hadn't become any less handsome, even at nearly sixty.

Mike stepped forward as if to embrace her, then stopped. He let his arms fall to his sides.

"You're looking well," Cynthia said. She stepped back to let him walk past her into the room. "I ordered room service. Help yourself." She took a pastry and sat down in one of the chairs. She took a bite, but instead of tasting butter and sugar, it was like sawdust in her mouth. She put it down and absently picked it apart.

Mike poured himself a cup of coffee and sat as well. "You're as beautiful as I remember."

"Don't be silly. I'm almost fifty-three years old and I'm bound to be a grandmother soon."

"I'm already a grandfather twice over. Cyn, I think we've progressed past social niceties. We had an affair. It was unwise, and selfish, and we produced a child. If I could go back and change things, I probably would, but regrets don't help either the living or the dead. I want to move forward, and I'd like to acknowledge that I have more than one son."

"Yes, well, you pretty much set that in motion, like it or not, by coming to the wedding uninvited. Apparently, Ryan noticed your resemblance to Tyler and told him last night, and the timing couldn't have been worse. Between this asinine video business, his house being vandalized by God-knows-who, his father having a heart attack, and this news, it'll be a miracle if he doesn't end up in the hospital himself."

Mike frowned. "I had no idea Tyler's health was that fragile."

She'd never told either Sophie or Mike about the worst of Tyler's childhood and adolescence. It had been too painful, too shameful to share. It wasn't any easier now. *Hey, Mike, yeah, you've got a son and look at the wonderful job I did raising him! I let his father do terrible things to him and now he cuts himself to cope with stress. Isn't that great?*

"I'm being hyperbolic," she said, and that was probably the truth. Ryan seemed to think that Josh had Tyler well in hand. Cynthia wasn't so sure, but at least if he did cut himself, there would be someone there to take him to the hospital. Then she remembered that Josh was a physician himself and Brad's matchmaking campaign suddenly began to make sense. "Besides, Josh is with him. At least he's not alone."

"I've seen the tabloids saying Josh is Tyler's boyfriend. Wasn't he Ryan's friend when they were teenagers?"

"One and the same." Cynthia threw on a blinding smile she didn't feel. "Congratulations. Your long-lost son is gay." *Also, prone to slicing himself open.*

Mike looked annoyed. "Cyn, you told me and Sophie that Tyler was gay when he was thirteen. It didn't bother me then and it doesn't bother me now. I thought you knew me better than that."

Cynthia felt stupid. She remembered it now, crying on Sophie's shoulder, Mike there in the background, offering advice on how to deal with Peter, not that it had done any good. "At the moment, I don't feel as if I know anything anymore. Everything feels unreal."

Mike shoved an envelope her way. "Read this. It's reason why I came. I promised I would deliver it in person."

Cynthia fumbled with the envelope with numbed fingers, eventually tearing it open and sliding out the letter inside. The paper smelled of Sophie—cinnamon and vanilla and underneath that something floral—and that was enough to make her eyes start to tear. "I'm not sure I can do this," she said.

Mike grabbed her wrist. It was the first time he'd touched her in over eight years and the tingle she'd always felt was still there, making her heart speed up. "Yes, you can. Sophie managed to write it and you will damn well read it."

"Of... of course," she mumbled and opened the letter clumsily, somehow managing not to drop the pages onto the floor.

Dear Cindy,

I expect that you won't want to read this, so I've told Mike that he must deliver it to you in person and watch while you read it. I hope you haven't made him jump through too many hoops to see you. The past eight years have been hard for all of us. Needlessly so, I think. Maybe now that can change.

I know why you left. You were in a difficult position and part of that was my fault, although I comfort myself that I wasn't the largest part of why you left, and I flatter myself in thinking I might have been part of the reason why you didn't leave sooner. I forgive you, Cindy, I did years ago, and I only regret that I never said so.

I know that you and Mike found each other in a time that was hard for all of us. I was half-dead from radiation and chemotherapy, Mike was half-dead from exhaustion, and you helpless to save either me or yourself. We were quite the pair, weren't we? Me a skeleton with no hair, and you with all those suspicious bruises. No one as graceful as you could ever be that accident-prone. I knew what you were going through, if only subconsciously, and I was too wrapped up in my own misery to help you escape yours. Too selfish, as well. If you left Peter, you would leave me as well, and I couldn't bear losing my best friend when it seemed like I was losing everything else at the same time.

It was probably inevitable that you and Mike would comfort each other. At times, I resented it, and at other times it brought me a strange sense of peace. I thought I was going to die — we all thought it, even my doctors who tried to be optimistic about my chances. I was glad that Mike would have you when I was gone, my children would have a second mother, and that you would have somewhere to run that wasn't back to your parents. It seemed that things would work out, for you two, if not for me.

But I didn't die. Every day was a gift, at least that's what they say. I lived to see my children grow up, but I also spent too many years doing nothing but lying in bed at home or in the hospital, in pain and wishing to die. My cancer was like a vampire, draining everything and everyone around me.

You stayed as long as you could. I know you both hoped for and dreaded my death. I understand, Cindy. I really do. I both hoped for and dreaded the same thing. Every relapse was nothing but misery and pain. Every remission felt like stolen time. When I was sick, Mike was miserable. When I was better, Mike was always waiting for it to come back. It wasn't fair to any of us, and I'll admit that it was harder after you left. I missed you. Mike missed you. I hope that you missed us.

I spent too much time after you left feeling angry at you. I know you tried to stay in touch at first, and I said things that made you withdraw. I'm sorry. I wish I could take those words back. You hurt me, Cindy. Yes, you slept with my husband, but more than that, you left me alone. It felt like a double betrayal when you left, and I was cruel. I'm sorry.

I knew from almost the beginning that Tyler was Mike's son. As a baby, he looked so much like my own Garrett that I just knew. And there were those bruises you had. Those bruises you tried and failed to explain away. What I didn't know about was what Tyler was going through, because you hid that too well. He had trouble in school. He was rebellious. He and Peter didn't see eye to eye. I didn't think anything of it, especially in those last few years before you left, given how sick I was at that time. I didn't put the pieces together until it was too late. I didn't know what made you run and when later you tried to explain, I didn't want to hear.

The person who explained it all to me was your son, Brad, believe it or not. Maybe six months after you went to California, I was in the hospital. Brad saw me while he was doing his rounds with the other students. We were surprised to see each other, and he came back later that day to visit me alone. I was still so angry with you for leaving me that I lashed out at him because he was the closest thing to you I had.

He stood there, let me verbally abuse him, then he let me have it right back. He told me about the harm Peter had done to Tyler, the cutting, the suicide attempt. He said that he'd told you that if you didn't take Tyler and leave, that one way or another he'd end up dead. So, there we were, both of us angry at each other and at you, and I realized how petty it all was. How petty I'd been. My anger was only one more thing that brought me misery, and after that day I could finally start letting it go.

After I went into another remission I tried to make amends, but it was too late and there was too much distance. I only wish I could see you one more time, that we could forgive each other in person. Brad is getting married this fall and you'll come back for that. I had thought maybe then, but now I know that's not going to happen. I've had my last remission and I've run out of time.

I had so many more years of life I didn't expect. They were hard years, bad years, but good years, too. There have been compensations.

Even in my despair, my darkest hour, and my deepest anger, I always loved you. I never stopped, no matter what I told you. I've missed you, Cindy, but you've always been close in my heart, and I know that I'll see you again one day. You and Mike both. It'll be like old times.

All my love,

Sophie

Cynthia folded up the letter and started laughing. She was crying, too. Laughing and crying and she wasn't sure she could stop.

"Cyn?"

"That bitch," she said. "Even from the grave she just had to get the last word in. God, I miss her."

"I know. She was ready to go, at the end. Too many organs had failed. They had talked about a kidney transplant, but she wouldn't hear of it. The bone marrow transplants were one thing, but she said she'd be damned before she took Garrett's kidney to the grave with her."

Cynthia smiled and wiped her eyes on a napkin. "That sounds just like her."

Mike put his mug on the table and leaned forward, taking her hand and enveloping it in both of his. "What now?"

"Well, I suppose we figure out how to explain to our son why I lied to him for his entire life. And then, frankly, I have no idea. I'm hoping he'll still be speaking to me by the time we're done."

"You want to tell him together?"

"I'm not sure I can do it by myself. If that's okay with you."

Mike squeezed her hand. "No. Together is fine."

ఌ౸

Sunday, October 2nd, 3:50 p.m.
En route to Josh's perfectly adequate condo
Evanston, IL

Cynthia read the text conversation over and over as Mike drove them to Josh's home.

Tyler: I need to see you. Where can we meet?
Cynthia: I can come to you, if you want. You're staying with Josh, right?
Tyler: Yes. Josh says that's fine. Come over around four. We should be done with his insurance company and the police by then.
Cynthia: Police?
Tyler: Josh's car was vandalized Saturday. I'll tell you about it later.
Cynthia: OK. See you at 4.

Cynthia: I love you, sweetheart

Tyler hadn't responded when she said that she loved him. Maybe she was being too sensitive. Maybe she was making something out of nothing. Still, it worried her.

Josh buzzed them into his building, then opened the door to their knock. He held his hand out to Cynthia, who ignored it and gave him a brief hug.

"I'm not sure if you remember me," Mike said, "but I knew your father, of course, from when I worked at the firm. And I saw you at the various family functions. But you were always..." Mike broke off.

Josh had been staring at Mike, but that broke his trance. "Always with Ryan, yes. Back in the day, where he was, I wasn't far behind."

"I'm sorry," Mike said. "It was rude of me to bring that up. I've been away from the Chadwicks long enough that I'd forgotten—"

"That some things are never talked about?" Tyler said as he walked over to join them. Cynthia went to hug him and he was stiff in her arms so she drew back. "Speaking of not talking about things, I didn't realize this was going to be a family reunion. I'm not sure of the etiquette in meeting your sperm donor, especially when you've already met. 'Hi, I'm glad you knocked up my mom' probably isn't appropriate, but I'm not sure Emily Post ever covered this situation."

"Tyler," Josh barked at him with a frown.

Her son flashed Josh a disgruntled glance then shared it with her. "Can I assume you're here to actually talk about things or are we going to ignore the elephant with my face in the room?"

Mike made a muffled noise that she thought might have been a snort. Cynthia wanted to pinch him. This wasn't funny.

"Ryan called me last night," she said, stung by the sharpness in Tyler's tone. She knew that caustic tone but it had never before been directed at her. "Yes, Mike is your biological father. If all you wanted was confirmation, I don't suppose we need to stay, but if you'd like an explanation, he's part of the story, obviously. Should we stay, Tyler, or should we go?"

Tyler blinked at her, raw pain naked in his eyes. "Am I not allowed to be upset? Is this going to be another time when I have to pretend things are just fine?" Josh grabbed Tyler's hand and held it tight. Josh's gaze, directed at Cynthia, was cold. She was being judged by Josh Rosen and she found she didn't like it. She still thought of him as that nice boy who operated as Ryan's shadow. This man was not that boy.

"Come on," Josh said, walking down the short hallway and taking her son with him. "If we're going to do this, let's at least not do it in my foyer." He led them to a Spartan living room, painted white, furnished with a long couch and two chairs upholstered in black leather. There was a beige rug on the dark hardwood floor, and a large black television hung on the wall above a sleek black console. The only color in the room was the artwork: a painting of a gnarled tree in autumn on one wall and a ship tossed by an angry sea on another. "Please, have a seat."

She sat in one of the chairs and contrasted this stark room to Tyler's house, where each room was painted a different warm tone and there was so much color everywhere, from his furniture to the clutter that was never quite tamed despite a cleaning staff that came twice a week. She couldn't imagine Tyler living in a room this sterile. He and Josh didn't fit. The two of them would probably end up killing each other within a month. Tyler was chaos and this was a room owned by a man who craved order. Even if they didn't live so far apart, it would be impossible. Brad and Ryan were insane if they thought the two of them would work as a couple.

It was going to end in tears, sooner rather than later, and it would be her picking up Tyler's pieces, as usual.

"Can I get you anything?" Josh asked, breaking into her unhappy thoughts.

Tyler sat on one end of the couch, then drew up his legs and hugged them. "Coffee, soda, something stronger? Only not vodka, as we are all out due to extenuating circumstances."

Josh shot Tyler an indecipherable look and hovered, looking at Cynthia and Mike expectantly.

"I could use a beer, if you have any," Mike said.

"Cynthia?" She shook her head. "Tyler?"

He waved a hand and Josh left and headed farther into the condo, presumably to the kitchen.

"So," Tyler said. "I'm a bastard. Officially."

"If you wish to be technical," Cynthia said, "you're not. Peter Chadwick is listed as father on your birth certificate. As we were married at the time, you are legally legitimate, not that it matters, as you well know, so being nasty is counterproductive."

Tyler closed his eyes. "Excuse me for being nasty. I'm still a bit overwrought. I can't imagine why. Do you have any idea how creepy it is looking at you?" This last was directed at Mike.

Josh walked in at that point and handed a beer in a dark glass bottle to Mike. He put his own beer down and handed Tyler a can of something. Even though he hadn't asked for anything, he took it and started to sip it slowly. Ginger ale. Since when did her son drink ginger ale?

"Yeah," Mike said, after taking a long drink. "I might have some idea. You look like my son."

Tyler balanced the can on one knee. "Well, yeah. That's why we're all here today, right?"

"No, I mean you look like my other son. Garrett. Your brother."

"No." Tyler's voice cut like a whip. "I have two brothers. Ryan and Brad. They're both pains in my ass, but they're my brothers and I love them. I don't even remember your 'other' son. He might share my face, but he's not my brother any more than you're my father."

Silence enveloped the room. Josh stroked Tyler's leg but said nothing. Mike looked at her, then down. Cynthia studied her son. "What would you have had me do?" she asked.

"I don't know," Tyler said, his voice cracking. He wrapped his hands around his drink, dropped his legs to the floor, and leaned toward her. "Make me understand, Mom. I need to be able to forgive you, I'm just not sure how."

Cynthia sat there and felt crushed under the weight of all her bad decisions. They had culminated in Tyler, the child she had sacrificed so much for, and it still hadn't been enough.

"I can't promise that you'll be able to forgive me," she said, "but I'm going to try at least to explain, so maybe you'll understand."

Chapter 35
Tyler Learns the Truth

Sunday, October 2nd, 4:28 p.m.
Josh's perfectly adequate condo
Evanston, IL

Tyler sat back as his mother started to tell his origin story. If this was a movie, he would end up being a superhero or some shit. Ordinary people didn't have origin stories. Or rather, everyone had one, but generally they didn't need telling. It was all that "when a mommy and a daddy love each other very much" crap that was boring, and thus only the participants cared. Tyler, however, had an origin story and it wasn't even something fun, involving industrial chemicals and ending with him having superpowers. No, his origin story was all about stupid drama, where the villain was his father and Tyler's only superpower was his ability to deep throat without choking. As superpowers went, it was pretty lame, and you could argue that his father, while a grade-A asshole, probably didn't deserve to be cheated on and have some other man's kid foisted upon him. Also, there were no capes, which was a shame, because capes were kind of awesome.

"I married your father, I mean, I married Peter, because he got me pregnant. I was seventeen, a senior in high school, and I went to a party with friends where there was alcohol and college-age boys." His mother gave a little shrug of her shoulders. "Peter was in his final year of law school and so much older than me. In the beginning, I don't think he even realized I was underage. We went out a few times, and it was nice, but nothing special. We both would have moved on, especially once he realized I was still in high school, but I found out I was pregnant. I had no idea what would happen when I told that handsome, rich man I barely knew that he was going to be a father, and I was terrified. I thought he'd get angry, or at least try to deny it, but he was ecstatic, and I thought that it must be because he loved me. Peter asked me to marry him right away, and of course I said yes. I thought I was living in some sort of fairy tale, even after his parents made me sign a prenuptial agreement."

"You could have challenged that in court," Mike said. Tyler's mother gave Mike a look and he didn't say anything more, just took another sip of his beer.

"It became clear to me early in the marriage that it wasn't the fairy tale I'd thought it would be, no matter that he swept me away and put me in a house right on the lake that looked like a castle. Once I'd given birth to Ryan, Peter pretty much lost all interest in me, but he did dote on our son, and I took hope from that. I tried to save my marriage, but there wasn't anything to save. I was a naive teenager that didn't realize until too late that I'd been bought and paid for only because I carried Peter's child. I had a hard enough time learning how to be Peter's wife in public; I had no idea how to do it in private. He had a mistress, or maybe several of them. I don't know. I just knew he didn't want me. I'd have never gotten Brad if Ryan hadn't kept asking for a sibling. He wanted a brother or a sister more than anything else, and so Peter decided to give him what he wanted. After Brad, we drifted into separate bedrooms and never drifted back. By the time I thought to try and reconcile with him, Peter made it clear that an heir and a spare were sufficient and the physical aspect of our marriage was over. I could either like it or lump it, but if I left, he would fight me tooth and nail for the boys, so I stayed."

His mother looked at Josh. "I'm sorry, but I would actually like some water."

"Of course." Josh rose and went to the kitchen.

"When Brad was in preschool, my best friend Sophie—Mike's wife—got sick. Thank you," she told Josh when he handed her a glass of ice water. "We found out she had leukemia. She was very ill with the treatments and we thought she was going to die. I was wildly unhappy. Mike felt the same. And we—"

"Got busy," Tyler said, not feeling particularly charitable.

His mother's eyes flashed at him. "We comforted each other."

Tyler made a rude noise. "Whatever. You had unprotected sex with your sick best friend's husband and got knocked up. Not that I'm ungrateful, but let's not dress this up."

Once you were old enough to know where babies came from, the next uncomfortable logical leap was to realize that your parents had had sex at least once. It was one of those horrible parts of reality that were inescapable, like gravity and death. This, however, was a step beyond, and Tyler thought he was justified in being pissy about it. Learning that you were the product of an affair, and a rather clichéd one at that, was more than he was prepared to deal with without snark. Especially since he was still semi-hungover and knew that none of this story was going to culminate with, "And that's why you're a superhero, here's your awesome costume, go save the world now, sweetheart." Which was a shame because his ass looked very fine in spandex.

Mike cleared his throat. "Not that it excuses anything, but that night the doctors gave Sophie a short time to live. I was distraught. That isn't really an excuse, just context."

"But your wife didn't die. I mean, not then," said Josh, king of tact.

"I remember her vaguely. The picture I saw last night jogged my memory. I know I saw her at the Chadwick picnics and parties. And up at Blue Lake, too. I think I remember seeing you up there as well, or am I not remembering that right? It was a long time ago, but I keep associating you with those summers up there."

Mike started. "No," he said. "You're right. My wife and I did spend time at the lake. We have a house up there, although we mostly rent it out now."

Josh gave him a look. "White marble in all the bathrooms?"

Tyler wanted to laugh, and he stuffed his hand in his mouth to keep it from escaping because he knew it would sound hysterical.

Mike looked confused. "What?"

"I think I rented your lake house two weeks ago. How many Michael Connollys could possibly own houses up there?"

"Not to mention conveniently close to our house," Tyler pointed out. His mother's insistence that they spend every summer up there made perfect sense now.

Mike blinked at Josh. "I rent it through an agency. I had no idea, Josh. What a coincidence. That's just—"

"Not really," Josh said. "I looked for rentals as close to the Chadwicks' place as I could find. Yours was the closest one available."

"It's a small world," Mike said with a lame smile. "Sophie and I bought the land at the same Peter and Cynthia bought their plot. We were all good friends at one point."

"Right." Tyler wanted to derail this line of conversation. It was leading him down paths of thought he didn't want to follow. "Back to your wife, who didn't die."

"Of course, Tyler," Mike said with the ghost of a smile that disappeared almost as soon as it came. "No, she didn't die. Not then. Her cancer went into remission and she made an amazing recovery. It was a miracle."

"Only there was this inconvenient baby," Tyler felt the need to point out. "Oops."

His mother frowned. "Mike didn't know, not then, at least. Your— I mean Peter knew you weren't his right from the beginning. We hadn't... so he knew the child couldn't be his. He said he didn't care as long as I told no one, but if it ever got out that there was a cuckoo in his nest, the interloper—his words, not mine—and I would be out on our asses without a penny. However, if I kept my mouth shut, you'd be raised as a Chadwick. He also warned me that there better not be any more surprises." She sighed.

"Why did you stay?" Tyler asked. "That's what I really need to know. I mean, all this ancient history is great for context, I suppose, but it still doesn't explain why you stayed as long as you did."

"You don't remember, because you were too young, but I did try to leave him. You were maybe two, and Peter smacked you when you were crying and you fell and hit your head. There was so much blood. I thought he'd killed you, but I knew you'd be fine when I picked you up and you started screaming. I got you cleaned up, and when the boys got home from school, we left."

Tyler gripped his drink so hard the can dented, the noise as loud as a gunshot in the silence. "No…"

"She did," Mike said. "She brought you and your brothers to stay with Sophie and me for a short time, but—"

"But staying with Mike and Sophie wasn't a long-term solution. They had their own family, and living with them full-time would have been difficult at best."

Tyler laughed. He couldn't help it. It had bad sitcom written all over it. Either that or a reality show on Bravo.

His mother frowned at him, then continued. "I talked to my parents, but they weren't prepared for me to bring three boys back home with me. There wasn't the room, and they didn't have much money. On top of that, Ryan wanted to go back home. He was so angry with me. He wanted his father and he didn't understand why we left. He said if we didn't go home he'd never forgive me and that he'd run away. And then your grandfather—Peter's father, I mean—contacted me. He said that I had to go back to Peter. Divorce wasn't an option. Your paternity would come out because Peter had vowed to fight for custody of his two biological sons, but not for you. Your grandfather didn't want any of the family dirty linen to air, so he cut me a deal. He had trust funds set up for Ryan, Brad, and you. Peter wouldn't be able to touch the money, and it would be yours on your twenty-first birthday. The only thing I had to do was go back to Peter and, as your grandfather put it, keep my damned legs shut. In addition, he made Peter promise to keep his hands off you."

"That sounds like him. Grandfather always was a tyrannical bastard," Tyler murmured. "So, you went back." *Too bad Dad didn't keep his hands off me, and I'd be willing to bet my trust fund you didn't keep your legs shut, either.*

"Yes, Tyler, I went back. Where else could I have gone? Ryan was furious with me at the idea of leaving his father, his friends, and his school. In addition, how was I supposed to support us? I never finished high school. Your father said there was no need, because he would always take care of me. I could have gotten my GED, sure, and then what? I had no skills other than what your grandmother taught me. I could be a society hostess, but there's not a lot of demand for that. In addition, I had a rebellious twelve-year-old, a rambunctious six-year-old, and a toddler. Who would take care of you while I worked, if I could even find a job? And that was if I got custody, which wasn't a sure thing. Money, Tyler, is important. So, yes, when your grandfather came to offer me that deal, I took it. It seemed like my only choice. And Peter promised never to hit you again."

Anger burst through Tyler. "Only that didn't last very long, did it? And yeah, I guess I can understand staying while Brad and Ryan were still at home, but once Brad left for college, we could have gone, too."

His mother frowned at him. "I already told you why I stayed. I made that bargain. I promised your grandfather to stay until you were of age."

"Was it just money? That's all? If you'd have ever bothered to ask me, I'd have told you I didn't give two shits about the money."

"Tyler, you have no idea what you're talking about. You've never been poor. Not one single day of your life. I know you like to say that you and I fled your father with only the clothes on our backs, but that wasn't true. You thought roughing it was flying economy. You had your college tuition paid for completely. Did you think going to university was free? You've never had to work to support yourself. The first job you ever had wasn't working at McDonald's. It was in a commercial *for* McDonald's. You have no idea what reality is. You don't know what it's like to worry that there won't be enough money for both rent and food. Your idea of economizing was buying a house in Burbank. It's easy for you to sit there, dressed in hand-tailored slacks and a cashmere sweater that I know cost a small fortune, and tell me money doesn't matter. I hate to break it to you, but it does. A lot."

Tyler felt like he'd been slapped. It was unfair to hold him accountable for choices his mother had made on his behalf. He hadn't had any control over any of it, from the arbitrary punishments he'd suffered under, to the extravagant presents he received at holidays and birthdays. None of it had been of his choosing. "If you'd given me the choice at thirteen between living with Dad and shopping at Burberry or living on our own and shopping at Walmart, I'd have picked Walmart, but you never asked. I would've told you the money wasn't worth it, but I guess I ended up earning every penny of it, didn't I?"

"Yes, you say that now," his mother said with an edge to her voice. "But who's to say you'd be better off in that other life, the one with Walmart and worrying about making the rent payment and hoping our lights aren't shut off because we were late paying the electric bill?"

Tyler pushed up his sleeves, showing the scars on his wrists. "I wouldn't have these," he said.

His mother looked at him and gave him a sad smile. "Or you'd still have them, but for a different reason. We can't know what would have happened, only what did."

She and Mike shared a look, and Tyler thought he understood

everything after seeing it. She'd stayed so long not, as she claimed, because of the money. No, even if she believed that, it was a lie. She'd stayed because of Mike. The two of them stared at each other like lovesick teenagers, and it made Tyler want to give his mother a good shake. Despite that lecture she'd just given him, the real reason she'd stayed with Peter was because if she left him, she'd have had to leave Mike, too. How hard it must have been, visiting Tyler in the hospital, and having to weigh her son's life versus her own selfish wants. He should be grateful, he supposed, that slashing his wrists had finally been enough to tip the scales in his favor.

"Well," he said, "I think it's safe to say that had we been poor I'd have never gone to Bridges, been raped four times, and then branded. That place was expensive." He gave his parents a wide, sunny smile. "And what a shame it would have been to miss out on that fun experience."

"Tyler—"

"Not to mention all those years I had with Peter Chadwick as my father. He ignored me, belittled me, mocked me, controlled me, and when that wasn't enough, he hit me. But, hey, I did get a brand-new Mercedes for my sixteenth birthday, so that totally made up for everything else that happened. And my shiny Blackberry absolutely was worth feeling that there must be something wrong with me because my father didn't love me." Tyler's fist clenched and the can dented further. He put the drink down before he ended up spilling it. The last thing he needed was to set Josh off by making a mess. Before Tyler could stop him, he'd be waxing the floor or something equally ridiculous, and Tyler didn't have the energy right now to circumvent him.

His mother started crying and Tyler tried not to care. She should be crying. He was crying, he realized, and as he angrily wiped at his stupid eyes that had no business leaking like this, he thought it was only fair that she join the waterworks. Mike—it was impossible to think of the man as anything but Mike—sat in blank silence. There was no way to know what he was thinking or if any of the accusations Tyler had spouted were news to him. Maybe his mother had already told him, or maybe he thought Tyler was being a drama queen, or maybe he just didn't give a shit. It was impossible to tell. Tyler found it funny that he couldn't read a face that was so like his own. Josh sat beside him and looked grim. He was probably wishing he'd never gotten involved with any Chadwick ever, starting with Ryan, and he'd be right to think so.

Tyler wanted to crawl into bed and forget any of this had ever happened. He wanted to go back to when his mother was a martyred saint, tied for years to marriage with a man she despised because of reasons that Tyler didn't know or understand, but nevertheless knew to be justified. Or, failing that, he wanted to sleep until he wasn't so angry with her anymore.

"But you did finally leave," Tyler said, his voice drained of emotion.

He wished this was over and done with so he could be alone. He felt Josh's hand on his leg and thought, *well, maybe not entirely alone*. He'd told Josh that if he couldn't forgive his mother he would have nothing left, but that wasn't true. It had never really been true. There was Purvi, his brothers, all his friends back home, and now Josh. "And I somehow kept the trust fund and got my college paid for. How'd you manage that?"

"While you were in the hospital in Wisconsin, after you..." His mother stopped, her uncertainty palpable.

"Tried to kill myself, just like I told you I would," Tyler prompted, merciless.

"Yes. I went to your grandfather again. I told him that we had to leave, that I had started divorce proceedings and Peter was fighting me on it and I wanted him to intervene. Staying in the marriage was no longer an option because you were going to end up dead if we didn't leave, and if you died I would make sure that every piece of Chadwick nastiness was aired. At that point, I'd have nothing to lose and no reason to remain silent. Your grandfather agreed to arrange for a quiet divorce from Peter. I would receive custody of you, enough money to support us, and you would get your college paid for and your trust fund. In return, I agreed never to tell anyone about my marriage and why it ended, that Tyler wasn't Peter's child, or that there had ever been any abuse." She waved her hand. "So, there you go. The whole story."

Tyler doubted that, somehow, but he didn't want to poke at it anymore. He'd heard enough. He looked at the man who had provided half of his DNA. It was unsettling looking at him, seeing himself in that older, yet eerily similar, face. "Do you have anything to add to this lovely story?" he asked Mike.

"I've known you were my son for a long time, but it wasn't something I let myself think about. Peter made it clear that he'd fight me if I tried to claim you."

"Why? He never loved me, never wanted me."

Mike shrugged. "Pride, maybe."

His mother nodded. "He didn't want anyone knowing his wife had been unfaithful."

"Yes, well," Mike went on, "right before my wife died, we went to a movie you were in. Seeing you on screen—looking just like me—was a pretty big 'a-ha' moment. There was no longer any point in pretending I didn't know you were my son."

"I bet that was super awkward," Tyler said, almost finding it funny.

Mike's ghost of a smile returned. "Sophie already knew. She'd known since you were a baby. You looked just like..." He paused, then decided to go on, "our son. Garrett. Who is your brother, biologically if not spiritually, and who remembers you even if you don't remember him, and would like to meet with you. As would my daughter, Gretchen. Brad probably remembers Garrett. The two of them are only a year apart and used to play together sometimes when they were young. Garrett's wife just had a baby less than six months ago. Your niece. And Gretchen has a little boy. You're an uncle."

Tyler wanted to clap his hands over his ears. He didn't want to hear about this pseudo-family that was his and yet not his. These people who thought they had a claim on him.

"I..." he started, then stopped. He took another sip of ginger ale, then put his can back down. "Not now. It's too much, all at once. I can't. Not yet."

Mike looked disappointed for a second, then he smiled and it all went away, almost like magic. "No problem. Maybe later."

"Maybe." It was weird seeing a smile he'd practiced in the mirror on the face of another person who, despite looking just like you, was a stranger. Tyler had heard of long-lost relatives being reunited with family they'd never known and feeling an instant connection, but there was nothing here. Not really. Just a sense of unreality.

"Great. That would be... just great. Whenever you feel you're ready, we'll be there. And if you're never ready, that's okay, too." Mike pushed his smile a little wider and Tyler knew with a start that it was an act because he did the same thing. It was the smile he wore when it was either grin or cry or scream yourself hoarse, or, in his case, find a nice spot to cut yourself.

He made himself smile back and it wasn't one of his scary ones. He found himself almost liking the man, even if he didn't feel drawn to him. Of the three people he could claim as parents, Mike had done him the least harm. "I need some time."

Tyler glanced over at Josh and saw him staring at his mother, a pinched expression on his face. He wasn't quietly disapproving of their family drama as Tyler had earlier thought. He was furious, and it was all directed with laser intensity at Cynthia. Tyler needed to think of a way to distract him, or Josh was going to end up exploding all over and that would be worse than him spontaneously waxing the floor.

"Mom, did Ryan talk to you about my theory on who stole and uploaded that video of me?"

She shook her head and looked surprised.

"The whole reason why Ryan felt the need to bust open this shit-show was because I told him that I think it was Dad who did it. I mean Peter, I guess. I'm sorry. I hate the bastard, but I still can't think of him as anything but Dad. Anyway, this is proof, sort of. He has motive. He's always hated me and now I know why."

His mother shook her head. "Your—Peter didn't steal that video, or have someone steal it for him, which would have been more likely. He was too angry when it went missing. Also, he wouldn't have released it like that. It doesn't just expose you. He feels exposed as well. Believe me, I got an earful from him earlier in the week."

That stumped Tyler. If his father—Peter—hadn't done it, then he had no idea who had. "What do you mean?" he asked.

"The video went missing a long time ago, just a few days after the police took it in. The officer who was dealing with the incident went to go get it so it could be destroyed, and it wasn't there. I assume the other parents were notified of the disappearance as well. I remember Peter was livid. He was sure the video would be used against our family in some way, probably for blackmail purposes, but who knows what Peter was thinking, and in the end, nothing happened. Well, not until now, I mean. At the time, Peter threatened to take legal action against the officer who misplaced the video, but the police chief talked him out of it. I'm not sure if the video was ever recovered. Most of what I know was what I overheard. It wasn't like Peter ever discussed things with me."

"So, we're back at square one," Josh said, and Tyler was relieved to see he'd stopped giving his mother the stink-eye. "We still don't know who released the video or why, but we have learned that your brother is having an affair with one of his employees and that your father isn't really your father. Oh, and your guidance counselor was killed in a car accident."

"Yeah. It's been an eventful week."

"Two weeks," Josh said, ever pedantic.

"Whatever. Mom, can we call it an evening? I think I've had about all I can handle right now. Stick a fork in me, I'm done. I cannot deal with one more thing thrown at me."

So, of course, his phone picked that second to start ringing.

"Oh, fuck me," Tyler muttered, and answered it.

It was Alicia. "I've got great news, kid! They want to cast you as Simon in *Jar of Starlight*, which, honestly, is a shit title and hopefully not firm. You must have wowed the hell out of them at your reading because they want you to sign a contract right away. If you agree to do this, and as your agent I think you'd be crazy to turn it down, then they'll need an answer soon. They want to start shooting in November."

"Great," Tyler said, trying to work up the proper amount of enthusiasm, but it wasn't easy. He was too tired and drained to be excited. "Send the contract over to Ryan and we'll look it over tomorrow, okay?"

"Sure. I think things are going to be fine, Tyler. I know the past few weeks have been crazy, but you've done a great job of handling everything. You should check in with Tom. He should be able to give you a rough timetable of how much longer you and that boyfriend of yours need to keep playing house. In no time, I'm sure you two can see about getting on with your lives."

"Yeah, thanks, Alicia." It had been easy to forget, in the flurry of activity, that there was a slight problem with falling for Josh, and now it had reared its ugly head. Maybe going their separate ways was what needed to happen. Living here with Josh was like living in Fantasyland. It was this nice little fake fairy tale world that didn't really exist. Tyler had a life. That life wasn't here. It was just hard to remember that when Josh touched him and the rest of the world fell away. Even now, listening to what should've been the best news he'd heard all month, Tyler's hand went to Josh and gripped his arm like he'd vanish if Tyler didn't hold onto him.

"No problem. I'm just glad things are going our way. I'll see you when you get back home, kiddo. All right?"

"You bet," was his dutiful reply, and he said his goodbyes.

He turned to Josh with a smile that he had to manufacture. "Guess what?"

Josh favored him with his own fake smile. "I heard. Your agent is loud. Congratulations. You got the part. This is great." He smiled wider and Tyler wished he wouldn't. It hurt to look at it. "I bet you can't wait to get home."

"Josh," he said.

"No, this is fantastic news, right? They picked you despite all the publicity. Or maybe because of it. I don't really get how it all works, but it has. Worked, I mean." Josh looked at Tyler, his face full of desperate expectation.

"Yeah," Tyler said. "It worked." He should've been happier. He should've been turning cartwheels around the room. Later, after he'd gotten some sleep and had time to think, then he'd be happy. He was just tired. That was it.

Tyler's mother stood, a concerned smile on her face. "Yes, this is wonderful news. Congratulations, sweetheart. I'm happy for you. Will you see Mike and me out?"

The manufactured happiness fell off Josh's face and was replaced with icy displeasure, focused again on Tyler's mother. He looked like he was about to object, so Tyler put a hand on his chest to keep him from standing. "It's fine, really," he said. *Down, boy.* And damn his heart for finding Josh's protectiveness, as unnecessary as it was, endearing in any way.

At the door, his mother told Mike to start down without her. He nodded, then shook Tyler's hand. "I'm sorry about everything," he said, and it occurred to Tyler that his mother had given him a long list of explanations and excuses, but no real apology.

After Mike was out of earshot, his mother took both of his hands in hers. "I know you're angry with me and you have every right, but I'm your mother and I love you. I thought what I was doing was for the best, but I know you don't agree, and I'm beginning to see that maybe I was wrong. I'm sorry. I only wanted the best for you."

"Oh," Tyler said, surprised. It appeared he was going to get something of an apology after all. He opened his mouth to say that it was all right, then closed it. It wasn't all right and he wasn't ready to tell her that it was. "Okay," he said instead. "I've got a lot to think about." That was the understatement of the year.

"About that," she said. "I have some advice for you, whether you want to hear it or not. Go home and take that role. Your life is back there, not here."

"I know that. I'm going to take the part. I'd be crazy not to."

"But?" Dammit. Why wouldn't she let it go?

"No buts, Mom. Why wouldn't I go back? Everything is going just the way it's supposed to. Things are working out perfectly." And fuck it, but his voice cracked there at the end. Some actor he was.

"Oh, honey. I won't tell you 'I told you so.'"

"You just did. I get it. I fucked up yet again, didn't I?" Tyler felt tears prickle in his eyes and he fought them down. He gave his mother a wide smile.

His mother raised a tentative hand and brushed his cheek with her cool fingers. "You're in love. It's written all over you. And normally I'd be thrilled for you, but..." She stopped and gave him a troubled smile. "Learn from my mistakes, okay?"

"Sure," he said, and allowed her to enfold him in her arms, just like she had when he was a small child.

It was just a two-week affair. It felt like longer, though. The thought of leaving a man he'd only been involved with for two weeks shouldn't hurt so much. It wasn't reasonable and it wasn't fair, but if life had taught Tyler anything, it was that life wasn't fair. Not by a long shot.

"I love you," his mother said as she pulled away from him.

"I love you, too," Tyler said, and the hell of it was that he still did.

Chapter 36
Josh and the Metaphorical Glass Loafer

Sunday, October 2nd, 5:15 p.m.
Josh's perfectly adequate condo
Evanston, IL

Josh had been a huge nerd as a kid. He was uncoordinated and skinny with thick glasses, braces (not the invisible kind), and an out of control Jewfro. He liked computers, video games, math, and visiting museums, especially the Art Institute, where he could, and did, go on and on about his favorite artists to anyone who'd listen. He got picked on quite a bit in school, especially middle school, which he was convinced existed to segregate children aged eleven to thirteen away from the rest of society in an environment not that dissimilar to the island in *Lord of the Flies*, which was one of his favorite books. He did not have many friends.

In middle school, he learned his hair was gay, his clothes were gay, liking art was gay, his glasses and braces were gay, watching *The X-Files* was gay, and getting straight A's was especially gay. That he had to concentrate in the gym showers to not get an erection was beside the point. Josh was so used to being called gay for every single thing he was and did that discovering he really was gay came as less of a surprise than it might have otherwise. It was pretty much the crap cherry on top of the shit sundae that was his preteen existence. He'd resigned himself to four hellish years of high school when a miracle happened: Ryan Chadwick insisted on becoming his best friend and champion right at the beginning of freshman year.

Everything changed for Josh then, because Ryan didn't tolerate anyone picking on him. Josh was invited to parties because Ryan wouldn't go if his best friend didn't go, too. He wasn't bullied because Ryan would've stomped down hard on anyone who even thought of trying it. Ryan persuaded Josh to join the football team, and while he was never much more than a bench warmer, he put on muscle and gained coordination. The coach noted the one thing he was good at—running—and encouraged him to try out for cross-country, where he excelled and won trophies for the school. Josh graduated in the top of his class and received a scholarship to Stanford.

By his senior year of high school Josh was no longer skinny or gawky, had figured out how to deal with his hair, found glasses that suited his face, grown several inches taller, and the braces had done wonders for his teeth. He became adept at politely turning down the now numerous overtures from Ryan's more desperate cast-offs, the less shy members of the National Honor Society, the girl in art club who'd been dumped by her girlfriend and "wanted to give cock a chance," several pushy cheerleaders, and even a few discreet and hopeful boys. Josh wasn't interested in anyone but Ryan, who was friend and lover and savior all rolled into one large, attractive package. He couldn't imagine ever wanting anything or anyone else.

Largely thanks to Ryan's looming omnipresence, Josh had never been beaten up for being gay, or hazed, or even ridiculed beyond juvenile insults. When he'd finally come out, no one except his parents had cared, and even they were only passively disapproving. They didn't disown him or stop paying his college bills or tell him not to bother coming home. Even if they didn't necessarily approve of him, they still loved him.

Josh was inordinately lucky. He knew that, but the knowledge had never really hit home until today, sitting next to Tyler and listening to his horror show of a childhood. Put together with what he'd learned from Rachel and Tyler himself, it was clear no one had ever sheltered Tyler. The man he thought was his father despised him, his mother failed him, and Ryan seemed oblivious. It seemed the only one who'd ever tried was Brad, and Josh felt a surge of affection for his friend.

"If my phone goes off again, I'm not answering it," Tyler said when he came back into the living room. "I am done for the night. Done." He flopped down on the couch and laid his head on Josh's thigh. "I don't care what the emergency is, either someone else can deal with it or it can wait until tomorrow."

Tonight, Tyler wasn't as beautiful as he'd been that first night in the rented house (*Michael Connolly's house, and how crazy is that?*) when he'd laid his head in Josh's lap. The skin around his eyes was pink and puffy and there were dark shadows under them. He looked tired and every one of his twenty-five years, plus maybe a few extra. But for all that, he was still achingly precious to Josh. He wanted to wrap Tyler up in cotton wool and protect him from everyone in the world, and he knew he couldn't. So instead he said nothing, but stroked Tyler's short hair and thought, *don't leave me don't leave me don't leave me*, while knowing that he would, soon, and that wanting Tyler to stay was way beyond selfish. He refused to be yet another person in Tyler's life who put him and his needs last.

"You're being suspiciously quiet, Dr. Rosen," Tyler said after several minutes of silence.

"I was just thinking that it's a miracle you aren't more fucked-up than you already are."

Tyler let out a quiet snort of laughter. "I know, right? I did warn you. I told you to run away while you still could and you said, 'no, Tyler, I could use some excitement in my life.'"

"'I am not a smart man,'" Josh said. He didn't finish the quote. It hit too close to home.

"Stop quoting movies at me. I know you're trying to make me feel better, but *Forrest Gump* quotes are not the answer. If you tell me life is like a box of chocolates then I'm going to have to hurt you, which would be a shame because I have plans for you."

"Plans?"

"Yes, plans. With a capital P."

"Good plans?"

Tyler yawned. "The best. I'll share them with you when I'm not so damned tired."

Josh grunted and ran his finger over first one of Tyler's eyebrows, then the other. "So, what now?"

Tyler closed his eyes. "I think I'm going to let you pet me for a while, then we'll see. This doesn't suck."

Josh ran his finger down the bridge of Tyler's lovely nose. "No, I meant what now for you and me in the greater scheme of things. Not just the next fifteen minutes."

"Only fifteen minutes?" Tyler pouted, pushing out his plump lower lip in the most calculated way possible.

"Tyler…"

Tyler opened his eyes and schooled his features into a neutral expression that didn't fool Josh for a second. That was the face Tyler wore when he was wary of giving too much away. "What?"

"Are we going to talk?"

"No!" It was said in almost a shout. Tyler closed his eyes again and lowered his voice. "I mean, yes, but later. Not now. Keep on with the petting."

"Yes, your majesty."

Not a surprising answer, but also not the one Josh wanted. He needed to know if there was still room in Tyler's life for a somewhat neurotic doctor teetering on edge of being middle-aged. Yes, there had been that declaration of love, but Josh had pestered him into saying it. Had practically begged for it. Other men had said they loved him, but none had stayed that way. Since Josh hadn't loved any of them back, it hadn't mattered to him, but this was different. Night and day different. There was nothing to indicate that Tyler would continue to feel the way he did now, whatever that even was. Tyler had said he was stupid with love for Josh, which, when he thought about it, didn't sound promising for long-term happiness.

Tyler would go back home, be in his movie, and with the distance between them, Josh would become less important. There would be other men, especially now that Tyler was so very publicly out, and one of them was bound to distract him from his long-distance relationship. LA had no shortage of attractive men. Tyler would find someone handsomer, younger, and more importantly, who lived closer.

Josh could and would visit. It was doable, he knew, but he kept picturing going into the grocery store, standing in line, and seeing Tyler on the cover of a tabloid with someone else. A model, maybe. One with no gray hairs yet. Or worse, Josh pictured himself flying out to California, only to be met at the airport by Tyler and his new boyfriend. "Oh, I'm sorry," Josh could imagine him saying. "You know how it is. We just clicked. I'm sure you understand. You can still stay in my guest room. I wouldn't dream of you staying in a hotel. You're family, after all." And then Josh would have to spend a week not killing some underwear model named Chet or Xander.

"Josh, why are you making a fist?"

Oh, no reason. I only want to punch your imaginary boyfriend Chet in his pretty face.

"Sorry," he said, and unclenched his hand.

"Do you really think I was chosen to be in the movie because of the recent publicity?" Tyler asked.

That was so far away from where Josh's brain had travelled that it took him a few seconds to think about what Tyler had said. "I don't know. I'm a dermatologist, not a media expert. I could do something about these, you know, if you wanted me to." Josh took one of Tyler's wrists and lifted it. He pushed up the sleeve of his sweater and touched the scar there. "I'm surprised you've left them like this. Give me six months and I could make them all but disappear." Josh put Tyler's wrist back down, wondering if he would be anything but a memory to Tyler in six months. "But I don't know jack shit about Hollywood. What do you think?"

"I think it's probable," Tyler said. "Why else would they have called Alicia specifically to make sure I was there for the reading?"

"Does it matter?"

"Alicia would tell me that it sure as shit doesn't matter. A role is a role, and it's not a terrible one. The script isn't awful."

"You don't sound convinced."

"Because I'm not." Tyler bent his knees and wrapped his arms around them. "This whole acting thing is precarious. I know that. Very few people are successful. For the ones who are, your career might stretch on for years, or you might make a few movies and then fade into obscurity. I have this face, a certain ability to act, and a bit of charisma, but I'm nothing special. There are prettier faces, better actors, men with more charisma than I'd know what to do with. There are actors who are nicer and taller and pretty much anything you can think of. The one thing I have is this recent burst of fame, or notoriety, or whatever you want to call it. I've captured people's attention, and maybe I'm seen as sympathetic enough that more people will forgive me than revile me. Being gay in Hollywood has gone from something you used to hide at all costs to something you go on talk shows to discuss. It's... I hesitate to say popular, because that's not correct, but that's almost what it feels like, and I don't like it."

Josh went back to stroking Tyler's hair. "Isn't that better than the opposite?" He was reminded again of his own high school and college experience. The way made easy for him by Ryan, and, ironically enough, all those girls Josh had loved to hate. No one ever questioned Ryan's sexuality. Nothing he ever did was gay, not even dragging his best friend everywhere with him, and by extension, Josh hadn't been gay, either. At least never to his face, not where he or Ryan could hear it.

Tyler shrugged, his shoulders bumping into Josh's leg. "I'm being objectified either way."

"How can you become a famous actor and not be objectified? Or, hell, Tyler. You've done modeling, too. They dress you up and take pictures and stick them in a magazine for everyone to see. How is that not objectification?"

Tyler frowned. "It's not the same thing. It's not about the model, it's about the clothes. The clothes are being objectified, not me. And just like modeling isn't about me, but the clothes, I want to be successful for what I do rather than what I am. I want to be known as a good actor, not a good gay actor, but I've lost that choice. It's gone now forever. Alicia would say it doesn't matter, and she's probably right. She usually is. Maybe I'm just looking for excuses."

"Excuses for what?"

"To not go," Tyler said. "Excuses to stay here with you."

Oh. That squeezed Josh's heart until it ached. "No," he said. It didn't matter how much he didn't want Tyler to leave, or how much he worried that distance would cause their very new and very fragile relationship to fray, then snap. He couldn't be responsible for Tyler giving up on his dream. Even if it was a potentially impossible dream. Even if it was a dream that Josh didn't fully understand.

"No?" Tyler said, sliding into a dangerous tone.

"Turn it down if you think it's going to be bad for your career, or if doing the role makes you uncomfortable, but don't turn it down for me. I'm not worth it. No one is worth that."

"Shut up," Tyler said.

"Excuse me?"

"I know you think you're being helpful, but you're not, so stop. Shut your gorgeous mouth or use it for something more productive than lecturing me on how I should feel."

That stung. He pulled his hand away from Tyler's head like it'd been burned. "That wasn't what I was trying to do."

Tyler sat up. "I know. Your shining armor is showing again, and I should find it sweet. Part of me does find it sweet, and that part is pissing off the rest of me. I'm an adult, dammit. I don't need you telling me what to do for my own good. If I want to shove a stake in my career, I should be allowed to do so."

"Not on my account." There was no way in hell Josh could live with himself if he let Tyler sabotage his career just to be with him. It would taint their relationship forever.

"No, not on your account, you arrogant asshole. On my own fucking account. Why is this your decision? It's my life. And if I want you, in all your priggish glory, then I ought to be able to decide that for my own fucking self."

"Tyler, that doesn't even make sense. How the hell did we get here? What am I saying? Every conversation with you is like this."

Tyler turned his body so he was sitting on the couch facing Josh's profile with his legs bent and held tightly. It was the position he always sat in when he was upset about something, although Josh had no clue what had set him off this time. The boy was nothing but a walking minefield.

Boy, his mind echoed, and the thought made him pause. Tyler wasn't a boy, and thinking of him that way wasn't helpful. Like he'd just said, he was an adult and deserved to be treated as such.

Josh took a deep breath, held it for a few seconds, and let it out. He looked at Tyler and saw his mouth was a thin line and his eyes were narrowed into slits. Josh had managed to piss him off royally not even an hour after his mother had destroyed the last of Tyler's childhood illusions. *Nice job there, Josh. Let's try this again and see if I can maybe keep my foot out of my supposedly gorgeous mouth this time.* "What do you want from me, Tyler?" He fought, he thought successfully, to keep his tone neutral. He wanted honesty, not a confrontation.

Tyler was quiet for a long time. "I want you to listen to me. Let me tell you a story. It might even be true."

Josh leaned his head back and closed his eyes. "Okay. I'm listening."

"Once upon a time in the kingdom of the North Shore there was a king and a queen who had three sons. The first son was the heir. The second son the spare. The third is always the unlucky one, have you ever noticed that? But he's the one the story is always about. He has trials to overcome and a princess to win. Or in his case, a prince, but the principle is the same."

"Of course," Josh said. "It can't always be princesses."

"Not in this story, at any rate. So, the first son had a friend. A page boy who followed him around everywhere like a devoted hound."

"Hey," Josh protested.

"Hush. This is my story and I'll tell it how I want. As the boys aged, the first son grew tired of the page boy and sent him away."

Josh's eyes flew open and he turned his head to frown at Tyler. "That's not how it happened."

Tyler laid his finger across Josh's lips. "Stop interrupting. The page boy took his banishment in stride and ended up becoming a successful healer, just like the second son. As for the third son, he had many trials, which he overcame, and many adventures, in which he was daring and brave and strong and true, just like all third sons are meant to be. But there was one thing missing. In all that time, he had not come across his true love. There were a few princes who tried to be that, but they were never quite right. Their feet never fit in that metaphorical glass slipper."

"Wait, wait, wait. Hold on. Glass slipper?"

"I did say it was a metaphorical glass slipper. Gah. Stop being difficult."

Josh forced his face into a scowl, which was hard because it wanted to smile. "Shouldn't it be a metaphorical glass loafer instead?"

Tyler rolled his eyes. "Fine. Whatever makes you happy. Where the hell was I? Oh, yeah. The third son and his quest to find someone to fit into the loafer. The metaphorical loafer. There was no real, and I can't stress this enough, glass footwear of any kind."

"Okay, got it."

"Fantastic. So, the third son, after many years spent abroad, returned home for the wedding of one of his brothers. And while he was going through yet another trial, or maybe an adventure, he came across someone he'd known before. The page boy, only now he was all grown up. He gallantly agreed to help the third son with his current adventure, or trial, and soon the third son wondered if maybe the former page boy might fit that glass loafer. Which did not really exist because it's a fucking metaphor and don't even start with me, Josh."

"I didn't say a word."

"I could hear you thinking it," Tyler said. "And had there been an actual glass loafer, it would've fit the former page boy perfectly because the former page boy was practically perfect in every way for the third son."

"Tyler..."

"Shh. I'm still not done. At some point during the adventure the former page boy fell in love with the third son after realizing he was no longer in love with the heir. Right?" Tyler's voice wobbled a little at the end.

"Yes," Josh agreed. He looked into Tyler's uncertain eyes. "The former page boy finally grew up. It took being around the third son to make him realize that he had grown out of what he'd felt for the heir. It was something that no longer fit him. If we're still talking footwear, the shoe would have pinched in the toes and rubbed a blister on his heel. That shoe was now too small for the former page boy."

"Really?" Tyler asked, the expression on his face making Josh's heart lurch in his chest.

"Without a doubt."

"Oh. That's... I mean, the third son knew that, of course, but he was relieved the former page boy had figured it out, too." Then Tyler's face fell a little. "Only the third son's life had changed him so that he could no longer live in the kingdom of the North Shore. At the same time, the former page boy had built a life, a good life, there and had no desire to live anywhere else. One couldn't stay and one wouldn't leave. So, do you know what they did?"

"Nope," Josh said.

"Me, neither," said Tyler. "That's the problem. I don't know what to do."

Neither did Josh, and that bothered him. "I don't like the way your story ends. It needs work. And I have a question."

"Only one?" Tyler asked, one eyebrow predictably raised.

"If the glass loafer is merely metaphorical, then how do you know that it would be a perfect fit for the former page boy?"

"Isn't it obvious?"

"Should it be?"

Tyler looked annoyed. "Christ, Rosen, how much more plain do I have to be? I take it all back. You are hopeless."

"I need you to say it, Tyler."

"Why?"

Josh pried Tyler's hands free from the death grip they had on his bent knees, then he pulled Tyler's feet onto his lap. He started to rub one of them. "Because it's important to me."

"That feels amazing." Tyler shivered. "Keep doing that and I will be your slave forever."

"Just answer the question, Tyler."

Tyler moaned with pleasure. "What question?"

"Now who's being difficult?"

"I'm always difficult. You should know that by now, page boy."

"Former page boy," Josh corrected. He started to rub the other foot. "Stop dodging. You should've gone into politics instead of acting."

"Okay, fine. The shoe fit because it was his shoe the whole fucking time," Tyler mumbled.

Josh stopped rubbing Tyler's feet. "It was his shoe?"

Tyler wiggled the foot in Josh's hand. "Keep rubbing. Yes, dammit. It was his shoe. Your shoe, I mean."

"Mine?" It seemed impossible to believe. "What do you mean it was mine the whole time? Plain English, please. No more fairy tales."

Tyler groaned. He started to pull his legs back, but Josh grabbed them and held on. "Nope," Josh said. "No pulling back, no curling up, no dodging. Explain, Tyler. Now."

"I... you..." Tyler flopped backward, and it was a good thing the couch was long because otherwise he'd have hit his head on the arm. As it was, his head barely cleared it. "I might've had a crush on you once upon a time. And I might have measured every man I've ever been with my whole life against you. You might be the Tyler Chadwick gold standard." He covered his face with his hands. "God. I can't believe I just told you that. How do you do that? I never tell anyone anything, but you make me spill everything. It's not right. It's downright unnatural."

"You had a crush on me?"

"Oh, man, such a crush. In retrospect, it's cringeworthy. I was this little wannabe baby twink dying to seduce you, and you, meanwhile, were completely oblivious. Which, now that I think about it, was a good thing."

"Just how old were you when this crush started, Tyler?"

Tyler's feet drummed against his leg. "Are you sure you want to know the answer to that?"

Probably not, but he was dying of curiosity. "Yes?" he said, and it came out like a question.

"Promise you won't freak out?" Tyler removed his hands from his face and blinked up at Josh, giving him huge, pleading eyes that didn't fool Josh for a second.

"Please tell me you were at least a teenager, Tyler."

"Um... technically, yes."

"Define technically." He should stop probing, but not asking was impossible, like ignoring a sore in your mouth.

"I was thirteen."

Josh winced. "That would have made me—"

"Don't think about it too hard, okay? It'll only give you a headache. This is why I didn't mean to tell you. It's all creepy and weird, knowing that your ex's teenaged brother was plotting to seduce you into taking his virginity. Stop looking at me like that. It's not like I succeeded. You'd have remembered. I am memorable as fuck."

"Great. Now I have this vision of mini you trying to get in my pants. I could've gone my entire life without that image. Wait a second. Tyler, you tried it at one of the summer picnics, didn't you? I remember now! You kept trying to get me to go off with you and I had no idea why. And it turns out you wanted me to fuck you in the botanic gardens. Ugh. I think I need a shower now."

Tyler kicked him, but carefully. "Stop being so dramatic. That's my job. Josh, my virginity was never in danger from you. Even if Brad hadn't intervened, you'd have never done anything with me. You were still too hung up on Ryan back then, not to mention too inherently decent to do anything with a teenager."

"In the great outdoors, no less. What were you thinking?"

"I was sixteen, duh. My dick was doing most of my thinking. If it makes you feel any better, I lost my virginity to someone approximately my own age a few months later."

"Approximately?"

"He was a freshman at UIC. Stop being so fucking squeamish. You had your cherry popped in high school, too."

"I am not discussing losing my virginity with you, Tyler."

"Just as well, since I already know who you lost it to. Right, then. So. That's all settled." He started to swing his legs off Josh's lap and again was stopped.

"No," Josh said. "Not a damn thing is settled. Tyler, if you stayed here, what would you do?"

Tyler stilled. "I'm not sure. I have a degree in theater. I could probably get a job at Starbucks."

"No, be serious for a moment."

"I am serious," Tyler said, sounding anything but.

"So am I. Have you considered actual theater? I know it's not like being in a movie, but it's still acting. There are a million theaters in Chicago. Well, hundreds, at least."

Tyler thought about it. "I did some theater work in college. High school, too, although I'm not sure if that should count. This thing I have..." he went from looking tired and a little worn at the edges to compelling. The shadows under his eyes made him look interesting rather than exhausted. He almost seemed to glow from within. Then it stopped, like Tyler had flipped a switch and turned off some sort of internal lamp. He went back to looking pale and drained. "That's really hard to do effectively on stage. It takes too much out of me. But on camera, it's so much easier, and I don't have to do it night after night after night. Some people get off on that shit. I don't think I'm one of them."

Josh nodded, still a little dazed. "Okay. Ty, I can't say that I understand, because that thing you do still kinda weirds me out a little. But if it shows up better on film than in front of an audience, then I think you should take the part in the movie. I know it's your decision, and this is just my opinion. Feel free to ignore me, but regardless of why it was offered, I think you should take the part. If you don't, all your adventures might be over, and I don't think you're ready for that." He scooted sideways on the couch, moving so he could pull Tyler onto his lap.

"I hate it when you hold me like this," Tyler groused, but he laid his head on Josh's shoulder anyway.

"Liar, you love it. And me, too, apparently."

"Apparently, but this isn't comfortable and I'm going to make your legs go numb. I know you like to pretend that I'm tiny, but I'm not."

Josh shook his head. "God, you're a pain in the ass. I want to hold you, so do whatever you need to do to get comfortable, and prepare to be held."

Tyler moved so he sat beside Josh instead of on him. He lifted Josh's arm and snuggled into his side. "How's this?"

"Perfect," Josh said, and it was.

"Good." Tyler yawned. "Josh, if I accept the part, I'll have to leave. I've gotten used to you. My cat has gotten used to you. Who will pester me to eat a sandwich? Who will hog the bed? Who will explain art to me in museums and compare me to beautiful statues? Who will talk you down when you start steam cleaning the curtains because you're stressed out? Who will take you to lunch at work? Who will you hold at night? Hint: if the answer to that last one is anyone but me I might get violent."

"You were always going to leave. We both knew that. But this kingdom has an airport, and phones, and Skype. The former page boy has a lot of vacation time saved up. We'll figure it out, I promise. Somehow."

Tyler sighed and didn't reply for a long time. When he did speak, it wasn't to say anything Josh expected.

"Why can't I let him go?"

Josh opened his mouth to say, "Who?" then closed it. There was only one "he" Tyler could be referring to. "Your father? Mr. Chadwick?" Even after all these years he couldn't think of the man as Peter.

"Yeah. Mr. Chadwick." It was said with a wisp of humor. "Knowing he's not my father should help, but it doesn't. I've been sitting here, thinking about him in that hospital, wanting to want his death and not quite making it. I think part of me thinks that if I leave and go back home, he'll die as soon as I get on that airplane, which makes no sense. I shouldn't care one way or the other. Josh, what the hell is wrong with me?"

Josh brought his hand up to stroke Tyler's hair. "He raised you. You thought he was your father. Love and hate can't be turned on or off like a spigot."

"I don't love him. I don't think I ever loved him. I used to think that maybe I was a changeling, you know, like in fairy tales, and one day I'd find out that I was really a fairy prince and not his child at all. And now it's all come true, except that instead of being a fairy prince, it turns out I'm just another Irish kid from suburban Chicago." He huffed, and Josh was amused to realize that Tyler was upset at finding out he was common as muck. He was, despite all his protesting, a bit of a snob. Like his snoring, it was another thing about Tyler he shouldn't find endearing but did anyway.

"You're my fairy prince," Josh said, applying balm onto Tyler's wounded sensibilities.

Tyler elbowed him. "Shut up. At some point in elementary school one of my teachers remarked how much I looked like my mother, and I saw how true that was. Same hair, same eyes. I knew I couldn't be a changeling. If I was my mother's son then I must be my father's as well, like it or not. Only now I've found I'm not, but I still can't let him go. Years of abuse didn't do it. Learning we're not at all related didn't do it. I just want to stop caring, Josh. It hurts too much."

"I think you're your father's son, like it or not, and you always will be. We're a product of our genes, yes, but also our environment. Peter Chadwick is your father. He hasn't been a particularly good one, but learning he doesn't share your DNA doesn't strip him of fatherhood. If it did, every person who ever adopted a kid wouldn't be a 'real' parent, and every one of them is as real as it gets. Mike Connolly might be your biological father, but Peter Chadwick is your dad, for better or worse."

Tyler banged his head several times against the thankfully well-padded back of the sofa. "How do I stop caring? How do I make him not matter?"

"I don't think you can. Or maybe it just takes time. I don't know."

Tyler moved so that he was back on Josh's lap, this time facing him. He grabbed Josh's face and kissed him hard. "Then make me forget. Please."

Josh took hold of Tyler's shoulders and pulled him back. The look on his face was heartbreaking. Josh wanted to give Tyler everything, but not this, not now. It might be what he wanted, but it wasn't what he needed.

"I think you need to talk to someone about this," he said.

"I was," Tyler said. "I have been. You."

"Not me. A..." Josh paused, then spit it out. "A therapist." Tyler stiffened, but Josh plowed on. "I know it hasn't worked for you in the past, but I think you weren't ready before, and maybe now you are. Therapy isn't magic or voodoo. It's just someone impartial who can help you sort things out. I'm not impartial. I'm about as far from impartial as you can get."

Tyler grunted.

"Does that grunt mean yes or no or maybe or fuck off?"

Tyler sagged on Josh's lap, laying his head on Josh's shoulder and melting his body into Josh's so that there was no space between them. "Maybe," he said. "But you'll likely have to bully me into it."

How Josh was going to manage that from clear across the country was anyone's guess.

Tyler let out a deep sigh. "If you won't fuck me, you could at least have the decency to rub my back."

"Yes, your majesty."

Tyler yawned and tried to snuggle even closer into Josh, a feat that didn't seem possible.

Josh dipped his hands under Tyler's soft sweater to stroke the softer skin underneath. Tyler hummed in appreciation but was otherwise silent.

Damage Control

After a while Josh noticed the change in Tyler's breathing and he realized that Tyler had fallen asleep on him, wonder of wonders. It was still early. They hadn't eaten dinner yet and Josh was starting to get hungry. Even so, he sat still and held Tyler and let him sleep. Just like Tyler had predicted, Josh's legs had gone numb, but he didn't care.

He wanted to protect Tyler like Ryan had protected him, sheltering him from every snub, cruelty, and humiliation that might come his way. That wasn't possible, though. Even if Tyler would tolerate it, which he inevitably wouldn't, he didn't need it. Tyler was more than capable of fighting his own battles and had been for a long time, even if he didn't always recognize that in himself.

Tyler needed a partner, not a parent. He already had three of those and he didn't need a fourth. Josh could suggest, he could facilitate, he could even cajole, but couldn't force Tyler to do anything. He found that he didn't really want to, either.

He'd promised Tyler that he wouldn't try to fix him. He hadn't promised not to try and help Tyler fix himself, though. That he could do, but again, not from two thousand miles away.

Josh looked around his home, the sanctuary he'd created for himself. His refuge, and if you listened to his sister, his self-imposed prison.

Maybe Tyler wasn't the only one in need of fixing. If Josh expected Tyler to take the first, uncomfortable steps toward fixing himself, maybe Josh needed to consider doing the same thing.

He weighed his options. On one hand was the safe, comfortable life he'd built around himself like a snug cocoon. On the other was a life where everything was new and unfamiliar except for the man he held in his arms. He couldn't have both, and it was past time for him to decide what he really wanted.

It's supposed to be a relationship, Josh, not a suicide pact.

Josh tightened his arms around Tyler. In his mind, he stood hand in hand with him on the edge of that damn cliff, wind whipping at their clothing.

Tyler's eyes sparkled a dare at him. *"Are you ready to jump? All you have to do is take my hand."*

"I thought we already did."

Tyler shook his head and pointed up. The top of the cliff was maybe ten feet above their heads. Josh realized that they stood on a ledge. The chasm was still far below them.

"You can climb back up and get behind that railing or you can jump the rest of the way with me, but you have to choose. You can't stay here forever. What's it going to be?"

Josh looked first up, then down, and thought about it.

Chapter 37
Princess Tyler Rescues Himself

Monday, October 3rd, 10:47 a.m.
A poorly secured parking garage
Evanston, IL

Tyler was in his own world, his brain far too busy with his thoughts to pay much attention to his surroundings. He'd walked to Josh's practice to get the Volvo so he could pick up Purvi at the airport. When he'd gone inside to snag the keys, Josh had whisked him into his office, locked the door, and kissed him senseless. Consequently, now he was running a little late.

Tyler was both nervous and excited to introduce Purvi to Josh. He thought they'd like each other. He needed them to like each other. He wasn't sure what he'd do if they didn't like each other. Purvi's flight was due to touch down in thirty minutes and it would take at least that long to get to the airport with traffic, giving him plenty of time to brood about things, not that he hadn't been doing that all morning already.

Josh didn't want Tyler to stay. Tyler knew, at least in his head, that it wasn't a rejection. Josh didn't want to hold him back or stifle his career and ambitions. He was being noble, of course, and reasonable, which was worse.

"*We'll figure it out, I promise. Somehow,*" he'd said. The words had comforted Tyler yesterday, but this morning he thought they sounded bleak, the sort of empty promise you give a child, telling them everything will be all right even when you know damn well it won't.

Tyler knew he wouldn't be satisfied with Skype and vacation visits, not in the long run. He didn't want Josh in the abstract. He wanted him in his house, in his bed, and underfoot, likely scouring the house before Tyler's cleaning service got the chance. He didn't want Josh halfway across the country and only seen over a computer screen.

Purvi said that she'd fix things, to leave it all to her. Tyler wasn't sure what she had up her sleeve, but at this point he was willing to let her play fairy godmother if it got him what he wanted. Purvi had worked miracles for him before. Maybe she could pull another one out of her ass and straighten this mess out.

As occupied with his thoughts as he was, Tyler didn't hear anyone approach and was caught unawares when arms came around him from behind.

For a split second, he thought it had to be Josh, the figure featuring so prominently in his thoughts, but he knew almost at once it couldn't be. It didn't feel like Josh, and the smell of his aftershave was all wrong. He stiffened, frozen with shock and fear. It couldn't be. It couldn't.

"It's me, baby. Did you miss me?"

It was. David held him tight. His breath tickled Tyler's ear, and he shuddered. He was in a nightmare. That had to be it. One of his stupid nightmares, brought on as usual by stress, and any minute now he'd wake up from it, safe in Josh's bed. Any minute now.

"Well?" David rasped at him.

"D-david," Tyler stammered, his tongue thick. "I didn't expect... what are you doing here?" The restraining order wasn't up yet, wouldn't be up for almost a month, but a fat lot of good that did him now, held so that he couldn't get to his phone in the pocket of his coat. He tried to ease his hand backward and David tightened his grip.

"You've been a bad boy, baby," David purred, and Tyler couldn't help his flinch. He knew that tone all too well. It always preceded pain. David would tell him how bad he was and then punish him, usually with his fists.

"No, I —" David's hand cut off his air. Blackness crept in on the edge of his vision. *No no no no nonononono.*

David had done this to him before and Tyler knew that after he woke from the blackout David was inducing, he would be somewhere he didn't want to be. He fought, or tried to, but David was stronger and taller. Tyler remembered Ryan wanting him to take self-defense classes and how Tyler had ignored him. Stupid, so stupid. Typical of him. Just typ...

છ૪ઝ

Monday, October 3rd, 10:58 a.m.
Inside Ryan's Volvo
Evanston, IL

Tyler came to, as he always had from David's little choking incidents, with a splitting headache. He didn't want to open his eyes, but he did so anyway. He was in the driver's seat of Ryan's stupid Volvo, and he could almost believe that he'd passed out and David had been merely a dream or hallucination, except he could smell him: Axe and Dial and sweat.

"I know you're awake, Tyler. Let's go for a drive."

Fuck, fuck, fuck.

"Um, David, you can't—"

Tyler's head snapped back with the force of David's blow, hitting then rebounding off the headrest. "Don't tell me what I can and can't do. I said drive."

The car was already running. Tyler itched to turn the car off but didn't dare. He tried again. "David, what do you think you're doing? You know you won't get away with this. The restraining order is still active and this is a third violation. You'll be sent to prison this time. Just get out of the car now, walk away, and I won't say anything, I promise. We can both get on with our lives. No one ever has to know."

David snorted. "I can't get on with my life. Not without you. Not anymore. I tried, you know. I did. But you just won't get out of my goddamned head."

Tyler started counting. It was either that or scream. When he spoke, he tried to keep his voice level and calm. "No, Dave. I'm not—"

David smacked him again, hitting his ear and making it ring. "Shut up, Tyler. Shut that ever-loving mouth of yours for once in your life. This is what's going to happen. We're going to back out of this space, and then we're going for a ride. I'll give you directions. If you're a good boy, I'll be nice to you and we'll do the things you like. If you're not a good boy, I'll have to punish you. If you're a very bad boy, I'll start with your face. There are things even the best plastic surgeon can't fix, Tyler. And then I'll come back here and have a little chat with your handsome doctor where I explain to him the consequences of taking what's mine. So, Tyler, are you going to be a good boy or not?"

White, hot, impotent rage filled Tyler, blinding him for a second. The panic that he'd felt from being at David's mercy paled next to his fear of David coming back and hurting Josh. He struck out at David, trying to go for his eyes, but his wrist was caught almost at once in David's hand. He'd forgotten how damn quick the man could move when he wanted. At one time that speed and dexterity had been arousing. Now it was just frightening.

"I could break your wrist so easily," David said. "You always were delicate." He squeezed, grinding the bones together in Tyler's wrist. He moaned, but refused to scream.

"Are you going to be a good boy or not? I'm getting what I want either way. The choice is yours."

Never letting go of Tyler's hand, David used his other hand to grab something down by his leg. When he brought it up, nervous sweat prickled on Tyler's temples. It was a gun. David had a gun. Tyler felt his breathing speed up and knew if he didn't do something he was going to hyperventilate, so he started to count slowly, breathing in on the odds and out with the evens.

"Are you going to shoot me?"

David gave him a sad, chiding look. "Baby, I don't want to hurt you. Don't make me have to."

Tyler knew then he was fucked. Completely and utterly fucked.

Stop. I can't panic. He wants me to panic. If I go along, maybe I can find my way through this. If I panic, he automatically wins, and fuck that. David does not get to win.

David placed Tyler's hand on the steering wheel. "Remember what they told you in driving school," he said with chilling cheer. "Both hands on the wheel at ten and two. Remove your hands from the wheel, Tyler, and I will make you regret it. Do you understand?"

"Yes," Tyler breathed.

"Yes, what?"

Tyler clenched his jaw. He knew what David wanted to hear and he didn't want to say it, but he wanted even less to provoke David. "Yes, sir." He didn't trust himself to look at David in that moment. His eyes would give too much away. Tyler breathed in and out slowly and made himself fall back into that younger man who had loved and feared the man sitting beside him in equal measures.

Once he had control over his features, Tyler risked a glance at David. He was left-handed and held the gun low, so that if fired, the bullet would hit Tyler's thigh. He wouldn't die, at least not right away, but he wouldn't be able to run, either. Tyler couldn't risk getting shot there. He needed to be able to run. While it was an activity he loathed, he was still in better shape than David, who had always emphasized strength training over aerobics. Tyler was sure he could outrun him, given the chance. He just needed to figure out how to turn things around in his favor.

"I'll be good," he said, injecting the right amount of humility and meekness into his voice. "Wh-where do you want me to drive?"

David reached over to stroke his hair. Tyler made himself keep still under his hand. "I knew you'd be my good boy again," he said. "Turn left out of the parking garage, then right onto Green Bay. That'll do for now."

Tyler automatically buckled his seatbelt, making David laugh. "Oh, I love that. You do want to live. I knew it. Yeah, you'll be my good boy, won't you? Of course, you will."

Oh, yeah, I'll be your good boy. Right up until the moment when I get the chance to stomp on your face.

The car let out a warning, indicating that the front passenger needed to put on his seatbelt. The front passenger ignored the noise.

Oh, yeah, thought Tyler. *That's not going to drive me insane.* He wished there was a way to disable it. He sure as fuck wasn't going to ask Mr. Mental Health to buckle up. Today, he'd be playing the role of broken and submissive boy, terrorized out of his mind, and incapable of doing anything but obeying. David had the upper hand, but only for now, and he would get complacent. Tyler needed to be patient. Not one of his better skills, but today he thought he could manage it. It was amazing how patient you could be with a gun pointed at you.

Carefully, Tyler backed out of the parking space, pulled out of the garage, and steered the Volvo into late-morning traffic.

"Watch your driving and that lead foot of yours," David said. "The last thing we want is to get pulled over. Things could get unnecessarily messy."

Tyler suppressed a shiver. His mind churned, going a million miles an hour but getting nowhere, trying to think of a way out of his situation. There had to be something he could do. Or maybe he could escape when they got to whatever destination David had in mind. He wanted Tyler to drive north on Green Bay. That would take him back home, or rather, back to the home he grew up in. The problem, though, was that Green Bay went north forever. Up into Wisconsin, all the way to the actual city of Green Bay, but Tyler didn't think they were on their way to see a Packers game. Tyler wished he knew where they were headed but was afraid to ask. Cowering, cowed Tyler should probably keep his mouth shut. He bit his lip and drove.

Out of nowhere, his phone rang with Purvi's ringtone. Shit. He'd forgotten about her in all the excitement of being kidnapped. His hand left the steering wheel to grab for his phone and he felt the gun jam into his leg. Tyler flinched.

"Hands back on the wheel," David barked.

Tyler grabbed the steering wheel tightly. His phone continued to ring. "She's not going to give up," Tyler said, loath to speak but knowing that listening to his phone playing Katy Perry over and over would drive him insane even faster than the car's persistent seatbelt alarm.

"Where is it?"

Tyler gestured with his head. "Jacket pocket."

Not taking the gun off Tyler, David snagged the phone out, turned it off, and tossed it behind him. The phone hit the rear windshield with a crash and fell somewhere far out of reach. The screen was probably all fucked-up now. He was going to have to get yet another replacement phone.

Fuck David. Fuck David so hard. Tyler wasn't sure how, but he was going to make David pay.

They weren't even out of Evanston before Tyler's nerve broke and he spoke. He couldn't help it. "Why now?" he asked. He did, at least, manage to keep his voice meek.

"Serendipity, babe. Pure serendipity. I was going to wait until November, but there you were, right in front of me, and I couldn't resist. It's like it was fate."

Tyler's stomach churned. Serendipity. That must mean he hadn't been there for Tyler at all. It wasn't a great leap to conclude that David had been waiting there for Josh, and it made his blood run cold. He'd nearly taken a taxi to the airport. Instead, because the day was so nice, he'd decided to walk to Josh's office. It had given Tyler time to think, not that he'd come to any satisfactory conclusions, but the walk had taken longer than he'd expected. He'd been running late even before Josh had delayed him, and then David had snatched him. By now, Purvi would be frantic. Would she call Josh when she couldn't reach Tyler? Did she even have Josh's number? Tyler couldn't remember. She was bound to call Ryan, though. Ryan would call Josh, and—

Josh. David had a gun. David had been waiting with a gun for Josh. For Josh. With a gun.

Bile rose in Tyler's throat and he swallowed it down.

"Right, Tyler?"

Tyler forced himself to focus. "R-right. Yeah. Fate." Thank God, he'd decided to walk and get the car. Thank God, the day had been nice. Thank God, Purvi was flying in today and needed to be picked up at the airport. Josh was safe and Tyler would figure this out, somehow, but the important thing was that Josh was safe. It must indeed be fate.

It also meant David didn't have a plan in place. That was good. Another point in his favor.

"I've missed you so much, baby. Did you miss me, too?"

Like a raging case of herpes. This would take a certain amount of delicacy. If he sounded too eager, David would get suspicious. If he sounded too diplomatic, David would get suspicious. What he needed here was fear mixed with desire and the tiniest flare of defiance. David lapped that shit up.

"You hurt me," he said, injecting what he hoped was the right amount of wistfulness into his tone, then he bit his lip for effect.

"Babe, I wanted to explain. You never gave me a chance."

Ah, yes. That was David's first violation of the restraining order, the one he didn't get caught doing because he'd left before the cops showed up. Tyler had watched the whole thing play out over his security camera, and later Brad and Ryan, who had intercepted David, had filled him in on the missing audio.

"They didn't let me. They made me stay in the house." Tyler cut his eyes over to David to see if he was buying that bullshit. It seemed he was.

"It was all for your own good, Tyler. You have to see that. Everything I ever did was for you! Ever since I saw the video, I knew we were meant to be together. You have to see that, too."

"The video?"

"Yeah. I didn't want to share it with everyone, but you didn't give me a choice. They had to see. You're mine. You've always been mine. Why is that so hard for everyone to understand?"

That didn't make any sense at all, but Tyler wasn't going to question him. Poking at the crazy man's delusions seemed like an unhealthy option, but getting him to monologue might be helpful. Tyler had seen enough movies to know that you always got the villain to talk if you could to buy time. He had no idea if it worked in real life, but it seemed plausible.

"I think... I think maybe I'm beginning to," he said instead. "A little." *Come on, dude. Spill your crazy-ass guts. You know you want to.*

"I grew up near you, you know. Or you didn't, because I never told you. Needed to keep it a secret, but I can tell you now. The cat's out of the bag, right?"

What? "Um, sure."

"Not here, though." David waved his hand at the window, referring, Tyler supposed, either to Kenilworth, which they were leaving, or Winnetka, which they were entering, or both. Maybe the whole damn North Shore. "I dreamed of living somewhere like this. I used to drive down Sheridan sometimes and look at the huge houses and think one day, I could live in one of them. But that doesn't happen for people like me. We don't get mansions on the lake, or country club memberships. I grew up in Highwood, you see."

The hell of it was, Tyler did see. A little. Enough to almost feel pity for David. Then he remembered the gun, and that he'd been waiting for Josh, and his pity was incinerated away.

"Highwood," David went on. "So close, but yet so far, right? Sandwiched right between Lake Forest and good old Highland Park, because the rich people need somewhere for their servants to live, right? Isn't that the old joke? Anyway, I ended up with a decent job, and maybe one day I'd make it into Highland Park, but not in one of those mansions by the lake. I was doing okay, though. Then I saw that damn video and I was that kid from Highwood again, wasn't I, nose pressed to the glass, seeing things I wanted but could never, ever have."

He saw the video? I don't think he means that he saw it three weeks ago. It's like he's talking years ago when he saw it. How? Doesn't matter. Keep him talking. "What things?"

"Growing up, it wasn't safe for me to be gay. Mom would've thrown me out of the house while praying for my immortal soul. My brothers would've kicked my ass and helped her. Some of us aren't as lucky as you, Tyler, and you don't see me being all emo about it. I learned how to get by, how to pretend, and I was doing just fine until that fucking video."

Again with the video. "I don't... I don't understand." Tyler didn't have to fake his confusion on this one.

"It fell into my hands, and I saw you, and you were everything I ever wanted. Those other boys, the ones who fucked you, I hated them. I wanted to make them disappear. But you? Oh, babe, you were perfect, and nothing I could ever have. Like that mansion on the lake. I watched you over and over and over. And then, years later, I saw you again and I knew it had to be fate. We were meant to be. Why can't you see that?"

They were already at Glencoe. After that was Highland Park and then Highwood, which had to be their destination. Tyler was running out of time to think of a way out of the mess he was in.

"Answer me, dammit," David insisted, his voice rising to hysterical levels. "Why can't you fucking see that?" He pounded on the passenger window with his right fist hard enough that Tyler thought the glass might break.

Don't hurt me don't hurt me don't hurt me.

Tyler shoved down his instinctual response, which was to pull into himself and wish he was far away. He couldn't indulge in that right now. He had traffic to contend with and a lunatic to outwit. He was glad he had the steering wheel to grip. He was sure that otherwise his hands would have been shaking too much to be of any use.

"You hurt me," he blurted out, his voice sounding like a wounded child's. A dispassionate part of himself thought he'd managed, on accident, to get the perfect note of terror mixed with entreaty.

"I never meant… it was for your own good, baby, always. You've gotta see that. Everything was for you, and for us, so everything could be perfect. Now we're together again and it will be perfect again, just like it was before. I'll be able to go home."

No no no no no no no.

Memories swamped him. His arm twisted painfully behind his back. The time David had tied him up and left him that way for hours, how everything had hurt and he'd thought that maybe David would never come back, and when he did, he'd cried with relief and shame and anger. He remembered all those decorative bruises, and how David would press them to get a reaction out of him. Tyler thought of how it had all escalated, slowly, how he kept crossing lines and then redrawing them, until that night. That last night, filled with so much pain, and the next morning, waking up with every breath an agony and blind in one eye and wondering if he would ever be able to see out of it again.

Tyler remembered every shot to his confidence, the sneers, the carefully worded insults. He also saw how he'd gone along with it so easily because it felt so familiar, so natural, so deserved. It made him sick now to remember how eagerly he'd let David ensnare him. He'd been such a naive little fool, and he'd paid dearly for his ignorance. He was still paying for it. He'd end up paying even more if he wasn't careful.

Tyler gave himself a mental shake. He needed to stay alert. They were already in Highland Park, driving past Ravinia. Time was running out. He was good and trapped, and he didn't have many options.

What do trapped animals do? They chew off their own captured limbs. I should know, I've done it before when I was sure there were no other options left. Maybe it'll work this time, too, and anything is better than letting him win. He's going to hurt me; there's no reason why I can't beat him to it.

Tyler glanced at David, who gave him a lazy, knowing smile. Chew off his foot to escape. How was he supposed to do that?

Then he remembered that Melissa Anderson's house was coming up and he knew.

He felt a little bad about the Volvo, but only a little, because he'd always hated it. Sometimes he thought the sole reason his brother had bought it was so he could foist it off on Tyler when he was in town. He'd never seen his brother drive it, and the mileage on it never seemed to increase in his absence. Maybe Ryan would replace it with something better. One could only hope.

As he drew nearer to Melissa's house, Tyler wondered if he was doing the right thing. There were so many things that could go wrong. Tyler was pretty sure this was an idiotic idea, suicidally idiotic, but it was the only idea he had.

Idiotic plan or not, I'm in control now, David. Me, not you.

He shot another quick look at David. He was still pointing the gun at Tyler, but his hand had sagged. If the gun went off, Tyler thought it might graze him, or maybe even miss him altogether. David seemed lost in his own world, and God knew what the color of the sky was in there.

The house approached and Tyler waited until he had a perfect trajectory, then he gunned the Volvo's engine, calling on every bit of the 400 horsepower the thing was supposed to have, and headed straight for the massive oak tree in the middle of the Anderson's front lawn. There was a noise he felt on a cellular level, then what sounded like an explosion, pain, and then everything went white.

Chapter 38
Josh Jumps off the Cliff

Monday, October 3rd, 11:10 a.m.
A dermatology practice
Evanston, IL

Josh was finishing up charting his previous patient when his cell phone rang. He glanced at the caller ID and frowned. It was Ryan. He considered letting it go to voicemail, but he couldn't imagine Ryan calling merely to chat, so he picked it up.

"Hey. What's up?"

Ryan cleared his throat. "I tried calling Tyler, but he's not answering his cell."

Josh glanced at the time. "He left here about twenty minutes ago to pick up his PA at the airport, so that's probably why he's ignoring his phone. Is there anything I can help you with?"

Josh couldn't help but remember the last call he'd had from Ryan, asking him to be his groomsman. Josh had been vibrating with nerves while on the phone that day, his heart in his throat, palms sweating so much that he'd nearly dropped his cell. Today he felt, well, not nothing, but nothing like the emotions that had swept over him just three weeks ago. His not-Ryan was still there, in the background, but it had faded into near obscurity, and the feelings it engendered now were closer to a sort of wistful nostalgia as opposed to the heartache he'd felt before.

"How's Tyler?" Ryan asked. "How's he doing?"

"He's coping remarkably well, all things considered. I think I might have him nearly talked into trying to see a therapist again."

"You… really?"

"I think so, yeah," Josh said. He started doodling on a prescription pad.

"No… um… incidents?"

"As far as I know, Tyler hasn't sliced himself open, no."

Ryan cleared his throat. "That's good to hear. Things are likely to get more stressful for him in the short-term rather than less. What we've uncovered in relation to the video is troubling. How much do you know about Tyler's former relationships?"

Josh tapped his pen against his desk. "A bit. The most recent one was Ethan, he's some sort of reporter, I gather, and he and Tyler are still friends. Before him was David, who from what I can tell was an abusive psychotic asshole of mega proportions. I have no idea who he dated before that."

"This concerns David. He lives here now, in the area. Did you know?"

"Not exactly," Josh said. "But we did have the dubious pleasure of running into him here. Tyler thinks he's the one who went after my car."

"That's probable. He's done that sort of thing before. We're certain, well, nearly certain, that he's the one who leaked the video."

"What? Really?"

"We discovered he worked for the Highland Park police during the time of the video incident. David wasn't one of the police officers involved, but it's telling that he resigned shortly after the video disappeared. There were rumors at the time that he was forced to quit or face charges of theft. It seems he was likely stealing from the evidence lock-up."

"So, he stole a sex video with Tyler in it and years later ends up dating him? That's not at all creepy and disturbing."

"Tyler's relationship with David was very troubling. In retrospect, we should have done more at the time to help him, but Tyler hid how bad the situation was for a long time. And that's neither here nor there. The important thing is that I'm going to make sure David is adequately punished for his crimes this time, but in the meantime, you and Tyler need to stay alert. Have you talked with the police about your car yet?"

"Yes, yesterday. We told them about our suspicions, and Tyler let them know about the restraining order. I guess it moves with Tyler, so it's active here, too. They told us that he might need to seek another one once the current one expires."

"I'm hoping it won't come to that," Ryan said. "I think we'll have David arrested long before then. But in the meantime, you need to keep your eyes open. I'm glad Purvi's coming into town. I don't want Tyler alone until we get this taken care of."

"Fine by me. Should we hire some sort of security, do you think?"

Ryan paused, thinking. "Maybe. I don't think Tyler would be happy about it, but it might be a good idea. I'll discuss it with him this evening."

There was a knock on his door. "Come in," he called out.

Nik poked his head in. "Your next appointment is in room twelve," he said, and left.

"I've got to go," he told Ryan. "I've got a patient."

"Give me one more second," Ryan said. "It's been brought to my attention recently that I treated you badly."

"I..." Josh stopped, at a loss for words.

"I'm sorry. You don't have to say anything if you don't want to. I just need you to know that I realize I treated you poorly and I am very sorry for all of it."

Josh sat there, stunned. "It wasn't all... you don't have to be sorry for *everything*."

Ryan was quiet for a second. "Okay," he finally said. "There are some things I'm not sorry about. And Josh?"

"What?"

"I'm glad you're with Tyler."

"Yeah. I'll take care of your brother."

"I know you will, but I meant... you and my brother...he's good for you, too." Ryan cleared his throat. "I just want you to know that I'm happy for both of you."

Josh thought he could hear a smile in Ryan's words, and smiled himself. "Thank you. I'll be your groomsman, by the way. That is, if you're still getting married."

"I... thank you. We'll discuss it later," Ryan said. "Didn't you say you had a patient to get to?"

"That I did. Goodbye, Ryan."

Josh sat there, dumbfounded. Ryan had apologized to him. Ryan. Apologized. He might have sat there indefinitely, lost in his thoughts, except Nik stuck his head into his office again and reminded him of his patient.

When he returned later to his office, Josh glanced at his phone and noticed he had three missed calls from Purvi. *What the hell?*

He returned her call and she picked it up almost instantly. "What the fuck did you do with my boy?" she snarled at him.

"What?"

"Where. Is. Tyler?" she bit out.

"Hi, you must be Purvi. I'm Josh. It's nice to finally hear your voice. Are you insane?"

"This is serious. Where the fuck is Tyler? He isn't answering his phone. No texts, no calls, nothing. He said he was going to pick me up at the airport and he hasn't shown up. I already called Ryan and he told me to call you. Brad isn't answering his phone. I don't know what to do!"

The last word ended in a wail.

Josh's heart started to pound. *Calm. You need to stay calm. Tyler is fine. His phone is probably fucked-up, but he's fine.* But what if he wasn't? What if... *stop it. Stop it right this fucking minute.*

Nik opened his office door after knocking and not getting a response. "Your next patient is here."

"I need a minute, Nik. Something's come up. Stall for me?"

He pursed his lips. "Okay. I'll let the patient know there's a delay." With a frown on his face, he walked out.

"Okay, Purvi?"

"Yeah?"

"Tyler was here about an hour ago to get the keys to the car so he could pick you up. When did you hear from him last?"

"We texted right before I got on the plane in LA, so hours ago."

Josh remembered Ryan saying that he hadn't been able to reach Tyler, either, and he started to panic. "Okay, so I was the last one to talk with him. Let me at least make sure he took the car, and I'll talk with the garage security. Maybe someone saw something. Then... I don't know. I'll call the police, I guess. You should probably get a taxi. Do you want to meet me here at my office?"

"Sure. That makes as much sense as anything right now."

Josh gave her the practice's address. "It'll be fine, Purvi. I'm sure he's okay."

"Right," she said, not sounding convinced. Josh couldn't blame her. He wasn't convinced, either.

He headed out to the parking garage, not sure if seeing Ryan's Volvo in his parking spot would be good or bad. When he got there, the spot was empty. Okay. Assuming it hadn't been stolen, that meant Tyler had taken it. There could be all sorts of reasons why he hadn't shown up at the airport and wasn't answering his phone. Maybe he'd accidentally left his phone in the condo, although that seemed unlikely. Then on the way to the airport, Tyler had gotten a flat tire, or maybe someone else had had an accident and he was stuck in traffic. Maybe he'd muted his phone without realizing it. Maybe he'd gotten pulled over for speeding. Maybe...

In the middle of walking back to his office while thinking up all sorts of scenarios, some more likely than others, Josh ran into Nik, literally.

After they bounced off each other, Nik grabbed his arm. "Hey. Where are you running off to? You've got a patient waiting for you."

"I know. Mary Bastock. Hives. She'll live. There's something I need to take care of first." He tried to pull out of Nik's grasp but the other man held on.

"What? You can't just leave a patient waiting like that."

"Let go, Nik. Tyler was supposed to pick someone up at the airport, and right now he's MIA and not answering calls or texts. I need to find out where he is. He might be hurt or in an accident." Josh wondered if the Volvo had a security system that could track the car. He needed to call Ryan. And then the police. Or maybe he should call the police first. No, Ryan—

"Josh, are you okay?"

Josh focused on the man gripping his arm. "My boyfriend is missing, not answering his phone, and left his best friend stranded at O'Hare. The car is gone, and since it's his brother's car, I have no clue if the security system could be used to track it down. I need to call his brother and the police, not necessarily in that order, so no, Nik, I am not okay. Now, excuse me so I can go and figure this shit out."

Nik dropped his arm. "Um... I saw him," he said.

Now Josh grabbed Nik by both shoulders. "Really? When?"

"Maybe an hour ago? I was on break and walking out to my car when I spotted him. There was some guy with him. They were —" Nik broke off.

"What?"

Nik looked annoyed. "The guy gave him a hug from behind, and Tyler kinda sagged into him. It looked to me like they knew each other."

Josh felt cold. "What did he look like?"

Nik shrugged. "He was a tall white guy with dark hair. Had some scruff. More than you. Like a closely trimmed beard."

Josh pulled out his phone and thumbed through his pictures until he got to the one of Tyler's ex. "Could this be him?"

Nik looked and shrugged. "Maybe. He was far away."

"Shit."

Nik looked startled. "Josh?"

"I have to... I have to figure this out." He started walking back to his office.

"What about your patient? Matt is going to be pissed."

"Fuck Matt and fuck Mrs. Bastock. If it was the guy in the picture, then it's Tyler's ex."

Nik scoffed. "And this is all because you're jealous?"

"No. Look, I don't have time for you right now. This is important, and if you don't mind, I have to make a call."

Nik looked like Josh had slapped him. "But—"

Josh's phone rang, startling them both. *Please be Tyler please be Tyler please be —*

It was Ryan. "I think David has Tyler," Josh said.

"How... Josh, there's been an accident. Tyler was driving and David was in the passenger seat. They hit a tree. Both have been taken to Highland Park Hospital."

"Oh, God. What happened? Is Tyler okay?"

"I don't know. I'm on my way to the hospital now."

Josh ran a hand through his hair. "Come get me. I've got no way to get to the hospital. Oh, and fuck. I forgot about Purvi. I told her to take a taxi to my office. I'm sure she's on her way here by now."

"That's fine," Ryan said. "The officer I spoke with said Tyler was in stable condition, so here's the plan. I'll drive to your office, we'll wait for Purvi to arrive, and then we'll all go to the hospital together. Okay?"

"Stable condition? Stable condition means dick. A coma is a fucking stable condition." Josh saw Nik flinch back and realized in a detached way that he was close to screaming.

"If Tyler's in a coma then fifteen minutes won't matter one way or the other."

"Fuck you, Ryan."

"Josh!" Ryan's voice snapped at him like a whip. "Get ahold of yourself. I will be there shortly. Purvi will be there as well. I need you functional, do you understand? You're no good to my brother in a hysterical state."

Josh gripped the phone tightly. "I can't lose him," he said. "I can't. I... I can't do it again."

He heard Ryan sigh into the phone. "You don't have the luxury of falling apart right now. You need to keep it together for Tyler. Can you do that, Josh?"

"Yeah, okay. I'm... fine. I'm sorry. I'm fine. How soon until you get here?"

"Twenty minutes, maybe."

"Okay. Thanks."

After hanging up, he looked at Nik. "I'm going to go speak with Matt. Can you see if one of the other doctors can see Mrs. Bastock, or let her know we need to reschedule? I'll be gone for the rest of today, perhaps longer. After I talk with Matt I'll see if Marisol can deal with the rest of my appointments. She can maybe get them rescheduled or something."

Josh left Nik in his wake and went to go give Matt the good news: he was going to need a leave of absence. Matt was going to be pissed, but Josh didn't give one single fuck.

ଅ୫୦

Monday, October 3rd, 12:30 p.m.
Highland Park Hospital
Highland Park, IL

The first person Josh saw in the ER waiting room was Cynthia, and he hurried over to her. "Is Tyler okay? Can I see him?"

"Right now, the police are speaking with him, so no."

"But—"

"Josh."

Josh looked over at Ryan. He realized that his voice had gotten loud so he lowered his tone. "Sorry. I'm just worried."

"We're all freaking out right now," Purvi said. "Cynthia, how is he?"

"He's a little banged up, but nothing serious. I'm sure you'll be able to see him when the police are finished asking him about the accident. He's been asking where you were from the moment I arrived." She gave him a wan smile. "I think he was disappointed I was there and not you."

"He shouldn't be speaking with the police without a lawyer present," Ryan said, looking irritated.

Cynthia flushed. "Mike's in there with him."

"And Tyler's okay with that?" Josh had a hard time picturing it.

"Well, no, he wasn't happy about it at first, but we convinced him it would be better than him talking to the police alone. I don't know exactly what happened, only that Tyler deliberately crashed Ryan's car into a tree. The passenger in the car, who is apparently his ex, was badly injured. None of this looks good, and when Tyler agreed to speak with the police, I decided using the lawyer we had was better than not using one at all. Luckily, I got Tyler to agree, and it was fortunate Mike was with me."

"Why exactly was he with you, Mom?" Ryan's eyes narrowed with suspicion.

"We'll discuss it later," she replied. "And then you can explain to me why you left your brother's wedding with one of your employees."

Purvi looked at Josh with rounded eyes but didn't say anything. The four of them sat in silence until two police officers walked out of one of the exam rooms and headed their way.

"Well," Cynthia asked, "is my son free to go?"

Ryan put a hand on his mother's arm. "I'd like to know if you're charging my brother."

"Are you Ryan Chadwick, the owner of the vehicle in question?" one of the officers asked.

"I am. What about my brother?"

"We'd like to speak with you. As for Tyler, things are complicated, but no, we won't be charging him at this time. Your brother is claiming he acted in self-defense and that he was under duress at the time of the accident. We're still gathering evidence, and I'm afraid your vehicle is part of that."

"Can we see him?" Josh asked.

"I imagine so," said the other officer. "He's in the first room on the left."

Josh and Purvi headed that way. Mike walked out of the room as they approached. He smiled when he saw Josh. "It's good to see you again. I wish it could have been in better circumstances, though."

"How is he?" Josh asked for what felt like the hundredth time.

"I think he'll be much better as soon as he sees you," Mike said, then went over to where Cynthia and Ryan were speaking with the police officers.

As they approached the door, which was only partially open, Josh heard a querulous voice demand, "Is he here yet? Can you go check again?"

"I've already told you that they'll send him in as soon as he arrives, I promise." The door opened wider and a woman in scrubs with a harassed expression on her face stood there. "Please tell me you're Josh."

"Is Tyler here? Can I see him? How is he?"

"Oh, thank goodness. He's behind the curtain and he's all yours." With that, she sailed out of the room.

Josh and Purvi approached the curtained-off bed. Josh drew the curtain back and there was his grumpy elf, looking very disreputable indeed. His face was covered in bruises and cuts. Most were small, but one above his left eye was large enough to be held together with three butterfly bandages. Otherwise, he appeared to be intact.

"I look like Frankenstein's monster," Tyler whined. "I'm hideous."

"Oh, shut up," Purvi told him. "On your ugliest day, you're still prettier than most of us mere mortals." She bent down and kissed an uninjured spot on his cheek. "You scared the crap out of me today, Tyler. Don't do that again."

"Well, since I probably paralyzed my kidnapper, I doubt I'll have to do it again."

Josh stepped forward and took one of Tyler's hands. It was ice-cold. "What happened?"

"He was waiting in the parking garage for you, Josh. With a gun. But I was there instead and David figured he'd won the hostage lottery. He made me drive and he had a gun and I have no idea where we were going because he wouldn't tell me but when we got to Highland Park I remembered Melissa Anderson's house, with that big tree in the front yard, and how her dad said one day some drunk asshole was going to hit it with his car and kill himself, so I got up to ramming speed and went for the tree and the gun went off and there was glass everywhere and everything went white and then I woke up here. Apparently, I have a slight concussion. And David, who neglected to put on his seatbelt, banged around the Volvo like a pinball and broke his neck. Isn't that nice? Even if I end up going to jail, totally worth it."

"You aren't going to jail, Tyler," Josh said. "Ryan would never let that happen."

"That's good because I'll have to become someone's prison bitch and I look like shit in orange."

"Do you think he's on morphine, Josh? I think he's got to be on morphine."

"They injected me with something awesome," Tyler said. "I can't feel my face." He poked at it with his hand, and Josh saw his wrist was in a splint.

"That's probably a good thing," Josh said. "Facial wounds are especially painful. What did you do to your wrist?"

Tyler pulled a face that would've probably caused him agony if it weren't for whatever pain killer they'd given him. "David happened to it. It might be broken and they want me to keep it immobilized. But look at my poor face! I'm going to have a scar. I'm sooooo hideous now."

"Harrison Ford has a scar and it didn't make him hideous. It'll give you some character."

"I think it looks manly," Purvi added.

"I won't be able to call you princess anymore." Josh reached over and stroked Tyler's hair.

"You call him princess? Oh, my God, that's the most precious thing I have ever heard. Princess. Holy shit. *Princess.*"

"Try calling me that, P, and I'll put Nair in your shampoo."

Purvi gasped. "You wouldn't dare."

"Try me, bitch."

"How come he gets to do it?"

Tyler smiled at Josh. "I love him. It gives him great latitude."

"Hey. You love me, too." Purvi put her hands on her hips.

"Well, yeah, but I love him more because he has a dick. You know how this works."

Purvi grinned at him. "Fine. Be that way. I'm going to go talk to someone about paperwork. They're going to want your insurance and I'm sure your stoned ass was in no position to give it to them." She kissed Tyler's cheek again and wandered out.

"I like her," Josh said.

"Seriously?"

"Yeah. She's funny and smart and loves you. What's not to like?"

"Oh, thank God." Tyler closed his eyes. "Jeremy, my boyfriend when I met her, couldn't stand her. He thought she was competition, like I'd decided out of the blue I was straight or something. Me. But he was convinced I was cheating on him with her. Then David loathed her and vice versa. She and Ethan didn't get along, either, but that was more of a personality clash thing. She thought he was a helpless baby and he thought she was a managing bitch, and they're both right. But you like her. Really?"

"Yes, Tyler. I like your best friend. Conveniently enough, you're related to mine, so that's all good."

"LA has the Getty," Tyler said in a rush.

"It... yes, I know that," Josh said, wondering if maybe they'd given Tyler too much morphine.

"My house doesn't have a view, but it is close to the ocean, and I can look for something that overlooks the ocean if you want."

"Um..."

"I know you don't like California but you followed Ryan there and I know it hasn't been very long for you but it feels like so much longer for me and he had a gun, Josh, a gun, and he was waiting for you and I can't go home if you're not with me. I can't. Not just for a month. He had a gun. And the Getty is a really nice museum. And the Huntington Library. It has all these rare manuscripts. There's all sorts of culture. You'll…"

"What?"

Tyler closed his eyes. "Nothing. Sorry, I know I'm babbling. I'll stop now."

Josh took Tyler's icy hand and brought it to his lips. "I'm okay. I'm here and I'm okay. And yes, the Getty is very nice. I'd love to go there again. I only saw a small portion of it when I went."

"Please come home with me. Otherwise I'll stay here and work at Starbucks and I'll be the bitchiest barista that ever existed."

"I don't think you're retail material, Tyler."

"No, probably not. Good thing you can support us and my cashmere habit. Also, Oliver does not eat shitty cat food. He is an expensive feline."

"About that…" Josh put Tyler's hand down and rubbed the back of his own neck.

"What?" Tyler asked. He opened his eyes and looked up at Josh.

"I quit."

"You what? You quit what?"

Josh rocked on his heels. "The practice. I quit today. Matt said I absolutely could not leave with a patient waiting for me. I explained you were in the hospital and I had to go. He said you weren't a spouse or family member so I… just… quit." It felt unreal, but he couldn't say he regretted it. Matt refusing to let him leave had made everything that much easier. "I have savings, of course, and I'm sure I can find another practice. One that's a bit more flexible, perhaps. And in another state. I'll have to transfer my license, but Purvi said she'd take care of all the paperwork for me and she'd start looking for practices that might be a good fit. I'm guessing LA could stand to have another dermatologist, right? And in the worst-case scenario I could be your house husband. I'm not the best cook in the world, but I will keep the place spotless and I'll make sure you eat more than just ice cream."

"That is probably the least romantic proposition I've ever received."

"It's just the morphine making you think that. I was romantic as hell."

Tyler snorted. "I'm not that stoned."

"Okay, fine. I love you, Tyler, and I quit my job today for you. I am willing to uproot my life for you. As much as I hate change and uncertainty, I am certain of you. Everything else will sort itself out."

"Are you sure?"

"Yeah, yeah, I am. I really am." Josh leaned down and kissed Tyler, but gently, because his lower lip had not escaped the devastation. "Are you prepared to put up with an aging neurotic doctor with a cleaning problem?"

"Forever, if necessary. Are you willing to put up with a mentally unstable, high-maintenance actor with nightmares, a cutting habit, uncertain job prospects, and a house with no view?"

"I left my practice for you. What do you think?"

Tyler smiled, and even with his face battered and bruised he was still beautiful. He reached his hand out to Josh. "Do you want to come home with me?"

In Josh's mind, he and Tyler stood on their ledge, hand in hand. Both looked down into the abyss.

"Are you ready?"

Josh looked down. *"Yeah. I'm ready if you are."*

They stepped to the edge and, holding hands, they walked off into thin air and an uncertain future. Together.

Josh blinked and looked at Tyler and saw his elf and his prince and his love. He took Tyler's hand and rubbed his fingers. "Always," he said.

Epilogue
Tyler Comes Full Circle

July, the next year
O'Hare Airport
Chicago, IL

There were no paparazzi waiting to ambush Tyler when he got past security at O'Hare, which was a good sign, not to mention a huge relief. He collected his suitcase and found the driver he'd hired. No one knew he planned on arriving today. It was so seldom that he got to surprise anyone that Tyler couldn't help but take advantage of the circumstances. He couldn't wait to see everyone's faces.

Or one face in particular.

It had been a month since he and Josh had been within touching distance of each other, and that had been when Josh had flown out to New Zealand to see him. It had only been for four days, but they had been four fucking amazing days. Tyler relived the memories late at night when he couldn't sleep, and made do with what they had until shooting on *The Golden Key* was concluded: video calls, dirty texts, and the occasional rambling email from Josh, in which he professed his love in the most roundabout way imaginable.

> *Tyler —*
>
> *I dream of you almost every night, and you're always doing crazy things. Last night you wanted to eat ice cream in the pool and I kept following you around, trying to talk you out of it, when all I wanted to do was fuck you — no pool, no ice cream — but you wouldn't stand still! I woke up aching for you, hard like a horny teenager.*
>
> *The house is so quiet without you. Purvi and Kevin come over to keep me company sometimes, and Ethan and Charlie took me to dinner the other day. Oliver misses you. He wanders around meowing, then looks at me like I've hidden you somewhere.*
>
> *I went running on the beach after work yesterday and stopped for the sunset. I watched as the sun sank out of sight, heading toward you. I wish I could follow it, but even you might find swimming across the Pacific a challenge.*
>
> *Miss you. Come home to me.*

Josh

Josh followed that up with a texted dick pic of his morning erection. It made Tyler laugh and got him through an otherwise grueling day of filming.

He fell a little bit more in love with Josh every day. Tyler had progressed past "stupid with love" and had drifted, at some point when he wasn't paying attention, into epic love territory. The kind of love they wrote horrible songs about. The kind of love people dreamed about, but seldom got. The kind of love Tyler wasn't sure he deserved.

It was one of the many things he talked about with Marilyn, his therapist. They had video sessions three times a week, where Tyler could talk about anything. At first he wasn't sure about it, but had agreed to it to make Josh happy. Now Tyler had gotten to the point where he looked forward to Marilyn's calls. She listened, didn't judge, and she could be very funny in a sly sort of way that Tyler appreciated.

She was the one he had first confided in, when the idea came to him.

"You seem very sure, Tyler."

"I am," he'd said. Then, "Yes, I am, I really am."

"And you feel confident this is what you want."

"Yes," he'd said. "Absolutely, yes."

Marilyn had gifted him with one of her slow, sweet smiles. "Then it's the right decision."

Even so, sitting in the back of the hired car, Tyler was nervous and felt his anxiety level rise. Along with it came that old desire, but he tapped his thigh several times, closed his eyes, and pictured his safe place. He sat on the rough boards of the dock at the lake house, Josh next to him, and they watched the still, blue water. By the time the car paused, stopping at the admission gate of the Chicago Botanic Garden, Tyler felt almost calm.

Tyler knew right where to go. The Chadwick picnic was held in the same area year after year, just adjacent to the rose garden. This year, for the first time, Peter Chadwick wasn't in attendance. His health was too frail, and he was confined to the hospital bed Ryan had gotten installed for him in the house in Highland Park. If it weren't for that, Tyler would've never had the idea to do this, and that would've been a shame, because there was a beautiful symmetry to today that pleased Tyler. Ten years had passed since the last Chadwick summer picnic both he and Josh had attended. Tyler wondered what his sixteen-year-old self would think if he could see into the future and see what his twenty-six-year-old self would become.

Teenaged Tyler would see a somewhat taller version of himself, height added by both the boots he wore and the topknot of blue hair on his head. Young Tyler might notice the scars, but only if he looked very closely.

They were fading; slowly, but surely. What Tyler hoped his younger self would see, more than anything else, was his older self's happiness.

Things get better, younger me. I promise. Now, just watch this.

Tyler saw Josh standing with his father, mother, and very pregnant sister. Brad came over and whisked Rachel off to the buffet. Josh's parents drifted away to talk with a few of the firm's lawyers and their spouses. Josh stood alone and scanned the crowd.

Tyler went over, walking quietly, looking only at his target. His hand stole to his pocket and fingered what he had in there. This was real, he reminded himself. As real as it got. Tyler got within an arm's length of Josh when those dark eyes saw him, really saw him, and opened wide with shock.

"Tyler? I don't…"

Tyler reached out and touched Josh's chest, his very solid chest, with one finger.

"Would you like to take a walk with me?" he asked.

"Oh my God, when did you *get* here?"

Tyler smiled and devoured Josh with his eyes. "Just now. Come on. I want to show you something."

Josh reached for Tyler and Tyler danced backward, out of his grasp.

"Come here, elf! I've missed you. Let me show you how much."

That made Tyler grin and back up a few more steps. "Follow me and *then* you can show me."

"Tease," Josh muttered, but obeyed. "I'd better get to kiss you soon."

"I think that can be arranged."

Tyler led Josh to the garden's waterfall, leading him up the winding, shady path, the relative cool a relief after the glaring sunshine. When they got to the top, there were a few people there looking at the magnificent view of shining water framed by verdant trees, but after a short time, they wandered off and left.

Once they were alone, Josh pulled Tyler to him and kissed him hard. Josh tasted so good. He was everything perfect and wonderful and Tyler could have kissed him forever. If home had a taste, it would've been Josh's mouth.

"I missed you, elf."

Tyler sucked a ragged breath into his lungs. "I missed you, too. So much. How have you been, Dr. Rosen?"

"Lonely. Horny. Are you going to explain why we're here and not California, which would make more sense? I've been wondering for over a week why you decided I needed to be here, of all places. What are you up to?"

"I'll tell you," Tyler said, "but first you need to sit down."

Josh sat on one of the benches and looked up at Tyler, brows raised.

"I love you," Tyler said. "So much more than I ever thought was possible."

"Okay, that's good, but I don't know why a trip to Chicago was necessary to tell me this. We could be doing this at home. In bed."

"Hush. These past several months with you have been among the happiest of my life. You know that this place is no longer my home." Tyler paused. "Well, neither is California."

Josh's brow furrowed. "What? Please tell me you don't want to move to New Zealand."

Tyler laughed. "God, no. That's not what I meant, but you always manage to distract me, don't you?"

Josh shrugged. "Turnabout's fair play."

Tyler dropped to one knee.

"What are you doing?" Josh's voice caught.

Tyler's hand fumbled in his pocket. "What I'm trying to say, badly, is that *you* are my home, Josh. Wherever I am, wherever you are, I want to always find my way back to you. Forever."

"Oh, hell."

Tyler frowned. "That wasn't the response I was hoping for." He worked the box out of his pocket and held it tightly in his fist.

"Tyler, you little..." Josh stopped, blinked a few times, then said, "Are you asking me to marry you?"

Tyler's frown deepened. This was not at all what he'd imagined. He studied his knee. "Maybe," he said.

"My God, Tyler. I'm sorry. I'm doing this all wrong. It's just that...I thought..."

Tyler looked up at Josh. "What?" he asked, heart in his throat.

Josh gave him a crooked smile. "I was going to ask you. I was waiting for our anniversary."

"Oh," Tyler said. "Really?"

"But this is better, elf."

"Yeah?" Tyler asked, knowing his heart had to be in his eyes.

"Yeah," Josh answered. "Definitely."

Josh hauled Tyler up and then pulled him down until he straddled Josh's lap. He took Tyler's face between his beautiful hands and kissed him again, over and over, until Tyler was breathless.

"Yes," he whispered into Tyler's skin. "Yes yes yes, of course, yes."

"I bought these," Tyler said, feeling pleased and ridiculous and thoroughly besotted. He handed the small box to Josh, who braced Tyler with one hand and opened it with the other. Inside were two platinum rings. "The larger one is for you, obviously."

Josh wore a grin wide enough to split his face. "Are you going to put it on me?"

Tyler rolled his eyes, while inside he was turning cartwheels. "I suppose. If you'd like." He slipped the ring onto Josh's finger.

"My turn." Josh slid the other ring onto Tyler's finger, then kissed it. "No backing out now."

"As if I would. Are you insane? I bought you a ring." Tyler couldn't believe he'd found his way to this point, but he wished his younger self could see it. "Same goes for you, you know."

"Oh, Tyler. You're never getting rid of me. Haven't you figured that out yet?"

"How about you spend the rest of our lives proving it to me?" Tyler raised an eyebrow at Josh in his most imperious manner.

Josh snorted. "How about we spend the rest of our lives proving it to each other?"

Josh drew Tyler's head down for another kiss. There was a smattering of applause and a wolf whistle. Both men looked up and saw that they had a small audience: Tyler's mother, Mike, Josh's parents, Ryan, Brad, and even Rachel, who looked hot, tired, and irritated, but still pleased. She sank onto the bench opposite them and groaned.

"You just *had* to propose at the top of a hill, didn't you?" she wheezed. "Never mind that I'm eight months pregnant."

Tyler and Josh ignored her.

"It's a deal," Tyler told Josh, giddy with love and relief and joy.

"I'm holding you to that, Tyler Chadwick, even if it takes sixty years," Josh said, then pulled Tyler down for another kiss.

The end

Afterword

For those who struggle with some of the things described in this book, there are resources available:

Self-harm:

http://sioutreach.org/

Suicide Prevention:

https://suicidepreventionlifeline.org/

or call 1-800-273-8255

Acknowledgements

I have way too many people to thank/blame for this book. Suzanne, this book would not exist without you. Courtney, Sam, and Sissy, thanks for giving me a chance and for being my cheerleaders. Jood, thank you for holding my hand and helping to keep me sane. Michele, you have been so helpful to me, especially finding me a cover artist! And lastly, Piper, you are sweet and patient and altogether wonderful.

Eternal thanks to my betas: Su, Courtney, Sam, Sissy, Michele, Brittany, Kyleen, Nick, Melinda, Jill, and Michael. You all helped to make this a better book.

I owe a huge debt to Amelia and Ed for being two of the nicest people I've managed to not yet meet. Thank you for everything.

Lastly, thanks to you, Constant Reader, for choosing this book and reading it to the end. I can't express how much it means to me, as a writer, that you stuck with me and my boys for the whole ride. I hope you had a good time.

About the Author

Lynn Van Dorn was born in Ohio and left it for the wilds of Chicago in her reckless youth. She wanted to become a fairy princess when she grew up, but since there are few openings for that position, she makes do with being a writer.

In her spare time, she drinks entirely too much tea, snugs her cats, loves her husband and son, reads voraciously, and avoids housework. She loves to watch anime, travel, knit, bake cookies, and conjure up happy every afters for handsome men who have trouble getting there on their own.

Lynn Van Dorn, Chicago, Il, August 2017

Made in the USA
Lexington, KY
22 September 2018